Praise for *A Ship of Fools*

Now, we must confess, *'A Ship of Fools'* is a book so audaciously original, so daringly unconventional, that it sent our usual roster of endorsers running for the hills! But fear not, dear reader, for we've managed to round up a few brave souls who dared to dive into the wild ride that is Tigran Haas's narrative and lived to tell the tale. So, without further ado, here are their ringing endorsements (and remember, any resemblance to actual persons, living or dead, or organizations, is purely coincidental).

"Haas's 'A Ship of Fools' is a narrative rollercoaster. It's a wild, unapologetic dive into the depths of human experience that leaves you breathless and begging for more." —Fictitious Famous Author, Stefan Ring

"'A Ship of Fools' is a bold, unflinching exploration of the human condition. It's a book that dares to push boundaries and challenges readers to do the same."—Fictitious Notable Publication, The New Yorker Times Review

"In 'A Ship of Fools,' Haas has crafted a narrative that is as thought-provoking as it is entertaining. This is a book that demands to be read and deserves to be celebrated."—Fictitious Prominent Critic, Michaela Katana, Literary Critic

'A Ship of Fools' is a captivating exploration of the human experience. Haas's storytelling is evocative and powerful, drawing the reader into a world that is at once familiar and utterly unique." —Fictitious Celebrated Figure, Opera Windblown

Quotes that inspire the Author

"Storytelling was a way to see the world bigger than the one you were looking at, and that had great appeal for me. I think, since that was part of my upbringing, it became part of me, and I wanted to pass it along to my kids and my grandkids."

—Robert Redford

"All knowledge, the totality of all questions, and all answers is contained in the dog."

—Franz Kafka, Writer

"Be careful, Michael; choosing not to believe in the devil doesn't protect you from him."

Father Lucas Trevant, Actor Sir Anthony Hopkins in "The Rite"

*"If you ask me, psychopaths are more talented than the rest of us... but they're still f**king psychopaths."*

—Jonathan Kellerman, Psychologist and Author of "Self-Defense"

"There are two things that are infinite, the universe and man's stupidity..... And I am not sure about the universe."

—Albert Einstein, Physicist

"All that is thought should not be said, all that is said should not be written, all that is written should not be published, all that is published should not be read."

—Menachem Mendel Morgenstern, Rabbi of Tomashov

A Ship of Fools

Behind the Doors of a Highrise

Tigran Haas

A Ship of Fools, Behind the Doors of a Highrise
First edition, published 2023

By Tigran Haas

Copyright © 2023 Tigran Haas

Composite Cover Art by Reprospace. Photos by Author and Fishki.net

Paperback ISBN-13: 978-1-952685-71-2

Published by Kitsap Publishing
Poulsbo, WA 98370
www.KitsapPublishing.com

Contents

This book is dedicated to all my four dear grandparents and my loving parents, as without them, I wouldn't be here where I am, and I wouldn't exist at all…I am because of them…my eternal love to all six of them.

*A special thanks goes to
James Howard Kunstler and
Ingemar Anderson for making this book happen for me.*

Foreword

by the Publisher

It is our distinct pleasure to present to you a collection of stories that chronicle an extraordinary journey through both time and space. Over the course of a decade, the esteemed author Tigran Haas has traversed the globe, immersing himself in the rich tapestry of life that spans from Zürich to Reykjavik, and myriad cities in between. Drawing inspiration from locales as diverse as Boston, Sarajevo, Dubrovnik, Stockholm, Split, Berlin, Miami, Prague, San Francisco, Bled, Tel Aviv, Detroit, Geneva, Vienna, Oslo, Zagreb, and Rome, Haas has crafted a series of tales that capture the essence of human experience in its myriad forms.

This remarkable compilation, entitled "A Ship of Fools," is centered around the microcosm of a helter-skelter highrise building in an unspecified Eastern European capital. Within its pages, you will discover stories that not only span the globe but also delve deep into the human psyche. Through his vibrant prose and masterful storytelling, Haas weaves together the threads of individual lives, unraveling the complexities of human connection and the universality of our shared experiences.

In "*A Ship of Fools,*" you will encounter language that is raw, explicit, and at times, potentially offensive. This is not a decision made lightly by the author, Tigran Haas, or by us, the publishers. The language used is a deliberate choice, intended to paint an authentic and unfiltered picture of the society about which Tigran writes. The characters in this book inhabit a world that is often harsh and unforgiving, and their language reflects this reality. It is a testament to the struggles they face and the environments they navigate. While the language may be challenging for some readers, we believe it is essential to the integrity of the narrative and the authenticity of the characters. We encourage readers to approach the text with an open mind, understanding that every word is chosen with the intent to immerse you fully in the world Tigran has so vividly created.

In an age where true storytelling has often been overshadowed by the instant gratification of digital media, Tigran Haas's work represents a triumphant return to the art of classic storytelling. This collection is a testament to the power of the written word, and it is our sincere hope that, as you delve into these pages, you will find yourself transported to the myriad worlds that Haas has so skillfully created.

The stories are set somewhere in a south-eastern central European major capital city (such as Sarajevo) between 1980 and 1990.

With great anticipation, we invite you to embark on this literary odyssey, and trust that you will find as much solace, inspiration, and delight in these tales as we have had the privilege of experiencing.

Introduction

"There might have been things I missed, But don't be unkind. It don't mean I'm blind. Perhaps there's a thing or two I think of lying in bed. I shouldn't have said. But there it is…"

… and so on, go the lyrics of "From the Beginning," a 1972 song written by Greg Lake and performed by one of my favorite progressive rock groups, Emerson, Lake & Palmer (ELP). Surely I would have missed a few, if not a significant number of things in the book, but every writer does; the key is to draw the line and be happy with what you got. All possible and impossible mistakes, omissions, faults, misses, and deficiencies in this text are mine and mine alone. I guess that was meant to be, and 'you were meant to be here' and read it this way, which brings me to language issues. It is vital, which is probably the understatement of the century, but that's how it is supposed to be, and it should be.

The book is based on a unique "holy trinity," immersed deeply into naturalism, an artistic, primarily literary, direction that continues on realism. The heroes of this book and many naturalistic novels are really, as someone has said, slaves to passion, prisoners of their unfortunate fate, and people burdened with hereditary traits. That is at least what some believe, and so do I. Although the nonfictional fiction book is also submerged in realism (at least bits and pieces of it in a worldview based on the real-world view that seeks to present reality faithfully, without passion, objectively and impersonally) and finally completing the trinity is the 'new primitivism' (a subcultural f**kabout reactionary street talk cultural movement or as Zlatko Gall depicts it vividly: "as possessing clear anti-intellectual traits, including the glorification of the streetwise local noble savage via humor that plays to the cheap seats and as such straddles, the thin line between allusion on one side and vulgarity and repugnance on the other depicts nature and man in the most vulgar and dark moments." There you have it. And that is why the language is obscene, vulgar, profane, derogatory at times, and often just plain f**ked-up due to the simple fact that reality was such at that time, in that specific place. Any other alternate state of things or the mind would be false and criminal to write (for me). It is all about the truth of the time and my vision and POV. So, accept it; you don't have many options. But of course, therefore, we have disclaimers, a need for parental advisory, and possible age restrictions, as you would find in movies or albums that are sprayed with explicit and vulgar content.

Truthfully, the irresistible stories must be passed along, retold, and kept alive. And amid that, am I! I am a direct participant, observer, and storyteller. Lastly, I regard myself much more as a storyteller than a writer. The writing experience came from my oral storytelling to my small cousins, family & friends, and other infantile acquaintances. The tales are known incidents with an additional spice produced by my vivid imagination and a touch of urban folk tales, street talk as we call it, but all based on actual events, even if some are recognized as urban legends. It felt like bedtime stories or sitting around an open camp picnic fire, with me as a personal storyteller and a congregation willing to listen and engage. The whole idea is that these stories-tales should suck you in immediately, not letting go, sweep you up, engage your intellectual curiosity or lack thereof, and immerse you towards a satisfying end or a shitstorm of laughs and cries every time they end.

The stories gathered in this book are engaging, as the decade between 1980 and 1990 was such engaging and f**king great! Most have the added thrill of being based on actual events, as told by me, to me, or through someone. They embody the time, the moment, the culture, the customs, the people, the beliefs, disbeliefs, the politics, the geography, the f**king everything via a wide variety of people I have met and lived with and played with. The book and stories lean very much on 'Observational comedy', which is a form of special urban humor based on the commonplace aspects of, in this case, everyday life on the streets and in the designated places. The idea was to provide a fascinating glimpse into a range of closed worlds within this array of peoples and destinies and a glimpse into a central-eastern European socialist-communist, westernized, and post-socialist atmosphere. So now you know…and if you have an opinion about this book, positive or negative, I refer you to the great quote of iconic Clint Eastwood (From Dirty Harry, Inspector Callahan): "Well, opinions are like assholes. Everybody has one."

Read me, please!

The man sitting across from me at the café (a simulacrum—open up a dictionary for this word, as I am sure you have no f**king clue what it is) of Starbucks was either thinking about quitting his job, robbing a place of wealth, maybe even killing his wife or mother or just putting a bet on a horse race. It was neither of those profound options but something completely different altogether. His face was becoming a tense bliss, as someone just about to pee in his pants and feel the spartan warmth of it all, not knowing the sticky and cold feeling that was about to enter right after that nor the aesthetics of one's pants. Instead, the "gentleman" farted pretty loudly, and for a moment, time stood still, and particles of dust froze in the air while the apparent gases came out. He sniffed once, twice, and inhaled the air around him. The smile that came afterward was the one you only see in movies. He was content with what he felt, smelt, and relived in those short minutes. But stoically, I endured and contemplated the reasons and desires of such an act of public display and airy ambition…and I am sure that Marc Antony would say this at that moment: "Yet Brutus says this man was ambitious; And Brutus is an honorable man." In farts, there's always a hint of wind coming over, and as the smell carried to me, a combination of onion, the sewer, green cabbage, and rotten potatoes also came with it.

Let me restart, folks! Well, fart or no fart, and the hell with this opening that has no meaning, this book is about storytelling. And what the f**k is that? 'Either write something worth reading about or do something worth writing about.' Kurt Russell uttered these words in the movie "The Art of Steal," Honestly, folks, this book of stories might just be that, or it might not. But what the heck? I know what you are thinking now and what is going through your head standing in the generic airport bookshop before your trip on the way to a crappy summer holiday destination with an airline you have never heard of but got the ticket for the price of a hamburger. Ah, here is an exciting book for a 30 dollars with a cool name, "*The Ship of Fools: Behind the Doors of a Highrise* or if you want to be in the rhyme and poetic mood its all about "*Behind the Doors of a Highrise, the Ship of Fools Disguise,*" an author no one has ever heard of, and a great cover of some mother f**ker jumping off a tower or a burning highrise. It even became a bestseller, shit! And while you are contemplating the value of a book packed with storie ssspread over massive 600+ pages and a few days of lazy reading, you may also think that 29.95 dollars could be better invested in a beer and pastrami sandwich that you will digest and crap out in a few hours. Or—and two pints of beer you will piss in a few hours, a small cheap travel gadget you will never use, or some other (un)needful thing. If you will not buy the f**king book, leave it on the shelf, and don't flip through the pages with your sweaty and greasy fingers from peanuts and dirty from the toilet visit just a few moments ago. Just don't frigging buy it. It's not a catalog with pictures, nor will a page or a few lines tell you the plot or change your mind about buying it. Wait! F**king buy it! Follow your gut instinct, buy it, enjoy the next few days on a beach in some God-forsaken place or overcrowded tourist dump, and read the best book of your life! Well, that was a frigging pitch…

I need to focus, folks. Well…How many stories do you remember from your childhood? Some many, none? Some for sure, and I can guarantee that you WILL NEVER FORGET THESE stories THAT HAPPENED! U bet! These good, bad and ugly, and beautiful as well (well, probably not) stories will help you remember messages of life for a lifetime. Storytelling in this book is also about a significant theme and development of characters and moral evolution and degradation. It's about asshole people and their f**king lives, and it's about an ordinary world with extraordinary events and themes, places, lives, events, moments, things, and all kinds of other elements that look and behave like a carousel. All these characters you will love & hate; they will be close and personal, vivid and elusive, and compelling and memorable. You should be activated and alive when reading this, associating yourself with the characters, and flipping pages in a frenzy to find out what is next…if not…

well f**k you! And by the way, if you expect a Happy Ending instead of an Inferno Apocalypse, you are in for a surprise, for this is not a frigging fairytale.

Why read all of this, you might ask? Aside from reading and holding a book that might help you look more intelligent and intellectual, it's much more than just Facebook, Instagram, TikTok, Spotify, YouTube, or Netflix, right? It's reading from a paper, reading a book, feeling past, present, and future, being in a place, and knowing something. Well, these stories (as in any "great literature") open and disclose freshly painted and refurbished windows and shed new light onto familiar subjects of life & death. They also treat the significant matters of life and death, as that is what matters, with un-sensational f**king simplicity and desire for nothingness – that sounds good to you? Yes, some of this material was harvested from different sources, and such is storytelling. Yes, it has changed a bit, morphed, and reshaped itself as it went from one to another timeframe. It feels like a flowing time-lapse, speeding up the passage of time so that events seem to happen faster.

Still, the book always kept the keen sense of the absurd and real-time feel, the wickedly silly and funny situations, the surreal and outrageous, the bewildered imagination, and the harmonic convergence of idiocy. Its curmudgeonly situational settings, satire, the playfulness of loneliness, joy, material nothingness, and psychopathic dances are always playful, like a naked butt on the roses of thorns. The book's blunt, primordial, (neo)primitive, and sometimes (the very) profane language of naturalism keeps evolving. My memories as windmills of the mind and bewilderment of love, hate, and revenge perpetually open themselves as we go along. Let's be frank, folks, these stories deal with a lot of crap, shit, craziness, lunacy, impossible situations, weirdos, and other stuff. The book deals with eternal philosophical, moral, and ethical issues that will always be relevant, regardless of the age they are written in or intended for. All of that is tied to the timeless human beings we are and to the eternal elements of human nature & soul. These things and persons are in our lives in one way or another. The cluster of relations, passions, drama, and psychological conflicts are there. As in life, love, faith, fear, hate, drama, adventure—all these feelings, emotions, and friendships are maybe given in a funny, harsh, and more visible light of another life or lives lived, but they are here.

I think Stephen King, in his "Everything's Eventual Collection of Dark Tales," mentions the practicing of an (almost) lost art of writing, that storytelling is as important as it is about life stories. This book is about LIFE and the feeling of belonging to a COLLECTIVE; the themes of our life, eternal issues we deal with daily, and dilemmas we go through every moment of our existence. But what about this place, then? Where does it all play out? There is something primordial here—a sense of place when people feel a longing for belonging towards a home, a building, a site, or a city they are familiar with. Associating this place with all the characters inside will be for all of you reading it like visiting a location for the first time, where you feel anxiety, nervousness, expectations, and excitement.

When you read this, it might be enjoyable, it might be disgusting, it might also be boring (for some of you assholes out there), it might be f**king hilarious (for most of you buggers), and it just might be damn good (for you, the enlightened ones). Whatever emotion it leads to, as a place leads to either positive, negative, or neutral feelings, you will never forget it. I promise you that! A sense of place that goes into the heart of darkness or light in any storytelling exercise, and so in this one, is when people feel a longing for belonging towards a place, neighborhood, building, or city they are familiar with. But I already said that…

If people enjoy their places of habitation or visit and it leads them to a positive emotion, they will re-visit or return to the area, either physically or in the windmills of their minds. So, the opposite will happen; places they hate, or places that make them uncomfortable will haunt them forever, even if they never return their memories, and the mind will experience the vertigo of nostalgic experiences. This sense of returning to the place frequently and having that deep connection with the site makes what the environmental psychologists and urbanists call: the 'space' becomes a 'place' of meanings and connections. You will want to revisit or return to these characters and settings. This sense of returning to the book stories unfolding and having that deep connection with the place makes the stories and storytelling even more compelling. It becomes a place of meaning and connection for you or any other reader, even if you have never lived in these places. Stories will forever be engraved in your cortex's spinal fluid, like it or not. It is essential to have these connections with fictional and non-fictional landscapes and geographical surroundings so that more of you guys create bonds, kites of your imagination, stories of your mind, and a sense of place with their environments and people that inhabit them. Well, I could go on and on, but I won't. F**k it! Buy the book and make your life better or worse. But most importantly, enjoy your frigging holiday! Ok? This book was initially envisioned for children, but now it is for kids from 7 to 97. A childhood remembered aura also compelled me to reveal a lot but not the actors' real names as some privacy needed to be kept. Also, the vocabulary is raw, naturalistic, and utterly free of snobbery of artificial and perfectionist English language that is only an end in itself, a tool for pretentious wanna-be literary masturbators…that's not the case here; here, it is a vocabulary for the masses and to be enjoyed and understood by all, even with its mistakes and flaws.

Also, I could have abstained from saying anything, but my big mouth and speed (As my grandma would say: Speed is Devils work, my son!) prevented me from doing that. I do not want to guide you through this book; I want you to discover it as a lovely oasis with clear water and consume it as a tasty cake. If you vomit or have diarrhea afterward, even better, then you won't forget it for a long time. And if you fart, pee in your pants from laughing, and dislocate your jaw in the process, then even more incredible! Frigging baloney! Enjoy the show evolving in front of you. It was a great time in a great place, long before the world we know now, which is the shitty world we live in. Some dude once said stories are not about beginnings, middles, and ends and are not just anecdotes and snapshots. I couldn't agree more! Why love this book? Just because! Remember the emotions we have. We attach emotions to events to create stories and memories. The gray matter in our skull has been manufactured and designed that way. So, storytelling is essential if you want to use gray matter and its undiscovered realms the way it's meant to be used (Like in the fantastic movie "Lucy" with Scarlett Johansson and Morgan Freeman). We remember the emotional, the particular, and the violent incredibly. We forget the boring, the general, and the healthful.

But there is one more selfish element in all of this, and it's not money and getting a bestseller on the shelves of airport bookstores, groceries, and internet shops; it's about nostalgia. Nostalgia has been part of my life forever and part of every human that is normal, and is sort of a sentimentality for the past, typically for a period or places with happy personal associations, but I would say for bad ones also. Remember what I said about the sense of place? Good and bad shit gets remembered. Having a vampire sucking your blood or a good tooth fairy granting you a wish is something that both will be recognized, although when you become a vampire, I am not sure what you will feel anything. Nostalgia is associated with a yearning for the past, its personalities, and events, especially the "good old days" or a "warm childhood" or those "happy times" but also the negative shit, situations, memories, and people. Once upon a time, it was described as a medical condition, a form of melancholy in the earlier modern days, a hypochondria of the heart (or, for some, homesickness). In 1688, Swiss physician Johannes Hofer published a report on this mysterious epidemic, naming the problem nostalgia, a mash-up of the Greek words nostos (a homecoming or return) and algos (which means pain). Nostalgia, of course, has come to mean something different now, but in storytelling as well as in this book, reliving memories may provide comfort and contribute to mental health or may not. So, there you go, with a bit of selfishness from my side.

It's this frigging dilemma, right—It's being sick for home (homesick) but also sick of it, same with the persons, sons, and characters. It took me almost two decades to remember its ugliness and beauty and all the characters and moments in time, but I managed in the end. These 30+ stories will touch your emotions and engage you, grab and maintain your attention; they will help you understand and remember or leave you ignorant and forgetful. Whatever happens in the coming 600-plus pages, you will be a part, at least during your crappy ten days vacation of cheap food and drinks and bad lodgings, an even worse airline company, of authenticity, participation, and engagement into streams of life like you never witnessed before. Let yourself go and enjoy this!

I bid you farewell, my dearest readers, as it's time for you to engulf yourselves in this carousel of stories – "A Ship of Fools." You might like or dislike this book, but I guarantee you won't be bored. F**k, I guess I can promise you that much. Now I need to go, as there is a beautiful and adorable Atlantic puffin on my windowsill in Reykjavík, probably from Dyrhólaey cliffs, watching me intensely with a mouth full of small fishes. It might grant me a wish, who knows, or at least a small fish, or I might eat it for dinner if I can catch it with my bare hands; the sky is the limit, folks…keep dreaming and reading.

Tigran Haas, Reykjavík,
Friday, May 17th, 2019, 17:54 Local Time

Wait, I wrote it again a month later. So please read me again!

Just in case you might be displeased with the original introduction and the Author's Note, here is an abridged, much more severe version, abridged, I promise! So, this book that you are about to chew, swallow, maybe digest, or spit out has been a product of 20 years of thinking and procreating and probably nine months of writing and execution within those 19 years. It depicts a time between 1980 and ca 1990 (take or leave +/- 2 years) with some extra things, such as people, places, and situations, situated in a central-eastern European Balkan country and one of its capital cities, that of Sarajevo. In many ways, this is storytelling of microhistories but with destinies and characters that are unique but still universal. The book depicts (and remembers) a time when things were quite different than today. A time when time stood still but also moved faster; people and situations that life was made of and that made life; a unique combination of events, planned and unplanned (in an almost Jungian atmosphere of synchronicity), that all these events were "meaningful coincidences" as they occurred with no causal relationship yet all of them seemed to be meaningfully related, in this collective state of mind and bizarre community socialist feel. Maybe I should have called this book of Stories simply SYNCHRONICITY (one of my favorite rock albums, The Police—Synchronicity from 1983, Aside from Asia's ALPHA also from 1983). Synchronicity was a principle that Jung felt gave conclusive evidence for his concepts of archetypes and the collective unconscious. It described a governing dynamic that underlies human experience and history — social, emotional, psychological, and spiritual. So, it has penetrated this book almost entirely. But still, *A Ship of Fools* epitomizes the spirit of the matter at hand.

Oh yes, reality. This is a nonfiction/fiction book as all stories are based on actual events and facts verified and unverified but wrapped in elastic-plastic of fictitious cellophane; otherwise, they would be unreadable. The book is what it is: a unique but hopefully universal picture of very different events, people, and places that we are usually accustomed to; an almost parallel universe of transverse situations; things that are impossible to comprehend today, and events that are so strange that they feel almost unreal today. Unfortunately, that time brought also an aura of darkness when it came to political incorrectness, homophobia, absence of LGBTQIA+ rights, racism, injustice, intolerance, brutality, discrimination, sexism, bullying, hate crimes & hate speech and other dark problems prevalent in societies of those times & age. Then those things were "normal" which was an abomination of all human and humanistic values, but fortunately a lot of that is gone now but still remains in minds, memories and souls of many that suffered such things during those times.

Political correctness, a forerunner of the cancel culture, is the hallmark of our age now. Aside from positive things it brought, especially when related to things I wrote above, it has also brought mob justice, a sheep mentality that just relies on "feel good terms" as the dominant discourse. As somebody from the literature world said recently, 'It is those who cannot defend their argument who seek to silence those who can. The cancel culture is born of the inability of an opinion to withstand the scrutiny of thoughtful debate.' Also, while writing this book, I learned & realized many things; it did help me sharpen my senses in one key thing: to discern good people from bad people – acceptable persons from evil ones, sane characters from insane ones, and most importantly, to devel-op one's Voight-Kampff machine for detecting psychopaths and other people in my life, past, present and future. Voight-Kampff machine was a very advanced form of a futuristic lie detector that measured contractions of the iris and the presence of invisible air-borne particles emitted from the body. The test was used primarily by "Blade Runners" (All from Ridley Scott's Blade Runner epic movie) to determine 'if a suspect is truly human (as opposed to a replicant) by measuring the degree of his empathic response through carefully worded questions and statements'. I didn't build a physical machine but more of a social science observational intuitive one that helps me, after some time, to detect the beasts, the predators, most dangerous of human beings, those of psychopaths. Finally, free speech, honest dialogue, hard talk, healthy debate with argumentation and free literary mind (full) writing in a respectful manner, is a must and if we cannot say or write what we think, soon we won't be able to think at all and then we are f****d for good! The base idea of this book was to create an interesting concoction, assemblage of tales and events, partly (very much) real and fictional, to present a larger story steeped in modernity as well as in near history. The stories are constantly hinting at real-life happenings and real-life events and characters in the Highrise captured in moments in time; having equal parts of truth and creativity mixed into it. Well, that's the hope anyway… Each story in this book can be read on its merit, but also the whole book and flow have, and I hope, follow some irrational logic.

What else is there to say? Not much. I already said too much. The rest could be found in the first author's note if you cared to read it. I suggest you do., I just wanted to write these few lines because the book was conceived long ago. The first lines were written in a Hotel in Zürich in the good old 1999, and I think it felt appropriate to end it there in 2019 in another hotel in Zürich, just a few days after the visit to Iceland, where I finished my author's first note. I thought that was it, the final lines in an ice island. But it was not. Switzerland had the last word on the matter; my favorite country in the world and Zürich, my most beloved city ever.

It's a beautiful evening on the 1st of June in Zürich's old town, 22C degrees with a light breeze…I feel I said what I wanted to say while the book was written in 20 cities around the USA and Europe, including Israel. Now I leave you with the task of reading, hoping you are literate; if not…well, buy the book anyway and at least recycle it when you go to the toilet.

Tigran Haas,

Saturday, 1st of June 2019, 2 PM local time, Zürich, Switzerland

What is a Highrise Building?

A highrise building is a multi-story structure that rises vertically and is taller than it is wide. While not as tall as skyscrapers, highrises are still considered to be tall buildings, usually used for residential, commercial, or mixed-use purposes. Highrises typically have a significant number of floors, with modern construction methods and materials used to ensure structural stability and efficient use of space.

As you embark on this literary adventure, I wish you an abundance of fun and excitement, and may the pages ahead spark your imagination and captivate your spirit! May the fart, oh sorry, the force be with you.

1

The Brain Man

In the modern-day age of multimedia telecommunications, fiber optic cables, and information technologies, yellow and white pages are becoming increasingly obsolete. Still, for some, it is the primary means of finding the telephone number and address of the loved one, a business friend, or just somebody they want to waste time within a telephone conversation. They still believe in the power of the written word and the power of the telephone book, comments, and numbers. All those hundreds and hundreds of sheets of names and numbers, of people you will probably never meet in your life, basically of ink print completely wasted and of forests chopped down for nothing. All those bulks dropped down every year in front of your door, all the problems created by it: "Where to store these damn 'books.' I just got no place for them". Well, you take them, or you don't!

In most cases, you do that. But these books were always considered a companion to your telephone, or shall we say to your 'far sound' as the Greek root of the word would cover it. It looks good to have it. It shows that you are connected, that you are modern, that you somehow know people and are not lonely – that you could have a social life – what a bullshit thing! There is also this great need to have it, even if you are going to open it a couple of times a year, maybe never.

For some morons, this represents a part of their essential home reading. Believe it or not, some people placed this in the most prominent aspects of their home libraries, even saving the older ones and showing off their 'encyclopedic value'! Well, they indeed had exceptional value, especially when being online was fantasy and fiction. Well, you must admit that these paper dinosaurs have their attraction value. All this discovering, rushing down with your index finger through new names, exciting family names, bunches of numbers, licking your fingers while turning the pages and leaving pieces of Mr. that and Mrs. that on your tongue…hmm…exciting! For younger generations, this was the oracle – the place for fun and games – and primarily for pranks. What a goldmine! There were thousands of potential victims out there. Names to be called, faceless people tortured by adolescent games, and hundreds of bucks piled up on parents' phone bills. When you look a little bit closer, they certainly had their value. Every year we see a change in covers too. Depending on the sponsors or the art style of the moment, we get to see 'interesting' stuff pop up on the front. Most of the time, it's just pure advertisement crap. Sometimes something exciting does come up. Well, this is the least essential thing in the bloody book, but still, you want to see something interesting that can sustain this thing artistically throughout the year. And every year, you seem to grow with them as they grow. Some people seem to grow even more. That brings me to one, Alex Dimitrov.

Alex was a special kind of bird. He was a troubled child from day one. According to his doctors, he acquired mental disorders early in his adolescence. God knows what they pinned down on him. His parents were conscientious about hiding all of this. Being part of the upper socioeconomic strata could have damaged their social status if it was revealed that their son was in the 'birdie land.' No sir! Hide it and tell the community he is a compassionate soul. Well, that can work, but how will you hide it when the 'bird man' grows up? Alex did grow up. When he reached 38, we remembered this enormous chunk of meat, weighing about 155 kilos. His vast belly was protruding from the pants, and if it were not for the tight leather army belt that he wore, his jelly belly would have probably spilled out on the sidewalk. He always wore khakis, light blue Armani shirts, dark loafers, and a gray Ralph Lauren jacket. The body was a combination of a hastily put-together snowman, an overweight Santa Claus, and a Sumo wrestler. His hair was full of oil and combed towards his left side to show, as his mother used to say, the 'high forehead of our ancestors.' His eyeglasses looked more like magnifying glasses that you get in your first biology class or your grandmother's jars with all the goodies stored for the winter. A huge bulky nose with tons of hair growing out of it dominated his face, which showed total confusion. Those dark, fast-moving eyes and elastic facial expressions always put you on guard. If you catch my drift, he swayed from side to side when he walked, sort of a penguin-duck walk.

He used to roam the streets very often but somehow spent most of his time, or it seemed like it, around our urban quarter. That's why we had a unique opportunity to learn more about him. He had this capability to be at every place at every time. As some used to call him, the fat ghost' was everywhere. As I said before, he was diagnosed with many things. Hyperactivity was one of them. It manifested in Alex's distractibility, restlessness, and inability to sit still, but he had no difficulty concentrating. This was curious. This minimal brain dysfunction (as some old geezers used to call it) was shoved under the rug, even though it indicated hereditary and family problems. He developed eating disorders early because he ate like an elephant at age 4. This led other doctors to believe that he had autism. A famous shrink named Leo Kanner was the first to identify autism as a mental disorder in children in the early 1940s. Alex was withdrawn and self-preoccupied but never fully fit into this category. He could communicate with his parents and sur-roundings but did reoccur in motoric movements. For example, he used to clap every five minutes or so. So the local shrinks identified all kinds of treatments and suggested spending considerable time in a sanatorium in the Swiss Alps.

No way! The parents wouldn't have any of that. Father, the city's most prominent surgeon, had his theories. Anxiety and social in-ability were one of them. Good grief! The problem was that autism and similar brain diseases were poorly understood then. One of the shrinks also discovered that he had a case of dissociative identity disorder. I am unsure if he was correctly diagnosed, though no-body gave a shit about that. Therefore, he was not a split personal-ity but liked to take the role of somebody else occasionally, usually a famous person. Still today, it is difficult to treat these kinds of problems. The kid was undoubtedly a multi-faceted case of disor-ders with unique talents. So maybe the Swiss Alps thing could have been a good idea after all. Oh yes! Here comes the significant part. Remember I mentioned the yellow pages? Well, Alex Dimitrov was the 'telephone book of the city.' Possibly being a byproduct of autism, Alex knew the white pages by heart. Holy shit! More than 450.000 inhabitants in the city, and Alex was your info, man! That was one of the reasons people liked him and didn't bother him too much.

As I mentioned, he had a habit of roaming through the city and visiting almost every café on the way. The guy just couldn't be still. He used to come in and sit at one of the tables. He usually dropped in this sleazy joint called the 'Two Fisherman.' Nobody knows how this shit place got that name. There was no fisherman in these parts, and fish was nowhere to be seen. The barman named Jeremiah 'the old tooth' Bricks would usually say: 'Yow, Alex, my man – your table is waiting.' Alex would reply: 'To you, it is His Excellency Mr. Alex Dimitrov, the Prime Minister of Paraguay.'

"Oh, I do apologize, Sir," the barman said. 'What would you like today, some sparkling wine or perhaps something else this time around?'

'Don't give me your usual shit; bring me champagne from the best, somewhere around Marne River from Château-Thierry, you know!' One thing you had to say about Alex Dimitrov was that man was a fountain of facts, not a synthesis of knowledge. He never went to school but had private tutors. How he learned things, at least some, remains a mystery to me.

The barman Jeremiah replied: 'Oh, that champagne. It will take a while to get it out of our cellar. I only have a couple of bottles left."

'Hurry, hurry…I don't have too much time to wait in your low-quality establishment'.

Alex was getting impatient now. Jeremiah was a mean son of a bitch. He is a strong guy in his early 60-s, always on guard, and never lets his customers out of sight. He had this Hemingway novel face: many old scars covering his sun-dried skin, whitebeard with a couple of homemade plum-grape brandy stains, a white ponytail to match the beard and almost dark yellowish eyes which could perfectly fit into a house of horrors in your nearby amusement park. It was an establishment with a whole gallery of winos, people from the sidelines of society, and even some crooks; you had to always be on your toes. He did like Alex, though. This guy brought some dignity to the place, although Jeremiah considered him a complete idiot.

'Well, if you are so impatient, Prime Minister, then I will have to speed up the process.' 'Yes, you do that and make it snappy,' replied Alex.

'Oh, I will make it snappy. Don't you worry about that,' Jeremiah thought.

While Alex was starting a conversation with the only female in the bar, one who looked like one of the vessels after LordNelsons' naval campaigns, Jeremiah was preparing Alex's "champagne." He poured mineral water into the bubbles, unzipped his pants, took his pecker out, and urinated into the glass. His piss only filled 1/3 of the glass so that the color would match champagne as closely as possible. Good grief, his piss had a dark yellowish color of a man in the late stages of rotting. It had more wine than anything else in it. In that sense, Alex was getting his 'sparkling wine.' Seeing this, Jeremiah added some of the house white wine, which had never seen a single grape and tasted like a package of aspirins.

Alex finally yelled to the dame: 'What's your name, milady?' 'Oh, nobody called me milady before.' That's because these visitors here do not have any manners at all. They don't know how to treat a lady', proudly answers Alex. You could hear some grunts, but most of the guests were half-dead, their heads buried in the alcohol remains on the table. Only the barman was grinning with the only yellow tooth in his mouth, protruding between his dirty white whiskers.

'My name is Sandra Myers.' Alex thought for about 2 seconds: 'Your telephone number is 765-643!'

'How do you know my number, you bastard' feverishly replied Sandra.

'Well, I know all the numbers of everybody in the city.' And then he started his usual clapping, which would last at least a minute or two. Sandra took this opportunity and went for the door. 'I will not continue to reside in your establishment, Bricks. You only have the perverts and sleaze balls here'.

'Whose going to pay for your drinks bitch? I'm going to kick your dirty ass with my baseball bat if you don't pay, screamed Bricks, the barman. 'Let the pervert pay,' and she vanished through the door. Now all the half-dead customers woke up and started chanting: 'Pay, pay, pay....'

" Pay, I will pay, pay, pay, pay, " exclaimed Alex.

'Sure, but first, you have to drink up your champagne. He brought him his glass, and Alex swooshed it down in seconds. 'That was excellent. It would help if you got more of these. Jeremiah was amazed. This idiot was immune to everything. Alex threw a bunch of money, and before he left, he checked four of the establishment visitors and reminded them, to their amazement, of their telephone numbers. He was probably the only person in the city that was the first to receive a copy of the white pages. His dad pulled some strings in the Telephone Company to make Alex happy. And he was!

Alex also had other psychological disorders. One of the numerous shrinks Alex visited diagnosed him with Echolalia, a compulsion to repeat all or some of the words he had previously heard. That's just what happened in the bar. But the worst thing was that he used to do this in other places, very different from the bar environment. One of his passions, or sicknesses, was to roam through the obituaries in the daily papers and pick up persons that he fancied in his confused mind. He would then go to all these memorial services and even attend funerals. This guy could be your worst nightmare in a more gentle way. He knew all about the art of disposing of human remains. He was the burial master. Not just that, he knew all the prayers, respective of which religious burial he attended. He didn't miss the atheist once, either.

It was not a rare occurrence that he would be thrown out of the cemeteries because of his constant repetition of prayers and clapping occasionally. Once he started repeating after the minister: 'ashes to ashes, ashes to ashes'…He couldn't stop for 10 minutes. Everybody was standing in shock. He was clumsy once he stumbled into the grave pit. The fall was so vicious that instead of him getting hurt, the wooden casket was severely damaged. His parents took care of the costs naturally. On occasions, being extremely good with numbers, he would calculate the dimensions of the grave and how much dirt was put in, what geometrical formulas they should use next time because the tomb was never perfect for him. He should have been consulted. He did all of this aloud. No wonder that sometimes he got beaten up in the process. To make things even worse, he also had this ridiculous laugh which he would practice from time to time. He would start laughing for no reason whatsoever. But he was that type of a guy. So, in most cases, people would be more in a state of shock or bewilderment than anything else, for that matter. As far as the memorial services go, he would behave strangely, attending these ceremonies, sometimes in homes or at the cemetery. He would cry the tears of a crocodile and would go around shaking everybody's hands and asking them for their names. Well, you know why: he could tell them their telephone numbers.

Alex also had a special kind of phobia – fear of small kids. I don't know the accurate medical term for this (maybe kidophobia), though I doubt there is one. As he used to hang out, always for a limited time, in our urban quarters, there was always a chance that small kids would surround him. He was strange, and being as he was, a vast bulk of flesh, he was undoubtedly an attraction to kids. When this happened, he would stutter, make strange, delirious sounds, and scream: 'Don't hurt me, don't hurt me.' You had to feel pity for the guy. The small, mean kid named Igor would often come to him and say:

'I will piss on you, you big monster, and then I will feed you to my dog.'

Alex would start to get tremors and run away as soon as he could. But he tended to forget instantly what happened. So he would go on and then find an obituary, usually placed on the door of the building where the deceased lived or on a tree or at a local public transport station.

Life was a sort of strange entrapment for Alex Dimitrov. Fortunately, he did not realize most of the things happening around him. He just lived on short-reflex activity actions. Telephone books, memorial services, cemeteries and funerals, bars and cafes, collection of strange and meaningless facts, clapping, and God knows what when he was alone in the privacy of his own home. He had his bubble, which you could not penetrate even if you wanted to. The worst thing is that his parents didn't give a flying f**k about it all. To them, he was just their boy, a big bulky plush toy you could take around and let loose occasionally in the city. They stopped being ashamed of not getting him proper treatment long ago. As the Pink Floyd song goes, they stopped caring and became comfortably numb.

In any case, in the vast services of today's emerging information technologies, you have to take one step back and say: 'Do I need the telephone book?' Maybe not, but people like Alex Dimitrov need this incredible book of facts as their survival food. You probably will never look at the white pages the same way again, knowing that there are Dimitrovs around, people whose whole life centers around things like that. And the world would be different without Alex and people like him. What would we do without people like Alex Dimitrov, our Brain Man?

2

100% Recycled

Recycling, waste management, and your old-fashioned-everyday garbage collection and awareness were not strong terms in those days when we were kids. People didn't care too much about these things, such as nature conservation, sustainability or eco-recycling, except for getting the bloody stink out of your house, the household waste, sometimes in any way possible. All of the recycling terminology, technique, and action came in the later days. But all of that doesn't mean that the waste was not disposed of. No, Sir, it sure was.

Separation of waste, a wholly foreign and unpronounceable word, was not considered, not at all. On the contrary, everything was being taken away, paper, glass, metal, household waste, etc. All of it is disposed of as one type of garbage. Separation was still in the sphere of future studies and science fiction in the line of deep space explorations. And we know at what stage that was. Nobody gave a shit about it, even those people that called themselves the protectors of nature and defenders of ecological balance and green survival. Those pricks were the worst ones. They had a triple moral when it came to waste. They were all bullshit and sweet talk on the outside, while on the inside incredible consumption, debris, and non-environmental disposal of garbage.

Now the big question you may ask yourself is: 'How did the garbage disappear?' There was a working force; people were getting paid for it and earning their daily bread. I can tell you that not too many people wanted to do this. Shit pay, lousy working hours, the stench penetrating every pore in your body, short vacation, no pension plans, social security, medical coverage nonexistent in this horrible profession. But still, it was a way to be employed and respectably earn dough, for some at least. And the most excellent kick was to drive the garbage truck if you had your driver's license. This was one of the reasons that diseases never developed. There were always these guys doing their jobs. There were challenging periods, especially during the hot summers when the garbage people decided to strike. Oh shit! When all kinds of household waste garbage pile up at 35-40 degrees, you can imagine what can happen. Suddenly you get whole new generations of Musca Domestica, or houseflies, reproduced by thousands. This new army of 'space invaders' is always in numbers when the shit hits the fan. Oh, but they were nothing. You get used to them hanging and walking on windowpanes, on your furniture, being a part of your household – becoming your very own pet.

In contrast with dogs, cats, birds, and household mice, this one does not need care, affection, worry, or food. They will find food themselves. Perfect companions, ha! Well, the household fly was OK, but the real problem was the whole families of these f**king blowflies, not blowjob flies. These buggers were mean sons of bitches. They all had these silver, bronze, and green metallic bodies, like Roman centurions, and made horrible sounds like airplanes before dropping bombs. This family included screwworms, bluebottle flies, green-bottle flies, cluster flies, and God knows what more. We were deprived of most of these family members, but we had some. And this is just the f**king predator-parasite aerial population. The ground forces, like sewer, tunnel, and construction rats – our proud and joy-junkyard dogs, lost. Wild cats, and all other small, medium, and significant members of the f**ked up part of the animal kingdom, would find great pastures and temporary residences during garbage crises. The rats already had permanent residency. They were legal squatters in many respects and considered the construction site on the side of the building their paradise turf. Fortunately enough, the outbreak of the garbage problem didn't happen very often, but when it did, it was messy.

As I said, this was not a pleasant job, not by a long shot. Waking up early, riding on the shitty trucks, getting back and having hernia problems, and if you were lucky, understanding the gypsy language. Most of the garbage collectors – the spring boys – were "gypsies" (called the Roma population today of course) anyway. The only Kings in this job, if there were any, were the guys behind the wheel. They had to operate all the controls of waste lifting and crushing, but they isolated themselves from the stench and shit around them. The garbage trucks were constructed in such a fashion to 'eat & crush' all types of garbage remains and then dispose of them at waste transfer stations and then to landfills. A driver and one or two loaders serve each collection vehicle. These were typically trucks of the enclosed, compact type, with capacities of up to 30 cubic meters. In this case, the loading was done from the rear. In this compact way, the volume of the shit in the truck was reduced to less than half of its loose book. They took the small trash containers with a unique scoop, which also brought all other bags, emptied them, and then started 'chewing' them. It was not rare that they got busted at the time due to the crushing equipment hitting concrete or other impossible stuff being thrown into the garbage by some Neanderthal.

We had our legal team of solid waste management collectors, and one knew the guys after a couple of visits. It was usually the driver and three guys hanging on the truck. The driver was one big mean guy which we only knew as Frank. The hanging guys were Zeke, Ivan, and Pablo. You had to have a translator when they started talking. Ivan was the one that boasted about his education. It seems he had two years of high school oriented toward educating and preparing people to be garbage collectors, gravediggers, and animal control officers. Good grief! Why do you need two years of school for these jobs? They always made incredible noises while collecting the garbage. Garbage was collected and taken away at least 1-2 a week. They never came more than two times.

Only when the decomposing process was unbearable, in the summertime especially, they popped up three times. The system was that the garbage was collected from silverish containers in the disposal rooms. The whole garbage system in the skyscraper was a combination of a considerable garbage tunnel with hatches, going on throughout the entire building and ending up in this room with moving containers. The tunnel was situated in a concrete hatch, not tightly pressed to it but done more loosely. The local cleaning staff of the skyscraper (which consisted of one person) would move around these 2-3 containers until they became full. By that time, our waste pals would take the shit away. The channel-tunnel garbage system was standard for skyscrapers and worked well. It was designed so that you should know how and for what to use it. But some people never learn, do they?

I remember somebody throwing complete bed madras into the trash tunnel. How stupid can you get, for God's sake? The madras got stuck on the 8th floor, probably 'flying' one or two stories. Nobody noticed until the garbage started piling up. Somebody triggered the alarm when it was packed, and you couldn't open the tunnel shaft lock on the 15th floor. In the meantime, whole colonies of insects began to occupy the premises, and the stench could turn your insides out. Those lazy bastards responsible for this couldn't take their fat butts down and properly dispose of this. To make things even worse, somebody set the whole thing on fire. All right, hurray for humanity! It was a warm July Saturday morning. Somehow you were trying to get over the stench in the hallway. The responsible real estate firm and the property and building block manager promised that things would be shortly taken care of. Yeah right! Take care of my ass! Nothing was ever done here. When the elevators got f**ked up, you had to wait days for the assholes to arrive.

As soon as you entered the hallway, there was a combo of smoke and stench. Damn strange! Even the visibility was getting low. Holy f**k – the building was on fire! That was the first thing on everybody's mind. The panic erupted immediately. In this situation, just as in the case of an earthquake or another natural or manufactured disaster, you see how folks behave. Everybody looks after his/hers own ass. Nobody gives a shit about anybody else. People were already piling up in the corridors, stairs, and elevators. Lots of shouting, yelling, swearing, and panic in general; Suddenly, one could hear a shriek that carried through the stair and elevator shaft throughout 18 floors: 'Calm, calm, the skyscraper is not burning, it's the damn garbage tunnel.' It was our very own president of the council of tenants (of our skyscraper), Mr. Arno 'the cockroach' Stockhouse. Everybody despised this slimy character, but somebody had to do this job. God knows that nobody wanted a part of this. He, on the other hand, thrived in his leadership position. It was his life, his everything. 'Get back to your apartments and stop shouting. I need a couple of good men to assemble on the 8th floor. That's where the fire is.

Each floor was equipped with a fire extinguishing hose. So the hydrophore, which was pumping water to the upper levels, had to work all the time perfectly. So it did. The assembled men took control of the job under the great general Stockhouse, who was directing, screaming, and shrieking simultaneously. 'Common, you cream puffs, you rookies – you can do better than that. When I was in the wars, we went right into the fire with our bare hands. 'Shut the f**k up, you little dingleberry freakazoid! If you don't, God helps me if I don't shove your skinny rodent ass down this shaft right this minute', screamed Al Durant, our local crook, hoodlum, and small-time mobster. Arno Zontag was a mouse. But most of all, he was terrified of Al. 'No, no, you are doing just great, fantastic as a matter of fact,' whispered Arno in an almost crying voice. The fire was being extinguished. Hoses worked on several other floors, pouring water down the trash channel. Finally, the fire was extinguished. The trash was somehow pushed down, and the madras, what was left of it, was taken out. The people were black from the smoke and completely wet. Everybody was pissed off and ready to eat alive the retards and crack brains who did this. Even calls for the Police were heard. This was the five minutes that Arno had waited for. The victory was achieved, and Arno felt like Napoleon at Austerlitz – a complete victor! The funny thing is that nobody called the fire department. Well, nobody would believe them anyway. The fire brigades were going to be engaged in a slightly different on another occasion. It seemed that things were under control for now. Arno calmed everybody, promised fast results and revenge, and justice would be served. I am not sure what he meant by 'or another.' Maybe we should all punch in with money and get a hitman to delete these, as he called them, 'worthless slime' off the face of the earth. He was already shouting and calling for retribution, penalties, punishment for crimes against the collective goods and society, and God knows what more. He didn't add the gulags, guillotine, or chamber, though. Zontag wanted blood; somebody had to pay for all of this. Everybody knew it would be just a matter of time until the cockroach man exposed the perpetrators of this, as he called it, 'hideous crime.' It wasn't good, but you shouldn't hang somebody for it. As I said, he worked on it, and people finally confessed. It was never revealed who it was, but as Zontag was a cunning small-time negotiator and relentless collector of fees for the building expenses, he squeezed money from them for all repairs and even more. But he also kept the information in a priestly, confidant manner. He also did a post-analysis of the happenings, being once a piss-ant cop, and discovered that the bed madras was the initial reason for this but that somebody threw a cigarette, which ignited thrown newspapers and then moved to the madras. The flames then engulfed the rest of the garbage, especially the PVC trash bags. God knows how he came to this conclusion, but everybody welcomed it to eliminate his silly investigation. If he felt like Napoleon before, he felt like Inspector Colombo now. He was at the top of the world. He also found the guilty party for the cigarette crime in no time. That part was a real tough one – but he managed it. Of course, nobody confessed, but the bills were paid, everything was fixed, and Arno felt so good. Fortunately, with some defects, the whole garbage shaft construction survived miraculously. Nobody cared for these defects as long as the shaft was operational, but they would play a significant role in what would happen later. Unfortunately, this was not the end. This was the beginning of the future.

A year or two after this incident came the final blow for the channel tunnel. It sounds like the one between France and England; this one was submerged, too!

The garbage collectors were at their usual place. It was a warm day, full of f**king flies and all kinds of garbage. Frank, the driver, was listening to his favorite country song on the radio. Ivan was approaching the job scientifically while Zeke and Pablo threw garbage into the truck so that all kinds of shit spilled on the pavement. Suddenly, an incredible roar filled the tunnel and the collection room. Everybody looked up. A colossal concrete block came tumbling down the tunnel and crashed into one of the containers. Soon after, a meteorite shower of concrete blocks, pieces, and construction material followed. 'What the f**k is this?' proclaimed Pablo. 'Cock sucking mother f**king sons of bitches', added so elegantly Zeke. Their language was constructed solely on swear words and some nouns and verbs they picked up along the way. Frank came out of the truck. 'What's happening? F**k, I can't even finish my tune in peace. You guys, you always have to f**k it up for me.'

'It's not us, the boss; it's some dirtball throwing concrete through the shaft. I don't f**king believe it, exclaimed Ivan amazingly. 'F**king slime, no good blancos throwing their shit on our turf.' Zeke was pissed off.

And now came the thunder of something collapsing, crunching, and being separated from the main body. The whole inner metal shaft of the tunnel was breaking into two. A massive piece of it collapsed, and the other blocked the tunnel. Later it would be discovered that another huge of concrete broke the inner shaft in two and was hopelessly stuck in a newly created internal post. It was a complete mess. The tube was already damaged after the fire was completely screwed up this time. Nobody could fix this mess.

'Let's get the son of a bitch!' said Frank angrily. Everybody made a run for the building. They got in, and Frank took the elevator while our three musketeers ran for the stairs. Eighteen floors – they didn't care. They had to get him. While they were running, Hanes Grubber, the taxi driver, continued to dump the construction material on the 11th floor. He was breaking up one of his walls in the apartment and doing some redecorating at the same time. Instead of dumping this in a proper place, he was throwing it into the shaft. It would have been better to leave it through the window onto the semi-abandoned construction site. Hanes was a tall, slightly overweight man with pale blue-gray hair departing from his skull increasingly. He had big hands with rock-hard fingers and nails, developed through generations of peasant ancestors working in the fields. Hi, was your 100% Bauer (peasant)? Driving a cab in the city and an urban setting didn't help me that much. The primitive genes of a couple of hundred years back did their tool. Even our garbage people had more urban brains than this guy.

Zeke and Pablo were approaching the Noise Hanes was making. Ivan was a couple of steps back. They all arrived on the 11th floor panting. Frank stepped out of the elevator and saw Hans approaching the shaft with a whole load of concrete on his wheelbarrow.

Now, this thing pissed off the guys. This guy was not stopping. Hanes looked at them in bewilderment, but when they started shouting and swearing, I think that is when some small watt bulb flicked on in Hanes's brain.

'You f**king worm, I'll f**k you up so bad that even your stupid cow mother won't recognize you,' screamed Pablo. Zeke added: 'You slimy vanilla trash. I will piss on your stinky bold head and show these wheelbarrows into your megaderm ass!'

'F**k you, gypsy man. You stinky piece of latrine shit lips'. What you going to do, you little worthless man?' Grubber was now looking fiercely at them. This was the last drop in the cup. The guys threw themselves onto Grubber. Zeke got such a blow into the head that he flew a couple of meters and crashed into the staircase railings. Pablo hit Hanes in the stomach, but he was like a stone. He took a piece of concrete and slammed it into Pablo. He fell in pain. Ivan jumped onto Hanes and started to wrestle him. That was a challenging task. Grubber was on top of him in seconds, choking him ferociously. Frank saw all of this as he came from the small elevator. He was approaching Hanes from a passage behind him. Not much time to think. He saw a steel pipe lying on the concrete floor. This was part of the old plumbing system in Grubber's apartment.

He took the bar and came behind Grubber, standing tall above Ivan and holding a concrete block over him. He, in the heat of the lunatic moment, wanted to crush the guy. Frank acted swiftly and slammed, with all his might, the steel bar on Hanes's back and head. He just fell like a concrete block.

Now the tenants were starting to come out. There was shouting: 'Police, call the police.'

'Get up, you sissies, and let's throw this piece of shit into the garbage. The guys were lifting with considerable pain. Frank and Zeke, whose head was pounding like an incoming freight train, dragged him to the big elevator. He was more or less in dreamland now.

When they took him out, he was showed in one of the small containers in the garbage room. The tunnel was history now. They dragged the container out and positioned it in front of the forklifts of the scoop at the back of the garbage truck. Hanes was coming to his senses now. 'What the f**k… What are you doing, ass holes?' Assholes ha! You will see motherf**ker! Frank put the automatic stuff in motion. The police were approaching now. Hanes started yelling and screaming now, and as the forks lifted the container and Hanes fell into the scoop, he started begging too: 'No please, don't crush me, no please don't.'

'Eat this motherf**ker, screamed Pablo as Hanes crashed into the waiting garbage. Now the scoop was lifting him and getting ready to shove him into the 'crushing zone.' You can imagine the terror and fear on Hanes's face. Frank said: 'Now you die motherf**ker!' He pressed the scoop button but didn't press the crushing mechanism. Hanes landed with screams, and he was sure he was becoming recycled refuse. Frank laughed wildly, followed by Pablo and Zeke. Ivan was explaining to the police officers, which just arrived, what had happened. The whole situation was comical. They got him out of the truck, entirely in a state of chock. After much hassle, they all went to the police station, and things were more or less cleared out. He was charged with destroying public property, and the attempted murder charges were stricken. Our trash guys got off too. They were even considered heroes in our skyscraper community. Everybody hated Grubber from then on. Ass hole paid for some damages but got off others on technicalities.

The worse thing was that the channel was so damaged that it was abandoned. After a couple of tries to fix it was all over. The result was that the trash channel was closed until further notice. That further notice became an eternity. The stench was so foul because the trash was not cleared. Folk threw garbage for days after the incident. The shaft doors on each floor, which were in a small room, were welded, and the rooms bolted. And that was the end of that. Initially, there were complaints, but later, people went with the flow. God knows what kinds of species of the animal kingdom were thriving in the sealed-up tunnel. One could get/smell a glimpse of that by just taking the garbage into the container room. Holy flies! You must get in underwater and hold your breath as long as possible. Our trash guys got unique masks for collecting shit in our building. Well, from now on, you must think about how much garbage and waste you will produce during the week. The more you did, the more often you visited the smelly kingdom.

3

The Street Hawk

His sharp eyes were focused on the environment below him. He was passing over the last remnants of the deep forest and mountain hillsides. Security and home were behind him now. There was always a chance to turn back, but the hunger was more robust. He felt sure of himself. Flying so high, one almost felt invincible. Civilization was getting closer now. Stacks of chimneys were appearing below him. Roads, telegraph poles, high voltage cables, traffic, and people were all becoming more apparent now. Suddenly he saw it. Not because they were the only or the highest ones but because they were ahead of him on his flight path. Four tall, yellowish skyscrapers in front of him and, by the looks of it – full of flying defenseless food! This was going to be a treat. It was worthwhile leaving the grandfathers' homes, if only for a while. He descended on the nearest skyscraper and took the highest peak on the ledge, just under the ceiling roof of the attic windows. And he waited…

As children, and I must admit, as adults, too, we have an incredible inner urge to fly. There is such unbelievable magic and beauty in it. To reach up where you don't belong, to go higher and higher straight above, further and further into the sky and the sun. It's no secret that many of us have constant reoccurring dreams of flying, namely that we can fly like birds, airplanes, choppers, or Superman. Who could forget Greek mythology and Icarus, son of the inventor Daedalus, who perished by flying too near the Sun with waxen wings? Even though the poor bastard expired, and that was his fault for flying too close to our shining star, it still is a fascination of just doing it. So even more, the incredible passion for flying creatures like birds may be one of the animal kingdom's most perfect and beautiful specimens. One of these Street birds was the city or street pigeon. This lovely but still shitty bird nested year-round on buildings and beneath bridges. They were a nuisance, a significant pain in the ass with their shit droppings and not-so-rare disease transmission. People used to call them flying rats. These sturdy birds may reach to live 35 years.

In other words, you could not get rid of them that easily. But you got used to them anyway. The domestic pigeon, as it was often called, or in Latin Columba Livia, is not a bird without history or tradition. I remember reading books about Mesopotamia from 3500 BC. You could find these buggers on various artifacts, coins, figurines, tablets, etc. They were also used throughout history as messengers and God knows what else. Food was also another thing they were suitable for, or so the ones that tried say. I doubt our city or skyscraper blue-gray pigeons were an excellent dish. Eating all kinds of shit and carrying God knows what kind of bacteria was not a good prerequisite for HQ dish.

Nonetheless, they existed and, on many occasions, presented a nuisance, not just in the dropping division but also in the vast numbers. Well, you know how the Darwin theory goes, and the evolution of species, especially the fantastic thing of 'the stronger eats, the weaker,' simplifying matters here now. So, at least temporarily, the 'judgment day' came for our domestic friends.

When I mentioned flying and the elegance of the craft, I was not necessarily referring to pigeons. Other beautiful creatures include the majestic American white eagle, the most beautiful bird. But there was another very much domestic in our highland parts, the peregrine falcon. This was my favorite bird of prey. Oh, yes, this was your full-blooded predator. This beautiful creature can be found worldwide but has come to the brink of extinction in many parts. Habitat destruction has also played a role in the falcon's population decline.

Fortunately, our forests and mountains had a few of these boys and girls left. If you open any zoology book and find this beautiful creature's description, they will be more or less the same and reflect real life 100%.

It is a gallant bird with bluish gray above, with underparts white to yellowish with black barring. Male peregrines range from about 42 to 47 centimeters, while females can reach up to 52 centimeters long. They are robust, endurable, and fast. His craft-full, almost fighter-like body and fantastic, glistening eyes give an impression of a universal soldier or a hunting machine. They fly fast, often high, and dive at tremendous speeds, with a noisy flapping of wings, striking with clenched talons and killing by impact. You could often hear his war-like recognition yowling, which sounds like 'kayak, kayak. He usually utters these sounds during the mating seasons. His prey includes ducks and shorebirds. That is why he is often called the duck hawk. Well, in our case, it would probably be the pigeon hawk. But I am getting to that. Peregrines inhabit rocky open countries near water where birds are plentiful. The usual nest is a scrape on a ledge high on a cliff. He rarely makes nests in urban areas but will hunt there if forced. The females lay two to four reddish-brown eggs; the young hatch in five or six weeks. He brings fear and fright into every body of winged creatures more petite or his size. He fancies high and dominant places, beacons, where he can control the area and potential victims. As I said, he resides in the forests and mountains around our city but never visits the city itself, maybe only occasionally, but always flying at high altitudes.

It was a rainy April, dark and shadowy gray for most of the time. It was one of those days when you could barely see one of our sister skyscrapers, not even the one adjacent to us. On one of these days, it must have been late afternoon, dusk almost, I get a call from my pal on the 15th floor, just one floor below me. Keke Tollberg looked like a red-haired Scott. His older brother Talis Tollberg also had that reddish hair and freckles. They could have well fitted in the highlands of Scotland or under the command of Braveheart. Keke yelled: 'For f**k sake, man, look out your window. You'll never see a bird like that in your life. A f**king eagle it is. It's on the highest peak on the other skyscraper, just beyond the attic windows, on the corner ledge.'

'What eagle, man? There aren't any eagles here,' I replied. 'It has huge wings, and it's bluish gray, but it ain't a f**king pigeon. That I know!' 'Ok, I will look. Stay on the phone, Bro'!

I looked, and there it was. F**king majestic! As the weather was shitty, I took my binoculars to get a better look. Oh, that was no eagle, but something even better, a hawk. Bringing back my knowledge from biology classes, one of my favorites, I remembered the Falco Peregrinus. Man, what a beautiful site. 'Yo, Keke, it's a hawk, and it's called the peregrine falcon.' 'Oh, don't give me these Greek shit names, man. What is it called, actually?'

'Shit, Keke, let's call it the gray killer hawk!'

'Yeah, Keke was getting excited now. I knew this son of a bitch was a killer. Man, he killed one of our f**king flying rats (pigeons). He is on the hunt now! Hurray!

I had never heard Keke so excited before. I could see his head below me. We were both watching him now. He didn't do more hunting that night but continued in the coming weeks.

Unbelievable as it seems, our hawk found a temporary lodging place. He used to go back to the high forests and come back again. Probably the food supplies are what got him so hooked here. And maybe he was preparing for the mating season. Whatever the reason, watching this beautiful bird day in and day out was a blessing. Seeing this creature in flight takes your breath away. He could spot things and movements in a matter of milliseconds. He is always on guard, and when it rains, he puts his head on his shoulders so that his throat disappears completely. Keke and I became his biggest fans and, it seems, the only ones aware of his existence. It suited us just fine. We were jealously protective of our new friend. And hey, he was cleaning the shit for us. The pigeon colony accumulated so many newcomers in their community that they became unbearable. Our hawk was a blessing in disguise. He was there to sustain the Darwinian theory and relieve us of the droppings and mess in the process. He shitted loads, too, you know. But being a gallant knight as he is, his shit seemed to always fall on the right place, on the construction site.

We were watching him on one of these highland rainy days with dark gray puffy cloud cover. Our hunter was standing on the ledge, preparing for the next kill.

A pigeon was flying near our bird; he didn't know better. Not seeing him has come way too close. The hawk opened his enormous wings briefly and stormed the innocent bird. Everything was happening blitz fast! He clutched the pigeon from the back with his paws and never let him go. The poor bird didn't know what hit him. A shrieking sound and flapping of the wings were all heard through the drizzling rain. The hunter, our predator, brought the still struggling but already semi-conscious bird to his ledge corner. The second phase began: the methodic and technological process of killing, dissecting, and consuming this prey. The pigeon's throat was cut, and the hawk cut fast with his sharp beacon to get to the meat parts. The feathers were flying all around and insides of the poor bastard. The brutal ritual was over even before it started. Pieces and leftovers fell to the ground. The hunter was satisfied, but not for long. He took every possible opportunity to make a fast and successful kill. There was no remorse in this guy.

The pigeon community, being extremely stupid, did not fully realize the full magnitude of changes that our friend brought about. He made more or less 30-40 kills in these weeks, sometimes 2-3 pigeons a day. These stupid birds did not realize that at all. But fear was coming in, and community members were disappearing. Sure, they saw all the kills, and when the killing did not stop – DANGER DANGER, GET THE F**k OUT OF HERE – was probably the sentence that started crawling into their tiny, miny bean brains. Maybe they developed Pavlov's conditioned reflex of seeing somebody get killed repeatedly until the logical conclusion would be: 'I am next; run or better fly the f**k away from here!'

The brutal killing continued until they began to comprehend the new, cruel reality on the ground, or shall I say, in the skies. You could almost say that the hawky boy was starting to disturb the natural balance. He was slaughtering these poor bastards by dozens. Although he was not a goose hawk, he rarely went into combat against black ravens. They are somebody you don't want to mess around with too much. They would all gather in flocks to counter-attack if he tried to attack. They would attack fiercely as Admiral Doenitz's submarine wolf pack in the II World War. They would produce all kinds of loud, shrieking gurglings and a sharp metallic 'tok,' calling their brothers in arms to join them in the struggle. This struggle often became a ferocious attack on the hawk, especially if his prey was entangled in his paws. These fearless aerial acrobats were daring when it came to our predators. So basically, he avoided them at any cost.

He has been a member of our community for some weeks now. This was his second season with us. Unfortunately, we did not know at that moment, nor did he, for that matter, that it would be his last. It was again one of those late afternoons but with much more visibility. Keke and I were 'birdwatching,' if you can call it that. It was more like watching Russel Crowe do his gladiator things, though our gladiator was not the defender. He was the attacker. You know the feeling: you can't eat the same food all the time, you need variety, change, surprise, a gourmet dish from time to time.

Most probably, the same thoughts were invading the mind of our flying ace. And the pigeons were not the only dish here. There were the rats too. Of course, our rats, the rats from the construction site.

As you know, this is a damn formidable force to be reckoned with. You don't want to f**k with these guys because they can f**k you back, and it can cost you dearly. The hawk, of course, did not know that he was dealing with a particular rodent colony, especially after his first rat kill, which he had made a couple of weeks ago. It was a medium size rodent, and I would even say a smaller rat that he deleted from the face of the earth. The rat made the mistake of coming out in the open, not staying in the well-protected and hidden part of the site with all the leftover and once-to-be-used construction materials.

He killed the poor bastard in seconds and boldly stayed on the ground. The colony was, of course, watching. As you know, it consisted mainly of gray, black, and Norwegian rats. In other words, the worst possible kind you can have. It's a pity we never had any rat expert come and examine this. It could have been a researcher's wet dream. The other question would be if they would ever get close to these savage inhabitants of the urban wild. Not to mention a whole range of mutants that developed with time. This was an excellent breeding place for these guys. Our urban predator did not know all of that. He was going against a much worse and more cunning kind than his. So Keke and I were watching his late afternoon hunting, looking out from Keke's window. He didn't kill one single pigeon that day. He was getting hungry and restless. That is when mistakes start arriving. Even if the margin of failure and errors was close to zero for our bird friend, there was still time for that first mistake and, unfortunately, a fatal one.

A giant rat was moving between the massive pile of bricks and approaching some abandoned construction tools, steel bars, wires, etc. It was approximately 20cm long, a typical size for our rats. Let me take that back: one of the medium-sized rats in our colony. The biggest ones were monsters 28 to great 35cm long. 40cm was the biggest motherf**ker you have seen, a black rat, which went by the name of Norwegian Dream. At least, that is what we all called him. This was a f**ked up mutant, a combo of black, gray, and Norwegian rats. I don't know how he came to be; probably from some incest, kinky relationship in the underground tunnels. But he was the natural-born killer, your natural Tarantino's reservoir dog.

You can bet your sweet mama he was always on the move close by, in charge of the colony. So it was on this day too. Our hawk saw the grayish shape move slower and approached the semi-open areas. This was it. The hawk decided to storm this nice chunk of meat. Hunger was eating him from the inside. He attacked just right after 17:00 hours. The rain subsided, and one could have a nice view of a beautiful post-rain approaching dusk. But it was still evident enough for us to see what would happen. He threw himself with guiding missile precision from the skyscraper ledge. With semi-folded wings, he descended and opened up just a few meters from the ground. He approached the rat at five o'clock. The rat must have spotted him, but he faced a pile of bricks in front of him, and the back was blocked. So the only way was ahead. But that was open land. The other option was right into the paws of the approaching winged beast. He ran for it and made the crucial mistake of not taking the logical cover of the brick world as tight as it was. Hawk anticipated and awaited this move. He caught him on a bunch of old wires with his sharp nails. The attack was sudden, swift, and deadly. He started attacking him and delivering fatal blows with his beacon. The rat was fighting back, trying to get the f**k out of there. The worst part was the loud squeaking noise that he produced in the process. Believe me, folks; you don't know how this sounds if you haven't seen a rat get killed or were not making the killing. It's just terrible. There was not much to do. This rat was not one of the fighting kind. The hawk was deep in his prey that he did not realize that the time on the ground was getting longer and longer. Nasty stuff, dude! From all of the struggling, he did not know that he was getting increasingly entangled in the wires. Now, something did blink, some backup alarm that he should get out and take the rest of his fat rodent to the ledge. His hoof got caught in a barbed wire protruding from the construction rubble when he was about to lift with his prey. He started to get up ferociously, not letting off his half-dead game. This proved to be fatal. He got more and more entangled in the wire. The hunter became the captive now. Now he was pissed off. The 'kgiak, kgiak' sounds were coming out of him now. A slight moment of DE concentration can cost one dearly. He fell to the ground in the tangle of wires. It's just un-believable how he got himself into this situation. At one point, he lifted partly to be entangled even more.

If one thing our rats have in common, it is a sense of collective reflex. Suddenly rats were protruding everywhere. One of their compadres was dying and bad luck! They didn't give so much shit about it, but there was food here, and it was big. Even though it had wings and looked like a badass wounded samurai, it was worth of attack. They were still hesitant about the flapping bird, but when the leaders of the rat pack started showing up, the collective courage was growing by the minute. The hawk was wearing out more and more. The rats moved in closer now. Hawk was aware of this. His eyes were like a carousel, scanning the area around him. And guess who showed up to lead the army into an attack, the Norwegian Dream. The big motherf**ker emerged suddenly from the considerable brick pile with two rat centurions by his side, two long knives, and a gray and black rat. Both of them measured at least 30cm in length. 'Keke, do you see what I am seeing' I asked in a panicked, excited voice.

'F**k yes, Bro. F**king A! We're in for a battle royal here'. And it was a battle. They attacked suddenly, without remorse or even fear. They were all over him. The medium rats assaulted them from the front while the big guys descended on him from the back and the sides. Norwegian dream was already on his back, known for his incredible climbing and jumping skills. He was cutting through the hawk's body. Hawk managed to give some deadly blows to the gray monsters before him. But, alas, there were two dozen rats all over him. He fought the best he could until the end, pinned down on the ground. What a humiliating lot! The beautiful bird tried to resist with his beacon, talons, and wings. He disposed of a couple of rats, but more were coming. This was Thanksgiving for these rats. More dead compatriots meant more food. The scene looked like when a colony of ants descends on a piece of bread or if a bunch of piranha goes on the attack. No mercy was shown here. The beautiful shining eyes of our predator were getting weary and tired. Life was slowly going out of him. The flapping became less frequent now. There were at least 7-8 dead rats around, but two times more live ones on the hawk. Norwegian Dream and his centurions were killing him off. After a while, it ended. The look in his eyes was gone now. It was just a memory, a dark bliss. The hawk died. We were, as in a dream, totally numb. Usually, we would react and at least throw some bottles at these buggers. I doubt that it would help, but nonetheless. We left to fate to take its course. And it did. The rats were now rejoicing over tons of food. They clawed their way into the bird's insides, and it was party time now. The other dead rats were being taken care of. Not buried, of course, but eaten. We couldn't watch it anymore. It was terrible. He came as a mirage, and he left as one. Unfortunately, he did not leave for better pastures but for darker rat bellies. He ended his life, far away from his natural hill and forest habitat, as pieces of meat and feathers in the dark and terrible tunnels of the rodent kingdom.

He promptly disappeared as quickly as he came from nowhere, from the hills and mountains nearby. A bold, brave, and ferocious highlander would never have believed such a destiny would await him. To disappear amid a stinky and shitty construction site, killed by a pack of dirty rodents, and, even worse, killed on the ground. He would have never dreamed of that. But if you want to f**k with natural balance too much and if you want even more, more than you should take, then destiny and Mother Nature could be cruel to you. Our hawk has learned that lesson. Unfortunately, he can only use it in the land of the dead or wherever the souls of the dead birds end up. His guardian day & night stance position on the corner ledge of the skyscraper will never be forgotten. Indeed, our streets or skies would never be the same again.

4

Luke the Nightwalker

He couldn't remember what it felt like. It was a terrible headache that felt like a sledgehammer slamming in never-ending shifts. His temples were pounding like a freight train on a course for a significant collision. The painkillers were wearing off more and more. The damn pills couldn't keep it together for a couple of hours. Sleep was just a good memory. Sure, he never got enough sleep. The job mainly was day and night shifts, but it was always reasonable and healthy when sleep came. Oh, how he longed for that telephone call in the early morning. 'We got another body Luke…it seems they are holding hostages…they cleaned the whole place up… The car was left some 5 miles from the scene…can you come down.' He would be out of his pajamas, kiss his wife goodbye and run for his car.

Downtown life was Luke's life. Sure, it was disgusting: rape, murder, robberies, drugs, etc., but that was the kick; that was what brought life to his veins, and that was what he was so good at. And that was all over. F**king retirement and such pension. Now he couldn't sleep, headaches were all over him, nightmares and fears. There was no time for these useless sensations while he was on the job.

There was no time to think about that. He was a complete power machine, always on call, always ready, never late, and never weak. Prozac! What kind of f**king name is that? Damn pills. He only knew about aspirins on the job. And there was nothing more. You swallow a couple of the police coffee and are set to go. Now the shrink tells him:

'Luke, you need o take 2 Prozacs a day. Then we will cut it down to one if you feel better.

His doctor, Harry Kislow, is a significant wimp and pain in the ass; if you ask, Luke explained the headaches many times to him.

'You have, what we say in the medical profession, a sporadic episode of headaches. They occur only irregularly. But the ones you have are not mild, as in most cases, they are. Your pain results from distension of the extracranial arteries or sustained contraction of the face and neck muscles.

Luke would stop him at that moment and say:

'Talk English for f**k sake, doc'!

Harry would blush all over, and his already long, pointed red nose, elliptic spectacles resting on it, would become even more reddish, like a fresh red Hungarian paprika.

'Well…hmm…simply saying, such headaches often arise from fatigue, mental stress, or aggravation. You feel frustration, resentment and, anxiety, even depression. I have seen and noted all these symptoms in you. This emotional situation in your life, retirement, your wife leaving you after so many years, and a daughter with problems have brought about worse headaches than you had before. Aspirins don't help, and your headaches have become worse. They've become chronic daily headaches occurring daily. But as I said, due to all the happenings in your life, the most common cause is a psychological one. As I felt anger, deepening depression, and frustration in you lately, I have put you also on Prozac, an antidepressant that can also treat chronic headaches. So this should help you get all the other painkillers out of your system. Don't forget that excessive use of these might have caused these prolonged chronic headaches.'

Luke has heard all of this before. And somewhere in his mind, he agreed with the doc. He was right. His life was a mess now. Everything was f**ked up. And it could get only worse. What the hell was he supposed to do with his life now? The streets and heat of the night were everything to him. This gave him a nickname in the force, Luke 'Nightwalker.' Now all of that was gone like a bubble of soap.

Luke Petrowsky was one of those people you never notice so much in everyday life but still have a sense that they are always present. Luke fits into the category of invisibly current tenants. He was a retired cop with a cheap gold-plated wristwatch and an average pension to show for it. He was medium height, highly fit 65-year old, gracefully bolding guy. Two large patches of gray hair were left on the sides. A very sharp nose and almost cat-like blue eyes were the two most significant facial features that Luke possessed. His earthly possessions consisted of a wife and a daughter (both gone from his life now), an old Fiat, two bedroom apartment, and his pride and joy, a 357 Magnum. Although 357 was not your everyday standard police equipment, Luke liked to have this weapon for household protection. When he worked, he always carried his Sig Sauer P228. He was one of the highest decorated cops on the force. There was a whole cupboard filled with medals and commendations that he had received performing in the line of duty for more than 30 years and always stayed on a detective level. He could have quickly risen in the ranks if it was not for his short temper and continuous lust for street work. He despised the desk and paperwork. His partners had to do this job. His world was his instinct, methodical police-investigating brain, long experience, animal reflexes, and holster. Sharp and brutal at times, but the job was always done. Even if it were a challenging case, he would work on it until it was cracked. One hundred thirteen instances in his career, all salved one way or another. But his personal life suffered in the end.

The wife left some 10-12 years before retirement. She couldn't take it anymore. They lost each other for years. Luke was unaware of that until she said it was over one day. She left him for a post office clerk, a wonderful caring person who fulfills all my needs, as she used to say. He was mad at hell and wouldn't have it. A couple of beatings worsened it, and court orders prevented him from coming close to her.

That was all...or was it. Some strange rumors were going around the building, mainly initiated by the "BBC World Service" (as we used to call the cotton-picking old retired girls' gossip network headed by Norissa Guzinski) that he was forced into early retirement. Excessive force, the problem with nerves, they say...who knows. Maybe the episode with the wife has contributed to that. The only daughter left home early at 18, never returning to her folks. She got into bad company, alcohol, crack, and petty theft. Luke helped her several times, trying to put her back on the right track, but it never worked. The wife blamed Luke for this too. He was now alone and forgotten. The headaches were there during duty years, but now they were unbearable. Now they would not go away.

Luke was the 18th-floor tenant. The attic floor was the only thing separating the 18th-floor tenants from the flat roof. Every tenant, that is, every apartment, had a shed in the attic (floors 10 to 18) or the cellar (floors mezzanine to 9). People usually store their old things there, such as furniture, old unwearable clothes, broken toys, and different kinds of shit and useless junk.

The attic was a maze of passages. To find your shed, you had to be Sherlock Holmes. Even Theseus would have more problems there than in Minotaur's labyrinth. Luke somehow thought it was his duty to be in charge of building security, which meant the "shed security," too. Security…Hmm…It would be difficult to imagine what possibly valuable could be stolen from the sheds. And even if somebody took that task upon him, he would probably call for help after being lost in the shed labyrinth. Poor bastard would be scared to shit, especially at nighttime when the attic was worse than the interior of the pyramids at Gizeh.

Be as it may, Luke took his job seriously. He controlled the locks regularly, the staircase steel bar door, and the attic entrance door. It was the only access to the attic as the elevators just went to the 18th floor. Maybe this work was his active duty again, even if it was only "security." It was better than drowning oneself in the bottle. At least the headaches would go away for a while. This would be a distant dream and remnant of the good old street days and the heat of the nights. Luke belonged to the pavements and city nights. Posted in front of the TV was not his idea of active life. At least the self-imposed security duties were something. He did this job voluntarily. This suited the council of tenants perfectly, especially its 'eternal' president, Arno Zontag, a small-time-small-town retired patrol cop. He envied Luke before, but now he was delighted that he was the man on top. But that was about it because Arno feared Luke and was terrified of him now when he was going through physical and psychological problems.

A friend from the 3rd floor Mike Gleisch and a couple of his friends decided to fix their bikes and mopeds in the attic on a fine afternoon in mid-August. They thought it was a perfect place for such a job. A couple of well-lighted connecting openings were among the maze of corridors and sheds. Quiet, no disturbances, they thought. Oh man...were they wrong.

Mike and his buddies brought the bikes in the afternoon and continued working into nightfall. In those days, it was a tremendous passing leisure activity; owning these bikes meant getting closer and getting the best babes. So the guys wanted to have their machines in the best possible shape.

Mike and his folks had a shed in the attic, which automatically entitled them to a key. So the whole group came in legally, opening the attic bolted door and entrance. They locked it meticulously after them.

So he worked with his friends near his shed on a larger opening in one of the mazes. They cleaned the bikes, changed some parts, and even took one moped apart. It looked like a scene from one of the MC biker movies. They even spilled some oil in the process, but they would take care of that later. Here you could yell and talk as loud as you wanted. Nobody could hear you downstairs, or so they thought.

Luke had already checked the locks on the doors to the attic earlier in the day, double-checked, and probably triple-checked. He didn't know about 'Mike and the mechanics' because they arrived a little later. And even if he had heard voices, it was customary for people to visit their sheds occasionally. So Luke retired to his apartment for the day. The headaches were back and pounding in a big way. A nice glass of sherry and some fisherman's beef could take mind of things. One thing must be said about Luke. He had a superb sense of hearing. This was a quality that helped him so many times in police work. It saved his partners' life once. When he was getting ready to watch his favorite late show on TV, a new episode of Miami Vice with Don Johnson, he suddenly heard some muffled noises above him. 'Strange,' he said, 'I must be imagining!' But after a while, he heard something that resembled thumping and loud footsteps. This was such a distant noise but to Luke's extrasensory hearing, prominent and close indeed.

'Somebody's walking up there.' 'What if it's a burglar or maybe a pyromaniac or, even worse, a terrorist'!

'I must be f**king imagining.' He returned to his program and the tray with the food in front of him.

'F**k, I am starting to imagine things. Maybe I am going out of my f**king mind'. He swallowed one more Prozac and a couple of painkillers. He was becoming a severe painkiller addict by now.

After a while, he suddenly looked up and saw a tiny yellow patch on the ceiling.

'What the f**k is that? I just repainted the damn thing a couple of days ago.

Was he thinking again as a cop now...or was he? Whatever he was thinking, he was thinking fast. He heard the sounds again. The patch on the ceiling was getting slightly more prominent. 'I am not f**king crazy. There's some motherf**ker upstairs.'

He ran to his bedroom, took out and loaded his 357 Magnum, took two pairs of handcuffs, and quickly went for the door. He was out the door and towards the attic in seconds, making no sounds. He knew the attic as his back pocket. If you wanted somebody to guide you through the mazes, Luke was your man.

'It is like being back on the force again,' Luke thought. His 357 Magnum was firmly in his hand. He entered the half-dark mazes. Small patches of sweat were breaking on his hardened face. His small blue eyes were adapting to the dark fast. He looked like a cat on the prowl. He had Nike's on and was sweating underneath his short-sleeved blue polo shirt. 'It's been a long. I am not the same Luke anymore. Shit, my brain is all messed up. No more time for thinking. I got to act now.'

He could hear voices now. They were coming from the intersection on the right.

'There's more of them, a whole gang, maybe? I'll bust their asses', Luke said quietly to himself. He knew all the shortcuts, and he had the advantage of surprise on his side. While Luke was approaching, Mike and his friends were smoking and taking sips of beer at intervals. They were talking more loudly now.

Luke slowly approached the small opening where Mike and his three friends worked on the bikes. He heard some mechanical sounds, making him believe they were robbing the sheds. It was time for action. 'F**king bastards, looting the honest people's properties. I will show you....' He could see now the opening and all the 'perpetrators.' He counted four. One of them seemed familiar. 'It must be one of the assholes I busted once. He must be out of the joint. The f**king system, letting out these f**kers on the loose.' It was Mike that he recognized, not as a criminal element, but as a neighbor's son. The problem was that the pills were taking control of Luke's brain. He was back on the streets and alleys. He was after the bad guys. This was his life. Luke was now waiting for the right moment. Suddenly he jumped from the dark corridor and pointed the gun toward the guys.

'Put your hands in the air, assholes, or I'll blow your f**king brains out,' Luke shouted commandingly. They were utterly taken by surprise and scared as shit. Still, with a steel wrench in his hand, Mike started to say something, but Luke cut him off: "If you don't put your weapon down, I'll send you to La-La land before you know it." He didn't even recognize him. He was entirely in another world now. He was making a bust, and he was the man in charge. Mike started to say: Mr. Petrowsky, it's me, Mike, from the 3rd floor, don't you remember?'

'From the 3rd floor of the state prison, sure I remember, I put you there, you son of a bitch. And now you are out and robbing again. No more, you and your Markie grass-heads are going down.' He was entirely in another world, a world of his own. The shirt was all wet, and he was looking wildly, ready any moment to shoot.

'Down on the floor, you bastards, and lower your weapons,' screamed Luke. The weapons were wrenches and screwdrivers.

One of Mike's friends, Ricky Salgado, was not going down that easy. He was a tough MC guy who thought Luke was just another f**king old pisser. Knowing they were dealing with a seriously disturbed individual, Mike and his friends did what they were told.

'I am not going down the floor, jerk! Go home, man. Try not to miss the toilet bowl when you are pissing tonight'. Ricky was holding a big screwdriver that looked like a knife, glistening in the subdued light of the attic neon lamps.

'What did you call me, you f**king skunk maggot? Luke was blazing with fury. Mike jumped in: 'Mr. P., he doesn't know that you are a cop.' 'A cop, you mean to tell me this old hag is a pig.' 'Hey, old pig, I bet that gun isn't even loaded, ha! 'Shut the f**k up, Ricky,' shouted Mike. Ricky was waving the screwdriver toward Luke. 'I am not kissing the ground for you, pig. You made a big mistake.

'Down on the ground, I am warning you. I will shoot.'

'F**k you, asshole.' Luke was in total blind rage now. How could this piece of shit insult him in such a way?

Bastards like these were responsible for his daughter's screwed-up life. He has been putting these characters behind bars all his life. And now this punk was ordering him around. Ricky started approaching now, and that was the mistake. Seeing the screwdriver and a big guy approaching him, Luke aimed the gun at Ricky, and the whole room exploded from a gunshot sound. Ricky fell in terrible pain. The bullet went clear through Ricky's right arm. As Luke's hands were shaking, so were his aiming skills. 'Oh for f**k sake, you shot him, man,' screamed one of Ricky's buddies.

'This wouldn't have happened if you just did what I said. I was just about to read you your Miranda rights, and you f**kers had to start it, didn't you? Now shut the f**k up, go down on the ground, or I swear I will kill every one of you.'

They instantly threw themselves down, putting their hands behind their back. Luke threw the handcuffs on the floor and told Mike to cuff his friends and then himself onto the pipes used for heating. Mike tried explaining that they were fixing their bikes and pleading with Luke again, but there was no reasoning with this guy. "How dare you speak to me, asshole? You even stole all these bikes." Ricky was screaming and bleeding at the same time.

'Shut up, or I will aim better next time.' All of them were terrified and in a state of shock. When he was sure they couldn't escape, he went downstairs to his apartment and called the police. He was so proud of himself, and a retired cop made the bust with no backup.

The police were already on the way. Someone called them when they heard the shot. Paramedics were on the way too.

The police arrived and checked the identity of the 'perpetrators.' The detective on site was a young rookie in Luke's days, Malcolm Pace. The paramedics took care of Ricky and took him to the hospital. The others were taken downtown. Luke was taken in for questioning. He was more than glad to go. When they checked everything out, especially when Mike's dad came up, and the bike's registrations matched, Luke's mistake was obvious, so they let the guys go. In other words, Luke f**ked up. Mike's dad was upset like hell, but they calmed him down. Being a good neighbor, he did not press charges, but the others did, especially Ricky's parents. They didn't go as far as taking him to court, but he had to pay all the medical bills and a hell of a fine. Community service was also a prerequisite for staying out of jail. As Malcolm and, more or less, the whole police core knew Luke well, they went easy on him. They took the gun away, and he was now ordered to get psychiatric help. He ended up spending a couple of months in the local nut house.

The guys were called to clean the mess and the oil they spilled. Luke came back as a half-vegetable from the nut house.

From then on, Luke was his usual self. He was much calmer and much more at peace with himself. Or it seemed on the surface. At times, he seemed like an old volcano, ready to return to life with a vengeance. The shed duty was abandoned. Luke did not seem to mind at all. The only sane thing he did was redirect the stairwell traffic during the burning inferno incident when he acted as the in-house cop. A few years passed after that, and the neighbors heard a gunshot from his apartment one day. Later he was found in front of the TV, holding the family photo from earlier happy days. It was Luke, his wife, and his daughter vacationing in Greece. Where did he go wrong? These were most probably his last thoughts. He left his gold-plated watch on the desk beside him and three photos of his partners throughout the good old police days. No letter, no explanation. None was needed. He blew his head clean off with his favorite Sig Sauer hidden in his apartment. It seemed that he was now finally at peace with himself.

5

Aerial Garlic

For construction and principles of fundamental structural theories, staircases, and elevator shafts in skyscrapers were usually placed in the core of the building. Such was the case with our tower and the three adjacent ones. This, in a sense, represented the very heart of the building. Unfortunately, the whole core was supplied with artificial lightning except for the 18th floor, which had a skylight above it. The entrée hall and the first two floors got some natural light while the rest of the skyscraper core was a light bulb and neon paradise. The elevators were, of course, used more often than the staircases. Only in the case of natural and artificial disasters, power shortages, repairs, illegal and sales activities, and other things were staircases the main lifeline. For folks living on the mezzanine and the first two floors, elevators didn't mean much, although even the mezzanine people used them on certain occasions. There were two of them, one bigger with a capacity of ca 600kg (6-7 person capacity) and the smaller one with Max. The capacity of 350kg (4-person capacity). They were usually called the 'big' and 'small' elevators. The small one was so small that there was no room to swing a cat in. Made in the mid-'70s, they did not present the state of the art in today's terms but still were doing their job. Elevators were also called lifts; in our case, that was what was written on them. These small moving apartments carried tons of people and freight daily in a vertical shaft between the levels of our 18 multistory buildings. I am no expert in elevator technology, but the internal structure of these babies consisted mainly of these small cabins propelled by electric motors, with the aid of counterweights, through a system of cables and pulleys. If they got f**ked for whatever reason, you were left to the mercy of repair people, the same guys that work for the company that made these flying boxes. Sometimes it could take a long time before that happens. As long as you got one working elevator, it's not a crisis. Passenger elevators were possible thanks to a visionary American, Elisha Graves Otis, who introduced a safety device in 1853. Let's clarify: This was no modern OTIS elevator, but it was not bad either. The company that made these things, called after its founder, 'David Left' (almost lift!), had 50% of the market while the other two, 'Mechanica' and 'Roger Dachster,' took the rest of the market. We were 'blessed' with Left's elevators. It didn't matter because all three sucked one way or another. Mechanica had the most progressive and modern ones, but they were expensive. So we got one of the other two. The advantage of these two was that they were adapted to the brutality to which they were fully exposed daily. These poor mechanical structures were prepared for the barbarian onslaughts on almost every occasion. Now you can ask how the hell you can destroy an elevator. Not entirely, but you can destabilize, pollute, invalidate, and paralyze it for some time. You can attack the interior environment at any time, and f**k up the electric system is also a possibility. People just did that for no reason whatsoever. The action of moving furniture was probably the worst period for the elevators. It was like stone quarry work for them. The difference between freight and passenger traffic was quickly forgotten and misunderstood. The interiors were made from a cheap wood imitation that, with years, looked more like a toilet in a sleazy joint on the city's outskirts.

They say: 'When in Rome, do as the Romans do.' So when you had visitors coming, they also behaved according to the environment around them. That's another story. There was also a mirror installed inside. It was stolen many times, so the repair people got tired and installed a pocket one instead. This ridiculous thing couldn't even reflect your nose correctly. It did stay for a long time, but one day even that miniature artifact disappeared. It was heavily missed in the skyscraper community. There was also neon lightning in the beginning. What luxury! Neon lamps disappeared within weeks of use, and of course, the story is the same as with the mirror. They were broken, destroyed, or stolen. This being an expensive thing in those days, was soon replaced by a lamp, which would proudly stand in any coal mine in England at the end of the 18th century. A steel frame protected this light bulb, and one could not steal or break it. It was an ingenious product for the Neanderthal age of using elevators. The shaft for the neon lamps remained on the elevator's ceiling to remind us of the old days.

The last interesting aesthetic detail was the control panel. It was equipped with a system of collective operation. The cabins answered all calls in one direction in sequence and then reversed and answered all calls in the opposite direction. Their memory capacity was quite OK. At least they could remember the first to press the single automatic push-lighted button on each floor. With years these buttons lost their light. The two elevators were somehow, in some understanding, operating within a specified operating interval in a timing sequence. Well, with years, that disappeared if it ever existed. These flying cabins became highly independent of each other. If they had any artificial intelligence, they would commit suicide by flying through the roof or crashing through the basement. Life was painful enough for them. Yes, the control panel. It was nice, with 20 buttons for all floors, including the lobby and mezzanine. There was a stop button (probably the most abused piece of plastic in the world) and an alarm button. Occasional pyromaniacs that inhabited our environments used to burn these buttons, so the plastic melted and looked like the remains of Chucky the doll. The panel was changed on many occasions. The earlier panels, with heavy black buttons, were later replaced by lighted ones. The attacks on the panel also affected the memory and electrical system, so the elevator behaved very strangely on certain occasions rebelling against the brutalism shown to him. This was one of the occasions.

Sonny, 'the garlic' Lazarus, had heart problems his whole life. He was a fragile child that survived well with the care and help of his parents. He was never put under any pressure due to a severe heart condition. This was also tuff on him as a child, not being able to participate in all kids' activities. Later in life, the condition improved, and he could lead an everyday life. He did stay on heart pills every day and was careful not to put himself under any pressure. His residence was on the 8th floor. He had a wife and a daughter and led a peaceful and serene life. Sonny was quite a literature soul. He used to write short reviews of books, poems, and some prose. Later he got involved with the funny side of life, writing and collecting jokes. Due to his heart problems, he ate garlic – tons of it! Garlic (Allium sativum) is a beautiful herb. I can't imagine a cuisine without this ingredient. In ancient and medieval times, and even today, garlic was prized for its medicinal properties and was carried as a talisman against vampires and other evils. Lazarus knew very well. I don't think he cared much about the vampires, but his heart was what he was concerned about every minute of the day. The amount of garlic imported into his body would have destroyed any vampire within a thousand miles. There was the only problem. He was overdosing on it. He was your 100% Garlic junky. He was even growing garlic on his balcony. The apartment was full of it. Being a good cook, he used, abused, and misused it in every possible way. So imagine when you get into an elevator with this guy, you are half dead by the time he reaches the 8th floor. This incredible overdose of garlic produced a wall of scent around him, and when and if you got into it, it wasn't easy to get out with a clear head. I have survived these encounters. I can't say I was the sole one, as others have relieved this encounter in various ways.

Sonny was in his early 50s, overweight baggy body structure, which didn't help his heart problem, old khakis, a worn-out casual jacket, and half shaved face with a touch of continuous nervousness about him. His dark hair was always nicely folded to one side, while the glasses were necessary for every minute of the day. He was think-ing of another poem while waiting for the 'big' elevator to arrive. There was no response. Well, the light in the call button died many seasons ago, but still. 'Shit,' thought Sonny. This wasn't good. The 'small' one was the only option if this one was dead. And that small bugger behaved strangely at times, even swinging as a pendulum at higher altitudes. No, that one was getting dangerous. He imagined all kinds of scenarios of elevators dropping from the sky like in 'Speed,' or cables popping out and Sonny being stuck in the small claustrophobic cabin for hours, maybe days. He was worrying too much. He moved to the left corridor in the lobby hall. It was a smaller passage with no light. The damned kids always screw with the electricity. Somebody should do something about it. He tried the tiny elevator, and then he saw a small piece of paper plastered over the reinforced glass window of the elevator door:

OUT OF FUNCTION!

NOBODY KNOWS WHEN IT WILL WORK AGAIN.

YOU CAN WAIT IF YOU WANT…OR DON'T

Who the f**k was screwing with them? Nobody knows…those damn assholes. As soon as the weekend arrives and if the elevator doesn't work, you can go and…you know what. This wasn't nice. Now he was utterly scared. Sonny was feeling pretty down today, which aggravated his focus on the heart problem he carried as an alien with him throughout his life even more. Suddenly he heard voices in the long corridor and the elevator door opening. He rushed from the small hallway to the lobby. In the nick of the second, he opened the door.

'Is it working?' Sonny said, amazed. The elevator was just boarded by my dad, Nathan Haas, and a friend of his, Mick Rowells. Mick's son, Harry, was a good buddy of mine.

'Yeah, it just came. Seems no problem with it, said Mick.

'It seemed that it didn't exist on the panel, nor could I hear any sounds.

'Well, you know our elevators. They tend to disappear in the shaft and come at will. It's a miracle that they work at all, added Nathan.

'I was slightly worried about all these stoppages lately.' It's the weekend so the repair guys won't be here until Monday.

'Don't worry, Mr. Lazarus, this one has many miles ahead of him.' Mick was a major, but also a doctor, in the army and had a strong confidence in every mechanical construction, especially if it was a company doing work for the army.

'We have a couple of these babies in our hospital, and they work perfectly.'

'I thought you guys had Mechanica elevators there,' said Nathan. Unfortunately, we have one of these in our Physics Department.

'Hmm…when I think of it, maybe you're right. Yeah, it's Mechanica, those soft black touch, and silent elevators. No, it's not Lefties….'

'I think we're not moving at all,' added Sonny impatiently.

It was true. All buttons were lighted on the panel, 8th for Sonny, 14th for Mick, and 16th for Nathan. Something was wrong. The elevator had an outer steel door with small reinforced glass panels, but to start it, you had to close a pair of old-fashioned wooden inner doors with similar glass panels without reinforcement. These could get tricky at times. You had to be very gentle, meticulous, and patient with them. If the elevator was not functioning correctly, then a way to start it often lay in these doors. Unfortunately, it was not the case this time around. The three guys tried all kinds of maneuvers, but alas. Nothing worked. Sonny was getting more and more nervous now. They tried everything, getting out of the elevator, meddling with the doors, and jumping slightly. None of them wanted to ride the stairs. Friday afternoon, a week of work has somehow entered their legs, which felt like lead anchors. Sonny didn't even want to think about such an option. No way, Jose! His heart would be damaged, and he wouldn't survive; they would carry him on a stretcher, and so on. It was all in his mind. He forgot the 8-12 hour power shortages that happened a few years back and stretched over almost one year. Then he was forced to walk. Nathan and Mick almost decided to give it up when little Moritz appeared out of nowhere. If tobacco companies wanted to have a role model and a cigarette enthusiast and fighter for their rights, they could have indeed found him in Moritz. No problem, he would have taken out Al Pacino and Russel Crowe in The Insider without a second thought. There was only one problem: Moritz was seven years old. He was on the path of becoming a 100% certified bum by the time he reached high school and would be dying from lung cancer, emphysema, or heart disease by his 45th birthday. He started smoking when he was four. All kinds of illegal activities were already passing through his head. He was heavily influenced by TV, old lousy company, cigarette inhalation, and no family values, and he was on a roll. Money, sex, drugs, alcohol, etc., were his favorite topics. It was incredible how much of that was compiled in such a tiny being. Even with all that, he was among the most exciting and sympathetic. His dad was a total bum, while his mom drowned in Vodka daily. The poor kid had to take care of himself, especially since his brother of 18 left home for better illegal pastures. He did spend a lot of time with Rock Curtis's (local 13-year-old gang lord) gang and wanted to be like him as soon as possible. If he had the possibility, he would undoubtedly manipulate the gene growth just to get out of this, as he used to say on many occasions, 'f**king doll body.' Sometimes you believed that little Moritz was from the dark side. He certainly didn't do anything else to deny it. They lived a couple of quarters from our building because he had a couple of buddies in the building, which was not to their parents' liking. Other small kids admired and saw him as their spiritual leader and protector.

They also supplied him with cigarettes. Moritz collected a fee for, as he liked to call it, 'tobacco and protection tax enforcement revenue.' It was sometimes unbelievable what came out of this kid. He was pumping everything with 'PG' and 'R' written all over it. Well, he was a blessing in disguise for the guys in the elevator.

'Hey, what's up folks? Having trouble with the elevator? Don't worry, and I know how to fix it.' Sure he did, all of them thought; this guy knew all the world's wonders.

'Hey, you are smoking. You can't smoke here', yelled Sonny.

'Didn't you know that the Aztec kings smoked a hollow reed or cane tube stuffed with tobacco?' This gives respect, man. Don't you know your f**king history? French and British troops in the Napoleonic Wars smoked joints. Respected people like Lucky Luciano smoked all the time. Did you know he was capo di tutti capi ('boss of all the bosses')? How could you?

'And it's none of your business, old man, what I do when and with whom I do it—comprehended Pancho! So the best thing is that you shut the f**k up, and I'll do something about the elevator.

Sonny couldn't believe his ears, and Nathan And Mick looked at each other. There was no point in arguing with this kid; they had tried that many times before. 'What the f**k, you little prick...' Sonny started saying when Moritz cut him off:

'Now listen. Something is not right with the elevator. It behaves strangely. But I found out how you can ride this baby. You don't stand on the floor. It won't lift while you are standing on the floor. It's that simple.' He looked at the three guys with his 'old-timer' profound look. A Camel cigarette was sticking out of his mouth and making perfect circles and other shapes with the smoke coming out of his mouth. Sharp green eyes, a hairstyle that reminded you of Prince Valliant times, t-shirts with heavy metal bands or proverbs like 'eat shit,' and dark blue jeans were the package called Little Moritz. Often he used to dig for slobber in his nose.

'You got to be kidding, said Mick.' 'How are we supposed to ride this thing then?'

'He probably thinks we should climb up on the elevator somehow,' added Nathan.

'Exactly, Prof.! You are a physicist, and you should figure it out.' 'There is something f**ked up with electricity and the gravity pull.' The last thing on Nathan's mind was to discuss the problems of gravity and Newton's laws with Little Moritz, but maybe the kid was right somehow.

'This is what you should do, guys. You see that ledge and the compartment placed for the neons on the ceiling. There is enough room to grab with your hands and lift your bodies during the travel time. A little bit of physical recreation will do you good. I will jump up and do it myself.

'Before you say no, look at the option: walking. There is no f**king way I will walk up to the 17th floor. You two who live on the 14th and 16th floor probably share my view. Let's play democracy now. Higher floors are in the majority, so Mr. Sonny, you decide – to fly for a while or take an alpine hike. It's your choice! You can also stay here and start drowning in Garlic. Mr. Sonny, you stink, man!'

On another occasion, they would probably argue with the kid or ignore him and start walking, but all three were tired and wanted to get home as soon as possible. What was wrong with some climbing? There could be no harm in it, primarily if it worked. And Sonny's smell! God, they don't need that now. Nathan and Mick said simultaneously: 'Ok, let's do it, guys!' Sonny was in total disbelief.

'Are you going to trust this small piece of dog shit?'

'Common Sonny, don't be a pain in the ass. Could you do it now, and no more complaints? It would help if you dealt with some people, like in the army, though, Mick. Mick was taking charge now.

'My heart, my heart,' Sonny kept repeating. 'Don't worry, and the walking would damage you much more. No, there's a hand and climb.' He obeyed like a petite schoolboy. There was no f**king with the armed forces, and he knew it. He climbed up as well as Mick. Nathan followed. They were distributed on three sides of the elevator now.

'Ok, I will close the door, and then we lift off.' Little Moritz closed the door in a yippy and jumped up as a spider on the ledge. The garlic smell was filling the cabin fully now. 'Lift off – F**king AAAAAAAAAAAAA! Moritz was excited. And what do you know, the elevator started moving, but only at half speed. This was going to be an excruciating trip. Eight floors to the first stop and salvation from the garlic attack seemed like an eternity. All four held, but Sonny began panting and whining like a pig.

'I can't hold on much longer. My heart won't take the pressure. This is so stupid. What have you done to me?

'Will you shut up!' yelled Moritz. 'Can't you see we are moving even though it's half speed? We are still moving, aren't we?

'For God's sake, can anybody help me' Sonny continued winning. 'If we help you, the elevator will stop because I, or Nathan, will have to jump down and hold your fat ass in the air. So get a hold of yourself, man.' Mick was pissed off but on the verge of laughing. Nathan was suppressing laughter because it would loosen his concentration. The garlic was everywhere, so all three were breathing through their mouths. At that moment, Sonny farted brutally and fell on the elevator floor with all his might. They just reached the fourth floor. He was crying now and winning even more. The elevator stopped. Little Moritz jumped as a G-man and shouted at Sonny: 'Look what you've done. We stopped because of you. You look like a pig that knows it will be slaughtered and served as Christmas ham. What is wrong with you?'

'Let's get him up. There is no point in waiting. We've stuck between floors anyway, so the only thing is to continue hanging for the rest of the trip.' With that being said, Nathan climbed down and tried to lift Sonny. He could barely suppress vomiting because the smell of garlic was everywhere. Sonny was still farting; this time, it was coming close to the inevitable – shitting in his pants. That would be a major disaster, especially if the elevator refuses to comply with this con flight. They knew what that meant – locked in a small cabin with garlic and shit all night. Add to that inevitable vomiting, and you will see Armageddon in a new light. That's why all three of them put all their energy into lifting Sonny. Sonny kept repeating, 'My heart, my poor feeble heart.' Little Moritz felt proud that he was an equal part of this tragicomic happening.

'Just hold on tight, Sonny. You won't fall off. It's only four more floors. Mick knew that these four floors would be an eternity. How the hell could they listen to that tiny monster? Staircase climbing felt now like an excellent idea. Too late! There was no turning back. Mick and Nathan looked at each other. Panic was evident, not of being stuck, but being together with Sonny.

'Keep it together now, Mr. Sonny! You can make it. Moritz was bringing in necessary optimism. The elevator started again. Three grown men hanging in the air in a slow-moving elevator, one on the verge of shitting his pants, and one little guy pasted like a spider in the corner of the ceiling. Their feet were dangling in the air. This was indeed a ridiculous scene. The garlic and terrible compound that farting produced have wiped 'clean' the breathable air the six-person cabin had.

'Hold your breath, everybody, because if the first one vomits, we're goners! Mick was trying to issue orders, but they were barely managing. The elevator was moving so slowly that they felt they were going from the deepest dungeons of hell and that purgatory would never end, but instead, they would be sucked into eternal damnation. Fortunately, the sixth floor was reached when Sonny suddenly farted his last one, which opened the valves. It was such violent diarrhea that it flooded his inner pants in seconds. Shit was poring everywhere. They never knew so much shit could get out. What kind of underwear was he wearing, for heaven's sake? Couldn't it stop some of this brownie avalanche? His socks were being filled with yellow-brownish fluid and complicated matter.

'Oh no, no, what's happening to me? Yelled Sonny. Nathan was the first to react. 'It's nothing, Sonny, just keep holding on. Don't let go. Our pants are full also. Don't let go.' Their pants were incomplete, but if Sonny fell again, they knew they would be full of everything during that night because not even a bulldozer would get him back on the ledge again. And besides, his pants were a couple of kilos heavier with brown substance. Amid everything that just happened, Sonny was still holding on. Little Moritz, who was in control all the time, suddenly, after a wild burst of laughter, fell into a catatonic stupor. He became a little boy again, scared of what might happen if this elevator stopped again and if it stopped for good. That cannot happen, though, Moritz. He was paralyzed in the corner, watching wildly a grown man full of shit hanging like a baboon while shit was pouring out of his pants. Yes, the air. There was no air. It was long gone. I don't think even gas masks would help at this moment. Mick, Nathan, and Moritz held their last breaths before an inevitable explosion. Then the elevator stopped. They looked in horror at the other panel above the door. That one showed the progression of the floors and, strangely, always seemed to survive the attacks. It was mostly intact, except for some holes punched out and became urns for bubble gum, cigarette stubs, or occasional food remains.

Number eight was fully lighted. This red light seemed like salvation for them, like an opening to the gateways of heavenly delight. Everybody scrambled down in a rush, except for Sonny, who was still shocked. He was also embarrassed. It was no problem with Mick and Nathan, but this little bugger Moritz will release this news like the worst tabloid. That was probably the last thing on his mind. He just wanted to get out of this as fast as possible. They opened the inner and outer doors showing Sonny as fast as possible. All the stench came out as a tornado swept through the eighth-floor corridor. There was no way in hell they would get back into that cabin. There was so much shit on the floor anyway; the smell would remain there for some time. The whole idea seemed crazy. How could they listen to Moritz? And look what happened to poor Sonny. While Sonny was slowly moving to his apartment, they checked on him and said fast goodbyes. Little Moritz, sensing that as much as he helped, he also f**ked up, ran fast up the staircase. He had four floors.

'If we came so far, we should finish this crazy trip. We didn't go through this for anything, to climb up the stairs again. What do you think, Mick?

'Ah, what the heck, let's do it!' Mick liked the fighting spirit. 'Don't forget to take a deep breath.' In a surprising move, they went back to the elevator. They were both excellent divers once in their youth days. This helped them to keep their breath in what felt like an eternity, part 2. Mick got out of the elevator on the 14th floor and saluted Nathan. Nathan continued for two more floors. Little Moritz was hidden in his pal's apartment on the 12th floor, no doubt recounting the events from the 'cabin' and portraying himself as a brilliant leader. There was no doubt about it, and the kid found a way to ride the flying machine even when it refused to lift off. He didn't know garlic, and other aromas can give you a different perspective and view of flying. He was meticulous when he farted next time, constantly checking his pants afterward. Garlic was something he despised for the rest of his life.

6

Shit Happens Only Once to Dancing Bears

In the case of our building, as it was with many others, the tenants were often visited by different salesman types, especially on the weekends and holidays. Not all of them were salespeople. You could also find and meet various types of beggars, mobile preachers, con-artists, different statisticians, people seeking donations, kids collecting cans, and "characters" willing to repair almost anything for a relatively small amount of cash. This last group, along with the beggars, was probably the most persistent one. All visitors, including these "repair people," used the two elevators for the ascend and the staircase for the descent during their working hours. When I say "repair," I mean tiny repair. In other words, these people repaired three things: umbrellas, scissors, and knives. The repair of the two latter ones consisted basically of sharpening. And to tell you the truth, they didn't do such a good job, but people paid them anyway. You always had a problem with umbrellas, especially if you valued them as an artifact, which could and should never be changed. Knives always needed sharpening, as it was a tool you didn't buy every day. The same thing was with the scissors. So basically, there was always work around. 99% of these "repairmen" were Romany Gypsies with slightly darker skin. Unfortunately, the beggar population also mainly consisted of this group. The sellers carried small workshops and were, in most cases, very persistent regarding repairs. Unfortunately, they were also persistent regarding some "other" things, diametrically different from repair.

The Romany (Roma Ethnic Group and People) used at least two names: a private, personal name in their language that was not used outside their community and a public name in the language of their country. So was the case here. The term "Gypsy" today is not politically correct. Unfortunately, that's what these people were called in those days. Gypsy, by the way, is the 16th-century English translation of the Spanish word Gitano. All gypsies originated in India. Some believed that they came from old Egypt, so the term Gitano. Later they spread all over the world. The term Roma or Romany Gypsies came into use at a later time. These people were not occasionally branded with bad, harmful, or evil things and doings. This led to an excuse for official and legal prosecution and the police's favorite leisure activity. Sometimes it was true, but they were often blamed on false grounds. Most of the Roma Gypsy population pursued occupations that allowed them to live oblivious lives on our society's 'outskirts and margins. Men did all kinds of things as livestock trading, animal training, small informal economy sales, metal smith and utensil repair, and music. Some urbanized gypsies found employment as car mechanics, auto body repairers, car washers, waste collectors, and parking attendants. The women population told fortunes (coffee, beans, crystal balls, palm reading, etc.), sold potions, begged, and performed other music-related activities. When it came to repairs of different utensils, they were the ones trusted to do it and were good at it.

As Sonny Lazarus, a publicist and freelance journalist on the 8th floor, often said, 'These people very talented when it came to music, dance, song and even some poetry.' It was true. We witnessed that primarily groups collecting money in trams or housing quarters playing different instruments accompanied by dancing bears. Different characters roamed the corridors and hallways of our housing quarters throughout the years. It was in the blood of these people to move. Through centuries they were always on the move as nomads, never staying in one place for too long. In our case, the exotic stereotype of the nomadic Gypsy often disguised the fact that fewer and fewer remained truly nomadic, a movable group.

Boboko, or as he called himself Sami at times, was operating alone or with his cousin contingency of Milosh, Putzina, and Bakro. Sometimes Yolanda went with them, but only on musical 'gathering' occasions. It was a warm August morning when you wanted to be a vegetable with enough water to keep you going throughout the day. The temperature was already reaching 25C, and it was only ten o'clock in the morning. By noon it will be over 30, and all hell will break loose. It was a Saturday morning, which meant 'repair' morning and maybe some entertainment for Boboko and company. As it was late August, they knew most people were back from the holidays, which meant only one thing: potential customers. They had their lodgings in a trailer in nearby no-man's-land. Oh, yeah, these lands were abundant in the city. The authorities didn't know what to do with them, and most were waiting for development, which never came. Usually, it was just patches of green spaces, abandoned buildings, leftover prefabricated facilities, or old warehouses. It was an ideal place for squatters of various kinds, winos, sociopaths, homeless, nomads, etc. Boboko and his contingency were lodgings on one of these green patches near the river. It gave reasonable control of the surrounding environment and strategic operating ground. One thing is sure, and this group worked hard for the money. Everybody was employed, one way or another. They even had ideas of settling permanently, but insufficient economic activity was available, which could support them in the long run. You can sharpen knives, fix umbrellas, and entertain people with dancing bears and music, but that's not enough in the bigger picture. Be that as it may, Boboko was not thinking of those things that Saturday morning. His target this morning was our city quarter neighborhood and the adjacent one. Putzina accompanied him. The rest would arrive close to lunch to earn money by providing the dancing bear entertainment. All this was illegal, but the authorities did not give flying a crap unless it became dangerous and over-disturbing for the community.

There was also another thing associated with these guys.

The fact is that repairman somehow thought that the elevators were moving toilets. Every time one of these gentlemen came to our building, he 'relieved' himself in the elevator. Sometimes it was a smelly pond of urine (piss), but most of the time, it was shit of different consistencies and smells. And when I say shit, I mean actual shit, not your everyday-ordinary shit, but shit of enormous quantities and various 'killer' stenches. It was totally out of anybody's comprehension how these people managed to shit so much in a relatively small, public, and fast-moving space. Probably they stopped the elevator between floors and did their 'thing.' However, there was never any proof for this, although it always happened when they were in the building. But this Saturday morning, things took a somewhat different turn of events.

Boboko rang and rang apartment No.5 on the 4th floor. Ms. Norissa Guzinsky opened the door. A widow of 62 years, she belonged to an informal group called the 'World Service.' She was their organizational and spiritual leader. The other two members were 3rd-floor power woman Fosha Shufflebottom and 6th-floor bitch, Pippa Pantoliano. They also had two more accomplices or adjunct members from the higher floors. This was important to cover the whole territory. The two old hags on the 11th and 18th floors were Olga Balescu and Blanca Parrayo. The service was a high-powered gossip machine, covering all kinds of dirty, sleazy, private, and other information. It functioned brilliantly around the clock. If you want fresh tabloid gossip, you turn to these ladies. Their main objective was building happenings and related issues and happenings in the quarter. On one occasion, they played a decisive role in an incredible event on the 9th floor. The essential thing was not to screw with these ladies, as they would come back with such revenge that you would have wished you had never whispered their names. Opening Pandora's box was the understatement of the day. If you crossed their lines, they would bring all kinds of skeletons from your closet, even if you had none. They dedicated their retired life to this, keeping their brains on constant alert.

Norissa was the wrong woman to piss off this morning. Bad headache from yesterday, undone hair and nails, not-so-good news from her son and his screwed-up marriage, and this bum standing in front of her didn't help. It just made them worst.

'What do you want?' came a sharp hissing question from Norissa.

'I sharp, I fix, I make things better, missus'!

'What things, what fix, what the hell are you talking about?'

'Knives, scissors, umbrellas, pots & pants, you name it.'

'I have all of those, you dumb ass.'

'No, I fix, not sell; I repair old stuff.'

'You want to fix my old stuff?'

'Yes, yes,' anxiously fired Boboko.

She was insulting this morning. 'I don't need any fixing, so piss off.' She knew and enjoyed it to the fullest.

'I cheap, fix cheaply. No worries, later, man. He was becoming very persistent now, almost blocking the whole door.

'I said I don't want any fixing. Are you deaf or just plain old stupid?'

'No, no, I do it almost for free. Only take a moment. Later you happy, all utensils sharp, sharp, sharp.'

'I don't want it even for free. I said, piss off, you asshole. Instead of living in the gutter and doing this shitty thing, you should make an all-out effort to return to normal society and contribute to its well-being and prosperity. She just loved when she could put these 'deep' thoughts forward.

'I don't understand. I fix, I help, I work.' 'Why won't you pay little money? You stingy, very stingy!

'What did you tell you, little sewer worm? Get off my door before I call the cops. But Boboko was getting more persistent and angrier by her behavior by the minute.

'I no sewer worm. Don't insult an older woman. I fix for little money. Give me some money.'

'What! Old! Money! Are you begging now? Wait here just one second.' With that, she left in a furry for the kitchen and took out the giant knife she could find, one that Mike Myers would have enjoyed if he had it on Halloween. She was back at the speed of light, waving the butcher knife in front of Boboko.

'Is this what you mean? Do you want to sharpen knives?'

'Yes, yes, that's it. I do a good job. I will sharpen it for you.

'Now listen, worm. If you don't disappear from my door at this very moment, I will shove this knife up your ass and 'sharpen' your insides out. You understand what I'm saying. Everything I have is sharpened and functioning properly, so get the f**k out of here – and I mean now!' She was yelling in a high, pitched voice now. Boboko was scared now, but he said: 'You'll be sorry, no way to treat people, you sorry.' With that, he ran away. He met with Putzina somewhere on the higher floors. He collected some small cash. Not much. Bussines was relatively slow. Boboko told him about his encounter with the old hag and the insults. They just wanted to fix things. Why the hell were they being insulted in such a manner? It was near noon, and they would switch to some entertainment to earn some more small cash. The problem was that they needed to go to John as fast as possible, but no one was around when they needed it.

Indeed, they were almost caught in the act on several occasions. Once, one of them even left evidence behind, pieces of a broken umbrella. One time a lady from the 9th floor entered the elevator right after one of these guys 'relieved himself.' She always wore nice and expensive perfumes and was sometimes unaware of some other 'scents' that existed in the real world. She almost fainted when she came out of the elevator; the only smell was of rotten shit.

This 'rebellious act and protest against urban culture and civilization,' as Zontag Windhorn, an anthropologist from the 8th floor, like to call it, always happened to us in our building. After a hard day's work, the flying cabin was the only shitting ground for them. Strangely it never happened in the other three sister skyscrapers. Could it be that the payments were so low here and that they found elevators as an appealing shitting ground, or was it the only place to do it after a hard-working day? Why not the greenery outside? Why the bloody elevator? Whatever the reason was, they always left a mess behind them. It was always cleaned up, but you couldn't eliminate the smell that easily. But you got to hand it to them; they always covered their pile of shit with newspapers and were never caught in the act. So was the case this time, almost.

Boboko couldn't wait any longer, nor could Putzina. They boarded the small elevator and stopped it between the 10th and 11th floors. Both took out their pants; they had no underwear anyway and started to shit brutally. Putzina had diarrhea, which worsened things, while Boboko shitted for two people. He fancied doing this in front of the old bitches door, but the shit couldn't wait. He would instead piss in front of her door. The whole elevator was covered in deep shit in a matter of minutes. They had some newspapers, which they used to clean themselves and to cover this mess. They almost ran out of the elevator. Boboko just wanted to empty his bladder on the 4th floor.

Moments after, Fosha Shufflebottom and Pippa Pantoliano tried to board the tiny elevator on the 6th floor. They couldn't wait for the big one. It was Saturday, and some asshole was probably moving furniture in or out. It took them only a moment to realize with horror that they were traveling with hard and liquid waste. The stench was unbearable, and the remnants of the diarrhea were spreading all around the floor. The paper didn't help things much; it was so dirty with shit anyway. Fosha even stepped into one pile and was screaming in disgust now. They both were. What seemed an endless journey to the lobby lasted only seconds, but it was a lifetime for them. They came out screaming and yelling all kinds of things. Suddenly they remembered they were supposed to pick up Norissa. Oh my, this was soul food for the 'World Service.' They needed to tell, confer and ask for advice from Norissa. She would know what needed to be done to stop whomever or whatever was doing these gruesome things. They were pale when they arrived at her door. She would know; she always knew.

Milosh, Bakro, and Yolanda brought him to earn some petty cash for the noon festivities. He was a shaggy-haired brown bear (Ursus arctos). This bear type is common in zoos and can be trained and easily managed. Formerly they were frequently trained to move rhythmically to music, better known as the dancing bears of European circuses, carnivals, and festivals. This one was a typical dancing bear. The poor bugger was chained and almost gagged with corroded steel. It was evident that 'Browny,' as they called him, didn't like this shit at all. Performing all kinds of stupidities for some leftover junk food was not worth doing. He just wanted to run to the forests. He couldn't remember it but could feel in his whole body that it was his home, his turf, not this shitty nomad and asphalt life. The plan was not to perform only in front of the building but also in the buildings themselves. Milosh, who was in charge of this outfit's musical section, devised this 'brilliant idea.' He played the harmonica while Yolanda and Bakro had all kinds of percussion instruments with them. The guitar section was Putzina's division, but he had other things to attend to this morning. They couldn't see Boboko or Putzina anywhere, so they entered our building accompanied by Browny and boarded the big elevator.

After spilling their guts out to Norissa and crying on her shoulder, the "World Service" was ready to act. Norissa had a pretty good idea who did this, especially after finding a pond of liquid in front of her door; she was ready for death penalties to be handed out faster than in Texas. She had already called the cops and wanted to wait for them in front of the building. The morning coffee and bagels would have to wait as an 'incoming world service dispatch' was coming. This one was certainly worth the wait. Fosha's and Pippa's story about the shit also grew to monumental proportions by now. They were all so preoccupied with what might happen next that they boarded the big elevator in a trance, not seeing who was inside or where the elevator was going. After the elevator started, Norrisa glanced at the people inside and realized, to her horror, that it was not just people inside but also a brown monster.

What was even this stupid elevator had a memory of its own and was going up instead of going down. She also recognized familiar faces of 'Saturday people.' It was the whole gang inside with, with a…a bear??!! The horror filled the eyes of the founding members of the World Service gild. What made it even worse was that the gypsy orchestra started performing in the elevator seeing potential customers in front of them. They did not realize these were probably the worst possible customers you could get. The music, singing, and shouting filled the elevator cabin, and the poor bear started dancing. The whole elevator began shaking. It was on the brink of stopping, almost overloaded with six people + a bear. The bear was jumping around and moving with the rhythm. The three women started screaming, and this soon became a tragicomic scene played out in an elevator shaft and a cabin running wildly toward the 18th floor.

'Let us out, help, help,' were the chorus cries of three women. Amidst all that, the bear felt the urge to empty himself in a big way. He started shitting all over the place. This just added to the horror that the ladies found themselves in. The screams intensified. Milosh, Yolanda, and Bakro didn't quite get what was happening, and this screaming was increasingly agitating the bear. At least the shit was behind him. Finally, the 18th floor arrived, and they ran out as soon as possible. They almost crashed with Boboko and Putzina.

'You son of a bitch', hissed Norissa, who was half mad. Realizing something wrong went down, Boboko and Putzina boarded the elevator and started their descent with the dancing bear party. The small elevator was the only thing left for Norissa, Fosha, and Pippa. It was full of shit, but they would survive. Fortunately, it was on the 18th floor also. They were arguing now in the elevator. Boboko was screaming at them for bringing the animal inside the building. They were yelling back at them for not being there, and so on. The elevator reached the lobby, and as soon as they got out, the cops stopped them. World Service also arrived in the 'shit evidence' elevator. The cops were tired of Norissa Guzinsky's constant reminders of how, where, and when the law should be administered. But they still respected her, especially when she was of help in a significant bust once. Everybody started screaming now, and the poor bear, out of sheer excitement or basic physiological need, started pissing on the lobby stairs. He didn't shit the second time.

Even the Boboko group was amazed by this move, as this 'trained' beast was not supposed to do these things. It probably had enough of everything, and as it was an older bear, some controlled actions were fading away as pissing and shitting. Poor guy! They started yelling and whipping it when the police intervened. The whole group was dragged downtown in a police van. Later we heard that the bear was released and donated to the local zoo as Boboko and the company didn't have any papers, and the whole activity was illegal. Nobody got to jail, nor were they fined, but all of them were ordered to move. We never saw them afterward. Boboko's gang had just moved to a different part of the city, a different suburb. They were others, but nobody liked this gang. 'The world service strikes again' was the word throughout the building. The three ladies were undoubtedly a force to be reckoned with.

7

A Valuable Lesson

YOU HAVE BEEN FARTED!

Shots on goal in handball must be taken from outside the goal circle, an area in which only the goaltender is allowed. Their best offensive player was coming close to that line. He went through the defense like an armored vehicle. One of Boris's teammates stopped the guy in such a manner, which caused the referee to signal a violation of the rules. This allowed the guest team to make a free throw with just 60 seconds on the clock. The match was tied, and the divisional title was on the line. Whoever wins this thing, the next stop would be the majors. Boris Duchovny was playing the match of his life. He was the best goalie in the division and probably one of the best goalies in the country. Offers were already popping up from Spain and Germany. Take it easy, he thought. There would be time for that. They just had to survive this. The guests were ready. The foul was played out. One of their best players made an unhindered pass to a teammate from a spot near where the foul was committed. This guy found an opening and was right in front of Boris. It was a cannon shot. Its sheer power almost swept Boris away, but he held his ground. He deflected what seemed a sure goal. The crowd cheered and roared. He quickly took the ball and found his offensive player. The ball swished across the court and found him. He scored a magnificent lob goal. It was all over. Or was it? The guests had only 15 seconds left. In a blitzkrieg attack, they went forward, and again, their best player came to the outside circle and got in. Just then, one of the defenders slammed him, and he tumbled down in the penalty area. With 5 seconds to go, the guest was awarded the penalty throw at the goal. This was usually awarded for more serious fouls. It was such a case this time. The crowd went silent. They knew what this meant. If the game were tied, the guests would reach the majors because of a better goal difference. There were no extensions, sudden death, or penalties in this instance. Penalties are taken from a mark just outside the goal circle. It was all up to Boris. Last shot. Last ball. Last game of the season. Last and only chance to get to the mayors. If they lose this one, the team will probably dissolve, and everybody going for the bigger ones, for money, better opportunities, and fame. He just had to defend this one. He just had to.

'What happened then? What happened?' All of us were screaming at him to tell us the last moments of this ferocious and nerve-breaking thriller.

'Hold on, guys, I am coming to that.' Boris was recounting to us the last moments of the game. We were all packed around him in front of our building, on our only decent patch of greenery. He just came from the game. Most of us watched the game on the TV, but we wanted to hear the story and the last seconds from his mouth. He was an athletic build guy, 1.90m tall, with solid hands, slightly dark skinned with black hair. If anybody reminded me of Burt Reynolds in the earlier days, it was Boris. He only missed the mustache.

He even got some offers for sitcoms, which he refused due to his tight handball schedule. He was the goalie for the local team, which played in division one. He loved handball.

Boris used to tell us that the modern handball game grew out of three independently developed sports in three countries: the Czech haze, the Danish handhold, and the German torball. Some of us used to disagree with him, saying that this sport could go back to ancient times, such as in Old Rome. He told us that we were just a bunch of idiots that mixed this game with something else resembling modern-day squash without rackets. Boris said those things were played in walled courts or against a single wall, with a small rubber ball struck with a hand or fist against the wall. You could play this in pairs or more. And besides, the court in handball is 40 by 20m. As far as he knew, it didn't have jack shit to do with modern handball.

I checked the books, and by God, he was right. When it came to sports, especially handball, there was nothing he did not know. He lived for sports day in, day out. The school suffered from that, but he didn't care much. Later in his life, he planned to study law, but there was plenty of time for that. What mattered now were the majors, a chance for the big ones. He was tired of the minors, petty divisions, and playing idiotic clubs with players without dedication or drive. There were exceptions, like the team they met in the divisional playoffs. But in general, very few of them wanted the big time! It was the only thing he thought about. As he was about to recapitulate the last nerving moments of the game, a small five-year-old kid named Igor Pavlov came to our group, that is to Boris, and began bugging him.

'Hej Boris, give us your ball to play, common man.' Boris brought one of the balls from the match with him.

'Hej kid, I don't have time for that now; get away.'

'Common Boris, give it to us.' Igor wore prescription glasses that looked more like magnifying glasses from a biology class. A small tiny kid, the type that can go on your nerves like a mosquito or a leach you cannot get rid of. He left, but not too far away. Boris continued his nerve-wracking account of the final moments of the game. 7-8 of us were all listening and waiting in anticipation.

'As you know, the goal in Handball is about 6 feet by 9 feet, and the goal circle has a diameter of about 20 feet. So this is not a rat hole.'

'Were you nervous, Bro?' somebody asked.

'Hell, yes! I knew if I blew this one, nobody would remember all the saves I did that day, and what's even worse, we would be f**ked. The whole shit was on me.' He was getting totally into it now, relieving it step by step.

'And then when this big guy took the boll and approached the penalty line, I knew…with that he was again interrupted by Igor.

'Hej Boris, what's this game you're talking about? Igor had a bunch of small kids assembled around him. They were all a pain in the ass. We want to hear too.

'Tell us. Tell us. No, even better, play ball with us. If you're so good, common and show us.'

'I said once, kid, piss off! I am tired and want to tell my close friends here something. Maybe some other day I will tell you and your friends. Now leave us alone. He left reluctantly again.

'So when this guy took the ball, continued Boris, It was like a ton of bricks on him too. He knew he had to make a shot; otherwise, they were goners too. The worse thing was that this guy was the best scorer in all leagues. He never missed a penalty during the whole season. And I saw on his face that he was not about to do that now.'

'I was ready, and so was he. Shit, I needed to gamble, so I walked out of the goal slightly, even more than needed. This made him think that a lob shot was possible. I knew deep down he loved those shots but didn't play them that much. He probably thought I was expecting a bomb, his usual shot. He took the ball, tested me with an empty move twice, and…' Igor interrupted for the third and final time.

'Hej Boris, commonly give us the ball. Stop talking so much about a silly game. Show us what you can't.' The small bugger was hanging on Boris's sports pants and wouldn't stop.

'You little rat. You can't stop, can't you? Would you like that?' well, I will show you what I can.

'Yes, yes,' said Igor. He was waiting for it. Well, what came was not handball virtuosity or similar. Instead, Boris took Igor's head by his giant hand ad redirected it towards his ass. His large hand had a firm grip on his head, like a ball in the court. He guided it deep into his ass with a fast move and farted violently. One factor that significantly impacts the volume of an individual fart is the amount of gas expelled, or so I heard. Boris certainly had enough gas to create the desired volume. A wonderful dinner after the game, with eggs and meat, was still being digested. So this fart was a combo of power and smell, and what was even more critical—of duration. It lasted for almost about four long seconds. Boris had an excellent position leaning on the side of the hood of the car to produce a fart of that magnitude where the dirty air forces itself through his butt-cheeks in the best possible way. The smell started to reach even us. Just imagine the poor kid whose head was still submerged in Boris's ass. He let go of him after a couple of seconds that followed the initial fart. A person produces about half a liter of fart gas daily, distributed over an average of fourteen daily farts. Boris has tried to combine all of them in one big, noisy, and smelly fart. And that one 'came through' all right! Releasing him, Boris added some of his poetry to the occasion: 'A fart can be useful, it gives the body ease, it warms the bed in winters and suffocates the fleas.'

'Well, my boy, you have been farted!' With that, we all laughed like a madman. Igor Pavlov was in a state of shock. He just moved away from Boris and us as in a trance. He didn't know what hit him. It was his first experience with a powerful fart. The other kids just ran. They thought more was to come.

'Finally, we are alone. Boris recounted the last details. Let me finish this thing, guys, and then I have to go.

'He took the ball after those false moves and threw himself like a bomb was on the way. In the last second, he stopped his hand in mid-air and threw a soft touch lob. Even though I knew it could be coming, I was not 100% prepared. With last bits of strength and stretching my body to the fullest, I twisted myself backward and barely touched the ball with my fingers enough to deflect it on the wooden post of the goal.'

'We won, guys! It was magnificent. The last thing I knew was that the whole team was all over me, and the crowd went wild. So that's the story, morning glory. I hope you enjoyed it, even with occasional disturbances.' With that being said, he gave a sort of crooked, evil eye to Igor, who was still standing on the side in a sort of autistic behavior. His face showed fear, anxiety, suppressed loathing, looming danger, terror, obedience, surrender, total crack-up, and God knows what more. Seeing Boris's look and pointing towards the ass again, he ran too. He would surely suffer for a long time, as I call it, a PTFS (post-traumatic fart syndrome). The urge for 'survival' was more potent than the kid's primal fear. He disappeared into the bushes with the rest of the kids.

Boris stayed longer to recap some of the other details of the match and post-match parties. After that, we all left. Myself, Boris and two other friends from the building went for the big elevator. We boarded the elevator, not seeing who was in there. Boris lived on the 7th floor, as did my best friend, Anthoine Scott. Guess who was in the elevator? None other than Igor Pavlov. The poor kid was with his two best buddies. When they saw us, especially Boris, terror spread in their eyes. Igor was only traveling to the 2nd floor, but the Journey could have been accessible to the moon. Boris gave him the evil eye and asked if he wanted to visit, as he called it, 'the monster in the caves' again. Boris farted again, not so strong, but firmly. It lasted eons for him...

'It seems the monster in the caves is getting hungry again. It's almost his feeding time now.' Igor started crying, as well as his other two buddies. They ran like hell when the elevator reached the second floor. There was no stopping them now.

'The poor kid thought there was a monster in the cave. Good grief! These kids today believe everything they hear. We all laughed. We said goodbyes on the 7th and 10th floors. Going up with the elevator to my 16th floor, I remembered a saying from an old and wise man about farts once. He said, 'Although the smell of a truly vicious fart seems to linger forever, it is a fleeting instant compared to the permanent brain damage it may cause.' I don't know if Igor suffered any brain or other damage, but one thing was sure. He has certainly learned a valuable life lesson.

81

8

The Medicine Man

Frank Costello was sleeping like a baby. The snoring could be heard even in the other division, where Evan Kapadia operated the pharmaceutical packaging machine. Frank was working in the tablet and capsule production division. Evan didn't give too much shit about that. He used the 'sleeping room' on many occasions. They were all buddies that looked after each other. The job wasn't that bad, tedious at times, but not bad. All kinds of pills, capsules, and tablets surrounded him. Some of them you could get high on. Those were damn good. He knew because he had tried them many times. He was once addicted to amphetamines. He thought that he was no junkie. The pills just took tension, anxiety, stress, and depression away. What the hell? He could stop using these things anytime, or so he thought.

Evan lived on the 1st floor of our skyscraper. Hi, brother was Memphis Kapadia or, as everybody called him, 'The Legend.' Memphis was one of the most respected people by us youngsters. He was the bullshit man. He was a con artist. He was the magician. He was the Joker. He was the man. Evan never had a job until the opportunity in the pharmaceutical company popped up. Bubba pulled some strings to get him there. So Evan Kapadia finally got a job in the local pill-making operation PharmaChemia Ltd. The company was one the biggest ones in the country. Shit, he didn't know much about the industry except what he read on the wall. It was some wording from WHO (World Health Organization).

The only thing that stuck in his head was the organization's definition of the pharmaceutical specialty as a simple or compound drug ready for use and placed on the market under a unique name or in a characteristic form.' He thought that was pretty cool. He was producing pills, for God's sake, and supplying them worldwide. The world would be much different without Evan Kapadias operating packaging machines worldwide. That fact made him proud. The company produced all kinds of pharmaceutical products and compounds. Their division was the most important one. There they produced various tablets, powders, granules, cachets, pastilles, and hard and soft capsules with soft gelatin shells. His machine packaged the solid dosages in the form of tablets. This had many advantages over other types of pills. For Evan, two were most important: smaller bulk and ease of packaging. Well, there weren't too many problems with capsules either, but he loved his babies more, his rugged tablets. He could operate that other machine too, but the big Italian machine packaging the tablets was his best friend. He knew it by heart and soon became a master in operating it. He became buddies with a couple of people there, Frank in the tablets and capsules, Joe Parr in the warehouse and transport, and Lisa Boyle in capsules. He had a hots for Lisa, but with Evan's looks, he was not going everywhere. He looked more like a 60's junkie than a pharmaceutical worker. Afro-styled hair and mustache accompanied by a pale, unshaven face, hawk nose, and non-expressive facial characteristics didn't help much. Memphis 'The Legend' was the complete opposite. Sometimes you couldn't tell that these two guys had anything in common. But Evan would keep trying on Lisa. You can't just give up that easily. Frank's snoring woke him from daydreaming and constant fixation on Lisa's ass.

Anthoine Scott and I were best of buddies. He lived on the 7th and I on the 16th floor. From day one, we became inseparable friends. I lived in the same building, went through elementary school together, shared the same high school and class, and played together as kids all the time. Unfortunately, we drifted apart in our later days due to our different paths and ended up in various corners of the world. But in those days, we were as one. One of the most incredible things in childhood and later teens were having a best friend, somebody you could share everything with. We were both lucky in that sense. Due to some changes in the system, high schools became very much specialized in those days. We were attending the one that still retained the 'old school tradition' of old-fashioned learning and quality instead of quantity motto. We took the natural sciences line with much chemistry and biology in the luggage. Thank God literature, Art, languages, History, and other social sciences subjects were still substantial. After 9 hours of chemistry, 7 hours of biology, and 5 hours of physics per week, you wished to know where Napoleon was pissing before the battle of Waterloo, how many mistresses Picasso had, or how you say 'fart' in Latin. But we liked our school. To become more specialized, ready for the real world, and operational in what we learned from books, the last year of high school included 'practical experience.' It was a lotto thing. Whichever company or institution offered places were taken, sometimes even if they had nothing to do with your school program. We were partly lucky as we got places in PharmaChemia Ltd. It didn't make much difference for me, as I had already decided on architectural studies. Anthoine was, on the other hand, going for Medicine, following in his father's and sister's footsteps. I had no interest in taking up my dad's (physics) or mom's (chemistry) line of work. But working one day a week for a whole year in a pharmaceutical company sounded cool. We didn't get any pay for it, but we got lunch coupons. So we were not hungry, at least. The worst thing was the working hours, where you had to start from six in the morning. That wasn't very pleasant, but we managed. We moved through different sections for the first few weeks until we came to production and packaging. We didn't have the slightest idea that we would meet Evan there. 'The Legend' did mention on occasions that Evan had a job, but where and which kind, nobody knew.

'Hey, you two. Come over here!' Frank yelled when he saw us standing in white robes and protective and sterilized garments on our hands and legs.

'Who gave you that bullshit to wear?' Frank was dressed more for a beer-drinking and poker-playing party than a tablet and capsule production line.

'You don't need that shit here. The girls over there in those closed glass rooms need to be careful. Here we mix ingredients, powders, and these solids. So who gives a shit?' He was a big, 1.95-tall man with bulky composure and a pleasant but mean-when-needed face. The last remnants of his blond hair were leaving his hair as desertification of his skull was happening rapidly. The yellow fingers pointed toward a chain smoker.

'So, get that silly clothes off and get over here on the double.' We were certainly not going to argue with this guy.

'Hmm…you are interns. That means you were shoved from division to division. He thought for a moment with a half-wicked smile. We were his now.

'Maybe we will have some use of you here for the rest of your internship.' He was already calculating how to put us to work and have more free time. He didn't give a crap if we were or were supposed to learn something. We didn't know that producing tablets was not Frank's only preoccupation on his mind. He was into other stuff too.

'You see my buddy over there, Evan? Anthoine will stay here with me while you can go and help Evan with the packaging. Later we will shift you guys around, but I think you could be helpful here. I obeyed, of course, and when I heard Evan, I hadn't had the slightest idea it was our very own Evan.

And to my big surprise, it was. He was happy to see me.

'Hej dude! What's up? Nice to see you here, man. I think you will like your internship a lot. He had the flu. His eyes were bulging out, red, and coughing and sneezing followed. The machine was a lovely state-of-the-art model. It was equipped with the latest electronics and gadgets. I just wondered who the hell gave Evan the responsibility over this thing. He did seem quite handy with it, at times rough. He gave me the runaround in a few minutes.

'So when I take a break, which could be a long one, you're in control, dude. Can you handle it?

'I think so. What if something happens?'

'Nothing will happen. If something goes, talk to Lisa over there. That's the babe with the nice ass.' It was supposed to be a semi-sterile environment. Evan was coughing like mad now over the packaging process. The machine made various noises, producing alarms and blinking LCDs. Evan just clicked on a couple of buttons, and it stopped.

'This thing pisses me off sometimes. It requires a clean environment, making noise whenever it doesn't like something. No wonder it made noises. Evan was spilling all kinds of germs and bacteria around with his coughing and sneezing. Even worse, he had no protective gloves or mouth cover.

'Maybe you should wear gloves or mouth protection when sick,' I said boldly. He actually should have stayed at home.

'Oh, f**k that dude. This is Proclain+. It's a drug for schizophrenia, and it's going to Russia, somewhere in Siberia. So who gives a f**k?' F**k the Russians; they can take any drug. Last week we had a strong sedative called Suplex2. That thing was exported to Albania. They won't mind.' I was just amazed by this guy. Holly shit! How the hell did this pass any internal control? And then the answer came.

'Yo, I will go now and nap in the 'sleeping room with Franck. You keep the fort alive and come and wake me up 15 min before the scheduled control comes. Have you got it?

'One thing more I forgot to mention. Every 30th or so package is 'crooked.' That means it has to be put aside. The bloody machine doesn't pack them properly, so the silver bottom doesn't fit properly with the plastic cover, the text is crooked, and so on. You just put those in the black bag on the side, and I will take care of them later.'

I acknowledged I understood, but I didn't know if this was a joke or not. Then I saw Anthoine guarding the machine producing the pullers and mixing other substances. That meant only one thing: Franck was in the sleeping room again. In a short while, one could hear a duet snoring. Lisa, who was close by, didn't give a shit about it, nor did the other workers do their thing. It seems more than one employee utilized the sleeping room. I wondered if Evan had flu or was on coke or heroin. Maybe he was back on amphetamines or, even worse, cocaine. I remember one time he almost had an overdose. Memphis saved him in the nick of time. In the '60s, he was high on the hash, as many of his friends were. One of the rare people that visited Woodstock, he continued this in the 70s and 80s. In the '90s, he went for the strong stuff, but lately, the talk was that he was cleaned up. Or was he?

Lisa was a babe. This blonde chick was in her early 30s looking great. This 5'11" beauty looked just perfect. She could have made any magazine cover with her slender legs, beautiful 34-21-33 body, deep blonde eyes, and long, black eyelashes. There was no way she would wear gloves with those long red nails nor a mouth cover to screw up the red lipstick that outlined her perfect pre-silicon lips. Wearing white, she looked like a nurse from a very naughty dream. It was no wonder that Evan couldn't keep his mind on work. She was operating the capsule machine. With a couple of friendly smiles and looks, I was melting like a snowman on a tropical day. But I had to keep my mind on this bloody machine. It was just packaging and packaging. Lisa climbed up on her capsule machine to insert a new set of capsules. It must have been a thousand or more. I looked at her again, especially her voluptuous breasts bulging from her white working robe. As she gave me another naughty look, her leg slipped slightly, and the pot with 1000+ capsules slid out of her hands and spilled all over the floor. Holy shit! It was like millions of worms appeared on the floor from nowhere.

'F**k, shit, f**king bitch what have you done? Lisa yelled at herself. She was not a cover girl anymore. Her expressions changed, and the language became a street one in seconds. She looked like Nikita, ready to blow away anyone who crossed her path.

'Son of a bitch, f**king capsules, mother f**king machine! Damn, control is in five minutes, and look at this mess. What a mess, what a waste. I have to put them back. Too bad!'

'I will help you throw them away before the control comes,' I added. I didn't quite get what she meant by putting them back.

'Throw them away! Are you out of your mind, little birdturd' Get a wiggle on! We don't have it all day!

She was ferocious now—no more, lovely cover girl chick Lisa. Mean Lisa was in control now. I was hurt. The bitch called me birdturd. I didn't look at her the same way. I hated her at that moment!

'Pick them up, and then I will put them back in the machine.' I was pissed off.

'You can't put these back; they are out of the sterile zone. Do you want to get people killed? Now she rushed to me and put her beautiful, mean face within inches of my face.

'You listen now, and listen, good buster! If you don't help me pick up these capsules now and you don't keep your big mouth shut, I swear I will pin this on you, and they will throw your ass out of this place, and your pretty ass will get f**ked when you come back to school. Maybe you won't even graduate? What do you think of that? Damn, she was beautiful even when mean. She knew it, and with that said, she gave me another smile.

'Did I make myself clear? I could have said and done a hundred things, but nothing came to mind. I was paralyzed.

'Yes, madam' was the only thing I blurted out.

'Call me Lisa. Now help me get this shit off the ground'. We started picking up capsules fast. I didn't have a conscious at that moment, or I was fighting with what was left of it. She sensed this.

'Don't worry, pretty boy. The people on the other side of the spectrum, the boondocks, won't mind. They usually take these anyway. It's some shit capsule for backaches or something. Anyway, the floor is clean, as you can see. You help me now, and I might help all of you later. The floor wasn't dirty, but it wasn't clean. Holy cow! We were working fast, and we just finished the thing and poured the capsules back into the feeding slide. What did she mean by 'helping all of us later'?

'Put your white clothes on you and protective garments,' she yelled.

'But Franck told me…' she cut me off, 'Screw Frank! He's an idiot. Listen to me! And get that bean head, Evan, here. I got him in seconds as I got in my white robe, protective gloves, and mouthpiece. I felt like somebody working in an illegal drug lab for cocaine lords of Colombia. Evan came looking like a Mack truck hit him at 100 miles an hour. Fortunately for him, he was all packed in white like an astronaut. He also added some glasses that must have been fake. He never wore prescription glasses. Lisa was already charming the control guys. They certainly were not looking at what she was doing but instead at what she had (or didn't have) underneath her white robe.

There were three big sacks of leftover pills. Two I haven't seen before.

'What's in the sacks, Evan? We only had one today, didn't we?

'You ask too many questions don't you dude? It's just pills, OK.' Lisa came by.

'Hey, maybe the kid can be useful. He could take the sacks this time, Evan. You have done it too many times, and your face is everywhere. That Jack character from control is getting more and more suspicious.'

'OK! The dude is cool. He knows what needs to be done.' here's the deal. It would help if you transported these leftover sacks to Joe Parr in the warehouse. He opened one of the bags and took two packets, which he inserted into an empty package of headache pills. He showed this into his pocket.

'Damn, bean head!' Lisa didn't like that at all.

'You're just going to get us in trouble, you f**king moron.'

'Shut the f**k up. I need this shit. You dig!'

'What the hell is inside?' I had a pretty good idea, but I just asked anyway.

'If this is illegal, you can write me off.'

Lisa was quick to answer.

'Now listen good! You're going to do this, and that's it. If you don't, I will burn your ass and get you into trouble with the local drug mob. I'll tell them all kinds of stories about how you were stealing from them, and that won't be the end. Evan will also get f**ked up because of you, as you are his responsibility.

'You can't do shit,' I started to say.

'Just watch me.' Seeing that look in her eyes, I believed everything she said.

'It's amphetamines inside. You know the three kinds: amphetamine proper—Benzedrine, Dexedrine, and methamphetamine –Methedrine. We got the first two. It's a goldmine with these babies. Then I remembered the theory.'

'But don't these things induce a psychosis that comes close to mimicking schizophrenia? Shit, these things are as much as dangerous as LSD. You know the expression 'Meth is death.''

'You watch too much TV, kid' I hated when she referred to me as 'kid.'

'Amphetamines produce drug dependency, physiological tolerance, and toxic effects, but no physical addiction. That's why they are goldmine honey'. Yeah, and that would make it all right, I thought. 'Honey' sounded good, though. Damn, I needed to get a hold of myself.

'What about toxic psychosis with hallucinations and paranoid delusions that they might produce? I asked.

'Will you shut the f**k up, dude? We don't need any pharmaceutical and toxicological lessons here. These babies can cure disease, too, and get you out of f**ked up mood stages. If it makes people feel good, so be it. We stream that along.' Evan made a point, which was, by his mind, sane. He (them) also made a bunch of money in the process. They didn't give too much shit what the pushers were going to do with this or how many people would get affected.

'Now get this f**king back to Joe, and if somebody asks, you will dispose of trash and leftover products in the special incinerators just beside Joe's place.'

Joe Parr was in charge of the transport facilities. He was the only person that could get this shit out of PharmaChemia Ltd., no questions asked. He couldn't take the finished packages ready to be shipped. They were all marked and counted. But the leftovers that Evan and Lisa produced were a goldmine. Whenever a pill, capsule, or tablet popped up with any drug-related effect, they ensured plenty of leftovers. There were careful there too not to overdo this scam. Evan was the 'Medicine Man,' while Franck and Joe were on the supply side. Lisa was the brain breaker. I met with Anthoine outside. He was also carrying two bags of leftover solids and powders. I didn't even ask. We could read each other's faces.

'Franck is also in on this.' It was self-evident. The 'medicine people' needed a chain to do this. Anthoine continued.

'He used me right away. He said if I didn't do what he asked, he would, and I quote: 'f**k my sister and kill my dog.''

'How does he know you have a sister and a dog?'

'It must have been Evan. It's unbelievable!' they are so bold with this, Bro.

'Tell me about it. You should have seen the chick. She is a master when it comes to cover-ups. Evan is probably high all the time.

'That fat pig Franck doesn't give a crap too much. He looks like a lazy collector. He was going on and on about how their wages were so low, and he needed to support his family and that if I kept my mouth shut, nothing would happen.'

'I got pretty the same story, Bro! Evan trusts us, and the chick thinks she's got me wrapped around her red nail fingers.

'What are we going to do, Bro?, asked Anthoine.

'I think we must take them down, but I don't know.

We entered the warehouse transport building. We went straight to the office area. The thing was to get rid of these bags ASAP! It seemed nobody was there. We heard some sounds from a room in the back of the hallway. It sounded like folk music. We slightly opened the door, and what we saw inside was unbelievable. A guy was sitting behind a big old oak desk. This must have been Joe. He was a guy of 250 pounds with dark skin and mahogany hair. His pointed nose and chin didn't fit with the rest of the fat face and small fox-like eyes. He was waving his stuffed arms, following the rhythm of the music. A bottle of J&B was on the table, and various brands of German salami, Greek Feta cheese, Spanish olives, and French baguette bread.

Coffee and cigarettes were accessories that followed. The whole room was filled with cigarette smoke, so you felt you were in a Finish sauna. On the other side of the room, an instead well-formed lady in her mid 40's was dancing on the table barefoot. She was wearing a red dress, and cellulite was trying to get out of every piece of polyester fabric. Her dyed blond hair, sleazy looks, and cheap seducing moves pointed toward specific previous jobs she might have had. The other two guys in the room were half singing, half eating. The fifth person accompanied the radio music with the playing of a small pan flute. It was not a lunch break. It just seemed that these people had a break all the time. Joe saw us, as did the rest. The others didn't move a zilch. The 'lady' just continued dancing and was fed some feta cheese and J&B by one of the participants in this underground show. There were remnants of plates filled with beans. That's probably why the whole space was filled with a smelly fart odor. Joe saw the black sacks. He had already gotten word from Lisa that the interns were coming.

'Hi, guys!' He got off his big ass and shoved it into another room, considerably smaller than the other. He was behaving like we were his pen pals for years. He just reminded me of those sleazy child molesters that you could read about in the papers or see on TV.

'Give me the bags now. I will take care of the rest. You want some booze, food, or something else. He brought a bottle of some strange pills. They looked like Ecstasy or Adam as it was called in States.

'This is the new shit. We just got it from States. Of course, this you cannot get on a production line. This will make you feel liberated and good about yourself.' He portrayed it as if it was just like using Prozac today. He became very persistent.

'Take it now! Anthoine reacted swiftly with a perfect lie.

'Thanks, Mr. Joe! We appreciate it. But my friend here takes amphetamines, and I'm into heroin, so we'll pass. As they say, we don't like to mix.' He kept such a straight face while I was getting nervous. Joe was suspicious, but he let it go.

'OK, then. That means you got your shit. Maybe next time, right? Now get out of here before someone sees you.'

This guy was a crony. There was no doubt about that. And he was delivering this to the intermediaries and pushers. But there was someone at the top; there always was. That somebody was taking the cream off. Where the hell was the local DEA?

The fat pig returned to his office and ushered everybody out except the dancing woman. Then he locked the door behind him.

We decided unanimously (like there was a bunch of us) to somehow report this to the authorities. Our only concern was Evan, as we knew him. He was the King of the transport & warehouse section. The poor guy would get into a shit load of trouble. But we decided we had enough. Evan would have to go down. The events that followed superseded our decision.

We were doing our mid-term weeks at the factory when Lisa approached me.

'Listen, I want you and your friend to move to another division today. You will go to the laboratories and do quality testing after lunch. I talked to a friend of mine there. I'll take care of Franck and Joe—Evan's no trouble.

'But we got two weeks left here.' I was happy to get out of there.

'Listen to me. I like you, and you were useful here to me. I'm an undercover agent working for DEA. We had these guys under surveillance for over a year. The feds have also been involved, as many people have been murdered lately. We will use a small timer like Franck and Evan to squeeze the bigger fish. The fat pig Joe will go down for murder.' Shit! I knew that guy was in deep trouble but was a murderer.

'There's some serious shit going to happen in the coming days, probably even in the afternoon. So I want you guys out of here on the double. I will probably call you later for more questioning, but you won't need to testify. We will cut a deal with small fish. You haven't done anything except protect your friend and do what I said. As I am an agent, it makes it OK. I knew you wanted to go to the authorities. We overheard you in the locker room. This whole place is bugged from top to bottom, guys.' Just keep your mouth shut and no word to Evan.

'What's going to happen to him?' I blurted out.

'Don't worry. He will do just fine. He won't be able to avoid a rehab clinic and a minimum security facility for a year.

I was taken by surprise. This great-looking babe turned out to be excellent in the end. She was a female agent as beautiful as one of Charlie's Angels. I was in seventh heaven. I just wanted to be 007 at that moment. As we were transferred, I told Anthoine the whole story. He just opened his mouth, saying all the time: 'F**k a duck, Bro; awesome! What a babe!' Yeah, what a babe, indeed!

As Lisa said, the equivalent of Feds and DEA came in storms in the afternoon. We were in the labs when it happened. Franck was taken away and cuffed, as well as Evan. They looked shockingly at Lisa when she put her DEA suit on. Joe was not that easy. The fat big barricaded himself in the room, taking the barefoot dancer secretary as a hostage. In the end, after some shooting, the dancer lost a piece of her ear, and a feds shotgun almost blew away Joe's right ass buttock, so he surrendered. He knew he would face drug trafficking and murder counts.

Indictments and arrests followed. Two more guys were picked up from two other divisions and people from all over. The whole network was busted. Small fishes gave out the big ones. Some fled the country, though, while most were caught. Lisa did her job with flying colors. Evan, 'the medicine man,' got what she said he would get. Memphis 'The Legend' later told everybody he took a job offer in Canada. We kept our mouths shut about him. I saw Lisa again when we answered some more questions. She was even lovelier than before. Their wonderful smile and business look woman made her look even more attractive. I understood when she had to play a nasty bitch, even when she did what she did with the capsules. The conditions improved dramatically in the packaging section. The environment became even more sterile. The sleeping room was used for different purposes. The dog and pony show at the warehouse, Joe's private amusement, was a thing of the past. Our 'professional experience' ended as scheduled. We have seen firsthand what kind of spin-offs the pharmaceutical industry can produce in a unique 'sterile' environment.

9

Peeping Tom

He was watching patiently for hours, waiting and waiting. Not a single muscle moved in his body. He looked like a statute from Michelangelo's times – unbelievably live and realistic but still frozen in time. Woody Lee had just bought new binoculars, 8x30. This compact, wide-angle model was ideal for bird-watching and sports. It had state-of-the-art multiple-lens ocular systems, offering a high-resolution flat viewing field. We never figured out the brand. It could have been a Nikon, but on the other hand, it could have been a military one from the Soviet Union block, probably DDR or Russia. It didn't make a big heck of a difference. As we found out later, he had a couple: a Vivitar, Zeiss, and others. I'm sure as hell that he wasn't watching birds or sports with his new binoculars. Bird-watching was just a cover-up. Let's be realistic. The only thing you had flying in the air besides occasional spit, paper, trash, pampers, food, and pollution were crows, ravens, sparrows, and flying rats (pigeons). That much of an enthusiast, he was not. A different type of – he was!

I guess every large apartment building in the city has its number of beautiful women. Some less, some more, and some, in most cases, have none. Well, we were pretty lucky there. Our skyscraper was blessed with three gorgeous beauties: a black, a blonde, and a brunette. Each of the girls had her own "special qualities." The blonde girl, Michelle, had a fantastic figure and a beautiful face that accompanied her "healthy body." She was your typical "pet of the month" girl with gigantic, full breasts, beautiful legs, and a nice behind. The black-haired girl was something else. Andrea was more like an Haute Couture figure, a Gianni Versace or Karl Lagerfeld model, than a Playboy or a Penthouse girl. She was a typical catwalk model with a beautiful cover-girl face and long, slender legs. The third girl, the brunette Sonia was a combination of two former girls. With an attractive face and a nice-looking body, she could have passed for a high-class hooker anytime. Every time we saw one of the girls, we stopped breathing.

The girls certainly enjoyed the stares and whistles. I can't tell you their exact proportions, but all three were in the 34-25-35, 5'4", and 115lbs range, so you can get a picture of what I am talking about. Because of their apparent attributes, the girls received much attention from male species of all ages. Besides being tenants in the same building and having gorgeous faces and "healthy" bodies, these three girls also had another thing in common. They all lived on the eastern side of the building. Two-bedroom apartments (apartment #3) were entirely on this side of the building. Michelle and Andrea lived in these apartments while Sonia was also in a two-bedroom apartment, but in the one that just partly had access to this side. The rest of the apartment was on the southern side. Michelle and Andrea even lived on the same floor, the 6th, while Sonia was on the 10th floor. My apartment was also on this side, even a couple of my friend's apartments.

It must be said that in terms of the view, our skyscraper was one hell of a building. Every side had excellent views of different parts of the city. Our site was particular because it had a nice view of the city center. The skyscraper was part of a complex of four almost identical skyscrapers. One of the sister skyscrapers was the only thing that partly blocked the view. The distance between the skyscrapers was approximately 50m. So naturally, the higher floors in our building had better 'strategic' views, not just of the city but also of some of the apartments in the 'neighboring sister buildings.' The same thing goes for the higher floors in that skyscraper. There was a difference, though, a big one. Out of all four buildings, ours had the best 'babes.' And above all, they all happened to be living on the same side, the side that was partly facing the other skyscraper. And on the 10th floor, Woody Lee lived in that building – our own 'Peeping Tom.' This was undoubtedly not a legendary citizen who looked out his window in the 17th century, nor was he looking at Godiva, an Anglo-Saxon gentlewoman famous for her legendary nude rides through Coventry. No Sir! He was that type of peeper, but he had something different to look at. The risk of being caught gave an additional element to the excitement of our voyeur. By definition, Peeping Tom is a person who derives sexual satisfaction from watching from hiding places as others take their clothes off (in most cases, women) or engage in sexual acts. Woody Lee wasn't a sexual maniac or pervert by definition, as far as we knew. He was in his late 20s, had his apartment and a girlfriend, and was a pretty average guy – or was he? Regardless of how well you think you know some people, they can be completely different.

So our peeper liked to watch girls, but not all girls. He chose the three gorgeous beauties in our building that I just mentioned. Hey, and who can blame the guy? Even if we all wanted to be peepers, we would immediately be out of a job. All the girls in the peepers building, especially the ones on the side that was facing our building, were ugly as hell! So there wasn't much to look at. The girls were not aware of Woody's presence. He watched the girls occasionally and was careful not to be spotted. It was mostly at night and sometimes in the morning, probably when the girls were dressed or undressed. He sometimes watched during the day. The living rooms and one of the bedrooms in apartment #3 had balconies. This meant they had more privacy than the other rooms, the kitchen and the bedroom. But the girl's bedrooms, and even Sonia's in a different apartment, were without balconies. This left them more "vulnerable" to eventual peepers. So our peeping Tom took this opportunity to invade their "bodily" privacy. He probably didn't possess, as usually peepers and voyeurs do, a large telescope or a camera with zoom lenses. His only peeping tool was a couple of good binoculars. He used them whenever an opportunity presented itself. Woody worked at the post office, but I don't know what he did exactly. One time I remember that he was in our building checking something on the telephone connections panel in the lobby. I didn't think of that much then. He always watched from his room, where he had the most privacy. We also occasionally watched him, especially when putting two and two together. He usually wore a T-shirt with inscribed text: "Back Off – I'm a Postal Worker." Well, he certainly didn't look like one. A combination of a recovered homeless guy, a wanna-be-biker, and someone going strong on Prozac was more of the way Woody Lee struck you. Black beard and bushy black hair, which was never taken care of properly, an unsporty skeleton and a face spelled out INSOMNIA gave him a very unattractive look. In a way, he was more of a conservative, shy peeper rather than an aggressive one. That's probably why none of us thought that we should report him to the authorities. He was not doing any 'damage' yet. And besides, he had such an ugly and unattractive girlfriend that, after all, you couldn't blame the poor guy. I can't say if we had any laws against this. I think we did. There were not of the American type that came into power in 1997. To my knowledge, a law in States would make peeping a misdemeanor carrying a $1,000 fine and a six-month jail sentence. According to that, it is now a misdemeanor to "look through a hole or opening, or use any instrument, such as a periscope or telescope, to spy on someone where that person had a reasonable expectation of privacy." Yeah right! That certainly did not apply to Woody. If it were all possible, in those days, Woody would have brought up his 'visual surveillance' to a different level by installing digital gadgets, cameras, bugs, etc., in girls' private places like bedrooms, bathrooms, and dressing rooms. One thing was sure, you could have filed for civil damages, but Woody's actions would not pass as a crime under the laws we had. So he continued to have a field day with his activity.

Our peeper, besides watching the girls in their underwear, half-naked, had another very grotesque habit. The balconies in the skyscrapers had unique rectangular flower pots. People planted different kinds of flowers and sometimes even some tiny vegetables. The peepers' balcony had all the balconies' lushest and most beautiful flowers. Sometimes even these flowers gave him cover for occasional peeping. This credit went to his ugly girlfriend, who wanted to find beauty and nurture it elsewhere, as she did not possess it. His mother was also doing a pretty good job with planting, but the flowers were still so fertile, super-fertile, to be exact. Were they using some new planting technique, or maybe they had a new fertilizer? Whatever it was, it was indeed working.

And then, one day, something extraordinary happened. The peeper was on the balcony, looking with his binoculars. My friend Keke and I were killing a dull fall Saturday afternoon. We were catching some sunrays and bullshitting around when we spotted Woody at his routine activity. He carried on with his binoculars when after a while, he started working on the flowers. He suddenly got very excited. He took the flower-pot boxes down from the railing, one by one. We thought he would water them, change the soil, or something like that, but he had something else in mind. He glanced and assured him nobody was watching, taking his pants and underwear off. Good grief! Although the thick-glass balcony railing gave you some privacy, there would always be a chance that somebody was watching you. Well, at that moment we were watching the peeper. He was excited, most probably by the nakedness of one of the women he was 'bird watching.' And, of course, we thought he would end his dirty daily routine by doing, well…you know what. No, he did something else instead. He was now half naked, from the waist down. Suddenly he started urinating (pissing) into the flowerpots. He was "fertilizing" the flowers!!! There were four flowerpot boxes, and the peeper methodically divided his piss among all of them. When he was finished, he put his underwear and pants back on. He had a face of a man going to one of his wildest wet dreams. My God! Keke and I looked at each other. This bugger was something else. You are wrong if you thought he pissed in the flowers because he was in a hurry. The man did this regularly, a couple of times a month. I don't know if he just got aroused from watching the girls or if he was some flower lover – a flower fetishist. Whatever it was, it was bizarre, even grotesque. What a guy! What a sight that was…

oh man. The "pissing peeper"! Was this a thing to talk about, or what!

But then, one day, things got slightly complicated and out of hand. They usually do when things like this and people like this are involved. It was a beautiful day in June. Sun sent gorgeous rays through the clouds, creating a heavenly array of light. The atmosphere was angelic. There was no wind, and you could almost feel the softness of the air. It was paradise for sunbathing and beer or Coke sipping. You just needed the ocean or the sea to fill in the picture.

"If this were heaven, I would take a long-time subscription, Haas!"

Keke was drinking a Coke on my balcony and enjoying the sun again rays. I was deeply involved in one of the Marvel Comics.

"Yeah, Bro! You got that right. I could go on forever like this. By the way, what's up with the Woody guy?" Woody was active lately, primarily since the girls used to come out more on the balconies as the sun and warmth drew them out like snails after rain.

"F**k! He is at it again! Oh…he's got a phone now."

"What?" I asked, amazed.

"F**king phone Bro. And you know what I think. I think the bastard is calling one of them. And it must be Michelle, as the other two are not in town." It was obvious that Keke was well-informed.

"How the hell do you know that? He could be calling anybody, for God's sake."

"No, no! Come and see, man. Keke gave me his binoculars, and it seemed he was partly right. Woody was watching with a telephone and stroking and rubbing his private parts. He was in a half-trance now.

"Keke, he must be calling the 070 number. Do you think she would stay on the line with him? He probably has free access through the post and doesn't pay any bills. But he must be watching Michelle. Let's call Gill and check it out"!

Gill was our buddy that lived two floors above Woody's apartment. Gill was a pig, inside and out. He used to eat all the time, on every possible occasion and at every opportunity he got. He weighed twice as much as Keke and I but didn't give too much shit about it. His parents were the size of polar bears, so I guess it ran in the family. But he was a good buddy. You could always rely on this guy, no matter what. He was digesting a large piece of a chicken club when we called him.

"Hey Gill, get that f**king food out of your mouth and help us catch a dirty guy!" Keke was excited, and so was I. We did not know what we were doing, nor did we care. Nor did we think of consequences either. We just took things and played along as the events unfolded and evolved.

"Get the damn binoculars and see what Michelle is doing!" Gill didn't need much to do that task. The keyword was "Michele." That could receive the highest of priorities and even bypass the best dishes that Gill enjoyed so much.

"Man, oh, Man…She is topless, boys, taking the sun on the balcony! We could see that Gill was drooling on the balcony. No wonder Woody is getting wooded! Holy cow – those breasts."

"Keep us informed, Gill." Keke was already thinking fast.

"Let's get the f**ker, Haas"!

"I don't think it's any of our business, man."

"No, but these are our women, man; what are you talking about." Keke was becoming very territorial now. They were indeed not our women, even if we all desired that. But on the other hand, he was right. This activity needed to seize. It was an infringement of people's privacy. Well, those dilemmas soon became history.

"I will call Michele now," screamed over the telephone Gill hung up.

"What…" I began to say.

"He's calling her dude. The man is a pig, but he's got balls of a buffalo." Keke was all hipped up. We watched Gill make the phone. During that time, Woody did not move an inch. He was again one of Michelangelo's statues.

"Hi, aaahhh, is this Michelle?" Gill was sweating like a pig, and his voice was trembling. But he kept the phone in one hand and the binoculars in the other.

"Yes, speaking!" Michelle had her wireless phone by her side. Gill just went for it. "A man is watching you from the opposite building, on the 10th floor. He has binoculars and his hand in his underwear. He urinates after that in the flower pot and does all kinds of things with his Willy. Oh yeah, he is a pervert, by the way." Gill blew all this information in one package, so Michelle was utterly unprepared.

"What the hell…Who are you?"

"Who I am is unimportant," Gill said, sounding like a secret agent. "The important thing is that this wacko has been watching you and two more girls, Sonia and Andrea, for over a year. And I must say, Michelle, that you have a fine pair of tits, and I am not an expert, but I think your bra must be a full 36D size. They look so good in the sun".

"You son of a bitch, you can also see me"…she immediately covered herself with a tee shirt and started looking at the apartments across. She was angry, hurt, and pissed off. Gill slammed down the phone and ducked behind the balcony railing. He was only two floors higher than Michelle in the adjacent skyscraper, and she could spot him easily. She was looking for our peeping Tom, and after a while, she spotted him. We saw this because he suddenly jerked and moved to the side, even if hidden. She was screaming from the balcony.

"You f**king son of a bitch. Damn, pervert! I will call the police, the army, and the Marines. No, I will kill you myself."

 She was like a raging bull. She knew now that she was watched when she had her boyfriend there or when she was undressing. She never really bothered to check if someone was watching. There was no privacy. What if this guy had cameras in the apartment, she thought?

Woody could hear this as the sound carried so far. She was so angry. Soon the neighbors started coming out. She disappeared from the balcony. So did Gill. Woody was nowhere to be seen. We were still watching, amazed.

"Far out, Keke! This is like a thriller. It was nothing like Sliver with Sharon Stone and William Baldwin, but it was improving by the minute. Things happened fast. We didn't know that Andrea's new boyfriend was a cop. Michelle was his good friend, and she immediately called him, explaining Woody's activities and pointing out that Andrea was probably the one most watched by this pervert and that cameras could be involved in the whole thing. She added fantasy and lies with it. So by the end of her description, Woody Lee probably looked like Charles Manson. Andrea's cop boyfriend didn't waste much time. There were three patrol cars there in a matter of minutes. It was a slow Sunday, so the cops didn't have better things to do. They came from nowhere and then went up the building. Very soon, we saw them on the balcony. Woody was also handcuffed while they were rampaging through his apartment. Search warrant – no…who needed that. The Police operated here in a different fashion, especially with perverts. We could see through the binoculars that Woody already had a couple of bruises. They probably gave him a couple of fast beatings.

"Holy f**k Haas, these guys are not kidding around. Woody is going out of business." Keke was right. Woody would be closing his shop soon, as well as his zipper. Suddenly the shouting started, and they showed him back in. Later two detectives arrived, one of them from the Postal Services. Michelle was nowhere to be seen. As usual, Gill was probably hiding in his mom's closet and sweating like a pig.

A couple of days later, we had some answers. All three girls pressed charges, and what was even worse, the Police found something in his apartment which was incriminating enough to put him in the can for some time. Electronic eavesdropping was the charge. Or, if we used legal terminology, it was the act of electronically intercepting conversations without the knowledge or consent of at least one of the participants. You have wiretapping, which monitors telephone communication. All of this shit was legally prohibited in virtually all jurisdictions. Woody Lee was not that sophisticated. He did wiretap her phone and bugged her apartment. They found all the gadgets and monitoring devices in his apartment. He was into electronics and portrayed this to his girlfriend as 'making new inventions for the postal services.' She was very proud of him then, but that suddenly changed. So he was listening to her. He fancied her most, as the two other girls only had bugs. How he managed to get this sophisticated equipment, nobody knew. They brought him up on these charges. Some jail time and fines followed. Contrary to what we thought;

Woody had a lovely large telescope with a camera with zoom lenses. It was even equipped with night vision. So he was watching all the time. How he explained this to his girlfriend nobody knew. Our three girls were much more careful now with reviling themselves. Who knows, there might be more perverts out there. Michelle knew at least that someone else was watching too. Gill was afraid to come out on the balcony for weeks to come.

Time passed, and he was moving to another city when he got out. He got sacked from the Postal services. We did see his girlfriend once or twice. Once she came out on the balcony, full of rage, watching the windows opposite and thinking of all those women he was looking at. She felt so humiliated. And the damn polluted plants and flowers. She just threw them all out from the balcony on the asphalt beneath. That was the last we saw of her again. We never saw him again; some other people moved in and started having their flowers and plants. I can tell you one thing: those new 'botanical species' on the balcony were never the same again.

10

The Shitting Birds

The rain just stopped. It lasted five hours like an artillery barrage before an offensive took place. It was so strong that we could not see the other skyscraper while it was pouring from the skies. Finally, it subsided. The clouds didn't have that ominous look like before, and there was even some clearing in the heavens above us. Now I knew what November rains meant. I always hated the damn rain. It brought foul mood, depression, restriction of playtime, and…well, it just sucked! Living in Seattle and Vancouver must suck big time if you hate rain. The rain in these cities seems never to stop. I knew about the November winds, but the rains? The day was ending, and the sky, as it was already dark, was getting darker even more. The streets seemed deserted. It all had a bizarre dark look. I hated going outside, but there was nothing to do. At least for the last five hours, I had an excuse. It was simple. Before nightfall, I had to cover my dad's car in the parking lot. The problem was that the adjacent industrial park, 'John Higgins Ltd' discharged, usually in the evenings, some industrial acid rain – as we liked to call it – 'rust rain.' It was some bloody type of rust dust (sounds like something you can get high on!), which stuck to the hood of the car, and it was almost impossible to wipe off. It wasn't that visible, but closer, you could see it was not part of your usual car gear. With the addition of rain, it had an even worse effect. As we know, the process that results in the formation of acid rain begins in most cases with the discharge of sulfur oxide & nitrogen oxides into the atmosphere. The combustion of fossil fuels releases these waste gases through automobiles, electric power plants, and smelting and refining facilities. That's how the textbooks define it, anyway. I didn't have a clue what this thing was. The affected parties (most of my friend's parents) tried to protest and do something about it, but it was more or less in vain. There were some promises that filters would be installed, which was done, but the rust rain continued at a stable pace. It was some 'steel industrial' process that was doing this, but what exactly, I can't tell you. The industrial park was restricted, and they did many things, some even for the military. Nobody cared; just the rust rain was pissing off everybody, especially the car owners. I wonder if anybody thought about the damage and impacts to the ecosystems around us, us being the most important one in this respect. Probably not! The looks of the hoods of the cars and the elimination of unnecessary cleaning labor were the #1 thing on the local agenda. Most of us knew that if we didn't help our folks cover the cars with the unique composite material that this tarpaulin had, we would eventually participate in the hand washing these vehicles as the automatic brush facilities found at the gas stations couldn't do the job correctly.

Some cars were already covered, and some were not. I took the car's keys and decided to do my duty as a good soldier. In the elevator, I meet my good friend Danny Slowitz. We covered two identical Volkswagen Golfs: crimson red and post office yellow.

'Yo Haas, you too!' Danny was in high spirits.

'Yeah, Bro, me too. What else can one do on a Thursday evening than fight the rust rain'.

'Heck, man, I don't think it's been so bad these last weeks. This covering shit is kind of unnecessary.'

'Well, don't forget, I started putting on a philosophical look that if it weren't rust rain, it would be crime prevention, protection of windshields from birds, or something similar.'

'Yeah, and in the summer, it would be the f**king sun rays destroying the inside furnishings. There's no way of avoiding this shit'.

'When we start driving these machines fully, we will probably continue this 'family tradition,' I added.

'The best thing is to get it over and go home.' Danny was determined to wrap this up as soon as possible. The probability of another rain shower was still very high in the rain. Somehow I had some strange chills in my body. I couldn't figure it out. The parking lot seemed pretty deserted and uninviting. Dark shadows were covering the leftover light traces after the rainfall. Nighttime was slowly creeping in. Cars stood like ominous shapes, piled like bodies in a mortuary, side by side. The number of covered cars made that effect even more robust, which reminded me of bodies covered by white sheets after or before the autopsy performed after some hideous crime. I think I was going over my head and having some strange attacks of dark episodes. Danny was excellent, as you can be in this simple-to-do action adventure episode. What action adventure? I must stop these day/night dreams.

We reached the cars, which were situated in the center of the parking lot. The tarpaulin—WATERPROOF CANVAS AUTOCAR COVER SHEET—was in our trunks. These beasts weighed almost 5 kilos and were made out of a combo of materials, waterproof rubber being just one of them. They looked like army tents ready to be assembled for a military exercise. While I was trying to get this thing out of the trunk, Danny was looking at the long row of trees facing the industrial park. He was looking and not moving at all.

'Hey, Bro! Weren't you the one saying something about efficiency and getting the hell out of this humid, sticky, and wet atmosphere?' Danny didn't reply. I turned around to see what had captivated his attention, and what I saw froze my insides instantly. Approximately 30 high Canadian Maple trees lined up in front of the long fence of the industrial park behind our parking lot. I could never figure out why they planted these trees here. It looked nice, though, hovering at about 30 m in height. Even though this tree is planted along streets and in parks, it didn't seem here at home entirely. I liked to call them Canadian maples as I always associated those trees with the flag and the country where I spent a year of my early childhood. This one was, I think, the Sycamore maple (A. pseudoplatanus), a critical shade and timber tree. Whichever one it was, it provided lovely shade for the workers taking a break in the industrial park open space and giving beautiful colors, especially in fall. My vision was not 100% clear but undoubtedly adequate to recognize the shapes topping the high branches and peaks of the high trees. They were full of crows. Yes, you heard me right – crows! Not one, not five or twenty or even a hundred. Over a thousand sinister black beasts must occasionally sit, flapping their wings but not moving significantly. I understood why Danny was mesmerized. So was I!

'Look at that, Bro,' Danny finally spoke. 'What a f**king invasion force, man.' Danny was obsessed with UFOs and all kinds of X-files terminology. He saw in every large grouping a potential invasion of small green men or whoever looked out of the ordinary.

They were crows, our animal kingdom neighbors. Together with pigeons, rats, stray dogs, and cats, they presented the most significant animal (in the world's most comprehensive sense) population. They were always there, moving around, watching, waiting. All these crows were about 50 cm (20 inches) long and had colored glossy black bodies with sharp, rather long beacons and two dead eyes that could quickly have emerged from the darkest rooms of Lucifer and his followers. What was even more chilling was that I knew that crows were omnivorous. The ones I observed in our surroundings feed chiefly on the ground, where they walk about sedately. They are gregarious, and at times they roost together in great numbers. Heck…this was a significant number, not many thousands like in record books, but well over a thousand, which was more than enough for us. Well, insects were a part of their diet, but you never know. I don't understand why we were…well…afraid. I think we were. Ridiculous, they were resting on the trees and doing nothing, but we had a strange feeling that they were watching every move we made. I felt that Danny was feeling uneasy as I was, but he wouldn't admit it. We turned to each other almost simultaneously and said: 'Do you remember Hitchcock's Birds?' We were supposed to laugh at this moment, but only an ice-frozen grim came out.

'Let's get this shit over with. We don't have a whole night'. I was determined to leave ASAP and was not at all interested in the intention of these birds or if they had any, for that matter. It seems he agreed with me and started immediately unfolding the tarpaulin I followed shortly. We forgot about the birds for a moment. About halfway through, we heard a hissing, flapping sound coming behind us. To our horror, the birds seemed to be preparing for the departure from their terminal. We didn't know the final destination, nor did we particularly care, but we were somehow afraid if there would be a stop in between or if we were that destination. Usually, when you think the worst, the worst comes knocking or even banging at your door. Our behavior was becoming tragic, and fortunately, nobody was there to see us. It was an eleven-hour decision to stop what we were doing and be prepared. We were working on a special kind of telepathy, remotely aware of each other's actions. Danny was the first to scream.

'F**k Haas, they are coming after us. Dug for cover, man!' We didn't know if that was true, if the birds were birds or some angels of death coming for our souls, if they were just tired to death and leaving now, or if we were just two chicken shit idiots with a half-lunatic imagination. There was no time to find that out as the massive wave of birds lifted instantly and flew to the skies. They made a half circle and then, looking bent on doing something, made a sharp swing towards us, flying at high speed and low altitude. We threw ourselves down between our cars and covered our heads. Crows are smaller and less heavily billed than most ravens, and they are named for their typical call that sounds like "caw" or "crah." Now we understand why.

The terrible shrieking sound filled the air, and what came after the whooshing sounds of a low approaching airplane coming in hundreds was a sound that we didn't hear before like somebody throwing something slimy at fast speed into a still object. It was a combo of artillery barrage sounds coupled with paintball thunder and hale coming down from the cloud cover. We knew we were goners. It was probably these black f**kers eating at our brains and chopping the pieces of our bodies. We felt no pain, though. After a couple of seconds, which felt like an eternity, we finally got up and looked at each other. There was joy, happiness, and embarrassment on our faces simultaneously. How stupid could we be? We were all in one piece, and the birds were back in their trees. Nothing was wrong, we thought. As we returned to the car work, we saw what the sounds we had heard a moment ago meant.

The cars were filled with bird toppings, or in plain language – piles of white, stinky crow shit. These bastards bombarded the parking lot, mainly focusing on us and the cars around us. Remarkably there was no shit on either one of us. Now we had to cover the half-shitted cars. Shit! That meant a whole lot of cleaning. How the f**k was one going to explain this? I didn't care. The only thing on my mind was to cover the car and get out of here smelling decent. Bird shit was one small bugger you couldn't get rid of quickly. I was in a hurry now. Danny had other ideas. He just wanted to f**k with the crows. Bad move!

'Get down from those trees, you damn, dark bastards! Come on down, and I will mop up the floor with you little bastards.' Danny was shouting, screaming, and even throwing stones across the street where the maples were.

'Stop it, man! We don't have time for this bullshit. Leave them be. Can't you see that these are the mean son of bitches.'

I wanted to get out of the parking lot in a hurry. Somehow I managed to cover the car, secure the tarpaulin, and was turning towards Danny when we heard the same sound again. It seems it was a cycle, or they were just pissed off at Danny's constant shouting. They were ready for another attack.

'You stupid f**k, look what you have done now!' I was pissed off at Danny, but there was no time for discussion. I helped him cover the car for what must have been 10 seconds. 10 seconds too late. We wanted to run, but it was too late. Danny was paralyzed, and I had time to cover my head and lean slightly to the car when the Crow Armada arrived. This time the shitting was brutal, violent, and ruthless. A couple of hundred birds flew over us and discharged their heavy load. Danny was covered in shit. Smelly crow deposits plastered his face, but no birds attacked us. They were around 80-90 droppings on Danny's face, hair, hands, and clothes. He was in shock. I survived with 10-15 due to the cover I had from the car, though I was pretty f**ked up and smelling bad. These buggers must have mutated somehow and adapted to the industrial spillovers in the air. Who knows, maybe they liked the rust dust. My imagination was growing by the minute. This was far from over. They were coming back.

'Run, man!' I screamed to Danny, who was waking up from his shock. The crows didn't return to the high maple ground but instead were making a larger circle. We could be 100% certain that they were returning to finish their dirty job and plaster us even more. Our feet felt like lead pylons. We started running across the green lawn separating two parking lots sets. After that, it was the parking street and the entry to our skyscraper – salvation! We were halfway through the narrow green lawn patch when the 3rd attack came. There was no room for cover as we were on the open now. I turned my head around just a second to see the incoming beasts, but a second too late. I tripped on a rock and fell with all my weight into a dirt hole filled with mud and rainwater. This was a great compliment to the already drying droppings. This thing did not save me from the 3rd violent attack that was commencing. Danny was in slightly better luck. He managed to slide between two cars when the shit hit the fan. I curled myself in the hole, which was a stupid decision, and waited. Instantly, I could hear the heavy shit rain falling on me from the dark flapping monsters above. They were flying low. I was literally in deep shit! Danny Boy got only a dozen or so. He helped me get out of the hole and sprinted for the last 25 or so meters. The black demons didn't follow. It seems they had enough or just ran out of shit. Satisfied, they returned to the high maple ground. We watched from the security of the covered staircase patio and entré to the skyscraper. In an instant, they all lifted a thousand or more. We thought they would do a kamikaze and splatter their bodies all over the entrance doors while spearing us with their beacons. None of that happened, though. They disappeared behind the maples into the dark, misty night like demons from another world. Only the shrieking sounds followed. They were laughing at us. We felt a chill in our bones, especially as I was soaking wet, full of mud, and plastered with shit. Danny mainly suffered in the first attack, and he looked like someone threw a can of white paint all over him. We looked at each other and just laughed our heads off as two madmen lucky to be alive. There was a hell lot of cleaning to be done. Ahh… November rains are something else.

11

Al Durant

'Get out of the bed, you stinking, no-good dirty bitch, and fix me a drink!' Al Durant was looking viciously mean this morning. His hangover was cutting through his whole body like a barbed wire. He needed a drink fast. Al was lying crosswise on the couch in the living room. There was also a bedroom, a kitchen with a small dining place, and a bathroom. The windows, which lost any remnants of transparency and cleanness, were positioned towards the construction site.

He was wearing his favorite flannel striped pants and a blue shirt with alcohol stains, patches of dried tobacco, some lipstick, sweat circles under the armpits, and some moth holes. The beard was a week old. It was a tough week. Two insatiable whores, surely 20 liters of solid booze, a whole week of poker, and his friends around him were the result. He was not the sole participant in that dreadful event. He had a gang of his old timers, four of them. They were all bums like him, but somehow he took the leadership naturally, being the strongest, most cunning in small-time crime, and having a relatively higher IQ than the rest of the gang. He didn't do any work, lived on social welfare, and had activities on the side. When you asked him what he was doing, he would give you a cliché answer: 'I am a businessman.'

Most of them have seen the inside of jails many times. This last week was though a fun week. They scored at a gas station some weeks ago. Al's motto was Lay low, don't get caught, and enjoy the fruits of success. The booze and the whores dried Al this time. He was rarely sober, and on these rare occasions, he always found time to exchange nice words with us youngsters. And somehow, on these 'rare' occasions, he always wore a jacket. A guy feared by most, not just by his mean looks but by the criminal stories and the company surrounding him.

His 'woman,' as he liked to call her, was lying in the bedroom. She was also a half-homeless street wino, and Al Durant used her simply as slave labor and sometimes, as he used to say, 'for desperate sex.' She was half drunk and snoring like hell when Al came from his buddy's apartment early in the morning. He fell like a bag of shit on the couch. Now he was half awake and angry as hell. 'Where's the f**king drink? Do I have to repeat myself twice bitch? You know what happens when I do. There won't be an intact part of your body when I am through with you.

She was getting up slowly now. Her baggy hair went well with her shaggy clothes and a hard wino face, which carried some timely scars. It is very doubtful that Bella, her name, ever looked like a proper woman. She was a huge woman. At one time, she used to carry about 120 kilos. She was down to 85 now, but we were sure that each of her sagging breasts took at least 20 kilos. When she hit the streets, and under which circumstances, nobody knew. She was hanging with Al's gang and was his general, not one for carnal purposes, more for filling up Al's belly. This suited her pretty much. She looked more like his mother than his babe. The time she stood still for most of her useless life. She couldn't remember when and why she got hooked up with someone like Al Durant. She only knew that he was the one that took her out of the streets and sheltered her.

Al was still lying motionless on the couch. He farted on with all his might. The harsh smell of combined alcohol, garlic, German salami, and simple rot filled the rum. Al was proud of his farts. They could bring the dead back to life. It showed that he was a strong male. He used to say that his ass muscles were 'high and dry.' I don't think he even knew what he was saying, but this sounded good for him in his limited preschool vocabulary.

Bella was slowly walking towards him. 'Where the f**k have you been all week?' asked Bella in a raspy, dry loud voice. 'None of your f**king business bitch'. I was with two whores, and they smelled nice, not like you. They did nice things for me. You are f**king walking sewage. Ha, Ha, Ha…Yeah f**king sewer rat, that's what you are bitch.'

'Whores, you have been with whores. And you call me a sewer rat, you smelly old no-good-for-nothing limp fart'.

Bella was pissed off, and she could get nasty if you f**k with her.

'I am not going to fix you any drink. I cook, I clean, and I wait for you. Drink your smelly piss for what I care. No more dirty old man, now you can go and f**k yourself.'

Al could not believe his ears. This piece of shit was on the attack. How dare she do this after all he has done for her?

'What are you saying bitch? Get your smelly ass over her so I can teach you a lesson.

Bella grabbed the first chair available. He was getting up and taking his belt from his trousers. His mind was unclear from the enormous amounts of alcohol, and he was a bit afraid of Bella. She was almost big as Al, if not even more prominent. And she could fight sir; she was damn good at that. But she had something else in mind. As with all his tough, macho fart façade was a coward deep inside, especially when it came to big Bella.

'Al baby, you want this on your back. Oh, no, even better. You don't need any cooking, so you surely don't need any dining chairs.' She was a strong woman, and with one swirl, she threw the heavy chair with all her might at the kitchen window. The window exploded in a burst of flying glass, and the chair went down three stories into the construction site. 'What the f**k....' Al was utterly taken by surprise. He didn't finish, and the second chair was going out.

We were standing outside the building when we heard the crash. We all knew it was Durant's window, but what was happening? Whatever it was, it was becoming exciting. Everything that had to do with Al was interesting. Having a local hoodlum living in your neighborhood could sometimes be a particular trait. After two or more seconds, two more chairs flew out of the window. Was it a fight? Usually, noise and screams accompanied fights. But this time, it was developing relatively quietly.

Durant was looking at Bella with glowing, wild eyes. He now resembled Jack Nicholson from The Shining. 'Leave it bitch', he screamed.

'F**k you, Al, I am stronger than your weakling ass. When did you throw furniture lately?

This was it for Al. He rushed into the kitchen but did not approach Bella, who was already holding a long, razor-sharp kitchen knife. Instead, he took the kitchen table and threw it outside the window. In that process, the other window exploded into shreds too. They were actually both still heavily drunk. Bella began laughing like a mad woman. 'Watch this, Al!' She went for the small fridge, wildly jerked out the power cord, lifted it almost professionally, and showed it outside the window. Al was petrified. If she could throw the fridge out like that, what the f**k would she do with him? But this was no time for weakness. He had to show her…

We just saw the last flight of the refrigerator. It crashed on the construction site. With it came some remnants that we could call food and a couple of bottles of booze. That was pretty cool, we all thought. More and more people were gathering. Even the people from the skyscraper across ours were looking through the windows. It was becoming a natural spectacle. The furniture was piling up on the construction site. Then came the bed, Al's favorite sofa, shelves, lamps, and God knows what else. Fortunately, they didn't throw out the dirty laundry. It was unbelievable how they quickly threw out all these 'artifacts.'

Al went for the living room. 'You want to see power bitch. I will give it to you. With an alcohol headache still pounding, he went for the TV. This was the worst nightmare for Bella. TV was the only shit worthwhile having in this horrible place. In those momentary lapses of reason, she enjoyed programs like the Wheel of Fortune and daytime soaps. Santa Barbara and General Hospital always took her to her dream world, which she would never be a part of.

Durant knew that this was her soft spot. 'Not the TV, Al, not the TV for heaven's sake…' cried Bella.

'Oh yes bitch, the TV is going down, and all your f**king shows.' 'You threw my favorite sofa, and now it's time for payback.' He lifted the 25" Philips (stolen) TV and threw it out as a basketball.

Luke Petrowsky, a retired and highly decorated cop, said we should call the police. He was ready to storm the apartment. Most people laughed at that thought. Anyway, Luke went for the phone.

'Hey, the man has a right to do with his furniture what he likes. Let him be!' said one of my friends. Another guy said: 'I need a f**king refrigerator.' Some people rushed to the construction site. Luke screamed: 'I will personally shoot all looters.' That helped things a bit. There were a lot of spectators piling up now, total strangers and by-passers attracted by incredible noise and flying furniture. It seems that people were enjoying this. And when we thought this 'bizarre happening' was dying down, the TV flew out and landed on the sofa. Believe it or not, it stayed intact. Unbelievable, the sofa buffered its fall. Bella was overjoyed. 'Now what asshole?' cried Bella triumphantly! Al was furious. F**king sofa saved the damn TV. This was ridiculous. But wait, he knew what to do. Bella started shouting and throwing plates and kitchen utensils at him. The whole apartment was becoming one domestic battlefield. Al rushed for the bathroom and took his tools from the cupboard. Bella was still enjoying her sharp laugh, which ended up vomiting on the only half-decent carpet in the living room. She was spitting her insides out, again because of heavy drinking and food that even the fungi avoided.

Suddenly Al emerged from the bathroom. He was all wet. Now 'I am going to f**k up your damn TV bitch.' In a half-drunk state, he disconnected the bathtub from the water system and dragged it out of the bathroom. Bella was watching dizzily with a stupid look and somewhat foreign interest on her face. 'You can't hurt my TV, Al; it's alive and kicking. Santa Barbara will be on in a few hours, and I intend to watch it.'

'Well, we will see about that, won't we?' Al dragged the heavy bathtub to the window, or more closely, a hole in the wall. Amid it all, he called Bella: 'Help me out here bitch, this is too heavy.' And guess what, she did. She brought her big ass up, vomit still fresh on her dirty blouse. 'Oh woman, you stink; what have you done?' 'Shut up, Al, I need to take a shit now, and then I will help you. She took her skirt down immediately and, in a split moment, had incredible diarrhea on the kitchen floor. Al has never seen this happen before. For his dirty mind, this was somewhat cool. It turned him on. New strength was in him. She was finished fast, and they were hurling the bathtub out momentarily.

The bathtub came flying through the window. We were all startled. How on earth did he manage to do that? We didn't realize fully that she was helping him now. They were both looking out the window now. The tub crashed on the sofa, and with that, the TV set exploded as the bathtub crushed it. They were both laughing like madmen. But when Bella realizes that her favorite utensil was destroyed, she turns on Al. Now the thing throwing, cursing, and cat-dog fighting started. Things were getting now out of hand. Suddenly a police car came. It seems that Luke did call the police after all. They rushed into the building.

We could hear the door banging, police coming in, and all kinds of noises following. After some time, the police came out with Al and Bella. They were holding their noses. They were not ready for the encounter with double jeopardy: vomit & shit. Al was handcuffed, just in case. Bella was somehow completely stoned now. They took them downtown so they would calm down. Al ended up in the temporary cage to cool off after this domestic shit. They knew he was a petty criminal, but there was no evidence yet. He had been on their 'waiting list' for some time now. The whole gang was becoming a nuisance now. They would have to wait for some hard evidence for some time more. There was some questioning which did not help much. Bella managed to vomit and shit once more. The smell was unbearable in the station. They cleaned her up and released her after a good night's sleep. They did the same with Al.

All in all, the spectacle was over. People dispersed in time. We all talked about it for some days. Nobody stole the furniture overnight. Luke made sure of that. Nobody dared to do it, not even the human sewer rats that would go to any lengths. Everybody knew that Luke would bust ass. There wasn't much to steal anyway. The next day somebody saw Duran and Bella picking up the furniture from the construction site. It seemed that the happenings from the previous day did not happen at all. 'Kiss and make up' was the key phrase until next time. And we all knew that there would always be a next time with these two characters. This was one of their rare sober moments. Collecting furniture brought them together. A new TV soon found a place in the apartment, informing from some warehouse. Life continued for them, though the furniture never flew out like that.

12

The Flying Cats

He was patiently waiting for her to arrive. A medium-sized axe was in his hand, and he looked like a man with a mission. Full of self-esteem, confidence, and ruthlessness Rock Curtis was waiting for the kill. At the age of 13, he had already acquired a look of a madman and a sparkle in the eyes that could freeze your balls off. With a compact composure, red hair, devilish blonde eyes, strong hands, arms, and thighs, he looked like a mutant between Denise the Menace and one of the Vikings from Chrichton's 'Eaters of the Dead.' Highly respected and blindly followed by a group of kids that have already decided not to have a decent future, Rock has created a power base from which he ruled. Their sole purpose was based on three things: complete disobedience of all authority, vandalism whenever possible, and torture and intimidation of all enemies (usually everybody outside Curtis's circle was an enemy). He didn't have much of a family in terms of love, affection, and upbringing. His mom and dad were interested in other things. These two characters ran joint outside city limits called the 'Sanctuary for the Unfortunate Ones.' It was supposed to be a retirement home, a service house for older people, and a shelter for low-income people who could afford it. Rock's dad was a sleazeball that could swindle almost anything. He even got funds and state money for refurbishing an old 6-story mansion and for the grand opening of this place. He was hailed as the donor and a 'big heart' community member. The joint soon became a cover-up for more lucrative businesses, such as money laundry, illegal gambling, and booze & tobacco smuggling. In due time they even started counter fitting money. But the biggest lunacy of all was that these two pretended to care for the old & helpless. Most of their tenants were not far from zombies. Their policy was to take the worst cases, such as those who could never speak, and see what was happening. Rock was helping out his folks, especially on Bingo nights. The poor bastards living there and paying money for rent in a house that looked something like from the Twilight Zone had no idea they were being robbed every day. The water didn't adhere to health or environmental standards and was being taken from a well underneath the house. There was a rumor that it had contact with the local sewage system. The electricity was only available for a couple of hours a day. During winter time, the heating didn't work for days. Some tenants woke up with their noses or limbs almost frozen several times. The toilets were few, kitchen facilities non-existent, staff minimal (most with a shady criminal past), weed and grass growing from the floors, and the rat population on the rise very soon after the hasty refurbishment. This fitted well with the type of people living there, namely that their children didn't want to know too much about them. While the checks were coming in, Curtis and his wife would call the tenant's children sometimes and write, sending phony pictures of their loved ones enjoying their retirement days. But probably the most inhumane thing was the Bingo night. Rock Curtis used to help his folks with that. There were about 25 tenants in this facility, and Bingo Night was every night except weekends. Two things connected: first, the participants had to pay to be a part of it, and second, if they didn't pay, they would be left out of the dinner. Wait! That's not all. Even if they paid, there were no guarantees they would win. Only three to five winners were chosen, meaning these lucky bastards would get something to eat. And the crown of the dinner would be tomato soup with noodles, so you can imagine the other options. All the others would have to wait for breakfast, which you usually serve to pigs. Lunch was a disgusting soup full of animal remnants, often stray dogs and cats and rotten fish and poultry. And the amazing thing was that this worked until Rock brought one of his disciples to help him on one of the Bingo nights. Unfortunately for him and his parents, this kid squealed to his parents, one of them working for the surgeon general's office. There was also a parallel investigation going on in district attorneys' offices. Rock's parent's illegal activities were leaking everywhere. What happened was that the busts and indictments came. The whole business went down the drain overnight. The health authorities were appalled when they discovered the flesh and bone tenants, survivors of the numerous Bingo nights, and their horrible environment. All the illegal money, some weapons, and even drugs were confiscated. Rock's dad has been busted, as well as his accomplices. His mom got away with all the money, and there was much of it. She disappeared without a trace, probably living on one of the islands and drinking cold drinks with colorful umbrellas. Rock's dad got 20 years, and Rock Curtis was given to his aunt for 'guardian and safekeeping purposes.' She wasn't thrilled at all. No wonder why. Rock Curtis was one of the most violent kids I had the displeasure of knowing. Maybe being abandoned by his folks had something to do with it, or maybe it was just in his genes. The school was a constant problem, but surprisingly enough, he could express himself in a rather well-structured way. Unfortunately, he took pleasure in every pain and misfortune he caused and enjoyed the suffering of others, whether from the human or animal kingdom. His favorites were stray dogs and cats. He disliked the sewer rats. Intimately he was terrified of them. One of his brutal attacks was aimed at a group of stray dogs that wandered around the neighborhood. He masterminded one of the attacks on them where one dog lost both legs, a large hammer bashed the other's head, one sick was stabbed by a syringe full of gasoline and rat poison, and the fourth one was thrown into a dark tunnel underneath our building. His hollering could be heard for nights to come. The one stabbed with a syringe died in horrible and monstrous pain. At that time, nobody could stand up to Rock Curtis; nobody wanted to. He was too f**king dangerous and evil. Fortunately for us, he didn't live in our skyscraper but was a frequent visitor to our highlands. There was always someone to recruit, someone to torture, or something to destroy. That day he wanted to kill a stray cat as brutally as possible. He had two right hands, Little Moritz, a seven-year-old on a fast track to becoming a certified criminal by age 15, and Andrea 'Fat ass' Domenico. He was the enforcer. Andrea would be the perfect man if somebody needed to be beaten up. Only 12 years old, he gave an impression of a 19-year-old monster wrestler. On that afternoon, only the inner circle of Curtis Rock's outfit was playing the game. They waited. Curtis was one with the weapon, and he wanted to smell blood. The other two could assist, only assist. The female black and white alley cat came behind the curb. She had to pass between two low walls, through sort of a tunnel. Curtis's axe was raised and waiting at the end of the tunnel.

The Alley Cats best fit the Domestic cat's group (Felis catus). This type of animal possesses the features of their wild and relatively larger relatives, in most cases flesh-eaters, remarkably agile, powerful, and finely coordinated in movement. Our alley cats were the opposite of that which made them perfect targets for the construction site sewer rats and people like Rock Curtis.

The ancestors of the other common household pet, the dog, including the alley dog, were social animals that lived together in packs with hyponymy to a pack leader. The dog has readily transferred its allegiance from pack leader to a human master. The alley dogs retained the blind leadership to the strongest in the pack, while the cats, domestic or alley ones, have not yielded as readily to subjugation. Compared to dogs, they are extraordinarily self-reliant and adapt to hostile environments more quickly and successfully than the most house or even some alley dogs could. But these cats didn't adhere to this principle. Instead, they became highly insensitive to all danger, reliant on garbage provided by tenants, and even, in some cases, had a leader. The black and white cat was one of those. She was rather fat, moving lazily, and indifferent to any nearby danger. It's just by sheer luck that these stray alley cats were not extinct.

She passed through the tunnel, and when approximately half of her body was visible, Cutis's axe came down with the butcher's precision and meticulous bodywork. He cut her clean into two pieces. The blood sprayed around, and the poor cat shrieked in utter pain for about a millisecond after she died instantly. Rock Curtis was proud of himself, and his two close buddies were full of admiration. They addressed each other by the terminology used in one of the old James Bond movies, Diamonds Are Forever, I think, and later used similarly by Tarantino in his 'Reservoir Dogs.'

'Mr. Curtis, what a clean and precise shot', remarked Moritz.

'True indeed, Mr. Moritz. She didn't feel anything. The makers of this axe should be commended. The weapon has passed the test'.

'Remarkable timing and showcase of the superiority of humans over animals, Mr. Curtis.'

'How very proper, Mr. Domenico. I think we made a critical scientific test today. We should be proud.

Then they went into a union of disgusting, shrieking laughter. It didn't last long, as Curtis was bored again and needed more challenges. Rock Curtis came to a sinister idea.

'Mr. Moritz, have you ever heard of flying cats before?'

'I believe I haven't, Mr. Curtis. As far as I know, they didn't exist.

Unfortunately, in some people's minds, they did, or at least they should exist. Rock Curtis was one of them.

'I heard of flying squirrels, Mr. Curtis'. Domenico wanted to show his limited knowledge of zoology.

'I think we should do another scientific test and see if we can make cats fly.'

Brilliant, Mr. Curtis, splendid idea!' yelled Domenico and Moritz in the union.

Finding cats was not such a big problem. Four to five breeding females around (called queens) were always in heat, as many as four to five times a year. It was precisely this time of year, and the tiny kittens were being produced. Usually, several small kittens were being brought to the world blind, deaf, and helpless. Curtis liked them when they were a couple of weeks old. With a large population of sewer rats, who lived on the abandoned construction site in front of our apartment-skyscraper building, there was a large contingency of cats. The problem was that, in due time, the cats stayed away from the rats when they became so dangerous, hungry, aggressive, and relentless that they started killing the cats. Curtis used to say: 'Where are rats? There are cats.' His two henchmen forced a couple of other kids to start hunting after the cats and put them into five medium and large-sized boxes they had. As the skyscraper, with its 18 floors, the attic, and the flat roof, proved to be an ideal setting for this great test that Curtis had in mind, so were the recruits from these premises. Unfortunately for us and two of my friends, Keke Rosberg from the 15th floor and Aaron Green from the 13th, we found ourselves in the wrong place at the wrong time and adjacent to the wrong company. They were surrounded in a flash when they saw us in front of the building. A circle of Curtis's disciples, some 6 of them, and Curtis himself, plus Little Moritz and Fat Ass Domenico, would be a too-tough match for us. We could go down in glory fighting, as we did once on a previous occasion, but this time the odds were not in our favor, and there was no help.

'Listen, you three assholes! You are going to do a favor for Mr. Curtis today. He loved to dominate and be in charge. You need to help us get some more cats for a scientific experiment we are about to do on the roof of the building, and then after assisting us, you will be free to leave.

'What if we refuse, little Viking man?' screamed Keke. He was the same age as Rock. We all were. That brought such a harsh blow with a baseball bat from Domenico that Keke almost fell in pain to his knees. We tried to stand up but were, in an instant, wrapped by the disciples that carried all kinds of homemade devices that performed unusually well as weapons. There was no point in resisting.

'One more word from you, Keke, and I will burn you, as I might add Viking-like red-brownish hair. Besides, if you don't do this, we could beat you up, and you could live with that and get out with the honor of this. I respect that and know you would fight and probably cause casualties, but we don't need that. Because if you don't do this, we will hurt the two girls you punks are all in love with, Laura, Maya, and Shelley. We can always get to them and play all kinds of games. The difference is that you can't always be there to 'protect' them. Do I make myself clear?'

I just wondered how this guy would be when he reached the age of consent. He will probably end up in the black chronicles or the most wanted list. We knew that Rock Curtis would do this, even though he fancied the girls himself, especially the lovely 12-year-old blond with curls, Laura. Laura and Maya lived in our skyscraper, while Shelley was in the adjacent one. We couldn't let this happen, so we decided to make a deal with the devil, even though we couldn't trust his word.

With all our hunting skills, we still needed three hours to catch these cats. Ultimately, we had around eight cats, three large ones, two medium-sized ones, and three kittens. Although the door to the roof was locked, there was always a way to get around the lock. Aaron Green knew how to do that. We needed first to get through the attic door. All three of us had keys. Rock Curtis counted on that. While there, we guided the whole group through the attic storage room maze to the point at one intersection, which led to the roof. Aaron climbed the particular flight of stairs and handpicked the lock of the roof door. After 5 minutes, he made it. Rock Curtis was full of admiration. He told his people they needed someone like Aaron in their group. Aaron's eyes rolled 180 degrees in his eyelids at the thought of being one of the disciples. Curtis's disciples also brought some cardboard boxes, tape, and rocks. We had no idea what these things were going to be used for. We could imagine the worst nightmare when Curtis was the director. Tension and excitement were growing amongst them. They knew their leader was up to something big. We were all now standing on the flat roof of our skyscraper. Rather ample space if you imagine the floor space of three 3-room apartments, two rooms one and one studio combined + the hallway space. The core, where the elevators and staircases were, ended up in small flat roof facility spaces. Electrical stuff, ventilation, water systems, TV & Radio antennas, etc., were also part of that. But there was rather ample space around. A medium-height wall and railing encircled the roof. We went to the eastern part, where we had a view of the construction site below.

'What you are about to witness today will be a scientific experiment that should prove that cats can/might or cannot fly. Whatever the outcome, we can be certain that what we do here today will be an important step for us and a long or perhaps short flight for others'.

'Well said, Mr. Curtis! Brilliant indeed', yelled almost simultaneously Mr. Domenico and Mr. Moritz.

'To summarize, we will venture into the animal kingdom and experiment. I can imagine how Icarus or the Wright Brothers must have felt. I wish I were going together with our historic flyers'.

After that cynical remark, the whole Curtis congregation clapped. We stood by the side, fully aware of what would evolve here. We wanted to escape, but Little Moritz and two disciples blocked the hatch. There was no help for the cats. Their destiny was sealed. The first historic test flight was underway. Two young disciples got the honor to orchestrate the 'first flight.' After getting a green light from Curtis, they took one of the skinnier cats, a brownish-black one, and threw her over the roof railing. All of us ran to the railing to see what would happen. The cat ('the black-brown eagle' as they called the first flying cat) did not perform the 'flying" part all too well, swirling like a leaf in the wind but falling much faster. The disciples watched excitingly.

She was more or less squashed like a bug, significantly because she fell on ample sharp steel support lying on the abandoned construction site. The cat was still moving or shaking for a while, which was hard to tell from the roof. If the height didn't kill her, the steel support would surely do that. We all knew that the sewer rats would take care of the rest in a concise while. One of the youngest disciples puked. He was immediately called a weakling and beaten up for a few minutes. Curtis was not satisfied with the experiment; he wanted more. Now they shoved the medium-sized cats into one of the larger boxes, filled them with rocks, and started taping them from all sides, so nobody would fall out or escape during the flight.

'Let's see how they navigate in the dark with obstacles in their way,' proudly proclaimed Curtis.

'The dark brings out the best of some, Mr. Curtis!'

'Right you are, Mr. Moritz. Let's see if the darkness can show them the path to the light. Are we ready, Mr. Domenico?'.

'Almost, Mr. Curtis!'

Mr. Domenico was orchestrating the whole thing now. Mr. Curtis was watching as the great commander-in-chief. All of the disciples were near the railing now. Only Mr. Moritz was left near the exit hatch. Our chances of escape were getting higher. We were forced to help out tape the boxes with the cats. The cats enclosed in darkness with huge rocks around them were doomed. In a matter of seconds, the boxes were in the air, with the cheers of the disciple crowd, and the cats were flying for the first and last time. They just fell to the ground with a tremendous thump, and some were broken. It was difficult to tell if there was any movement. Most probably, there was none. To the dismay of the disciples and Curtis's inner circle, the cats were not flying. They all unanimously decided that the time for extreme measures came. The kittens remained, and a large fat cat. The one who undertook this last task was Mr. Moritz. Now the exit hatch was unguarded. Mr. Moritz took the remaining kittens and put them in cardboard boxes. He didn't tape them. There was a chance for escape.

'Let's see how they perform as parachutes, Mr. Curtis.'

'Well thought out, Mr. Moritz. You have taken our experiment to another level. Well done indeed!'

'If this doesn't work, Mr. Curtis, we should try using dogs the next time,' exclaimed Mr. Domenico.

'A point has well taken, Mr. Domenico. We certainly should try!'

Moritz was eager to try this out. He threw the box over the railing, but it went to the left a bit too much. What happened was that the box fell into a dark smaller pit, a hole we called "the tunnel." It was a concrete pit some three meters deep, which led to a tunnel that came out just outside the industrial plant. Nobody ever ventured there because of the rats and because there was a word that a re-al-life boogieman was living inside. These cats were gone for good now.

'These cats just can't fly Mr. Cutis', was Mr. Moritz's comment.

'If God wanted cats to fly, he would give them wings, Mr. Moritz!'

'Absolutely right, Mr. Curtis!' was Mr. Domenico's observation.

'Well, we should wrap this up now. My dear disciples, take care of the last standing cat. Let's show that we, as scientists, have given a fair opportunity to our volunteers and that nothing is left to chance. Rock Curtis always had a way with words, which made him even more potent amongst his followers. The disciples were more than eager to fulfill the wishes of their master. Mr. Moritz was back at the escape hatch, but we decided it was now or never.

The last to go classically was an old, fat cat. She was named 'Big Bertha' immediately. Curtis commented that she was a slightly better flyer. At least she had consistency in speed, which was probably due to her fat-body composure. The cat was even doing some gymnastic salts in the process. But as all 'good things end, so too did this flight. Bertha, unfortunately, fell on two exposed steel bars from the reinforced concrete block. She had a similar destiny as the first flyer. All the limbs were probably broken in the process, but that did not make a big difference to the rat colony. They were there in relatively strong numbers, already attacking violently on the remains of the unfortunate flyers. Although we know that cats are good jumpers and land on all fours, this flight was a little bit too much, as were the others performed that afternoon. The rats were enjoying a free meal now. We ran at full speed towards the hatch and crashed with all our might at Little Moritz. He was taken entirely by surprise, as were the other disciples still looking over the railing.

Little Moritz has shoved aside, and Keke gave him a blow in the groin while I destroyed in the face one of the disciples that just appeared from nowhere. My hand was hurting like hell, but not much as his face. Aaron went for the hatch, and we climbed the exit staircase in seconds. They all stormed after us, Mr. Domenico leading the pack and waving his baseball bat. Curtis was furious. We didn't want to be a part of this crazy thing anymore, and we couldn't trust Mr. Curtis's word that he wouldn't hurt the girls. A deal with the Devil was never a good one. Aaron stayed behind, and we realized he was missing at the end of the attic maze. Fortunately, he appeared from the darkness.

'Where the hell were you? We were worried, man. Let's get the f**k out of here. They must be after us.'

'Don't worry, Haas, I did some lock picking, guys! Damn, I didn't know I was that good. Maybe I should join Mr. Curtis after all. The hatch is closed. Can't you hear the banging?'

We could hear the banging and muffled screams and curses from the roof. They were locked up on the roof.

'Too bad Luke Petrowsky is not alive anymore,' said Keke.

'Yeah, if he were still here, he would hear the banging and think it was a bust or something. He would just blow the lock with his Magnum and storm the roof and blow away the f**kers for good', added Aaron.

'Not just that, I threw in a while running towards the stairs; he would also take no prisoners or hostages. You would have corpses up there piling faster than the cats they killed today.'

Rock Curtis was furious as the worst red Viking that you could imagine. He was mad at himself primarily for allowing himself to be trapped like this and his two helpers, Mr. Moritz and Mr. Domenico, for being so passive. He had to set an example for the disciples.

'When I get my hands on these three assholes, I will clobber their heads with my bat,' screamed Domenico.

'I will cut their eyes with my Swiss Army knife and feed them to the pigeons,' added Little Moritz.

'You will do no such thing. They outsmarted us, and I respect that. I will deal with them at a different time and a different place in my own, different way'. Rock Curtis suddenly had that crazy gleam in his eyes again.

'Mr. Moritz and Mr. Domenico! Find us a way out of here. You have 5 minutes to figure out something; I will do what you want to do those three. Get to work now!' Fortunately for them both, Little Moritz remembered the particular door to the staircases and elevator shafts. They busted the locks, and after half an hour, they were home-free. The disciples were tired and scared, so they dispersed immediately. Rock Curtis thought they were useless anyway. This type of situation brings out the selection of species too. Heck, he admired the Aaron guy. He probably came up with the idea of locking them on the roof. Brilliant! They went home before somebody reported something. Rock Curtis was already known as a minor offender, and one or two more wrong things and the juvenile home would be his permanent home. The strange thing was that nobody from the skyscraper or the one adjacent saw or heard anything. A flying cat would be a new site for the eyes, but these first 'test pilots' just fell and fell fast. As for the flying boxes, they fell into the category of garbage in those days. And flying garbage from a skyscraper is not extraordinary and foreign, especially after the garbage disposal tunnel was broken. We dispersed to our apartments after the escapade on the roof, hoping that there would be no repercussions. There was going to be none, but Mr. Curtis was never going to keep his word. In due time his threat would be fulfilled, but in a slightly different manner than he expected. We knew these guys would somehow escape and hopefully disappear, at least temporarily. As for the unfortunate cats, the stench from the boxes and the corpses inside and around them was a different story. The sewer rats climbed into them during that afternoon and evening, headed by the 'Norwegian Dream' mutant rat, and simply said—cleaned the house. There were only some bones and cat skulls left behind. There were no wings found anywhere.

13

We Called Him Pépe

Necrotizing fasciitis (NF) is a medical term given to the so-called "flesh-eating bacteria." This does sound kind of drastic and overdramatic, but essentially, this little bugger does eat flesh. It attacks the soft tissue, which then becomes gangrenous. The infection moves swiftly, usually under the skin, where one can't observe it. Once tissue becomes dead, it has to be removed. It doesn't make any distinction between ages, sexes, or races. It just attacks without warning when it sees an opportunity to penetrate. For that, it has to have an opening, a cut, or an abrasion to enter the skin. You also have to get into contact with the carrier of NF bacteria. This invader usually doesn't attack muscle or bone, but it's known for doing that too. In really shitty cases, major limb amputation is necessary. In other words, you are f**ked! This flesh-eating disease has one primary target – the flesh! Suppose you get saved, and the skin gets removed. In that case, you are in for one hell of a ride because when the recovery process starts, it's long and involves lengthy physical therapy plus long-term psychological, emotional, and spiritual recovery. The fasciitis bacteria is truly one mean son of a bitch. Everybody believed Pepé had it. Initially, we called it simply faccia (meaning face in Italian), but at a later time, somebody, and things like this usually happen, found the name in a medical lexicon – fasciitis. Poor Pepé, with his remarkable medieval-type face resembling the priests in Umberto Eco's 'Name of the Rose,' wasn't happy with this choice. He didn't have this disease, but the whole facial appearance gave that look as something in the transition from decay to recovery of post-trauma sense. Two small hilly bulge-swellings on his forehead, which re-sembled tiny horns, a very sharp pointed nose, grayish eyes, and a dark complexion, gave Pepé a look of a servant from the dark side but one of lower stature. The bacteria story just gave toppings to the cake. Pepé's true name was Zachariya Belinski. Nobody called him Zachariya, not even his parents. He was proud of the Pepé nick-name, how he got it, and for what reason beats me. Whatever it was, it couldn't have been to celebrate something positive. On the con-trary! His dad Hicory was a professional alcoholic but could still do his job as a mechanic in a large cargo and trucking firm. His mom Morena worked in the housing company responsible for our sky-scrapers. She was in charge of the cleaning operations for our sector. Pepé was on his own for most of the time. They occupied one of the studio apartments on the 10th floor. Pepé is a character that is extremely hard to define. He became the mascot of the skyscraper and later, with all the stories accumulating about him, became one of the urban legends of our district and some parts of the city. It went to the extent that even comic books (independent homemade production) were being made to celebrate this person. The legend had nothing to do because of heroic deeds, his looks, his brains, or anything similarly noble or normal. It happened for all the wrong reasons, and for all possible and impossible negative, funny, clumsy, unbelievable, and outstandingly silly things he was involved in. He also had the gift of producing a thousand faces quickly, which was the main reason he got his second nickname. In the end, everybody was sure that this eating-flesh bacteria became one with Pepé, made some union with his face, and decided to live happily ever after. His teeth gave a final touch to the face growing and going in all directions. He wore shorts for most of the time and 2-checkered shirts. Pepé was always full of bruises, mostly because he fell off his bike (a homemade production done by him and his dad) 5-6 times a day. It would take miles of text and a trilogy of books to compile everything said, told, spoken, and thought about him and what was happening around him. Still, it would be impossible. Though some things stand out as memorable moments in time, left there to be remembered and told afterward. One was one of the Hollywood production moments, which came to our skyscraper at one point, although slightly deformed and with a different purpose.

'No, please stop!' The chorus singing of all actors involved in this movie sequence muffled his screams. The whole elevator shook badly from the violent vibrations in its interior. Most of you have probably seen the famous movie about boxing, "Rocky" with Sylvester Stalone. A couple of sequels followed, all of which were not so good. Well...there were also independent productions of Rocky being illegally made in some parts of the world. This didn't exactly involve accurate movie shooting or real actors. The production site and the movie's "real" theme differed immensely. The leading role was not given to an actor but to a particular individual named Pepé. He had a slightly different role than Sly, or the roles have been switched. Our skyscraper had two elevators, something I mentioned somewhere before. The big one could take more folks and was more spacious than the little one. It also gave room for more extensive operations where specific movements were necessary. The elevators were real heroes of our building. What these two machines endured through the years and decades was quite unbelievable. Just to mention hundreds of people using them daily, people moving all kinds of furniture through the years, kids' playgrounds, various types of vandalism performed in and on them, and God knows what else. They have been, quite unbelievably, also used as public toilets. Some individuals also used to stop them between floors to perform other things of a more intimate nature. However, their most bizarre use was probably as a setting for a movie about boxing with numerous sequels. The production was low, the cast was always available, and there was no budget but a lot of will, dedication, and brutality every day in boxing movies. Even though Pepé got the leading role, I doubt he was enjoying his 5 minutes of fame. Initially, he was excited about the whole thing, not knowing what the movie was about. Soon he changed his mind after a couple of these shootings.

The producer and director of this low-budget-cast production were Norman "Stone" Podworsky," the strongest kid in the building. He used to hang out with a character called Rocky (what a coincidence!), who had the hobby of going around local schools and beating up kids he disliked. There was a whole bunch of those. Norman was his right-hand man, while his left hand was a dark character called Spiro Guilee. Strange rumors went around about him. He strangled his grandmother, his soul guardian and relative, and cooked her afterward. When she died, he inherited her retirement money according to her will, written on toilet paper. Anyhow he was not someone to mess around with. Spiro collected the money for Rocky while Norman "Stone" did the beating part if needed. Rocky would jump in only on important occasions. Their biggest scam for extorting money from scared school kids was the 'house scheme,' where they sold parts of construction materials, usually bricks, to the kids. The idea was that each kid who bought a brick would invest in their future home and construct their "future" house. The brick(s) was usually taken back and sold again. Those that refused to pay or return the bricks were being taken care of by Stone. This lucrative affair was Rocky's brainchild. The whole close-circuit deal with bricks and other extortion was pretty good for the trio and gave them an image that was not easily forgotten. In other words, nobody could resist these guys. Having Norman "The Stone" in our skyscraper had its advantages. He had his assistants in this movie operation: Ture Tollberg and Mike Gleisch. Sometimes Boris Duchovny jumped in for Mike or Ture. They always participated in this movie and most of the sequels. This was Norman's brainchild. The rest of us were film crew and extras. We all changed, and rarely, it was always the same extra crew. The rest included most of my friends from the skyscraper. On this particular occasion, it was three of us: myself, Danny Slowitz, and Daren "The Head" Capouya, who had the "honor" of being the "cameraman" of this show. I delegated the responsibility of the "lighting" technician, while Danny was to produce the "sounds." Including Pepé were 8 of us in the elevator, which was just on the border of the elevator capacity. The show was about to begin.

He could not have refused, even if he wanted to. It happened all too fast. Norman and the rest of us were bored and decided to go for a session of Rocky movies. Usually, Pepé was taken by surprise in the elevator, but this time he was swiftly dragged to the entry hall. He resisted but to avail. His bike, a story by itself, was left outside the skyscraper with many others. We all boarded the elevator under the firm command of Norman "Stone" Podworsky. Pepé was everything else but ready to go into showbiz. We all asserted our places, and Norman began to direct the movie.

'By the time we reach the 10th floor, you will be a star, Pepé, screamed Norman after all of us boarded the elevator at the entry level.

'No, no, I don't want to be a star. I did too many sequels. Why can't we make some other type of movie?

'Hmmm…maybe you are right. Maybe we should produce an agricultural documentary about different fruit and vegetables. How about…' Norman was thinking and then…' the theme of showing different fruit into your asshole. That should be fun!' Pepé was shit scared.

'No, not that, please!

'Yeah, maybe you are right. We stick to boxing. I love sports anyway, so this should be fun. OK. Enough talk; let's act! Everybody, please take your place!

We were all in position. The shooting was about to start. As soon as the elevator started the ascent, Norman screamed again: 'Lights, sound, camera, and action!'

Daren started rolling the camera, which was nonexistent, but he was good in pantomime; Danny started producing all kinds of technical sounds while I covered 75% of the light in the elevator (which came from one coal mine type of lamp) with my jacket. This one replaced the neon lightning, which was, God knows how many times, destroyed in numerous vandal attacks on the elevator. In this dark, lightning atmosphere with half shadows moving and strange sounds produced, make-believe movie history was happening.

'Actors action!' Norman now directed Ture and Mike to act. Acting consisted of beating up Pepé in the make-believe ring. The trick was doing it quickly and swiftly before the elevator reached its destination.

'No, ugh, stop, ugh, no, ahhhh, help'! These were some of the different cries that Pepé was listening to while the 'gentle beating' started. Pepé was a veteran now in the movie business. This was his 7th or 8th shooting. The 1st time he was extremely eager and happy to discover that he would star in a new movie. After the 3rd and 4th shootings, he lost all of his enthusiasm when he found out that the sequels were all similar, the scenario was always the same, and he was the leading actor. The extras changed, but it didn't make much difference.

The supporting actors were doing the same thing all over again. It was total darkness in the elevator now. I was ordered to cover the whole light. Danny was making all kinds of mechanical sounds, and when Pepé cried out, he began to scream and add to it. We all screamed and yelled simultaneously, so it was a madhouse controlled superbly by an experienced director like Norman. The only light was coming from the passing floors. The beating was in the middle stages now. What should have been a couple of minutes' ride (as the elevator's stop button was pushed so many times in the commotion and on purpose) was like a lifetime for Pepé. There was no escape. Everybody was hyperactive and pretty excited. After all, this was a Rocky movie. Pepé was screaming and creating some strange out-of-this-world noises. During that time, the whole elevator was shaking and swirling like a leaf in the wind due to the incredible commotion and movements inside with all the beating and running that was going on. The whole construction seemed to be cracking up.

'Be brave now! I feel like the stuntman in Hollywood action movies. Imagine what they have to go through?' Norman was doing his finale.

'Camera close-up!

Daren was close to the commotion around Pepé.

'Now, all jump! Commanded Norman. After that, we all jumped on one pile in the center of the elevator. You can imagine who was the person underneath – Pepé, of course!

'5th round is finished' were the last words given by Norman when we reached the 10th floor. Pepé looked like a larva of a giant butterfly, rolled up to cover the shots. He was squealing like a pig before the slaughter. Mike and Ture were exhausted as they had all the work to do. The only ones were willing to do the action part of the movie. After a few more kicks and punches, Pepé was kicked and thrown out on the 10th floor. He quickly tried to crawl to his apartment, his only sanctuary. He was pretty beaten and shaken up. After all, the guys were "considerate" and "careful." They didn't want to damage their main star too much.

'Oh no, you're not going anywhere.' With those words, Ture caught Pepé by his legs and dragged him back inside. Part II of this sequel or mini-series was about to begin.

The elevator took its descent to the entry level. Everything was happening faster now, and the director lost control. The darkness was complete so that even the cameraman got a blow in his face at what he became angry and started delivering fists all around. Soon everybody was fighting with everybody. The elevator was swinging like a glider in the air. I was sure the cables would crack, and we would all die as fearless stuntmen of this ridiculous production. We were already at the entry level when the order was returned. It was just a bunch of us entangled in a big mess in the elevator. The funny thing was that Pepé somehow managed to get out of this, and as soon as the elevator came to a complete stop, he darted from it like an arrow from Robin Hood's bow. Pepé was a fiery bullet. Norman was the first to come to his senses.

'Get him! Get the little bastard; no actor will run out of my production. No, never! We ran immediately after Pepé, who had just boarded his homemade bike. He was pissed off, everything in a sort of humorous way.

'Possy, let's get a posse after the fugitive,' screamed Ture while still jumping from the stairs of the entry to the skyscraper in the hope he would catch Pepé.

'Brilliant Ture! Let's go after him, guys!' Norman boarded his bike, as well as Ture and Danny. We didn't have our bikes out, so running was the only viable option. Staying behind was out of the question, at least while Norman "Stone" Podworsky was in command. The troubles just began for Pepé on that humid, late August afternoon.

He wasn't quite sure where to go. The idea was to run, run and run. His homemade bike was a wonder of technological inventions. A galvanized slim water pipe and parts of refrigerators supported the whole frame. Other parts include electrical equipment, leftovers from the construction site, all kinds of ridiculous gadgets that didn't work, and tires that suited more of a truck than a bike. Pepé was probably the only person in the world to manage this monster creation; to everybody's surprise, he could also acquire unbelievable speeds. The pursuit was on, but Pepé was already gaining speed. He took a sharp left turn, speeding like mad, rushing past the joint fish restaurant. As he was about to turn again to the left and pass between the grinds separating the civilized world from the eternal construction site, he crashed at full speed into a pregnant woman moving a child carriage. He didn't fall from the bike but made a somerset in mid-air, and somehow half crashed behind. The woman fell, and all her bags spilled on the pavement, with eggs breaking and milk spilling. The carriage skidded some meters down and overturned. She started yelling and crying. Norman, Ture, and Danny were already there. Ture's bike came crashing down over the milk and destroying whatever was left in the bags, while Norman crashed into Danny, who screeched brutally on his brakes. They all went down in a bundle when we arrived. While we tried to help the screaming mother and her kid, the three guys on bikes tried to scramble back on track. Pepé was already accelerating and turning a sharp right into the shopping boardwalk. He started speeding at an incredible acceleration. The guys were already losing him. Unfortunately for Pepé, he tended to look elsewhere and everywhere. I could bet you a hundred bucks that he had a head that could turn 360 degrees. He turned around and screamed in his harsh, highly original tone, accent, and sophisticated dyslectic manner:

'Ha, you can't catch me, bastards. F**k you, all of you! I am a faster biker, haha!

With that, he turned around and saw another woman holding a small child pace away. In some incredible animal reflex, Pepé unusually swung his monster bicycle to avoid the collision, which could, at this speed, probably cripple all the parties involved. What happened instead was quite a treat for the eyes. Only one alternative left for Pépe – going straight for one of the shopping windows.

This one had the whole array of bathroom appliances and gadgets on display. The move was so swift and sharp that Pépe didn't know what hit him. He crashed into the shopping window at full speed, destroying the glass into thousands of pieces.

Furthermore, he trampled with his bike over the window sill, and the violent shock left Pépe flying in mid-air and landing into an open toilet bowl on display. He banged his head into the raised seat, and the whole toilet bowl overturned and crashed. He just ended with a couple of bruises, bumps, and cuts. It's funny how these events attract humans like flies are attracted to shit. The guys were coming closer now. Suddenly a bunch of people started assembling in front of the bathroom shop. The shop owner was in shock but already on the move to bash the head of the idiot that did this.

'You damn moron, I will submerge that shitty head of yours and spool it with piss water. Look what you did, you idiot!'

'Sorry, Mister, so savvy, don't be mad, Mister...' Pépe was already on his feet, boarding his miraculously new bike and escaping this crime scene.

'Stop him, stop the bastard! The owner kept shouting in vain. Ture took the other road back to our building to cut him off. Pépe was gaining speed, but now Norman and Danny were just meters from him on their bikes.

'Now you are dead meat, pal!' Norman wanted Pépe's ass badly, but Pépe was a better biker than us. You couldn't take that away from him. He was already making a considerable distance from the guys. He was speeding at an incredible acceleration. He swooshed by the social security and Retirement Fund building, by the AURORA cinema, and down the basketball alley road towards our building.

They say that shit, mischief, and lousy luck never come alone. They came in triplets when Pépe was concerned. What he didn't see, of course, because he had eyes on the back of his head, was the delivery truck coming from the right side access road. He was just about to swing in Pépe's direction when the driver saw something like an ugly troll from Tolkien's novels speeding on a contraption resembling a bike. The trucker's mind didn't work that fast, especially after having four beers for breakfast that morning. He stepped on his braked but too late. Pépe did the same, but it was also too late. He crashed into the front part of the truck at full speed. The guys saw this from a distance, and everybody just held their breath.

'My God…he was squashed like a bug…he must be dead! Norman was in shock as we were, the rest of us arriving on foot. Well, Pépe wouldn't be Pépe. He certainly was knocked off and in temporary dreamland. The driver was in shock. We all gathered around. There was no blood, no nothing. The bike was FUBAR (f**ked up beyond any recognition), as Norman used to say. Suddenly he just woke up and got up. His troll head with two excerpts of horny-like structures seemed intact. He just made a face that would make the piss run into your pants as on autopilot.

'Hej yaa! Wats' up, guys? He was still not sure what had happened when it hit him. He started running from the scene, leaving his destroyed bike squashed on the pavement. We were all surprised by this phoenix rising of Pépe, the magician. We were all sure he was a goner, but no…he defined the laws of physics and medicine so many times. His head must have been made of lead or strong materials like concrete or titanium. He was running to our skyscraper now. Ture was waiting in the entré hall for Pépe. He had no idea what had happened. Someone else was also waiting, looking, and stalking – The Usurper family, retired husband and wife – Mortimer and Gloria. Mortimer looked like he was born dead. A walking corpse, thin, white, almost transparent color with high pitched nose and pointed cheekbones and small, tiny weasel-like black eyes. Gloria was the opposite. With some 150kg, she looked like a gigantic human snowball, always full of makeup that couldn't do anything to deflect the sheer horror of her hideous face. She always wore those silly net things on her head so that her made-every-week-at-the-same-time-hair wouldn't be affected. They got the name usurpers when they illegally acquired two cellar sheds without permission. Every apartment is entitled to one; those living on higher floors get the attic one, and those living below get the cellar one. The usurpers just moved in and took two empty sheds that were not used. Word spread fast, and they were branded for life. So when Pépe approached the building, Gloria was waiting. She hated him, mainly because he screamed at them all the time:

'Usurpers, f**king usurpers…cellar takers, soul takers, damn usurpers…."Usurper Gloria, usurper Mortimer!'

He always used to yell when he saw them hanging on the window of their 4th-floor apartment, just watching the day and people go by. Gloria was also an associated member of the gossip and information channel that ran through our skyscraper, headed by Norissa Guzinsky. Now she had a large bowl of boiling water with some of Mortimer's smelly urine, so when Pépe arrived, she would be ready. As Pépe approached the entrance, he saw the usurpation. He slowed his pace seeing that we were left behind, and started yelling at them.

'Shitty usurpation, shitty you…Usurpators…' he didn't quite finish the sentence as hot, boiling water splashed on him. He was taken by surprise and started screaming.

'Good job honey, that's what the little monster needed. Maybe it will straighten that ugly face of his…he…he…' Mortimer was admiring the targeting qualities of his monstrous wife. Pépe ran inside, still hollering at the top of his lungs. He would soon be in the safety of his 10th-floor apartment. Not really! Ture was waiting for him, and when he got into the elevator hallway, he grabbed in his favorite swift, athletic move.

'Now I got you, little prick.' 'Shit man, you are so wet and smell like piss.' Boris Duchovny's older brother, Roger, was passing by. He was Ture's best buddy, and he loved good pranks.

'Hej Ture, what you got there, a troll or a pig-goat mutant?'

'Ah, man…We had a Rocky session, and our star actor decided to split on us. He did some serious damage on the way.'

'Maybe he needs some reformation in the way of musical therapy'; Roger said I just got something perfect for him.

'What do you mean?' Ture was utterly puzzled.

I presume there is a bunch of guys on the way. Give me Pépe and then come to my apartment when you all assemble.

'Right on, man.' Ture ran out to get the rest of us. Pépe tried to resist, but Roger was a big guy who trained in Judo in his spare time. There was no bullshit with this guy. He brought him to the apartment and took him to his room. He took Pépe and handcuffed him to his bed. His mom worked at the customs and once brought this home. He and Boris always had the latest state-of-the-art Hi-

Fi equipment. Roger began using it with his various girlfriends. It came in handy even now.

'Now listen, Pépe! I will help you through musical therapy. You can listen to the latest song from a very influential European group called LAIBACH. The song is "Live Is Life." I will play it for you 20 times. It should be enough at level 10+.'

'No, please don't,' Pépe was begging now as he knew Laibach was a sort of industrial heavy theater rock with many noises. He couldn't stand it, and if the volume was 10+, he knew he would die with that.

'Don't worry, buddy, you will be cured, and maybe it changes your face in the process. With that said, he adjusted the volume and closed the room leaving poor Pépe handcuffed to the bed and his legs tied together. The horrible song started, and the room was filled with a wall of sound. The glass and the walls felt like vibrators. Everything was moving. Roger knew he could do this for max 20 minutes as the neighbors would start complaining. He also knew Pépe would be a vegetable if he left him there longer. At that moment, the crew of the Rocky movie arrived. We were all there, spearheaded by Norman, Ture, and the rest. We all piled up in front of Roger's room, where Pépe was locked and screaming. His agonic cries were muffled by the crescendo of sounds coming from the two gigantic 250W loudspeakers. The whole apartment felt like an earthquake had hit it. After 10min, we heard some thumping sounds, probably coming from the neighbors. After 15min, we got in, and Roger shut the music down. Pépe was shaking his head in agony and hallucinating. Then he started screaming again and shaking the whole bed he was handcuffed to. Roger uncuffed him, and Norman got him out of the room.

'I hope you have learned an important lesson today. You can't just leave the film set and create havoc on the way. You almost got killed today. We can't have that, man. Movie directors invest a lot in their actors. My reputation is on the line. But as you went through an ordeal today, we won't be shooting anymore. How does that sound?'

After hearing that, Pépe ran like a rabbit outside the apartment and up the stairs to the 10th floor. He was screaming and repeating the words of the song "Life Is Life."

'I think you did a good job Mr. Psycho,' Norman said to Roger.

'Yeah, it seems the kid is cured. Good! I am glad I was of some help.

After that, everyone laughed and didn't give too much shit about poor Pépe. We were all glad the movie's shooting ended, as it was becoming a significant pain in the ass. After the whole episode, the movie thing lost its appeal. The whole story seemed to wrap itself up, and there was no point in doing this as this unique experience was a gem in itself, left to be treasured and not copied. This 'action' movie was repeated on some occasions with some other people, and some other times, a whole surplus of sequels was made later. But none of them could beat the Pépe one; probably the only satisfaction and consolation for Pepé were that he made more parts than Sylvester Stalone in the original Rocky movies.

14

Meet the Doctor

Most of the people I knew, which probably includes most of you reading the story at this very moment, go ignorant through life, not noticing the little, unimportant things around them. Not everything is about big solutions, significant decisions, crucial questions, and our problems. It's also about looking around and noticing the 'other' things and persons that exist. In most cases, it's just a waste of time. I would agree with you there. Why should I give any attention to every asshole sitting on a bus beside me or take notice of all passengers at my airport gate? I can't analyze every tiny detail that draws my attention, a peculiar-looking character passing by me on the street, an interesting-looking woman behind a supermarket counter, a man talking to himself on the train or just remembering what some persons had on them, where I saw a drunk take a leak in the park or why those movers of furniture look like they could have a criminal record. But sometimes, remembering a specific detail or just simply remembering a name or event that might be of importance can be important as hell. The brain stores and accumulates all this information like a hard disc. But if you don't use it, all of this information in some way gets cleaned or gets stored in some far-away place in the depths of our still, in many respects, enigmatic brain. This information can sometimes erase the important one or temporarily push it aside. All kinds of things could happen. But if you are made from what you are, there is not much you can do about it. Noticing every possible detail, every strange and different looking face, every movement, every possible action and inaction, mimic, smile, laughter, a gleam in the eye and possible…something, it's not an easy task, folks believe me. It also creates pain, not the one that hurts, but the one you don't feel, but your subconscious registers it repeatedly. With everything being said, I consider this a gift. Don't get me wrong; it's not an exceptional talent but something a few people possess in large quantities. Sometimes I thought I had a surplus of that and was proud, but I was pissed off at myself on other occasions for storing so much of this useless information. Many notice, observe and conclude, but only a few try to see it all and see 'all' kinds of things possible and impossible in that 'all.' Unfortunately, my best friend Anthoine Scott did have a piece of that, but not as much as I did. It almost proved fatal for him on one dark afternoon in early May.

It was just one of those dull days when you had to look, listen, observe, and remember. There were too many of these lunatics to remember anything. The subject/theme/discipline/field was psychiatry. The word was not used in medical circles, but he and all his student colleagues at the faculty of medicine didn't have any other appropriate word to depict what they were seeing. The task was to observe all the different types of interviews that their teachers (clinical shrinks) had with an incredible rainbow palette of all kinds of people that were just not right in their heads. In other words, they were all f**king crazy. In that month or so, they were forced to look and listen to all kinds of mentally disordered and demented people, a rare multiple personality case, a whole bunch of schizophrenics, psychotics, dangerous psychopaths (or as society likes to use the language correctly term these days, sociopath) variety of hysterical neurosis cases, couple of suicidal maniacs, and a whole spectrum of deranged people that can all be found masterly depicted in Kaplan's Psychiatry Book. Anthoine and his friends were tired of watching these crazies perform their unique acts during the shrink sessions. Women pissing on the table, people thinking they are great states-men, generals, philosophers, or surgeons (one of them calling him-self the doctor), those that just cram into the corner of the room and watch your every move with a lunatic gleam, dangerous serial killers that were abused as children, and so on. There were too many of them, most appalling and disgusting. If it was interesting the first week or two, it was undoubtedly torture the last days.

That Thursday was a shitty day. Anthoine just lost count of all these 'lunatic sessions.' He had three notebooks full of notes knowing that the exam would be tough as hell. Danny Slowitz's dad Ivar, Anthoine Scott's close floor neighbor, was a strict examiner too. Anthoine forgot many things that day, but the worst was getting a signature from Dr. Ivar for all his exercise sessions. Without this one, there was no way he could participate in the exam. He barely missed him at the clinic and returned home hoping to find him. Danny opened the door instead.

'Hi, Bro! Looking for my dad? Shit man, he left 15min ago.'

'Where to man?' Anthoine was in a panic, knowing that he had to have the signature by 18:00 hours to deliver it to the bureaucratic clerk at the faculty of medicine.

'I think you need to go to Birdland, Bro'!

'What the f**k are you talking about' replied Anthoine nervously.

'Yeah, he had a couple of patients to check out tonight. They weren't feeling all that entirely well. You know, with the full moon and all this.' Anthoine had a strange feeling Danny was enjoying his misfortune at the moment.

'Birdland! F**k, double f**k! Birdland was the city's biggest loony-tone house. It was situated on the outskirts of the city center, but one still had a feeling it was in the middle of nowhere, especially if you didn't own a car. There was no public transportation to this facility, and it was also a security joint, above all things. Anthoine knew that to get this, and he would have to be a speedy Gonzales or Road runner, not to mention that he would revisit the Birdland after all those horrendous interviews, where some of which were performed there too. Prof. of Medicine Dr. Ivar worked as a part-time psychiatrist in Birdland, aside from his faculty job where he was teaching psychiatry.

'So get him, champ! I will call him on my cell and tell him you will arrive, Anthoine'.

'Thanks, Bro. I appreciate it! Tell him to tell security that Dr. Scott is on his way.'

Anthoine's dad was also a doctor and a professor at the faculty. If Ivar thought his dad was coming, he would speed up the security. He knew what to do. He had one hour to do all he was supposed to do, or his ass would be psychiatry grass! Anthoine was already flying out the door.

Birdland was the final destination and frontier for many people in society who think and function differently than most. In other words, they have certain foreign formations and networks in their brains which disable them from participating on the same level and in the same fashion as the rest of us. Some have extremely high IQs and, at first sight, look typical and even more expected than others. Unfortunately, in the next second, they could strangle your mother, throw themselves off the roof, eat live chickens, drink their pee, or just think they are Richard Nixon or David Letterman. Birdland was about helping these unfortunate souls reach an average functioning level or somehow redeem their souls.

The results are usually miserable, but society needed a place like this. What would have happened if there were no Birdlands? One doctor said in a drunk state once to Ivar, then all the crazies would get wings, and we would have to shoot them out of the skies, one by one. We don't want that, do we, concluded the drunken doctor. Birdland had about 80 permanent lunatics (I use this term to simplify matters for you as a reader and myself as a writer) and some ingoing and outgoing temps, as they were called. It was a massive facility with a big nurse and orderly staff available + security with alarms and dogs. There were about 4+1 shrinks available at all times. It seemed enough for these poor souls. Now Anthoine had to visit the cuckoo house at night, the prospect which he disliked utterly. He had these thoughts and others when he approached the building driving his blue Fiat. To pass the controls here, you had to have special permissions and all kinds of rubbish. Anthoine realized that if he wore a doctor's gown, and a white mantel, the chances of passing through security much faster would be more significant. He took his dad's robe and a fake ID, which he was a master at, and put on serious glasses. He was 185, as I was, had dark coal hair, and looked like a twin brother to the actor Jimmy Smiths from LA Law and NY Blue. With the robe on and glasses, he would pass by any guard and win the heart of any nurse. He was stopped first on the outer gate by some freshman guard. It took but just a second to pass him. The one outside Birdland was trickier. At first, he didn't believe him. Then Anthoine took a more rigid stance.

'Listen, you asshole and I can't wait! Let me through! We have a severe case on our hands.

'I can't do that, doctor. I need to check with the higher-ups, and please mind your language. The guard was rather big and looked meaner by the minute. The name on his tag read BUTCH. He had a rottweiler or a Doberman pincher by that name.

'Didn't you hear from Dr. Ivar Slowitz that I am coming?'

'Yes, but that was not announced in time. A procedure must be followed, and I can't do much about that. Besides, I have never seen you here before.' Now Anthoine went to the last resort.

'Listen, you f**king prick. I just had about enough of you, Butch. If you don't let me through this minute, I will call your boss (he made it his business to know the name of the boss of the security firm), Mr. Radclife, who I know, and tell him what's going on. Do you want me to disturb him with this and suddenly find yourself at the unemployment desk tomorrow morning? Now open the f**king gate, and I may put a word of commendation on your behalf to Mr. Radclife!'

Butch couldn't believe his ears. It was easier to let this son of a bitch through than to get in trouble with Mr. Radclife, who was one sorry, mean son of a bitch.

'I still have to make a note about this,' he replied robotically.

'You just do that, but now open the damn gates.' The gates opened in an instant. Anthoine was in Birdland. He was worried about finding Ivar. The lunatics and the 'estate' dogs were the last things he had on his mind. Birdland was divided into two wings (ironic, isn't it?), one for the softer lunatics and one for the hardcore ones. If these permanent tenants wanted to escape, the only thing that could help would be a pair of wings. Otherwise, the chances were minimal, considering the mad dogs, voltage guy bouncers, and frying fences. One guy did escape, though. Two Doberman Pinschers and one pitbull terrier caught up with him after 900m and almost ate him alive. See, the thing was that these dogs were fed not too often and always with fresh, live animal meat. Anthoine needed to go to the east wing where Dr. Ivar was. The real mad people were there too.

The nurse in the reception was a beautiful, young creature. She looked like the nurse you would like to have around 24/7. She wore a tight uniform, probably three sizes smaller, with her large breasts bulging. With Scandinavian blonde hair, red lipstick, dark blue eyes, and lips that looked like natural silicone, she could cure any patient's impotence and bring him back to life without Viagra if necessary. Her tag read LINDA. Strangely, one of the local, more revealing XXX magazines didn't pick her up. Anthoine knew why it was worthwhile to study medicine, amongst other, more obvious reasons: for the nurses and constant hard-ons and multiple one-night stands. He was lucky. The head, nurse Hilda was not at the post. Anthoine took a strong stance. He wanted to get to Dr. Ivar and knew he was the only physician in the eastern wing tonight. The other doctor came down with the flu. They were still expecting his substitute to arrive later that evening. It was still quiet, though the full moon was up.

'Good evening, my dear. I am Doctor Scott. They are expecting me. I need to see the doctor immediately.'

" I can't find you on the list, doctor, " the nurse said shyly, blushing. Anthoine would have loved to fool around with this one, but there was insufficient time. He would have to remember to take her number later on and teach her some gymnastics and anatomy.

'I am not on the list as this was an emergency. I was called from outside as this is not my regular post.' There is a problem with one hard case in the east wing, and they are summoning us up.

'That's why I don't recognize you, doctor. I should wait for…', she started to say when Anthoine cut in fast:

'No, there is no time to call Hilda. I am late as it is. If we delay this further, you will also get in much trouble, my dear. We wouldn't like that to happen, now would we?' He looked at her seductively, scanning her whole body with a cocky smile. She was all red in the face now but enjoying the apparent attention she was getting from this handsome young doctor. Besides, he couldn't take his eyes off her breasts. Maybe later…He abruptly cut her daydreaming, knowing that Hilda would be back soon.

'Listen, Linda, take me to the doctor now! Please!'

'To the doctor, THE DOCTOR (she raised her voice on this occasion), at this hour! Are you sure, Dr. Scott?

'Of course, I am sure. That's why I am here, for God's sake, woman. The doctor needs me, and I need to see him urgently. I told you we have a problem in the east wing'.

'One can't see the doctor at any time, but if you have a problem with him... Now I understand. He is a rather difficult case'.

What the hell was she talking about? As much as he liked her physically, she seemed a total simpleton, an idiot with no brains. Doctor, complex case?! There was no time to ponder over what she said. He leaned on the counter and looked into her dark blue eyes.

'Let's go, Linda, take me to the east wing now to see the doctor.' She didn't dare argue anymore but looked a bit scared. She led him to one of the elevators on the right side. Each wing had its own, as they called it here, set of feathers. There were four of them. Each one corresponds to a particular floor. It also corresponded to the level of lunatics held there. The fourth was on the top floor, where the worst cases were. A chill passed through Antoine's backbone. He could see several nurses and orderlies flowing through the corridors they passed. The elevator was glass and could only be operated by a particular card and key. Linda was getting more nervous. They came to the floor now. She took him to the desk of the primary nurse for that floor. She spoke briefly with her.

'I will leave you here now, Dr. Scott. He was about to say something to her and ask for her telephone number when the floor nurse appeared in front of him. She looked at him once more and left in a hurry, her beautiful peach behind swinging in the air.

'I don't know anything about this, but Linda said the doctor on duty and head nurse Hilda cleared it. Nobody said anything to me, which I find very strange.'

'Listen, this was an emergency. I need to see the doctor. That's why they called me, and the head of the clinic Dr. Mazurski, my personal friend, asked me to come here as soon as possible. I don't have time for small talk, nurse. Get me to the doctor now before it's too late!' This nurse felt it and didn't ask any more questions. He knew he could get into trouble and probably would, but obtaining Dr. Slowitz's signature that evening was the most important thing for him. He was looking mean and determined now.

'OK, I will take you to the doctor. How many orderlies do you need, and will you wait for the others?

'What orderlies, what others. I don't need anybody. I will take care of this myself. Do you understand?' She was astonished to hear this.

'But nobody goes without the orderlies inside to see the doctor.'

'Rubbish! Nonsense! What is this place anyway? Let's go; we are just wasting time. She was not going to argue anymore but would undoubtedly check this immediately.

They passed three particular security doors, and the last one was guarded.

'Are you sure, doctor, you will go inside alone?'

'What is the matter with you people? What's going to happen to me there? I will see the doctor and take care of what I was called here to do. He didn't know what to say anymore as her questions became more enigmatic. What was Dr. Scott doing so deep in this building behind many security doors? He could already hear sounds and distant voices and cries of some (probably) lunatic patients. Shit! Was his office close to the crazies? That couldn't be! He didn't want to ask the nurse any more questions to avoid losing his soft cover.

'Ok. Let's get it over with. Open the door!'

'If you need help or when you are finished or for whatever reason, we will come and assist you. There is a whole range of closed-circuit cameras around there. There are also special orderlies on three points. And if you....' Anthoine cut her in half.

'Yes, nurse, I know all the f**king procedures.' He didn't know shit, but that was the only thing he managed to say. She went to see Hilda immediately. She didn't like this young prick doctor, and all of this shit was highly suspicious. She opened the particular door, and the guard let him in. She closed the door with a bang behind him. He felt like he was in a dungeon with a one-way ticket.

Anthoine was in. Now he had to find Dr. Scott, get the damn signature, and get away from Birdland as far as he could. He was getting more worried now as the shouting and screaming intensified. The first orderly came to him. They all looked alike, big, nasty, with tiny teeth and probably low IQs. All carried a particular type of voltage gun, probably to tame the crazies. It was like the whole bouncer population of the city gathered in this birdcage. Anthoine started to remember the movie with Jack Nicholson, 'One flew over the cuckoo nest,' a famous Milos Forman movie set in an Oregon psychiatric hospital. Even more, cold chills started to run through his body. The scene he was about to see looked much more like the one from the nine monkeys with Brad Pitt and Bruce Willis.

'Take me please to the doctor.' Even this man, with the probably low IQ, looked at him strangely.

'The doctor? You want to see him. Shall I go with you?'

'What is with you people? No, I don't need anybody to go with me. I can do I by myself. And what the heck is this, is something wrong with the doctor?

'You will see when you meet him. He will be coming to the room adjacent to the main hall room. You can wait for him there. It's dinnertime. He likes to eat there with some of his friends. But we keep an eye. It's these new stupid experiments that the staff is doing to create a social environment. It's all lunatic if you ask me. They should be locked up in their cells around the clock. This guy seemed not so stupid after all.

'What do you mean, the doctor eats together with all the other lunatics?', Anthoine asked, amazed. The orderly extraordinarily looked at him.

'Of course, he does, not with all of them but with a couple of his buddies. Besides, we do not call them lunatics'.

'He's got buddies amongst the patients?' Anthoine couldn't understand a thing.

'He is a f**king patient!' the orderly answered angrily, looking dumbfounded at Anthoine. At this, Anthoine started laughing, taking this as a joke.

'That's great, man, a real good one. Yeah, I get you, a f**king patient. That's what they all become here after a while.' The orderly didn't respond with much.

'Yeah, whatever, doctor. Be careful and howl if you need the guy on the other side or me. They are also two more orderlies during feeding time'.

'Why should I need you?' The orderly thought for a second that he was dealing with a nutcase.

'Have you ever met the doctor?' he asked finally.

'Of course, I have; what a stupid question.'

'Then you know what I mean'!

'Of course, I do,' Anthoine answered, not knowing a f**king thing what he meant. Nja, this idiot was simply an idiot. Has Dr. Scott gotten mad?

'OK, let me in now!'

The orderly opened the bar gate, and Anthoine walked into the paradise of fools. Once more, the door was closed behind him. What he saw made him think of how great it was to be sane. About 30-35 lost souls were in front of his eyes, positioned in different parts of this enormous room, or as they called it, 'activity and belly space.' Some lunatics, as to Anthoine's mind they all were, were sitting watching TV and chewing on whatever was given to them in this God-forsaken place. It was doubtful what they saw and if they understood a thing. Some were talking to themselves, and one female patient was pissing on the table and screaming 'anesthesia' while the other was clapping and congratulating her on the act. One guy was holding a book, what seemed to be a Bible or some other holy testament. He was clumped into a corner and recited some verses, probably from the book. He was expecting someone, maybe the prince of darkness. It was so much noise in this place that he could barely hear himself think. Anthoine was in shock, moving slowly between these shadows of people. Whatever they had before was gone now, if anything, was gone now. And he was sure if you had any sanity left, this place would instantly delete that. A guy was eating his food, and after every portion, he showed into his mouth, he would scream: 'Now I fart, and nothing beats a good fart. Fart, Fart, Fart!' He would repeat that over and over again. They were all kinds of lunatics here, young and old, male and female, and all ethnic and racial groups. Everybody was mixed up. What the f**k were they doing here. Shrink engineering! This cure, or whatever they called it, looked more like a disease. Suddenly Anthoine's inner observations were broken by some very harsh voice:

'What'ya want? I paid my taxes.' I paid my taxes; I did, I did; no mortgage, rent, or nothing. Wife gone, kids gone, parents gone.

He was about 50+ years old, utterly bold with Holly Buddy-type glasses and stale sweat that turned your stomach around. His shirt was in various colors, presumably from puking different meals on various occasions. He had an old IRS form and chalk. How this two worked together was an enigma for Anthoine.

'I need to see the doctor. I am not from IRS. Where is the doctor? Can you show me? We have to deal with a patient.

'Doctor, doctor. Yes, the doctor. He is a very busy man. I did pay my taxes, you know, I did, I did. No mortgage…', Anthoine cut him off, 'Where is the doctor?'

'He there eats alone. Our Doctor is an important big man, a privileged man. I did pay my taxes, you know…' Anthoine was already moving towards the room to the left where the doctor should be. There was an orderly mimicking him if he needed assistance. Anthoine just waved his hand and said everything was OK. He came into the room, and what he saw was certainly not Dr. Scott having a meal with the patients. Instead, there were three persons in the room. One on the top of the table was wearing a white robe, while the other two on his side were in their regular Birdland outfits, which consisted of Chairman Mao Communist type of clothes for the males (light blue) and a similar one, slightly more feminine, for the women (light pink).

'I am looking for the doctor, Dr. Scott. Can anybody help me? We need to attend to patients as soon as possible. I had information that he eats at these premises. That comment from Anthoine made one gentleman standing on the left side of the table to begin laughing like a lunatic. He didn't have any teeth. Later it was explained to him that it was Rooster Barnsley, a serial killer of 11 children. He ended up here as a result when the police wounded him during the last atrocity he committed, one of the victim's parents, a doctor, performed a lobotomy (or some similar thing) on him as revenge. Now this monster vegetable was sitting here. The guy on the right side stood up, came to Anthoine, and saluted him. This was an army captain who, by mistake, ordered his soldiers to walk into a minefield during a training exercise. Five of them died, one being his youngest son. He lost his mind completely soon afterward. There was another creature sitting in the corner of the room. Anthoine didn't notice him at once due to the dim light in this windowless and what appeared to be an airless room. It was a younger man, maybe in his late 30s, lying on the floor like a baby sucking his thumb. Anthoine thought at he was autistic, but it was later explained to him that he was suffering from a form of schizophrenia characterized by a tendency to remain in a fixed stuporous state for long periods. In his case, catatonic schizophrenia, as it was called, could give way to short periods of extreme excitement. Only the person in the white robe was eating, while the others became amused by Anthoine, except the fellow in the corner. Anthoine repeated his question with a slightly higher voice. Nothing happened. When he did it the third time and was about to leave, the man in white suddenly rose as a spring puppet from his chair. That was when Anthoine met 'the doctor.'

'Dr. Scott is not here, nor does he take special care of attending to those in need in this outfit. I certainly have much more important business to attend than giving sessions to these people. There are so many of my patients I need to attend to now. By the way, young man, my name is Ricardo Turow, a professional surgeon at your service'. It was incredible how this individual instantly changed from just sitting like a zombie at that table flanked by two, more or less half, vegetables. The child killer, the Rooster, was still laughing.

'Stop at this instant. We will not have that anymore!' The doctor's voice seemed to have some special command over these lunatics. He stopped an instant. Also, the captain went back to his table. The person in the corner didn't move an inch.

'How may I be of assistance to you, doctor?

The doctor was three inches from Anthoine's face. He was a thin man with a pointed forehead, high eyebrows, and a goat beard. He could have passed for a lab scientist. His dark coal eyes, though, had a very sinister gleam. Anthoine didn't feel entirely comfortable with this individual. He seemed familiar, and maybe he had seen this guy somewhere before. It must have been at the clinic. But there wasn't a surgeon in town by that name. Oh, f**k…who could remember every damn face and event. Anthoine didn't want to spend time on things irrelevant such as those.

'Oh, I was just looking for Dr. Scott. Maybe you can help me find him. I didn't know they had surgeons on the staff here.'

'Oh, indeed they do. It is quite a facility. We perform all the necessary operations.

'I have a feeling we met somewhere. I had some pains, and maybe the best thing is to take it out.' that reminds me, Anthoine added in passing as a side joke, I should check my appendix.

'Certainly, doctor. Excellent idea! Why have this unnecessary burden? All these useless organs should be immediately eliminated. Surgeries are the best solutions, small, medium, or big ones. For example, why have women suffered hours and hours in labor when you can take care of it with a caesarian? It should always be performed. Anthoine was getting even more uncomfortable.

'I think we should look at your appendix state now!'

'No doctor, that won't be necessary. It's nothing. I only feel some reflexes from time to time.

'There is nothing called it's nothing. I insist!' He was now face to face with Anthoine. Suddenly Anthoine wanted o run out of the room, but he realized the captain was blocking it. What was even worse was that it was closed. How the f**k did he get there? Anthoine knew that this could be trouble. And who the f**k was this doctor.

'Excuse me, and I must go now; please move from the door.' The captain didn't bulge for an inch and said, ' The doctor gives orders here now.'

He didn't finish the sentence, 'What doctor, you mother…'. A sharp blow on the back of his head muddled his vision, and he fell to the floor in pain.

'Some patients never learn. Captain, please put him on the table, and Rooster gives a hand here —now!

How the catatonic man stood up and followed the doctor's orders like a robot was incomprehensible to Anthoine. He could hear this, but his motoric was half dead. Whatever blow he got must have paralyzed him temporarily. Before he started shouting, his mouth was gagged with a dirty cloth smelling urine and presumably last night's leftovers. He had the urge to spill his guts at that very moment. Where the f**k was the security. They should be coming in here now. Then he remembered that this f**king room had no camera. What kind of bullshit was this?

Four firm hands lifted him to the table and held him there.

'Good, now we are going to perform a fast checkup, and then we operate!' the doctor said. He opened Anthoine's robe and tore his shirt meticulously, killing off all the buttons. Suddenly a flash of memory passed through Anthoine's brain. The doctor – f**king doctor! Now it came to him. Somehow the fear pushed this information out of his hard-disc brain. It was that damn lunatic they had for display in one of those sessions. There were so many of them that he forgot, but this was a unique split personality combined with an anal-retentive personality, a rare case to which he should have paid more attention. Namely, according to all the books he read and Dr. Scott's explanations of the case, this was a rare mental disorder in which two or more independent and distinct personality systems developed in the same individual.

One was the normal him – Jeffrey Ivy, a former postal clerk, who was harmless. The other was the makeup person of Dr. Ricardo Turow, who killed his wife and two children at the makeup operating table, believing they had some organ failures. Each of these two personalities alternately inhabited this guy's conscious awareness to the exclusion of the other. In his case, there was no dominant one. They shared their time equally; neither remembered nor knew anything about the other, primarily while the other was operating. It was temporary amnesia. The other surgeon personality did the gruesome family operation, while the postal clerk didn't know a thing. In this case, these two personalities didn't differ in outlook, temperament, and body language, but they gave themselves different first names. Dr. Scott observed that this condition was scarce, and only a few hundred cases have been reported. According to him, this 'doctor' developed the formation of multiple personalities to cope with or escape from inner conflict, in this case, triggered by trauma experienced early in life, being abused as a child by his father and mother. How he came to be a surgeon and killed his family as one was out of Dr. Scott's comprehension and lecture notes. Anthoine doubted that he knew anything basically and that this case was much more complicated than it seemed. If so, what the f**k was this guy with a criminal mind doing alone in this room without any security ready to operate on him. That damn idiot and his social experiments. Even worse, it was mentioned that this guy was 'blessed' with a personality characterized by meticulous neatness, suspicion, and reserve. This was also formed in early childhood by fixation during the anal stage of development. In his case, it was a consequence of strict and harsh toilet training, where his mother would do all kinds of things to him if he missed peeing in the right place or if there were patches of yellow on the toilet seat. God forbid he didn't flush. This post-personality analysis was broken in Anthoine's head when he heard a door open, and someone came in. He was saved! Alas, it was another lunatic called Jizzard who joined the party. He tried to wiggle and move, but these two guys put on a firmer grip. The doctor finished his check-up. Anthoine thought that he was much more f**ked up than stated by this multiple personality shit by Dr. Scott. F**k! F**k! How could he forget this? The guy was called 'the doctor.' Instead of Dr. Scott, he ended up with this lunatic.

'I conclude that an operation is needed, doctor. Don't worry. We will take the appendix in a matter of seconds! Now Anthoine was in total panic, sweating like a pig ready to be slaughtered. This f**king Dr. Giggles was about to cut him open, and he didn't have any degree to back that act up. At least Hanibal Lecter was a highly educated man. Where was f**king Dr. Scott?

'Oh, Elsa, nice of you to join in. You can be the anesthesiologist, and Jizzard can apply the antibiotic saliva.'

Anthoine's eyesight improved, and what he saw was a sight to remember. He would probably have laughed if this was on TV, not on his skin. His chest and abdominal part were exposed, and the place where the appendix was supposed to be was covered in something yellowish. It was mustard. It was placed on the wrong side, opposite the appendix. Jizzard unzipped his pants, took out his huge erect penis, and started to masturbate. It was insane! In moments he came in white gushes all over the exposed body. It was disgusting. The doctor was thrilled and thanked Jizzer for applying the antibiotic so thoroughly. This guy was a total lunatic in both personalities. He remembered to make a mental note of that if he survived this. The doctor wore gloves, a plastic knife, and a corkscrew. Anthoine was scared as shit now. How did he get these things? Oh, no…God forgive him for everything he has done wrong. He just prayed to get alive from this tragicomic mayhem. Elsa climbed on the table above his head, drew her skirt up, and started pissing on Anthoine's head and screaming 'anesthesia.' The urine was coming down as torrential rain on Anthoine's head. It was terrible. The doctor hit Anthoine with the plastic knife. It made only a superficial wound before it split in two. Anthoine's muscles were tense as hell, especially in the abdominal area.

'Shit! They don't make these instruments as they used to. Let's try the other one instead. Before the doctor could apply the corkscrew and inflict some real damage, the young catatonic schizophrenia boy in the corner suddenly got to his feet. He started screaming in such a high voice that windows could explode. Even the doctor and the lunatics around had to put their hands on their ears to cover the unbearable noise he was producing. Only the pissing dame seemed unaffected by this. She was still gushing urine like Niagara Falls. Anthoine saw his chance at that moment. He rushed from the table and passed the captain and Rooster, who let go a second before. He went through the door violently that they fell out of their hinges. He looked like a lunatic now, mouth gagged, draining in piss, half naked with mustard all over his body. The boy's screaming filled the room in an instant. He wasn't stopping. This triggered all kinds of lunatic cries and screams. Alarms went off. Anthoine kept running through the crazy crowd. Orderlies were coming towards him with voltage guns. Someone was shouting behind them, coming through the security gates. It was Dr. Scott, nurse Hilda and one more doctor with many orderlies. The last thing he knew, before he collapsed, out of exhaustion and faulty voltage zapping by one of the orderlies (thinking that he was a crazy escapee), was the IRS lunatic guy saying: 'I paid my taxes, I did, I did. No mortgage, no rent, no nothing….'

Anthoine Scott woke up in the nurse's room shortly after that. Beautiful nurse Linda was with him. Seeing her lips and breasts, he thought he had arrived in heaven. There was no sperm, urine, or lunatic doctor upon him. Yes, little prematurely, but worth it. It was a good ticket. Sister Hilda and Dr. Scott soon broke that picture of erotic heaven. The whole thing was resolved. No scandal happened, and Anthoine got what he came for – the damn signature. Dr. Scott was furious, but when angry, Anthoine pointed out some security breaches and lapses in the medical profession; his escapade and break-in into the Birdland were forgotten. The lunatics were brought to order soon, and the 'doctor' was dealt with in a little bit different fashion. How he had control over the two lunatics was out of everybody's comprehension. Anthoine was escorted out of Birdland, which looked more like a maximum-security prison to him, by guards and heavily armored dogs. Fortunately, he got Linda's number. He didn't forget that. He swore that day he would remember things better and register details. Yes, remembering those small and sometimes insignificant details may be of help somewhere down the road. Anthoine Scott knew that very well now, or at least until the following incident appeared. We are what we are, nothing more, nothing less.

15

Memphis "The Legend" Kapadia & The Mineral Water Heist

'Oh, that's a f**king big head she's got, guys! Poor girl!' holy macaroni looks like a genetically mutated and orchestrated potato from some lab.

Memphis was smoking his fifth Camel of the afternoon and observing a small child that came out of the skyscraper to play with her friends. She carried an enormous head on a relatively small body that could barely support this humongous topping. Her name was Miriam Capouya. Her whole family was suffering from this deformity. It was not a disease or a genetic fault, but Mother Nature took her to bless this family with oversized heads. Supporting brain structure wasn't planned, so these people had to carry a large volume of air or something similar. Her brother Daren Capouya was a good buddy of ours. He had the most significant head in the family. Being almost an albino with small dark blue, sort of fox eyes, a colossal potato nose, and red hair, he created a formidable site. He was also the chairman of the red dragons, a club for supporters and fans of one of the rival soccer teams in the city. To be that, you had to have the power, authority, tenacity, leadership qualities…well, you know all that bullshit. But mostly, what brought him the leadership flag was his enormous head. Other fans thought that behind this was a genuinely remarkable brain, and it was if you compare it to the rest of them where the quality of the IQ was measured from back to front. He was also a colossal man, which allowed him to carry his big head majestically, unlike his sister, who had specific problems at age 6.

'Hey girl, how do you carry such a big head?' Is it difficult for you, honey? I don't know what I would do if I had one. Holy shit!

'The Legend' was pounding at this topic. Everybody was enjoying this, of course. Her brother Daren was not there. I don't think 'The Legend' would push this subject too much f he was. Every time Memphis 'The Legend' emerged from the skyscraper, we all came to listen to his dialogues or monologues. We felt a little bit like being in Old Greece and having him as an Aristotle in his school of philosophy. 'The Legend' was our genuine Socrates and Plato in one. And we were his disciples.

Miriam was playing amongst the cars with her friends, trying to perform all the same moves and works as her companions. That presented a slight obstacle. The head!

'Hey girl, 'The Legend' was getting to his important remarks; you defy all laws of nature. With that head, you should have been flat on your back a long time ago. I must hand it to you – you wear it well, girl!' Customary ovations, clapping from our side, thundering laughter, and unavoidable 'hear hear' always followed his remarks.

He enjoyed this very much. The poor girl didn't have much to reply to this. She knew life was difficult when you carried an XXXL head on your shoulders. She had a darker complexion than her lighter brother, with huge ears and oval black eyes. Her haircut looked like it was done under a shit and piss pot. She was a carbon copy of her who was a tall guy, some 195cm. He liked the booze a lot, which his girl didn't experience yet. Daren was 199cm and mom was 198cm. Aside from being the 'headmasters,' they also commanded the 'aerial boundaries.' The girl was probably going to reach those heights soon. There was no stopping her or her head. Fortunately, the body caught up at some point in life with the head in her family's case. 'Caught up' should be taken here as a relative term. Still, the head was huge.

'I think I should take you along when I go to Canada. That head will scare any f**king moose. Shit, it looks like it weighs more than 800kg, more than a f**king moose!' There was no way of stopping 'The Legend' now. He was on a roll.

'I am no f**king cook or culinary expert girl, but you had is one f**king leavening agent.' Somebody asked: 'What's that Memphis?' He looked at him scornfully for asking an apparent well-known fact in the 'The Legend' philosophy school.

'The girl's head is proof that it is a combo of substances causing expansion by releasing gases and then finally producing f**king baked products.' He saw this and took a more severe stance in front of us. Nobody understood what the f**k he was talking about.

'My friends, my friends, I am talking about air, steam, yeast, and f**king baking powder, and baking soda. This girl is f**king 'baking soda'! Yes, she is a f**king 'baking soda girl'! Now the ovations followed this deep intellectual analysis and observation. One more thing was certain – poor Miriam got a name she carried for many years, or till that day when she was almost 2m long and could beat up any of her girlfriends. Then she was not called that. Now 'The Legend' has spoken, and baking soda reference was being repeated in a whisper as one of the decade's most divine, breathtaking, and enlightening remarks. Aristotle's disciples would probably eat their hearts out. Her brother wouldn't have liked this at all.

Miriam was on the verge of crying but bravely held her rank and head. She seemed tired now of playing with her friends and 'The Legend''s sarcastic comments. She ran around the cars after her friends once more and then came to a blue Volvo with a large hood, then leaned slightly and positioned her huge head on the hood for obvious reasons – to rest this huge bulk and to rest her body of caring this. We never saw anything like it before. Some nine or ten of us, including the master, 'The Legend,' were completely surprised. It was a moment of silence. Nobody spoke. Memphis' Camel fell out of his mouth on the pavement, still burning. We all turned to Memphis 'The Legend' for words of wisdom. But none came. She rested there for a few minutes, then got up and continued playing. We were still amazed by this unbelievable site outplayed in front of our eyes. Finally, Memphis 'The Legend' spoke.

'Mark my words, fellow friends; this girl can reach an enlightened mind, not by her sheer size but by the inner doings in her head. Baking soda has shown us here by her head-hood act a certain mental tranquility, fearlessness, and spontaneity in her action. All of that leads to Zen, my friends.

He was still contemplating what he said, sure that it didn't bear any relevance to f**king fact that the girl had a huge head that needed rest, which was already weird and strange by itself. But 'The Legend' needed to make a point and finish this exploration into the unknown.

'She has just broken the boundaries of ordinary thought and pure logic. Man, she is something. 'F**king A' baking soda! You are the girl of girls! That head could be worth something, but it might not. It depends on which astral projection and the zen road you take!

We clapped in unison, celebrating the wise words of 'The Legend.' It was a crescendo of ovations, which Miriam thought pointed toward her. She smiled, revealing a set of giant teeth too. We didn't even want to speculate what kind of implications the growth of these would have. 'The Legend' picked up his still-burning Camel and made a final remark looking bemused at the blue hood of the car where Miriam's head was just a few minutes ago.

'The Ancient Romans said Populus vult decipi (the people want to be deceived), my friends. Let us not be deceived by the voluminous matter in front of us; let us take a moment and rethink the whole business of size, matter, and structure!'

We were looking at Memphis 'The Legend' with colossal respect, even though we didn't understand the f**king thing he was saying, and that, again, it had little to do with the matter in question.

'But, as the US Marines had that advertisement of looking for a few good men, so should the baking soda guys do with looking for a few good heads. F**king A girl! Awesome!'

A final roar of laughter and ovations followed 'The Legend''s final and unequivocal comment. He was indeed a Zen master.

Memphis Kapadia, or, as everyone called him, 'The Legend,' was one of the most respected people by us youngsters. He liked the name 'The Legend' after someone told him it means 'the man.' That someone was not a language expert. Our 'The Legend,' he was the bullshit man. He was a con artist. He was the magician. He was the Joker. He was the poet. He was the thinker, the most significant natural street philosopher, the talker, the doer, and the mover. He was the man. The point is that Memphis was the character of all characters, a Renaissance man (for all the wrong reasons) and the man for all seasons and all places. He was the man of the world. I doubt he saw himself in that light, but he certainly loved being in this limelight we projected and created for him. He truly deserved it. He was the hallmark of our skyscraper. A man of 25 years, he was also an attractive bloke. Sort of Italian-looking guy with a bit of spice of darker skin complexion and an athletic body. He won many ladies' hearts. He always dressed casually but elegantly. Crystal blue eyes and highly dark wavy hair, which he attended to hourly, gave him the unmistakable look and presence of a Latin lover. Sporadic jewelry, dark glasses, and expensive watches gave him a slightly pimpish look. He always had money. How he did it, nobody knew. He was also full of shit. Little education, as he bragged about it – a couple of hours and some morning breaks and maybe an excursion, a whole string of jobs (24 in 4 years!), no plans for the immediate future, or any future, even less for the present and finally a chain of very suspicious contacts and dealings. All legitimate, according to him. Even with this being said, he was the only soul provider for the family. But folks, don't be fooled. Memphis read stuff. He bought a couple of books. One was on Zen Buddhism, the other on the art of making love, the third was about politics, and the fourth was a book of sayings in Latin. He also had a collection of collected works on Calvin and Hobbes, The Peanuts and his pride and Joy – two Milne's A. A. masterpieces – Winnie the Pooh and The House at the Pooh Corner. He read these 11 times and was astonished by the depths he found in them. His mom used to say that these books were so empty, which was why they were so deep. Deep empty, she used to say. After those remarks, Memphis never raised questions of literature amongst family members. They didn't understand. The Zen part was the one that turned women on, not the Pooh one. His brother Evan Kapadia was a 100% certified bum by all standards, which gave his mom a premature heart attack. Memphis 'The Legend' found him a job in a local pharmaceutical company, ending in a drug enforcement agency bust. Evan went off easy with a rehab program and a year in a minimum-security facility, primarily thanks to one good-hearted DEA female agent. He finally quit drugs and remained a bum that slept 16 hours a day while the rest was spent on sitcoms. His stepfather (the Kapadias lost their dad to excessive alcohol abuse when they were 7) hated Evan's guts and would have kicked him a long time back if it wasn't for Evan's mother, who was so protective of her bum son. He had no problem with 'The Legend,' as he always brought fast cash. The stepfather was driving a local bus in three suburbs; not much to say about him. 'The Legend' didn't like him too much, but at least he gave Mom security, something she couldn't rely on from her flesh and blood. And she was not alone. At least they watched the damn TV every night and even went to see a movie occasionally. Life was not that bad if you were satisfied with the minimum everyday small shit life provides. Memphis always had bigger and greater plans. One of them, actually a life's goal, was to move to Canada, to Toronto. Why he got this idea? Nobody knew. He once indicated, though, that he once saw a magazine from Canada, and there was a fashion piece on some model called Julie Orlowski. He instantly fell in love with this heavenly blonde and decided that he would have her and that moving to Toronto was the only viable option. He wanted enough money before that to give her the life she deserved. Somehow he started writing to her and probably lying tons. He never got a reply until he sent her his picture. Then she got interested. But 'The Legend' had a long way to work to reach Canada, and he knew that. But he was always working on that, or at least he portrayed that picture. He once said that she was deeply impressed by his Zen attitude and views.

Back in the old days, a couple of years after the skyscraper was built, Memphis 'The Legend' was the initiator of the club called 'the Club of Procrastination and Rationalization.' It was his brainchild. He considered it a philosophical forum and resting place for all the 'mother f**king lazy assholes,' as he liked to call them. He also coined the term, which was hanging as a mantelpiece in the main room of the rented spaces for this short-lived club: "FJAKA" – A complete state of physical and mental listlessness or suspended apathy with the potential urge to do absolutely nothing. This brilliant piece remained as Memphis 'The Legend''s greatest saying. Somebody said the idea came from France, from some philosopher. People didn't give a rat's ass hair about that.

The candidates were streaming from all parts of the city. The spaces in the basement of the building were used for these purposes for about two years or so until Arno Stockhouse, the chief of the tenant's council, evicted everybody with the help of the police. 'The Legend' wanted to chain himself down with some of his pals from the club but decided against it as he always proclaimed peaceful means. The rooms were sold to a profitable Italian private company selling clothes & shoes. While it existed, the club attracted many members. It was said that at one point, it had over 343 members. The fees were outrageous and paid monthly, collected mainly by 'The Legend,' but it was a privilege to be a part of this original and soon very snobbish club. There were always those that could pay. The idea was straightforward, as all 'The Legend' had, but it proved lucrative while it lasted. Forty beds would fill the big room in the half-cellar space, and the members would only need to sleep when they arrived or just lay there doing nothing. As there were so many members, the spaces were used in shifts during the month. Memphis 'The Legend's brother Evan took care of that until he f**ked up and was replaced. 'The Legend' called it the Zen arena for contemplation and cleansing of the soul. There would be two film performances twice a week. All on sleeping, that is, they had to depict someone sleeping for 6-8 hours. They were all home videos, and the members were required to bring these. They ranged from normal sleepers to those hardcore snorers to children sleeping or, the best, action ones featuring people talking in their sleep or farting. For farting, one had to wait a couple of hours to happen. Mostly all of that watching was fast asleep by then. Soon pornographic movies came in, just those involving the bedrooms (most of them do anyway), booze, and even some drugs. 'The Legend' killed even more money on this, and what was even more critical, he penetrated the city's underground. He was paying off the right people for the protection, which worked. The illegal doings, mostly the drugs, ultimately killed the club. He did spend most of that money later on some horrible deals. Regardless, Memphis 'The Legend' cashed in on this deal in a good way, and what he earned there, at least a small part that was left, helped him later in life.

'Now listen to this, guys!'

Memphis 'The Legend' was scribbling something on the paper for the last half hour. It was almost 38C degrees, and we were all sweating like pigs while the noon August sun penetrated our skins even through the roof of the entry staircase where we were killing time on that bloody Sunday.

'This one commemorates this f**king hot day and all the pains one has to endure under such an ordeal. It's called a Hot trip! 'The Legend' stood before us in black slacks, light black loafers, and a black T-shirt. He started reciting his poem. It was a big moment for all of us to hear live poetry from 'The Legend':

Hot Trip

Once I took a f**king trip across the stinky desert. It was so hot! The temperature must have been 105 degrees F. I had decided to wrap my stinking socks around my asshole hair. I burned my dirty nails while walking on the shitty desert sand. All I could think about was some slimy and greasy, frozen urine to drink. In the distance, I thought I saw a pool of blood and tears. I laughed and cried. I was disappointed to find it was only a toilet bowl. Suddenly, slimy worms were puking around me. I shitted and pissed brutally, not wanting to show my f**king potatoes. In the nick of time, I heard a fat, sweaty voice behind me saying, "Pick up your hemorrhoids, punk." I stupidly turned and saw it was a eunuch. "Thank God, I cried. I am saved at last…."

Moments of silence and moment of truth were soon exchanged for a roar of ovations, applause, laughter, and general admiration for the poetic justice coming out of 'The Legend.' Somebody remarked that those Brits, Shelley, and Yeats should bow hearing these words of wisdom and beauty spoken by one of our very own. 'The Legend' calmed the crowd down and toned the exclamations of joy and admiration. He said he was a humble street poet, philosopher, and thinker. We all nodded, of course. He probably pinched keywords from some developing Mac Software program, but who cares. Why everybody was there at that time in that heat is still an enigma to me. It must have been the mentioned condition of FJAKA plus the presence of 'The Legend.' Lately, he was not spending so much low-quality bullshit time outside the skyscraper due to his 25th job in the wire factory driving the boss. Suddenly a tiny truck came out of the main street and turned into our neighborhood. It was written on its side: Ice Cold Mineral Water – Mountain Delight! F**king delight – Ice mineral water on a day like this – oh yes. We were too lazy to move our butts to the store or the apartments to get something to drink. So we watched this like in a dream or a Coke commercial. The truck was just about to swing to the left, down the basketball street towards the leading Supermarket, when something broke, and the truck stopped frozen, almost like its cargo, on the curb. It broke down, and it happened on our turf.

The mineral water (bulletproof) plan immediately began to develop in Memphis 'The Legend's head. He was just plain thirsty, and it seemed much more logical and more accessible to rob this truck than to go home two floors up to his apartment and drink the same thing from his fridge. No, the Zen ways worked differently. This was here to be taken, was Memphis 'The Legend's comment afterward. The drivers got out, cursing and kicking the truck like it would change something. The whole truck was out of commission. One left for the nearby phone booth to call in the shit that happened to them. It would take at least an hour to two for the other truck to get there, empty the cargo, and deliver it to the supermarket. The other driver soon returned, and they sat in the truck sweating like pigs and slowly dosing off in the horrible heat.

'Ok. It's rather simple, 'The Legend' was getting into gear now.

'We are thirsty, and what better opportunity than this broken truck in front of us? The guys in there are half-dead anyway, so it will be a piece of cake. The key is not to f**k it up.'

'How are we going to open the side doors to get the mineral waters' Mike Gleisch asked.

'The doors are permanently unlocked. They never lock this while delivering on short distances and to many shops. It's just to open the unique lever.

We all looked at each other and realized that 'The Legend' has done this before, probably much worse things too.

'But there is a point there! The back door is the electrical one, which is f**ked up now, so we have to use the side ones anyway. The problem is that they could see us in their side view mirrors, especially if one of these idiots wakes up. We will need a slight distortion while the door is open, and we will take one case out. We are after just one case. It's the question of thirst and making the point that nothing is impenetrable under any circumstances.'

None of us thought out this. It seemed pointless. It was bloody warm, and 'The Legend' controlled things.

'What will the diversion be?' I asked.

'Aha…the best and most reliable thing in the world, pal'.

'A bomb,' answered Pepé in a hurry.

'Brilliant, Pepé! I knew you were a f**king moron, but that stupidity can go to such degrees I was truly unaware of. Maybe you should be the diversion instead. We can start beating you up in front of the truck, and then the drivers will be amused and maybe even come out of the truck and help you.'

Pepé was shit scared now. He once remembered Memphis 'The Legend's words that unspoken words are worth gold, stupid ones even more.

'Sorry,' he uttered in a shy way.

'No problem. Just don't come up with any more brilliant suggestions. No, I had something different in mind. You will see. He disappeared into the building. We were all waiting nervously for what the idea entailed. Memphis 'The Legend' was a practical man. Some parts of our group diminished suddenly. The realization that this small job was illegal and could be pretty dangerous if we got caught vaporized our ranks. Some also took the opportunity to say that 'The Legend' was gone. What remained was Mike, myself, Anthoine, Pepé, Ture (Keke's older Bro), and Alan Meehan from the nearby Redbrick apartment building. The other 4-5 were long gone. After 15 minutes, 'The Legend' appeared, and he planned to take our breath away. In everyone's wet dream, the blonde girl, Michelle, was there with him. They were school buddies, at least the eight compulsory grades that 'The Legend' attended. Afterward, he thought high school would be a waste of time. Michelle's fantastic figure was accentuated even more by a Versace T-shirt, which must have been X-small size because her beautiful breasts were ready to explode. Her face and long blonde hair looked even more wonderful without the usual makeup. Calvin Kline could have easily made a commercial for a pair of jeans at that very moment. Our eyes just passed from her top to bottom like a good HP scanner does these days. This girl was something else, and she knew it. How she agreed to this with Memphis was unknown. We knew he had a flame with her until she moved to more stable and profitable harbors. His was very uncertain and, at most times, under heavy winds and rains. Memphis broke our daydreams.

'Michelle will help us to do this. But we have to move fast. I can see that some of the general population has deserted us. Don't matter – more ice-cold stuff for us. Alan will go after the door as he is the handiest here. Mike and Ture will go in and get the case closest. You, Haas, and Anthoine will take it from them and slide it into nearby bushes. After that, we will join you and drink the stuff up.

'What about me?, asked Pepé.

'You will be on the lookout if the police come, the red cross, the army corps, or our local types of FBI, DEA, DIA, NSA, CIA, or any similar problem.'

'F**k, I can't deal with so many problems.'

Memphis 'The Legend' just wanted him on the sidelines, so there wouldn't be any f**kups. 'Don't worry, pal, we will back you up if needed. You will be commando outpost guy'.

This importance of the task appealed to Pepé, who made a couple of dozen extraordinary faces in the process. He moved to his position.

'That guy can make faces. Holy shit. We should get some TV one day here. I could earn some money from him. I will watch Michelle's back if you wonder what I will do. It was closer going to be her ass he was going to watch. She did have one of the finest pieces of ass we ever saw. This was destined to work even before it started. Michelle went towards the truck while we took our positions. The drivers were half dead but not asleep, so Michelle was severely needed. The plan was that as soon she started talking with the driver, we would go to the other side of the truck facing the green space and the parking lot beyond.

'Hi there guys, are you hot in there?'.

Michelle was displaying all her charms now. The driver and the co-driver were the two biggest hillbillies you could find. The co-driver looked like he just came from milking cows, and the driver looked like someone growing up and going to school for Grizzlies.

'No miss, yes miss!' The driver looked at her like the only man on a stranded island with 50 Playboy playmates.

'We are warm, miss. The truck broke down. It will be fixed. We will fix it. Well…fix it.' He couldn't take his eyes off her. She started licking her lips seductively, in an erotic fashion, and inserted her middle finger into her mouth.

'I can get you something if you want, poor dears!'

'Oh yes, no thanks. Well…Maybe…'. The driver was losing his speech capabilities. The co-driver was half awake and came closer but could only see the bulging breasts: Wow, beautiful cows they have here and what milk they produce!' The driver turned around and slapped him over the face like a sledgehammer.

'F**king idiot. That's a lady you are talking to. Apologize for this instant. Sorry, miss, for my rude and primitive friend.'

'I am so sorry.' The co-driver came close and realized it was not a cow but the goddess of fertility he was looking at.

'That's OK. I was raised on a farm, too, and I love cows and all those excellent dairy products.

'It seems they did well to you, miss. You do look wonderful. Like a spring angel', added the driver.

'Oh, thank you, you are such a gentleman.' Michelle played with a gold chain around her, stroking her breasts and hard nipples slightly. The two mesmerized drivers by the heat and especially by the blonde pet angel in front of them didn't realize what was going on. In those 3-4 minutes, the operation went swiftly with Swiss precision. Alan opened the door, and Ture and Mike got in and got one case of drinks. Anthoine and I took it from there, finishing the operation. The case was then delivered to our entry by exchanging hands and keeping out of sight. Pepé stood in the middle of the street, making faces and waving his hands like a lunatic.

'Who is that? Asked the driver; Michelle needed an escape fast.

'Oh, that's my brother. He is a bit crazy, you know. They let him out of Birdland yesterday. He killed our parents when he was 16 and raped me. I had a child with him. He looks young, though, but he is already 38. He also tried to strangle one guy in the Birdland Hospital. They think I can care for him as he is fully reformed to return to society. It isn't easy, though, as he still breastfeeds at his age. He also screws with animals, mostly cows, when we go to the farm. I need to attend to him now. Sorry guys, bye now!' She lied tons, and it seemed to work. She went and took Pepé off the street, to his delight. The goddess touched him. He was still making strange moves and faces.

'F**king shit, man. Did you see and hear that,' said the driver.

'Breastfeeding at 38, raped and killed people, and she's got a kid with him. F**king monsters, man, that guy is like Mike Myer's character from Halloween'! Added the co-driver.

'Screws with cows on the farm. Was she f**king lying, man?'

'I don't think so. Did you see how that guy looked and behaved? They suddenly lost all desire for the fertility goddess. What is this world coming to? When is this damn truck going to arrive so we can get the f**k from here, said the driver nervously.

Inside we laughed like a madman when Michelle told her story. Pepé was not amused at all. Memphis calmed him down when he explained that he worked for the common good. Michelle didn't kiss him on the cheek. That would be too much to ask and a sacrifice for her. She got two ice-cold bottles, and we divided the rest into 10. Memphis, 'The Legend's plan, worked out. After half an hour came the new truck. We were outside when the drivers called us to help them unload the stuff and load it into the new truck. We obliged regardless of the heat, as this was a good cover-up. Pepé was not present as they knew him by now. They asked more about this guy, and we added even more lies, some of them to do with Michelle doing some witchcraft and voodoo shit on the farm. After a half hour of moving the cases in the blistering heat, we were rewarded with two cases of mineral water. Well, Memphis's plan was brilliant. We felt shitty, but Memphis 'The Legend' said that the thing was there to be taken, and we needed to see if we were ready and determined. More important things would come along, and this was a test. We wondered if he was talking about legal or illegal stuff at that point and if he was referring to himself or us. We were soon to find out.

She was soft as the finest satin sheets or your favorite silk underwear boxers treated with a super softener. Beautiful silky black hair fell on her creamy and nourished face. Her lips looked like a Cover Girl lipstick commercial, and those green eyes took you by storm. She was also the director's mistress, somebody you didn't want to fool around with. Memphis 'The Legend' did, and he banged her on every possible occasion. He was irresistible to her, and she was irresistible to him, not just because of her fantastic body with all the accessories included but also for her inside information. Namely, during one of their romantic meetings, she slipped something out in the heat of the moment about a significant cash transaction that would happen soon.

The director spilled his guts on her while being submerged between her breasts and other parts of her body. He was to receive an extra payment from one of the partners. In exchange, he was to give them exclusive rights for some product promotion for a couple of years. It was also an entry for money laundering schemes. The wire company was doing exceptionally well, and big money was being turned over. He was getting half a million bucks for this and promised her beautiful presents and trips. This was illegal as the people providing this money were connected to the regional mob. 'The Legend' knew this when he heard which actors were involved. He persuaded Tina, that was the mistress's name to steal the money together and move to Rio de Janeiro. He also lied about another half million he had stashed away from previous business deals. Tina was instantly hooked on living in style in Rio with 'The Legend' but was also afraid.

'Don't worry, 'The Legend' was saying, and we will make it as if he stole the money from these guys, and the blame will fall on him. You will only have to tell me exactly when the money arrives and how.'

'He will stash the money in my apartment. He keeps a safe there with some money and all my jewelry. I will be the suspect immediately, and he will kill me when he finds out!'

'Don't worry, dear. We will catch an Air France flight to Rio in Paris when he finds out.

'I wish it would be so easy as you say it, Memphis.'

'Yes, it will, dear. Just trust me. Ok!' He was already undressing and kissing her all over in the back seat of the black Mercedes in a suburban park. She agreed to everything. Memphis 'The Legend' also had the director's confidence as he drove him to his mistress every Friday at noon. That Friday was different as the director received a Samsonite silver case with the dough. He was very nervous and told Memphis, 'The Legend,' to hurry up. Tina had already alerted Memphis that the money was arriving on that Friday. What happened afterward nobody knows for certain, but after some years, parts of the story and the puzzle were received from rumors. If you combine all of it and trust the sources, the story develops in the following way. Memphis told Tina to keep the director occupied while he emptied the safe. Unfortunately for them, the director, in the heat of the passion, went to get an ice cold drink and saw a man in the hood and gloves in the living room opening the safe without any tools – which meant that he knew the combination and which also meant that he knew Tina. He didn't have much time to do anything, and while putting two and two, Tina hit him with a bottle on the back of the head and went into a hysteric attack. Memphis calmed her down and told her that this was even better. Although Memphis knew the director didn't see him, he would put two and two together. He also paid his friend to take his place as the chauffeur, and his records of working in the company were long gone and exchanged for his friends. It would be the director's word and a word of a semi-hore. The police could follow it up, but the mob would never believe this, especially after he calls them. He had the plan to take care of it all. They tied him up, and he told her to wait until 19:00 that evening, take the flight destined for Paris, and then go to the gate where the flight for Rio was going at 22:30. He had already bought her the ticket for Paris. He showed her his later ticket (which was for an earlier flight) and said he would bring the Rio ones with him. He needed to clear some business up and take his dough (which didn't exist). He also would take the Samsonite case. She didn't mind, been half scared, half in shock. They made love, and he comforted her once or twice more and left. The director returned to his senses, watching her prepare for the trip. He tried to move and wiggle out, but Memphis 'The Legend' was a master at knots. Memphis 'The Legend' didn't plan to care for any business or collect some non-existent dough. He owed some people money but had 85.000 dollars stashed away. With that money, he had already paid for all the expenses this scam required, especially for the false passport and other documents. That took almost two weeks and was damn expensive but essential. He had planned this out from when Tina told him about the money. It was a chance in a lifetime. He went straight to the airport to catch the early flight to Paris. He took the boat to England and caught the last flight to Rio from Heathrow airport under a new name, not to Rio but to Montreal, Canada. From Paris airport, he called the local police and told them about the mob money they would launder and the director's involvement. He gave them the address of her apartment. He also took care of the mob through an underworld acquaintance. They got an anonymous tip that the director and mistress stashed away the money and outplayed the whole farce blaming a non-existent chauffeur. He was skating on thin ice and playing a feeble story. But it worked out. 'The Legend' was a damn lucky bastard. As she was about to leave the apartment, the police busted her. They found the director tied up there and her fingerprints on the safe and bottle. 'The Legend's fingerprints were nowhere to be found. The bogus chauffeur played his role masterfully. Memphis 'The Legend' paid him off nicely. He was a brother in blood from long ago. The director was taken to the police van suffering a frenzied attack. Tina was crushed. She was not a stupid girl. When she saw the bogus chauffeur, she put two and two. Memphis Kapadia has f**ked her, not just literally but in a big way. She was a stupid fool to believe and even fall in love with him.

The 747 British Airways Jumbo Jet was on its regular flight to Toronto, Canada. Rick Montana just had a shot of Chivas Regal in the business class. He bought three books on the airport: English in six weeks, Guide to Toronto, and a book about Canada in French. He would have to repurchase his old books. His English was close to zero, and his French was below zero. He knew a couple of pick-up lines, mainly used for prostitutes. He would try to master it in due time. He was reading about Canadian mosses and how they could reach the weight of 850kg. He thought briefly about Daren Capouya's sister and her enormous head. That put a smile on his face. Soon it disappeared when he thought about Tina and how he f**ked her up, and how his family was left behind. He would find a way to send them money from time to time when things cool down.

They usually do. The flight attendant brought him another scotch. She had a fine ass and long silky legs. There would be time for that. He was sitting all alone in his row. He looked at the seat beside him. There was a silver Samsonite case lying there. He looked at the case and the flight attendant's ass again, then dozed off with a smile. He was a Canadian citizen by the name of Rick Montana. Memphis 'Memphis, 'The Legend' Kapadia, was history. Life was damn good.

The police talked to the stepfather and Memphis's mom, who almost got another heart attack. They didn't know anything. Stepdad was full of criticism, saying that both kids were bums. He was confident that Memphis had no brains to pull anything off like this but that he probably ran because he owed some people money, and these people were not friendly. Evan was a hard case. He didn't say anything. He was in some catatonic stage. We were disappointed that Memphis disappeared like this but were also happy for him. All kinds of stories began circulating about him being an international agent to a mastermind criminal. He probably achieved his dreams and goals, but not how we expected them. Police asked all kinds of questions, but we remained silent and ignorant. The truth was that we knew f**king zero, so there was not much to tell. Every story pointed out that we knew very little about him. His nickname, 'The Legend,' was never mentioned. The 500.000 dollars were never recovered, of course. The Interpol in Brazil was contacted as the local feds have been after the mob guys for some time, and this was one of the links they needed. Brazil's search turned out zilch! Memphis Kapadia certainly had a flock of loyal disciples.

The mistress eventually escaped the prison after a lack of evidence was deceived and left behind. The poor, beautiful girl was found overdosed in her apartment a couple of days after that. It smelled more like a homicide. The director was still serving his sentence for embezzlement and some other charges. He never spilled his guts on the people that gave him the money. He knew better. Unfortunately, that didn't help. At some point, he suddenly exited prison for strange, unknown reasons and maybe a lack of good evidence. A couple of days later, he was found dead in the local sewer system with wires protruding from his mouth and ass hole. The people that provided the half million were pissed off for losing the deal and pulled some high strings to get him out. After finding nothing from him, he was disposed of. The whole scam left a bloody trail behind and two dead bodies to show for it. The mob never believed their story about the chauffeur. The double-chauffer held his ground and was known in mob circles as a reliable chap. They believed him. After some more years, when everything cooled down, we got a postcard from the United States. It was addressed to Daren Capouya, of all people. The postcard depicted a Canadian moose. It was posted from Miami. There was nothing much written on it except:

'The inner self has been reached. Disciples no longer have to be that; they are to become masters. 'The Legend.' PS Baking Soda – F**king A!

We never knew if it was real or not. Although we knew what it meant and knew 'The Legend' found everything he dreamed of. If he ever met, the model was doubtful, most probably not. He was enjoying his solitude. Losing Memphis, 'The Legend' also meant closing the informal philosophical street school. At that stage, we graduated, as 'The Legend' pointed out, and were searching for our inner selves. Memphis 'The Legend' remained a legend until he resurfaced IN THE AIR, many years after…

16

A Night to Remember

The banging wouldn't go away. A monotonous, unbreakable chain of somebody or someone banging on a door, bum! Frank Gleisch had a dreadful headache from last night's poker game. He couldn't remember how many beers he had, but it couldn't have been this bad. The banging wouldn't stop. His wife Maria was deep asleep. She was always a better sleeper than him. He was fully awake now, and the banging was more precise and louder. It couldn't be his head, Frank thought to himself. Somebody was banging on their apartment's front door on the 3rd floor. He turned around and saw 02:15 on his bedside Sony digital clock radio. What the f**k was this?

Frank was a big man. Almost 98 kilos of solid fat and going strong, he had a giant beer belly and seldom shaved. This gave him a very worn-out look of almost a recovering alcoholic. His kids, Mike and Sabrina, always scowled at him for this and often called him a bag of beer bottles and human fat. His colleagues at the city's electrical utility company didn't mind. Most of them were like him anyway and played poker with him every Friday night. Bowling was something they did every second Saturday. The banging continued. Fortunately, the kids were on a camping trip. It was bloody warm, almost 30 degrees, and the f**king middle of the night. Frank hated the summer in the city. It reminded him that decent, hard-working folks couldn't afford to leave and spend a few weeks on some tropical island or drive to the coast. His wife worked almost 10 hours daily at the textile factory, and he worked 7-8 hours. Still, they couldn't afford a decent holiday every year. Their two-room apartment wasn't much to show for. He often considered himself a loser and his whole life a complete failure. At least he had a good marriage and two solid, hard-working kids. Fortunately, they saved money to send the kids away for the holidays. That was life, shitty and unfair to some and glamorous and healthy to others. He couldn't do much about that. The banging was growing louder.

'I'm coming; keep your pants on!'

'What's going on honey,' asked his wife Maria, half awake.

'Go back to sleep, darling, and it's nothing. Just some bug that needs to be exterminated.'

With that comment, Frank made his way toward the hallway and the entrance door. He was wearing a white T-shirt and Hawaiian motive boxers. Patches of sweat covered his armpits and the vast valley forming his ass. It was a bloody hot night. Still, in a half-awake-half-asleep state, he forgot to see who or what it was before he opened the door. What he saw took him entirely by surprise. She was around 23 years old, blonde hair in a mess, eyes all watery, dripping with makeup, and with one eye blue and puffy. A rather big, fresh scar was covering her left cheek. She had a beautiful face, but one currently stricken with fear, panic, and pain. Her clothes were half torn, and she was almost fully exposed in the upper part, which was nice. Only remnants of a white blouse and white bra remained. A red skirt and red high heel shoes accompanied the rest of the outfit, though with one heel broken. His hands were covered in blood.

'Help me please, please, mister, I need help! They will kill me if I go back; please help me.'

'Who is going to kill you? What's wrong? Are you OK? Do you need medical help, lady?'

Frank was getting more apparent now. He saw a terrified young woman in front of him, covered in blood and in need of serious help.

'Please help me. They killed her; now they are going to kill me. I can't stand the pain anymore, please....' She ran her hands down his T-shirt. It was not white anymore. The marks from her fingertips and nails were blood. She fell to her knees in obvious pain.

'It's too early to give a free blow job to the neighbors, honey,' a harsh male voice said in the hallway.

At that moment, the studio apartment door on the other side of the corridor opened. A younger guy in his late 20s in leather pants and wearing nothing except a couple of dark motive tattoos came running towards them. Before she could escape, he grabbed her and pointed a large kitchen knife toward Frank.

'Listen, Fatso, you back off now. This is none of your business. That was her name. Lola had more to drink than she could handle and had a little accident in the kitchen. So get the f**k back inside on the double if you don't want to get hurt!'

The guy had written 'CRIMINAL' all over him. His face was mean and dangerous, and obviously, he had a lot of booze and drugs in his veins but was still in dangerous control of himself and this situation.

'But, it seems the lady needs medical…' he was cut in two.

'Didn't you f**kin' hear what I said? Get back into your shitty apartment and shut the f**k up! And you bitch, you are coming back with me.'

He dragged her back by her hair to the apartment. There was a lot of noise coming out from there. Frank thought they had a party earlier in the night as he could hear music muffled with Women's voices and different screams. As it belonged to Al Durant, our local small-time and medium criminal, he didn't think much of it as Al had these parties occasionally. Complaining would not do much with Al. This asshole with all kinds of criminal activities wouldn't care much. Fortunately, the noise was bearable until now. She was opening her mouth and making only out words with no voice: please help me! The leather guy dragged her back into an evident cheer of the presumably male pals inside. The door slammed behind them. Frank watched for a few seconds, unsure what to do. He finally decided to call the police.

Lola was her name, and prostitution was her game. She was one of the most beautiful whores in the combat zone. Rather expensive, Lola was in high demand, mainly by the criminal community. She did have a past and a violent one. She barely survived marrying a local crime baron as a very young girl. The guy just took her as another trophy in his collection. Through his criminal activity, he almost acquired everything he needed to put him in the yellow press: fame and fortune, booze, drugs, gambling, and infidelities with a string of violent marriages. Lola was one of the last 'pearls' in that string. He wanted to be her provider, sugar daddy, and she would be his love slave, only his and nobody else's. He was both gentle and brutal. Beatings were not a sporadic event. He took her off the streets and now owned her. She got pregnant after a while. Soon after that, another rival gang attacked his home. Three of his bodyguards were killed. He was tortured and brutally killed, while Lola was severely wounded and barely survived. She lost her child and could never have any children again. She escaped from that life but responded to the call of the wild again – she returned to the streets again. There she sold her body and everything that came with that to the highest bidders, and there were quite a few of them. Al Durant wanted to have Lola for a long time. He was captivated by her looks and the fact that she belonged to one of the strongest crime barons in the business. As his operations mainly dealt with petty crime, some extortion, and small-time robbery activities, he was not playing in the same league as Lola. And frankly, there was never enough money for her. Besides that, she despised him and found him revolting in every aspect. Only a high flow of dough could serve as a buffer for that and the golden key to Lola's heart, not heart exactly but something else. Finally, that day came for Al Durant. He robbed a local post office with four long-time partners and accomplices. They were all disguised as a postman with pig facemasks. The post office had no surveillance or cameras, so they quickly got away with it. The employees didn't even push the alarm button in time. Nobody knew what the sum was, but it was rather large. They were supposed to lie low for some time, but the carnal pleasures didn't allow that. They needed fun and lots of it. His four pals Ron (the young leather man) and his brother Mick were coming strong into the crime world, Frazier, a mean bastard who used to serve 12 years for triple rape in state prison, and Pappa Joe, an old retired ship captain who used to throw his sailors off the board for subordination, wanted a deserved fun after a healthy job is done. The idea was that they meet that Friday evening in Al's studio apartment in our skyscraper. Ron and Mick would provide the drugs, Pappa Joe would get the booze, and Al and Frazier were to get the women; in Frazier's case, that was a dangerous prospect. Al had his eyes on Lola. He knew he could never have her for always, as it would be a ride down the highway to the heart of stone. But having her for one whole night would be good enough now. If the business continues this way, he could see her even more. They needed to get two more girls besides Lola. It was not difficult. They found two brunettes in the combat zone, ready to do anything they desired. Lola needed persuasion but didn't think twice as Al started flashing large money bills. She wanted an outrageous sum, half now, half later. Al didn't care. He was prepared to pay for almost everything. All of a sudden, Al didn't look so revolting to Lola. They all meet at his apartment for a night of fun & games.

Malcolm Pace was smoking his favorite slim cigar. Being a young rookie under the late Luke Petrowsky and later becoming his partner, Malcolm was one of the best cops out there. He was a detective now, and this was the late night shift. He was cruising the streets with his partner Rico Horta when he got the 911 call. The young female operator's voice broke the night silence and the accessible listening radio station.

'Reports of domestic violence, possible rape, and general disturbance of law and order in the voluntary donors of blood street 31, 3rd floor. Suspects are considered armed and dangerous. Approach with caution. Nearest car, please respond.'

'Car 65 on the way'!; responded Malcolm on the police radio.

'Shit, Rico, I thought we would have a calm night. Now we got some f**king rapist on the loose.'

'Well, as my old man used to say, shit strikes at most unexpected times.' Rico looked at the watch. It was 02:30 in the morning.

'Isn't that the street and the skyscraper where the late Inspector Petrowsky, your partner, used to live?'

'Yeah, Rico, you're right. The poor guy lived there. We wouldn't have to take this call if he was still alive. He used to take care of these things even when he was retired, though he strongly believed in having a backup in his earlier days. But at the end, he went over the edge. Poor bastard blew his head off.'

'We will be there in five minutes tops, Malcolm,' concluded Rico when he pushed their new 300 BMW series car into 5th gear.

Everybody was already there when Al and Frazier arrived with the three broads. The apartment was full of booze, cocaine, ecstasy pills, and food. There were even some guns spread around to impress the girls. These whores were used to this anyhow. Ron and Mick were already half drunk, and Pappa Joe enjoyed a Cuban cigarette and a glass of brandy. Frazier couldn't take the hand of one of the brunettes. Lola was off the limits, at least for now. Al wanted her first. The party started with relatively loud music and booze. The girls were soon under alcohol and drugs and pleased the two brothers. Frazier immediately joined in the fun. Al was making out with Lola in the kitchen and later in the bathroom. She didn't like him at all but pretended. The dough that flashed in front of her smelled so lovely. Pappa Joe was snoring on the couch and was uninterested in the women. His artificial right leg was hurting quite a bit. The story was that a giant white shark chopped it off while he was a vessel captain in Indonesia. The other version was that he lost it in a poker game, namely that it was blown off with a shotgun when he refused to pay. The whole thing in Al's apartment looked like a scene from some Roman Caligula orgy. After a while, Frazier became so violent that he slapped one of the girls and made her do things she didn't want to do. Ron, the guy in the leather, joined in with Frazier, and after threatening her with a long knife, they had their brutal way with her. This was history repeating for Frazier, who had a baby face and angelic falcate voice. He was a rapist and was always going to be one. No jail would reform him. Although Ron thought he was hurting the girl, as evident from her muffled screams and pleas for help, he liked the whole thing and backed his partner in this sick game. Ron's brother, the ugly-looking Mick dressed in a Marlboro man outfit, was unhappy with the other brunette's performance. He took an empty bottle of B&W and slammed it on her head. Blood erupted immediately, and she fell unconscious. He then joined the other two in what was a brutal rape. Al came in with Lola after being satisfied and throwing her into the room.

'She's all your boys. Take care of her now.'

When she looked at what was happening, she started shouting.

'You f**king pigs, what are you doing? What the f**k have you done to her?'

She was referring to the unconscious brunette, Milo. The other girl, Donna, was in obvious pain. Frazier was making horrendous sounds raping her. He sounded like a pig being slaughtered.

'Leave her alone, you f**king rapists. You bastards are killing her.'

Ron looked at her. He was mean and dangerous now. He saw a beautiful blonde that needed to be taken before him. She tried to escape, but he was all over her and his brother Mick.

'Do something, Al, do something, you motherf**ker', screamed Lola.

'Sorry honey, it's their turn now. I can't do much for your darling. He had his favorite striped pants and a pink shirt. His appearance presented a picture of a sleazy, worn-out pimp. He went over to Milo, the unconscious brunette. With a bucket of ice, he woke her up. Ron and Mick went brutally to Lola, who resisted as much as she could. At one moment, Ron cut her face with his long knife and threatened to cut her breasts off if she didn't comply with their demands. They raped her in every possible way. Frazier was killing the other brunette, Milo. He had his hands on her throat and was violent as he could be. Pappa Joe woke up and joined the fun. He suddenly had an urge for a woman. He and Al took Milo to the bathroom and tied her to the bathtub. There they had their way with her, whipping and beating her. After a while, Ron came to them. He left Donna in the room to the mercy of his brother and Frazier. The other girl, Donna, was dead. After having their way with her, Lola became unattended for a moment. She saw that the brunette Donna was dead. That lunatic Frazier strangled her at the end. With tears in her eyes and panic and horrifying fear in her heart, she went for the door and entered the hallway on the third floor. She needed help. The closest door was the apartment of Frank Gleisch. She started banging on it.

Malcolm and Rico arrived in no time. They took their automatic 38 calibers 9mm guns from their holsters and ran up the stairs. As soon as they were on the 3rd floor, they heard loud music and something resembling muffled screams. They went to Frank Gleisch's door. Frank informed them of what he saw and what he thought they might expect inside. According to him, there should be 3-4 men together with Al and an unknown number of women, probably two. Frank gave them a little bit of background on Al.

'Maybe we should wait for backup Malcolm. These guys could be dangerous?'

'Nja, I think we can take them. We don't know if they have any guns except for that knife'. It's just a couple of assholes having fun with these women and getting rough.

He didn't think as Luke Petrowsky taught him to do. Instead, he did what Luke did when he went to the Loony side. Rico felt this was a mistake but didn't want to go against his partner. They approached the door casually, and Rico rang on it.

'Police, open up. There have been complaints about noise and violence. We want to talk to you.

Nothing happened, and Rico repeated the same thing, just banging this time. Suddenly the music stopped, and there was a half scream violently muffled. Malcolm and Rico suddenly became more cautious, but it was too late. Rico was overexposed at the front door. A thundering shotgun sound exploded in the middle of the night, ripping through the hallway air, the door, and Rico's belly. He never carried a life vest on these occasions. Malcolm was surprised when his partner fell in pain, holding himself to his bleeding stomach. He fell on the cold concrete glazed hallway floor. Malcolm started shooting towards the door, and there was some commotion and curses from inside. He called for backup.

'Officer down, I need help; I need backup and paramedics. This is Detective Pace. Rico is down. Send somebody now. These people are armed heavily. Fast!'

Three cars were dispatched immediately. The operator knew precisely where they were. The highest officer in charge that night was a seasoned veteran inspector named Jerry McLaughlin. He used to work with Luke Petrowsky before but despised him and his methods. He handled situations differently and was in a mess like this before.

Furthermore, he knew Al Durant. More importantly, he knew the two brothers he hung out with even better. They were under suspicion for three murders already. He also knew that one of them, Mick was a sociopath who most probably killed his mother when he was 11. His mom was a whore. There was no bullshitting with these guys. Possible rape was mentioned, and his instincts were right; if rape was in the air, John Frazier couldn't be far away. Jerry personally put this bastard behind bars. What the f**k was Malcolm doing getting in there without backup? He immediately sent a local SWAT (special weapons & tactics) team. Everything happened within half an hour. The events started unfolding like on a movie reel.

Ron brought her back to the apartment. No screams were coming from the bathroom except for some sobs. Milo was alive but hurting everywhere. Frazier was smoking a cigar on the couch. Pappa Joe was arguing with Mick about the death of the second prostitute

Donna. They were too drunk to realize that Frazier had strangled her. When Ron brought Lola inside, Al was angry as hell.

'You damn whore. You thought you didn't have enough with a real man, so you had to go and have more from fat pigs like Frank Gleisch. You will need ours, and only ours!' you have been naughty now, and you need to be taught a lesson.

He already had his pants down and was moving towards Lola. Ron was still holding his knife to her. Suddenly everybody joined in. They wanted to take care of Lola. Suddenly there was someone at the door, the police. She started screaming, and Ron hit her with all their might with the back end of his knife. He instantly broke her jaw. Mick picked a shotgun from the floor and pointed it towards the door. Now the banging and police voices came again.

'Eat this motherf**ker pig! With that, Mick pumped the cage of the shotgun and shot Rico Horta through the door.

'What the f**k are you doing?' shouted Al. It was too late. Smoke came from Mick's gun, and Rico's insides were spilled on the floor outside the door.

Malcolm kneeled and came to Rico. He was losing blood fast. How stupid could he be? He should have waited for backup. He should have called for backup first. Rico was in pain but still conscious.

'I'm so sorry, Bro. I didn't want this to happen, said Malcolm.

'It's OK, Malcolm. Just get these bastards and get that girl alive from the apartment. I will live.' He knew the chances of that were getting smaller by the minute. He took the whole shot into his guts, and it ripped through him. Now the neighbors were waking up and showing their faces through the door. When they saw Malcolm and

Rico in a pool of blood, they disappeared as a house mouse when discovered in the middle of the night. The SWAT team was on the way with their man in charge, Joe Ramirez, and Inspector Jim McLaughlin. The SWOT team was ready to bust ass. They charged the stairs with their masks and lights like a party in search of dangerous alien species – to kill & destroy – was written all over these guys. Two sharpshooters were immediately posted in an apartment facing AL Durant's in the other skyscraper. They didn't have a clear view of the situation. Al and his pals were so drunk and unaware of the whole mess that they didn't realize what had happened in less than one hour. The lights were still on, but the light curtains were drawn. The sharpshooters reported back to the SWOT team that approximately four persons were on the move in the apartment. They couldn't see more. They also couldn't see Pappa Joe sitting in an armchair, scared as shit, and his artificial wooden leg hurting like hell.

'You stupid f**k! Why the hell did you shoot? Screamed Al at Mick violently. Mick wasn't paying much attention.

'You shut up, asshole. If it were not for your carelessness, this bitch Lola wouldn't have alerted the police, and we wouldn't be in a mess like this, yelled Ron at Al.

'What f**king mess, you asshole?

Ron was pointing at the pool of blood coming underneath the door. 'What do you think that is, idiot, cranberry juice flowing underneath the door? Mick shot that pig. And besides, we have a dead whore on the floor there. One of us got her'.

'She wasn't good enough. She didn't want to stop screaming', said Frazier.

He was filling his M3 submachine 45-caliber gun. There was nothing they mainly wanted to discuss with him at this point. Ron's brother Mick still held the shotgun, looking wildly at the door. Rico's blood was coming more and more underneath the door math now.

'It's a whole different ball game now, Al. You play, or you pray. What is it going to be, said Ron.

Al was just now realizing the mess they had created. This was not supposed to be like this. He needed to escape this fast and eliminate his 'pals.' His only close friend here was Pappa Joe. They needed to get these other three out of the equation somehow. Selfish as always and never thinking of consequences, he started thinking fast now. Ron looked wildly at Lola and turned to Mick.

'All right now! We need to get rid of this bitch. She is a witness. We can't have her talking, can we?

'What the f**k are you talking about? Then we need to kill the one in the bathroom too. That would be three homicides, you idiot', pointed Al.

'This one was an accident. Mick's shooting was self-defense, said Ron.

'Ron, you are a f**king moron. What self-defense? He shot the guy in cold blood. His only sin was ringing the bell and saying he was a policeman. You are a f**king idiot, Mick, don't you know that? Frazier was looking now at Mick and Ron.

'Actually, both of you are complete idiots.'

'Take that back, you mother f**king rapist. You strangled that whore, and we can pin this on you too. That could be a wonderful idea; what do you think, Al?'

That was the last mistake Ron made and the last remark he made that evening as Frazier just pointed his M3 at him and, not thinking at all, started shooting. The leather brother was directly hit in the face and the breast by submachine fire. Lola, who was beside him, took a bullet or two also. Lola was just hit superficially. They both fell, Ron dead as the meat was transferred daily in the freezer to the nearby market.

Mick turned on a spring and fired two shotgun cartridges at Frazier. One blew his left cheek clean off, and the other ripped his left shoulder. Still half-conscious, on the fast track to the nearby waiting room for the gateways of hell, he pressed on his submachine gun once more, spraying the remainder of the bullets everywhere. They were darting all over the place. One hit Al in the butt and one Pappa Joe in the artificial leg. None hit Mick. Mick leaned over his dead brother's body and was cursing and screaming. Lola was on the side, just lying down, seeing that was the best thing to do. Besides, she was hurting like hell. Pappa Joe was frozen with panic in the armchair. He still had his gun in his left hand. Frazier was still alive, but blood was gushing out of him like Fountain Di Trevi in Rome. Al was screaming like a baby. The other whore was still tied in the bathroom but alive. What started as a sick orgy party quickly ended in a horrible pool of blood. The whole skyscraper was waking up now. Mick started filling up his gun again. When he was finished, he went to the balcony.

The shooting started in the apartment. Jim McLaughlin and Joe Ramirez checked with the SWAT sharpshooters once more and told them if they had a clean shot at any of the bad guys, they should take it. Shot to kill, if necessary, were Joe's words. Jim gave the green light to Joe Ramirez to take his men inside. He liked the tactics of combining sharpshooters and SWOT cavalry simultaneously. Something not found in the books but proved to work for him every time he utilized it. He trusted his shooters like nobody else. He knew Joe Ramirez trained these guys like super commandos. There was no time for any negotiations here. He would have done it otherwise. Everything was happening too fast, and the shooting started almost immediately when the SWOT guys were in position. Malcolm wanted to enter, but Jim forced him to take a vest. The SWOT guys crashed the door right after Mick entered the balcony and the almost unlighted apartment. They could move quickly with their masks and lights. They didn't throw any gas bombs as they entered. The break-in was so suddenly done and performed so swiftly that Al and the others, still standing, were shocked. Joe was screaming: 'Hands in the air assholes, down on your knees, this is the Police SWAT, you are all under arrest!'

He put his hands up in the air immediately and kneeled. His right butt cheek was in the blood and hurrying like hell, but he was alive. He already had a story that would pin down everything on Ron, Mick, and Frazier. He didn't do any shooting at all. Neither did Pappa Joe. As for Pappa Joe, he put his hand in the air, but in one of them, he had a gun. One of the SWAT guys saw this and started shooting with his Heckler & Koch automatic gun. He blew away Pappa Joe's artificial wooden leg into splinters and cut three of his left-hand fingers where he had the gun. He fell screaming into the chair in pain. They checked Ron's dead body and Lola's. They got her out of the apartment and Al and Pappa Joe. They also found the dead whore, Donna, on the floor strangled. Milo was screaming from the bathroom now. Frazier was sitting on the sofa like some abomination from hell. Half of his face was missing, and a massive hole in his left arm. They thought he was dead. Not quite! He raised his M3 submachine gun once and for the last time and shot at two SWOT guys before him. Even though they had a vest, they fell, one wounded in the head. What followed was a barrage of fire from the others. Frazier, the rapist, soon became a target range. Malcolm put the last bullet in his forehead. After that, he ran to the bathroom, checked on the whore, and got word from the sharpshooters that a guy was on the balcony. The sharpshooters had a clear shot on Mick. They got the order to wound him if possible. Mick wanted to climb down the balcony to the second floor and, if necessary, jump into the back alley street some 7-8 meters. He didn't get too far. They shot him in the leg, and the arm, but none of the bullets were lethal. He slumbered down in pain on the balcony tiles. He was filling his shotgun in panic. At that moment, Malcolm appeared at the balcony door. Mick turned wildly and pointed the gun at Malcolm. Detective Pace was much faster.

'This one is for Rico, you bastard!' That said, his 38 calibers 9mm gun made three holes in Mick's skull. He finally took the fast train to hell. The whole mess was not over before 4:50 in the morning. The street was filled with police cars; paramedics, the coroner, and forensics were on the way; the SWAT guys were resting beside their truck while Al Durant and Pappa Joe were handcuffed downtown. Many skyscraper tenants were lined there as spectators to watch this incredible scene from an action movie being outplayed in front of their eyes. It was a night to remember. The ambulance took Lola and Milo. They both lived. So did the two wounded SWAT officers. Rico Horta didn't die. He barely survived and was temporarily paralyzed from the waist down. The shotgun bullet splintered parts of his spine. After six months of rehabilitation, he joined back the force. The coroner took care of 4 bodies: Ron's, Mick's, Frazier's, and the dead whore's Donna.

Malcolm could never forgive himself. He resigned from the force and started a community service to prevent crime in neighborhoods at the youth level. Rico forgave him. They stayed best friends, after all. Lola started working in the center with Malcolm after she recovered. The other whore, Milo, went foolishly back on the streets again. She died of an overdose two years after. Al Durant and Pappa Joe got eight years of prison. It was a relatively light sentence considering the whole thing, robbery, rape, shooting, killings, etc. Mitigating circumstances for both were that they didn't shoot anyone or carry any guns at the robbery. Rape was the worst charge of all. They also pleaded guilty, giving them a compromise deal with the DA's office. They gave testimonies of different murders and rapes on the three dead stiffs. Al Durant was 55 years old when he went for his most extended prison term. Pappa Joe was 65. They were out after four years for good behavior. During that time, Al's woman took care of the apartment for him, waiting for her man to return. And surprisingly enough, he did it together with Pappa Joe. Was he reformed? We were soon to find out...

17

Don't F**k with the Circus Clowns

We were out there in full force: Keke and Ture Tollberg, Danny Slowitz, my best friend Anthoine Scott, Boris Duchovny, Harry Rowells, Mike Gleisch, Norman Michaels, Pepé, Alan Meehan, myself, and a bunch of our friends from the other skyscrapers, as well as some guys from the adjacent low red brick apartment buildings. It was the big Saturday soccer game played out in the big parking lot some 200m from our Skyscraper, a group of friends playing the critical game, defending the colors of their skyscraper and turf. It was 11 against 11. The parking lot was under construction, so we were playing at the 'green' patch of land, dividing it from our skyscraper and its parking lot. This patch was maybe 1/3 of the size of the actual soccer field, so you can imagine how many bodies intermingled in this small space. Due to heavy rains the week before, the green patch looked like everything other than green that day. It looked more like American football at times than soccer. The whole field turned into a muddy, clay arena where the biggest winner at the end of the day would be our mom's detergent and washing machines.

We played on small goals, which made scoring even more difficult, but we loved the game, and to miss the Saturday match would be blasphemy. Our opponents were a combo of guys collected from surrounding skyscrapers and buildings. The score was even coming to the last minutes of the first half. Boris's dad, Lech Duchovny, was the official umpire, but later on, his other, older son Maurice, took over. We collected the last energy atoms for the conclusion of the first half when the circus announcement car arrived.

Philip Astley, an English trick rider, wanted to try something else that morning. It was a wonderful sunny day outside of London. The year was 1768. He was working on this for weeks, and the time was right for the final test in front of his friends and some well-known and respected folks in the community. He made a provisional ring with a covered roof and a small seating part. There were about 25 people invited. A lot was lying on the shoulders of his best rider, Charles Hughes, who was supposed to put Astley's ideas into practice. They had done many things together already, but this day mattered. Philip knew if this worked, he could implement his most significant idea into a lucrative and never seen practice.

Astley's arena was beginning to take shape in his imagination. Yes, it was going to be a success! If not, well…the horseman with a British dragoon regiment would not falter that quickly. What followed was one of the most brilliant displays of theory & practice. Charles showed in practice that Philip's discovery was authentic as it gets. Because of centrifugal force, standing on his horse's back was reasonably straightforward while it galloped in circles around a ring. The visitors were amazed, as well as Charles, who didn't know if he would pull this one off. He did! On the other hand, Philip always had a bee in his bonnet and believed this the impossible, demanding that acts of magic be performed to make it possible. Indeed, Astley thought, great times were ahead!

The circus (in our modern sense of the word) was founded on that sunny day. Three years later, his dream of Astley's arena was complete. He exploited his discovery, building seating stands and a roof for his performance ring to attract London audiences. He performed stunts, the famous being with one foot on the saddle and one on the horse's head while brandishing a sword. In time, he expanded this idea, gradually including other equestrians, acrobats, rope dancers, aerialists, clowns, and the first recorded circus freak show.

On the other hand, Charles established his ring nearby in 1782 and called it the Royal Circus, giving us, for the first time, the modern use of the name. Philip's idea came to life, and he didn't confine himself only to England but also to Europe. He traveled widely in Europe, spreading the circus idea and building many himself. Astley influenced local artisans in the process. 13 was his lucky number. It became almost a hallmark for the ring's dimensions, and Astley built 13 permanent circuses in his life. His whole family got involved in it. The whole idea exploded worldwide, in States and Russia, making circuses the biggest attraction of the times. Throughout the years, the circuses went through crises, showing signs of the times and changes in entertainment preferences. Regardless, the idea is still alive, and the medieval way of entertainment still works for many people worldwide.

International pan-European Circus 'Avalon' was in the city that month. It was one of the most famous attractions in town for a long time and one of the most acclaimed shows in Europe. It already had tens of thousands of visitors, and more were still waiting to get tickets. Kids wanted this, and parents were there to fulfill their wishes. Consult the books, dictionaries, and encyclopedias. You will find, more or less, the exact definition of a circus: an entertainment or spectacle usually consisting of animal acts and human efforts of daring, presented in most cases in a circular performance area called the ring, and frequently including other attractions. Clown performances, animal stunts, flying trapeze, magician craftsmanship, pantomime acts, other acrobatics, etc., were all parts of the show. Side things like parades, sword-eating stuff, fire throwers, bearded ladies, fakirs, things of the occult & macabre, giants and dwarfs, and extraordinary acrobatics were also parts of the shows. And let us not forget the music and the performers.

Circus Avalon had it all. Not much has changed from the days of Philip Astley. The same magic of the circus and the entertainment it involved remained. The most significant difference was in size and mobility. It had an excellent combination and variety of performers, artists, animals, acts, and sideshows. Circus Avalon had the advantage of swallowing up, during the years, a large number of smaller troupes to make it what it was. They traveled by big lorries and trucks and visited larger centers for more extended stays. Unfortunately, due to unprofitability, the smaller communities suffered. So if you want to see the show, you must travel too. If the circus didn't find such facilities like you have in New York (Madison Square Garden) or the Moscow Circus building, they reverted to the old fashion of raising large tents and small adjacent ones in the cities they visited.

Jack Astley, grand-grand-etc. The Son of the famous Philip Astely had a hangover. Lying in his trailer, he could only see black spheres and kaleidoscope images changing in front of him at the speed of light. He was always confident that the booze could never get to him. 10 shots of Vodka was not much for Jack. He was a survivor, a fighter, a real man. He could barely remember the whore from last night. She was blonde or something. She did smell good, though, and certainly knew what she was doing. But…somehow, he lost part of the night in a black hole. It must be the combo of pot and booze. Well, the only thing left was his grandpa, a famous tightrope walker, anti-booze drink. He couldn't comprehend how Grandpa Victor could do both: Drink as an elephant and master the rope better than the famous Charles Blondin, who walked the tightrope over Niagara Falls. F**k him, thought Jack; the Astleys were the best. Grandpa's drink was the elixir he needed.

Jack was a master. He modeled his acts by the best in the business and studied clown history in detail. His role models were the legendary Fratellini Brothers. He devised a three partite combination of Fretellini genius: of brother François who retained the traditional role as the elegant, pompous, white-faced clown, of brother Albert, as a miserable, ragged one with grotesque makeup with high black brows, an exaggerated mouth, and a bulbous red nose and of brother Paul that joined the act in a new role, the notary, with little makeup and a comic style midway between those of his brothers. He had all three of them combined and varied during the show. Jack was one of the clowns and a rather good one, for that matter. He was one of Europe's finest.

Being the last of the Circus Astleys, he carried the tradition which would undoubtedly die with him as he had no wish for stable family life, including having kids. He swore he would never let his kid into this business, even if that happened. There were better ways of earning dough, and more of it than this. This life suited him pretty well. He was good at his job, still attractive at 42, well built, with sort of Russell Crowe and Brandon Frasier physique, and looked combined with a thick dark mustache which gave him an additional look as a clown. Due to this type of life and other things, he never had a stable girl. He did have a go with all the trapeze women, which did not work out well. He reverted to local whores, and that suited him perfectly. His motto was diversity and change. He certainly had plenty of that. But this morning, he was in a rather foul mood due to the shitty hangover, and the appearance of the circus director, a confident Alan B. Moseley, didn't make it even better. Jack hated the bastard. He had nothing to do with the circus business, no tradition, NADA! I just wanted to earn money – f**king leach! But he was the dough provider, so it's better to keep quiet.

'You have been drinking again, haven't you, Jacky boy?'

The sheer mention of 'Jacky Boy' made Jack's blood boil to the point that he could strangle this bastard.

'Just a couple, nothing I can't handle, boss!'

'I hope it was only a couple for your sake and tonight's show.' Fortunately, he didn't know about the whores, thought Jack. Or maybe he did but just pretended. He knew Jack came from a long tradition of circus people. Hell thought Jack, we practically invented the circus! He could never lay him off, no f**king way.

'I need you and Jose, one of the side act weight lifters, to take the announcement car through the new part of the city. Roberto is down with the flu, and I can't find Mike. The other car is in the old city.' Jack was about to protest, but when Alan B. Mosley's eye gleamed, he knew the boss would love disobedience. He would not give it to him, at least not this Saturday morning.

'Sure, I will find Jose, and we will do it.' Alan couldn't believe what he had heard. Good! Obedience. This asshole will soon show respect if he wants to retain this job.

'Good! That's settled, then! Good luck with tonight's show. And keep off the booze, Jack – your grand-grand fathers would be more proud of you that way.

Jack still had his Grandpa's shotgun. Maybe if he loads it in time, he could split this bastard in two…hmm…maybe not today, maybe tomorrow, or some other day. He hurriedly left with that cynical remark, not giving a millisecond of response to Jack.

He found Jose lifting weights and training for the afternoon sideshows. They found the orange Volkswagen beetle in the circus park. It was a vast circus with a large drive park too. They had two of these refurbished cars. One was already out in the field. A substantial double-coned, silly-looking loudspeaker was on the top of the hood, making him look like a mutated Dumbo. They had to ride in this silly vehicle for an hour or two and play the pre-recorded circus invitation and promo tape. What the heck? Maybe the headache will go away. Jose was not much of a talker. With the looks of a used-up wrestler, with no single teeth left in his jaw and a face that would match any police precinct wanted list, maybe the silence was good. He was a lovely guy but did not have much of a brain to complement that. He wore a jeans mechanic uniform, still sweaty from the weight lifting sessions. Jack had his casual wear on. They were approaching the curb, which led into our skyscraper complex.

'Give me the ball!' screamed Keke to Alan. He had a clear shot on the goal. Alan masterfully passed the ball between two players, and

Keke took it. Instantly he made a shot at the goal and scored. The goalie didn't stand a chance. The score was 3:2 in our favor. We all gathered in joy around Keke. At that moment, we heard the noise: "Circus Avalon is in town, the biggest attraction in Europe. Come and see why! We have it all, trapeze, wild animals, and blah, blah, blah…We recognized the circus announcement car, and all turned around to see it. It was the Beetle with two funny loudspeakers on top of it. It was driving now alongside our field.

'Let's turn up the volume, Jack; some kids are there.' These were the only words Jose spoke during the last hour's drive.

'Yeah, you are right. They are playing soccer. Cool!'

Jack pumped the volume to the max. These shitty loudspeakers were a disaster. He told their pompous boss that new equipment was needed. A single loudspeaker (in this case, x2) could not fully reproduce the entire frequency range of recorded sound. He told him they needed some state-the-art stuff with woofers and tweeters and possibly with "subwoofers" and "super tweeters." Jack like the Hi-Fi stuff a lot, which could make a difference. The boss explained that they had audiences even with this equipment and that unnecessary spending was not required. Bullshit, thought Jack! This loudspeaker was making so much additional noise that it was sometimes horrendous. Just imagine how it sounded outside.

'What the f**k is that? What noise, man, this is bad!'

Keke and Ture were laughing their asses off while most of us were watching in the maze., Norman Michaels, the most muscular guy in the skyscraper, was watching this with a grim face. Anthoine, Mike, and Alan covered our ears while Pepé made strange faces. Danny Slowitz was looking at the car, Volkswagen vehicles being his obsession, while Harry Rowells and Boris Duchovny had something else in mind. It was evident in their body language. Their actions and brain connectors started working towards the same goal independently. As soon as the circus vehicle passed our field and was some 50 m in front, Harry and Boris bent down, as in an automated fashion, and started forming balls of greenish-gray mud, which was formed from heavy rains and clay. It formed very quickly into dangerous ammunition. When used by pros, this thing could be very lethal. Harry and Boris were good. Boris was the handball goalie star, while Harry's biggest dream was to join a sniper school someday. Only Alan Meehan was more precise than these guys, especially in wintertime, but he was not participating.

'Let's get the mother f**ker circus clowns,' yelled Boris.

'I'm with you Bo-Bo,' screamed Harry. A few years younger than Boris, Harry always looked up to him. They never invited any of us to join, nor would we, I think. They were in their world. None of us did anything nor said anything to stop them or to support them. All of it was happening too fast anyway. Even Norman, the oldest one in the whole bunch (the difference in age here varied from 3 years to a couple of days, and we were then in our late teens), didn't blink an eye. The mud was well formed now into medium-sized bullets. This only took a couple of seconds. The car was going at a slow pace anyway. It was about 80m from us when Boris and Harry ran some 5m ahead and discharged their bullets with crystalline precision, military accuracy, and complementing all laws of physics.

The mud bullets were on the dot, spot, and money. Two hand-propelled mud rocks hit the back loudspeaker going directly inside the cone and destroying it. Abruptly the sound started to waiver and flutter, and finally, it broke down. If this was not enough, they propelled two more mud pieces that followed the first ones, as did the German torpedoes, following each other closely in the battles in the Atlantic in the Second World War. This made the damage worse and broke the back windshield in the corner. The tape stopped, and the noise was horrendous. Jose and Jack didn't quite get the whole picture until the explosion of the rear back windshield. They stopped the car and got out. Seeing the damage and the two perpetrators holding mud bullets in their hands and having a ready battle stance, they got pissed. We all froze. You didn't need to be a Nobel Prize winner to guess what would happen. Jose opened the front hatch and took out a medium-sized sledgehammer while Jack took a crowbar from the rear seat. They both started running towards us. Harry and Boris's balls froze in that instant.

A system of survival, a streak of guilt, and terrible fear took over. When you have two big, mean guys after you with weapons that can kill an elephant, the only thing to do is – RUN! And they just did that, ran towards the skyscraper. Jose and Rick were halfway through the green patch. None of them did anything, primarily run, which would be a terminal mistake at that point. It would mean we did something wrong and are in some union with the culprits. Everything was happening so fast that any decision was impossible to take at that point. The best thing was not to move. We were all paralyzed except for four persons running after one another. Harry and Boris reached the skyscraper-like two sprinters, ran up the stairs, and continued running. Jose and Jack followed closely. Jose took guard and watch off the lobby and elevator entrances while Jack took one of the lifts to the 10th floor. That way, he would descend the stairs and try to catch them. He was gambling. Boris lived on the 7th floor, and Harry on the 14th floor. It was a good gamble, especially considering Harry's and Boris's state of mind. They were running like madmen.

'Wait, Boris, wait, man. I can't run so fast!'

'F**k that man; I need to reach the 7th floor. I can't wait for you. Screw that.'

'No, no, please. Wait! We can take an elevator somewhere. I can't run to the 14th floor'. There was some logic in what Harry said. They were on the 3rd floor, and Boris was running out of steam, and he knew Harry couldn't make it to the 14th floor at this pace. He would probably get caught, which didn't make much difference to Boris, especially if Harry kept his mouth shut! They came to the 5th floor and went for the small elevator.

Meanwhile, Jack was descending at a fast pace from the 10th floor. He was already on the 8th floor. Where were these buggers? He was so mad he could tear their heads off. Unbelievable what today's generation is doing! No respect for the fine arts of the circus anymore.

Jose was impatient. He boarded the small elevator and decided to ride to the 5th floor and wait for Jack. Little did he know that his prey was coming to him. The guys were such haste and panicked to board the elevator that they didn't see the enormous bulk occupying the cabin shaft. When they finally did, it was way too late. When Harry saw Jose come out with the sledgehammer, he fell half unconscious to the ground. Boris tried to run for it, but at the helm of the staircase, he was caught by Jack and got a sharp blow with the crowbar on his thigh. He went down in pain.

'You little dirty bastards, you thought you would get away with this, did you know? No, nobody gets away from us, do they, Jose?'

Jose brought Harry now and was grinning, showing his toothless jaw. Harry returned to his senses, and both, though petrified of what could happen next, tried to keep a stiff upper lip.

'What are we going to do with you now? Shall we bash your heads into the concrete, put you in the elevator, and destroy you with the sledgehammer? Amazingly Jack's headache was gone, and he was thinking very clearly now.

'The lions didn't have anything to eat this morning, Jack!

'What a wonderful idea, Jose! Let's feed them to the lions; they can feel what it is like in a coliseum.'

'You can't do that. It's against the law', said Boris.

'Besides, I haven't done anything; he did it all.' He pointed the finger towards Harry, who was still in shock and even more significant now, seeing how his friend played the whole blame on him.

'He did, did he now? If so, he will go first, and as I hate rats that squeal on their buddies, you will follow him. How about that? Nobody will know what happened. You will disappear, and there won't be any trace of you except some bones in the cages. But those we have all the time, don't we, Jose?' Jose was enjoying this a lot. Boris realized he had made a huge mistake and tried to run for it again. Jose caught him by his steel fist.

'You run again, and I will snap your throat like a chicken. Understand, little man?' Boris remained still during the whole descent. We were all assembled in front of the building when they finally got out holding them, waiting to see what happened. Boris was limping, obviously scared, and Harry looked like he survived the whole Scream trilogy.

'Get the f**k out of our way,' yelled Jack, waiving his crowbar.'

According to medieval circus laws, these dirty rats will get what they deserve.' They were none, but intimidation was a nice thing to use anyway.

'What's that? Alan yelled.

'We will feed them to the lions, of course. Jack had a severe dead face, and there was no reason not to believe him.

'You can't do that,' Boris yelled again.

'According to international circus law, we can. If any of you try something or contact the authorities, we are coming after you, one by one. So end of discussion now!'

None of us did anything nor moved an inch. These two guys looked so mean that any discussion would be fruitless within seconds.

They took them to the car, threw them in the back seat under the watchful eye of Jose, the 'sledgehammer man,' and drove toward Circus Avalon.

By that point, our opposing team had dissolved and disappeared. We just watched, amazed. Could this be happening? We were left there to think about what to do next.

They reached the circus after a 15min ride and horror stories from Jack and Jose. Jack was amazed how Jose became talkative and could wave incredible stories of what they did to people that didn't behave in various cities. By this time, the guys were utterly numb, waiting for the executioner in the black hood. Harry and Boris started crying and screaming. To make things worse, they took them to the lion's cage, opened the door, and showed them inside. There weren't any lions in there, but the small opening brought the beasts.

'It's their feeding time now. They will be with you in a couple of minutes. This will teach you not to do this again…which doesn't matter as you will be ground meat soon'.

With that, Jack and Jose left laughing. The guys were so scared that no sounds came from their vocal cords when they started scream-ing. Suddenly they heard a sound behind them. The door opened. Boris apologized to Harry, and they both waited for the final mo-ment. What came out was not a lion but a giant pig with a clown's hat and nose. The pig came close to their shock and farted violently in front of them.

After 10 minutes, Jack and Jose returned with the boss, Alan B. Moseley. They looked tired but relieved with the giant pig. The guys have pissed in their pants by now.

'Well, we have decided to spare your lives, and you will do some good deeds instead. Until the end of the week, I want you to dis-tribute around 1000 leaflets to kids to attend the shows, and you are also cleaning the animal leftovers until the end of the week. Considering what you have done, we decided that feeding you to the animals would be a too easy punishment. So you need to do this if you don't want us to press charges and put huge fines on your parents'.

'I hope you will have more respect for circus and clowns from now on,' added Jack. Jose patted them on the shoulder and told them they could call their parents and tell them they have a one-week summer community service job now. They obeyed. We also got the news before we decided to do anything. We laughed our asses off. Heck, this was a circus worth seeing. Jack got his wish for new loudspeakers and did a great show that night. Philip Astley would be surprised at the evolution of the circus profession; on the other hand, he wouldn't.

18

The Meaning of Life

If you got the hang of it, tying a good sailor's knot wasn't challenging. He wasn't planning on a sailboat career, especially after today, but the manual was good enough for this purpose. The guy in the nautical shop told him this would suffice for making all the basic knots when tying a sailboat. Little did he know! He didn't reveal his real purpose for the need for the manual, though it wouldn't make much difference by the looks of that salesman. The guy seemed like someone who didn't care about anything or anybody. He hated that type of person. How can you go through life living indifferently? He couldn't comprehend that. The rope was rather expensive, but it didn't matter much. The credit card invoices, the bills, credits, and everything else would be history in a matter of moments. Even his new Pierre Cardin suit he bought for the occasion was worth it. Well, he was not going to lose time on useless thoughts now. Captain Jack would always say, 'Let's be practical, yes practical!'

He looked above him. The hook on the ceiling could take around 100kg, which would be just enough. He has calculated this many times. He gained some weight in the last month, probably out of stress. Some people lose weight, and some gain. He fitted into the second category. Being over 89kg wasn't pleasant, but nothing mattered. Captain Joe was gone. His soul was in another world, dimension, sphere, or God knows where else. The days after Joe's departure from this world were the hardest in his life. It was incredible that he survived the event. There wasn't much left. It was time to join Joe wherever he was and continue the dialogue. He climbed on the leather office chair and adjusted the colossal rope. It looked like the one they used in hangings throughout history, from medieval times to Sergio Leone's Spaghetti Western movies. The rope fitted his head like a hand in a glove. He thought momentarily about the cake with rat poison that he had left for his wife and daughter in the fridge. There was so much poison there to kill a herd of rhinoceros, although he thought his family was even worse. He took his glasses off, looked at Captain Joe's picture on the wall for the last time, murmured a silent prayer, and kicked the chair underneath him. The common shakes and twitches followed this act of hanging. Some gurgling sounds came from his throat, and a couple of violent moves. After a while, everything was quiet again. It was Sunday morning, so nobody could hear him in his office room, even if he screamed from the depths of his body. The faculty was deserted on weekends. Therefore, he chose the office instead of his apartment on the 10th floor of our skyscraper. It wouldn't be until Monday evening, when the cleaning staff arrived, that he would be found. By then, everything would be over. After a couple of minutes, the shaking stopped. Mathematics Professor Daren Voinea hanged himself and was on his way to join Captain Jack.

There was no point in prolonging life. She didn't want him, and there was no way he would change her mind. She wouldn't even let him come near her. He tried everything, courtship, gifts, poetry, love letters, etc...nothing worked, and in the end, she even asked for a restraining order.

Why was she doing this, calling him a lunatic and a psychiatric case? Why, of why? And who was that ugly, hairy man by her side that was ten years younger than she was? There was nothing to do at this point except suicide. If he couldn't have her, was there no point in continuing this miserable life? This was going to be his 5th attempt. The other suicide attempts had particular reasons, and it seemed it could never work. He tried with the exhaust fumes in the garage, but the car broke down, and he woke up after 12 hours. He tried pills that were not sleeping ones but those that helped you against constipation. He took 20 of them. The result was everything else except a suicide, and it was messy. The third time he tried with his father's old gun. The damn thing exploded and injured his hand. And the last time, he wanted to jump from the roof of the faculty but just couldn't. This time it was going to be different. It was going to work, now or never. It was after work, around 18:00 hours, and he stood on the 5th floor overlooking the enormous atrium. There was not much there: marble paving and grass with two cherry trees. It would be perfect. He would fall on the marble, break his neck, and probably squash his brains everywhere. He needed to do this, or he would end up institutionalized somewhere. He wrote her a letter. Maybe she will understand, and maybe she will be his somewhere in the heavens. He also considered taking her along, but she was so young, beautiful, and full of life. Besides, there was no way he could get close to her now. His death will be enough punishment for her and her nightmare for years. He was sure of that. He wore a light khaki jacket with a short-sleeved white shirt and light brown colonial pants with antelope loafers. He loved wearing this outfit during summer; it was perfect for this occasion. Professor Voinea's assistant Mark Dimitrov climbed the railing and stood there as the world championship swimmer ready for another race, another record time. He looked at the marble pavement and the clear blue sky above. It was a wonderful Monday evening. 'Unfortunately, his right foot slipped and fell immediately without preparation. This took away his wish to go farther and over the cherry trees. Instead, he fell violently in a humorous way and fell directly on one of the trees. The result was two broken legs, an arm, three ribs, and a severe concussion. It was not Mark Dimitrov's turn to die today.

He recovered after some time. The only two persons that visited him in the hospital were Prof. Voinea and Dr. Ali Alzhemi, his closest older colleagues. He liked Prof. Voinea and was sad to hear of his death while in the hospital. Mark Dimitrov didn't have much of a family. He used to sing to himself often: 'Didn't know my Dad, Mom was all I had....' Their Mom died when he was 18. Lung cancer ate her up. No wonder she used to smoke 70 cigarettes daily and spend her life waiting for her husband, who ran away before Mark Dimitrov was born. After two weeks, Mark was checked out of the hospital and went home to recover fully before they committed him. He had just one wish on the day they came to pick him up and put him in a straight jacket to go to the faculty again. They climbed the 5th floor, and he came to the same place on the railing where he attempted the unsuccessful suicide. The two orderlies grabbed him.

'What do you think you are doing, man?'

'Don't worry, guys. I just wanted to see what I did wrong.'

'What do you mean' asked one of them, bewildered.

'Where I missed when I wanted to kill myself. Yeah, the f**king cherry tree, f**king tree stopped me. I always hated the damn simple cherries. Full of worms, not like wild cherries, f**king cherry tree!

The orderlies looked at each other, thinking how long this guy would survive in the nut house.

Dr. Ali Alzhemi also worked in the same department as Professor Voinea and Mark Dimitrov. He was renting a second-hand apartment on the 18th floor of our skyscraper. Dr. Alzhemi was a 100% certified schizophrenic with a tendency toward painful death. He attempted suicide only once and failed. Some months before that, he proclaimed to everyone that the famous scientist Sir Isaac Newton was an idiot and everything he did was, more or less, false. His primary concern was Newton's work on and his creation of a fundamental mathematical tool-calculus and his work in physics, namely his three laws of motion and his principle of universal gravitation. In discussions with Prof. Haas, my dad, from the Physics dept. And Prof. Miller from the same dept. Of mathematics, he realized after long discussions and full rebuttal of all his lunatic thesis by these two, especially his five new laws of motion, that he was an idiot. For a lunatic to realize this was not an easy thing.

Dr. Ali was intelligent enough to see that the argumentation between two colleagues was flawless, and there was nothing else to do about it. He didn't want a second opinion because he probably wouldn't find two other people who would take the time to listen to his crazy ideas. This was the final drop for Ali. He went early one Saturday evening to the nearby railway crossing where the trains take their final fast lap before entering the station. He was waiting for the intercity train 341 to approach underneath him. It was some minutes late. He was already passing through the gate and entering the restricted zone when it came behind the curb. Just as the train neared him, he threw himself from the 2m high ledge above in front of the locomotive. Although he was a mathematician, the fall was not calculated correctly. He fell down and unexpectedly rolled on the side of the tracks to leave his left hand on the rails. The driver saw him but couldn't stop the train in time. It roared passed him, cutting his arm clean off. He was unconscious immediately from the terrible pain. He survived thanks to the swift intervention of the train staff and the paramedics. The next thing he knew, he was in the hospital recovering. It was not heaven or hell but a plain hospital room, to his dismay. The irony was that he got a visit from Prof. Voinea, who was preparing for suicide. Ali was pretty calm, under the influence of painkillers and sedatives. Surprisingly he was relatively straightforward.

'How are you feeling, Ali? I heard about the terrible accident.

'I'm OK, Professor, as you can be in this situation. I was hoping for a better end, not an armless epilogue. Death was taken away from me. But it seems that you are not feeling well. I can see it on your face.'

'Yes, you are right. I'm not feeling well.'

'I heard about your mother passing away, Professor. I am so sorry. You must have been close to her.' Voinea looked at him blankly.

'Not really, I have taken it well. I didn't feel a thing. Her death created many problems for me, including the costs involved, burial, reading of the will, etc. We were close, but I have taken it well.

'Oh, I'm sorry anyway,' replied Ali shyly.

'It's OK. But when Captain Jack died last week, I understood for the first time that there was no point in living and that meaning of life had a considerably different perspective now.'

'Captain Jack, who was he, your brother?'

'No, no, he was my parrot. Without him, there is no life; every day passes like an empty album of photographs. He was the only one who understood me; we could communicate better than anybody else. He was my Prozac, my relaxhab. In other words, he was my everything. Plainly said, my family is useless and evil. But all that will end soon, and I will visit my dear Captain soon.'

At that moment, Ali knew that there were cases that required shrinks first aid help sooner than him. Professor Voinea was undoubtedly one of them.

Among all the 'psittaciform' birds (parrots, lories, and cockatoos), Africa's gray parrot (Psittacus erithacus) is unsurpassed as a talker. Captain Jack was a gray parrot and also a male. The male may perfectly echo human speech. Captain Jack was very alert for a captive bird and, for a parrot, relatively good-tempered. Prof. Voinea bought him on one of his rare trips abroad to Africa. The guy who sold him told him this bird was talkative and clairvoyant. The bird had to wait in quarantine for some time to get the green light so he could be imported into the country. He was 35 years old and about 33 cm (13 inches) long when Voinea got him. Now he was reaching 65. His complexion was light gray except for its squared, red tail and bare, whitish face.

Eating fruits and seeds is expected for this species, but Captain Jack enjoyed occasional sweets and even some alcohol on special days. Voinea wanted a male-speaking companion, someone he could confine with and share his thoughts, desires, and dreams with. It was impossible to do that with his wife and daughter. They never really understood him.

'Are you still talking to that stupid bird Daren? You spend more time with that bird than any of us.' don't you have anything else to do? Get the damn garbage out and make yourself useful.

'You can't talk to Captain Jack that way, Maria. I think you owe him an apology.

'Yeah, right!' She came into the room all dressed up, smelling excellent, and still having a bust of a 30-year-old woman. She was looking good for a 48-year-old. Voinea was nearing 60 and had become uninteresting for Maria. She had needs, and she knew a younger man that could fulfill those needs. Daren was out of the game and was spending time with his stupid parrot. And they enjoyed it.

'Where are you going all dressed up like that?' asked Voinea, not wanting to hear the answer.

'It's a girl's night out, honey, don't you know?'

For Maria, almost every night was a girl's night out. It was ridiculous and so transparent. Lately, she was not even trying to hide this. He hated her guts. F**king whore! He took her from the streets to give her a better life, which was how she repaid him. She even had the nerve to bring a guy once and do it in the kitchen with him while he was watching the news. That was when he came the closest to killing her. He even raised an axe over her several times that night but couldn't go through it. He was not a killer. Her punishment would come in the afterlife, where she would go to hell, her final dwelling place as one of the damned after the Last Judgment. Her foul soul would burn forever within the gates of hell. At this point, he didn't give a shit anymore. It was 20 years of living with her that just took away the edge now. He was just 'uncomfortably numb' now.

'I need to run now and don't know when I will return. Please don't wait on me. I prepared some food for Captain Jack. You got some leftover frozen TV dinners. If Linda comes home, make her something nice and tell her to bring out food for Jack! Bye, for now, lover.'

With that last cynical remark, she left ready for another hot lovers' afternoon. He used to boil inside before, but not now. He also knew that people in the skyscraper knew his students and colleagues at the faculty. He was not worried about that, not anymore. Captain Jack was his friend, his only friend.

'Life better, much better! No worry, no worry. Everything better in the morning Professor!'

Captain Jack was putting these things together. He was a remarkable bird who didn't just copy what others said but seemed to have an analytical and logical mind to go with that. Voinea was sure Captain Jack understood him better than anyone else and knew what kind of a bitch his wife was.

'Linda junky, Linda loves drugs. Others screw Linda. Not Just Linda, Maria likes it. Maria likes men. Men like Maria. Maria is a bitch. Maria burns in hell'.

'Yes, Captain! They are bitches, and they will burn in hell.' Captain Jack never spoke much in front of those two. He knew they didn't like him, so the only one he did speak to was Voinea. He loved this. He couldn't imagine life without the Captain. At that moment came Linda, the daughter or alleged daughter of Prof. Voinea and Maria Kowalsky. Lately, he was not sure. This teenage monster couldn't have been his. Maria also showed signs of that, and the 'thing' didn't resemble Voinea. It must have been a bastard, an offspring of one of Maria's playboys.

'What's for dinner, Mom? Is the old fart at home?'

'You mean your old man or your stepdad, perhaps?'

'Shut the f**k up! She came through the door looking like a leftover Goth that converted to hip-hop and punk but decided to be a Jim Morrison disciple instead.

'F**k you, shut the f**k up, mother f**ker, crazy bitch, pierced nose bimbo, bitch, bitch, bitch…' captain jack was running on six cylinders now.

'You dirty pigeon, you shut your mouth now before I make a birdy/fish soup out of you, and one of these days, I will!'

Voinea looked at her madly: 'You hurt Captain Jack, and I swear I will cut your f**king head off and throw the rest of your body to the local zoo animals.' He had the sparkle of a madman at that moment, and she didn't have any reason to disbelieve him, although she knew that she and Mom had already decided to poison the feather bastard. She was supposed to give him the food and get rid of him.

'And besides, you could read a book instead of pumping so much acid and amphetamines into you every night and learn the difference between pigeons and parrots and what a fish soup includes.' She was mad as hell and boiling like an old steamboat. Her face was pierced all over, ears, mouth, tongue, lips, nose—you name it. All of that gave her a horrendous look. But she had to keep her calm, just a little bit longer. If they could get rid of the parrot, they certainly could get rid of 'daddy.' She decided to take on another approach.

'I'm sorry, Dad. I apologize. Things have been going on badly lately, and I haven't been myself. Voinea couldn't remember when she was her 'real self.'

'Captain Jack, my apologies, Sir! I didn't mean to mistreat you.'

'Apologies, apologies, only apologies! Captain soon hungry! The meaning of life, life, life, life… Meaning of life – hunger, not poison, just hunger.'

Captain Jack was getting restless now. Voinea appreciated the new change in his alleged daughter, even though he was not sure it would last. He couldn't quite understand Captain Jack's final remark. He behaved a bit strange, though, unlike his usual self. Voinea needed to eat something, and why not do it with Linda? One could make bury the hatchet for a little while at least.

'Mom said something is in the fridge or a frozen TV dinner, and I am unsure.'

'Don't worry, and I will prepare everything, Dad.'

Mom prepared some Mango for Captain, and I got you his favorite beer. The Mango and the beer contained a particular type of deadly poison that was very hard to detect. Linda's current boyfriend was a chemist, and he gave her this after Linda persuaded him. He was reluctant in the beginning but later decided that taking a life of a parrot was not such a big deal after all. The poison had an after-effect of 24 hours, so no suspicion could be raised. That evening they almost ate as an average family. Captain Jack ate his Mango and drank his favorite beer. It seems he was not clairvoyant enough.

Maria and Linda were there with Voinea. He died in horrendous pain some 24 hours later. The veterinarian didn't know what was wrong. The last words that he uttered to Voinea when they were alone in the vet's room were:

'Figure the meaning of life. Hunger, not poison! Follow the path. Voinea friends, friends till the end. Not all Captain's friends. Hunger, not poison. Careful, careful; we are all not careful.

What were the last famous words from the Captain? Voinea cried like a baby. His only friend was gone forever. He was devastated. When he exited the emergency room, he saw a strange gleam in Maria's and Linda's eyes. It seems they even enjoyed this. Then he remembered Captain's words: 'Hunger, not poison, not all Captain's friends.' What if these two bitches had something to do with it? He didn't say much when he saw them or say more in the coming week. He found the leftover Mango in the fridge that Linda somehow forgot to clean up and took to his colleague at the biology department. After testing, he told Voinea that this poison was so bad that it could have killed a flock of birds and reacted in the body after 18-24 hours as a sort of a particular virus. Voinea took it all calmly. He suspected this. How could he trust any of the two bitches. He could strangle both now, but that would be too easy. Blowing them up with a shotgun would be too primitive. He remembered his colleague Prof. Firtz, who used to get away from his horrible family to a small cottage in the forest he had. Voinea asked him how he dealt with pressure, anxiety, and stress. Firtz told him that he strips naked, climbs the highest oak tree on his small patch of land surrounding the cottage, and shits violently from one of the branches.

He also told him that during the crap session, he often screams and howlers. For him, the falling of shit from the high ground and the feeling of aerial non-boundaries was the most glorious moment in life. Firtz believed that this process cleanses his soul. Voinea thought about other things being cleansed, but the soul?! He had to deal with this in another way. These bitches have crossed the line for the last time. Nobody was getting away with murder in the first degree. Voinea decided to use his opponent's weapon – poison. He told his friend at the biology department that he needed to get rid of giant rats in his summer house but wanted them to suffer badly. His friend knew exactly which poison would fill that criterion. It was undetectable for the victim at the time of consumption, a liquid that could be inserted into the food of choice by a syringe. When the pain started, it would already be too late to save the rats, and they would die in horrifying pain a couple of hours later. His friend didn't know what kind of rats Voinea was aiming at.

He took care of other business that week. He changed his testament leaving everything to the local ZOO, their bird section. He left the rest to charity and his summerhouse to his favorite assistant Mark Dimitrov if he ever gets out of the nut house. He was even charming to his family. He took them out for dinner, movies, and ice cream afterward. He promised them a vacation and that he would spend more time with them, which they didn't like. The change in attitude was new for them, and killing him would be slightly tricky now, but it had to be done anyway. It was Linda's birthday that Sunday, and he said he would buy a lovely cake for her. He also added that they should eat lunch without him and celebrate, as he had to work with his assistant the whole weekend on a project that they were already behind. They didn't mind this one bit. He was dead meat the following week. They decided to poison him one week after. His friendly behavior should be rewarded. Little did they know!

Professor Voinea also visited the cemetery and made specific preparations. Captain Jack was buried a couple of days before under a ceremony only attended by Voinea. He also bought a burial spot for himself, so Captain Jack was cremated and put in a unique urn above Voinea's 'future' head. The tombstone was already done, and everything was prepared. The tombstone read: best friends forever. He assured himself through his lawyer that none of his family could do anything to disturb this. A lot of money was enough insurance for that. He found the best chocolate cake, such that both women adored and knew the beasts would eat up wholly and immediately. He inserted 35ml of the poison into the cake. According to his friend, this would be enough to kill an army of sewer rats. These two were worse than an army, thought Voinea. The cake looked great. He bought some more packed food and beverages and left a birthday note for Linda. He also paid a guy, some small-time swindler and thief, to call precisely after 18 hours (when the pains start) to his home phone and tell his wife and daughter that Captain Jack says hi and wonders if they like the cake he prepared. It should taste as good, if not better, as the Mango and Beer he got. Then he should hang up. For 100 bucks, the swindler was more than happy to oblige. Voinea wanted this revenge to be served as a cold dish.

That Sunday morning, he finally went to his office, for the last time, with his new navy rope neatly packed in his favorite brown leather attache professorship-like briefcase. The fresh wanna-be Sacher chocolate cake was waiting in the fridge. He was sure that the two monsters would digest it in no time. He could hear the Captain clapping his wings on the other side … they will soon meet again …

all will be like before, just in a new serene setting without the two witches … just him and the captain … All of these things and final thoughts put a smile on his face. Life certainly had a meaning.

19

Sole Survivor

The Russian troops were advancing more and more now. There was no way of stopping them. Couldn't it be this bad? Somehow there would be a chance to get out of this mess alive and see her again. He was holding her photograph in his shaking hand. It was the picture of them spending one of their last pre-war winter holidays in the German Alps. She looked so beautiful, pure, and innocent. Perfect blond curls were falling on her cashmere sweater, smiling round face with those deep blue eyes. He knew you couldn't see it in a black-and-white photograph. He could see his beautiful wife in all her glowing colors. It was love at first sight in a cozy Hamburg Pub. She gave him an eternal smile of pureness and innocence. And from there, as they say, the rest was history. Else was an angel that gave him the only light in this stinky bunker, waiting to be slaughtered by the advancing Red Army troops. Colonel Günter Brandt was afraid for the first time in his life. Everybody knew that these were the final moments and that the orders from the high command were clear and short, to fight until the last bullet. It couldn't have been a worse part of the year. Bloody winter of 1942-43, damn months of December and this terrible month of January. He loved winter so much, and now he hated it. Frozen, beaten up, demoralized, and hungry soldiers and comrades. Almost five months of the worst carnage he has seen in his life. It was a terrible sight for a professional soldier and a patriot like Günter. He had his first hateful thoughts about the short man in Berlin. Does he know what's happening here, does he care, and why the f**k doesn't he do something.

Surrender, which seemed like mortal sin before, seemed like salvation now. His whole panzer division was stuck. For days, this was not the idea to fight in the city, block by block, house by house. It used to be a straightforward warfare with tanks advancing and capturing terrain, open spaces where the enemy got crushed, and where you fought battles. Here the soldiers were dying from dozens of snipers, fire, sudden attacks, and, even worse, all kinds of diseases and the bloody cold. The f**king temperatures fell below −30 C at times. This is not how a war should be fought. That damn pig that called himself Reich Marshall didn't deliver. Supplies were practically non-existent lately.

The Russians were attacking again and again. They were firing from all sides and coming from all corners. As soon as our soldiers made progress, there was a counter-offensive, and so on. Now we were the only ones being pushed back. He started trembling every time the pounding of grenades would start combined with the Russian soldiers' bone-chilling cries of 'Hurrah.' They were not able to hold them back anymore. Well, the angels of death were circling closer and closer. The awful carnage of death and killing on both sides turned Günter's stomach inside out. It was not just plain killing. The worst part is that these desperate days of war brought all kinds of dark and menacing actions by some soldiers. Brutal killings, looting, devious crimes, rape, and God knows what more. It was only a few, but it will leave dark spots forever. At least he was in command now at this part of the front. God knows what was happening elsewhere.

Last bullet. His soldiers were beyond desperation, hungry, disillusioned, and left like lambs for slaughter. The starving soldiers were forced to slaughter their horses and dig up their frozen carcasses to eat the bones. But the morale was still lingering on. Unbelievable! He was fighting with the best soldiers that he knew. He would never forget. Was this going to be the end? Else, what about the love of his life? He would never touch her beautiful body, and they would never make love in the early morning hours, touch each other for hours. It was all a distant memory now. He tucked the half-worn photo into his pocket. He touched his Iron Cross, pride and joy once, now just a reminder of this terrible campaign. Why wasn't the little man in Berlin listening to General Paulus and the great von Manstein, his hero? Why weren't they doing something else?

Has he gone mad? The whole 6th army was in shambles and on the way to destruction. His division was about to perish now. The Russians broke the line and were only 50 meters from the bunker. It was all over now. His soldiers were half dead anyway. There was only a handful alive. All others have perished. The whole division was wiped out. Their hands were so cold that they couldn't even shoot anymore. And they will never live to see daylight again. Günter took out his last cigarette. Even though he was an officer, he followed the 'one cigarette per day' ration. This could be the last one. It felt so good. He took his gun from the holster. What an irony; there was only one bullet left.

Lieutenant Mikhail Rabinovich, who was fighting under an already legendary General Chuikov, decided not to blast the bunker with grenades and flamethrowers or overrun it with panzers. Instead, he wanted to take it with human resources. This was one of the command posts. They must have heard the news of General Paulus's surrender. These soldiers should not be a problem. Why should they fight anymore? No reason whatsoever. It had to be handed to these guys, who have resisted incredibly, fighting to the last bullet and not retreating. They were nothing like those Romanian renegades. Oh, he badly wanted to get his hand on them, especially that mysterious f**king rapist and bone collector that was roaming around the outskirt villages. According to their intel, it was a Romanian seducing, killing, and robbing women. He was also looting the dead soldiers on all sides. Even the Germans and Romanians were looking for him. The worst thing was that this guy was a higher-ranking officer. Damn, bastard! As they were advancing towards the bunker, some of the troops already coming in, he saw the white flag from one of the openings.

Tisa Morencai was wearing his best aftershave ever. Now, a new job, opportunity, and endless possibilities were in front of him. Freshly dry-cleaned brown suit and a matching tie were shining on him now. His black mustache was meticulously trimmed to the last hair to match his wavy black hair. He was of medium height, half athletically built. Rip Kirby's type of glasses were proudly resting on his 'Celtic' type of nose. He could be considered a handsome middle-aged man with excellent manners and an exciting story. He was collecting the monthly TV subscription fee.

I can't quite remember when Morencai took over. A young girl was working before him. She was so bad that they had to sack her. Not once was the money lost, and things got completely messed up. Tisa was the total opposite. He was extremely cautious not to make any mistakes and took a long time to complete the TV task. Each of these collectors had its own 'regions' of operation. So he used to spend almost a whole working day on a job that should take a few hours. He did this once a month, but it was a week sometimes. People were late with payments, reluctant to pay, out of the apartments, and God knows what else. He was in charge of our block, namely our four skyscrapers.

New opportunities, you bet! Morencai was not just your ordinary TV fee collector. He was also an incurable womanizer. The new job presented him with a stock of opportunities, a range of women his age, and his favorite target group. He would not just go at widows, unmarried, or other free ladies. He would also spill his charms, do some serious 'deep flirting' with married ones, and then go for the kill when the opportunity arose.

So was this time too. Our skyscraper had such a population that suited Tisa perfectly.

Günter sat at the kitchen table drinking his morning coffee and listening to the German international radio. He tried to stay in touch with happenings at home. He was at the early dusk of his life, tired, full of memories, and full of 'what ifs' and 'what if it could have been.' Stalingrad was a distant memory now, but not a forgotten one. How could he forget all that happened there? How could he? So many good people died there for all the wrong reasons and were driven by a lunatic and his suicidal visions, but they still died for their homeland and died as soldiers. How he survived, he could never really comprehend. He was extremely lucky that the attackers didn't clean off the bunker. They captured them with respect. The Rabinovich character saved his life. He was about to blow his head off when the Russian officer came in, and he was Jewish above all.

What horrible things we did as a nation to Jews thought Günter, the Holocaust, 6 million Jews brutally murdered, annihilated in the worst genocide in history…He remembered the number to have first been mentioned by Dr. Wilhelm Hoettl, an Austrian-born official in the Third Reich and a trained historian who served in several senior positions in the SS. In November 1945, Hoettl testified for the prosecution in the Nuremberg trials of accused Nazi war criminals. Later, in the 1961 trial in Israel of Adolf Eichmann, he also submitted to a lengthy series of questions from the prosecution, speaking under oath from a courtroom in Austria. Horrible, Günter could never forgive himself or his people for this. It will take decades and decades to heal within and outside, or maybe, probably never. And 20 million were killed in Russia, good God! As an officer with an iron cross, he was deported to a labor prison camp after the war and so on for years. A couple of years after the war, it was hard work in Russian camps and some more. The return home was a difficult one. His beloved Else was killed in the battle of Berlin. He was a crushed man afterward. Due to his engineering skills, he got work and started to move through Central and Eastern Europe as a representative for a construction company. He somehow worked with one of our local firms and found the new love of his life. He was 45 then, and life began again after all the pain and sorrow. Gertrud was a lovely 36-year-old blonde girl. She reminded him of Else in many respects. It was new love discovered. After a couple of moving, they settled in the new skyscraper, our skyscraper. He mastered the language in due time. Russian was a big help. It was a good life, and the past was behind us. He was not ashamed of it, a professional soldier that did his job and paid his dues, but he rarely mentioned it.

The doorbell rang amid Günter's 'down the memory lane day-dreaming. Gertrud went for the door. Tisa was all smiles. It covered and stretched all over his face. His clever, cunning late middle age attack was about to begin. 'Good morning to you, madam; a wonderful morning, isn't it?' He was slightly younger than Günter and did all kinds of things to keep ahead of the coming old age. Gertrud was slightly startled. 'Oh, good morning to you, and you are…?'

'Tisa Morencai at your service, madam! TV collection at your door, anytime, day or night, whenever you need it.' He was an offensive line, but somehow he never perfected it; there was never a need to do it.

'If it is a bad time, I can come again some other time, or you can pay the TV fee in installments during the whole month if you wish.' This is how one catches fish. Tisa knew that this line one was one of his small favorites.

'Oh, I don't know, that sounds great. I will have to see about it with…' Tisa cut her off: 'Oh, I do apologize, madam. I haven't noticed how beautiful you look in the early morning hours. My wife Maria, God rest her soul, was never a woman of the morning. If I may say so, madam, and my apologies for being too personal, you are a morning angel to an old soldier's eyes. Gertrud was blushing now. She hasn't blushed for years. Even if this was slightly rude and straightforward, she liked it. Getting compliments like this in the early morning from a lovely middle-aged gentleman was not bad. Günter was her love, but he seemed to forget recently that compliments and even man and wife flirting and casual sweet talk were necessary and, honestly, a need. A slight warm shiver went through her body. Tisa knew this. He was a special deep magnet for women. That was his gift, this was his game, and the mastery of skills would bring his prey. But what he did not know, and the information he used to scan and gather didn't cover it, was that Gertrud's man was home.

Günter was already slightly irritated by this sweet talk and Gertrud's evident paralysis and mesmerized behavior at the door. 'Maybe you would like to come for a coffee, Mr. Morencai? Gertrud was like a hypnotized woman. Yes, Tisa was also known. It isn't easy to know if this was true because of his exceptional skills as a kid living on a farm. He hypnotized small animals, cats, ducks, chickens, and all kinds of things to them. He later moved to humans, especially women. Tisa bragged about this to some of his friends. Probably it was not true, but there was some strange effect that his sharp dark eyes and almost a satanic type of smile had on women. He reminded me of Al Pacino playing the devil in that movie with Keanu Reeves; what was the name? Oh well. It just worked.

He was scanning Gertrud now in her morning gown. She looked wonderful. Beautiful face and figure with full breasts slightly showing underneath the gown. This was his favorite type. And it seemed so easy. Hell, he worked fast. It was already time for coffee. As he was about to say an enormous YES to the coffee offer, Günter appeared at the door. 'Is there a problem, honey?' Gertrud was caught off balance. 'Oh no, Mr. Morencai is collecting the TV fee well. He is kind and says we don't have to pay right now.'

'Oh, did he now?' Gunther was analyzing this character in front of him. He was no particular expertise in human behavior but certainly didn't like what he saw in front of him. He could almost scan this guy. Tisa became slightly uncomfortable. This was not part of the plan for this bloke to appear at the door.

'Well, we can pay you now if you like. And then it will be easier for you later; you won't need to come in again.' Günter was going to get rid of this gut ASAP.

'Oh, no problem, it's OK, I can come gladly again. That is my suggestion. It is an excellent deal, especially since TV fees are so high. Take three installments.

'Oh honey, I think Mr. Morencai is right.' 'Oh, please call me Tisa,' he added very slickly. Günter was going to play this differently now. He could see that Gertrud would oppose a different solution and felt there was more to this guy than meets the eye. 'Sure, we will take the installments, but unfortunately, no time for coffee, Mr. Morencai. We are in a slight rush this morning.' Saying this, he squeezed Gertrud's hand. She almost wanted to say something but decided not to. 'Honey, please get the money.' He then turned to Tisa. 'It seemed you mentioned that you were a soldier. Was it in the 2nd World War? Tisa knew that Günter had a German background, but not that it was high ranking army one.

'Oh yes, I was. Believe it or not, I fought on the Stalingrad front on the German side. Well, I was a soldier then, and I just followed orders. I didn't think much about politics too much at that time. But I did fight for a great army if you know what I mean? With that, he gave him an eye.

'Hmm, what a coincidence, I was an officer on the Stalingrad front serving under General Paulus. Terrible times, never to be repeated, I hope. But we served our dues'. He became even more uncomfortable. Oh yes, many good boys died in that campaign. I was wounded in a couple of places.

'If my memory serves me right, the 1st Rumanian Cavalry Division and 20 Rumanian infantry division were fighting there, as well as the 3rd and 4th Romanian Army' Yes, Tisa was quick to add, I was part of the 20 infantry division, exactly that outfit. Proudly to say I was one of the officers. Colonel, I might add. 'My, that is incredible, another coincidence. So was I', added Günter in a half-wicked voice. Ah, so your commander was probably General Niculaie Verzeanu.

Exactly, a heroic and brave man indeed! I was fighting by his side. I was one of the sole survivors there. Some good men left their bones on that battlefield.

'What a f**king liar,' thought Günter to himself. There was no such general. This guy is lying as a rat or hiding something. Their commander was General Nicolae Tataranu, also a holder of the Ritterkreuz. He didn't fancy the man too much. His only admiration in the Romanian officer ranks was for Major Gheorghe Rasconescu, General Mihai Lascar, and Günter's personal friend Colonel Ion Hristea. All three showed heroics in the field and got the Ritterkreuz as Günter. Tisa was getting more and more nervous again. He knew he lied, but he needed to get rid of this damn nosy guy quickly. Fortunately for him, Gertrud came back with the money. He changed back to his slick behavior again. This woman was worth fighting for.

'Oh, madam, thank you. Here is your receipt, and I will be back in a month for the next installment. I need to rush off now. I am in a bit of a rush this morning. Won't you stay for some coffee and croissants, Tisa? Oh, please do so we can continue our exciting war memories, added Günter. Didn't you know that Mr. Morencai was in the war and fighting close to me? Imagine! Tisa was coughing and excusing himself, 'Oh, we must take that again. This was his exit line. Gertrud looked disappointed. Tisa said a fast goodbye and disappeared in the shadows of the skyscraper staircase.

Almost 800.000 of their soldiers perished in the operations, and Russian casualties almost doubled. What was left of German troops in the Stalingrad pocket after December 18 was approximately 249,000 officers and men. Forty-two thousand sick and wounded were flown out of that number before the last airfield fell. Another 85,000 lay dead on the battlefield. What was left was about 122,000 German soldiers, plus Italians and Romanians. They all surrendered, of course. Only about 6000 soldiers returned alive from the Stalingrad pocket carnage. The remaining ones left their bones in Mother Russia. And that this damn weasel was somehow part of the actual army fight is something that Gunther could not digest. Gunther could always smell a rat. There was something about this guy, but he couldn't figure it out. But he will — he made a mental promise to himself.

Tisa was pissed with himself. How could he get himself lured into the war shit talk? Damn! He should have just waited until this guy went to work. Ah, he was slipping. This didn't happen before; no more mistakes. He wanted the woman. That lovely piece of ass needed to be conquered. He wanted to feel the warmth of her body, her breasts. There was a time when he needed to do some other things with these women, some gruesome things that belonged to the past, or so he believed. That was all over now; he was cured, thought Tisa. No, the error must not be permitted anymore. There were other fish to reel in. Six more ladies in the quarter, four potential, one already hooked. When Bella Norton opened the door of her apartment on the 9th floor for Tisa, he knew they would be in bed within a quarter of an hour. She was a damn good-looking widow, already seduced and succumbed by Tisa's devilish charms. She was in her bathrobe, still smelling from all the lotions and herb shampoos. It was only a matter of time to reel in Gertrud too. He will have to visit her apartment on the 12th floor soon.

Günter didn't rest. He tried to collect all the material he could from the war archives, all kinds of bits and pieces of information on the Stalingrad battle, especially on the Romanian troops. This task was not easy, leading to a dead end after a while. He roamed through all the books and articles written on the subject. He also looked into some of his old contacts in Germany to get something. He was not even sure what he was looking for. For God's sake, who would have ever found a character like Tisa amongst hundreds of thousands of soldiers? He even tried to contact the families and colleagues that were still alive of some of the Romanian officers he knew. He was looking for anything or anyone suspicious in their ranks. Some of them said that they would get back to him. It was all a very long shot. Damn, he was getting obsessed with this. One thing was sure. The dirty bastard was probably going under a false name. But then it came. While they were getting ready for bed one night, Gertrud started reading aloud an article about some Nazi criminal that was finally caught after so many years. He was being deported from some banana republic. Mossad, the Israeli secret service, finally caught up with this guy after months and months of surveillance. And that's when it struck him. What if this guy was just a damn war criminal. He is not a big fish, though, but. There was something so sinister about him. He didn't tell Gertrud anything about his obsession, as she could spill all of it to God knows who. Calling Mikhail Rabinovich was his immediate thought. Even better, see him! He was going on a business trip to Moscow next week. He could meet his old friend with whom he kept contact after the war. They were just two damn good soldiers, and the war and its reasons were forgotten many years ago. If someone could help, it was Mikhail. Before leaving for Moscow, he did some small detective work, being very careful not to be spotted. A few photos of Tisa with Günter's new Nikon lens camera wouldn't hurt. Oh, yessir, Bob! Not at all! It could help him and Mikhail to find a perfect match if there was such. Shit, he must have changed. But we will see. He got a couple of good shots of Tisa. The damn guy was collecting money again. It wasn't a whole month. He felt uneasy leaving Gertrud all alone with this sleazeball. All that was going through his head while his plane descended towards Moscow and Sheremetyevo Airport.

Tisa was on the move again. He found out somehow, don't ask me how that Günter is away on a business trip for a week. Yes! That was when he needed to make a move. He was banging Bella already, but he needed more. It was rough sex by now, and she didn't like it. He didn't give a f**k. Damn bitch resisted him the last time, so he showed her. She said she was going to the Police and reporting him for rape. The hell she was. He had to deal with her. Disposing of the body was more arduous, but he did it. Before that, he cleaned her of all the valuables and savings. The stupid bitch kept everything at home. There will be some time before they miss her; by then, he will be long gone, with no way to trace him to her. He knew what he did, and he was proud of it. Thinking of it just gave him the giggles. He also remembered all the other women, most of them in another world now. But that was history. He knew better. He was just after their flesh and their savings. He knew he couldn't control it again. He rang the bell of Günter's and Getrud's apartment.

Günter met with Mikhail. He explained the reason for his suspicions and gave him the blown-up photos to Mikhail. He was looking at them for a long time, studying, looking again, going silent for a while, shuffling through his papers. Old memories were brought back, and the guys had much to discuss.

'There is something here, Günter, something I can smell. This face I have seen before, as a much younger guy. You say he is Romanian. Damn it, and I just can't remember.

'Yeah, I think that is the only true part about him. I can sense his accent, surely Romanian, no doubt about it.'

'Then I will check some of the war archives, and I have a friend at Army intelligence, as well as KGB. We can see if there was anything fishy on the Romanian side during the Stalingrad campaign. There could be something. Shit, there was something in those days, but I can't remember now. I also have Simon, who works for Mossad. He moved to Israel after the war. We were in the same outfit. He might know something!'

'Have you tried with the Romanians, Günter?' 'I had some contacts, but you know how they are. I hope to find something from a good friend still alive in Bucharest. We will see if anything pop's out.

'I will do everything I can here, and maybe my feeble brain will return to operation and retrieves some of the old intel I had in those days.' This was good news for Günter. Something might resurface. Shit always comes to the surface at one time or another. So it's just to wait. He had another job to do and then to get home as soon as possible.

Gertrud blushed all over. 'Oh, it's you again, Mr. Morencai. How nice to see you.

'Tisa please, dear Gertrud. No need to use last names. First name basis, please; we are old friends by now.'

'I just learned you can save even more on your TV subscription. Isn't that great!' if you accept to receive some free information from a certain number of companies, you will be entitled to a month of free TV viewing.

'As soon as I heard about this offer, I remembered you.' Flattery of this kind will get you anywhere—was Tisa's critical thought. He showed Gertrud that he cared, and that is where women are incredibly vulnerable.

'Oh my, you are so sweet and considerate, Tisa. That's wonderful.' She was almost ready to kill. 'Would you like to come in.' Oh, thank you, I would love that more than anything; I mean to spend time and talk to you. It would be such a pleasure for a lonely man like me.'

'Oh, I don't think you are lonely. A handsome man like you must have women all over him. With that said, Gertrud blushed even more. What the hell was she getting herself into? She hasn't been this frivolous before. But she was attracted to this guy. He could smell it.

'I will collect some fees tomorrow evening, so if you are not busy, I could just come by after work.'

Not thinking again, she blurted out, 'I can make us a light supper so you can tell me all about you and your army career.' Her heart was racing now.

'Great! I will be here after seven'. With that, he said warm goodbyes and disappeared. When Gertrud closed the door, she realized that a stranger was coming into her house, and she would let him in. Ah, the excitement was overwhelming her. She couldn't remember when was the last time somebody cared so much and gave her so many compliments, not even Günter. What harm can a light dinner do?

It was all there. This was amazing, scary, and terrifying at the same time. Could it be true? He could not believe his eyes. Mikhail was shocked when he made the perfect match in the end. They got in touch with Günter's friend from Bucharest. He also found something based on the pictures he faxed to them. The best stuff came from Mosha in Israel. According to him, this is the guy they have on file. Simon Wiesenthal's center also had an open file on him as this monster killed over 100 Jews during the war. So the Israeli's never closed the book on him. Whoever got to him first was going to eliminate him on the spot. It was triple-checked now. There was no doubt. The famous phantom robber, rapist, and murderer of Stalingrad's fields and outskirts remained alive. His real name was Teodor Radulescu. The bastard was caught once as a deserter and was not shot at sight by some miraculous event. An officer deserting was a thing for court-martial. The worst thing was that he escaped and was seen by later witnesses coming out of houses where people were looted and murdered. His Romanian past came after him. It was discovered that he killed more than a dozen women hideously and always escaped. The Phantom of Bucharest was a nickname this person got. Changing his identity and taking another guy's, a colonel in this case, an identity he got into the army. What he didn't know was that he was going to end up at the front. Of course, he did the best he could to survive. When it became unbearable, he somehow, and this was the unique part, got out before the worst happened. Wherever this man went, killings continued. God knows how many and where. Nobody kept counting, and it was impossible to catch this guy. The whole thing went into total oblivion at the end of the 50s. The tracks were lost. But where are they? Both Günter and Mikhail felt horrified but happy at the same time that this might be the real guy. They checked the pictures over and over again. Teodor had police records and, fortunately, an army photo. There was no doubt about it. A lot of time passed, but this was the guy. He had that sly smile, the Celtic nose, and incredible evil and devilish confidence in his eyes. Even the hair was the same. He has probably changed his looks many times, but somewhere in the end, you stop caring. How the hell did he end up at Günter's door? This bastard has traveled throughout the whole of Europe. Günter thought of Transylvania and vampires momentarily, and a cold shrill shook his body. This was a vampire, but a real human one. For this rodent, crosses, garlic, or stakes will not be needed. One clean shot will take this bastard to the la-la land. They decided not to contact any police or authority as that would create a mess from which Teodor, alias Tisa would undoubtedly escape. Günter decided to deal with this scum of the earth on his own. It was a question of avenging all the innocent victims and all their comrades, German, Ukrainian, Belorussian, Russian, Romanian, and others that gave their lives serving in both armies just to be robbed and looted by this monster. All those poor women in God knows how many countries! Günter decided to leave immediately, four days before scheduled. Gertrud was in terrible danger, and he knew it. Mikhail decided to come with Günter.

A box of chocolates, a bouquet of fresh lilies, and his best perfume were the hallmarks of the moment for Teodor Radulescu, alias Tisa Morencai. He was going to have her tonight, and if she resisted, he would have to teach her a lesson. That would be her last lesson, but that's life. As his mother, a hooker by profession, used to say to him: 'Tisa, all women are whores, and they need to be taught a lesson.' Well, he taught his mom a lesson. He was sick and tired of her whoring. He was back again. That idiot shrinks in Salzburg did not know anything. He was too shallow to understand the deepness of his intellect and his mission in life. The hell with him; there was a job to do now. Gertrud opened, looking more stunning than ever. Hair, makeup, a fantastic dress, and an incredible body were all Tisa needed. When he came in, and the door was closed, he started to approach her devilishly.

'My, you look wonderful tonight, Gertrud. God has granted you all wishes: grace, beauty, elegance, and wholeness of your soul and body.' These 'poetic' words took her. Günter was never like this. 'Let's sit down, and I will bring some sweets and coffee, Tisa.'

'I was thinking we could slip coffee and get to know each other better.' Gertrud turned around as Tisa was already putting his hands around her waist. 'What do you mean Tisa, you….' She didn't finish the sentence because Tisa was now all over her, kissing her wildly and caressing her. She became scared all of a sudden.

'Please stop, Tisa; you don't know what you're doing. I am a married woman, and you misunderstand things.

'No, I am not, you f**king whore! You are all the same bitches, resisting in the begging but begging all the time to do it. I will show you how Tisa does it.' At that moment, she started yelling and resisting Tisa's attacks. He slammed her over the face.

'If you don't shut up bitch I will kill you on the spot. You're going to open it when I desire it. Keep your dirty mouth shut. One more word from you and you are dead'. That said, he took out a medium-sized pocket sharp bowie knife.

'See this bitch! You are going to die as all the others do. One word, and I cut your breasts. She was petrified now, unable to say anything. Drops of blood were dripping from her mouth. He tore her dress and began cutting her underwear.

'Wonderful, wonderful, you are nicer than I thought. Now you are going to let Tisa inside, won't you?' She uttered a hollow scream, and suddenly the door burst open on its hinges, and Günter and Mikhail rushed in. Tisa looked wildly. Will he kill the bitch right away? No f**king time. Damn, Krautz was here and some other asshole. They have a look on their faces as they know. But how is that possible? I should have disposed of the motherf**ker on time. Damn, damn, too many mistakes. He turned wildly to them. It was too late. Günter was already flying through the air. He crashed into Tisa and gave him a fist blow. Tisa managed to cut Günter's left hand. It was a deep cut. Mikhail joined in and grabbed Tisa. The fight erupted. Gertrud was screaming now. Tisa's brain was running fast. Somehow he got out of the fight entanglement and ran for the door. Mikhail couldn't grab him.

'Stop, mother f**king murderer!' Mikhail was yelling now and running after him. Günter checked on Gertrud. They embraced. After seeing she was OK, he followed Tisa and Mikhail. There were 12 floors of stairs to go. Tisa went down right away. There was no f**king chance of getting an elevator. He was almost caught by two f**king amateurs. After all those years, after all those women, just f**king incredible! He was running like a madman. Mikhail followed with a bad breath after him and Günter slightly slower. He was heavily bleeding now, but he just didn't give a f**k. All this yelling brought some of the tenants out, but as they saw a wild man running with a knife, they disappeared as rabbits into their holes. Somebody did call the Police, but it would be an eternity until they came. By that time, Teodor alias Tisa would be long gone. He came out as a bullet through the entrée hall and double doors. In the process, he almost bulldozed a poor kid in his way. With this, he lost a precious second or two, enough for Mikhail to gain on him. He was only 10 meters behind him. They were running towards the construction site and the fastest city road lanes. There was a tram track there too. He wanted to outrun them and disappear. The roads were so busy he could leave those two behind if he made it during the red traffic lights. There was no f**king chance they could cross for at least 5 minutes. And he would be long gone. He knew how to run and, more importantly, hide. He was thinking of his next town, even a new country, when suddenly the tram came.

Eddie Bartoly was on his first week at the new job. Driving a tram was not his goal in life, but it was an excellent way to earn money, finally, get credit, and buy the racing car he dreamed of. Getting a deal with a sponsor would be easier. Eddie was a natural. Rallycross was his life. He used to test cars for some drivers and was a talent. His parents didn't approve at all. They thought Eddie was too brilliant for this job and that he was ruining his future. The most significant support he got was from his loving grandfather, who passed away some years back. He used to tell Eddie to follow his star and to do whatever he feels is right. He also told him often to enjoy life to its fullest, even if it means driving a rally cross race. There was only one life, and you never knew when someone could come and take away your dreams. There was nothing Eddie couldn't do with a machine in his hand. The tram was similar, though you couldn't get out of these damn tracks. But he understood vehicles like nobody else. It was green for him, and he knew the damn light would change soon at that intersection. And there it was for eternity until he got a green one again. What the f**k, he thought; let's see what this baby can do. He gave all he had – full power. The electrical tram was shaking but was responding. It was rushing like a silver bullet now. Oh yeah, he was going to make it. This streak was meant for fast driving, but not as fast as Eddie was doing.

Tisa didn't see him; his looks were on Günter and Mikhail, who were lagging now. These two are slow. Tisa trained every morning while these two probably couldn't get out of their couches. He was more and more confident now. Giant oak trees were covering the sight of the tram crossing, and a slight curve blocked the view just a little bit. Eddie saw two guys running wild, but they were at some distance.

'Some people don't get it, do they? This is no tram station, just a crossing. Must be foreigners.' He told his pal, who was leaning on the railing and smoking as a chimney.

'Hey Eddie, maybe you should slow down some.' 'Ah f**k that, bro, I'm already there. With those words, he froze in horror when a running man appeared before him. Even if you have time, it's those moments when the brain activity freezes, and you are paralyzed and incapable of doing anything. He just froze, and the last thing he saw was the horror in that guy's eyes. Tisa saw him. It was too late to do anything. Tisa didn't have time to think about it 'too late.' The only thing he whispered was, 'Holy f**k!' He was instantaneously splattered like a bug over the tram's front side. His brain splashed all over the beacon and the windshield of the tram. The tram continued rolling, making Tisa's body even worse. He was uttering the last horrific screams of a dying man in horrendous pain.

Eddie finally stopped the tram couple of hundred meters down. Günter and Mikhail were there. A few cars stopped but had to move on due to the fast traffic flow. Eddie got out in total shock. He couldn't believe what had happened. How the f**k did this guy pop up in front of the tram? I should have slowed down. These were some of the things running through Eddie's head. Günter and Mikhail were leaning over Teodor Radulescu's severed body. There was barely life in him. He was trying to say something. Blood was gushing out everywhere. Good grief!

It was a terrible sight.

'How did you find out, why?' was what he was repeating. Mikhail said in Russian to him: 'Your killing streak has ended. You got off easy, but all those soles from Stalingrad to now that you robbed and killed will rest in piece. We were there, comrade, both of us. I knew about the phantom and wanted to catch you at any cost. So many years now, but the hand of the law is long. Nobody escapes!' There was incredible horror and unbelievable appalment in Teodor's eyes. He understood Russian as well as German. Günter added in German:

'May you rot in hell, and may your soul never find a resting place to be cursed and damned forever. Oh, I was there too, in Stalingrad, I mean. You didn't fool me, you bastard. Should have learned your history and names better.' 'How many did you kill, you bastard?'

This was the last thing Theodore heard. He smiled and mumbled in Romanian: 'You will never know, will you…' and was gone forever. Günter and Mikhail did not have any mercy left. This monster has done too many bad things to be forgiven. Eddie was in total shock. Russian, German, Romanian…what the f**k was going on here? Are these people spies, criminals, or mobsters?

'Who was this man, he asked Günter?'

'He had caused misery and pain to many innocent and honest people. But at the end of the day, life comes back with all the receipts you forgot to pay during your life. He got what he deserved! Thanks for driving the tram just as you should have and a little faster than normal.' With that, he just smiled at Eddie. Eddie couldn't quite figure out this whole mess.

The police were already arriving. Günter slumped down on the ground. He has lost a lot of blood. The story never became a story, though. They found Bella strangled in the bathtub, and that was the only thing pinned down on Teodor as well as the attempted rape and murder of Gertrud. It was for the better. Günter and Mikhail never revealed the thing about the phantom. It would create havoc for the local police and open Pandora's box that would never be closed. All those victims, wherever they were, could rest in peace finally because the monster was gone forever. Not for their families, though. They would live with their grief for the rest of their lives. Günter came out of the hospital in a couple of days. Gertrud was fine, shaken up badly, but sure to pay the TV fee through the post office from then on.

20

Resurrecting Evil

"I will pray for your sorry souls, and I hope God washes away your sins of evil, backwardness, and hollow existence. Sinners, may you suffer the eternal fires of hell! When judgment day draws near, the dead will rise again to be judged, as well as the living, but you devil worshipers will never die or rise again. Instead, you filthy souls will swim in the rivers of fire and burn in hell for eternity...May the floods of fire wash away your souls forever."

–Unknown Priest, Lombardy 1234 AD

At various periods in human history, devil worship and witchcraft became significant for individuals who were wholly disillusioned and dissatisfied with the existing religious institutions and their heavenly representatives. The lure of the demonic spirits and black magic appealed to many people, even those in the religious structures. These same institutions, often in those times, fought back with tools like inquisition and exorcism. In the first 25 years of the 17th century, the witchcraft delusion in medieval Europe, especially in France, reached its highest peak of intensity and devil-mania madness. Cases of demonic possession involving priests and nuns were one of the highlights of those times. Demons of all kinds, shapes, and intentions were believed to be attacking humans everywhere, obsessing and darkening their minds and controlling the bodies of victims into whom they had entered through the small bodily openings. The medieval church fought back with a vengeance in a reign of terror against every form of demonism that materialized in the rather lethal Inquisition. By definition, this was a judicial papal church institution that fought heretics and witchcraft, plus all kinds of sorcery and magic. It gained considerable power in medieval and early modern times in its attempt to withstand what it believed to be a mass assault aimed at church and society by the Prince of Darkness – the Devil, working through his agents and worshipers, such as sorcerers, witches, and others. The name is derived from the Latin inquiro ("inquire into"), which emphasizes that the inquisitors did not wait for complaints but sought out heretics and other offenders. And they certainly did not, as many medieval cases bear witness.

Father Henry LeMuir despised the Inquisition but was fascinated by all other aspects of the medieval ages. For him, for all the wrong reasons, the period was the true renaissance of the European spirit, of the black and dark spirit. He also liked all mythology that had to do with the dark side. What is even worse, in practical terms, is that Henry LeMuir believed that he was the true reincarnation of Prince of Sorcerers, Father Louis Gaufridi, the 17th-century parish priest of Accoules in Marseilles, France, who was accused of witchcraft, subsequently tortured and burned. By many accounts, it seems Father Gaufridi was nothing more than a plain womanizer or a medieval gigolo in priest clothes. According to others, like Grand Inquisitor Sebastian Michaelis, victor of a thousand battles with Satan, Father Louis was the dark devil worshipper, wizard, and soul taker, especially of poor nuns' bodies and souls. At least that was what his confessions said produced under the excruciating torments of the inquisition, which probably even the famous inquisitor from Umberto Eco's Name of the Rose, Bernardo Gui, would have been proud of.

Father Henry LeMuir obtained copies and read all his confessions where he signed the pact with the devil, ate live babies, celebrated a black mass at the sabbath—a nocturnal gathering of witches where he held the rank of dark prince, sprinkling the witches with consecrated wine. He had exercised his magical and carnal power over women, especially nuns blessing them with his dark seed. Henry was living proof that these black ideas knew no historical boundaries. He believed everything he read and saw it in his nightly visions, often combined with other supernatural visual notions. It was found out later that he had a massive brain tumor that developed over time and was the leading cause of these dark visions, plus the fact that he was an abused child, often whipped by his father and tormented by childhood scenes of seeing his younger sister sexually molested by there, so-called dad. It all ended tragically one day when their mom killed herself with sleeping pills. Soon afterward, they murdered their father with the brown-bulky spider from the deadly Atrax family. Henry somehow got a hold of this venomous Australian spider and left it in his father's room. He died in excruciating pain, and when they were almost sure he was about to die, the ambulance was called. It was too late for the antidote anyway. The inquiry was made, and many suspicions were raised about why such a spider was kept in the house and how he escaped.

Police looked through their fingers, knowing what kind of savage father this guy was. And it was impossible to pin down anything on these two angelic kids with demonic smiles. Henry was 16, and his sister was 15. They had no relatives, and the house was sold soon afterward. After a hazy period of foster home-parents moves, his sister Isabella moved into a convent, and Henry decided on priesthood. She never got over her mom's suicide. They thought peace was to be found in the divine, but it was not to be so, especially for Henry. They rarely kept in touch, and Isabella moved to a mission to South America, and soon afterward, they completely went their separate ways. Henry changed parishes like someone changes underwear, but there was no inner peace, plus bizarre rumors followed every one of his premature departures from the religious communities.

Henry was the tenant of the smallest one-room apartment on the 18th floor, the last floor in the skyscraper. He mostly kept to himself and didn't bother much about the neighborhood population. A tall man with high eyebrows, dark and highly focused eyes, and an elegant bolding head presented a highly striking and respectful figure. Everyone knew he was 'the preacher' as the community called him. For some reason, he didn't live in his parish outside the main city perimeter, nor did anyone know where the church was where he was doing his services. He was quiet and didn't talk much about it with his neighbors. If the talk somehow resurfaced, he would always present the story of moving around the parishes and doing scholarly canonic work for the monasteries. We all thought he was some big-shot papal secret representative on a secret mission for the church. He was about to be banned from the church following bizarre events in the small parish where he had worked for the last 2-3 months. That was also the time when his tumor grew. The visions increased as the tumor pressed some parts of his right lobe side, and bad things were about to happen. He was unaware of the tumor. Henry never went to a doctor and just took painkillers all the time. Father Henry LeMuir was almost sure that he was Father Louis Gaufridi that came back, resurrected in a new century, with a new purpose. All of this was not quite in line with the beliefs that Henry was taught to follow, practice and preach, but Henry was not himself anymore. He believed that the forces of evil, which were more robust than the divine ones, were guarding him, and they were indestructible. The divine ones did nothing for his sister and his mother. But the evil ones took his father away. He should have realized that years ago. He had a new purpose in life now. He was entirely obsessed with every dark aspect of world mythology. Not just that, as it was later found out, he was also mastering the black arts of various devil worshippers throughout the ages. His library contained some 1000 rare books in alchemy, the occult, transcendental meditation, poisons, charms, spells, Egyptian black magic, and burial techniques. He accepted the bad guys from every world religion and mystic belief. When and why exactly all of these loony tune ideas came into his head, nobody knew for sure. Things were not that simple and unclear, at least not to us who lived in the skyscraper and knew almost nothing about Father LeMuir's dark ideas. As often happens, the most complicated and bizarre things end in a precise and sudden moment. In his case, it happened one gloomy and dark September evening in 1985. Things in Henry's troubled life came to an abrupt and strange end after an unbelievable, mystic, and almost bloody trial that took only six months to develop after his visions, which I tend to call chapter, verse, and visions I, II, and III.

Chapter, verse, and Vision I

The headaches were almost unbearable by now. With these constant pain attacks came visions that seemed too honest at times. There were short ones, but also the long, significant ones. Those were the ones that counted, and that made the difference. Three of those visions shaped Henry LeMuir's end of days, but not in the sense he expected and hoped for.

He was the dark prince flying above the Département du Puy-de-Dôme in Auvergne, France. Invincibility was flowing through him. His huge spear-pointed tail flowed in the air, and he had a red masculine body and great wings. Dark red eyes were glowing in the night. He could see the gathering in the middle of the night, the black Sabbath underneath him. It was ideally situated in a secluded part of the forest with an almost impossible opening, something like Leonardo DiCaprio's Beach. There were a couple of hundred participants with candles and in black robes, all waiting for him to arrive. Some witches, warlocks, and sorcerers were still arriving riding on goats, rams, and black dogs provided by the master himself. The huge Pentagram was lit with candles, and a young, naked woman's body served as an altar. His mouth was already watery. The rite was about to begin. He landed before the altar, and everyone moaned in appreciation, fear, and obedience. They all kneeled in front of the master. Soon he changed shape into a giant black wolf, jumping on the altar and licking the back of the girl's body, tied and sedated with special potions, so she was enjoying this and willing to join in union with this black monster. She was very young, and she was also a nun from the nearby abbey. All kinds of elements of satanic magic were used during the ceremony, such as philters and spells. Now Henry changed to a body of a beautiful young male, much as the Greek God Apollo was depicted in various statutes. He was going to have indiscriminate black intercourse with this lovely creature. He drank a magical potion that arose the sexual power of 1000 gates of hell within him. The poor nun was doomed. After he had his way with her, they all jubilated in union and gave her the final poison potion. She was taken away after that. The feasting and dancing began, and Henry changed his shape back to the Prince of Darkness again.

Black bacchanalias were reaching their peak. The masses were chanting:

'Beelzebub, Beelzebub, they shall not die; they shall rule the world of doom. Beelzebub, Beelzebub, thy time is here and near.'

Suddenly a witch brought a young baby wrapped in a black cloth. It was a baby girl. Henry's eyes burned red again, and he knew the child's sacrifice would be the highest moment of this evening. The baby was placed in the pentagram's center, and the chants and rites began. The baby was smeared with different potions and herbal oils. The creature extended its wings, flew over the innocent child several times, and descended in a lightning landing before its tiny feet. Its horrible face and the foul stench made the poor baby cry again. The creature extended its long nails and made a surgical incision, swiftly taking the heart out of the chest. The heart was still pumping and instantly became dark red and glowing. The creature took the heart and flew away into the darkness of the warm French August sky. The black union screamed in one continuous voice a hundred times: The Black Sabbath was over.

'Beelzebub, Beelzebub, they shall not die; they shall rule the world of doom. Beelzebub, Beelzebub, thy time is here and near.'

Father Lermo Petronius heard sister Sylvia Freund's confession. That bastard Henry LeMuir has molested her and raped her over and over again. He didn't know what to do. There was no proof, and Sylvia would not tell a living soul. She was too close to a complete collapse and breakdown, and Father Petronius feared she might do something to herself. He had to act. He never liked LeMuir. That man was the devil himself. Something was very wrong and ominous about him. Lermo feared him. He felt that LeMuir was following him like a shadow of the devil. Still, he had to do something.

Chapter, verse, and Vision II

It was dark, and the parish looked demonic at 03:00 hours in the morning. The small stone church from Romanesque times looked like a small beacon in the light of darkness engulfing the small compound. The old graveyard was to the left of the main church building, while the tiny house of the local priest was connected to the church building. The bell skyscraper was crowning this small but beautiful piece of church architecture. It was one of those places that retained quality and value over time. Henry, or as he taught of himself as Father Louis Gaufridi resurrected, was flying high above the darkened sky of someplace in the south of France. He was uttering the old bible name for the prince of the devils, Beelzebub, in verse:

'Beelzebub, Beelzebub, they shall not die; they shall rule the world of doom. Beelzebub, Beelzebub, thy time is here and near.'

In some religions like Hinduism and Buddhism, a sacred utterance of a word or verse like this means that the user believes in the verse's mystical or spiritual usefulness. These mantras are either spoken aloud or merely reflected inside in one's thoughts. Father Louis Gaufridi (Henry) repeated them continuously at times, while sometimes he spoke them once. This had an effect on black distillations of spiritual wisdom for Louis. Before his night flying, he was already meditating on this particular mantra. This brought him to a trancelike state, in his case, a hazardous higher level of dark spiritual awareness. Instead of using this to protect himself from evil psychic powers, he was becoming instead one with them. He was nearing the church now. A small light was burning in the house. He knew that Father Gandolfino (Italian by ancestry) was in there. He wanted his soul; he wanted to punish this priest for accusing him of witchcraft; although he wasn't far from the truth, it was much more than Gandolfini knew, and besides – he was a strong and dangerous adversary propagating the light side. Louis was going to change that. Gandolfini was examining an old, beautiful illumination he received from a crusader during his travels to the Holy Lands. He was 76 and in fragile health, rapidly getting older every day. He knew that the call of the other world was all too near, but there were still many things to be done, especially for the young. That evening he couldn't sleep—a needful activity and dire requirement for a man of his age and health status. He thought that a glass of warm milk and an old book might bring him back again to the temporary and inevitable but highly needed world of nightly hibernation. As he was about to finish his second glass of warm milk, he heard a strange sound on the adjacent roof of the parish church.

Though the soul may wander involuntarily when its owner's guard is at its lowest, like in sleep or when sneezing or yawning, Louis's soul was wandering due to soul loss in its enticement and capture by the dark side. He wasn't just leaving his body; his soul was leaving slowly too. Father Louis landed on the roof. His separable soul, capable of removing itself or being removed from a person while still living, was assuming a different form now. This most usually occurs in sleep. While detached, it may be placed in or assume the form of an animal or a thing of some kind. While in the air, it took the shape of a black crow; now, on the roof, it assumed the form of a black cat. He landed with a thump on the small grass patio before the church. Now he took the shape of a big black dog shaped like a rottweiler, but much more ominous, a hybrid creature from the depths of hell. Father Gandolfino heard more noises, and even though he was not scared by nature, a sudden cold shiver spiraled through his fragile spine. Regardless of the sudden streak of fear that took him by surprise, Father Gandolfini was no coward. He took his nightgown and an old oil lamp and almost ran outside. At that moment, the church doors opened with a thump, and something like a swirl of black sand entered the church, and the door slammed again. Gandolfini was scared now but decided to go in anyway. If we relate this to American horror movies, it could be called curiosity and stupidity, which would cost you your life in 99% of cases. Gandolfini opened the door and entered the church. What he saw inside froze the blood in his veins. Louis was standing at the altar, hanging upside down as a bat but in the form of a giant winged creature. His eyes burned yellow, and the church instantly smelled decay and death. Moths and cobwebs covered the walls and columns, and the usually beautiful vitrages were glowing now and depicting scenes from hell.

'Whatever you are, leave these holy premises now and return from wherever you came from,' screamed Gandolfini as loud as he could.

The response came from the creature in a clear and human voice of Father Louis, who Father Gandolfini knew too well:

'Beelzebub, Beelzebub, they shall not die; they shall rule the world of doom. Beelzebub, Beelzebub, thy time is here and near.'

'You think you can harm me, old man?' You will see the end of days sooner than you think, parish priest. The lord of darkness is near, and through me, he will fill your heart with wrath and death until it becomes black, and it brings you a free ticket to our dark realms, those that you fear so much!'

'Louis, is that you inside? The devil has taken you, but there is still time to get out, Louis. Can you hear me?, pleaded Father Gandolfini. He accused Louis of witchcraft and knew there was no hope, but he still tried. His fear was gone now. What remained was the will to save someone's soul. But Louis did not need salvation, not in this form anyway. He made an anti-clockwise turn in the air and flew to half of the central nave in the church. Gandolfini could smell the foul stench much more now. What appeared in the creature's hand was a vast cross taken from the altar table, the mensa. It was a medium-sized gold cross with a ruby in the crossing and fine handy work by an old artist from Venice. It was a heavy one. It looked like a toothpick in the creature's hand as it toyed with it. It was utterly black now with the ruby burning. The demonic winged monster looked like a ghost of dark and thick sand, constantly moving but with precise contours. Its small horns and burning yellow eyes gave it an ominous look of a disciple from hell. The only human thing about it was the whispering voice of Father Louis:

'Beelzebub, Beelzebub, they shall not die; they shall rule the world of doom. Beelzebub, Beelzebub, thy time is here and near.'

In this case, he had a bad premonition. 'Wake up, come back from the dream, son,' pleaded Gandolfini with the Louis soul creature. He soon started reciting the bible and even the parts used in exorcism, which he had performed several times before. Nothing was going to work as this didn't seem real, or was it all just a bad dream? It felt all too bloody real, as he soon found out.

'Time to die, old man.' No more talk. Now it is time for you to feel the pain inflicted upon your body and soul in my father's dark realm! He turned the cross upside down and swirled it with such velocity, power, and precision that Father Gandolfini had never seen before. And that was the last thing he saw, not even having time to pray for his soon-to-be-damned soul by creatures' standards. The last thing he said was:

'Damn you, may you burn in hell.'

'I am already there, you stupid old man,' replied the creature grinning.'

The cross went directly through Father Louis's old body and sliced his breasts like a knife through butter. He fell on his knees, blood gushing through his nostrils and mouth. He collapsed on the central nave's stone floor, grabbing the cross around his neck with his hand for the last time. Father Gandolfini was dead. The creature took his body with a swift move, the cross still inside it, and hurdled it with one swing towards the church apse, where it landed on the back wall and somehow clung in the air with the cross protruding out of, now late Father Gandolfini. Father Henry LeMuir woke up on the stone floor of the room he had in the monastery of his parish. He was shivering, and his clothes were in rags. He looked at his hands: they were covered in blood, but not his. He screamed with the sound of 1000 voices from hell.

Crimen et poena (Crime and punishment)

The local police soon found the body. The caretaker of the church grounds alerted the authorities when he found Father Lermo Petronius (Father Gandolfini in the vision)dead behind the mensa table with a golden cross protruding from his breast. There was an enormous pool of blood underneath him. He was the priest of one of the neighboring parishes where Father Henry LeMuir used to work. He was undoubtedly genuine and had nothing to do neither with the Middle Ages nor with accusing Father LeMuir of the disappearance and death of Sister Sylvia Freund. After forensics took care of the crime scene and the preliminary reports, the police brought Father LeMuir for questioning. They knew that he could hold a grudge against Father Petronius and that he was a prime suspect in the disappearance of sister Freund (as a couple saw him as a witness before the event with the sister) but were released due to lack of evidence. His fingerprints matched those found on the cross, and the DNA analysis pointed out that the skin underneath Father Petronius's nails was no other than Henry's.

The bloody robe was found in the cell full of Petronius's blood. Henry didn't have time to burn it in the monastery incinerator. When the police broke into his apartment in our skyscraper, they found an already three weeks decaying corpse of a six-month-old baby missing a heart nailed to the floor in the center of a Pentagram. It wasn't enjoyable. Later, the body matched the description of one missing baby girl from the town's northern suburb. For this carnage of evil to be complete, the police found the human remains of a poisoned young woman buried in a coffin, in a marked grave amid a forest 20 miles outside the city limits. The grave was marked with the words Beelzebub, Beelzebub. This piece of information came after Father LeMuir's confession. Well…none of this ever came out for, as the inside information said: the 'sake of public safety and unnecessary spread of fear.' But information leaked, as it always did, from one person who was high-ranked in homeland security (HM) and spilled his guts to our very own Luke Petrowsky, who was that time, one of the senior detectives (just before his retirement) and a good friend of Mr. X in the HM department. Surprisingly, nothing leaked to the press or was ever found out except that the three murders came out as solitary events by no means linked. What was linked to Henry LeMuir was the rape and death of Sister Freund, a crime of passion, and he was to receive a life sentence. But he was soon proclaimed insane due to all these unrevealed circumstances and events; I just portrayed above, his visions being the critical element. It seems he became an interesting case for the homeland security dept. And he was shipped to a very secluded military place (another leak that we came about from one of the high-ranking military officers living in our skyscraper). In this particular hospital, they kept an array of compelling cases, and God knows what kind of human experiments were performed. They didn't want to operate and remove his tumor but wanted to know more about his black visions. He was soon to die, but not from the tumor (which would have been the case some weeks or a month later). Instead, Father

Henry LeMuir was soon to leave that place and never to return…
yeah, you guessed right…another leak…

Chapter, verse, and Vision III

This vision was all too clear now. He was standing in front of the grand inquisition. It was all coming to an end now. He was standing in human form, the prince of darkness. His soul was eternal, so this petty gathering of clowns was just a mockery for him and the dark side. The inquisitorial procedure is quite detailed these days. Father Louis Gaufridi (Father Henry LeMuir as resurrected as Gaufridi in his vision of the Inquisition) knew that very well. But, in general terms, it gave a person suspected of heresy time to confess and absolve himself. Failing this, Father Gaufridi was accused and was thrown before this grand inquisition. They interrogated him for days and tried and tried, with the testimony of the so-called witnesses. Gaufridi was brought into court completely unshattered by the mental anguish and physical tortures performed on him in prison, especially the exquisite torments reserved for him—the strappado and squassation. He seemed almost dead after each torment, but when his captives came to his cell in the morning, he was regenerated – almost better than before. This was alone the proof the man was the devil himself, and the witnesses saw him change forms and chant on occasions:

'Beelzebub, Beelzebub, they shall not die; they shall rule the world of doom. Beelzebub, Beelzebub, thy time is here and near.'

He was always silent and knew that he could change forms and disappear from his cell, but this was supposed to happen – this would bring him to the ultimate goal – the eternal soul of the light and dark world. He will be more potent than ever when they burn him at the stake. At least, that is what he believed in his vision. He would let this go until he wanted, until the end when he decided it was time to end it. This day was going to be the one. Nicholas Eymeric, Papal Inquisitor of Aragon, was instrumental in relaxing torture regulations. In 1376 Eymeric wrote an inquisitorial manual called Directorium Inquisitorium. This work was a forerunner of the famous Malleus Maleficarum, a detailed legal and theological document dating from 1486 and regarded as the standard hand-book on witchcraft. Unfortunately, in Gaufridi's case, there wasn't to be any relaxation. The grand inquisitor Michaelis was glowing that day. He was going by the book, following Eymeric idea all too strictly that all forms of demon conjuration and Satanic pacts were to be condemned. Oh yes, thought Michaelis to himself, he would condemn them in the worst possible way. He made the final remark in a loud, banging voice:

'You, Father Louis Gaufridi, are condemned for practicing Dev-il-worship and witchcraft, making sacrifices, and singing satan-ic prayers.´ You are also condemned for summing Black Sabbath with witches and sorcerers and going against the church and our religious beliefs. God and the church condemn you of black magic and summoning devils, changing into satanic animal forms, tracing magical signs, placing children in the middle of devil circles, and seducing and sexually using women. We condemn you to eternal hell...'

Eternal Hell...that sounded good. The fool believed he was the vic-tor of a thousand battles with Satan, but little did he know thought Louis. The honest Satan was standing in front of him now and was going to be more assertive a 1000 times more after this, and then Michaelis and all these guys will burn in their unique ways, in the ways of the dark. Michaelis was determined to take down Gaufridi that day. Louis gave him that pleasure. The result was all too predictable. Standing in court in Aix that August afternoon in 1611, and although he could not at first have realized it, the priest's doom was sealed, but not the way his vision was pointing at. That afternoon he signed the confession and added a hundred things more that made the bodies of all present shiver in fear, even the great Michaelis. He wanted to burn this beast as soon as possible. Gaufridi was found guilty and condemned to suffer death by fire. He would be burned slowly over a pyre of bushes instead of logs to prolong his anguish. Michaelis and his tormentors gave him no last peace, nor Louis wanted any for that reason. Before taking him to the town square, they showed no mercy – he was tortured and beaten again and branded like a cow.

The vision continued more vividly now. After this final torture, the almost shredded body of the still living Father Louis Gaufridi (our Henry LeMuir)was dragged on a hurdle through the streets for five hours, escorted by archers. When Louis arrived at the place of execution, where all the city officials and the grand inquisition were waiting with Michaelis in the forefront, the priest was granted the unexpected mercy of strangulation before the fire was lit. Louis declined in an almost unearthly voice, the voice of a thousand deaths and nine circles of hell. His eyes began to narrow and light up, glowing fiercely in the daylight. The mass of people that came to see this spectacle and fulfill their craving for blood now started to move in fear. Seeing that the demon must burn fast, the executors returned the logs so Louis would burn quicker, thus escaping the ultimate horror of slowing burning. Suddenly, they wanted to get over this final act as soon as possible. His lifeless body was coming back to life again. The fire was lit, and the vast flames engulfed the logs and firewood in a second. First, flames were attacking Louis. He was screaming out now in a demonic voice:

'Beelzebub, Beelzebub, thy shall not die; they shall rule both worlds. Beelzebub, Beelzebub, thy time is here and near.'

'Beelzebub, Beelzebub, unite the light with the dark and bring the world of doom. Beelzebub, Beelzebub, thy time is here and near.'

Everyone was watching this scene in horror. Suddenly there was a black wind swirling around the execution square. Clouds began forming darkly and ominously. Louis watched it with ecstasy – he couldn't feel the pain coming from the flames anymore. The black wind turned and suddenly swirled with a howling sound toward the burning stake passing through Louis's body. With that, a final scream came from him, this one being the worse of all. His body became numb, the wind left, and the clouds dispersed before they assembled. Father Louis Gaufridi's body was then burned to ashes.

Lost souls

The last vision was not ending as Henry LeMuir expected it. Something very wrong was happening. He was not being transported to the Elysian Fields. He was hoping for where he could rule the light and dark together in a union of doom. He lost his body, which he didn't care much for, but his soul was redirected elsewhere. After the black wind took away his soul, everything became pitch black. At that moment, which he felt lasted for eons, but only lasted for a lighting, unearthly, heavenly moment, he felt excruciating pains. Finally, the pain was gone. As his visions were a mix of religions and different eschatologies, suddenly, two forms appeared before him, a blue and a black angel—Munkar and Nakir. Munkar spoke first:

'You damn soul, you are here, and you will be soon there to be nowhere'!

'Please, what is going on? Spoke Henry (Louis), where is my kingdom?'

'What kingdom you have forsaken soul? There is no kingdom for you, and there shall never be.

'I felt so much pain, spoke Henry, who was now just a lost soul spirit frozen momentarily in place. The angels brought him physical form and came to him even though there was nobody, burial, or similar.

Munkar spoke again:

'The Angel of death arrived when you were burning. It sat at your head and addressed your pitiful soul.'

Nakir added:

'As you were a wicked man, so was your soul. He has been instructed to lead you out and that you should depart to the wrath of God.'

'This cannot be true; it cannot be true, my visions…Louis started to say…

Both angels cut him off and said in union:

'You feared what awaits, so you screamed with the 1000 depths of hell. That is why you screamed in agony, and your soul wrapped in hair cloth has the stench of a decomposing carcass. Your soul sought refuge throughout your body, but the head angel of death had to extract your damned soul like the dragging of an iron skewer through moist wool, tearing your veins and ligaments.

'No, please, there must have been some mistake. I was going to see the light and dark together…I was going to….'

They cut him off.

'Enough! You have resurrected an evil soul and done evil and horrible deeds. You will have the pleasure of eternal hell'.

Henry LeMuir thought for a second that this was not so bad. At least he will be joined with the eternal darkness and with the grand master himself, Satan. But the final comment from the two angels took that away.

'We are not here to give you a trial and ask questions. You have been condemned before you thought you were resurrected. The verdict is final, and you have failed the test you never allowed yourself to have. God and his laws will punish you. Your soul will never have peace, and you will end up in between worlds, only feeling pain and anguish. You will be a soulless soul. The torments you will feel will be nothing compared to the wraths of hell. They will be million times worse. You will always get a new body to feel the pain and then lose it again. And you will never regain your soul. You will burn even when the end of days and the final judgment arrives. You will fail judgment day and die a second time and then again and again. The psychopomps will always guide you to the underworld as you will be alive, dead, and undead. Finally, we will be there every day and beat you to death until you rise and die again….'

With those last words, the angels left, and Henry didn't quite understand but was feeling the horror of things to come…the vision was a never-ending story now…Suddenly he was in a grave and had his body back…the torments began…suddenly the door opened in the tomb, and Henry was suspended with cries and screams of anguish into the heat and smoke of the inferno…

Henry knew that according to Chapter 125 of the Egyptian Book of the Dead, those who failed the judgment would 'die a second time' and be cast outside the ordered cosmos. But this could not be happening. The visions have brought him to eternal hell…

He saw all of them in his vision, as listed in Enoch 1:20: Uriel, Raphael, Raguel, Michael, Sariel, Gabriel, and Remiel – the arch-angels. They were all watching him. Suddenly only four were left, like in the Books of Enoch: Michael, Uriel, Raphael, and Gabriel. Henry thought this could be his salvation, but soon they all disap-peared except Gabriel, the angel of heavenly revelation. He came close to Henry and said:

'You are forever damned, and your soul will be taken over and over again.'

'No, please, screamed Henry….' As Gabriel disappeared, another fallen angel, Azazel, passed by and swished through Henry's virtual body and soul. Henry screamed in agony as the evil demon spirit ripped through him…

The angel of death, 'Izra'il, appeared out of nowhere and without warning. It carried 4,000 wings, and as many eyes and tongues formed its body as living beings. He was a horrible sight for Henry. He was standing with one foot in the seventh heaven and the other on the razor-sharp bridge that divides paradise and hell.

'I can see your name circled in darkness, and I can see that you are damned. Soon I will come for your soul and rip it out of your body, and then it will be returned for something or someone else to take it away. Henry screamed yet again, a scream of many more to come…a scream of endless screams…

Henry was standing in a barren field with only traces of black grass underneath his bare feet. There was no sky or land. Somehow it seemed that he was in an in-between world. The Shaman, or the spirit who knows and can journey at will to heaven or hell, appeared from nowhere. It took the shape of a common raven (Corvus Corax), not one, but thousands and thousands of blackbirds. In their magical flight, they were supposed to guide and escort Henry's undead soul back to the underworld. These psychopomps, or the soul conductors, were instead a symbol of dark prophecy for Henry—of death, devastation, and eternal pain. They took him by the thousand winds, and they swarmed him. The attack was so violent. During the flight, they guided him to the underworld. They savagely chopped him during the endless trip, like Zeus had his vengeance on Prometheus and had him chained and sent an eagle to eat his immortal liver, which constantly replenished itself. So was Henry's soulless body replenishing itself after thousands of bites…

The creature was laughing at him. It was a bulky older man with massive hands. His head was something like a face from Stephen King's horror tales. His skin seemed to be decaying by the minute and then renewing itself. He was carrying Henry on his shoulders through a pitch-black tunnel descending at least 70 degrees downwards. There seemed to be no end to this tunnel.

'Where are you taking me? Let me down', shouted Henry.

The giant just looked at him with his vast and demonic eyes.

'You will pay the ferryman, you will you know. Nobody goes free over the river…that wouldn't be good for business.

When he spoke those words, the stench from his mouth burned Henry's insides like sulfuric acid. He cried in anguish again. Finally, they arrived from the tunnel to the banks of what seemed like a river. Its water was black. The creature dumped Henry and left. At least the pain was gone. Out of nowhere, a silhouette appeared. It looked like a ferry with a ferryman steering it. It could take only one passenger. In the next moment, he was on the ferry or what seemed to look more like a wooden dingy. The black water was boiling underneath him, and he could see arms, legs, eyes, and other human remains floating. He was on river Styx, and the ferryman was not Charon. It was a dead demon in a black robe and a hood. He could see the glowing reddish eyes underneath the hood and the skeleton hands maneuvering the ferry. His duty was to ferry over those poor souls of the deceased who had received the burial rites. He should have received the coin in the corpse's mouth for payment. At least, that was what Henry thought; he might be on his way to hell. At least there was a chance he would get there. A smile appeared on his soulless face, frozen instantly as TV dinners usually are. Suddenly Charon spoke in a whisper:

'You poor soul, you thought you were going somewhere, going places, ha? No, my friend, you are not going anywhere.

'But you got pain, your gold coin…said Henry in a terrified voice.

'The coin is to be placed in the dead person's corpse, and I don't see any corpse in front of me…replied Charon.'

'But there is; look at it!' Henry was touching his body and pleading with Charon, who was blind.

'You might think you see a corpse or body, but I only see a soulless soul which has to be returned to limbo.'

With that said, Charon took out a big silver hammer underneath his robe and smashed it into Henry with the might of Hercules. Henry was thrown into the depths of the black river and instantly dissolved by acid water, creatures, demons, and the living dead underneath.

'Next time, die properly so you might get somewhere.' With that said, Charon left, leaving Henry to dissolve…Henry screamed in horrific pain again, a pain of many more to come…a pain of endless pains…the vision was a constant one…he couldn't wake from this endless dream anymore…Henry LeMuir was doomed, and he knew it.

Salvation

Father Henry LeMuir didn't escape the military compound. He went completely insane. His last days were spent in fear and horror, followed by screams that no sedative could stop. Somehow he wanted to end his life in torment and found a way to light himself up…the story was that he hurdled himself from the hospital rooftop. He was already burning from the gasoline that his body was soaked with. He fell and broke his spine, and the story went that his head was turned backward 180 degrees after the fall. The face had such horror that no medieval sculptor could ever portray…… yeah, you guessed right…another leak… How all of this happened, nobody knew.

21

A Flyer
with (no) Desire

Many individuals who lost their lives due to attempted and successful suicide must have asked themselves this relatively simple question: Is life's meaning defined by its duration? Some others might have thought about the hopelessness of the future, failures of the past, and emptiness of the present. Then some didn't think about the philosophy of life and death so much but rather about when and how to kill themselves. They could have acted rationally due to guilt, shame, economic disaster, etc. They were making a very sound and rational decision, at least in their minds. And yes, there is always that biggest bunch of poor bastards that do not overthink or instead have an open or blocked cerebral exchange. For those poor souls, suicide is a decision, like buying a cone of ice cream on a hot summer day for most of us. Don't overthink, go ahead and do it, is their motto. Ok...Ok...I know things are not as simple as portrayed above.

Science does not look at that in such a simplified street life manner. Some theories have been developed to explain the causes of suicide, from sociology, psychology, psychiatry, biology, etc. Different studies have claimed that among suicides, about three times the rate of mental disorders as people with non-suicidal natural deaths, something in the ratio of 77% vs. 25%. Most theories and studies point at mental disorders (schizophrenia, psychosis, etc.), alcoholism, alienation, residence in big cities, other physical illnesses, childlessness, out of passion, economic depths, etc., as the leading causes of suicides. But even if averting suicidal acts is much better today (maybe) than 50 years ago, no single theory, method, or approach can completely stop those individuals from wanting to end their lives prematurely. There will always be those men and women who have already decided it is better to be dead than continue living as they are. Something like a song from Rod Stewart: "Better of Dead"...

Whatever the reason for suicides, this act of voluntarily or intentionally taking one's own life is inevitably an ongoing process with no end. I guess I am probably trying to make some explanation or justification or simply introducing the suicides that happened in our neighborhood. And there have been a couple of them, some 8 to be exact, in those ten years. Oh yes, the name of the 'game' was: suicide. The place: the skyscraper(s), and how this was performed: jumping. But that was not the weirdest thing associated with these suicides; some loony aspects went along with these fatal acts of flying, although they all fell under various explanations of why people commit suicide.

***

They awoke relatively late that Saturday morning, at 10:00 AM. The plan was that the whole family would go to the Grandparent's place, a beautiful red house in the mountains near a lake, some 30 miles driving from the city. The kids ran to the bathroom, and the wife did the breakfast chores. One could already smell the fresh fried eggs and bacon penetrating slowly, but indeed through the apartment. Gerome Supilo, the head of the family, stayed in bed.

'Honey, aren't you getting up for breakfast?' asked Natalie, his wife.

'No, I think I will stay put here.' He was lying in bed, sheets covered up to his arms, and had a distant, worried, and sad but very determined look on his face.

'So you want to skip breakfast? You look a bit tired, dear.

'I won't just skip breakfast, but I will skip the Grands' trip altogether.' He liked calling Natalie's parents Grands. The kids did that, so he accepted it as a cool thing. He liked those two, and they liked him back. There were never any tensions.

'Oh, no, you can't; you promised to go. They will be so disappointed.

'I think I am coming down with flu, and I must miss this to return to work on Monday.' What he wanted to say but could not be that he was coming down, but not with the flu, that he would miss a lot more than Grands', and that there won't be any work on Monday.

'Oh, the kids will be so disappointed, you know...' she didn't finish off as Gerome cut her off gently:

'Please, Natalie, it is better this way. This is for the better. Let's not argue, dear, as I know myself best. It sure wasn't for them or him, but he was determined.

Between 10 and 12, Mike and Cindy were disappointed but not to the point of disaster or hysterical crying. It was decided that Mom was driving them and that they would stay until early Sunday, not late, as Dad was coming down with flu. It was a well-organized family, Gerome, a banker, and Natalie, a real-estate lawyer. Everything functioned as a Swiss watch but with room for necessary improvisation. They lived in the 3rd skyscraper, where we had direct visual contact. That skyscraper was also housed on the ground level of the Fourth Private Inter-Bank, which would file for bankruptcy on Monday. Gerome was its 3rd president. They said goodbyes, and you could see the kids glowing with anticipation of rediscovering mountain wildlife and running on a huge 3-acre estate with a beautiful stream. Gerome looked at them: two beautiful kids, both going after their mother, who was the epitome of beauty with her long blonde hair, slender body, and refined, almost Renaissance face. In her early 40's, she could still outmatch any younger famous Hollywood actress. It will be difficult to leave them, but there is no other way. The disgrace to the family was too big, and by his act, he hoped to redirect everything in one channel. His last hope was that the channel would drain soon after that, and his family could continue living normally. But nothing would be normal after this, would it be? Nobody analyzed Gerome's face that much, not even Natalie. How could she know? She thought he was sick. She had no idea about the problems in the bank. All hell was going to break loose on Monday. He managed to freeze things until then. But then the shit would hit the fan, and the press would have a field day. He was responsible, oh yes. He should have never made a pact with the devil, a pact with the local mobsters. He couldn't believe it had gone on for two years. He had no choice. They said they would harm his family, take away his kids, and particularly have fun with his pretty wife. Running away was out of the question. If he went to the authorities, the same would happen. But they also gave him his large cut for this. He didn't want to have anything with the money, but it still piled in his account. Money laundry went through his bank, and God knows what kind of other dirty deeds. The IRS, the local Feds, and all kinds of authorities were after them. The mob connection would come out unless he did something. He was an extremely skillful banker who managed to cover all mob connections, redirecting all of it – or as he thought of it – to him. The authorities would have difficulty believing this, but the mob would be protected. He had to save his family. The local mob, which had a code of honor and kept its word, would not touch his family. The money intended for him would be directed to his wife on a far-eastern offshore account. When things cooled off, his wife would find out about the account. He hoped he would have moved out of the city and country for good after the soon-coming events. But he had to pay the price for all that: saving the family and protecting the mob – he had to kill himself, a suicide, to make things look 100% genuine. If not, the mob would liquidate him and his family. So this was going to be a fatal, involuntary suicide. So, how his family, and especially his wife, could know? He kept it secret and would die with it, though things would come out. He was leaving a suicide letter for the public and authorities, which his wife would find. He had already sent the other one for his wife and kids to a trusted friend who would give it to them after six months. The bank would collapse; with all that dirty money and other dubious investments frozen on Monday, they would probably lose all. Fortunately, Natalie had wealthy parents who would take care of her until she received the letter with the explanation and the hint of security for the future. There would be the account number inside. Just to be sure, she would get another letter after one year with the same information. He took care of that. They would be secure for life, and their children would have a good education. Maybe Natalie would remarry, maybe not. He couldn't worry much about that. He would miss and see the kids grow, but at least they had a future. He had none. Good thing his folks were dead, so they couldn't suffer the pain and shame that was about to come. It was time to get ready. The story would probably break out in the evening news, more things to come on Sunday, and then the Big Bang on Monday. The Dan Rather look-alike would probably bring the news. Too bad he wasn't going to be there to see it. To see one's death. That would be cool. A cold smile passed over his stiff lips for a second. It was soon extinguished by the task ahead and a non-existent future.

He remembered what his dad once said: remember the past, but don't collect it, be aware of the future but don't expect it, son. That was about what he left him in his inheritance. He was an alcoholic and died at 45 from the most common type of cirrhosis, Laënnec's cirrhosis. In Dad's case, the primary cause was excessive and chronic alcohol consumption, bottles and bottles. His mom soon followed from a weak heart. He would never forget that gentle creature. His uncle raised him and made him what he is today. He accomplished a lot, but if he were alive now, he wouldn't be very proud of what Gerome was about to do. Maybe his dad was right: he just believed in the present, and the present was shaped like a bottle. There was neither past nor future for him. His letter was written, sealed, and left on the Petrof piano in the living room. He looked at the picture of Natalie and the kids again and started crying like a child. What was he about to do? Being a very rational man, he dispersed those 'irrational' thoughts very soon, cleaned himself up, showered, dressed up in his best suit, looked at the mirror for the last time, and walked out on the balcony of their 17th-floor apartment.

Dragizha Sergeyevich was looking from her 17th-floor apartment in our skyscraper straight at Gerome's building. She was completely drunk. At age 78, she didn't give too much piss about that. Life sucked anyway, and soon; she would be in the other world. Until then, alcohol was the best option. At age 78, she still had impaired vision, which could damage not even the Georgian brandy she was drinking. She saw a guy standing at the railing. She must wait for that lovely gentleman with white wings to see her again.

'Heck, what the hell is that guy doing in a suit on the balcony railing? It looks like he is waiting for a cab. But there are no cabs on the 17th floor'. She laughed wildly and took another big sip from the brandy bottle. After a moment or two, the guy in the black suit fell with a crash into the bank.

'Holy shit, doesn't he know banks are closed on Saturday? Some people can't wait for their cash withdrawals. Ha, ha, ha'. She looked once more and closed the window. The lovely winged gentlemen didn't arrive today. Maybe tomorrow…She was in no hurry…

Gerome Supilo looked down on the Fourth Private Inter-Bank. What irony! He would jump on his bank. He climbed the railing with the help of their dining table chair. It was a long jump. Gerome Supilo felt afraid for the first time now. He hesitated for a moment or two, so his left leg slipped a bit, and he didn't jump as he intended to. The plan was to direct toward the flat roof, not the glass ceiling roof window. He still cared for his bank and didn't want to mess it up. He fell unprepared, and a natural reaction came from him: he screamed in horror. He fell like a ton of bricks, breaking the ceiling glass panel window into a thousand pieces. Gerome fell directly into the main room, hitting the glass teller's window with his head. His head was severely cut, and he broke every bone. He died instantly, not knowing what hit him.

Natalie Supilo tried calling her husband in the apartment many times, but there was no reply. She was worried. Her parents turned on the Local News at Noon. The volume was at the highest level as both had the typical old timers' hearing loss. The first headline spoke about a suicide of a prominent banker who jumped from his apartment balcony on the 17th floor of…When she heard the news, she ran into the room. She screamed and fainted instantly. She knew when she realized it was their building and Gerome's bank.

***

Former Army Captain Ahmad Baba woke up a very determined man on that humid Monday morning. He was about to kill as many people as possible. Baba was honorably discharged from the military for showing excessive brutality over his subordinates and being involved in an extraordinary but unclear sexual relationship with the brigadier general. His ass became grass, and the army got rid of him. To make things worse, his wife left him after the incident and the brutal beatings. She couldn't take anymore. She disappeared without a trace one morning from their 11th-floor 2-bedroom apartment, taking their five-year-old daughter with her. Life just turned its back on Captain Baba, and he was left alone with only his defragmented thoughts as a sole companion. The wife made sure she was never to be found.

On the other hand, he thought he would find her and then kill her. But that had to wait. He wanted revenge first. In his somehow delusional mind, military action was the solution. If he was diagnosed correctly, God knows what kind of mental problems the shrinks would find. Nobody knew what he wanted to accomplish afterward, but it was hard to get into his mind then. He was blinded by rage, hate, disillusion, revenge, retribution, and injustice, all blocking the positive and rational thoughts that might have been flowing in his brain. This river of darkness just extinguished any light left in him.

When he climbed to the roof of our skyscraper at exactly 7:30 AM, he surely wasn't thinking of one Charles Whitman, the famous Texas Skyscraper sniper in Austin. Namely, Charles managed for incredible 96 minutes to shoot and kill 15 people and wound 31 before a police officer killed him. Public space was considered a haven until then, but that all changed soon. All kinds of acts, from lunacy to terrorism, occupy our daily lives and spaces. Ahmad Baba would add more on the subject on that Monday. Ahmed made no special preparations for this act as Charles did. He didn't give a rat's ass about food. He could survive without food for days. He only brought up on the roof was 2 gallons of water and enough ammunition to kill at least 1000 people. He stole everything from his base. As far as the weapons are concerned, he was very meticulous: an AK-47 assault rifle (the AKM version) with tons of 7.62-millimeter ammunition, five grenades, a Russian shoulder rocket launcher, the same type as the famous M9A1 'bazooka,' his handgun – a Sig Sauer P228 + the most important thing: his 22mmm semiautomatic hunting rifle with a scope, his pride, and joy. He was after serious blood. The reason for having a bazooka was to shoot against possible helicopters or any large group of uniformed men. I don't think he had any idea what the grenades were for or why he even had an assault rifle with enough ammunition to deplete a whole village of its human population.

The roof of the skyscraper was flat and done as most of the sky-scrapers were with necessary construction and materials. There were two other one-story high block-shaped constructions on top. One was the ending of the elevator and staircase shafts, and the other was connected to it – some electrical and heating storage. Below that was the story with the storage cells each apartment from the 10th floor and upwards had. The roof had a protecting ledge or semi-high molding. The roof was a popular place for pigeons to shit and mate and for occasional teenagers to smoke if they knew the way around the roof hatch lock. There were also a couple of sub-stantial strength roof antennas there. Ahmad Baba Bobby trapped the hatch with two grenades. Three, he left for later. Kill them all and let God sort them out was his favorite motto. His wife was ap-palled when he used the term, but with further protests, she could only receive a beating. There wasn't much discussion with Baba. Cook, clean, take care of the child, don't talk to men, and be ready for physical services to your husband was Baba's philosophy. Incred-ibly, she endured that long with the guy, but unfortunately, so many women do. As long as women are willing to take that, there will constantly be beating husbands around. Baba was such a husband.

He couldn't predict what might happen that morning or how long he would endure up there. Indeed, he had no plan for escape, nor wanted to run away. It seems he just wanted to start and end things up there. Our skyscraper remembered for a long time what hap-pened in the following moments. We had a 'night to remember with Al Durant's battle zone apartment,' and now a 'day to forget' came with this incident. People were starting to go to work at dif-ferent shifts, so Baba had a lot of innocent and unwillingly potential customers. He knew he had to shoot well to get people's attention. He strapped the three remaining grenades around his waist, pushed his handgun into the holster, and put the assault rifle and bazooka on the side. First, he wanted to make some noise, so he took the Russian version of the rocket-propelled launcher. This was developed primarily for attacking tanks and fortified positions at short range. He also planned to turn this against a chopper if such came and was in direct line with him. He loaded, adjusted, and aimed the launcher toward the same roof blocks on the adjacent skyscraper. It launched a 3.5-pound rocket. The rocket carried 8 ounces of potent explosive that could penetrate as much as 5 inches of armor plate. There was no need for that. The blast almost destroyed the service building on the other skyscraper rooftop. The blast was so hard and loud that it must have been heard through half of the city. Baba was happy. He quickly turned to his AKM rifle and started shooting wildly across the windows, trees, parked cars, moving trams, and innocent bystanders. Fortunately, nobody got poorly hurt except three people that suffered minor wounds. That was unbelievable as the AKM magazine, which holds 30 rounds and a cyclic firing rate of 600 rounds per minute, was empty. Chaos erupted on the streets and in the other two skyscrapers. Screams were heard and shouts. Baba was glowing. Now they will listen, and now they will come. He gave them some 15 minutes. By then, he could hear police, fire brigade, and ambulance sirens. He didn't hide at all behind the ledge or the service structures. He walked proudly, smoked his Camels, and wore his military assault uniform. He had his green baseball cap turned the other way around, as the SWAT guys do. There was always a Camel showed behind his right ear, a habit he couldn't get rid of. A well-fit man with a typical military stance, he was a force to be reckoned with. People from the other skyscraper were watching him now, hidden from gun sight. Now he got ready to kill people, or so he thought. He took his 22mm semiautomatic rifle with the scope and aimed over the ledge toward a guy crossing the street, who was still oblivious to the things happening in the aerial zones. He aimed and went for the head. When he clicked the trigger, something happened to the gun, and the whole thing exploded in his face, leaving him bloody and scarred, temporarily blind in the left eye. He would lose the right one as it was soon becoming jelly. He shouted and screamed in pain and agony. Somehow in all of this confusion, he thought he was in combat, already in the deranged state he was, and started to climb over the ledge, thinking it was a bunker hill he was going over. Someone heard him scream: 'Shoot 'em All, Shoot 'em All.' I don't know if that is true, but it made sense when he was questioned. Instead of rolling over a mound, wall, or whatever he thought it was, he was in thin air. The fall was fast and straight. He fell directly on the eternal construction site, a few feet from the massive pile of brick where rats loved to reside and some feet from the remains of an abandoned construction site yellow crane. One grenade fell during the flight and didn't explode. The other did severe damage to him when he fell. Somehow they exploded, or he triggered them in some final suicidal attempt. Whatever it was, he was everywhere. The explosion also made a hole where he fell. Police and ambulance were shortly there.

SWAT made sure the roof was not booby-trapped. They soon disarmed the grenades holding the rooftop latch and secured the rooftop. Rest is history, as they say. Malcolm Pace, the first detective to arrive at the scene ensured the CSI (Crime Scene Investigation) folks had space. There were soon going to match the remains with those of one Ahmad Baba. The weaponry would find its trace too. Malcolm Pace had gloves on too. A couple of feet from Ahmad Baba's shattered and splattered body, Malcolm saw a human ear and a small piece of the lobe. He was disgusted. It looked to have fresh blood, and skin remained connecting it to the rest of the head. The funny thing was that there was a cigar still attached to it. Malcolm came close, and when nobody looked, he took the cigar from the ear. It was a Camel, his favorite. Although he quit smoking, all these fragmented pieces of this guy's body made him nervous. He showed it into his mouth, lighted it, and took the first smoke. He felt better. Damn, that was a fine cigar.

***

Dragizha Sergeyevich was an incurable alcoholic. She was always red in the face, and her nose seemed like the marina for every plague known to men. A flowery scarf covered her fast-balding head, and she was somewhat overweight from all the food and alcohol consumption, where the alcohol always won 5 to 1. She was too old to go to any rehab or treatment clinic. Besides, she didn't want to. So her son didn't push too much. At times he took a sip or two together with her. What the heck, he thought, if she lost her husband and she was already old, what harm could alcohol do? Well, in her case, it did. Her dosages were incredible, even for the most seasoned alcoholic. If the producers of the Georgian Cognac Ahtamar knew about her, they would have used her in their campaigns. But unnatural and over-human consumption of alcoholic beverages can bring you into trouble. After some time, after passing through miles and miles of intoxication and hangovers, Dragizha Sergeyevich ended in the worst extreme of alcohol withdrawal syndrome: delirium tremens. She somehow survived the first one, by some miracle and the treatment received. Her son got her into the hospital in the end. But it was a different story when she fell into the second one. That was about the time she started seeing the winged gentleman. He always came in the shape of some angelic figure, looking like her husband. He never said much; he just hung there in the air outside her window. She knew that he would call her to come with him and she would come. He was genuine, all right. In her eyes, it was a sign from the heavens of new and exciting things to come. She usually talked to him for hours, but he didn't respond. This Delirium tremens was a terrible one. She was trembling, and her brain was in a complete mental cloud, disorientation, and hallucination. She was hallucinating visually and through auditory. This lasted for several days. In these cases, doctors usually report fatality rates ranging from 1 to 20 percent. She also developed an acute alcoholic hallucinosis that wasn't going away. One fine afternoon she heard the flapping of the wings of her familiar friend. He was waiting for her outside her window. She was in horrible, hallucinating shape. Dragizha opened the window and greeted her friend.

'Hello, my winged friend. How are you?' There was no reply, and he was flapping his wings, all dressed in white with hands on his sides. She rambled for a while until suddenly the winged man said:

'Dragizha Sergeyevich, your time has come. Come with me and join your husband Fodor in gardens of peace and delight'.

She was stunned. He spoke, and he mentioned Fodor.

'I knew you would take me to my loving Fodor.' Oh, thank you, thank you. I need to pack for the trip now….'

'No luggage, Dragizha, you won't need any luggage where we go. Just come with me out the window, and we will fly away. I will show you the road….'

'But I can't fly, she added in some rare shriek moment of clarity.

'You can, Dragizha Sergeyevich, you can. Just trust me. Walk out now and join Fodor; join him very soon.'

The winged gentleman seemed very respectable, and she wanted to leave anyway. Probably she would get wings too. Without hesitation, she climbed through the open window and just jumped.

'Fodor, here I come.' She didn't get any wings, as you might have suspected, but she did fly, for a while at least. Her body crashed at full speed into the construction site. Dragizha Sergeyevich ended up in the cabin of the abandoned construction crane. She was dead, of course. If she joined, Fedor is a difficult question. The winged gentleman was nowhere to be found.

I was playing Poker with Danny Slowitz and Alan Meehan at my place on the 16th floor. Dragizha Sergeyevich lived just one story above me. We opened our kitchen dining room window and heard Dragizha Sergeyevich talk to herself. She is talking to some guy with wings. We didn't listen anymore as it was becoming like a broken record. She was losing her mind.

'Did you see that? Shouted Alan in his familiar sharp voice.

'See what, brother Meehan? Responded Danny in an absent manner of a seasoned amateur poker player.

'Yeah, I saw something too,' I added.

'Someone must be throwing garbage again, said Danny, not moving his eyes from the cards he held so dearly in his hand.

'Let's see; it could be that old hag Dragizha throwing bottles and other leftovers. She is half crazy anyway.

'She is a notorious alcoholic, I added.

'My dad says that alcohol brings loony tunes to you too, and for free.
We laughed together at Danny's comment.

'Let's see, guys, I said.

We went to the balcony and leaned over, scanning the construction
site for new bags of trash or other remains. And we did spot remains; Alan was the first.

'Hey, you guys, look at that construction crane!´

Alan took my binoculars and looked down. Inside the driver's cabin
was a body in a fetal position, the intact part of the crane with a
glass window still standing (at least a couple of seconds before). It
seemed to fit nicely inside the driver's seat.

'What do you see, Alan? Danny and I yelled in one voice.

Alan was silent for a moment.

'It's Dragizha Sergeyevich. She looks dead!

And guess what: she is smiling!

***

He thought he could fly. So do we all, in our dreams. But for Mikael
Slowitz flying was an apparent reality. He was standing on the balcony ledge of his 13th-floor apartment in the adjacent skyscraper.
He had acute psychosis and was also diagnosed as schizophrenic.
That day he probably thought he was Icarus, who would not perish
by flying too near the Sun with his waxen wings. The difference
was that he had no wings and that he would perish. He was in his
pajamas and was flapping wildly with his arms. Again the landing

ground was the construction site. There was no plan from his side at where he should land. He just thought he could fly.

What was different here was that he attempted this at nighttime. He was the 1st and last suicide night flyer. He jumped like a butterfly swimmer attempting to break the world record. The only thing Mikael broke was his complete body. He landed like a ton of bricks on the rat's brick pile. He died. The rat community didn't take long to smell blood and attack. Nobody knew he was gone for hours, as it was nighttime, until his wife came some hours later and found him missing. They found him later on the brick pile, half eaten by our neighborhood rodents. Dasha Makarov, thrown from the balcony in the latest incident, landed on concrete and died but did avoid the rats. My friend Danny Slowitz's dad, Ivar Slowitz, a pathologist MD whose cousin just took his life, told a couple of people that he met outside the building who just expressed condolences on the tragic death of his relative:

'For heaven's sake, when will these people stop jumping from our skyscrapers? Can't they find some other place to do it from? I have to analyze and put them together again for the damn reports. What a f**king mess they leave after these jumps, frigging assholes!'…

***

22

Don't Piss on my Skirt!

I saw them from the corner of my eye. They were approximately the same size, one slightly taller than the other. The taller guy wore a black leather jacket with some cheap replica silver chains hanging from his shoulders and had the typical hard rock, heavy metal hair of the 80s. His eyes didn't give anything out, just that he was alert. The other one was in a Marlboro man outfit, except for the hat. He had the typical Marlboro man mustache and seasoned face. He wore a shirt underneath that said: 'I kill chickens for fun.' I believe he did. He also had a mean look about him. Two gigantic fellows that seemed displaced from some sleazy late-night joint. Somehow these bouncer-type characters were beamed on the entry stairs of our skyscraper. They went inside the building. It's true that all kinds of people pass by and visit folks in our skyscraper, but these two somehow didn't click at all. There were a lot of us youngsters and teenagers playing outside. I kicked a ball with Boris Duchovny, Anthoine Scott, Danny Slowitz, and Pepé. We were killing some time on that autumn Saturday afternoon. After five to six minutes, the two guys emerged from the skyscraper again. It seemed a mighty short visit wherever they were. They took their place outside the entrance doors and waited. Whoever they were looking for was not home. My other friends also saw the characters. We continued kicking the ball. After a while, Al Durant emerged from the direction of the adjacent skyscraper. He was strolling towards the skyscraper. He must have seen the guys but made no reaction whatsoever. On the other hand, they became agitated and suddenly started walking in his direction, passing us by. I could hear Marlboro man whisper to the complex rock character: 'That must be the motherf**ker....'

*

Al Durant was free from prison after the incident in our building some years back. He did his time together with his pal Pappa Joe. They never returned to challenging crime activity as they had before. The death of their pals, Mick, Frazier, and Ron, must have taught them a lesson. Prison indeed had its contribution too in their 'reformation.' But as someone said: 'Once a criminal, always a criminal,' was partly true in their case. It was some small stuff now, petty things that could pass by from the hand of the law.

Pappa Joe was there to assist if needed. Mainly these small-time scams consisted of ripping people off. My favorite was the 'temporary' renting of Al Durant's one-room apartment. I remember when Al rented his apartment to 4 Egyptian exchange students. They had fast cash, and he promised the place for six months. He took an advance in US dollars, no questions asked. They were happy to find a place on such short notice, and squeezing into that tiny apartment didn't bother them. After only a few days, Al returned with Pappa Joe and some other shady character and told them to get out, that the rent was terminated. Of course, they wanted their money back, but as this was a 'gentleman's agreement,' there weren't any papers signed. The explanation was that foreigners were not allowed to rent in our district, which was complete hogwash. When one of them protested, Al and his other pal beat the shit out of him. Others watched in horror as Pappa Joe had a small shotgun aimed at them that he kept in his hollow wooden leg. They beat the guy half to death and threatened others they would kill all of them if they went to the authorities. They never did; we know they left the city and the country altogether. And there were other times when Al let the tenants live peacefully, depending on the rent duration. He would let them be if it was a shorter period or Al couldn't beat up the new settlers. He usually took up residence with Pappa Joe in his small and stinky place in the old part of the city or lived in the sublevel of our skyscraper where tenants up to the 10th floor had their storage cells. Rarely any of them ventured often their. These spaces were places you visit only when you move in and want to get rid of stuff you can live without if it gets stolen. And most of it does. Some stuff got stolen by organized robbers, some by petty criminals, and some by our law-abiding and decent neighbors. To get around the locks was child play. The president of our tenant association, Arno Stockhouse, didn't look favorably at Al using this space and making a second apartment. But he knew better than to get into trouble with Al. As long as Al was there, he knew the robberies would cease, although there was not much to take away, and he only slept there. After leaving prison, Al devoted himself even more to his favorite leisure activity – drinking. He was mostly drunk when he ventured into the basement for the night's rest. They usually rented the place several times a year and hoped that 50% of those tenants could be ripped off. They usually knew how, when, and most importantly, who to rip off. In the case of the girl in the red skirt, Anita made a massive judgment error, which Al had to pay dearly for.

Anita and her roommate were hoping for a break in the apartment search, and they got it. They found Al's advert in the paper:

A one-room apartment for rent: Students that can pay beforehand are preferred. All utilities are included except the phone. 3rd floor with a view. Room, kitchen, bathroom, balcony, and closet. 15min from the city center by tram. Contact Bella.

Then the advert gave the telephone number, address and price, which was a bit high but acceptable. There was the prospect of the balcony and a view. What also gave security to the girls was the mention of a woman's name, Bella. That meant no sleazy, horny, and unpleasant gentlemen. As always put his dame Bella up when he needed to rent the flat. She could be nasty, too, if needed. The girls grabbed the opportunity and made contact with Bella. They were disappointed with her as she wasn't the Queen of perfection and cleanliness. So wasn't the apartment either, but Anita knew she could fix this place with her friend Maria in no time. Anita and Maria were best friends from the same village. They grew up together, went to the same school, and now the same university. They planned to get jobs close to each other, get married, and have children at about the same time. They were rather good-looking, Anita Blonde and her friend a brunette. Both wore nice clothes, especially Anita. Everyone remembers the lovely red skirt that she often wore, which reflected the shape of her body so nicely. The girls attempted to bargain, but Bella wouldn't budge, and money was given for an entire year ahead. It was no problem for Anita. Her father owned a butcher shop outside the city's biggest village and would not spare a dime when his precious daughter was in question. He wanted to buy her a flat, but she insisted on building a life independently. The compromise was that he would pay a year's rent for whichever apartment she found. After that, she would have some part-time job that could cover the apartment, and as a student, she should be able to stand on her own two feet. Her father knew he would buy her an apartment after the first year anyway. He would also give her the bank account number he had just opened for her. Why not, he thought? He was the wealthiest man in the village and could afford it. He also owned the most prominent restaurant and bar in the village. Anita would have none of that, at least not for now. She wanted to try it on her own. And this apartment was the first attempt. She told him about it, and he was a bit suspicious on hearing that the rent was paid for an entire year ahead. But after a while, he let it go. Both girls were pleased. They soon moved in. Bella was going to be the contact person for her husband, Al. The girls didn't have many suspicions as this seemed an exemplary married couple, though Bella was odd. Al and Bella were not married, of course. Two weeks passed, and nothing happened. Al was with his pal Pappa Joe getting drunk every night. Some days he went home, not to the apartment but to the cellar. He would drop down in front of the cells and fall asleep. When he was less drunk, he would pull out a mobile bed from one of the cells. There were all kinds of things you could find there. Even rats! Al had no problem with our rodents. They avoided him at any cost, as he smelled worse than any of them. He was probably potentially poisonous with all that alcohol in his blood. The rats tried to attack but never in an organized manner, as only one or two ventured into the galleys below. They kept to their hunting grounds in the construction site, the abandoned tunnel, and some other passages underneath our skyscraper and the sewer system. Somehow they were not interested in the cellar, not even when Al Durant was snoring. He was a bit lucky. Our rat colony had a whole hierarchical system and chain of command. All kinds of gray, black, and Norwegian rats were around with varying sizes and shapes. The worse was the giant rodents of 30cm and up. We concluded that the most prominent and probable leader was the harsh and mean Norwegian dream mutant rat. He was ca 4ocm long, with a huge tail, eyes, and teeth from hell. There were a couple of similar ones, a bit smaller. They were probably his first officers. These guys never went to the cellars. It's the smaller ones that did. But on one occasion, one medium-sized gray and hungry rat did. He found the snoring Al on the ground barefooted. Before Al woke up and managed to murder this rat with a sledgehammer, the gray rodent ate up Al's left leg toe. He was so drunk that he didn't feel anything until it started to hurt through the 'alcohol anesthesia' he was under. After that, he became more careful, so he told Pappa Joe. He was tired of Pappa Joe's place and the wet and dark cellar. It was time to evict the girls.

Al took Pappa Joe with him that Monday morning, three weeks after the girls settled the rent, which was supposed to last for the entire year. They were going to throw them out, plain and simple. Al wore his nice striped suit. He would respectably do this. He grinned to himself. The girls were still in the apartment. Anita opened the door.

'Oh, Mr. Durant, what are you doing here? She asked surprisingly.

'We got some problems that we need to deal with.'

'Yes, we certainly do,' added Pappa Joe like he had some claim on the situation.

Anita was reluctant to let them in, especially seeing the dirty older man with the beard and what appeared to be a wooden leg. Al didn't wait for an invitation. He pushed the door open, and they barged into the living room. Anita's friend came in from the bathroom with only a towel covering her shapely and nicely tanned body. Anita was entirely still in her morning gown. She went to the solarium every week.

'Nice, very friendly, said Al, observing Anita's roommate wildly. Seeing the wild look in his eyes, Anita's roommate pressed the towel around her even harder. He remembered the days when he forced himself on girls like this. Now he had to be careful. He didn't want to spend the rest of his days in the joint. It was safer to pay for sex. But the craving was still there.

'What do you want? Are we all ready for classes? Anita was worried.

'Well, my dear, I am sorry to say that you have to leave the apartment as of today. We have rented to another person, and he is paying more.

'No way, you can't do that; we agreed and paid one year ahead.'

'What agreement? Durant growled; I always have the right to cancel the rent within three weeks.

'And there is no refund,' added Pappa Joe.

'Who is he? Asked Anita's roommate.

'He is my legal counselor. He knows everything about the law and your rights. You need to leave. I will give you until 16:00 hours today.

Anita's friend became very angry.

'You cannot do that, you f**king bastard. We had a deal, and you will keep to it. If not, we want our money back. Trying to be aggressive, Anita's friend hid the fear slowly encircling her. She was suddenly terrified of Al Durant. So was Anita. She suddenly felt fear and nausea. In a split second, Durant was in front of the towel roommate, breathing at her face. He smelled rotten fish and old garlic.

'What did you say bitch!' he yelled. He instantly produced a medium-sized switchblade from his pocket and pressed it on her towel, sliding it down to her breasts.

'Do you want me to cut these two nice melons you have, sister? He was looking wildly at her now, and she was speechless. Anita tried to say something and even intervene, snapping the kitchen knife on the table before her, but Pappa Joe produced a small shotgun from his wooden leg and pointed at her.

'Don't you make a move now, pretty one? If you do, you won't be pretty anymore. Put it down. Now!'

She immediately dropped it and started shouting:

'You can't do this, you bastards. I will call the Police.'

'Shut up bitch, or I will cut your roommate's throat.' Her roommate was frozen entirely, and Al violently tore the towel from her. She was completely naked now.

'Uh nice, so nice,' said Pappa Joe.

'Yes, you are a very nice piece of ass, my girl,' whispered Al moving his knife across her breasts and down her stomach. She thought of resisting, but it could worsen things as this guy was dangerous. Suddenly Al remembered why they were there and gave a full smack across Anita's roommate's face. She fell in pain.

'That was for calling me names bitch. Now cover yourself!'

He turned to Anita.

'And you bitch, how you dare point a knife at me. I should rape you here and now just for that. Pappa Joe was grinning with his half-toothless mouth.

Anita was still angry, even with the mention of rape.

'You can't throw us out. I will call the police, or my dad will deal with you.

'Police, they don't give a shit about these minor things. And if you do, remember that I will find you and your nice roommate, and then we will rape and kill you. On second thought, we might rape you now and kill you later. Pappa Joe laughed. Anita's roommate was holding her check and crying. It was turning blue fast.

'And as for your daddy, let him come, and he will suddenly find himself having two assholes instead of one.' Pappa Joe laughed again.

'You dirty old f**k, you can't…' she didn't finish her sentence as Al was now in front of her like lightning, and the knife was at her cheek. She tried to scream, but nothing came out of her vocal cords. His eyed were glowing violently, and she knew he was measuring her body underneath the morning robe. He made a small cut on her face, and she grunted in pain. He slapped her even harder, and she fell in pain like her roommate.

'It's your lucky morning bitch. Otherwise, I would have my way with you, and you would simultaneously scream in pleasure and pain. And then I would cut you to pieces.'

He was over her, still holding his knife, and gave her a sleazy, aggressive kiss. She spat, and then he hit her again, harder this time.

'F**king bitch! If you are not gone by 16:00 hours, I swear you would wish you were dead first before I have my way with you. He looked at her roommate, still on the floor, petrified with fear.

'And that goes for you too, missy. I will bring three more guys to rip apart your tanned body and cut your pretty face. And then you won't be pretty anymore.

'Don't f**k with us, or you will be dead!' said Pappa Joe in the closing statement. The girls believed this.

'Don't even think about calling anyone, or you are dead!

Al moved to the center of the room and saw the red skirt on the sofa.

'Nice skirt bitch. It would help if you looked pretty in it.

'Leave it, please,' cried Anita. That was her favorite skirt she got from her mom a year before she passed away.

'Oh, I will leave it for sure, but not before I leave something for you.' He then unzipped his fly and took his penis out. The girls were frozen in place. After a second or two, he began urinating wildly on the skirt. It was becoming wet and stinky.

'Stop, please…stop pissing on my skirt, you animal', she begged. Al looked at her and hollered like a wolf.

'Now it will be nice and fine, wet and smelly!'The pissing would not cease. It seemed he had gallons of urine in his bladder. She tried to make some move, but Pappa Joe just came closer and pointed the gun again. He also watched her friend, who was entirely quiet now.

She had no intention of speaking. She just prayed these two animals would leave. Al stopped urinating and zipped up his fly. The skirt was soaked with his piss, and by the contents of it, there was no way any detergent would clean it. She had a better chance with acid than Al's piss. He also took his knife and made ripped the back zipper off.

'This is for the afternoon if you don't leave. First, you will wear it, and then I will take it off easier from you without a zipper. Both men laughed.

He was content now. It was time to leave. If they didn't leave by the deadline, he promised to beat them up badly and, yes – have his way with them.

'Remember, he said in a commanding voice, out by 16:00 hours'. Do you hear? With that, the two men left. They still stayed silent for a while, unable to move an inch. Both of them started crying. Anita looked at her destroyed dress and cried even more. Her roommate came to her senses, got up in a frenzy, and started packing.

'What are you doing? Said Anita.

'What does it look like I am doing? Packing! This is a f**king maniac'. We got to get the f**k out of here, or we are dead meat in the afternoon.

'But we paid, and it is our place.'

'Are you out of your mind? We need to save our lives.

'He won't do anything,' Anita protested.

'Oh yes, he will. This guy is an animal, and he is done it before. I have seen guys like this. I won't stick around to see it, and you are coming with me!'

After a while, Anita also agreed and understood they would risk their lives. They wouldn't contact the police, but she would tell her daddy. Daddy always knew how to handle things. In an hour, they packed and called the cab. It took them to her daddy's house in the village.

Anita's father decided to take care of his little girl. The girls were in shock but all right. Cuts and bruises would heal. The apartment was already bought, and she would get the keys and the bank account number. It was in the old city center 5 minutes from her university building and 5 minutes from all the night places in town. The girls would get over the initial shock of being evicted. Dad gave Anita and her friend a sermon about all the wrong 'apartment people' out there trying to scam two nice girls like them. It was better that he looked after them for now. That would work nicely, he thought.

Now there was only one more thing to deal with. The evictor had to pay dearly for what he did. The girls won't know anything. He just promised them that this guy would never bother them again. Anita knew her father always kept promises. He called his son, who ran the restaurant and the night bar. He wanted him to fix two 'good fellas,' as he called them, from outside (that meant outside the city and village) to show this Al Durant character a lesson or two, so he would never repeat anything like this again. He didn't care for the money Al took. He just wanted him never to forget. His son said he knew people who knew good people and that it would be taken care of. It could cost, but he knew Dad didn't care about that, just that it was correctly done. After four days, his son's friend called and told him that he had 2 'good fellas' that would take care of this. The next day two guys walked into the son's restaurant. One looked just like the clone of the Marlboro man from the billboard but without the hat, and the other was like a guitarist of a disbanded hard rock group.

*

Marlboro man and Hard Rock guy were now within a few feet of Al. Al looked at the two individuals in front of him. He didn't know them. We all turned and looked there as if knowing that something was about to happen. The two guys had the man's description but had to be sure. When they were almost face to face Marlboro Man just asked for two words to get the final confirmation:

'Al Durant…?'

'Yes,' Al answered automatically and looked straight at them. Quickly, two alley cats, Marlboro Man and Hard Rock Guy grabbed Al by his shoulders and, without considerable effort, span him around and flung him hard on the asphalt ground. A crash hit him.

'What the f**k?, he started to say…Marlboro man cut him off.

'This is for Anita motherf**ker'. With that being said, Marlboro Man, with incredible speed, kicked Al in the head with his heavy camel booth. We thought Al's skull was going to break open. The hard rock guy hit him directly in the ribs with such power that we could hear the bones breaking. He also had those sharply pointed leather boots that rock musicians like. Al wasn't a great fan of them at that moment. He tried to stand up even with the pain and was about to deliver some punch into empty air when the Marlboro man retook the stage. He took his hand swiftly and then, with total weight, landed on his chest with broken ribs. Al cried in anguish and horrible pain. He then kicked him in the stomach once more and moved away. Hard Rock fellow stepped in. He kneeled and started kicking Al on his mouth and teeth.

We just realized that he had a glove on his right hand, which was abnormal. For all we know, it could have been full of steel or lead. Al became a punching bag. The hard Rock guy was delivering blows at an incredible speed and accuracy. Al couldn't even open his eyes between the punches. The two guys were cursing at him all the time. Suddenly Hard Rock moved aside, and Marlboro Man came and picked Al like he didn't weigh more than a box of matches, lifted him in the air, and tossed him like a tennis ball on the ground. He came down with another crash. Then they started the accurate hard kicking again. They were using their legs, and Al was crouched on the ground. The ribs were paying a huge price again, but the kidney area suffered a major onslaught. An occasional punch would be delivered to the head. Al was not moving anymore. He seemed stone dead. They must have delivered 70-80 punches within 2-3 minutes. The hard Rock guy kicked him between the legs. The blow was decisive, accurate, and rugged. Al's body shook a couple of times, and he uttered something. They shrieked with a short laugh and started kicking him in the head again. He was entirely still now. They kept pounding him even more, only using their legs. They sure as hell could have been good soccer players. Nobody came to the rescue, nor did we do anything. They were now directly in the middle of the parking space, slightly closer to the left row of cars. Surprisingly enough, nobody walked by, and some people there just looked at this in amusement, morbid curiosity, and fear. The two guys were wrapping things now. They knew it had to be finished soon before somebody interfered, but by the looks of these two, no one would dare. We just watched this in complete shock. Nobody could move or do something, even though nobody was willing to contemplate that.

We just stood in a frozen union looking at a live beating event some twenty feet from us. We could have quickly passed for stone sculptures frozen in place by the Greek mythology monster, the Gorgon Medusa. Marlboro man was down and was lashing Al's face with his left blow. There was some groaning coming from Al, but it soon vanished. Blood spurted everywhere, and a small pound was behind Al's head. They seemed to work well these two. It was evident that they had done this kind of work before. When it seemed that one was trying to calm the other, the other would start punching even more. It was a strange kind of tactic that they enjoyed. It all took 7-8 minutes. Al wasn't moving at all. We were sure he was dead. Blood was pouring over his chest and his rather sizeable belly. Marlboro, as with delight at the final act, kicked Al three or four times more in the kidney area and stepped on his left hand, breaking a couple of fingers. If Al survived this, I was sure that he wouldn't be an organ donor in the future. Suddenly Hard Rock guy unzipped his fly and started pissing fast on Al's face. Urine got mixed with blood.

'That's for the skirt motherf**ker', yelled the Hard Rock guy. Marlboro man spat on him, and it seemed they were finished. Their faces were lashed with anger, and sweat was breaking from their foreheads. They looked in our direction, and their eyes were glowing like demons. We were sure as hell not going to say anything. And as we thought they were about to leave, they turned to Al again and took his Swiss knife and wallet out of his pocket. Finally, they delivered 6-7 strong leg punches into Al's abdominal area, cursed, and spat some more. The apocalyptic butchering was over. Al was lying on the ground like a broken sack of potatoes, most of them smashed. They looked around once or twice and left toward the low red buildings and the local cinema. They never turned around. A Marlboro man lit a cigar while the Hard Rock guy was fixing his curly old-Michael Bolton hair. We never saw them again.

We finally came to life when these two characters were at a safe distance and darted toward all who were utterly silent. Neither of us said a word. Boris and Anthoine leaned over to check him. Danny checked his pulse while I inspected the blood damage. He had a pulse which meant he was not dead. Pepé was running around and telling people what he saw. More people gathered now, as in Westerns when the bad guys usually leave or get killed. Some older guys appeared, boasting they would kick ass and show these bums if they were there. Sure, they would. None of them would lift a finger, not even the most muscular guy in our building Norman Michaels who was screaming at us for not doing anything. He was even suggesting some posy but soon quieted down. He arrived at the scene some 10 minutes after the beating duo left.

Norman didn't give much thought or shit about a half-criminal character like Al. Neither did most of us, but the guy required immediate medical attention. We were not going on a crusade for him, especially not against Marlboro country and Hard Rock people, but we would help our neighbor. Boris, Anthoine, Danny, and I took Al to the 400m nearby emergency room. Norman accompanied us as the self-proclaimed leader with no intention of helping with the carrying. We lifted him and started carrying him as a fallen hero or someone to be taken for sacrifice. The guy must have weighed a ton.

What the hell was he eating? What should have been a fast trip took us a century. Al's blood was all over us, and the Hard Rock guy's piss started stinking. During this trip, a can of tuna and a screwdriver fell out of Al's pocket. We had no intention of picking it up. The emergency room was a relatively new red brick building. With the shift away from general practice, more and more emergency rooms were popping up. For many, it became a primary source of health care. I have never seen it as such. None of us had any use, which I guess was good. Al was a primary case for this. He didn't need immediate paramedic attention, but he had severe wounds. There were no ambulance cars outside. We came in. The whole place seemed deserted. There was only one guy at the admissions reading Playboy magazine. He was profoundly studying the new pet of the month when we barged in with Al. We almost dropped him on the floor because most feared getting a hernia.

'We need help. Man is seriously injured', yelled Boris, sweating like he ran the New York marathon.

The guy at the desk didn't move his eyes from the babe on page 35. He replied lazily:

'There is nobody here right now except one doctor and nurse, who are busy with some patients. All our staff is on the field. Our emergency transportation is being used for the ill and injured to the hospital after the industrial blast'.

We heard about that on the radio the same morning. There were some killed and injured people in a chemical plant.

'Well, for f**k sake, call someone; the guy needs help,' shouted Danny.

'Keep it quiet, and this is a hospital.' You will have to wait or take him somewhere else. The prospect of taking him somewhere else was a daunting one. I think we would be dead after a mile.

The fat guy finally took his head from the pet of the month and looked at us with stupid ignorance and lazy amusement. He was chewing on a toothpick and had a severe attack of pimples on his forehead. Norman stepped in.

'Get your f**king pimple face out of your asshole and call for the doctor, or I swear every bone in your body will be crushed to ashes, and I won't need an incinerator to do it!

Norman was massive and robust; you knew and feared it when he was angry. He was also twice the size of the fatso.

'Get the f**k up, and now! Screamed Norman. The fat guy leaped from his chair, and we could see his unbuttoned pants. We all laughed, knowing what he was doing. He blushed and started sweating like a pig.

'Ok, I will get the doctor and the nurse in a moment. He rushed up to fetch them. Al was still not waking up. At the end of the corridor, we heard some screams and moaning. We lifted Al onto one of the mobile emergency beds and went to see what the commotion was about. A guy was lying on one of the same beds screaming in pain. He was about 40, and we could see no physical damage. He was naked except for a pair of boxers and strapped. It looked like a crazy case. He continued screaming. It was like the horns of Jericho. We neared him.

'They are here; they will get me, don't let them take me, please, please....' He started to scream again.

'Probably a nut that attempted suicide or something,' said Danny. My friend Anthoine was more concerned. Suddenly he was an expert in Psychiatry.

'What's wrong with him? Asked Boris.

'There is no physical damage, at least not on the surface,' I added another 'expert medical opinion.'

'He must be in pain' was the conclusion from our very own Dr. Danny. He started screaming again and lifted his head and torso. Norman had had enough. He delivered a heavy and exact punch into the guy's head. He fell unconscious. We were all stunned.

'F**k, I couldn't listen to this shit. They should have given him some anesthesia or painkillers. At least he will be quiet for a while.

In this entire crazy situation, we couldn't help but not to laugh. Norman Michaels indeed decided what kind of treatment this guy needed. At that point, it was better than the one he received at this macaroni. On the other side of this guy was a half-dead bloke with an axe protruding from his head. He was still alive and murmuring something. He was dressed like a lumberjack. Some tree chopping went seriously wrong, or a fight ended in exchanging axes. By the looks of it, this guy didn't do so well. We weren't sure he would see the next day's light, especially in this place.

The young doctor finally arrived, also buttoning, not his pants but rather his shirt. He was full of sweat even though it was a rather chilly day in autumn, and he, as hell, didn't do any carrying. He also had some lipstick on his right cheek. We doubt there was any medical operation in progress. The blonde nurse followed shortly.

She was also sweaty, and her uniform was wrongly buttoned as if something was done quickly. Also, her left stocking was not pulled up correctly, as the hanging garter indicated. You didn't need to be a mathematician to combine two and two. We just looked at each other and wondered about the practices in this medical institution. It was certainly nothing like Steven Spielberg's ER. We just hoped and prayed that if we needed urgent medical attention one day, the ambulance would miss this place somehow. The doctor asked questions, and we gave the basics and information on Al. Somehow his ID card survived the theft of his wallet. Soon more staff appeared, and the ones assisting the chemical plant accident were coming back. Al was taken up somewhere, and so was the axe guy. After that, we just left. The fat boy looked in fear as Norman departed the building.

*

Miraculously Al Durant came out of the emergency room the next day with only a massive bandage on his head and a smaller one under his swollen left eye. He had bruises and scratches on his face and hands, plus support for his neck. Otherwise, he seemed ok. We saw him walking toward the skyscraper, a bit stiffer than usual. He said the usual pleasant hellos to us. We were too speechless to react. How could he recover so fast? Half of his ribs must have been broken, and the internal bleeding must have been massive, or was it? It was incredible. When he reached the glass entry doors of our building, he took a piece of paper and some scotch tape from his pocket. The paper was an ad for an apartment for rent. His left hand was bandaged. He was putting up something. We thought it could have been that he wanted to leave the town altogether after the incident. We should have known better.

23

Dead Don't Fart (False Paradise)

Eleanor von Hedwig was sitting in the Zürich Kloten International Airport Business Lounge, looking at the arriving International flights. When she closed the door of her 6th-floor skyscraper apartment that Friday, she knew it would be for the last time in her life. No regrets, no last thoughts, no memories anymore. She erased everything, or so she thought. She remembered her late mother saying that memories don't expire like dates on milk cartons. But she tried. Eleanor knew it would take time, but she had plenty of time now. The fascination grew by the minute, watching the global scene evolve before her. Was life exciting as these people were? If so, then there was a lot more to live for. They seemed to be from all corners of the globe, Africa, Asia, the Americas, Europe…She never traveled in style, never traveled at for actually. A bit of nervousness, light stress, and anxiety were going through her. It was natural, and it was my first time abroad and the first time amongst classy people. She wasn't sure what was offered, what one should do, and what you should and should not ask. Was she wearing the proper clothes, did she look right, and did she behave appropriately? All those thoughts were roaming through her head and making her a bit nervous, and they were also bringing a light breeze of relief and warmth – the warmth of happiness for the first time in her miserable life. The man across her aisle gave her a pleasant look or two. She blushed slightly, and warmth swept through her body. She was still attractive at 52, and why shouldn't men give her a look or two? Within time she will accept it and probably very soon desire it. She enjoyed the black leather chair and all the drinks and beverages. It felt like a world of its own, of chosen individuals with a purpose and goal. Different people were going places, meeting people, and doing things. All colors and races were represented. Cities changed like commercials on TV as the screens were electronically announcing departure and arrival times.

All names she had heard of but had never been to Beijing, Rome, New Delhi, and Sydney…all she heard of. She was going to travel and see it all. A promise she made, one she would keep. She watched, amused and with awe when a giant Japan Airlines 747 Boeing skidded into gate 31. It was soon followed by a vast Swissair plane, a type she didn't know. Most people didn't watch. This must have been a regular occurrence for them. She suppressed herself, not staring too much and looking astonished. She only saw them in magazines. Some were using their cell phones, and some even had small computers, two inventions taking over more and more at the end of the 80s and the beginning of the '90s. Some good-looking and probably important gentlemen were enjoying their club sodas or single malt whiskeys. Women were browsing through magazines or looking at essential papers. Others were reading papers and magazines from all parts of the world. There must have been dozens of languages spoken in this place.

An International TV program was adding just another one. Eleanor was just satisfied to watch them for now. She giggled inside. Life would be fantastic, and she knew it. It was an antidote to commonality and poverty. She was sure that this will and had to be her future life. An occasional dark thought passed her mind, and she suddenly became startled. Somehow the banging of the cane, the tiny golden bell, and her late mother's cold, shrieking voice could be heard in this beautiful lounge. Was she here? She looked around and realized that it was just a dark thought. They will surely come and go. Who was she kidding?

All the 50+ years of her life could not be erased overnight, just like that with a magic wand. It would haunt her for years and years to come, probably never go and fade away. All she could do was resist and push it away with warm, pleasant thoughts. She would work at it and fight it. She took a sedative and swept it down with Schweppes Bitter Lemon, fast becoming her favorite drink. She would also have to get off these pills, another promise she made herself. The list was growing by the minute. The good-looking gentleman moved to a place beside her. He smiled at her, and she smiled back. She was suddenly becoming warm again. You never know. Life was full of surprises. She would now forget the banging, cold voice, dark shadows, and spirits. For now, she would start a conversation with this gentleman and live life for the first time. After all, she was free and would make the best of it. Too many 'she would,' but what the hell, it was more than four hours to her Miami flight. More than four pleasant hours…She knew she would also find Helen; yes, she would find her.

***

The bell started ringing again. It was 03:30 in the morning. Just 15min before that, she was woken up by the cane with a brass-plated finish. When combined, these two sounds were unbearable to the normal human ear. But for Eleanor, it was the music she had to live constantly with, at least these last eight years when her mother had the stroke from which she recovered almost completely but decided to remain firmly in bed. Elizabeth von Hedwig's mother was of nobility, at least on paper. They used to have a huge house in the finest part of the city center, a wonderful villa on the coast, and a good mountain cottage in the nearby woodlands. Her father, Richard, was wealthy but also very careless with money. They almost lost everything in a string of faulty investments and several embezzlements. He soon afterward killed himself. Eleanor always wondered if it was done out of financial misery or just the misery of living with her mother. It must have been both. Eleanor was the oldest of all three children. Two sisters and a brother left in time and didn't become enslaved as she did. They build up their families and usually come to see their mother on holidays, such as Christmas and her birthday. Even though they never really cared much for her, nor Eleanor for that matter, Mother always bragged about them and was very proud that they made careers and got kids (some of them monsters mind you). They despised her and were always untruthful to her. Bribing her with one small present and empty words of praise didn't bother their mother. Either she was living in denial, or she just thought they were pure good compared to Eleanor, who was always not good enough and had evil intentions toward her. Even though she has put her whole life into her mother, never married, never worked, although was allowed to graduate history of art, always been there like a slave, obeyed every wish, and took all the blame for all the bad things life bestowed upon the von Hedwig family and even being blamed for her father's death occasionally, never – never was there a word of praise, and not just that – a warm smile or look of love. She sacrificed her whole life and was always the anomaly that was not supposed to happen. All these thoughts ran through Eleanor's head when she went towards the bedroom where Elizabeth had her domain. The apartment was bought from what little money was left after the bankruptcy, and the estates were sold. They also had savings that mother administrated rather well, and Eleanor was doing extra work on some art books and student literature, which gave them extra income. She also had an early pension, although without a single real day of work. Mother fixed that with some doctors and other close family and friends to keep her at home as an enslaved person. The funny thing was that her aunt used to say that, after which mother terminated all relations with her; she loved her and had a heart of gold with almost no impure thoughts. Of course, at times, some would creep in occasionally, just when injustice came to such a limit that your only option would be to jump out of the 6th window floor. Eleanor remembered when her sister and brother came with their spouses and monster-screaming, stupid children. It was one of the Christmas just after her stroke hit Elizabeth. They missed the last two, mother always trying to find excuses for it, but this one, they stormed like griffon vultures (Gyps fulvus), expecting to distribute and divide the prey. They both thought her days were numbered and that the apartment plus (whatever was going on in their sick and materialistic minds) the leftover from Daddy would be divided – amongst them, of course. There were no leftovers, just a bit of saving Mother had made herself and smartly left in the bank for years. That extra interest rate and chopping off from the little savings helped them survive all these years. Eleanor's artwork (as mother forbid and 100% engagement) produced not so much, but still a good little pot over all these years. Mother had that in an account, surprisingly in Eleanor's name, as the family lawyer suggested it as a smarter option. That money was never to be touched, although Eleanor always wondered why not, although she didn't care about anything anymore. Life was just a blur, with no excitement, no image of reality, and any real surprises or elements of change. Every day was the same. There were no travels, outings, or events to go to. The only thing was to show face at times, make cocktails and dinners for distant family and friends, to give a false aura of appearances and something that was and will never be again. During my father's time, things were different. Mother was engaged in various social activities, presenting her nobility (although father was the noble one – not she) every step of the way. After he was gone, Eleanor became the scapegoat, the evil child and the enslaved person supposed to pay for all the evils that came upon the von Hedwigs. And she did; God knows she did. And then when her brother and sister that Christmas started telling her that mother needs to be put in a place where she will enjoy the comfort of the social world close to her (retirement home) and that they should take care of all the money as well as dispose of the apartment, Eleanor could not tolerate the injustice anymore. She would not let her take a mother away and throw her out in the street. The alternative was that they would rent her a one-room apartment on the city's outskirts and be pitiful that she was all right and forget about her. At times she could not believe that these people were her flesh & blood, but then again, Elizabeth was her mother – she couldn't believe that either. She attacked them verbally that Christmas, and in the end, her mother blamed her for destroying the family and being a crazy, unmarried spinster-bitch-witch.

"You little witch, you think you will take this place from me and send me to a forgotten home…."

"That's where you are wrong, lassie, you will first burn in hell before that happens, and my other two children will never allow it, never…I didn't know I had a snake in my home, but I know how to deal with snakes…."

Any attempt to defend herself or explain that this was the other way around would even anger mother more, and in the end, it was hopeless. She wouldn't talk with her for days but would expect all service and more. She was not allowed to read too much or watch TV or do anything for that matter which would not please her mother. This was not just in the periods of anger after some unjust confrontations like this; it would be everyday praxis throughout all the years. It was just hell. Eleanor thought of running away but knew her mother had powerful connections and would find her wherever she went. Her so-called brother and sister would probably testify in court that she was crazy and needed to be locked up. Still, not before the mother was gone – as someone had to care for her, it was good to have the enslaved person around. Mother used to poison her at times to keep her in control. Minimum traces of strychnine were put in the food at times when she wanted to be in control. Later, she found out about that when she found the bottles and consulted with some doctors. Eleanor wondered at times how her dad killed himself or did he? In any case, there was no escaping from the hell she was in. Every day was something new, and cycles just went on and on. She was 45 now and could not imagine where all the years had gone. A beautiful girl and a woman once now closely coming to the darker shades of her life that could have been nice if she wasn't slowly decaying in 25 years of torment. The only refugee she could find was in religion, believing that God would help her one day and that mother, however horrible it sounded, would never deserve any gates of heaven, that she would be in paradise lost for all the sins she did. She had to hide the religious part of her as her mother despised that, and at times she thought she was much more affectionate to the devil than God. She loved to do the séances with some of her close lady friends where ghosts would be summoned, and evil words would be read. Eleanor was never allowed to participate. She sometimes thought of herself as a captured bird in a cage, but not allowed to sing and say what she thought, nor sleep when she wanted – all of it was controlled.

After the stroke, things worsened, and she didn't mind cleaning, cooking, buying, and taking care of a sick person. But with constant humiliation, occasional strikes with a cane, and torture in the way of waking up every 15min or hour, she didn't have any perception of time anymore. Add to that deliberate urinating on the floor in the bed, or even worse; it made her almost half mad. She didn't mind the first year, thinking her mother was sick, but then she realized the stroke was never really an actual stroke, more of a seizure, and even when she recovered, the torment continued for four more years. She was crazy, Eleanor – she used to think that at times. There was no will in her to fight back and do something. She used to remember her youngest sister Helen at times.

Helen left home a couple of years after her father died and never returned or talked to any of them. Eleanor had little contact with her and knew about the injustice done to Helen, something she couldn't and didn't do anything about. Helen worked for a relief agency somewhere in Asia and enjoyed the solitude and nothingness of that part of the world. It also helped her forget home, forget all the beatings she got from his mother and all the sexual molestations she received from her father. Oh yes…that dark tale was never brought up, always to be forgotten and stowed away. But Eleanor knew, and mother knew she knew. The other two were her mediocre brother and arrogant, unjust, wicked sister, even if they knew they didn't care. Helen, the most beautiful of all, was destroyed for life, and Eleanor never forgot that and promised herself one day she would somehow make it up to her or make right a little bit of horrible injustice and pain inflicted on the young girl. Maybe Helen was better of.

The banging of the cane became louder and louder. Now even the bell started ringing vigorously. The lights were out, but she knew her way through the apartment. She went through the kitchen and the anteroom (a little half room where she was ordered to sleep most of the time as her room was made for mother's afternoon naps – and this was 15 years ago) and reached the bedroom. She felt an incredible stank. Eleanor knew her mother liked to fart at all times and then scream at her for not having enough air and cooking such lousy food. Eleanor thought she just farted ten times more than needed, which often resulted in her shitting instead. But this stench was horrible. As soon as she stepped into the room, her leg slipped on something liquid and solid simultaneously. She slid on the floor like an ice skating ring banging her head on the mother's bed railing. The light came on suddenly, and mother was sitting straight in bed with red, devil's eyes burning.

"Look what you have done, you stupid twat, you degenerate. Look at you all covered in shit and piss…but that's what you are – same as your father." Eleanor was covered with her mother's exhaust particles. The whole floor was in shit and urine. It's just incredible how much of it was there. And she was here just two hours ago.

"Clean it up bitch, clean it up, you lazy no good for nothing woman." She struck her with her cane on her forehead on the same spot where she had banged her head. She struck once again. Suddenly Eleanor stood up and took the cane from mothers hand.

"Never, never again will you strike me again, you devil abomination, it's enough" She raised the cane in what seemed a move to strike her mother, but she never intended to do anything.

"Ah, Elizabeth started screaming; now we see the real you, murderers; you would be struck and kill your helpless mother. I will tell all my children about this, and they will know what kind of snake I have to feed and care for.

"Tell them, tell those triple-faced monsters that would rejoice in seeing you dead and that lie in your face every time they meet you. They can't pay for or substitute the 'moral mistakes' they make by giving money and presents. Nice presents so easily buy you and false words, tell them for what I care, but by God, you will never strike me again, or I will be gone forever".

"Where would you go, you little nothing? You are nothing without me; nobody would want you, you hear: you are nothing without me". Eleanor was already leaving the room and going for the cleaning liquids. It was going to be a long night. Such was that night, and probably 800-900 similar ones in the next four years. Eleanor didn't go crazy. The lawyer, Mr. Andrew Steadway, was an old friend of her dad. Mother never trusted him but was compelled to use his services, especially since he stopped charging after his father's suicide. He often came and saw the misery in Eleanor's eyes and how she treated her. But he couldn't help. He only knew it was good that Eleanor had an account, even though she couldn't touch it now. He promised himself nobody else would, as this was Eleanor's money earned with blood, sweat, and tears. The vampire brother and sister already tried to poke around, but they could do nothing. He would make sure of that.

The window was always open in mother's room and in Eleanor's, which was occupied by mother now. Pigeons were frequent guests on the window sills, and mother didn't like them. She even killed one pigeon with a glass crystal ball that Eleanor got once from her father. She loved that little piece, but her mother did not. Still, the pigeons came and came. Pigeons mate for life and rear their broods together, although the other will take a new mate if one dies. Eleanor remembered once that a pair made a simple nest on the balcony, and the female laid eggs. Mother found this and destroyed the nest together, killing the female, a beautiful black and white pigeon with the crystal ball. She was reluctant to destroy this as life was being created before her.

The male pigeon, who was also similar but white, more grayish in his feathers, used to come after that for many days and stand in all kinds of weather on the railing, waiting and waiting. Eleanor never really knew if he knew what had been transcribed there. She was somehow sure that he knew about the murders. Eleanor remembered quite well that morning as she recounted the whole thing to their lawyer, Mr. Steadway. It was all as usual, as on any day in this miserable life. One thing was different. There was no ringing of the bell or cane was not thumping on the wooden floor. It was a bit odd. Eleanor was a light sleeper. She couldn't be anything else in all those years. Although she did take a glass of white wine before bed and finally after mother went to sleep. Mother sometimes allowed this luxury, although she didn't allow it all the time. All products were checked, and all receipts were closely inspected as she kept command of the money and what would be bought. That morning was very still. Eleanor remembered she left the window open as the days and nights were getting stuffier and even more as July approached. When she walked into the room, she was frozen in place. Mother was lying in a pile of shit and urine, white as a candle, with a horrified look in her, still open eyes. Her mouth was open, and from it was protruding what seemed to be half of a pigeon and one wing. The other one was obviously in the mouth. It was a scene from hell. Mother's fingers were all crooked, the hands and the legs one. It seems she didn't utter any sound as Eleanor would have heard otherwise. The room was filled with feathers, white and grey. The pigeon reminded her of the one that lost his female not so long ago. She rushed to her mother and tried her pulse. Nothing. Heart -nothing. She seemed dead for hours and was already cold. Eleanor couldn't just take the pigeon out. Suddenly a resounding fart came out of mothers ass. She froze and collapsed on the floor, and fell unconscious. She returned after some minutes and struggled to her feet to the telephone. I called 911, and Mr. Andrew Steadway just sat on the floor and wept.

The police came, as well as the coroner. They did everything by the book. Cause of death was natural, a heart attack. The pigeon thing was not mentioned, although it remained a baffle. Eleanor gave a statement and left together with Mr. Steadway. They gave her some sedatives, and she would come to the station later if needed. They took Elizabeth in a body bag. The pigeon was, of course, removed. Later they had tea in a lovely café near the police station. He told her then of the savings in her name, and that he had also invested some money for her, so it tripled, which all came into a nice sum that could take care of Eleanor until she died – she could have a friendly and good life and enjoy everything she lost in her last 25 years. She cried for her, for mother, for life – lost & found, and then she laughed. She was embarrassed, but Mr. Steadway knew. This poor creature went through so much. The vultures rest of the family gathered soon after and tried to grab as much as they could – or as they thought it would be. They started accusing Eleanor and the lawyer of foul play and murder, and just when Mr. Steadway warned and threatened them that they would see hell if they continued, they stopped. They were satisfied enough that mother left everything to them (hers) in her last will, including the apartment. She even wrote that if Eleanor dies by some chance after her, she should be put in some red cross place or, in the best case, to find a one-room apartment, but that she could not keep anything or inherit anything. It was a horrible testament that Eleanor looked over and over again when it was opened. Fortunately, her mother always pointed out that her belongings and money would go to her other two children. Still, Eleanor had an account in her name, thanks to Mr. Andrew Steadway, who created half of the earnings she made through her art book work and then tripled thanks to the wise investments of Mr. Steadway. The vampire sister and brother could not touch that and had no idea how much there was. It was Eleanor's money, money she paid in blood, sweat, and lost years for. She threw the testament and left crying, not so much for not getting anything. She knew she would never get a penny of the money or the apartment, and she didn't care. But what struck her as a poison arrow through her heart was hate and lack of all love from her mother. It was like she was not her child. She knew then heaven was a utopia for Eleanor von Hedwig. She would never see a glimpse of it…and didn't deserve any.

When Eleanor locked the apartment door with Mr. Andrew Steadway, she felt she could still hear the farting from mother's ass, even though she was not there. She remembered Helen, her sister, telling her when they were small that dead don't fart, but they do; Eleanor knew that now. She also knew that mother wouldn't fart in paradise but probably in some darker and meaner place.

24

Your Move, My Move, Our Move!

He was walking fast, almost running. Professor Janus Stromsky was squeezing hard his dark brown leather attaché case. It was an old vintage model, a seasoned bag with many papers and files visiting her. Janus was a left-handed man who always carried the bag in that hand. Grains of sweat were popping up on his high forehead. He was nervously looking at his Omega watch. The dials showed a couple of more minutes before 11:45 this Friday morning. He was going to make it, but it would be tight. There were two more crossings to conquer before he would be home free or at his crossing. And then, it was off for the 12:30 station meeting. He didn't know that Andrea Macaroni, a small-time crook, was watching him from a distance. Andrea operated in different parts of the city, usually stealing wallets, purses, or an occasional suitcase from the train station or the airport. He got busted several times but always returned to the same line of work. That was the only thing he knew how to do; that was his life calling. Andrea was a seasoned professional. At age five, he stole his grandmother's monthly pension and sold her jewelry when he was seven. Later it was a string of thefts, juvenile homes, short prisons, thefts, and so on, a closed circle of petty crime. The only life he knew. He has observed Janus for some days now.

The man was in a total frenzy. He was at certain places at certain times, and you could set your watch by him if you had one, which Andrea didn't. All the watches he stole he sold. This time it would be different. He would snitch that nice Omega watch from his and that leather attaché case. He was squeezing it so tight that it must contain something valuable. Or that was what Andrea thought. Professor Stromsky was always going to a crossing at 11:45 and then to the train station at 12:30 and 17:30 every day. He never missed, regardless of the weather or any other obstacle. Andrea was sure this guy would still be there if the city were being bombed. Andrea was also convinced that something smelled here, which was some dirty business. The bag must have been filled with money, drugs, or something else. The only thing that baffled him was that Prof. Stromsky never met anyone or exchanged anything at his usual spots. He must have been a real pro or a complete idiot. Andrea couldn't figure out what, but he was sure of one thing: Janus would be robbed this morning, and he, Andrea, would have a nice Omega watch on his right wrist and a lot of goodies from the bag that certainly would be worth something to someone out there. He would follow him and take him out at the train station. Andrea didn't realize that Prof. Stromsky was also being followed by three guys with altogether different intentions than his. Zed Creek, a half-friend of mine, and Hasslya Mazzlum, a half-half-friend of both of us, wanted to know precisely where Prof. Stromsky was going. We thought he might have been some spy or just plain nuts. We had no idea Andrea Macaroni would be there, and all of us ended up there for different reasons coming to more or less the same conclusion at the train station.

As you know, our skyscraper has 18th floors, each comprising six apartments. Each floor plan is identical. These apartments are numbered from 1 to 6. Apartments 1, 2, and 3 are two-bedroom apartments, 4 and 5 are bedrooms, and 6 are studios (one room). The distribution of social capital was quite a thing here. Apartments #2 and #3 were inhabited by university professors, doctors, lawyers, engineers, or some wealthier people who bought them instead of renting them. Army officers mostly occupied #1 while #2 was at times mixed. People of all other occupations, mostly blue-collar workers, lived in #4 and #5. Studios were mainly inhabited by older people, single people, some surprisingly large families with low incomes or socially unjust positions, and some total losers. Was this (re)distribution of social strata in our skyscraper engineered or not by the housing authorities? It was a debatable issue for sure; it was probably the case. One thing was certain though a social mix was achieved (God knows, with all kinds of bizarre consequences), and it was never dull, as you might imagine. Professor Janus Stromsky lived on the 18th floor. He taught philosophy at the local University. He was a very nice guy, though slightly shy and drawn back. He was not very friendly and had a bit of agoraphobia (afraid of people and public places) but fulfilled his minimum of pleasantries when confronted with another human being. He was unmarried and lived with his sister, a person we could never see. She maybe didn't exist at all, for that matter. She did, but in the end, she left Janus. Janus was a very tall and skinny man. Over 1.95m, with bizarre hair that looked like he was hit by 500V, with a deep and sometimes frightening voice and a strange John Cleese—Monthy Pyton's type of walk, always in the same dark blue trench coat. Professor Janus Stromsky was sometimes a scary sight. Sometimes he just had a divine aura like Gandolf in Tolkien's The Lord of the Rings, and sometimes, he looked more like a robot than a human being. He always had his faculty attached case and sometimes a dark blue umbrella. Well, all of that wouldn't matter much if it wasn't for one strange thing we discovered one day, purely by accident: His mania of being at a certain place at a certain time. I discovered this with a half-friend of mine Zed Creek who lived in the adjacent skyscraper. We both observed the Professor on many occasions and had a similar view of the crossings from our high-positioned apartments. Once, we saw each other watching and just signaled for the phone. After that, we decided something was wrong. And there he was again, our very own professor of philosophy, standing at the crossing, not far away from our skyscraper. He was standing there, totally frozen, doing absolutely nothing. People crossed the two streets whenever the crossing lights changed, but Prof. Stromsky didn't move at all. But when the next day came, and the day after that one…and who knows how many more days, we realized that this was a pattern and something was deeply wrong with the professor or that he was on some mission. He was standing at the crossing at precisely the same time every morning, regardless if it was a working day, holiday, or something else. Soon we became pretty sure that he wasn't waiting for somebody because, after 15 minutes of standing still, he was off to work or in the direction of the train station, which was even more bizarre. The whole shit was pretty weird, indeed! But that was not all; more was yet to come. When Zed told this to one of his friends, Hasslya Mazzlum, a person of great curiosity but a tiny brain. He told us he saw the professor at another crossing before his faculty. He did the same thing, but this time it was at lunch break, around noon. What was he doing? He was behaving like a programmed machine or a robot. Okay, let's say that this was part of his everyday working routine and that he couldn't work without "visiting" his famous crossings. Sounds silly. Well, whatever he did during the weekdays, he certainly didn't do over weekends and holidays. Instead, he did something even more senseless, absurd, and idiotic. He did his normal routine on Saturdays because he was a man who liked working six days a week. But on Sundays, some special Fridays, and every possible holiday he took his attaché case and umbrella and walked in an unknown direction. Zed and I were not keen on wasting weekends following him; Hasslya Mazzlum didn't have anything better to do with his life, so he did it. His report was quite interesting. Professor Janus Stromsky was differently "programmed" on Sundays (and don't forget the holidays). Instead of walking to the faculty, he went toward the railway station. When he came to the station, he went straight to the platforms. He did his usual "frozen man" routine for about half an hour there. During this time, two trains arrived and two departed. After 30 minutes, he left. Hasslya Mazzlum was baffled and followed him back home. He never met with anyone or spoke a word. He followed him again the next two Sundays and concluded that he was "meeting" and "seeing off" certain trains. This was complete bullshit, but even with his little brain, Hasslya was very convincing, and this kid never lied. We were all curious about where this was going and for what purpose he was doing it. Maybe it was a covert operation that was so sophisticated and engulfed in a series of muted actions. In any case, we had to check it out. Zed and Hasslya made a unanimous decision to follow him that morning. We wanted to check the pattern of crossings out, and then, as Hasslya Mazzlum said, this was a special Friday in the month. Every third Friday, Stromsky continued after the crossings in the direction of the train station to catch the fast intercity train at 12:30. And so we did just that, we were going to follow in his footsteps. Although this was an invasion of the professor's privacy, we didn't think he would mind or, for that matter, have noticed us anyway. That was what Andrea Macaroni was thinking, too, watching following the Professor. He was so much in his world that there was no way he would notice Andrea.

Professor's sister Hedwig Stromsky took care of Janus her whole life, but she was close to the expiration date and at the end of her life energies, in the end, like most things do anyway. She couldn't take it anymore. She remembered when he was a kid. He was a complex piece of psychiatric work. He suffered from the hyperactive disorder, a hyperkinetic syndrome, as one of the doctors called it, or something in the bag of tricks called Attention Deficit Hyperactivity Disorder, better known to ordinary folks as ADHD. All kinds of diagnoses were given to him by all types of doctors. Dr. Patrick Dixon, who was the best expert in the country, referred to this as obsessive-compulsive disorder, or as he called OCD, a type of anxiety disorder and phobic neurosis. It was not a common neurosis Hedwig was hoping for. This shit was much worse.

Dixon tried to explain that Stromsky had a molecular and chemical dis-balance in his brain and that he had to do these repetitive, purposeful, and intentional actions that were an action to respond to an obsession with a specific time & place. Hedwig wanted a 2nd opinion, not wanting to trust or accept Dr. Dixon's evaluations. Stromsky never wanted to commit to institutions or happy homes; no way or anyone could force him. He was OK at work, did his tasks, and functioned satisfactorily, and that was it. Hedwig didn't want to talk about the doctors until the thing became public knowledge, something we found out later. In any case, he was diagnosed with all kinds of things. Other doctors said Janus was delusional. Delusions are false beliefs that remain unchanged despite proof to the contrary, such as a conviction that anyone wearing a cowboy hat was trying to kill you. Well, Janus didn't have that, not at all times, Hedwig explained. Other shrinks have said he had hallucinations or false perceptions. Hedwig used to say that he was hearing voices and seeing things that weren't there. In psychiatry, both are critical features of psychosis, which can be defined as a disconnection from reality. Well, that was the general feeling that Janus was under psychosis. One thing was sure – the family did have a string of mental problems. Their younger brother Michael was a tough case at 22, diagnosed with a history of mental health problems, at 23 had been seen by a mental health professional, at 24 had been prescribed psychiatric drugs, at 25 had undergone a previous psychiatric hospitalization, and at 26 had tried or thought of suicide. At 27, he exhibited paranoid talk. And finally, at 28, he was put for good in a psychiatric institution in another county. The worse thing was that their father, while openly talking about his hallucinations and mental disorders when he shot his wife, believed that the real culprit for his actions was a black-winged demon that came into his room every night and persuaded him to commit a crime. Soon afterward, he shoots his wife and kills himself. So from that tragic story, Hedwig and Janus survived, but in what shape? Hedwig was known to have drinking problems, which she said began partly as a way to "medicate" herself to deal with her and her brother's manic-depressive symptoms. Dr. Dixon's diagnosis was the only one with strong scientific backing, but the others fit partly into the picture. In any case, Stromsky was one f**ked up pilgrim.

We didn't see Andrea Macaroni at first. He was hiding behind one of the massive pillars in the train station, a beautiful airy space at the turn of the 19th century. There were too many people that Friday, and we could hardly keep pace with Janus, who was almost running. Andrea was close to him like a sewer rat sensing a piece of rotten meat nearby. We came out on the railway tracks and saw Prof. Stromsky struggling to see which platform the fast inter-city train would reach. He was very nervous and puzzled as they switched the train from platform 3 to 5. That meant he had to take the underground tunnel, and the train was already approaching the station. He ran. We followed, and so did Andrea Macaroni. There were even more people at the platforms than at the station. It looked like a war scene where everyone was trying to catch the last train to Katanga. We crashed into a couple of people and, with the usual curses and swear words, managed to get out somehow. Janus was already climbing the stairs.

Andrea Macaroni was 3-4 steps behind him. The train was already at a moderate speed when he reached the platform. He was trying to position himself on the platform concrete floor in a specific spot, what looked like a white circle. While watching at the circle, Andrea Macaroni jumped like an alley cat, and in an incredible artistic move, he grabbed for the bag and, at the same time shuffling with Janus, who was by now wholly startled, he managed to take off his Omega watch. He smiled through his yellow, corroded teeth for being such a cool cat. The bag was out of Janus's hands, and he was shocked. We were already at the platform, and seeing what we had seen, we started shouting with all our might: "Stop the thief!"

Hasslya Mazzlum was the loudest, having a shriek that could wake up a 1000-year-old corpse. All the people at the platforms turned their heads. The roar of the train was getting louder. Andrea Macaroni was running and not looking where he was going. Instantly, he crashed into a huge fat guy who heard our shouts and tried to stop him. It was like hitting a block of concrete. He swirled, lost his balance, and being too close to the platform's edge, he fell directly down the tracks and hit his head on the railing. The bag also fell, opening itself, and tons of papers flew out, mostly train schedules from 5-6 years back. Andrea Macaroni was frozen. He forgot all about the train and his spinning and muddled head and just watched the bag in bewilderment. There was nothing in it. He didn't even see the train coming, and fortunately, he rolled partly off the tracks, and only his hand remained on it. He was such a pickpocket and hands artist that he slipped the watch on his hand while running. Andrea now watched as the Omega piece was broken. The mineral glass was cracked and seemed to read Omegan instead of Omega. A f**king copy! Asshole Professor! Those were the last thoughts before his arm was sliced clean off by the fast train coming too fast into the station.

Andrea Macaroni started screaming. Professor missed this train and sat inside his circle in a catatonic stupor. He was petrified. Andrea Macaroni was still screaming down there. Tons of people were coming close to the platform. The train stopped. Train security and police were on the way as well as the ambulance. We came to the professor's aid, who was like a piece of rock now. Andrea Macaroni was unconscious and was soon taken away. They operated, but his arm could not be saved. The train severely damaged the chopped part so severely that there was no way they could put it together. The worse thing for Andrea was that it was his right, the stealing one. He survived and got ten years in the can for attempted murder and stealing. They let him out after six for good behavior. What became of him after nobody knew? Professor went to significant psychiatric decontamination.

****

Professor Janus Stromsky was always so prompt, not ever missing one of his trains, except for that one morning. One could constantly adjust his watch to the professor. The poor guy was suffering from a syndrome of "compulsive actions," In other words, he had to be in a particular place at a specific time. There were no obstacles for this guy. The weather, the time of the day, the holiday season, his health, and all other factors were secondary to him. The only thing that mattered was to be "there" on time. It was never any of our, or any other's, business. If the man wanted to have his "fun" with the trains and crossings, let him have it. He was undoubtedly never bothering anyone with it or creating a public problem. The world is full of all kinds of weird people anyway. And besides, the professor was a very civilized and taciturn man. His students liked him. We liked him. Professor Stromsky was living in his extraordinary private world.

The Happygarden psychiatric institution in the nearby county was close to the local train station, and Professor Stromsky had a window directly facing the platforms. The only problem was that he did need psychiatric help and care at the end of the day. Now he had that, but that didn't stop him from seeing his trains come and go. Years passed by, trains went by, and in the end, Prof. Stromsky died peacefully one day, probably satisfied that he always made it on time. How he managed the problem of not being at the crossings daily still baffles me. He never missed any of it. Except for that one occasion at the station, he never missed a single train. One always wondered: What would happen to the professor if the railway employees went on strike? Fortunately for him, they never did during his time, at least not while he became a permanent member of a friendly mental institution community.

25

The Disappearance of Laura

Laura Hamilton, a beautiful girl with a beautiful name; Every time I saw her, my heart was swept away, I was frozen in time, lost in the moment and forever enchanted by those blond curls, blue eyes, and seductive look that she gave to just about every teenage kid in the building and our surroundings, and that made me mad. Christopher Cross's song "Think of Laura" was playing on the 80's hits radio station, and my memories went active again. I remember her so well even today, after so many years, filled with different distractions, passages in time, moments overturned by joy and sorrow, and a mass of other essential and not-so-important stuff – but I still remember her so well. Why not just me? Why not just me and no one else…well she knew she could have any boy she wished for and that they would drop down to the asphalt for her like crap came out of Canadian Geese…well, that was not the best of analogies. I was madly in love with her, or whatever love meant in those teenage, inexperienced years. At least I knew that when I saw her, my heart stopped, and butterflies filled my stomach while the rest of my body went numb, and when she was not there, I did think of her a lot. I was not alone. All the kids probably did the same, though we had some other OK girls in the building worth all attention. But Laura seemed unique, probably due to teasing and our inability to get to her…

I remember that spring afternoon looking at her…she was so memorable and unique, like the first flowers and plants of spring, like the first drops of rain after a hot summer day, like the soft breeze wind that surprises you in the evenings when the day is still humid…I don't know…damn she was something. The face of an angel-covered girl, hair and eyes of blue, satin blue…and those eyelashes; Everything seemed so perfect about her…She was so beautiful with her elegant stroll, yet sporty light dresses, and the way she smiled… boy did she have a smile…

"Wake up, bro; you are making an embarrassment of yourself! Man, oh, man… Daydreaming about Laura again, aren't you?"

David Green, a good friend from the 5th floor, looked at me in bewilderment.

"Even Laura and her girlfriends are laughing at you, bro. At least close that mouth, man, or your tongue might fall out!"

I looked at David, who was chuckling now, and the girls, some 10m standing left to us, also chuckling. Laura was amused and knew how she attracted attention, and now another teenage boy made a fool of himself. I didn't realize I was completely gone, frozen in time by watching here. David and I were sitting on the stairs of the entrance of our building. Fortunately, he came to my rescue.

"Sorry man, I was just lost in thoughts,"...

"Thoughts, my ass, you were lost for that girl boy; that's what you were, huh!" He had a joker's face on him, and he enjoyed this...

"Common David, can't you see that she is...I was cut off.'

"She is what, empty, shallow, utterly uninterested in the sublime qualities of this complex world...now I cut him off.

"Common man, she is 16 years old. She is not a rocket scientist."

"Well, I could give you some of those that did wonders in her age... oh well, I suppose she is nice." David smiled. He liked her too, but his ideal was beauty combined with intellect, and Laura lacked the latter. David was brilliant as it gets. IQ of 180 and a mind that can dazzle you and make you wonder if 16 is his actual age, David was a wonder to behold. I was not wrong; damn, she was pretty... I always knew David would go places and make something out of life given to us. He did well after some years, very well indeed. But he was not interested in Laura. His mind and reasoning were working faster than his heart, and when he put all the pros and cons, the result would be: No, not Laura. I thought a bit differently; my heart was taking charge in this case or something, emotions, I guess.

"Listen, bro, you will never get that girl, and I wouldn't be so depressed about it. You are too good for her. That shallow bimbo will end up with a football player or a gangster by the age of 21. She knows what she looks like and will be interested in attending with money, a lot of both. You might give her attention initially, but when you see how empty she is, that will fade away. Plus, unless you rob a bank or go into sports and film, I am not sure the money will work out for her. I know, I know what you are going to say – 16, she is still

16, yes, but she is already formed, man…could be some salvation for her in 2-3 years to turn her around and reeducate her in the real meaning of life but honestly I don't have the energy nor the will to do it!" We both laughed our asses off to the last comment. David always knew how to close things off, so I liked him and many others. He was a great pal and an excellent person to be with.

The girls were now looking at us and wondering why we were chuckling. They were standing just close to the boards that were separating the construction site from the parking and the beginnings of a shopping center that took almost 20 years to complete after it began. Some foundations were laid out on the site then, and soon after, it stopped and was dead for years; it became a humongous breeding ground for rats and mutant animals. Even the cats were weird, and it was understandable with the type of rats down there, especially with the mutant rat, Norwegian Dream, and his centurions ruling the underworld. That fellow gave me the chills… one means f**king son of a bitch mutant rat what he was. But that was not the only thing there. Word had it that a strange caveman was living in the tunnels. A few tunnels were made under the construction site and to the industrial complex on the other side. Many concrete hallways were made for different infrastructure systems that were never laid out; at least most were not. Now all lost, forgotten, and home to God knows what…but some say to a big man living down there. Nobody cared nor did anything about it. But the mystery remained…some say trash disappeared with some animals too into a giant 15 meters hole, sort of a shaft that led into the tunnels. Nobody even tried to climb down there with the little steel rod stairs constructed within one side of the concrete wall. It was dark, moist, and stinky there. The shaft was just close to where the girls were standing, and usually, it was behind the boards that were set up there, but one of the boards was missing today, so the access to the hole was free. People took all kinds of material from here, even these boards. At least the construction company fixed these after they were gone – that's just about what they did, no less, no more.

"Look who is coming, whispered David…."

Rock Curtis and his two cronies, Fat Ass Domenico Little Moritz, were approaching the parking lot from the west side. That always meant trouble, waste, and destruction of property or human beings.

"Look at these three, said David. These kids are out just for the fragmentation of everything urban, bro. They are a pure menace to society. It seems almost like they were born with a grudge toward life or something…

"I think they had just one f**ked-up upbringing, bro," I added rhetorically.

"You got that one right, bro, man… they are something". The three little monsters closed up, and Rock's eyes immediately locked onto Laura, like a predator locks his radar on a prey waiting to be slaughtered. They ignored us. I knew Rock Curtis would do this, as he fancied all the girls, especially the lovely Laura. He liked that all kids were scared of him, and girls liked his dark and invitingly nasty power. David and I were disgusted when he started flirting with them, and they responded.

"You see, David began his oratory sermon, that's women to you, man. Even though that piece of shit is one stinky, stupid, and mean bastard, they still like to flirt with him; incredible, knowing what he is. That's women for you, bro". David was almost right. Rock became pretty aggressive and started physically touching Laura, wanting to get a forced kiss or something. She now resisted, and his cronies didn't know what to do, nor did her friends Maya and Ashley. Laura resisted, and so no several times, but he was adamant about getting what he came, or what was given to him as he thought. He didn't have much brain, but the force was his companion, and he thought that would be enough to put anyone in submission. But Laura fought back, and I saw another side of her. He showed her almost to the ridge of the concrete shaft leading to the tunnels. I instantly moved towards him without thinking at all, and David followed.

"I don't think this is a good idea, bro." David was a pacifist like myself and didn't believe in force, but when confronted with morons who only understood one thing, you were forced to act in their way.

"There are three of them, but that fatso Domenico doesn't count, and Moritz is cunning but too little to do any harm. Rock is a problem as he looks like one nasty Viking warrior".

"I know, David; let's bust their asses."

"Yeah, right, though David and looked at me in his curious way…

"What do you want, assholes?" was Rock's elegant reply to our ascending to the scene.

"Leave her alone. I think she said NO to you! Does that mean anything to you…

"Who the f**k do you think you are, asshole?! Move before I bust your head open…Without warning, I did something stupid and hit him in the face with full force. I thought I broke my fist and, indeed, his face. He was more than startled and was in some pain, but nothing could damage that steel caveman jaw of his. He became all red in the face, utterly shocked that I dared to do anything like this. It didn't take long for him to react. I felt a sharp pain on my back as Little Moritz clubbed me with some massive piece of wood that came out of nowhere, and then Rock hit me with all his might into my gut, where I lost all my breath and collapsed to the concrete pavement. David was there in an instant hitting Moritz with two fists at the same time and crushing him on the ground. David was a karate apprentice for years and an admirer of the eastern ways. Before you could blink with your eye, he gave 2-3 punches to Domenico's fat areas but hit where it hurt as he crashed to the ground too. Before Rock could get more blows on me while I grasped to regain air, David was in front of him, his eyes burning. Rock was startled by this swift power that David excreted with cold precision on his soldiers, which was winning with pain on the ground. I was up and threw myself on Rock, hitting him with anger everywhere. He was much more robust, so I was thrown to the ground again, but his face was bleeding now, and he was furious. He also struck David in the face and said, "I will eat you alive, you pieces of shit. You think you can attack … before he finished, David swiftly leaned down and took something shiny behind his back, packed behind his jacket tightly to his spine. It was a shiny, more miniature Katana warrior sword. I was completely numb. Where did he get that?

"You say one word, and I swear I will cut you to pieces, screamed David…Curtis was taken by surprise but still furious and ready to strike. David slashed with his sword at Curtis in two lightning moves and cut his black hood jacket across his breast and along one hand. Precision shots are not intended to hurt but to paralyze. David was damn good. I had no idea he was so good at swords. He had a bunch of Katana swords hanging on the wall in the apartment, but this was something else. Curtis was cemented to the floor, and fear overtook anger. He was afraid of David and the sword. Moritz tried to get up, but I clubbed him with the same piece of wood he crashed into my back. Domenico was brilliant and stayed on the ground.

"If you move one inch, I swear I will cut your body in two, Curtis, and then you can pick up the remnants of your tiny brain from that stupid skull you call your head. He didn't move as David was dead serious and dangerous at that moment with his silver sword extended toward Curtis. All that was broken when Maya screamed, looking at Laura. From all the pushing, fighting, and showing, Laura moved further behind as our bodies blocked her retreat to the girls. She was on edge, unaware of the dark concrete pit behind her. She lost her balance, and her shoe slipped on the ridge. She screamed too and fell directly into the 15m dark hole, screaming while falling. We all watched in horror how she disappeared into the hole, her voice disappearing as she descended. It took us a few minutes to recover, and I was the first to rush to the hole, David behind me. Rock was still cemented, with his cronies watching in horror from the pavement. The girls were screaming now. In a few moments, the scene was swarmed by other kids attracted by the fight and especially by the screams from the girls, which was quite a shock now. I leaned over to the hole and shouted Laura's name several times. It was pitch black. No way one could see anything after a meter or two. I feared for the worst. She might have broken her neck or just died as this was a huge jump – 15m, for God's sake. My heart was in my throat, and I felt responsible; we all did. The only way was to immediately descend the stairs down the moist, damp, cold, and cobweb hole. We were arguing and thinking about what to do, and time passed. After 15 minutes, I decided, a bit too late.

There is no sign of life from her." "I am going down, David. We can't wait for the f**king ambulance and firefighters. It will take an hour before they are here, you know that!"

"We should send this piece of shit down there." David looked furiously at Rock Curtis, who was close to the hole.

"But he is too scared to go down there, all muscles but no guts and brain." Rock didn't respond. He was utterly silent. His cronies looked at each other. Rock was never scared of anyone before, but David was someone you did not want to f**k with right now, and Rock knew that. I began my descent into the bottomless pit…I was unafraid as the fear for Laura engulfed me …was she alive? Son, I disappeared. David turned to Rock…" This is all your fault, you piece of shit. If something happened to Laura, you will end up in jail and probably continue the fine tradition your family keeps". I am going down, someone calls the fire department and police", shouted David.

"No, I am going down; get out of my way David." He looked determined and ashamed as his cronies were losing faith, and he had to save face. He had to go down; he had no choice. None of us were equipped with any flashlights, I didn't have time to think, and Rock was not into thinking. We were going into the dark abyss.

Meet The Tunnel Man

When I was about to reach the last few corroded metal bars that represented stairs, my leg slipped, and I fell a few meters. Instead of falling on the concrete, I fell on what seemed to have been a pile of mud and grass which softened my hard fall. My first thought was of Laura. This must save her life, and she was not here, all splattered and bloody on the concrete. I could hardly see the dim light atop the shaft opening. It was pitch dark, and my eyes were beginning to adjust to the blackness around me. Where the heck was Laura? Maybe she was hurt and crawled as long as she could, and now she is unconscious and lying in a pool of blood. Cold sweat emerged on my forehead, and chills went down my spine. I started screaming and shouting momentarily:

"Laura, Laura, are you OK? Laura, are you, heart? Where are you?" My voice started echoing into the tunnel maze. There was no reply. I suddenly remembered I had a mini flashlight attached to my keys. It was a keychain, but the light was compelling and somewhat purple. One of those everlasting lights, or so do box instructions, said – yeah, right. Still, it was a light in the dark. I switched the little light on, and it gave a lovely glow in front of me. I started walking into the damp and somewhat windy tunnel. My heart was already pumping in my chest and beating like a drum. I almost hit my head on an overhead beam that was very low. The light saved me. Shit. I could break my head into two if I were running. After some 20 meters, the tunnel was separated in three directions. Great! I was always shouting Laura's name, but there was no response. I was paralyzed in front of a three tunnel crossroad, so I had no idea what to do next. I just heard some sound not so far away from the tunnel on the left side. I started shouting Laura's name again, hoping that it was her, but the response I got was all but human. It was a deep growl muffled by some language articulation and a weird voice followed by heavy footsteps and some other sounds coming fast my way. The shit froze in my asshole, and the only logical way thing to do was run the hell out of there. That was not Laura; it was something else. I ran the tunnel to my right with my little light bouncing around. I had no idea where I was going when suddenly I tripped over something and almost broke my neck. I saw stars and blackness as I hit my head on the ground.

Rock Curtis was almost at the bottom of the shaft when he heard noises down there. He became shit scared but knew two people were already there, Laura and myself, so he continued. He descended on the mud and grass landing and realized we were not there. He shouted my and Laura's name. There was no answer. He had no flashlight or idea where he was going, but he had his lighter, which accompanied a two-pack of camel cigarettes, always with him as two revolvers were with a cowboy. He thought: "F**k, I got nothing to be scared of; I can even be a hero and save these two. There is nothing done here except dampness and maybe rodents. He hated those buggers but continued down the 20m long tunnel. He also barely missed the beam as he strolled and had his lighter. Finally, he came to the crossing, which had some extremely faint glow, and the breeze was a bit stronger now. As his eyes adjusted to the dark, his lighter suddenly went out. Shit! As he tried to start it again, he heard a silent growl, and a horrible stink carried towards him. He looked straight – there was nothing – he looked right, then to the left, to the third tunnel, and heard the sound even more, plus the footsteps. Something was very close to him. He shouted my and Laura's name. There was no reply. He tried again, but still no reply. And when he wanted to do it the third time, his lighter came on, and he pointed it toward the tunnel. Some 5m from him, a tremendous shape came quickly towards him with two glowing eyes and a growl that seemed inhuman. He froze in his footsteps. The thing was coming towards him, what looked like a hairy thing carrying some wooden club in his hands. Rock Curtis's reflex was swift. He immediately turned around and started running as a bullet toward the faint light at the end of the entrance tunnel. He didn't get far, crashing his head into the concrete beam. He was lucky. It just knocked him down, leaving him half-conscious. He was also seeing start and cursing in the process. A silhouette appeared over him and soon materialized into a giant with broken yellow teeth, terrible stench, and massive hair with glowing eyes. It was the Tunnel Man. Rock screamed and instantly passed out.

I started to come to my senses and realized I had tripped over something furry and significant. My head hurt like hell, but I knew I needed to get my butt up and find Laura. I switched the light and flashed it towards the pile behind me. It was a dead rotting junkyard dog in the decomposition state but also ate up pretty well. Something took care of him but left some parts. Probably this thing was sick and not a very tasty meal. I was just about to vomit when I heard a faint sound some 20m ahead in the tunnel. I shouted Laura's name again, and it seemed the sound was there again. I got up and started to walk down the corridor again. In the meantime, the tunnel man took Rock's body and, with such ease, like dealing with an insect, lifted it and started to carry it down the corridor. I finally reached a point in the tunnel where a faint glow came from the left side. I cautiously approached, and when I reached the door, I saw some kind of room, not too big or small, furnished with all kinds of leftover stuff, old pieces of construction material, old furniture, and other garbage details. In the middle was a bunk resembling a bed, and Laura was alive. Her leg was tied up, and her head was bandaged, but it was unclear if blood was on it. She was awake and screamed when she saw me. I ran and was so happy to see her.

"Are you ok, Laura? Oh God, you are alive!"

"I am fine, but my leg is broken, and my head hurts like hell." She seemed happy to see me. Her blonde curly hear a mess, dirt, and mud all over it, and her dress was shambling, but she looked ok. It was a miracle that she survived the fall.

"It felt like Alice in Wonderland falling down the shaft."

"I can just imagine Laura! It must have been some ordeal". "Your head is bleeding, she said.", looking at me intensely now. The light was intense now, coming from a kerosene lamp that looked like something out of Jack London's novels. The whole room felt like it was 100 years old.

"I am ok, just a little blood." But there was a cut on my forehead that was bleeding.

"I had no idea what happened after the fall, just that I woke up here and screamed when I saw him, but soon it was ok."

"Saw who?" I was worried now.

"The tunnel man, He helped me!"

"What tunnel man? What are you talking about, Laura? There is no tunnel man here; it is just an urban legend".

"No, no, he lives here…and he is…before she could finish her sentence, a colossal creature came into the door carrying what seemed was Rock Curtis. I started screaming, and Laura followed automatically, but she stopped instantly.

"What are you doing? He is ok"!

The creature responded with some soft growl and wording:

"No screaming; I won't hurt you, me friend."There was even a smile with all those broken yellow teeth and that huge hair that looked like a forest on his head. The beard was huge and dirty too. Probably this creature never took a haircut or bath. I stopped screaming and became utterly numb. The tunnel man put Rock on the ground.

"He is ok; he just crashed his head; he will be fine soon. He started putting another bandage around his head. Looking at this vast creature, I was still completely frozen in time and space. Laura seemed to like him. Finally, I mumbled:

"We need to get you out immediately, Laura so that a doctor can look at you."

"You go soon; I help you to come out, the other side"!

On the other side, he must have been talking about the exit on the other side of the street, just adjacent to the fence of the industrial complex. He was going to help us get out! Who the hell was this guy? Rock was coming back, and as soon he saw the tunnel man, he started screaming, and the tunnel man followed, and we all did. Soon we all stopped. It was mass hysteria. This guy was living too long here. Nobody knew that, but when you think of it, the New York underworld is full of people. Our tunnel man was surviving somehow. We all calmed down. Rock was scared as shit, I was half numb, and Laura was alive. That was just about it.

"Maybe we should go now, Mr. Tunnel," I blurted out stupidly.

"My name is Jack; call me Jack. We go soon. You rest first".

Rest first, we needed to get out of here now, but this guy was in control. Suddenly he turned around, walked out, and stood at the entrance sniffing the air like an animal or a predator. He did for a few minutes and then returned or rushed into the room.

"We go now; they come, danger comes, they smell you"! He was alarmed and letting out some non-human sounds, excited or worried about something.

"Who is coming? Murmured Rock, what are you talking about?"

"What danger? What's going on" I added urgently.

"Rats, rats are coming. They smell you; they eat you alive…they are huge. Many are coming, can't eat all, can't protect you. Big one, nasty, nasty, dangerous, kills, kills." He extended his vast arms and depicted the size of the rat. According to that, that one must have been the dog's size. I didn't want to find out if it was true or not.

"We must go, now!" shouted the tunnel man, Jack.

We just looked at each other in horror. We were f**ked!

Norwegian Hunger

Norwegian dream was sleeping in one of the rotten pipes near the tunnel maze. He was surrounded by his pack of followers and a bunch of female rats, probably his groupies or harem. The rats ruled the underworld of the construction site and ate all that moved. This was the 40cm most giant motherf**ker rat you have seen, a black one, which we all called the Norwegian Dream. This f**ked up mutant somehow crisscrossed from black, gray, and Norwegian type and became what he was. He was huge with a body and a long tail that would be every man's nightmare. Claws on his front and back feet and two sharp ears like satellite dishes made him a nasty rat.

The Dream was in charge with a couple of his centurions by his side and hundreds, thousands if you will, blind followers. Well, humans were excluded from these attacks, but there were some stories, although I cannot verify them. Most of the cats and junkyard dogs were brutally murdered and cannibalized horrifically. Their strength lay in the fact that every attack was well coordinated, and they always stormed in packs, like when the street hawk was murdered. Mike Zito, a kid from a neighboring building, once said they jumped in a baby carriage and ate a baby while the mom fainted. Aside from the fact that Zito was a pathological liar and that no missing kids were reported, these f**kers could just jump, squeeze through, and almost move anywhere when they needed to or when hunger pushed them to. They rarely left the underworld because of the general fear of the humans, but when hunger was so insatiable, they ventured out in search of food, and they didn't give a rat's ass about any people. When that happened, you had to keep clear and get the f**k out of their war path. Norwegian Dream suddenly woke up, his 250 senses all on alert. He started sniffing the air and looking with his dead black eyes. His teeth were sharp as steel needles and strong as hell. He started producing squeaking sounds and getting extremely agitated. He smelled blood, people, new people; he smelled FOOD! They never touched the Tunnel Man, the crazy monster living there. Sometimes they attacked each other, but the rats kept away as the monster killed a few of them and had those ugly solid teeth and demanding wooden clubs that broke many of the spines of Norwegian soldiers. Besides, the hairy f**ker was a toxin, eating all kinds of rubbish that made him an unwanted piece of unhealthy food. The time will come when they will deal with him, but he was helpful in now bringing all kinds of dead animals down there. Norwegian Dream hated eating leftovers. After the almost complete massacre of local cats, the food market has lost dramatically on its appeal. This was different now…there was fresh food almost on the table. The squeaking was more intense now, and some other giant rats assembled.

It was battle time. Norwegian dream rushed, followed by dozens of rats. As he moved down the steel pipes and small concrete shafts that led to the tunnels, the rats grew increasingly. His blind followers were assembling like a coven of monsters of the underground. Amid this world that grew up underneath the construction site, a lake was also created, a lake of toxins, waste, sewage, and God knows what else. It was a black lake that became a breeding ground for them. It was hard to say how many rats lived here. Numbers widely went from a couple of hundred to ten thousand. Nobody ever counted, but there were many of them, and they bred and mutated quickly. Now hundreds joined from the direction of the lake summoned by their master and sensing close blood – fresh blood. They all remembered that glorious day when two sheep somehow got into the tunnels and lost their way. They were slaughtered by the lake and eaten up in minutes. They were now coming in from different directions, smelling the victims, following their savage leader. The packs were assembling now and coming close to juncture points. About 600 hundred rats were assembled in minutes, and some 300 came in the other direction. They were trying to block the passages. They were smart. Norwegian Dream was heading for the largest group, and they were only 50m from us now. They were closing in, hungry, starving, and merciless. The Dream sniffed the air and gave some last command before charging down the tunnel with his armada.

Our Ass Was Grass…Well Almost!

The tunnel man assembled us somehow and took Laura in his arms as she was the weakest link. We didn't even try to protest, trying to get ourselves out with him. Rock was still half tired and hurting, and I saw a lot of double images, and the blood was still running. He had some kind of a burning torch, a stick with a cloth dipped in kerosene. I got one too. We needed to get out now. We took a left and continued down to the tunnel, taking another left and a right. Now, this became a real maze as new and new corridors opened up. The tunnel man, or Jack as he called himself, obviously knew where he was going. He stopped suddenly listening to the sounds. There was a strange sound coming left, right, and behind us. It was the sound of something moving in large quantities, something strange, not flapping but like a river coming towards us, but not a natural river, something else. It didn't take long for the long-tail monsters to reach us.

"Hurry, hurry, we must go to the shaft; go with the straight tunnel. Just 50m more." Fifty meters felt like 50 miles for us. Rock and I could barely walk. We were helping each other now, forgetting what happened upstairs and why we ended up here in the first place. He was bleeding again, and so was I, but we didn't give a shit. There were more significant problems to worry about. Rock and I turned and knew we froze as the tunnel was well-lit. A river of rats was streaming towards us, and a vast fat rodent in front of them, like a giant cat or a medium dog. Was that a rat??? The Norwegian dream was looking at them now, his black eyes glowing yellow now in the illuminating light of the torches. We were very close to being slaughtered. We sprinted and reached the exit's opening or shaft. It was precisely the same as the entrance one. We had to climb, and Laura was hurt. Then we heard a scream. It was Rock. He fell behind us, and the rats were closing on him. One of his sandals was stuck in construction debris, and he couldn't get out. The Dream was just 2 meters away now.

"You take her up; you do now," said Jack in his strange, mixed-up lingo.

"I go get the boy; you get the girl. NOW". His voice was commanding, and there was nothing to talk about. You just had to do it. I took Laura and told her to hold tight. She put her hands around my body strangely, but they held. In the depth of this underground drama, it felt nice to have her close to me. I started ascending the steel rod stairs. There was 20m to cover. Jack ran down the tunnel. More screams were coming from Rock, now much more intensive than before. Long-tailed rodents gave it all. They launched their coordinated attack from three sides, joining into one flow at our backside. Fortunately for us, they didn't block the exit and the tunnel shaft as there were none there, but there were tons of them now in one endless stream like a sledgehammer waiting to strike upon us. It reached Rock Curtis first, unfortunately. He was stuck with one lag entangled in concrete and wires while the other was free; his sandal flipped to the side.

The Norwegian dream attacked his barefoot immediately and started clawing at his toe and other fingers. Chris took a piece of wood and defended himself from other rodents attacking. He was in a stream now. The Dream chopped two of his fingers. Rock was screaming in agony now. Some 50 rats were picking up at him from all sides. Suddenly there was a scream and a howl from the Tunnel Man. He landed at the scene with his massive wood plank and started hitting rats everywhere. They were flying in all directions from this giant. Jack was crushing them, chopping their heads off with his teeth. Rock could not believe what he was seeing. The Dream jumped from Rock and attacked Jack with 5 of his centurions.

"Run screamed the Tunnel Man to Rock; Run now!!!" I will be fine.

Rock didn't need to hear it twice. He got out from the pile of rodents, bleeding everywhere, without 4 of his fingers on the left tough, eaten by these monsters, and cut around. He looked horrible. He ran limping to the shaft and started to climb up, followed by a dozen hungry rats. I was halfway up with Laura hearing all the commotion and screams, unable to do anything, even if I wanted. Laura was cinching at me as best as she could. I could hear Rock screaming with pain but climbing and a battle happening not so far away. I looked up and saw what seemed to be David's face. He opened the shaft.

"I am coming down, bro; help is on the way; the ambulance is here." He swiftly started climbing down, and when we were some 5 meters from the opening, we met.

"I can take her now, bro."

"No, go and help Rock; he is in deep shit, and Jack, the tunnel man…:

"The tunnel man? What the f**k?"

David swung around, letting us pass, and went down as a bullet, a sword shining on his back. I was all out of energy, half dead. Somehow I reached the top, and the ambulance people helped us up. We both collapsed on the ground. David went to Rock, who was swarming with rats; he sliced swiftly like a Samurai on the run and cut some 30 f**kers helping Rock.

"I can't climb, man; help me out…."

"What about the Tunnel Man?"

"He will be ok, don't worry. If we don't move, we will be dead."

Rock was right. Although David killed some rats, hundreds and hundreds were climbing the shaft. It looked like it was being filled with black water. But they didn't move up more than 3m. David had to make a decision. Going down would be a suicide, and leaving Rock here would be wrong as he would slide down and get eaten up, so he helped Rock and hoped the Tunnel man would be ok, whoever he was. They made it to the top, thanks to David. They closed the shaft as rats were still climbing. We protested, but the cop who was there wouldn't have it – when he saw the rats, he was shit scared. We wondered what happened to the tunnel man, if he was ok, and where was he anyway?

In the tunnel, Man, Jack battled the Norwegian Dream and his most potent rats. There were hundreds of rats around him. It was going to be tough. The only thing was the fire. Jack took the torch and set himself on fire, his thick furry clothes. He became a burning bowl and ran through the rat meat. Rat started squeaking and running away. The Dream got off to, burning his fur slightly. He disappeared in pain with other rats. Jack ran and turned to the right. He knew he had little time before the flames got to his skin, hair, and beard. He ran to the end of the tunnel, opened one little shaft on the wall, and jumped inside, sliding down directly into the black lake. He crashed into it like a cannonball. The fire got extinguished somehow in the lake, though it was a miracle it didn't get on fire – all of it due to so many gases there. Well, faith would have it differently. After some moments, Jack came up, smoke coming from him. He was ok, a little burned here and there, half his beard was gone, and some hair, but ok. He looked around, and there were rats around, but no danger. He found his way back and disappeared into the tunnels. He knew this place as well as the rats. It was his home, his habitat. The Norwegian Dream went back to his layer, licking the wounds and cursing the bad luck they had. At least he had four new human fingers in his tummy. That felt good. The burns did not. That tunnel monster will have to pay one day; he just will.

WHERE ARE THEY NOW?

Laura Hamilton became a different person from that day. She went to med school and became a doctor. She married David Green, but the relationship never survived to see any offspring, which was good. Soon after, she started working for Médecins Sans Frontières (Doctors without Borders), helping the weak, needy, and landless. Soon after, she gave that up, found a wealthy businessman got two kids, and ended up on Prozac and booze. Rock Curtis became an exterminator, killing all possible rodents in households he could handle. He became very influential. He never got his left rigid fingers back, though.

David entered the IT business after finishing all their university degrees with the highest honors. He started working with a small IT firm, married Laura, and soon discovered it was not. He joined Apple, fell in love, and later built his own company in Silicon Valley. He became a multi-millionaire. As for the Tunnel Man, or Jack, as he called himself, he returned to the tunnels. Nothing was done that day or any other day about the tunnel. People didn't give a shit. Nobody found out about Jack. We knew he survived, but what became of him, no one knew. Some say he runs a Kendo training school on the outskirts of L.A. Others say he joined the Krishna people in Detroit… nobody knows.

26

Breaking into the Matrix (Spy Games)

Outside the Matrix

So many bullshit sayings or proverbs don't mean anything in our life. But on the other hand, some tell the story in so few words. One of them is when you hear sometimes people say, especially the old & the wise, that 'the devil is in the details.' Some would say that this proverb means that even the grandest project depends on the success of the minor components. When I remember those days surrounding my and David's entrée into network espionage, I would say that the proverb implies that even minor details might cause a significant f**kup in a project. And that happened on that warm 21st of July afternoon of 1985. You always wonder and have that brilliant phrase: "What if?" What if I had been there at that moment? What if I talked to that person? What if I had taken that Bus instead of the other…what if…what would have happened then…I don't know. I think about such things every day and sometimes, in a masochistic way, torture myself to death with these irreversibly unchangeable thoughts. As you get older, they become more and more part of your everyday life. We were 18, respectively 17 then, David Nathan and I sitting in front of our skyscraper, and had no such thoughts, none whatsoever. Especially on that warm day with the scorching heat of 35C, our brain matter was more like pudding, and we didn't have much say. Still…If it weren't for that most minor of details, a movement in space & time, and a minimal but still significant brain and reflex reaction to it that made such a difference, I wouldn't be telling this story. But then again, what does one story mean in the greater scheme of events, in the greater scheme of life? Maybe nothing, but this one certainly did make all the difference.

As I said, it was bloody warm, and we were killing time after spending three weeks of a nice vacation on the Mediterranean coast. Now we had the whole of August before school started and so much time to deal with time. There were a few friends on the stairs, most of them panting from the heat and trying to replenish themselves with what was now lukewarm water from the bike bottles. Everyone dreamed of ice cream but was too lazy to go for another round to an ice cream stand some 900m away. Still, we knew that it had to be done. Before we were able to muster any thoughts for such a complicated action of getting replenishments in this unbearable heat, one of our friends Joe Brown broke the silence:

"F**k a duck, guys; here comes Lolita with a pink ice cream stuffed in her mouth."

We instantly turned to our right and saw the sexiest but also the blowziest girl in our building. Shit…Every pure thought we might have had just went out the window. The only thing we thought about when we saw Lolita was to do with impurity. All our hormones went 1000% up. Lolita had a white laced dress that brought out all the gifts God gave her, primarily the physical ones. The dress was made for her, and her perfect body, full breasts, and fantastic tanned slender legs were all aligned. Why wouldn't they be? She was a sight for the eyes with white high heels, a white Gucci purse, and a white ribbon in her curly blonde hair. We all lost our breath, especially watching her suck the pink ice cream frozen stick… looked like strawberry with hints of vanilla, but who cared. She was swaying slowly and in rhythmic motion towards us with a walk that reminded me of catwalk models but with much more sex appeal than that. But then again, Lolita was a prostitute, a call girl, and an escort lady – have your pick. Heck, everybody knew that…not an open affair. Still, it was well known she brought a lot of different men into her one-bedroom apartment on the 12th floor and that she was also seen at many parties with other men, all in a relatively good material position. Oh, our Lolita was not the cheap thing… she went for the well-off stuff, being a sort of escort prostitute on her terms. There was much gossip around here, and God knows the old hags from our building would have loved to see her burned at stake or deported, but we were living in different times, not those of the inquisition. Besides, she was also an elementary school teacher – of Russian. Man! I didn't like the language nor the 'Soviets,' but damn if I hadn't forced myself to learn or take it as a different subject just to have Lolita as a teacher. Those kids were so fortunate. Well, she was safe. Because if she were a high school teacher, that would be a different story. So the woman paid taxes, and if she had extra curriculum activities, so be it. Nobody spoke of it, and nobody knew if it was true. But then again, it must have been, or otherwise, she was an insatiable sex machine and a nymphomaniac. The funny thing was that besides being so attractive, she was so pleasant. And that's what we all liked about her. Nobody knew her background, just that she spoke Russian fluently, her parents died in a freaky airplane accident when she was very young, and her aunt raised her until she died. Lolita Petrovna was already 22 then and started working as a teacher after studying languages. At 24 now, she was a sight for the eyes and all the senses, for that matter. She finally came close to us, and the ice cream was all sucked down her throat. She stopped at the brink of the stairs to adjust one of the straps on her high heel shoes. Our hearts stopped. She knew this and liked being watched. She raised her beautiful head and smiled at us with long eyelashes and dark cobalt-blue eyes. Her lovely freckles made the picture complete. We observed all the details of her strapping back to the left high heel with her long fingers and polished white nails. She was half bent while doing this, and her body's contours made us gasp with amazement wildly when Joe Brown somehow muttered that she didn't have anything underneath her dress. I guess he was referring to the lack of her underwear. There was no time to analyze that fact as she went for the purse and in trying to get her pack of Moore cigarettes (you know, those sexy long brown ones that you can't find anywhere today). While getting these out, watching us partly, and trying to be sexy as she could, something hard and shiny fell onto the pavement. We all scrambled in a second to help her recover this thing and almost crashed into one another. She was just startled a bit but gave a naughty chuckle. The shiny object was pushed from all that commotion to David, who didn't move an inch but just watched us in amusement. It landed in front of his shoe, and he picked it up. It was a lighter, what looked solid silver with a plaque of 18c gold, not a plated one. It was wonderful. The rectangular plaque had some crest with what was at that time a soviet emblem, and a sword was coming through it. Before David could see the letters in the bottom, which were very small, he felt a warm hand with beautiful nails on his wrist. He looked up and saw Lolita touch his hand, and he felt her warm smile but very focused eyes. She carried a scent of fresh apples, cinnamon, ginger, and some other misty fruits and herbs…must have been her perfume. She locked her eyes on him, and he was hypnotized.

"Oh, thank you…you found my lighter. How clumsy of me… thanks…It always falls on the heavy side".

She took it from David's hand and shoved it back in her purse with the cigarettes. She never lighted one. She turned and gave a smile to all of us.

"Thanks, guys, you are so adorable." After that, she climbed the stairs and disappeared into the building. We were all in a dreamlike motion.

"Man, David, did you see the body of this girl," I asked.

"She is extraordinary;" those guys are so lucky, added Joe. Bob Mackie and Mitch Zalewski both agreed. They lived in the tower next door and always enjoyed the occasions when Lolita passed by.

"Man, we don't have such babes in our building. If we did, I can guarantee that all the male tenants would be at her place 24/7", concluded Mitch. We all chuckled. David was silent. He was still looking at his hand like something was taken away or as if something was not in its place. I knew that look when I saw it.

David Green was a special guy, probably the smartest of all of us with an IQ of 175, but more importantly, a spectral mind, intuition, and intellectual curiosity rarely seen. You can have a high IQ but still miss out on many things. Not David. He had it all, + that he was a great person. He lost his mom to cancer when he was only five, raised by his dad, who never remarried as he always said—there was no or will ever be a woman like his mom, Sarah. David's dad, Steven had an IT company in the US and Israel, so he was away for most of the year, but his mom took care of David. Steven always felt terrible about this and promised David they would move and stay permanently in the US as soon as he finished high schoolmates. And so they did, to my considerable dismay, as I lost a great friend. But that's life; we all move on.

"What's up, David? You barely looked at Lolita, bro!"

He turned around and looked at me. I always felt he liked me the most of all his friends, and he once said he respected me the most. This was coming from him meant a bundle. I felt the same way. With Antoine, who was like my brother, David was my second one. Unfortunately, in two years, we would part ways.

"Tigran man, I did notice and smell her, and she aroused almost everything in my body but…but what…I asked. "She is all perfect, man, right."

"When was the last time she stopped and talked to me, man? She never sees me or any of us, for that matter. Sure, she smiles and likes to be watched, but you are the only one she talked to once, and if you were a bit older…who knows…she thinks you are good-looking, bro! I blushed immediately but was also flattered…

"Lolita thinks I am cute." I was mesmerized.

"I didn't say that, but screw that man…this is not right".

David stood up and walked in front of the entry stairs. He started intensely analyzing the north side of our skyscraper tower, especially the 12th floor and one of the windows with what seemed to be a sizeable circular radio antenna and a little coned one attached to it. To the left of the window, as the one-bedroom apartment had the east side openings in the form of the living room balcony, David saw an even bigger satellite dish. It was one of the rare ones that our skyscraper had. People were starting to acquire these 'windows to the world' contraptions.

"This is not right, bro, not right at all."

"What are you talking about, David." He wasn't making much sense.

"Listen. Something never really clicked here. I have been watching Lolita a bit more, bro". "Oh, have you now, man"?

"Not the way you think, man; this is different." David was getting more severe by the minute, which meant it was serious shit he was talking about.

"This was just the last piece of a puzzle that I have been putting together, and I still can't figure it out, but at least I am coming somewhere." I was utterly bewildered. "You are not making much sense, bro; I don't dig anything you say."

"He turned to me, looked at me intensely, and said: Common, I know you are not stupid; on the contrary. Listen, I have a theory, and you will help me crack it, and if it is right, we will test there. I need your help too. But this stays between us – you hear?"

"Sure thing, man," I said. I had no f**king clue what he was talking about.

"Firstly, why would a hooker, even a bit higher class one, have so many antennas in her apartment? She is rarely home; when she is, it's bunny hopping with the customers. Sure, she might like TV, movies, and even radio, and God knows what else, but why three antennas? You know we have a huge one on the roof for basics and radio, and most of us have another one on the balcony; few have a satellite dish, and none have one that looks like a military, commando desert antenna with a little space machine attached to it. As far as I know, she is not an amateur radio operator and usually gets clients by phone. To make things worse, there are probably tons of monster cables, as I can see on the balcony. And then again, the north side is fascinating as we have the big radio and communications tower – the beetle on the hill above the city. Interesting! Secondly, all her clients never say anything. Yes, I know what you are thinking. You won't say much if you go to an apartment to screw. True, some of them sometimes speak, but a majority say very little, which brings me to my third point. David was just getting winded up. I started to listen more intensely. Knowing David, the best was yet to come. I wouldn't be disappointed.

"All of them have foreign faces that are not our faces, and it's always the same type of anthropological configurations and layout of the facial structure and even body language, not to speak of the odor – they are east European, probably Russian, as I heard one speak once when in the elevator with them. Lolita didn't like that very much and, even then, looked at me intensely as I looked at the guy myself. I am not saying you cannot screw foreigners, but common – all these Russians,". I interrupted. "Well, you don't know if they are Russians, plus foreign people are working in the city and…."David cut me off. "Common, and they would all have a conference in her apartment. And finally, the last piece that got me, even more is the bloody lighter she had and dropped today. I looked at it, and it was not something a woman would have nor would get a present from a man, at least not from a civilized one, as this was one heavy son of non-feminine lighter. "Maybe one of the clients forgot it, and she took it, David?"

"Maybe, but you know what – I think this is hers?"

"So what's the deal then?"

"That lighter bro had a golden crest with some Russian Cyrillic letters inscribed. They were so small that I couldn't see. The crest had a sword and something else that looked like a hammer, but I cannot remember what as she took the damn thing from me. I am sure I have seen that crest somewhere; I am sure of it."

I still couldn't figure out what David was coming at.

"So what's wrong with that, crest, sword, gold, Russsian. She speaks Russian, is probably of Russian descent, and bought it there; who knows".

"Exactly, she is Russian, and she has been there, and she goes there, Moscow mostly. You know that she gives this bullshit story to her neighbor, and then all know that she has an aunt in Finland and likes to travel a couple of times a year, probably eight times. Finland that's just across the street from mother Russia, the bro.

"David, what are you getting at her?"

"Those antennas, that lighter, those Russian guys, those travels, the secrecy that surrounds Lolita, her erotic sex cover and her customers as well as her background, her zero or almost no communication with the rest of the building. She has done that swiftly, elegantly, adroitly, and you know what – she is getting away with it". David read my mind. He was steamed up, and I was still in the Land of Confusion.

"You are confused, yes! That's the best place for a man with a mission to be. And that's what we are."

"Common David, I think you have a vivid imagination."

Yes, there is no scientific investigation or real intellectual work without imagination. This won't be easy, bro!"

"I am sorry that I must ask this again – but what is your point, Lolita – what's so wrong with her except for being perfect." David looked at the apartment again and at the hill with The Beetle – the radio transmission tower. Then, he pointed at the industrial complex below that started with an iron, 24/7 camera-watched electrical fence—'John Higgins Ltd.'

"John Higgins Ltd, what's up with them? They produce some precision mechanical stuff, some turbines, some…I didn't finish as David completed, "some parts for nuclear power plants and some shit that is super classified. My dad used to work with these guys."

"Ok, what the f**k does that have to do with Lolita, man"?

"Everything! Man, it is no coincidence she has the apartment in a straight line with the industrial complex and radio relay station and that all three plus f**king antennas are pointing exactly there, not into the air where they should be if one is looking for TV or radio stations". David was right. The antennas were all at 25 degrees, pointing downward toward the complex, even the ones on the east side balcony.

"Still, that is not real proof, David."

"There is more, bro. I have seen several of her customers, particularly two that regularly come. Interestingly, they are always there on Tuesdays and Thursdays, like Swiss clockwork at 21:00, stay until 22:00, and leave. Some stay a bit longer. I don't claim she is not screwing these guys, but there is more to that. I think she is a f**king spy with some badass electronic equipment in that apartment for bugging, and God knows what. Industrial, military, political espionage…you name it. That is one of the only plants in this part of the world that makes these things. So it wouldn't be surprising – ha?"

As far-fetched as it seemed, there was something to this, especially for the fact that this was so God damn important industrial complex that anything could happen – but Lolita?"

"I thought our federal security service (FSS) had that covered, David?"

"What, surveillance of these characters? Those lazy bastards have their heads so far in their asses that they can't recognize their assholes from their noses. They sleep, bro. Do you think those bureaucratic f**ks give a rat's ass about Lolita? Well, they couldn't know, but there is so much information going out and in here – I am so sure about it. And Tigran – now he looked at me more sharply than ever before – what the f**k is Lolita doing teaching Russian and English to employees of the John Higgins Ltd, twice a week after 17:00 hours. If you catch my drift, I can guarantee she is screwing someone from there and extracting more than bodily fluids." Now this incredible story and David's wild idea were starting to make, however weird it might have sounded, make sense as his points converged, still without evidence.

"Well, you got zilch evidence, and even if we wanted, we couldn't get any. Maybe you should present this circumstantial evidence to the FFS.

"Screw the FSS. The Agency for Industrial Espionage (AIE) is what we need to look for – we need to find someone there. But you are right – we need evidence, hard evidence. And we are going to get it one way or another."

"What? You must be joking, man?"

"No, I am not, bro, and if you look up now, you will see our lovely Lolita looking down at us like that falcon that used to live here before the rats f**ked him up. I looked up, and David was right. She was intensely looking at us. So beautiful…damn! David suddenly waved at her and sent her a kiss with his hand. She grinned for a second and disappeared.

"What the f**k was that, David?'

I couldn't believe what he did, as this was not his style.

"She is already suspicious, and this was the only way to distract her. She doesn't like me much as I am the only one analyzing her and her clients. You guys look after her body parts. I am looking at the bigger picture".

"Get the f**k out of here, man," I said. We both laughed, but soon David became severe again.

"No, we need to get to the bottom of this shit, as I am sure this woman is bad news. God knows how much she has already sold to the Russians. My ass – aunt in Finland – bogus; that's just a way to get to Russia so that nobody will suspect her here. And the lighter, the lighter, where the f**k have I seen that crest?" David was biting his lip almost to the bone, and I knew he wouldn't stop until the mystery was solved.

"Well, she has been here for some time, and I know that people, especially the conservative ones, hate her, but still, a lot of people, especially men, respect the fact she teaches in school and gives lessons to people, so maybe the whoring part is just made up jealousy thing, although I don't buy that as nobody can have so many male friends, not even the most vibrant single woman."

"You are right, bro, and you know that saying that—Politicians, ugly homes, and whores become respectable with time if they last that long – Well, Lolita won't last that long, we will see to that – we will have to get inside that apartment!"

"How the hell do you intend to do that, David? Don't get me wrong, I hear all you say, and I think there is a lot of logic and truth in your words. Last I heard, breaking is a felony, and I certainly don't want to end up in a stinky prison because of a whore that might be, in some far-fetched universe, a spy. But man, imagine if we are wrong, boy we will be the laughing stock of this neighborhood and city, for that matter, for decades to come".

"What if we are right and do nothing, Tigran? What then? She will continue selling, giving, trading, milking, or whatever information about that facility is national security. Who knows where and what the Russians or those who speak Russian are doing with that? They could also be from one of the Soviet republics. God knows who could buy this stuff from them. I don't know…we might be saving lives at the end…this is nuclear stuff, man…these are parts for nuclear power plants but even more. At that time, the terrorists were more into political assassinations and less into weapons of mass destruction, but David seemed clairvoyant.

"What if some crazy mother f**ker gets hold of this technology, man? You can never know, and we will never be safe. This shit needs to be under control!"

My dad never spoke of his work there, as I think much of it is connected to the military, so I don't know. We need to break this espionage matrix, man; we must! It might be nothing; it might be something or everything".

Espionage matrix! David was in fantasy land and LeCarre and Forsyth novels. But I liked David's last comment. Something or everything! Where there is smoke, there must be fire, and there is undoubtedly smoke here.

"So what do we do, David?"

"I have a good idea of how to get into the apartment."

"What is it?" I was damn curious.

"Simple, you are going to pay her to have sex with you as I think she likes you, and that will brush off any suspicion of us."

"What? You must be f**king joking, right?" My mouth and jaw were about to drop.

"No, I am not, and close your mouth, please." He chuckled…and with a devilish smile, he said:

"Common bro, it's time you get in the sheets with a real woman who will be your best teacher ever." I was already blushing like a Tuscany tomato in a high summer morning sun.

"Why not you? Why don't you do it?" I mumbled.

"Not possible, bro! First, she doesn't like me and is very suspicious, and you are better looking". He grinned.

That boosted my confidence and moral and sexual arousal.

"Common man, that is hogwash…whores don't give a shit how you look; they just want your cash". Besides, Lolita must be expensive as hell. What are the rates for this?"

"Don't look at me, bro; I have no idea. But this one might do it free for you, kind of an educational pro bono case" He laughed.

"Thanks, David! I wasn't even pissed off, as this whole conspiracy was becoming so amusing. Plus, deep down…well…spy or no spy…having Lolita as a teacher wasn't a bad idea after all. But typically, this was Sci-Fi land. She wouldn't do it, or would she? We decided to go for it, and the sooner, the better. David would contact the Agency for Industrial Espionage (AIE), and the man, his father, knew a capable, rising young star, agent Jerry Matsui. His dad told him once that Jerry was the best of the best, once working as the head of security for the richest Japanese Businessman in Tokyo. He was now in charge of all the agents in AIE. But before Jerry came onto the agenda, we needed to go in and break this matrix that Lolita has created, one just under our noses, in our backyard. We both decided that the bitch (however sweet and peachy she was) was going down.

Towards the Matrix

Getting inside Lolita's apartment would never be easy, but it had to be done. It seems sex was the only solution if our premises were proper that she was an escort service, prostitute, or a whore, which all, at the end of the day, boils to one thing – carnal pleasures for money. We had no way of knowing if she would let us in and, if so if we would find anything. That was our weakest link –the idea was weak anyway, so who cared? David was putting the penetration structure into the apartment in his 24/7 working head. I was supposed to get into the apartment (on the condition Lolita would let me in) and…well, let her be in charge while David would get into the place and search for clues and evidence that this was spying. Man, how stupid would she be to have this stuff lying around? But then again, those antennas? We hoped the reimbursement would come from AIE if we paid for this visit. Yeah right! This was based on David's hunches, assertions, premises, and conjectures. We had zilch evidence…but when David was on the track of something and knew it stank, he was usually 99% correct. Ok, so we went with that, and the whole thing was so full of risk, but then again, a lot of risks could mean a lot of rewards but could also mean a lot of shit droppings. David had it all planned out, and it was going to work. At least, that's what we thought and hoped for.

David's idea centered on the fact that she was somehow attracted to me and that getting into her skirt and bedsheets would work, with or without paying. We were hoping for without. I frankly didn't even know what I was hoping for. Sure, the idea of getting into the apartment of this so-much-talked-about beauty and man seducer certainly had its appeal, although I was nervous and wasn't sure if I could get through this. In any case, David didn't care much about that now. He just wanted to attract Lolita's attention, precisely what he did. He followed Lolita everywhere in the coming days, but just letting her see him at some timers, and when she came to the building, he was always there watching her. He even planned to board the elevator and always continued after her 12th floor, although he lived on the 5th. Of course, she became very suspicious. Finally, after David carefully planned it, he positioned himself on the 12th floor one Monday afternoon when she was going for the night language sessions at the industrial complex. She almost crashed into him when coming out.

"What the f**k are you doing here" she blurted out, unable to hide her anger and annoyance with David.

"Oh, sorry, I was just in the neighborhood," he said casually.

"Neighborhood, my ass, you little rat." She suddenly became another woman.

"I have seen you following and watching me for the last two weeks and always behind me like a leach, you little pervert. What do you want, damn you? I don't like you, you hear!" She grabbed his arms and looked into his eyes like a wildcat. Although David was 17, he was even more significant than me, some 188cm, and much more athletic. But at that moment, he felt petite somehow, especially when she, in a blitz of a second, took a small sharp knife out of her purse and put it at the tip of David's Adam's apple. With the other hand, she pressed it and clutched David's balls into a knot. He squealed from pain and fear.

"What do you want, ferret? Why are you following me? What do you know?" She was furious.

Even with the accelerating pain, David knew he was on track for something as she did not have the moves and strength of a typical hooker, and the line "what do you know" was an indicator.

"I am sorry; please let me go; I don't want anything."

"Liar, liar, I will crush your balls and cut your throat if you don't tell the truth, little rodent." She wasn't f**king around and gave a camel's piss if someone would find them here. That's just what exactly happened. Zinka Dubai, an old hag and one of the critical links in the gossip chain of our fine establishment, came out from the apartment just next to Lolita's. She heard the commotion and squealing. She had just finished doing her hair and had some artificial contraption that was holding what was supposedly her hair and head. But she was nosy and always wanted to see what was going on to spread it through the rest of the gossip network in the building. Besides, she always heard (or at least that is what she said) the breathing and panting of Lolita's customers and her moaning. She saw Lolita with David squeezed into the wall when she opened the door. She saw no knife but her hand squeezing David's genitals.

"Ah, I finally caught you blasphemous little whore! Shame on you, now you are off to adolescents, you good-for-nothing slut. I knew it". She was glowing in thinking that she had caught her in the act. Lolita suddenly turned around, not letting go of David's balls or the knife for a second.

"Get the f**k back into your apartment, you ugly cow. If you don't, I will f**k up that thing you call your hair and will rearrange your face so it does look like something, for a change".

Zinka was shocked, and her mouth fell open, disclosing a platitude of rotten, broken, and missing teeth. She was numb and unable to utter a single word. But when she saw the wild predator looks in Lolita's eyes, she knew it was better to get the f**k out of Dodge City.

"The authorities will hear about this, you whore; I promise you bitch", and then she ran back to her lair. Fearlessly, she slammed the door and bolted her locks and keychain.

Lolita suddenly turned her attention back to David.

"Now I won't ask twice, and I will cut you like a sewer rat and rip your balls if you don't answer me – why the f**k are you following me?" David knew he had only one chance, and the squeeze was getting more challenging than the following pain. So it was easy to start crying, and he made it even more dramatic (although he was a bit scared as this got a bit out of hand) when he started to sob.

"I am so sorry, Ms. Petrovna, but my friend is so shy and likes you so much that he wants to sleep with you but doesn't know how to ask about it, so he asked me to ask you, and I didn't know how…I am so sorry. He started weeping now. Please don't hurt me, and forgive me. I mean no harm; my friend wants it so much and is like a brother to me". David was quite an actor, tears running down his cheeks and trembling.

She looked with a suspicious blink in her eye but relaxed her muscles a bit.

"What, your friend wants to sleep with me. You have to be f**king kidding me".

"No, I am not, I swear. I am so embarrassed!" She moved the knife from his throat and let go of the groin. That was when David slid down on the concrete floor of the staircase hallway.

"We thought you had so many male partners, and my friend has never had a woman before, so he wanted someone to teach him the art of love and sex."

"What, you think I am a prostitute?" she said surprisingly.

"No, not that; we just thought you had many men coming to your place…the rumor goes around the building, you know…." David didn't finish the sentence, and she was down with the knife again, a bit of suspicion in her penetrating blue eyes. David had to strike it now.

"I am sorry, please don't hurt me, but we heard you are an..well… an escort service lady, so maybe if we pay, you would sleep with my friend. He has saved some money. She faced a problem now. We have seen you bring so many men here. So we thought you were what you were – a prostitute. Please forgive me; I am so sorry". David covered his hand and started a low sob.

Lolita couldn't believe her ears. What the f**k! She started thinking about this and how to tell this guy and his friend to f**k off, but if she denied it to this guy, even if he was shit scared, the probability that he maybe would follow her again was significant. And who knows, maybe even go to the police at the end. That could not be compromised, especially since they had to transmit a bunch of crucial material next week, as well as the coordinates of where the truck carrying the materials will be. She decided to go with the escort thing and clean away any suspicions this damn boy had. Besides, a younger boy could be a nice thing for a change. She chuckled inside.

"Get up and clean yourself, or someone else might come around. She tucked the knife into the purse.

"Sorry that I came at you like that. I have to be very careful, as men find me attractive, and there are many evil men out there; not all are good or pleasant. And I am not a prostitute. Let's say I like men and their company. If you wanted something, you should have just asked me. Ok? She completely changed, and her composure was relaxed. She was a different woman now. David just nodded, looking at her and standing up, his back against the elevator door.

"Your friend is the cute guy that always blushes when I pass by; Tiger something, right?

"Tigran, yes…David now put on his hopeful face and looked at her.

"We have some savings and can pay Ms. Petrovna so you can teach him the art of love for one evening or something." She laughed so hard. "You mean to teach him how to screw? Right…"You two don't have that money, nor would I take money from you." She was all pleasant now and a different person.

"This is what I will do. I will give him 45min of my time and teach him some things that might be useful with girls. I guess he was never with a woman before?" David nodded. She blinked her eye at David and smiled.

"He will get the best lesson of his life." But after that, I want you to leave me alone and never speak of that to anyone, or I swear I will tell the Police that you are two perverts and offered me money for sex".

"No, I swear, Ms. Petrovna, we won't!" "Call me Lolita," she said. She would not tell the police or anyone else, which would be too dangerous. David knew she was dirty and that her apartment was a nest for something highly illegal and dangerous for our city and security. He needed some ice pronto, as his balls were turning blue.

Inside the Matrix

I was shit nervous after David told me what had happened. A few days passed, and D-day was coming near. We decided it would be a Thursday night when she finished her class; I would get my 45min of pleasure right after that. Man! Meanwhile, David was preparing whatever strategy he had. Just the afternoon before we were supposed to do whatever we were supposed to do, he rushed into my apartment right after school. His eyes were shining like two comets, and he had that body language about him which meant he was in control of things or he just made an extraordinary discovery. It was to be the latter.

"I know what the thing on the lighter was, Tigran. I f**king remembered, and it took me three hours last night to get through all the emblems, insignia, and crests I could find in books. And I found it in one of our old books on signs and symbols. It's a KGB seal with a shield and sword. That was a f**king KGB lighter that Lolita had.

Now I am sure something is happening, and the two guys we see more than others are dirt". David was referring to the blonde giant, a sleek, haute couture-dressed darker man of slim but still strong composure and bodily structure with a ponytail and was in his later forties while the blonde giant was probably around 35.

"Anyway, bro, all is fixed now for next week. You will have Lolita for 45min and leave the apartment door unlocked. She will presumably have you in her bedroom, as I think the equipment must be hidden in the closet as that is the only logical place. She cannot have it where she has sex as it is too dangerous. They probably take it out when needed. The antennas are in the living and bedroom, and there must be some monster cables. While you are indulging in sensual pleasure, I will snoop around. I know this electronic shit better than anyone, so I will find out if something is fishy. And I won't stay more than needed. No worries, I won't peek into the room". He laughed.

"Man, what if she sees you? Then we are both f**ked, well…at least we will be both dead. If she doesn't get us, the guys will". I was worried.

"Don't worry, nothing will happen, and the guys don't come around on Thursday night. They never do". That's what David thought, at least.

As two skilled operatives whose training and experience were extensive, André Veselovsky and Vlad Karpov knew that Lolita had to be watched at all times. There was just too much at stake, and not that she was unreliable; on the contrary, she just had too many things going for her, and the cover-up with men was not all that great as there was too much traffic in her apartment at some times. They didn't like that, especially André, who began to fancy Lolita more and more. He had his way with her, and she gave him pleasure that he utterly enjoyed, but now he was getting annoyed by the other man, and that meant only one bad thing in this business – he had feelings for her. Both of them just came unexpectedly that Thursday afternoon, as if they had a hunch, but they just wanted to check everything and the equipment for the transmission that was going to happen that week as well as the triangulation they were supposed to do of the truck carrying THE LOAD which was going to be intercepted by another team as soon as they delivered. More than anything, they did not trust Lolita.

I had a wrong hunch about all this, plus I was so nervous standing there in front of Lolita's door while David was behind the stairwell-reinforced concrete wall. I had my best outfit, perfume on, a hot steamy Turkish bath, and all the confidence and coolness I could muster. My palms were sweating while holding a small bouquet of roses. This was my idea. David didn't give much shit to romantic expressions of desire, lust, or love. This was a job that had to be done. Full stop! But who was I kidding…I was nervous as hell and burning with desire as hell at the same time. WOW…I thought of her fantastic body, forgetting that this was the devil's lair and I would eventually be eaten up. I rang the buzzer several times, and Lolita opened the door. She came home a bit earlier and looked terrific, wearing almost nothing. A silky peach negligé and beautiful high heel shoes were there. That was about it. Yes, her beautiful blonde hair was loose and had more curls than ever. Blonde eyes were more penetrating than ever, and the make-up was a sublime combination of Loréal, a Cover Girl…I almost fainted when I saw her magnificent naked figure and those fabulous breasts underneath. I was in heaven.

"Hello sweetie, common in…flowers…that is so nice…you are a sweetheart!" She closed the door and walked to the kitchen. I will be back in a second with the drinks. Gin and tonic are okay. I murmured something…of course, anything is okay, even the most potent alcohol. One thing I did remember, as my brain and concentration were melting in seconds, was to unlock the main door slowly. Otherwise, David would have been f**ked, as being a locksmith is not one of his traits.

She offered me a drink, vodka Stolichnaya and after 5 minutes of chit-chat, she took my clothes off and led me to the bedroom and the bed covered in satin. I had just entered the seventh heaven, and there was no way I would return. I didn't even have time to be nervous or blush; I just wondered about all the lucky men who entered this paradise. Now I was one of them. Instantly I forgot about the spying, the KGB guys, the agency, David, and this stupid mission. I was thinking and seeing Lolita in front of me.

David waited some 15min and decided to go in. The door quickly opened, and it didn't produce any cracking sound. It was brand new and steel reinforced with three locks inside and a steel bar. Miraculously Lolita just locked one Wertheimer lock and left the others open. The number of locks suggested something more than usual household security. It was a pleasantly furnished apartment, something from an IKEA catalog, nothing lavish but nothing out of proportion or a good sense of taste. Lolita had style, and it seemed she liked to live comfortably. David knew there was not too much time to spare as God knows how long or abruptly my amorous rendezvous would last. I was on the sheets learning a whole bunch of new things. David heard the moans and movement from the bedroom and just smiled. "That lucky bastard,"…he thought. There was no time to waste. He hurriedly moved from the hallway to the kitchen and then to the living room like a cat on the prowl. He saw the monster cables and another wiring intelligently "connected" to the large Sony TV, JVC Video, and Hi-Fi Stereo. If anyone had any suspicions, they would fly away as this was the best home entertainment set David ever saw. There were around six loudspeakers. It was all probably a camouflage, but maybe it also worked. He had no time to check it out. After checking all the cables and writing some stuff on his little black notepad, he traced several cables leading to the bedroom but very nicely hidden. The main antennas were outside the bedroom window. He couldn't get in there, not yet, anyway. The closet was next. He got in and turned the light, all without making a noise. He was hoping I would not screw up and she would be in the closet at any moment. It was full of beautiful clothes, shoes, accessories, and you name it. David scanned the little room like a laser, and it took him 5min to find out that there was an anteroom hidden behind the last line of clothes. Something was behind it, but he had no idea how to get to it or open the door. The whole panel seemed okay, but to a keen eye, it was misplaced. It was newer than the other walls and fit in this closet.

Time was running out, and David began to sweat. The moaning was more apparent now. There must be a button in here some-where. SHIT! He was getting frustrated more and more. Suddenly his heart stopped. There was a ring on the door. Did he hear it right? Yes, it was crystal clear. He heard some movement in the bedroom, and Lolita was probably startled to hear that too. David was frozen in place, but his mind raced fast. There was no chance to get out of the closet now, and where the f**k would he go. He looked inside the closet and saw the upper cupboards resting on a solid reinforced parapet. There was not much time to think. This was it, especially when he heard the main door open.

Two silhouettes were outside Lolita's door listening to some muf-fling sounds from within. Vlad, the curly blonde guy, was a giant. I remember seeing him come to Lolita's place without looking into his eyes. He always looked around like an animal, looking for prey or being on the lookout – like he was being hunted. His looks were precisely like those of a former Russian heavy-category boxer with blonde peroxide hair who could have just been a KGB agent, a little golden earring, and a suit that looked like it was put over a wood log. He was a 100% peasant but a dangerous one. André was a sharply dressed man with three pieces of pink stripe suit and a paisley tie. A gold ring with a massive stone was on his left middle finger, and a Rolex Oyster watch was on his right hand. The man was all about looks, and he seemed to be the intellectual piece of the duo, the brains, while Vlad was the muscle. He spoke first.

"Some sounds are coming from within, and she has no customers today, and that is not the TV. What the f**k is going on!" He rang the bell and instinctively went for the door knob. It opened quickly as butter. David made one small mistake, not locking the door behind him. He knew that and was biting his lips behind the cupboard-closed doors, lying with the linen on the top shelf and praying that this wooden structure would hold. He was only 60 kilos, so maybe it would. Who knows. André was distraught now as this was not one of Lolita's traits – sloppiness! She would never leave the door open, never! Vlad was already going for his hidden holster and his huge Glock. They got inside the apartment, scanned the living room and kitchen in a second, forgot about the closet and bathroom, and swiftly went to the bedroom before Loilita could manage to get out. She was standing naked and sweaty, trying to cover herself with her nightgown, and I was looking behind the sheets like a scared church mouse. When I saw the two guys, my heart stopped; I remembered them instantly. They were in the apartment, and David's theories were now falling into place more firmly.

André spoke our language but with a broken accent with Lolita, sometimes switching to Russian…What the f**k do you think you are doing with that teenage boy? Are you out of your mind, you…" he wanted to add bitch, but restrained himself. He was furious as he saw that I was not a client and this was not the visiting day. She tried to explain.

"I know he looks young, but he is 21, and he is a friend André!" "This is my brother André, and he worries when I go out with strange men or when some of my friends come for a drink." She was trying to salvage this, trembling in her voice and trying somehow to hide the fact that she had customers and that this was not her brother. She turned to me graciously, adapting to the situation immediately.

"Yes, I am f**king pissed off, yelled André. Mom told me to watch over you and what you bring her, young students or what the f**k… You know you belong to only one man, and that is your fiancée!" He was raging, furious. There was no fiancée, but only André. He was mad as she had brought someone young this time, obviously not a customer, and broke the rule of bringing him on a sacred day when the transmissions would take place in the evening and leaving the door open. She would be taught a lesson! Then Vlad spoke: "I will crush your bones, little man. You have nothing to do with my…he hesitated awhile…friend's sister…."

Before he could finish, there was a slight noise around the door. Someone else opened the apartment with a key and walked casually in. The blonde guy Vlad and André turned around like two animals going for his pocket, probably for a gun. I was shit scared and suddenly freezing under the warm sheets. "What's this, a congress? Asked the visitor; it was an older gentleman with grayish hair and a fine mustache, looking a bit oriental but more Middle Eastern, also nicely dressed and very cool. The two goons eased their guard when they recognized the man. Lolita intervened immediately: "This is my father, Bruno, Michael." There was no Michael here…I guess it was me. She looked at me with her penetrating eyes. "It's time for you to leave now; please take your clothes and go." He just smiled and gave a cold grin to Lolita and looked at me with dark, almost inhuman eyes but with a crooked smile. It was time for me to get the f**k out of there. It wasn't very comfortable, and I somehow got out, collected my clothes, and took them to the living room, dressing in a flash, still with a considerable sex appetite. All that time, the two big guys watched me, which made it even worse, but the man they called Bruno, the dad, smiled again, relaxed and even more remarkable. I think he realized that there was no real danger here, just a teenager with his pants down with a huge boner, experiencing some of the pleasures that Lolita provided. Good for us that he was partially wrong. After 25min, it was all over for me, and my heavenly gates collapsed. I was back in the real world. Now I just thought about David. I couldn't see him anywhere. So he must have gone out…I hope!

David was keeping his breath and tearing the skin from his lips. There was another visitor. Shit! His mind was racing like an Indy 500-speed car, hoping this blonde Kazak monster Vlad won't start looking through the apartment. Why would he look around? Hopefully, they will be satisfied with me getting kicked out. The whole thing was so suddenly f**ked up beyond redemption now. Instead of me staying in the warm sheets with Lolita and David leaving the apartment, it would be the other way around. However, David was squeezed into a cupboard instead with three perilous individuals and a lady that lost control. He was stuck in the apartment for now. It was so f**king dangerous, but it was worth gold, and David knew it. He just hoped the wood would keep him in the air now.

When I was gone, Vlad bolted the door, checked the kitchen and the bathroom, and opened the closet door. "All clear"! André began to say something, fury still in his eyes, but Bruno cut him off.

"Not now. We have work to do. We will deal with this issue later". He grinned and looked at Lolita. "So you like them young, don't you? I don't blame you". He looked towards André with a dose of satisfaction as he knew he had the hots for her. "What you do on the dates allocated to you, it's your own business, but if it collides with the task ahead of us, then it is my business. You also left the door unlocked and brought a teenage customer. Both of those things are dangerous, especially nosy kids." She tried to say something, to explain the door, as she was sure that it was locked, but Bruno just waved his hand. "Later, now let's talk about Jim's information and the truck. Later tonight, we will transmit. Vlad, check the equipment. And you, he pointed towards Lolita, who was still trembling on the bedroom door, get dressed and get us some drinks and food. We will deal with security issues later, and besides, this thing will be over in a few days, and we will be all gone, except for you, my dear, as you will have to stay six months longer here not to raise any suspicion". With that, they went to the living room. Vlad opened the closet, and David's heart stopped in an instant. There was a little crack in the cupboard door, and David could see Vlad going towards the false panel behind the last line of Lolita's clothes. He turned an almost invisible little know hidden behind one pair of shoes, and the panel opened. David was angry at himself for missing that. When the panel opened, he saw the most sophisticated piece of electronic equipment, things he had just heard from his dad that were being developed. They were already here, and Vlad just turned some stuff on to see if it worked, and it did. Hundreds of little lights, transmission systems, strange communication blocks and packets, little screens and other devices for tracking and triangulation, digital transmission, and even jamming devices – holly shit! There was much more here than David knew, and he knew quite a bit about electronics. He couldn't see much, but this was first-class military hi-tech. Where the f**k did they get this. He couldn't see more as Vlad closed the panel and the closet door. Fortunately for him, Vlad didn't look too much into the closet, plus the closet didn't have that tremendous acoustic capability (to stop the sound), so David decided to do dangerous and stupid things. He got out silently while they were talking loud in the living room and pressed his ear to the door so he was able to hear the parts of the conversation, the most important ones. It was a gamble, as they could open this door again, but David would hide behind the clothes on the left this time. Or get caught…Shit! It lasted about an hour, and he could hear that Bruno was about to leave with Vlad. André had some unfinished business with Lolita, and he would stay. They left, and fortunately for David, no one looked inside, and he heard André telling Lolita to undress and shower. He was going to join her. She went to the bathroom, obviously reluctantly, to take a shower. As soon as André joined her, David heard that wild things were happening, physically, verbosely, and sexually. He didn't have time to think about this. It was his exit time. He just prayed that they won't pay too much attention to yet another unlocked door, maybe not.

I was out of my mind. David was nowhere to be found, and I just had dreadful thoughts. After three hours, just before nine o'clock, he arrived at my apartment door, locking it behind him, white as a ghost but looking OK. He spoke in a very composed manner in the hallway. My folks were watching TV in the living room.

"I know what they are up to. They will hijack the John Higgins Ltd special transportation truck carrying some nuclear material and transmit the key information for Hi-tech and weaponry blueprints in which John Higgins Ltd industries are secretly involved. They will transmit this to "Bruno's" people, whoever they are, and they are badasses, bro, badasses."

"Oh man, are you ok, David? I was scared as hell. Shit man! You were in the apartment all the time. Holy shit! He told me how he hid in the closet, the electronic equipment he saw, and the gadgets, cables, and talk they had with Bruno. All of it! He was ok, more excited than scared. He jokingly said that he was sorry I couldn't get the complete 45min treatment with Lolita and that she would be in trouble for this, as André would see to that. I was now scared for Lolita, even though she was an accomplice in this badass thing. The next day we went to Agency for Industrial Espionage (AIE) to Jerry Matsui and told him everything we heard and knew about the transmission and the heist that would take place. He knew David's dad well and believed us when we presented the thing. It was time for the pros to finish up this thing. Jerry took all of it well, was angry a bit as we could have compromised his investigation but commended us on the job well done. It seems they had these people under the looking glass for some time. John Higgins Ltd was going to send the scheduled truck, but not with the cargo of sensitive material that the crooks were waiting for but something else. Jerry was going to see to that. We have all the info on when they would meet for the vital transmission and triangulation, and Jerry told us to stay away from this one now. We happily obliged.

Outside, Looking in—Seaside Matrix

It was Sunday evening, and the transmission would occur in a few minutes. Jerry Matsui was cold as sushi. Special agent Matsui was always concentrated, always on the lookout, sharp, and ready to act. He had five agents with him, and they were top notch four men and one woman. Three more were waiting by the car, while another group of ten was at the stand-by inside the empty truck, which looked more like a Trojan Horse, ready to surprise the visitors intending to hijack it. Jerry's man all carried 38mm silencers and Uzi's, just in case this whole thing got out of hand, which would happen. After all the intel David gave them and the description of the guys I gave, after drawing the photo robots myself, Jerry was able to find, with the help of Interpol and the American CIA, that they were dealing with the same two ex-KGB rouges agents that they were also following and that was no shit. There was also a third man, a shadow figure who went by different alias, Abdul, Bruno, Gerry, Serim, etc. But he was impossible to track. They just had a photo of him. Jerry was convinced, especially that the intel he collected coincided with David's information and my descriptions from the hot afternoon in Lolita's apartment. He was now tracking a group of ex-KGB and other agents working for some rouge nation and selling industrial and other military secrets. David was clairvoyant at the end. This was probably just a part of them, but apprehending them would be worth gold, plus the girl involved. The shadow man was essential, but he was nowhere to be seen. Somehow they popped up in our country, in our city. Still, Jerry just could not put all the pieces together, especially the place they visited, the place where information was being sent from, the place where the information was being milked from, from people revisiting Lolita's always warm satin sheets, the place, an apartment, an enclosure within which something wrong originated. Evil developed—the industrial espionage matrix – Lolita's apartment on the 12th floor. He would get all that when apprehended, together with the group going after the John Higgins Ltd truck. All those things were going through his head while small grains of sweat were emerging on his forehead. The heat was unbearable outside, and it was even warm even in our staircase elevator shafts which were always cold. Still, Jerry was a bit nervous. The two former KGB guys under surveillance for more than six months were there with this hooker Lolita, starting their transmission at any moment. A few days ago, they got Lolita in and pressed her with a life sentence if she did not cooperate. She was a mess and totally flipped out, but in the end, she went along as she didn't want to see the bars of a cell her whole life. She was still young and wanted to see life & sun. A minor sentence in a secret prison was promised. After that, she would get a new identity and money to go wherever she wanted. She was thinking of Tuscany. All that went through Jerry's mind when he pondered if Lolita would leave the door unlocked for the 2nd time. This time for real! Jerry had no intention of knocking on the door or blowing it up. There was no kidding with these guys. It had to be swift. At exactly 22:00 hours, they went in. The door was unlocked as promised.

They say that memories don't have expiration dates like milk cartons. Here I go again with sayings, but this one stuck to Lolita when a 55 caliber hit her right shoulder, burying itself deep into the flesh and bone. The other bullet missed just by an inch to her left temple, and before the blonde ex-KGB guy Vlad could send the third one with his silencer between her eyes, Jerry Matsui took his Uzi and popped it into the giant's body. André emerged from the closet room with his gun and saw Lolita on the ground and Vlad full of bullets. Two of Matsui's agents were down, one dead, one wounded, both struck by Vlad. Andrej emerged from the closet and saw that Vlad, even though critically wounded wanted to put the last bullet into Lolita, who was bleeding a bit now. He took his gun and shot Vlad right in the head. Andrej wanted to do something about the others in the room, but he already knew it was too late. What was done was done.

As soon as they entered the apartment, Vlad knew that things had gone wrong and they were compromised. After shooting two agents down, he turned his anger towards Lolita, knowing she must be responsible for this shit. The rest was history. When Lolita fell to the floor carpet and closed her eyes for a second, as the pain struck her hard, she wanted to be back in Russia with her grandmother, who was no longer alive. She was only five years old and playing in the dining room. Her grandmother was weaving and looked up at her. My dear child, what would you like to do growing up?

"I would like to be a ballerina grandma, or maybe an actress, something sweet and airy, with many nice people around me…." So you shall, my child, so you shall, said Grandma. Lolita looked at Jerry Matsui leaning over her as a knight in shining armor…he picked her up, and the paramedics arrived soon. There was a lot of commotion in the building, as this does not happen that often. Dead and wounded is not precisely your everyday tower life, though we had our fair and square share of that in the past.

Jim, a guy on the board of directors in the John Higgins Ltd company, was the mole, although he had no idea who was behind the whole thing, as the former KGB agent, André, would not speak. After a while, they attempted to deport him back to Moscow, but they failed. The agency wanted all of them to pay for their crimes here, and they also had double citizenship, which made things easier. The other two who were trying to hijack the truck were local nationals, and they got 15 years of hard labor. The "Seaside Jail," as it was called, on a small rocky island in the Mediterranean, soon became a relatively permanent home for all of them. At least André got 25 years, a long time in God's forsaken place. Vlad got the cold ground and eternity in hell, probably. Jim, the guy from the company who supplied all the hard cash info, joined them for the same duration. The agency was merciless and swift when it came to executing the law. No judge would go against this state within a state body. But the worst thing about being outside the law is that that same law does not protect you. So these guys paid a considerable price but never gave up on the critical guy. The man they called Bruno was nowhere to be found. It was hard to tell if he was the critical guy, but he was most cunning, leaving no trace behind him, none whatsoever. As for Lolita, she talked as much as she could, although she didn't know the making of the top either but gave all the rest she could. They went a bit easier on her. 8 years in a woman's prison, and then she would find another life and heal her wounds…

We were happy that this thing was over and that we could never be connected to it as Lolita never found out anything. I was just a happy customer, after all! We never told anyone and kept our mouths shut but were happy deep down that a patriotic favor and deed to our country was made. There was no recognition or commendation. That part went to Jerry Matsui, not to us. But we were ok, especially David, who was so happy that his premises, conjectures, and assertions proved correct. Damn, the guy was good and could have easily been the director of any spook agency. I was frankly happy on an entirely different level. To have been for 25 minutes in the satin sheets with Lolita before the two Russian goons came in was paradise. I Didn't get the full instructional ca 45 minutes, but still, it was worth it, and she showed me things I will always treasure. David always said I should be thankful to him for opening Lolita's gates for me, as that was worthwhile in the long run. He once told me often laughed thinking of that story but was sad about how Lolita ended up.

As for David…well, my friends…he is a wealthy and successful man, running his two IT companies, one in Silicon Valley and another in Tel Aviv that his father set up. In Tel Aviv, he gave the name 'Balagan Tech,' a Russian-derived Hebrew word for "mess." Israelis are very familiar with this concept and have the cause to use the word often. It applies to anything from a disorderly desk to geopolitical woes. David said it reminded him of the times with Lolita and the spygame we played. We kept in touch for some years, but the wings of time took us in different directions, so we didn't see each other that much. But when we do, we think of the crazy events in our tower, this incredible shooting, and David's ingenious systemic mind. Of course, my encounter with the romantic Lolita… oh yes, we think of that…often.

27

Saturday Night Tapes, Diamond Cow Blues, & Carousel of Fools

The scene resembled something from an Italian B family feud or mafia movie, a bad Soprano scene, or a segment from the LA Riots. It portrayed a bundle of individuals involved in a street fight that was rarely seen, even by the standards of our unusual tower. Hair, teeth, clothes, and God knows what else was being torn, broken, and flying all over the parking place. It was an assemblage of ca 100 people, men, and women, young and old, able and disabled, massed in one huge angry body mass, not knowing what the f**k they were doing here in the first place nor what started all of this and what will end it. The only thing that mattered at that moment was that someone was an asshole, idiot, whore, criminal, liar, cheater – you name it! Screaming and shouting were followed by some weird shuffling sound from so many hands and legs moving in a constricted space of the main oblong parking. The police were on the way, foot police, although this scene required riot police or even the National Guard. It's hard to believe what harm and damage a diaper full of sepia-colored baby shit, forcefully thrown from the 18th floor by a significant peasant character, can do. This diaper had such a massive impact on the condition of the human state that particular September afternoon, which inevitably created a chain reaction of violent events that led to a violent street shuffle of grand proportions. And they say shit doesn't make a difference! Yeah, it does – SHIT HAPPENS, and it happened in a big way that day! But it wasn't that frigging simple. The grand finale of the day had its precursors and leading actors. The combination of these some-how bizarrely unrelated events united by a heap of pooh-pooh in a rather stinky fashion led to one major havoc that even got a few lines on page six in the local newspaper "Morning Sunpost."

***

Dan Saltstone's criminal career shortly began after graduating with honors from the medical-dental school at the local university. Soon after, he became a dentist and a practitioner with a medical diplo-ma and a dental surgery diploma. He also had a special certificate for two years of studies in dental medicine, which put him magna cum laude, the best in his graduating class. His parents were in-credibly proud of him, especially his dad, who was also a dentist. He was always dressed nicely, a tall man with deep brown curly hair and a tanned face; well-fit was the ladies' favorite. Their younger son Mischa was a disappointment and a half bum interested only in Volkswagen Beetle cars and Pink Floyd music, plus going out with a peasant girl that had no school whatsoever and behaving and looking himself more and more like a hillbilly every day. With long curly hair, yellow submarine glasses, and hippy clothes, he looked like a used-up version of John Lennon, just fatter and even paler as he never saw a ray of sun, spending his time mostly inside and during the night.

The younger lad didn't show any genuine interest in pursuing an academic career (or any career for that matter), at least one of dental medicine, the 'science of the mouth & teeth' as Dan proudly called it. Dan soon realized another aspect of dental professions – the smuggling of diamonds and other stuff in the mouth and teeth. After a visit to South Africa at one point and a raise in customers at his private dental firm, which was suddenly opened, the raise also became evident in his lifestyle, where cash was being generated and spent simultaneously at the speed of light. Everyone thought the business must have been a blast, but the real business was blossoming. The diamond trade was so bloody lucrative that Dan was in paradise. He could afford just about anything. Some gold on the side and teeth fixing were excellent, but diamonds were the real deal. Miraculously, after a full year of operation, he didn't get caught. Somehow, somewhere – I guess out of sheer stupidity and greed – he got involved in a car-tape-recorders-heist-scheme that his idiot brother Mischa was running. The heist of tape recorders was high, and Mischa had a very swift gang of under-aged kids pinching this stuff professionally. They were ripping everyone and most of us from the building. Mischa didn't give a shit who it was that owned the car, just what was in the car. He even pinched by mistake his parents' car! Any alarm system was hacked and bypassed, and any car with a music system inside was in peril. Everyone was in danger. They were operating in some districts in the city, never getting caught until. Dan was a bit worried for his brother but didn't say no to some extra cash plus, Mischa was also up to his neck in helping Dan with the diamond and other precious stones illegal imports.

The ultimate mistake both of these made was to get involved and personally pinch the new CD audio stereo car-system stuff that Saki Debanov (the proud owner of the new fish restaurant, just opened in the back side ground level of our tower) acquired. He got this (one of the first in the city) from Japan and paid bundles of money, plus having it installed in Germany for his brand new 500 series BMW car. Saki was riche-nouveau, getting rich on tomatoes and potatoes, extending his business into fish restaurants, cafes, storage facilities, energy, and close connection with the local hoodlums. He was on the fast track to becoming a good fellow himself. The man was someone you did not want to f**k with, certainly not to steal his new car Sony CD High-Fidelity Stereo Surround Equipment with a 9 CD changer in the rear trunk. He brought prosperity and busi-ness to the neighborhood. That he was not far from a mule when it came to brains and that six of his teeth were made of gold didn't matter to anyone. His money did!

***

Salihi Saaban and Tito Pantaglione pinched the wrong car that night, Mischa Salstone's car, to be exact. The 'Saturday Night Tapes Session,' as Salihi and Zed used to brag and talk about, ended in a badass way. The night began with the traditional dope session for Salihi, which consisted of taking a Prozac type of drug combined with inhaling some glue shit that, again, according to Salihi, had a remarkable healing effect. I don't know what he was getting healed from, but Salihi was more or less high every night of the week. The dope combo worked wonders for him. Usually a tall man with decaying hair on the sides and red, sort of Anjou or Burundian nose bordering on Albino complexion, Salihi was even taller and a noticeable site when on drugs. That evening he and Tito, whose shady character and domino crime effect doings were well known around our part of town, went for a nite-ride. Tito was a short guy, always wearing a small Fedora bucket hat, the so-called French Connection movie hat that Gene Hackman (Popeye Doyle) made world famous. He was nothing like Popeye Doyle but did his best to emulate the great role model on the other side of the law. His hands and legs were also short for a 16-year-old, and they had no intention of growing further as all of that stopped when he was 13. He was a formidable force with a very mean, dark complexion face and narrow but sparkling black eyes and teeth like a sewer rat. Everyone knew he was already doing chores for hoodlums and setting up some small-time action for himself. Salihi was a good partner, an almost complete idiot, doped most of the time, and obedient to Tito as a junkyard dog. It must have dated to when they visited the local ZOO as younger kids to see the animals. The ZOO was the epitome of its true purpose: a facility where wild animals are housed for exhibition. It was also a prison for these poor creatures, an inhumane resting place until their death. With its idiotic name: "The Valley of Living Nature," it was one hell of a place. A couple of animals tried to run, and some committed suicide. Everything was better than spending time in cells four by 4 feet or slightly larger, depending on the animals. Wolves had it the worst; four were stacked inhumanely or in animal conditions. The oldest went slightly mad and made crazy circles in his little cell. The birds and monkeys somehow survived the best out of the whole lot. Larger animals of prey had it tough. The lions were so worn down and senile, probably even blind, that they didn't care anymore or react to anything. The same was with the tigers. The Zebra pair was long gone, as they committed suicide. There were some other weird animals, but they were not worth mentioning. But there was a grizzly bear that was still somehow active and energized. The story was that the ZOO keepers were giving him some drugs just for fun – keeping him high all the time. He couldn't even sleep and made all these ridiculous sounds during the night, which would piss off the monkeys, and then the birds would join in creating a sick animal farm symphony. Anyhow, a horrible place by all standards, but one which Salihi and Tito enjoyed visiting time after time. It was a great place for them to smoke cigarettes, later pot while teasing the animals until insanity. They loved pissing on monkeys, farting at the wolves, throwing tomatoes at Lions and Tigers, shouting, and cracking jokes at the bear. Once, the bear was so pissed at Salihi's shouting that he almost chopped his head with his claw, as Salihi loved to come close to the bear through the steel bars. If it weren't for Tito's swift move, Salihi would have surely been without a left eye, cheek, and ear. The revenge was merciless. Tito first reacted by drawing the bear near the steel bars and then placing a horrid tuberculosis type of yellowish-green mixture of his spit into the poor bear's left eye, which might blind him temporarily. After throwing stones at him, they came one night and tried to burn the poor thing's fur. It caught on fire his back, but fortunately, the night watch prevented the bear from burning to death by hosing him with water. After that historical incident, the two became blood brothers. Salihi never forgot what Tito did and stayed loyal to him, always. Those two were a strange site and a weird feast for the eyes, a giant and a dwarf. But mind you, laughing at those two could cost you a broken nose, jaw, or lost teeth. Both of them had major hill-Billy bums for parents and didn't give a shit about anything, especially school or any future for that matter. They just enjoyed the tastelessness of the moment. We always treated them respectfully (everyone was afraid of Tito, and Salihi was so unpredictable that one moment he might kiss you and the other blow your head off) and laughed at Tito's jokes which were never any good. Unlike Salihi's Soviet training overalls dress code, Tito was all wool, cashmere, fine slacks, polo sweaters, and pink stripe blazers. He dressed like a 50-year-old mobster-wanna-be, not like a 16-year bum kid. That's why they got involved in stealing all kinds of goods. The mistake was to start getting into the car stereo stuff, as that turf was already occupied. After robbing several cars and stashing it all in their Fiat Topolino, they went for a ride. The car broke down that evening at 03:00 AM after a lunatic drive through one of the neighborhoods. The car crashed into a ditch and lost both front wheels. Salihi was driving, and somehow both of them survived in one piece. As both were high as a kite, the only "rational" thing was to find another car and transfer the stolen goods. The decision fell on a Volvo 850 that they saw nearby. They didn't know this was Mischa Salstone's car parked outside his girlfriend's apartment. He didn't have time to get rid of the stolen stuff in the trunk, especially the CD package they pinched from Saki Debanov's BMW. Salihi and Tito had no idea until the next morning when they popped the trunk in Tito's garage.

***

Saki Debanov's rise to wealth began with taxi driving, or to be more exact dead bodies' taxi smuggling driving across the border. In some weird scheme, he was helping out people (for bundles of cash, of course) to transport their dead loved ones that perished in another country by putting them into empty dishwashers, machine washers, or stove cartons that would be mounted on the top of the car and then smuggled somehow over the border. Or that was the story. The story also told of his dropping the whole thing when his car was stolen, including the dead customer in the above box. After that, as you can imagine, the entire thing was dropped altogether. What he did not have in his brains, Saki compensated in hard 16h work per day, and cunningness was rarely seen in a human being. Before you knew it, he began the FISH RESTAURANT "Pisces the Fish" chain, which became the talk of the town. As he lost several teeth in some whore house fight, and to show off his new wealth, 18K gold teeth soon arrived on the scene. He even got a nickname, "The Goldfish." Aside from a beautiful 19-year-old girl from Moscow, his last acquisition was a brand new CD player in the car with changeable discs in the rear trunk. This was state of the art then and just hit the markets in Europe and the US. Saki had to have it, and he was in love with it!

***

Bob Bondarenko was the ultimate peasant. He was the epitome of the word, meaning, the social phenomena, its history – you name it. The man was the closest thing that came to a domestic animal. He was short in composure, bald with highlander red crimson color from centuries of ancestors plowing the fields, hard nails on his fingers that could dig wells, and a robust bulky body with all the touches of a Neanderthal dressed in civic clothes. He came from the hills, occupied an empty apartment on the 17th floor, and never refused to leave. This somehow worked. Aside from his peasant wife, Broccoli, he had two children, a little infant named Zlatan and a teenage daughter named Zlatania. After the year, the family was enlarged by the fifth member of the household, Bob's new crown possession, brown cow Maria. He needed to feel at home and the free milk, so Maria came along. Maria lived on the balcony, and she ate and pissed there. Bob also took her down to graze our patches of grass and shit and piss even more. He usually took the large elevator where she could fit in nicely.

Sometimes when that thing was out of order, the stairs were used. This incredible livestock tenant brought consternation to the whole tower, and attempts were made to remove this creature that was pissing and farting and shitting on the 17th-floor balcony, messing up the façade and presenting a health hazard in the process. Everything went through Arno Stockhouse. Weeks and months passed, and nothing was being done as Arno had an ulterior motive for squatting in this issue. President of the Council of tenants (of our skyscraper), Mr. Arno 'the cockroach' Stockhouse, was getting the free milk from Bob Bondarenko and closing his eyes on this potential health haphazard as the cow was pissing liters and liters of urine down the balcony and the eastern façade of the tower. All the complaints from the tenants were brushed off as long as the milk flowed. Nothing would have happened if it wasn't for that afternoon on September 15th when a shitty diaper changed many people's faith.

***

The diaper gained speed as it fell from the 17th floor with high velocity. Dan's son, the little peasant Zlatan, was still in diapers. As the boiling milk was covering the stove, his mommy Brocollia did not have time to dispose of the diaper properly, so she just threw it with all her might out the open window down the street, not thinking for a second where the thing might fall. The diaper, usually a white garment consisting of a folded cloth which was, in Zlatan's case, a bit faded and brownish (probably due to being rewashed sometimes), is drawn up between the legs and fastened at the waist. When hoisted out the window, it kept a compact shape as Brocollia just robustly took it off her kids' ass. Worn by infants to catch excrement, the diaper was never meant to be a flying object, let alone to carry so much human waste as Zlatan crapped mightily into it that afternoon. When Brocollia realized what she did, she screamed, running to the window and ignoring the burning milk on the stove:

"F**k, f**k, she was cursing; I could have used that thing a couple more times, dam it! I need to fetch it back, son of a bitch." She was adamant about retrieving this worthy possession. She looked down the window, saw the thing fall on some guy's head, and saw her daughter Zlatania standing nearby.

The diaper landed, with all its might, onto Mischa's head as he was silently arguing with Dan over the disappearance of the car and the major f**k-up that was going to bring.

'What the f**k' screamed Mischa! The thing did not hurt him that much, as it was soft, but it opened up a bit in the flight and twisted around, so the shit partly came out when it hit Mischa's head and smelled like hell!

'Motherf**ker, motherf**kers, f**k', he was screaming, realizing what had happened. Dan was shocked, and for a moment, he forgot the problem they had hand and began to laugh.

'F**k man, this shit can only happen to you, my brother.'

Salihi and Tito arrived at the scene also. They were able to stash the car in Tito's garage after the heist the night before, and now they needed some extra time to think about what to do. They were surely going to sell a hell of a lot of things from the trunk but getting rid of the huge Volvo 850 that belonged to Mischa Salstone (they realized that instantly) was another matter. What the f**k? They would take it out of the city and sell it. F**k Dan and Mischa! Salihi was doped and blurted out – 'F**k you, you got your CD stolen, man… now you are covered in shit…you motherf**ker, man, you are a piece of shit, you deserve it! Now they saw Mischa covered partly in diaper shit, and they could not stop to laugh madly.

Dan was startled, and so was Mischa, when they heard,

'What the f**k, how do you know…' and then they realized in an instant…

'What the f**k, you stole our car, you motherf**kers!'

***

Zlatania was down there as she was playing with some other kids, and she noticed the crashing diaper and instantly recognized it as her brother's. Also, her mother yelled from the 17th-floor window at her – 'pick it up, Zlatania, pick it up, I dropped it, honey'! It had all the signs of heavy usage and was full of shit which could only mean one thing – it was her brothers.

'Sure, mom, no problem.'

She took the shitty diaper, it was half empty now and started to fold it so she could carry it home for more use.

'What the f**k' Mischa said in a startled voice when he saw Zlatania go for the shitty diaper. He somehow forgot in a second what he had heard from Salihi and Tito.

'What are you gonna do with that kid!'

'Oh, mommy asked me to bring it back. She threw it out accidentally but still wants to keep it as Zlatan will probably use it a couple more times.' With that, she picked up the shitty diaper in her hands.

No one could believe what they saw. The girl was a f**king moron. Mischa saw the creature with dirty flaxen black hair gesticulating from the 17th floor. He got mad now.

'You f**king peasant cow, you f**king Neanderthals!'

He looked at the creature upstairs, and the girl, again raging mad, grabbed the diaper from Zlatania, opened it thoroughly, and plastered it all over the head.

'Here, you f**king peasant, eat this, you a little piece of shit.' He pressed it even more violently, and the poor girl fell on the asphalt with the diaper smeared all over her head.

But Dan didn't take his eyes off Salihi and Tito, not for a moment, not even when the diaper was used again. He started yelling at Salihi and Tito, calling them names, and threatening to kill them when they put 2 and 2 together. Dan also knew that someone was skimming their operations, and it made sense that these two clowns were involved as he caught one little thief that implicated Tito in a recent car tape player heist. After applying the shitty diaper onto Zlatania's face, Mischa soon joined in, ready to bust their ass. Brothers were both significant in complexion, Mischa looking more like John Lennon, but some 50 pounds heavier, and Dan was fit as a kite with his every morning workout session and running 10 miles.

Salihi was not thrown off track and made things even worse, absolutely denying nothing but confessing all of it proudly.

'F**k that, and you deserve it, man…you f**king shitheads…like the shithead you are for stealing the CD from Saki, man. Everyone knows Saki has the hottest shit, and you don't pinch Saki, man. You f**k, you asshole, you f**king amateur!' Salihi was rocking' rolling' now, but Tito realized they should have. Salihi kept their mouth shut after all, as this was getting out of control, plus too many people were hearing it. Salihi was going at it again…

'I saw it in your car, dude, in your f**king trunk, man….' We got your f**king car man, your f**king stuff, Saki's f**king CD and…' he didn't finish the sentence as Mischa, with his glaring eyes and look of a madman, long hair covered partly in shit, attacked him viciously turned around. The battle royal began where one fist blow led to another and another and another…

***

Saki was just on the way to open the fish restaurant for dinner when he overheard the brawl between the Salstone brothers and Salihi and Tito. He just picked up the line about the CD player, his name mentioned, and the four assholes responsible for this. Saki was a man of action, not of words and thinking. He had his four guys with him, working in the restaurant. They looked more like gorillas than waiters. He just ordered them into this brawl.

'What the f**k, how do f**k do you know…motherf**kers…you assholes did it. You pinched my new CD stereo car! Now I will f**k your asses'! Everyone was startled but already in a fistfight which meant only one thing – more fist-fighting! They started beating the shit out of everyone they could lay their hands on, especially the four main characters. Screams were heard and yelling as some of Salihi and Tito's pals were coming to help, as well as Dan and Micha's. Somehow the number of people involved was growing exponentially by the minute.

***

When Brocollia saw what happened to her daughter and that she was lying on the asphalt covered with a diaper full of shit and screaming and crying wildly, she called for her husband Bob to straighten things out and help the daughter. Bob was in a foul mood anyway, and he took a substantial wooden stick and his cow Maria (that needed a walk always) to the already forming battlefield at the parking lot.

'They should know better not to f**k with Bob as Bob will f**k with them!' With those words, he rushed out in aid of his daughter. Maria, the cow, followed obediently – Bob wished he had a bull. Broccolia, half-mad, followed directly to help out, taking the infant Zlatan with her. Zlatania was hurt, and they were going to pay!

***

Our Pepé's proper name was, as you know from before, Zachariya Belinski. Nobody called him Zachariya, not even his parents anymore. His dad Hicory was still indulging himself heavily into the intricate paths of alcoholic pleasures but still was vivaciously doing his job as a mechanic in a large cargo and trucking firm 'We Carry It All". That day he came a bit earlier from work, celebrating something with his co-workers and being pissed drunk as usual. Hicory Belinski stepped onto the developing scene, holding three Chiquita bananas. He just saw Pepé was involved, and some bald peasant guy was shouting at him. He saw Salihi and Tito's fist fighting Dan, Mischa, and Saki in the middle. There were others and more of others who seemed involved in a physical brawl where hits were delivered in the groin, across the back, on the legs, and across the face. Spit was used as firepower, and fists took the scene in a complicated way. Women were ripping each other's hair. Hickory joined in, trying to give an inspired speech that nobody noticed. He finally got into the fight armed with three bananas. Soon he was being blasted by fists and disappeared in the cloud of rampage dust. One thing led to another – the shit truly hit the fan.

***

It's hard to describe the scene and how and why so many people got involved, but it was your perfect chain reaction. Everything was happening so fast, and in minutes, more than 50 people were in the parking lot, busting each other any way they could. When one found out about the other and the other found about the first, the stolen stuff, the diamonds, the heists, the dead bodies in trunks, the frozen fish served instead of fresh ones, the cow and the milk, the hoodlums, the whores, and God knows what, all hell broke loose. Dan and Mischa were in a direct fight with Salihi and Tito. They were all backed up by their gangs, affiliates, and supporters who flocked to the scene within minutes of the eruption. I always wondered how this was possible in that time and age when the cell phone still did not enter the scene. Battle Royale was going on! It must have been animal instincts and some wild telecommunications. Saki's pals joined in, the servers from the restaurant, some people passing by, sons and daughters of all, and, of course, their wives and others that just wanted to humiliate, spit, piss other people off, and bust asses. In the midst of that, Dan's wife, Brocollia, brought the cow down, and the poor thing was in the center, letting sounds out from her mouth and the cowbell hanging from her. Blood, Sweat, Pee, and even Shit slowly covered the parking lot.

***

Some of us were already there, even before the mess began, but now we quadrupled in numbers. This frigging bunch of mad people, filled with peasants, was a feast for our eyes, at least a few of us that did not get involved but barely followed this from the (front) sidelines. They were beating the shit out of each other with fists, bricks, wood sticks; you name it. The macabre scene, developing so vividly right in front of our eyes and initiated by the peasant wife of Bob Bondarenko and his kid's shitty diaper, brought me back to that bizarre but extraordinary lecture given by our history professor in the first year of high school.

Professor Rodolfo Magruda was in the midst of a lecture dealing with 1300's middle age Europe and life in the cities when one of the students came late 15min into the talk and just walked in and slumbered into his desk without saying anything. If there was THE gravest of sins, you could commit during the lectures of Prof. Magruda; it was not to come on time and, on top of that, show no respect whatsoever for the act itself, not even a simple apology or remorse for being late. That's what exactly happened when John Forestcreek came in, an ordinary chap with curly blonde hair, a vital complexion, always wearing a happy face with those red cheeks burning at high altitude levels. Magruda looked at him and said: "Glad you could join us, Mr. Forestcreek, as we are about to touch upon a subject, apparently very close to your heart and, shall I say, probably your DNA, the questions of peasants. I wasn't planning to go into this, but somehow you provided a needful inspiration this morning, and I am very grateful for that".

John smiled back and had no idea what to expect except that he was deep down rejoicing in this rare moment where he was the center of attention. None of us knew what would come and what we would be enlightened about. We all, especially John and those individuals who recognized themselves in the speech, would never forget that morning. Somehow I remembered everything he said (word by word), as we also took extensive notes during his flashy presentations, but especially now, looking at this lunatic carousel evolving in front of me and the vast number of peasants involved in it, I could not help myself of reconstructing the whole speech in my mind. The whole part of the lecture came back in a split second and opened my eyes again, but now for different reasons. Finally, I fully understood what Rodolfo Magruda was talking about that morning, a man from a 700-year-old line of ancestry that was part of the civitas, belonging to the urban, to the city. He had a clear, deep, and balanced voice that was lifted only when necessary and lowered only when appropriate:

"The invasion of the peasants into the civic life, their movement into cities has throughout the history of Europe happened in a continuum with higher or lesser intensity, depending on country to country, from people to people showing some interesting general and common characteristic phenomena. The commonality is there, regardless of historical epochs, types of cultural matrixes of different countries, or times of urbanization, industrial revolutions, duration of feudalism, bourgeois revolutions, wars, etc. We could add to that the phenomena of forced urbanizations that result, as it is in our case, my dear students, of totalitarian regimes and dictatorships in Central and Eastern Europe as an already lost race with the departing industrialization of others".

We had no idea where he was going with this, but it was already in the realm of 'politically incorrect lingo.' It was just getting better by the minute. He continued:

"The other thing is the massive impoverishment of the peasantry masses like in the Latin American countries. Well, so much for some shallow socio-historical background here. I won't go deeper into this as this is such a difficult, complex problem that one should analyze the deeper historical, sociological, cultural, economic, political, civilization, and God knows what other reasons and backgrounds for the fact that peasants have flooded the urban cores of humanity". He looked at us with hesitation. "But, I think you might deserve to get a bit more. Trust me; it will come in handy in life". He made a sour grin on that last comment and continued:

"Nonetheless, a short overview of the universal characteristics of these phenomena is needed here, but just in a free, bypassing fair reflection of some socio-psychological, moral-emotional, and cultural aspects is a must. The big question, my dear fellows: what is common for all peasants worldwide? – this form of a human being that continually moves away from its original habitat—the hinterlands, orchards, plow fields, and domesticated animal kingdom they have created for itself—to the cradle of civilizations and the epitome of urbanity – the cities."

He raised his voice now to make a point. "That unfortunate social and human phenomenon called THE PEASANT – with this sheer and deliberate action of moving into the cities, which of course didn't happen overnight, but was a protracted as a steady process throughout the history of humanity, puts the burden on the cities in 2 ways: with the biological surplus—the exodus and export of the humans from villages to the cities—and by radiating its specific psycho-mental structure on the urban realm and civitas. And this second one is much worse; trust me on that! So why is the peasant a sorry form of existence and human being, one to be saddened over more than angry? Why? Because it is a tragic figure that is, in historical terms and rules, destined to disappear and dissolve in the city without being created into something or creating something for that matter. He is only being transformed but not transmuted in the city. The only thing he brought from the villages is his practical culture, the handy work of the mind but the not-that-fine abstract part which is required to be a part of the civitas, and the culture of the city with its civic-urbane population and class and its material and immaterial cultural and spiritual heritage that civilizations bestowed upon it. No, he didn't bring that…how could he…" Magruda paused, his back turned to the blackboard, before continuing. "With its practical culture, the peasant has been grounded, metaphorically and literally. His connection to the fields and orchards, the earth that produced the results of his physical labor and his domesticated animals, and his practical knowledge of the work and chores had nothing to do with the realm of abstract, sophisticated, and enlightened thinking, knowledge, and doing. Instead, the peasant carries within him hereditary millennia burden long of masochistic scars due to the generational exploitation, persecution, humiliation, and contempt from the merchants, the urban civic population, the power structures in the city, and their ways of living, demands, and production. This has been going on for millennia, growing out of the dark slavery periods of our history. So that has left a deep and irreversible element of masochism in the peasant structure. That is why we must be sorry for him, but still… Therefore, the City has and is, for a peasant, a dark and ominous alien force, full of threatening elements and things that will never be accomplished within the matrix of its urbanity. In a certain way, he begins to lose his whole being in the city due to increased despair, suffering, and non-adaptable behavior toward the requirements of the sophisticated. That produces a feeling of hate, hatred, strange and negative behavior, even destructive towards the city – its urban, cultural and civic qualities." Now Magruda raised his voice even more to grab our full attention: "The peasant mutates into a being of weird sadistic behavior, not literally (at least not in all cases) but more in terms of his mental and psychological apparatus. With that, we get the sadomasochistic version of the peasant, the wanna-be-quasi-citizen, the damn first kitten! He doesn't get much help here with his 'sound plow field mind,' his simple and plain numerical logic, his practical village culture and customs, and his so-called natural intelligence that all animals are born with. But do not be fooled; the lack of synthetic intelligence and the finer mind, the peasant will compensate with an efficient logic and a high dose of cunningness." Some students were now paying even more attention while some dropped their mouths even more.

"Everything that has even a little foothold in the abstract culture is for him alien and weird, impractical, unnecessary, a surplus, a nuisance and extremely annoying, like a smaller size of shoes that he might be wearing and that were a pain in the ass. That is why he is always, and I always say, suspicious and distrustful with a strong dose of hatred towards everything that represents urban, that which is colored with the delicate, sensible and sensitive, romantic, complex, ethereal, sublime, refined with the nuance and sadness of the millennia development of the civitas—something that he can never understand or reach". Magruda moved between rows of our desks, getting increasingly involved with his body language.

"He hates abstraction, speculation, scholastics, imagination, philosophy, artistic expression, dreams, visions, aesthetics, the fine touches of fashion, the refinement of urban forms, high culture, etc. What he likes and feels good about is the basic and plain logic and proof of his inner being, 2+2=4, verbatim, simplicity, singularity, straight line things, and he needs to verify just about anything you say to him, checking it in several places until he is sure that black ink is on white paper. He is always full of very simplified self-security and what I would call the flatline behavior outlook on life, which is one characterized as mostly positive in all instances, regardless of how complex and tough life can be at times, without the more difficult doubt and questioning of the inner-self and everyday life that an urban soul has. Life is not simple, nor is it always sunny, nor is it easily calculated. It is full of difficulty, hesitation, doubt, and hard obstacles. So you can't just look at it with a happy, shiny people's attitude, John!" Magruda was looking straight into John Forestcreek with his dark brown penetrating eyes. "No, John, you cannot, or as if you do, then I will doubt your intelligence…although it is very little, I see there anyway." This last line, he said in a shallow voice. John was dumbfounded. "But out of all of that, continued Magruda, what he utterly despises and hates is the 'flight of the true urban soul,' characterized in imagination, dreams, visions, fantasies, artistic expression, things that Carl Jung – I hope you know who this chap is – thought to be the key elements for achieving a great self-awareness of an urban mind & soul."

Wow, we were all mesmerized and in awe. This has taken shape no one expected, and you could see that the classroom was a moving, fluid matter now. Some students were uneasy, some were surprised, some were lost, and some wanted even more. Oh, yes, more surely was to come.

"The aesthetic sense of the peasant is pathetic and is reflected in the way he dresses, where a small detail can show the essence of things – like wrong shoes, lack of tie when needed, and whatnot, in his mannerism, in his speech, in his body language, in the sensibility towards the cuisine, in art, in music, and so forth. I could give you a million examples, but we have no time. Therefore, for example, a peasant from Northern Europe, which is more developed and advanced than his kinship from the Center or especially the South, where we are, still shows the 'Chairman Mao' way of dressing and way of collectivist life, equality in the lowest level where all species are the same, lack of taste and accumulated brand of minimalism that makes you nauseous, one which only village mentality can provide and create, one which city and civitas can never except. That is why the social being of the peasant, like the one in Eastern Europe and the Balkans, for example, is perfect for totalitarian societies and societies with a false sense of democracy, due to peasant's allegiance of a subject mentality."

With these last words, Magruda looked at us with a dose of resignation, sadness, and optimism, as he could see some of us looking at him with sparkling eyes. This was something different. Oh boy, it was. A part of the class started to slowly grumble and vibrate, probably from realizing they were the people he was talking about. Magruda was a tough cookie that goes straight at you, regardless of how much the truth must hurt or how much you can or cannot handle it!

Finally, he looked at the watch, which showed 2 minutes to 12, and he knew he had to finish with a blast as he moved to the window and pointed to the cityscape outside:

"The peasant in the city is also 'weak' regarding the sense of place, urban geometry, culture, and social and physical space enrichment. He does not feel the space as such; for him, it becomes just a void that needs to be conquered, as the villages and open acres of agriculture and forest land allow. Space needs to be crushed where only moving is essential. In contrast, the participants in space are not, so pushing and shoving are expected as he has grown in such a void, unregulated space in the hinterlands. That is why I am being pushed and shoved so many times in the grocery stores, bookstores, and cinemas because there are so many damn peasants out there. So the peasant finally loses the sense of feeling for the actual urbane elements and civitas and the people and culture of that realm. He does not care for such a complex space. So at the end of the day, he doesn't give shit how he looks in the eyes of others. Also, as the hallmark of human finesse, humanity, life, and aesthetics, language is not essential for the peasant. He is rude in his expressions and mannerism; he is deaf for all of that, loving to be part of the sheep, the herd, the masses, the flock, and the collective good. He feels secure there and only there, despising all elitism, individualism, higher quality, education, and the culture of civic society. He is not an individual that builds and participates in the intricate urban patterns which create a civic human being. He can never be that. Yes, it's easy to create a good functioning scientific and technical intelligence from a peasant. Still, the culture, the humanistic discipline, and the arts need millennia of civic and family tradition. My dear students…he paused, tired of this spontaneous, mesmerizing speech…It doesn't happen overnight…

We were all just numb, some comfortably, some not. The bell rang, and Magruda took his papers and notes. Before he walked out, he looked at us. He said: "So when you go out into the city, into your daily lives, look around you carefully, and you will recognize that the peasant is everywhere around us…he might be easily recognized by, for example, having hard and blown up nails or skin that is immune to the rays of the sun, both from millennia of working in the fields or it can be a modernized and hidden peasant, repackaged and transformed on the way of becoming a citizen. And if you get involved with one, get a husband or wife or someone you will live with, don't be surprised that after a while, you will begin to copy some of his or her characteristics, regardless of how strong your will is. Yes, salvation might be in the fact that they are becoming boiled into a real citizen and that all will be ok, especially if they have children one day. Well, it isn't going to work like that. That is a long process that might take decades or hundreds of years to succeed. But, even if it does, you can always detect him by just some of the things I mentioned today…and don't be naïve, my friends…if one thing is indestructible, it is DNA, which stays for eternity…."

Magruda walked out and closed the door. Sitting at my desk, Roger Rogerson, who used to cut his nails with a bowie knife, turned to me, showing his hand into my face, and asked: "Hey man, what about my nails? You think they are hard and blown up, as this mother f**ker said?"

***

I awoke from daydreaming by howling sounds that sounded animal-like but were made by this typhoon of humans entangled in the battle scene. Prof. Rodolfo Magruda nor Roger Rogerson, nor John Forestcreek were here. Still, the dreadful scene made me realize even more that we were dealing with a massive bunch of peasants as the main actors and some half-citizens in supporting roles, and a handful of extras, us the citizens. The tumult lasted for almost 30min now and was gaining intensity, where even more people were getting involved in one way or another. The spectator arena was getting larger, too, including all those from the other side of the looking glass – people watching from their windows and balconies from both towers that shared this common parking space. It was now an urban gladiator arena, a public space to the fullest. Bodies were messed up with each other, fists and teeth were flying everywhere, and screams and cries and animal howling were echoing through the spaces. Finally, the police arrived, a dozen of them, and surprisingly enough, were able to disperse the crowd in minutes. They kept and booked the main vital actors, Dan, Mischa, Salihi, Saki, Bob, poor Hickory, and a dozen others, including Brocollia, one of the most violent actors in the street brawl. All kinds of confessions followed, and this mess was somehow entangled. Jail time was coming to Dan and Mischa for their diamond. Tape heist f**k up, as the police gathered all kinds of evidence, plus Salihi and Tito, to avoid juveniles home spilled their guts over the stolen goods in 'Diamond brother's car,' adding a significant number of fictionalized crimes in the process (where some of them did correspond to the truth, believe it or not) and thereby really screwing Dan and Mischa plus Saki added his weight to the matter and his connections. Due to the severe Diamond business, the brothers were looking for some hard time behind bars, Dan several years more than Mischa. We never saw or heard about any of them after that.

The rumor was that they both moved to South Africa after their sentences expired. Their parents were so ashamed they moved from the tower very soon after the whole thing and died miserably in a nursing home on the coast. Saki was released immediately, retrieving his prize possession – SONY CD Player – and buying lunch for the whole police core. Poor Hickory and others were released as light bystanders and passive participants. History demanded that he gets his bananas back. That wasn't possible. Pepé was impressed by his dad's bravery, standing for the right things and defending him in the brawl.

Salihi and Tito got off on probation from the juvenile home. They were going to be watched closely. One wrong move, and they were f**ked. That didn't stop Salihi from doing himself continuously. Arno Stockhouse was trying to incriminate everyone and was snitching on all. He was especially viscous to Saki, becoming now the new defender of health and crusading against having animals-live stock in apartments (or balconies in this case). The truth was that Arno realized his face needed to be saved, and there would not be any milk. That, of course, didn't work out. As the President of the Tenants Council, his authority was highly damaged in not preventing or stopping this tumult. But he didn't get any jail or penalty time. He was stripped of his council duties which caused him to have a heart attack soon after that. He survived. All of the actors, some 65, were bruised and battered. Almost 150 people participated in this brawl. It was something else, folks! The rest was more or less cleared up except for the cow. Oh yes, the shitty diaper from the scene mysteriously disappeared (as crown evidence).

***

The cow was slaughtered sometime after the incident, but not before the doomsday inferno hit our skyscraper tower (in a distant future). Someone from the health inspection ordered the cow to be removed permanently from the 17th-floor balcony. Bob Bondarenko protested and even tried physically to stop the inspectors, chaining the cow to the balcony. In the end, Police came, the cow was released, and Bob was apprehended and released. He was somehow compensated, as he claimed that this atrocious act would viably damage his livelihood. The truth is he never could get over his favorite cow, Maria. The story was that Maria ended up in one of Saki's restaurants as steak & beef soup (as sort of revenge for the diaper shit thing), although everyone knew that he only served sea, river, and lake dishes in his restaurants. This was, of course, never confirmed. The other version of the story was that Maria was stolen by one of the health inspectors who picked her up and has now found a new home on the 13th floor in another tower on the southern outskirt of the city. Aside from the milk, the health inspector found some new profit in arranging tourist visits to this single animal farm specimen. If the story was true, it was an excellent site. Truth can sometimes be twisted, but twisted people flourish everywhere! Oh yes…you are probably wondering what happened to the shitty diaper…I have no clue!

28

Winter De-Lite

(The Snowball Siege Chronicles)

In those good old days, they said that while the climate may be pre-determined, the weather remains uncertain. Now it is all screwed up, and nothing can be predetermined anymore, and everything remains uncertain except constant nasty surprises and f**k ups that weather brings. Guess it's the damn global warming, greenhouse gas effect, and this entire climate shit we humans caused. It's kind of nature's revenge upon us as in the last decades, we have multiplied by hundreds and hundreds of millions; we are in billions now. People continue producing little toddlers with no respect for the globe's future. There won't be any tolerance level left, and we will all go to hell. That will be "nice," As Borat would say – "Sexytime"! Yes, sexytime indeed! But this is now. Then, in the good old days of the mid-80s, we lived in a Shangri-La, and seasons were predictable as morning piss or hard-on and brought what they were supposed to bring. In winter, cold and snow, and in summer, warmth, sun, and other seasons, you know what comes along rain, wind, leaves falling, spring flowers, blah, blah.

Nowadays, kids are so frigging stupid that they don't even ask you about the simplest things – what is this f**king snow, what does it mean, and how is it made? The things you are more apt to hear are, will this impact the global cycles of whatever? How will it affect people experiencing poverty, and what about the endangered species? Give me a break! Who gives a shit! Everything has an impact on everything, so who the f**k cares.

On the other hand, it isn't always easy to remember simple stuff. That morning when I walked out of the skyscraper on the parking lot completely covered in fresh snow, I remembered the physics and chemistry session in high school that week. Snow on the ground… hmmm….well, it was like snowfall remains on the ground until it melts. In colder climates, snow is lying on the ground all winter. That wasn't the case with our place. We were not in the cold polar circle but had a harsh winter due to mountain terrain and real alpine winters. So we did share something with the polar lands or, in a slightly different way, the snowpacks—Snow that persists over a long(er) time. The deepest snowpacks occur in mountainous regions like ours. It is influenced by temperature and wind events determining melting, accumulation, and wind erosion. That was the book stuff. What I was seeing in front of me was playtime, f**king playtime! Even if someone passed by a little kid and asked me if I knew what snow was, I was ready for that: Boy, snow is a type of precipitation in the form of crystalline water ice, consisting of many snowflakes that fall from clouds. Since snow is composed of small ice particles, it has an open and, therefore, soft structure, and when it falls, it melts or doesn't, and then it makes piles of snow. But forget that, kid – it's puffy white matter that you can take into your gloves and hands (when it's ready to be used) and make a snowball out of it, form it, and hold it a bit until it gains strength. Its shape takes the perfect round form and then throws in the hope of hitting or breaking something with usually and preferably dire consequences. Yes, well, it went something like that. Snow was there, and that was great! Some of my friends were already out, indulging in the glory of white! The problem was that aside from me, there were only two individuals there, Daniel and Patrick. Daniel was already bored.

"I made myself a snowball out of piss

Just as perfect as frozen piss could be.

I thought I'd keep it as an iced tea

And let it sleep with me…

I gave it some love & heat

And a catheter for its leaking beat.

Then, last night it melted away,

But first −it salvaged my day!

F**king ice yellow snowball:"

Daniel recited his new poem repeatedly, in some perverse attempt to kill the mid-morning passivity and stillness of what was supposed to be a winter de-lite day.

"Will you shut the f**k up, Dan" yelled Patrick, the red-haired guy from the neighboring brick building. He was dressed in his winter parka with a Norwegian wool cap and those shiny, reflecting cheap Polaroid wants-to-be sunglasses. Although it was still early in the day, he wanted something to happen, and everyone did. It was a glorious New Year's Saturday noon morning, and the snow has been on the ground for a few days now, some 5-6 inches of great snow, that wonderful half-wet kind that makes the best snowballs ever! While the climate may be predetermined, the weather remains uncertain, or is it the other way around? Well shit, in those days, you could predict climate, nowadays with all this global warming stuff…I don't know. Still, the weather remains elusive. There was a bit of flurry in the air, and some snowflakes were coming along, which meant we were in for some more snow later in the day or none at all. Everyone was bored to death, and it was only 11:30 in the morning. It was Christmas Day, and the idea was to do something memorable on the first of January that year. But somehow, ideas were lacking, or we were just wide asleep. There was an occasional snowball or two on innocent passers, but that seemed a bit stupid, and some wrestling in the snow was soon abandoned. There were 6 of us, myself, Daniel, Patrick, Pépe, Keke, and Zito, a new kid who moved in three weeks ago. We were all sitting on the staircase of the Highrise with no clue what the next move or action should entail in the coming minutes and hours.

I looked at this glorious day with the blue skies and snow, thinking about why white and why blue. No, the snow isn't white at all. It is made of ice crystals, and if you come up close, very close to the micro level of these buggers, you will see the individual crystals. They look clear, like glass or something transparent, a diamond. But if you pile them all up in a large stack, a snowball may be made of snow crystals. They will look white, something like the salt and sugar white phenomenon. At least, that's what my 5th-grade physics teacher used to say. And there was something with light reflection and retraction, which made this white color deep down blue. But who cares! Well, the blue sky phenomenon is a neat thing too. Mr. Newton said something about that somewhere: such a clear, cloudless daytime sky like it was this Saturday is blue because molecules in the air disperse blue light from the sun more than they disperse red light. So, in other words, the f**king sky and the air molecules are hit by the blue light from the sun, which then scatters, and our eyes perceive it as blue. That's it! I was saying this aloud, and the others watched me dumbfounded with a specific grain of amusement but more concerned that I might have flipped a little. It must have been from all that stillness in the air…nothing…there wasn't a single sound except the thundering noise from the left side of the Highrise, the road connected to the construction site.

A vast white cement truck passed by every 30min as the eternal construction of the shopping center continued. As we used to call it, our construction site has been where Babylonian towers would indeed have been erected sooner than this shopping center, which was already taking 11 years to build. There was a still mate for some years, and only weeds, trash, and the urban animal kingdom prospered. Somehow there was a lot of activity that year, and foundations were being laid. Some construction was being erected, which also meant the departure and death of the rat population, a long-standing and 'distinguished' pillar of our community. It seemed a private developer had taken over and was ready for heavy investments. Cement trucks were coming one after the other from the main boulevard into the collector road in front of the industrial compound, swinging into our little back alley street and pouring the stuff into the construction site. Regardless of the season, it was happening all the time, which was the case this morning.

They also say that 'everything comes to those who wait.' That was damn sure that day, I'll tell you. Snow was there, something we all had been waiting for weeks. Winter was in full swing, but there wasn't that white coverage we needed and that specific type of snow we longed for, until that Friday morning, when after three days of snowfall, there were tons of white crystals on the ground, snow that meant only one thing: SNOWBALLING OR A SNOWBALL FIGHT!!! To top that off, it was school recess time – f**king A!

As it was the case on several jolly good occasions (when f**kups of the highest order were going to happen), that Sunday slowly brought out not just me but most of my pals, friends, acquaintances, and lads I had never seen before in my life. It started slowly with a few of us testing the snow, throwing snowballs at each other, rolling in the white seas of white and eating snow as much as we could! We started as only a few, but then in a matter of 45 minutes (I was first out at 09:00), we gathered in this winter de-lite atmosphere in full force: Keke and Ture Tollberg, Danny Slowitz, my best friend Anthoine Scott, The Kapadia brothers, Boris Duchovny, Harry Rowells, Mike Gleisch, Norman Michaels, Pepé, Alan Meehan, Shaki Badouro, myself and a bunch of our friends from the other skyscrapers, as well as some guys from the adjacent low red brick apartment buildings and more or less – all the young f**kers mentioned in this book so far! The entire bunch was engaged in a (so far) friendly snow fight on the grounds of our adjacent skyscraper. Danny somehow took control of things to let's have a revolution! The word spread fast, and with that, the number of 'revolutionaries.' At the end of the assembly, there were some 65 of us! Welcome to the revolution mother f**kers!

As I said before, construction time again was the year's theme, especially during these winter months. Namely, our never-ending-story-about-a-fairy-shopping-center-that-was-going-to-be-build-soon was taking shape after some 12 years of construction or, more like it – nonconstruction. The site was left in such an unfinished

mess with tons of material spread around; some foundations started, the ridiculous crane that stood there for years and then collapsed, plus some other shit. All this was a paradise for all kinds of
crap, rat kingdom, wino sanctuary, disease and rape haven, gang and
lunatic transit stop, and you name it! All that was becoming history
and the center was being shaped again. To all our dismay, the toxic
and dangerous site was cleaned up, and the rat colony (containing
mutants of the highest order and some endemic species) was erad-
icated. In other words, all of it was becoming history. A new crane
was erected, and as I mentioned, numerous cement trucks were delivering goodies for almost a hundred workers on the revived site.
The wooden board wall that separated the parking space from the
site (one that withstood the test of time and vandalism of the first
order for 12 long years) was taken down. Although it was damaged
incorrectly in some places and looked like a separation line between
two warring factions in a 100-years wall, it still stood there, never
faltering. In many ways, this ugly barrier was a cultural heritage
artifact and a historical monument, at least for us. Although, nobody tried to stop its demise, and I think most people were happy
to get rid of it. So no one minded the rumble of the cement trucks
as they did their business daily. So it was this winter morning; two
came after the other in intervals of 35 minutes each. It was tough
construction time again, even on a Saturday morning!

Jeremiah Bielinski was an old f**ker, an asshole that was way passed
70 but still going strong. He always smelled of piss, but unobtru-
sively, it was some wayfarer perfume. He did tell all kinds of bullshit
stories about his, probably 99% invented travels. Everyone called
him THE PILGRIM due to his numerous rehashes of his "holy"
travels to the Holy Land. As with all his lies, he was probably never
there. But nobody cared, as everyone liked this f**king bugger. He

rarely came out of his stinking hole on the 12th floor, the one-room shitty apartment which, according to the gossip tower network, was a shop of horrors. As long as we knew him, he was retired. However, his story was that he was honorably discharged from the armed forces after being a decorated war hero in almost every conflict from Vietnam to Lebanon. He was sober that morning when he stepped out on our "grand staircase" of the skyscraper, inhaling the fresh winter air into his rotting lungs, which would soon be replaced by the killer penetration of the Strong French Gitane cigarettes that he always carried and smoked. His brother lived in France, and this was the only thing he sent him every year in large amounts. The pilgrim thought yellowish beard and mustache, small black eyes, and a nose size of an apple, or a mandarin at least, with a funny Norwegian red Polar hat with some stupid rain deer woven on it and wearing a winter parka that must have seen the whole cold war but was still hanging on proudly with those matching green heavy wool slacks and combat boots. The hat covered his huge, yellowish thick curly hair that was never introduced to a barber or shampoo, let alone to a comb. Most were stuffed under the polar hat, but tons were still coming out. He was a site to behold, a sort of a derelict Bad Santa figure or a Santa reject that looked like he was all covered in piss. He always said he would sell or donate his underwear of 20 years stature! Imagine if EBAY existed in those days! Good grief!

Nonetheless, we keenly listened to his 'wise' words when sober. He looked at the scene in front of him, the white snow coverage, a mass of youngsters (some 30 by that time) involved in a snowball fight or something similar, the never-ending line of mother-f**king-cement trucks that Jeremiah utterly despised, and a racket (that we were making) that his, still not sober, ears could not take. He lighted his

7th Gitane of the morning, inhaled deeply, and spoke in his harsh, whiskey and smoke commander of the seas resonant baritone voice:

"Listen up motherf**kers!" It was after 9 a.m. on Friday, and he was not drunk (not totally, at least) and had something to say. In an unusual moment of collective unity, we all stopped what we were doing and looked at THE PILGRIM with intense curiosity.

He continued scanning the ground and looking harshly at the cement track just passing by our western tower wall on the street that led to the entrance of the construction site and our fish restaurant.

"Snowball fights are known to have been a medieval pastime. Are you f**kers in the Middle Ages? Ambrogio Lorenzetti, in the 1300s in the middle of the frigging dark f**king bullshit ages, depicts his personification of winter as holding a snowball. Give me a f**king break! For this geezer, that was the high point of entertainment – snowballing each other. F**k! Is that the best you can do like that f**ker Ambrogio!

On the other hand, on March 5, 1770, the pelting of occupying British soldiers with snowballs eventually led to the Boston Massacre, which helped spark the American Revolutionary War. And these things can have consequences". I wasn't there, but I knew that this was the cause.

He cleared his throat and continued.

"When I was 1959 at Yale University in New Haven, for those of your f**kers that don't know where that is, it's on the east coast or eastern seaboard of US of A! The so-called "snowball riot" was there, and we did a lot of damage. Yes, we surely did! We attracted national media attention, and it was a kind of town-and-gown riot.

F**k, those were the days and….” He didn't finish the sentence as a good friend of mine, Alan Meehan, interrupted him.

“Pilgrim, what the f**k is that you are saying? We are not getting anything, man!”

“Old age comes at a bad time. Of all the things I've lost, I miss my mind the most, maybe my liver and kidneys too. Wait, those I still have” With that, he started to laugh like the old geezer and looked at Alan and all of us listening to him.

“F**k! F**k, f**k the duck. Man, you yellow geezers. Some people are only alive because it is illegal to shoot them. We shot many of you motherf**kers in Vietnam, Chad, n Lebanon. You mother-f**kers are so f**king stupid! What the f**k do you not understand! Fight assholes, start a f**king war!

“F**kin A, guys! Make this a frigging combat zone and attack all those f**king cement trucks, all the motherf**ker vehicle owners, the buses, all of them – put them under siege with snowballs. Re-member Boston 1770?”

Someone said: “Are you crazy old man, nuts or what the f**k”!

“I'm not a crazy asshole; I've been in a bad mood for 60 years. F**k it, f**k all of you, you chicken bastards. Errors have been made, and errors will be made. Others will be blamed. Show some f**king balls, cohunes, you motherf**kers! F**k this; I need a drink”. Yeah, f**k this shit'! Carry on my wayward sons and…he paused…looked at us again and said….”And you know what… f**k all of you! He laughed once more, and with that last comment, he left for the near-est bar, “Owl the Insomniac” (I could never figure out that name, but the owner was a nut case, so I guess that explains it). In a few moments, we continued with what we were doing and instantly forgot the old f**ker, except for one person. Alan Meehan was lost in thought and looking sharply at the collector road, the construction site, the sky which has produced this fantastic wet snow and finally murmured to him: "The crazy old man didn't make any sense, and he always sounded as a compilation of different disconnected sayings, but you know what – he is damn right!"

The Siege: The Cement Truck Attack

After Pilgrim's wise words, the first strike commenced, and the target was the two cement trucks! Surprisingly enough, it was only two trucks, but as it was Saturday, it was to be expected. Coming in intervals of 35 min each, they were an excellent opportunity to test the fantastic snow that fell on the ground during the night and early morning. These ugly Russian-made trucks produce cement, and for those who don't know what that is, it is a building-construction material that is a powder made of a mixture of calcined limestone and clay; When used with water and sand or gravel, it can produce concrete and mortar. So, in other words, it was critical for the functioning of our construction site. A rolled concrete mixer is a significant challenge to remove, as the load quickly hardens and, with its load, is too heavy to the right. The ready mix truck maintains the material's liquid through agitation or turning off the drum until delivery. Rear discharge (or "butt dumper," as some call it) trucks require both a driver and a "chute man" to guide the truck and chute back and forth to place concrete in a manner suitable to the construction site. Ray Bitko didn't have the Chuteman.

Ray Bitko was in a foul mood that morning. He slept poorly, took two sedatives, and had two shots of Vodka before work. He didn't shower and was smelling bad, dressed in a moth-eaten wool sweater from the 1960s and a heavy Romanian Parka that he pinched from a homeless guy last winter. His black curly hair was thick with grease, as was his deep bushy mustache, and their eyes were red colored with insomnia. Alcatraz polyester hat was on his head, upside down. He hated his job, he hated his construction site boss, he hated this damn cement truck, he hated his f**king cheating wife, he hated her lover, he hated his two loud, screaming kids, he hated his brother, he hated his sister, and he hated his parents. Ray Bitko was a man with a lot of hatred and problems, but in a nutshell, he disliked people in general – your 100% natural-born misanthrope. The damn truck was loud, producing all kinds of sounds from its corroded funnel; the Cement mixer was even louder, and Russian-made things certainly didn't pay too much attention to noise levels. You can go depth in a year driving this piece of shit. Unfortunately, it was a job to be done, and it paid off the monthly expenses. It was mainly for the kids, as the wife got dough from her lover monthly. Their marriage was soon ending, but ray was clinging on as much as he could…he didn't really know why as he hated all of them, so he didn't care…but that was the stale dynamics of life.

The whole damn thing was full of corrosion and rust, but as it was built for -45 weather conditions and war-like situations, it still ran well. The front was white with the painted logo and name of the company, while the cement cylinder was filthy gray. This rear-discharge concrete or cement truck was one of 20 the firm had. They called them the Concrete Mixer Trailers. This concrete or cement transit-mixing trailer was a variant of standard concrete transportation. It was used to supply short loads of concrete for our construction site. It has a concrete mixing drum with a capacity of between 1-yard and 1.75 yards. It was made by some factory in Siberia and had a 100-year lifespan –right?

All of those things and a lot of nonsense was going through Ray's head when he pulled from the collector road into our one-way alley street that led to the entrance of the construction site. After some 50m, a thunderous salvo of incoming snowballs hit the windshield, the side windows, and all possible parts of the truck. Ray thought he was in a combat zone. He had no clue what was going on. Looking to the left window, he saw many kids throwing what seemed to be…snowballs! They felt like rocks pounding on the truck, and there was no stop. We were throwing multiple salvos from some 70-80 hands and a bunch of stored snowballs lying on the ground. We also had a little clearing where this "white water" stuff was stored. There was just tons of yelling going on and screaming and pounding…Ray just passed through this snowstorm and didn't give it much thought. They were working on a small segment of the construction site, and only two trucks were needed. Soon Mike, the other driver, would be bringing his truck. He hated Mike, also. The same happened when Mike passed – he was brutally attacked from two sides as we placed ourselves on both sides of the one-way street, some urban Mini Park, an anteroom to the two colossal parking spaces. He was shocked when he arrived and heard from the construction workers that Ray got through the same shit. Ray got back again (in the switch mode with Mike) and was greeted with the same shit again. He let it pass. Finally, he would not take a fifth pounding the third time he came around as some small pride was left in him. What he didn't know is that slippery when wet is a thing you must be careful of… Mike Gleisch and Daren "The Head" Capouya had something else in mind. It was partly Memphis Kapadia's wild idea to pour water from the fire hydrant hose in the wall of the building onto the street and, yes – produce Ice. In a diabolically minded fashion, they wanted people to break limbs and cars to swirl and maybe crash. Some of that happened, and several individuals fell like logs and concrete on-ice part of the road… it wasn't funny at all, but we all enjoyed it immensely. Even if one protested, they were greeted with an incoming salvo of snowballs. In general, we also pounded all unfamiliar individuals that passed through – that was like a practice range for the vehicles. People just ran and passed away quickly, not wanting to stand up to what looked like an almost 100 kids' angry snowball mob! Mike Gleisch and Daren "The Head" Capouya did one more 'sprinkle' of the road when a ray appeared on the horizon.

"Motherf**kers, I will show you who is in charge," thought Ray. "I will f**king drive at a fast speed, and they will get scared, and then I will stop and get out of the truck with a huge French Wrench key I have in the truck. That will scare the living daylights out of these little shitters!"

That was what Ray thought. No harm in that; scare the little buggers. Ray admired what they did. He was like that when growing up. In those times, kids from one urban quarter would meet another neighborhood quarter and beat the crap out of each other with bricks, stones, steel bars, etc. Man, those were the days when you came home with a blue eye, missing tooth, or broken hand. So it would be simple: fast turn, brakes, stop, get out, scream, and leave. Well, the story played a bit differently than Ray, or we thought, certainly not even what Mike, Daren, and Memphis Kapadia could dream of. Ray was driving too fast on the collector road, reaching 85 on the speedometer and swinging into the one-way road with

90km/h. What he didn't anticipate was the ice road created by my buddies. The snow salvo started (we were throwing everything at the truck), and Ray was driving mad. Suddenly the Cement truck started swirling around, sending some of them in a panic to the parking space, and Ray wildly tried to maintain control over the monster vehicle. We could see the driver all over the driving wheel, turning it on all sides like he was in the final leg of America's Cup or Volvo Ocean Race. Finally, he hit the brakes with full might, sending the vehicle to the right side into the small urban patch of grass separating the parking and the street. He was lucky not to hit anything. "Motherf**ker, f**king shit," Ray was screaming inside as the truck slid off and crashed onto the grass with the cement drum creating a massive sound, still swirling and doing some damage to the pavement and grass and the truck, of course. The scene was a bit comical, too, like from the cartoon or movie world…the huge Russian/Soviet-made truck crashing down on our turf. We felt like we killed an elephant, a dinosaur, or a mammoth in the old hunting days of our civilization. Something ancient and primordial came in as we started producing these Neanderthal voices, screams, and hollow shrieking-piercing sounds. It reminded me of when we demolished, stoned, and finally burned down a bus from a foreign football club supporting fans, and they had to get another bus. Our club lost that match, but we rejoiced in breaking up their supporter's transportation. That was the time I heard these howling ice age sounds. The staff was pouring from the cement cylinder, and a few pieces of supporting machinery were broken. Glass also shattered on the windshield, leaving three huge cracks, and the right window exploded. The poor driver must have been shaken-up.

Ray Bitko was shaken & stirred, as 007 would say. He was glad he was ok, nothing seemed broken, and the truck's engine stopped. He shut down the damn cylinder and other stuff and climbed out on the left side, opening the door and standing on the truck like Indiana Jones, wild-faced and bewildered. He was holding the French Wrench Key in his left hand and shaking his right fist but also scratching himself as he had a slight discoloration.

"You bastards, you malignant rats, you slime f**king worms, I out to bust up every one of…." There his words stopped as he saw almost 80 kids looking at him with no fear holding the snowballs and yelling and shouting some wild scorching sounds. "F**k this, he said to himself, man there are so many of them." Mike, Daren, and Memphis were the first to react. "F**k you and your shitty truck," screamed Daren. Memphis yelled: "Snowball, this piece of shit!" We all followed as one. Some 50 snowballs probably hit Ray, and in a matter of 20sec, as he stood his ground, he lost control, slipped on the side, and fell with all his might on the icy street.

The nose was bleeding, and he was yelling in pain. Somehow he stood up and took the key in a lame effort to retaliate. Alas, that made things even worse for him, as David Nathan took control now and bravely led a dozen 'snipers' into the attack. Another salvo of dozen frozen snowballs hit Ray, and man, that must have hurt as hell. He couldn't catch his breath from all these attacks and uttering something no one understood. He stood up, but David relentlessly pounded at him, and I joined and a few more. Now two dozen of us attacked. Ray was lost. He just said: "F**k it," and started running towards the construction site. We ran after his part of the way throwing all we had…when he came to the enormous wooden gate of the construction site (some workers came out to hear what all the noise was about, seeing the truck and a wild bunch of kids) Ray thought he was saved and in some small gesture of Pyrrhic Victory showed us the middle finger and yelled: "F**k you little assholes"! We let it pass, except for one person, Alan 'Spitfire' Meehan. The man could hit just about everything at any distance, and once he bragged how he hit a seagull shitting in mid-air in such a fashion that he fell in the air hitting his shit coming down. He also broke 2 of his sister's front teeth, hitting her from 50m with a micro-sized rock. Believe what you want—this was 150m distance, and Alan was the sniper. He looked at the sky, the wind, the velocity of the snowball, proportions and threw this ice bullet from his hand.

"Get this motherf**ker", Alan yelled as he threw this like the best pitcher of the MLB World Series Final. Snowball flew like a small rocket in the air, stopped high, and came down with military precision of missiles in the Gulf War. It was incredible. Ray saw the little white spot and laughed – "Yeah, right; what can that little thing do." It was the size of a mandarin (how Alan liked those best), and it gained in speed coming down. It was completely frozen, and when it hit Ray, it almost broke and separated his nose from the rest of his face. He howled in pain and was hurdled inside the construction for first aid. We screamed another howling round of battle cries. Alan did it again. He was the man.

The Siege I: ATS540 Crane Truck

After Ray left, patched up and pissed off, catching a ride with the other cement truck, we slowly returned to the crime scene and admired the result! A colossal cement truck was lying on its side, overturned by us on our street! We all yelled satisfactorily – it was a war cry, and this battle had been won! After a while, the other cement truck never appeared again. Guess they were finished for the day or kept at the construction firm for their good, as one truck was already lying on its side; the driver probably told them what happened. They would turn it over and return it for repairs (if any were needed), probably on Monday. Nobody was going to do anything on a Saturday. However, they alerted the cops, a fact we didn't know then. Still, it would take them another 1.5h to get there. In the meantime, our legitimate target was gone. In a matter of minutes, thanks to the excellent organizing capability of Alan Meehan, Norman "Stone" Podworsky," and the seasoned Evan Kapadia, who we all respected – a new idea (and new target) was born & found: THE COLLECTOR ROAD SIEGE! The collector road-street "Ivan Mishkin the Black" (name derived from the filthy and heavy industry facility across the road) was going to be attacked with full force, in a sort of medieval fashion, not sporadically as now, but with all our might, well planned, coordinated and executed to the last detail! Just in the right moment and in the nick of time, Memphis Kapadia, Evans's brother, arrived at the scene and immediately took command, exerting enormous respect from the troops on the ground. A massive Snow Fortress-Barricade snow/ice wall was erected with the help of water, which soon turned it into an impregnable fortress and a tremendous defensive outpost on the other side of the street. Boris Duchovny, Harry Rowells, Pépe, Evan Kapadia, and Daniel Kehooe were in charge of that side, with 40 troops under their command. On our side, Alan 'Spitfire' Meehan, Norman "Stone" Podworsky," Danny Slowitz, and Memphis Kapadia commanded the troops where I was and my best friends David and Anthoine. We had the entire flank of the automobiles in the parking space, which provided excellent cover for our troops, dividing us ca 50/50 on both sides along a 75m white Maginot Line. Salishi Troika, Joe Brown, Little Moritz, Patrick Payson, Fat Gill,

Keke, and Ture Tollberg, with Moustafa Haider, covered the empty spaces in between, in front and at the rear being special forces and the lookout posts having a dozen 'soldiers' under them.

The attacks that commenced were both brutal and indiscriminate. Everything on wheels was under siege and attacked, and we pounded our snow ammunition at a constant rate, never faltering to give up. The drivers were shocked, and none dared to venture out of the vehicles (those that did were attacked even more, so they fled the scene in their cars in a panic) when hit, and even if they did, a salvo of white balls would crash upon them like a punishment from heavens. It looked more like a road to hell than anything else. We were about 75-80, going steadily towards 100, and this frequent medium road was an incredible battleground. Nothing was allowed to pass without punishment. Harry Rowells and Boris Duchovny reacted immediately when a Truck-mounted crane appeared on the horizon…."Welcome to the f**king revolution,"… screamed Boris! "Everyone, get ready; here comes Big Momma," yelled Harry, and we all turned to see what was coming our way.

Generally, these truck cranes are designed to be able to travel on streets and highways, eliminating the need for special equipment to transport a crane to the construction job site. This incredible mobile invention could be moved from place to place. The one appearing on the horizon was a German Made KEMPMANN with the letters ATS540 painted on it, a bright yellow color with four pairs of heavy tires on each side, totaling some 16 tires if my math serves me right. It was a colossal SOB! This crane truck also had moving counterweights for stabilization beyond that of the outriggers. According to the specs, or as we heard from Fat Gill's dad once, who used to drive one of these monsters, loads suspended directly over the rear remain more stable, as most of the weight of the truck crane itself then acts as a counterweight to the load. Truck cranes range from about 14.5 US Tons to about 1200 US tons. I had no idea how much this one was; nobody did, nor did anyone care about that in the heat of the moment. There was also a command cabin for the crane with some dude sitting inside and two drivers in front. This one was a target that was not to be missed. The truck was driving steadily, and had no clue what would happen.

Hans Svensson was smoking a second joint of the morning. They had a tough Friday on a construction site some 30 miles from the city, and the truck had to be returned to the main garage this morning. He was sitting in the small cabin of the crane truck as that was the place to be. Sitting in front didn't allow indulgence in vices; the damn driver was such an asshole conservative, and I would report him immediately. He opened a window even though it was cold, but his boss and the driver, Max, didn't particularly like hash, so ventilation was necessary. Hans also played with the crane's controls, accidentally releasing the thing. Max saw some people on his left and right sides, just 50m in front of them. They all wore wool caps; most wore gloves and looked with mean faces towards them as if waiting for the right moment to do something.

"Hej Hans, are you awake"? They had radio contact in the truck.

"Hej man, wake up; what the f**k is that ahead of us?"

"Can you see it?"

Hans was already in the clouds.

"See what, man?"

"Left and right, Asshole; what are those kids doing?"

Hans took notice of the scene in front of him, putting his hand out to throw the small piece of joint that was left.

"Nja, a lot of snow and cars, Max, and some demonstration, I guess." He also saw a significant bunch on both sides of the street.

"Nothing to worry…." He didn't finish the sentence when an enormous salvo of ice, melting, wet, puffy, demanding, and you name it, snowballs started to hit the track from both sides…It hit the driver's cabin like the worst spring hail creating judgment day sounds…" What the f**k is going on…" yelled Max, who tried to steer the enormous truck but still moved from one side to the other. Alan 'Spitfire' Meehan and Harry Rowells were in high spirits, and they both saw with satellite precision the open window, the dude smoking inside, and a target that could not go to waste! Incredibly enough, their ice snowballs hit the target with 100% precision.

Hans just felt an incredibly sharp pain on his forehead and cheek, making him scream and clutch to the controls and steering wheel of the crane. As the crane was released, it swung wildly on both sides, swinging the large steel hook in front that crashed into a trailer in the parking space and breaking a windshield of a large SUV type of car. If that was not enough, the giant crane destroyed three street lamps in a row before somehow stopping to a screeching halt down the street. Max was in shock, and Hans thought he was flying if it was not for the pain that was getting worse from the ice bullets he got into his face. The whole truck was pounded by white powder. We all hid behind the white wall and the cars. There was no need to agitate these two, especially after the damage these two dudes did, or we did! It seems they just thought the same. Max and Hans were both out of the truck assessing the damage and looking at some people passing by and taking notice of the f**k-up. The damn kids were nowhere to be seen.

"Max, let's get the f**k out of here, man; we busted two cars and three street lamps. Boss is going to kill us if he finds out!" He was clutching his face in agonizing pain.

"You friggin asshole, it's all your fault; if you hadn't released the damn crane, none of this shit would have happened." Max was angry as hell.

"Get a grip, man; who the f**k knew these mean toddlers would be using us for practicing range…? Man, those snowballs were like rocks. I would strangle these assholes myself, but they are gone. Plus, I say let's get the f**k out of here before something else happens or someone sees this shit we made and reports us. I ain't paying shit for this".

Max thought for a second or two, and they both looked at a considerable cement truck lying on its side in a side street. They looked at each other like thinking: 'We are not that bad after all.' What the f**k was going on here.

Max decided without further thinking on the matter.

"For once, you are right; let's go! We came out and let out a victory cry again! They secured the crane and got inside, this time in the driver's cabin, and got out in a hurry from the collector street, soon disappearing into the main avenue.

Hours slowly passed, and we were in full command of the street. Everything that passed was attacked with such vigor, ferociousness, and simple precision never seen before. The scene resembled a combo of medieval siege and French Revolution barricades; all stuff traveling on gasoline was considered an enemy. The white wall and the cars provided protection and a temporary hideout when someone decided to see what was happening, which was rare. This time, we let be the innocent bystanders that used their legs for transportation. Alan 'Spitfire' Meehan was responsible for artillery attacks and fine-tuning snowball shooting. As you guessed, everything was hit with the bull's eye precision.

The Siege II: The Shattered Windshield

The moment of truth was coming near to me. I contemplated the existence of this particular snowball I held for almost 35 minutes and suddenly realized its time had come! It was a piece of rock, ice, and a weapon, a bullet, an incredible byproduct of nature ready to be let out in the world and make its historic mark on the environment. I threw a lot of snowballs that morning and added to the combined power of the attacks but haven't hit anything significant, i.e., destroyed or hit myself only. That was soon about to change. A small mini-combi van-truck just entered the collector road, approaching us at 75km per hour. It was evident due to the horrendous orange paint and giant black letters denoting the name of the business it was in: "White Recycling Construction Ltd." How ironic! Two guys, Mike and Bo, riding inside had already heard that this was a shitty street and everybody was being attacked. They got word from the sister company that owned the cement trucks. Something weird was going on, and the cops should be here soon. But they were not scared – these two dudes were ex-military, and they knew shit when they saw it and never ran from anything. We lose 15min and try to bypass this road…how bad can it be? This isn't the damn Bulgaria or Angola, this was their city, or at least they thought so.

I was thinking of what I had in my hands—A snowball! It is a ball of snow, usually created by scooping snow with the hands and compacting it into a roughly fist-sized shape of a ball. That was it! The snowball is necessary to hold a snowball fight or attack. Everyone knew that! The pressure exerted by the hands on the snow determines the final result. Reduced pressure leads to a light and soft snowball. Alan "Spitfire" taught me that part! Higher pressure causes the snow to melt, turning it into liquid water. Once the pressure is removed, the water turns again into ice, leading to a more compact and rugged snowball, which eventually can be considered harmful during a snowball fight. That stage was where everyone wanted to get to. Our high school professor said the melting and refreezing process is called regelation. Well, so much for the scientific minute; I picked up in physics, or…was it chemistry class? My 'scientific' daydreaming suddenly stopped due to the sound of this incoming vehicle. I could see now that it was a small orange FIAT half-delivery truck and two dudes inside. I decided to throw my snowball and this little truck. It was my best throw of the day, robust, precise, and direct. I threw it in a long, sharp loop, letting the truck pass a bit, and didn't think much of it. It seems my geometrically calculated throw found it the target. Until I heard Alan's voice screaming, I had no idea where the snowball went.

"Man, you broke the f**king windshield"!

"F**king awesome, Haas, you busted the truck with that Ice rock," added Norman. They all looked at me in awe and then at the truck again, which abruptly stopped in the middle of the street. After some 30 sec, nothing happened, and we were all frozen in our footsteps. Then two dudes walked out of the truck, and suddenly with six sense of urgency (or he knew this from before experience), Evan Kapadia screamed at the top of his lungs:

"Run for your f**king lives!"

A couple of snowballs hit the sides of the truck doing no damage at all and producing classic sounds, except for one. Mike and Bo heard the explosion when an ice bullet hit the windshield. It exploded into 1000s' of pieces, and they were fortunate not to get hurt. It took them half a minute to catch their breath and realize what had happened. It didn't take long for these two ex-militaries to take a decisive course of action.

"Let's get these f**king toddlers, Mike; they screwed with the wrong dudes today!"

"I am with you, mate; let's bust their asses!"

The two guys out of the orange looked like mean sons of bitch-es and carried both rusted crowbars. They didn't yell or scream or anything like that. They stopped the vehicle, regained control, took two crowbars, and started running towards us as African long-track sprinters. We were 100 meters from them. After Evan's words, we all started to run on all sides. In the tumult that followed, where there was a lot of screaming & shouting, those of us that ran into the skyscraper made the biggest mistake, as we were not thinking at all. Instead of hiding in our apartments, we ran like crazy mice in a maze – up and down the staircase. Mike and Bo went for the skyscraper immediately, Bo running the staircase and Mike board-ing the elevator and cutting us off on the 1oth floor and then going down the staircase. I was caught on the 7th floor, Mike on the 5th, Anthoine on the 6th, and David on the 9th. No force was needed, but one look at the crowbars and these mean dudes made us all realize: Don't f**k with the duck! They took us one after another to the apartments, to our parents, where psychological and physical punishment came from our kin (well deserved) and where short-medium and long-term grounding happened to most of us. Bo and Mike meticulously took all information and left as good citizens uttering as few words as possible. When they were done, they came down, scanned the area, and took off in their broken truck, first removing the windshield pieces. They drove off in silence.

We later discovered that a little weasel called Patrick Payson, a geek kid from the adjacent tower, squealed on us when Bo and Mike caught him downstairs on the tower's grand staircase. He didn't participate in anything happening that day but was watching the whole thing instead. Patrick gave up at least two dozen names, and the two dudes collected all on paper, plus some kids that surrendered out of fear were interrogated and freaked out when Bo and Mike raised their crowbars. Later we all had to pay fines. The incredible thing was that Bo and Mike didn't use any force or had to beat up anyone; they just did it with ease but with a commanding stance and some intimidation. That was enough! The guys were vast and robust, plus angry as hell, so nobody wanted to f**k with them. Patrick the Weasel was dealt with later, being locked for 12 hours in a cellar shed full of rats in which we all shitted first, so the smell was unbearable…don't worry, he survived and learned a most valuable lesson not to squeal, ever again. He never wanted to visit the smelly rat-infested cellar shed again! Patrick got what he deserved, and those are the most valuable life lessons – through suffering, pain, and anguish (and even some light torture) comes a fresh and healthy dose of self-realization and self-purification. This is how Boris Duchovny explained it, and we naturally agreed as it made complete sense in light of the recent events. Of course, we all learned a lesson too. But it was not over. There were more things to come.

The Siege III: Bus 435

The final scene played out some 30min after I and some of my friends were picked up. Half the gang ran home or hid in various holes and never returned. After Bo and Mike left and alerted the police, of course. Still, some 20 kids returned to the scene, although not in command anymore by the illustrious and braveheart Kapadia brothers, who called it a day. Norman "Stone" Podworsky" and Boris Duchovny took command of one final attack with this little group left. "Let's finish this off, brothers, in one bang, shall we?" "For all our comrades and fallen heroes, and those asses that didn't come back—let's bust some ass!"

Norman was determined to close this with a victory, and you didn't need much persuasion when Boris was in question. Situations like this were for him like a pond was for a frog. The leftovers screamed in one voice: "Let's do it!" The idea was to attack one final time, whatever appeared on the horizon, and very little appeared at all. They took unprotected open ground, abandoning the barricades and the parking lot. No more hiding! It was the entire front without cover!

Nuruda Chello was a cousin to a guy that lived in our apartment building and drove a cab, Sherif Chello. Nuruda came out of the mental institution recently and was rehabilitated, according to his doctors. He was called Nuruda "Fangio" Chello, getting the nickname after the driver Juan Manuel Fangio who dominated automobile-racing competition in the 1950s, winning the world driving championship in 1951, 1954, 1955, 1956, and 1957. He had won 24 world-championship Grand Prix races when he retired from racing in 1958., making him a legend and a grand F1 racing champion. On the other hand, Nuruda was not an F1 champ; instead, he held the record for fast-driving city buses, busting 5 of them in the last five years and destroying some property in the process, making him a legend in many street talk circles in the city. Driving with Nuruda was always a special treat, as you had no clue how and where it would end. So finally, at the Bus firm, they decided to give him one more final chance and the most tedious and harmless route, Bus 435, where there was a minimal possibility for actual speeds and harm to be done. Or so they thought. He was driving that damn red bus that morning through that damn street. He hated this part of the city and hated this line. Nuruda loved boulevards, wide streets, and even steep roads where he could practice his driving style. Instead, it was this shitty part with low-speed limits.

Additionally, he had a middle-aged woman asking him every 10sec when the station was coming and that she needed to go out. He tried to explain that there was a long stretch, almost 2 miles, before the next stop as this bus worked/covered only a few stops on medium distance. She wouldn't budge, and Nuruda was losing his nerve. She was at it again:

"When is the next stop? You need to stop soon, and you need to let me out. You are driving too fast young man. You are a bad driver. Where is my next stop? When will you stop?"

It just wouldn't stop, and Nuruda was gaining in speed when he entered our collector road; he realized it was built for speed. It was almost a mile and a half long, enough to burn some tires, thought Nuruda. Who the hell was going to check? The sooner he reaches the Bus stop, the sooner this old hag will stop winning. He pressed the gas pedal, let the clutch go, and the bus accelerated with people clutching to the interior bus steel bars and posts more intensely now.

Boris and Norman saw the red bus coming and got ready. When the bus arrived, the cannonballs started hitting it on all sides, especially the windows. This was the best target possible as usually they never stop because of the passengers and time schedules (though busses were always late), and they provided a huge body to shoot at metal and glass – it couldn't be better! Everyone had two (ice) snowballs in their hands and some two dozen ready-made on the ground.

Nuruda saw many kids on the two sides of the opening and didn't realize anything until snowballs impacted all parts of the bus. People started screaming inside due to the combined speed of the vehicle and the relentless pounding of white ice powder on the windows. Cracks came on the glass, and one part shattered. The windshield that was heavily cracked and never fixed by the damn company was also attacked, as was the left and right flank. It cracked even more now on the left side. It was like a scene from Clint Eastwood's movie THE GAUNTLET, but you had ice and snow combined instead of bullets.

Nuruda was in shock, and the woman beside him started screaming and yelling, "Stop the bus, let me out, my station is here, let me out, stop the bus," and the screaming continued. Suddenly Nuruda said: "F**k it, you want your station bitch; here is your stop!" He violently hit the brakes with a screeching sound. The bus went almost 100km/h and did not slide, spin, overturn, flip, or anything. It just stopped in an incredible momentum, causing people to fall on the floor and out of their seats, and the woman that complained and wasn't holding on to anything flew right out the windshield breaking it entirely on the left side. She was fortunate that the windshield was already messed up. Otherwise, her destiny would be like a smashed potato or crushed tomato inside the bus. She went out like a bullet traveling 100km/; suddenly, a body was bloodied and broken on the street a few meters from the bus.

Nuruda watched in horror and couldn't utter anything except: "F**king A man…She shouldn't have asked me to stop, and she shouldn't have asked me to stop…she shouldn't have…."

Nuruda Chello wasn't hurt as he always had two pairs of security seat belts on him as military pilots have, but soon after the event, he went into a catatonic state for months. The doctors said it was the shock. The ambulance arrived immediately from the ER, not far down the road. People were coming out of the bus, some still screaming, some yelling at Nuruda, some at the kids. The woman was miraculously alive but broke up pretty badly, with two limbs, two ribs broken, a heavy concussion, and a partly cracked skull with small hemorrhaging. It could have been much worse, and what happened as she went through the windshield as a bullet was no wonder. After a few minutes, all the remaining 20 or more kids ran in all directions like rats fleeing a flood. This was way too much, and the best thing was to get the f**k out of Dodge City. Norman and Boris were running like rabbits and disappeared instantaneously from the scene. After that, most of the kids dissolved, fearing being picked up for this, while some came back to the scene, coming out of hiding or just pretending they had nothing to do with it when cops and ambulance were about to leave. After that, the mayhem was over. All this lasted until 17:00– 5 hours of relentless attacks until cops showed up after the ambulance and bus 435 episode. Two patrol cars and a minivan called "Gretel" (from Hansel &

Gretel Fairy Tale – please don't ask me why I don't have the faintest clue!) came to pick up the anarchists and rioters as the word spread that some activist revolutionaries were trying to take control of the street and neighborhood. That's usually how stories change their content & form. They realized it was a much more 'benign' thing than thought previously, though people were hurt in the process, one even seriously.

After gathering information and getting the bits and pieces from eyewitnesses and the people in the bus and from dispatch (Mike and Bo and busted Ray Bitko + Hans, and Max they finally came clean with what happened as the crane truck suffered damage that could not be hidden) they finally left. The traumatized woman was taken care of in the ER and released a week later. Another bus came and picked up the stranded folks. Nuruda was taken to the Police for questioning, but nothing happened as he was speechless. He would soon be committed to Birdland, the city's biggest loony-tone house. Just before the whole thing was wrapped up, another can-didate for Birdland, Jeremiah Bielinski, "THE PILGRIM," came back from his compulsory Saturday drinking session and seeing all the mayhem and mess in front of him, he just said: "Kill em all and let God sort them out." No one paid much attention to this.

It was all over, and heavy fines were being processed, but no legal action was taken as it was hard to get any witnesses to this whole mess which consisted of a chain of violent episodes involving more than 100 people. Some local cops were reprimanded for not coming to the scene earlier when reported by Ray Bitko. They never took any serious notice of that call, which proved a mistake.

Post-Siege: The Midnight Hunt

I know what you are thinking: "Is there anything more possible in this story? What the hell can be added to this story."

The day was not over, nor was this story. What happened at the end could not be found in any sane tale or script. Well, when everyone thought that this was it, when almost all dispersed and the cops and ambulance left and normality returned to the street and neighborhood, some of us were already paying the price of 'going to war' and others, people like Ray Bitko, Hans Svensson or Nuruda Chello thinking WHAT THE F**k HAPPENED that day, something incomprehensible was going to play out like there was room for more lunacy that day…it seems there was!

Remember the Usurpers, Mortimer and Gloria? Those beings on the 4th floor wrongfully and illegally seized and held the cellar shed of another tenant. They got the name usurpers ('supplanters') when they illegally acquired two cellar sheds without permission. The usurpers just moved in and took two empty sheds that were not used. I wrote about this in another story. They were watching this scene and probably writing down everything for post-gossip shit as the female head of the family was part of the enormous tower gossip network headed by Norissa Guzinski. Gloria was probably calling the Police too, but they didn't pay much attention to it as she would call even if a sparrow shitted on her window. The problem is that Pépe liked to tease them at times; well, we all did. But this was neither the time nor the place (after such a day) to start anything like this. He and a few others gathered again in a small group outside the tower when all mayhem passed. Pépe saw Gloria pasted onto the window sill, looking at them and making notes. That ticked him off.

"Shitty usurpators, shitty…Usurpators…", Pépe was at it again, but Gloria did not react; she just drew the curtains and seemed unwilling to participate in a feud.

"Those are weasels, the tip of the Police, the Gossip Channel; they stole cellar sheds, and they are mean and hate us," proclaimed Pépe to the small group around him, pointing in the direction of the 3rd, instead of 4th window floor apartment. What happened is a bit uncertain. It seems Moustafa Haider, Little Moritz, and Fat Gill, that stood there with Pépe and wanted some extra kick and more mayhem, just decided to attack the Usurpers window with a cannonade of snowballs. Little Moritz was, of course, in charge of this violent move. What they did was hit the wrong window on the 2nd floor. Ice snowballs shattered the glass pane instantly. They did hit the target, but in the whole confusion, the wrong one, partly thanks to Pépe pointing wrongly. They just wanted to empty their last salvo of the day on, as they thought was, the evil usurpers' window. Fat Gill suddenly realized as he lived in the tower aside from Pépe – "F**k man, that is the wrong window! We just broke a f**king wrong window Pépe! "You f**king moron, that was the wrong window!"

Pépe also realized this with delayed brain reaction that they crushed the window just below the usurpers on the third floor where a mano-depressive-schizophrenic-clinically diagnosed and deeply depressed John Adams Forestbird lived with his wife Keisha and their 22-year-old weirdo daughter Larna. Everyone knew that John Adams was a damn weird bird that is best left alone!

His wife Keisha used to say to John Adams frequently and to pick it up from some TV Soap Opera: "What do you hear from your brain, as empty as it is? An occasional thought must creep in it sometimes, John Adams?" he didn't even get upset. Of all the things John Adams Forestbird (or 'JAF' as we liked to call him) lost, he missed his mind the most. JAF consistently reiterated that some people are only alive because it is illegal to shoot them. He often thought, 'When he was young, and without this damn family still in control of his mind, his favorite pastime activity was wild animal hunting.' But all of that was gone now. The only thing remaining was the empty nothingness of life. When the window shattered, JAF argued with Keisha and was near a nervous breakdown, probably the 100th in a row. She was going about how crazy he was, that he should be committed, and how she could have married a better man. The explosion of the window glass triggered something inside him. He started screaming, "I'm not crazy; I've just been in a very bad f**king mood for 45 years, and now I am going to kill someone, at least when I cannot kill you and our stupid, moronic daughter"! He went to the broken window and saw a small group of kids looking in fear. His eyes were burning red. JAF was a small man with a strong body, an almost egg-like face, and a bulky chest. He was short but could walk and run as fast as hell. He said to them in a calm, almost ominous voice, but still loud enough to hear:

"I will kill all of you, and I will do it now." he then disappeared into the apartment and took his loaded shotgun, came back to the window, and said:

"Yes, I will kill you one by one with this shotgun." He then went and put on his parka, wool cap and gloves, and hunting boots and walked out of the apartment carrying a shotgun in his hand and a

5-meter rope in the other. Keisha was screaming behind him, but he didn't hear. He didn't care and was deaf.

It was just after 20:00 hours, and the darkness was beginning to fall deeper and deeper. Pépe and Moustafa ran in one direction and Little Moritz and Fat Gill in another. They didn't think the crazy guy would do anything, but when they all turned to see if anyone was following, they saw JAF exit the building with a gun and rope. At that point, they were shit scared and lost all orientation and reason. Fear gripped them entirely as they knew this guy was a lunatic. Eyewitnesses say that JAF hunted the kids until midnight (this was never confirmed). He did hunt them until he got them. However, Pépe could hide in some concrete pipe at the construction site and almost froze to death when he got out at 03:00 in the morning, unable to move from fear that petrified him. Moustafa Haider, turning to see if he was being followed, fell into a ditch and broke his leg, so JAF let him be after first terrorizing him for a quarter of an hour, saying, 'The last thing I want to do is hurt you, you little weasel, But it's still high on my list.' After that, he left him there.

In the end, he caught Little Moritz and Fat Gill. They were running in strange circles and hiding in the nearby construction site and park and then, in desperation, ran to another park some 3 miles away. This was done primarily on panic; these two could not outrun JAF. It never crossed their minds the best thing was to go home. JAF had the hunters' noses and was determined to catch his prey. His mind was a mess, but he was a man with a gun and a mission. Some people called the Police when they saw a guy running like a rabbit with a shotgun. He constantly changed pace and looked like a ridiculous figure in the night, crouched like a hound dog, trying to find and kill foxes. He was running around like a lunatic, talking to himself and then shouting some incomprehensible word occasionally and gesturing with his hands and arms. Police finally apprehended JAF when he tried to terrorize Little Moritz and Fat Gill after tying around a tree in an adjacent park. He was probably unsure what to do, nor was he in control, but the gun was loaded, making him dangerous. They were both in total shock, and it took them weeks and months to recover fully. JAF was taken away, and he soon after joined the Birdland facility. With that, the incredible and long day came to a fitting end.

EPILOGUE – Our Crimes & Some Punishment

I was grounded for two weeks. Most of my friends suffered the same faith, and we all had to pay for the damage to the windshield of the orange FIAT vehicle, busted cars and street lamps, bus damage, and even the cement truck damage, plus damages to public property and ER costs for the lady that didn't have full medical insurance. We have certainly learned a valuable lesson and our parents an economic one. But it was the sweetest grounding, and we were heroes of that part of the city and a cluster of neighborhoods for a few weeks as the word spread like lightning. I especially had a privileged position for busting that windshield with one shot. Man, we did significant damage that day. I thought The Pilgrim was correct when he said, 'Errors have been made, and errors will be made. Others will be blamed', After that day, I wasn't so sure in Pilgrim's words, especially that we all should be killed…but who was? Sometimes his words were as helpful as a grave robber in a crematorium, but at least he triggered the white inferno that day and all the crap that happened after that.

They say that 'everything comes to those who wait.' Boy, was that true that day? Each revolution and war has casualties and collateral damage. After the mayhem, we caused to public transportation, Bus 435 that looked like a remnant from the LA gang wars, The Kempmann Yellow Crane truck attack, The Cement truck spitfire shooting and crashing on its side, and the actual catch of the day – the breaking of the orange Fiat mini truck windshield and tens of dozens of innocent automobiles, people hurt in the process and public property was damaged. Fortunately, nobody died that day or remained brain-dead or paralyzed. The finale was coming up with the unexpected midnight run and shotgun episode! THE SNOW-BALL SIEGE CHRONICLES, the name that this event became legendary and famous for by the local community and actors themselves, was over.

We became unique and known for this. The important part was that there were no casualties, not real ones. Some got committed to institutions, like John Adams Forestbird, for the first time, and others got there for life, like Nuruda Chello. As they say, errors have been made. Others will be blamed. Others have been blamed. We have been blamed. I have been blamed. We got f**ked, all of us – one way or the other, but boy, was it worth it—damn worth it! I was the hero of the block for bustin' that windshield—at least for weeks. I became part of a legendary group of lads that defied the weather, vehicles, traffic, construction, police, transport planning, physics, and good behavior conduct! We ruled that day, and the local community members never forgot us. Tales were told, and stories were passed along for many seasons and winters after that, but such a day never returned. It just lives in the memories of the white winter veterans and our chronicles!

***

PS Some of the Legendary Heroes of Snowball Chronicles day: KUDOS TO ALL OF THEM!

Alan 'Spitfire' Meehan; Norman "Stone" Podworsky"; Danny Slowitz; Memphis Kapadia; Anthoine Scott; Mike Gleisch;

Daren "The Head" Capouya; Boris Duchovny; Harry Rowells; Pépe; Evan Kapadia; Daniel Kehooe; Alex Hermon; David Nathan; Boris Rohas; Tigran Haas; Salishi Troika; Joe Brown; Little Moritz; Patrick Payson; Fat Gill; Keke and Ture Tollberg; Moustafa Haider and some 60+ others which names I cannot recall anymore…sorry guys!

…And, of course: Jeremiah Bielinski, "THE PILGRIM," the old f**ker that started it all…

+

Red Bus Line 435, Heavy KEMPMANN Crane Truck ATS540, Small Orange FIAT Mini Van-Truck, Tens of dozens of automobiles

…And, of course—the f**king Russian-made Cement Truck!

29

The Newest Bohemians

On intersecting lives of five people united by music as contemplation on the significance of human life & death…

When he stepped forward and gazed into the city's concert hall main stage, Lucio Tassone didn't know how many people would be attending that evening's performance of Donizetti's Opera Don Giovanni. At that stage, the music and everything surrounding his work were based on tradition, respect and loyalty to his profession and himself as a first-class performer. Every time he performed or was about to enter the stage, a sense of adventure, purpose, and even renewal overcame him, and he was sure that very few people felt that in their everyday lives & jobs. He was a fortunate man, lucky that God granted him this unique gift, the gift of an opera singer. When he entered the stage, thunderous applause erupted, and everyone stood up and watched him in awe; all his young friends from the world of art & literature were there. He was an inspiration to them in many ways. Lucio Tassone was in seventh heaven…

Aside from Bohemian being a native or inhabitant of Bohemia in the Czech Republic, the word is used differently today, at least in the everyday vocabulary. A Bohemian person is a nonconformist writer or an artist, painter, musician, poet, architect, etc., who lives an unconventional life in a " bohemian lifestyle." You could say that is what Lucio "Caruso" Tassone did. He got his nickname from the outstanding Italian operatic tenor that lived from 1873 to 1921, still (most probably) the best, Enrico Caruso. He wasn't quite like Caruso regarding his looks or voice range, but Lucio was still a great opera singer and respected throughout the city and country. Medium height, a balding gentleman with relatively solid eyebrows and a year-round tan circling a pair of cobalt penetrating eyes, Lucio was a charming and handsome gentleman that many women desired. Add to that a great sense of wardrobe and impeccable manners, and it was no wonder many ladies were interested in this 47-year-old bohemian of Italian ancestry. Unfortunately for them, Lucio enjoyed the comfort of men, especially young ones, sleeping around all the time but only, as he would say in private, with those that would give him enjoyment, softness, and mutual artistic pleasure. Lucio had the reputation of a gentle but passionate southern lover, and being a sort of celebrity, there were a few gay men in the art-music-media-literary circles that could resist his charm. The private, official part of his life was a disaster. He married early to a woman called Diksha Pathak, a mediocre chansons bar singer with a dubious past but rather good looks. It was more of a marriage of convenience where he wanted to satisfy his parents. She sought a safe and prominent harbor after a few disastrous relationships and one capsized marriage. The problem was that he discovered soon after they got married that he was gay and could not stand women anymore as physical partners. The only woman he slept with was a young girl by the name of Dasha, who married Makarov, who was, believe it or not, living in the same building, our skyscraper, with her husband, Viktor Makarov, a polished Neanderthal, but a very successful and well-off situated salesman who gave Dasha a taste of the good life. They had only one son Yevgenij, who didn't resemble the father and was a musical and artsy soul. Lucio met him at a Bohemian party and slowly fell in love with the young boy. His parents had no clue Yevgenij was also gay. To make things even more complex, Mathew Panduro, a folk song performer and recording artist (and a bachelor living on the 9th floor of our skyscraper), was screwing Diksha Pathak, Lucio's wife. Lucio knew this and didn't care a bit. As mentioned, Diksha was also a performer, but of a different kind. She sang chansons in three jazzy, bohemian restaurants near the main square in the central city. She always wanted to be a first-class chansonnier like the great Edith Piaf was. She was eons behind the French lady in talent and performance skills. That is where she and Mathew met. Music and sex connected them and kept them together for almost ten years. Strangely enough, Diksha preferred it that way, not to leave Lucio but to continue hanky panky with Mathew and keep the good appearances, especially at social gatherings. Many people knew and suspected that they had parted ways and that Lucio was gay, but it was never brought up in public. Being a wife of a first-class Opera singer suited her snobbish character and gave her the upper hand in some circles, not to speak of the skyscraper gossip network she was a part of, headed by Norissa Guzinski. Diksha was slowly losing her good looks and voice, so it was essential to continue 'pretending' to be something and someone. She knew after a while that Lucio was gay but didn't give a rat's ass about it, and it also gave her a bit of the upper hand in the, more or less, arranged marriage. But deep inside, she cursed the day her best friend set her up with Lucio, a young, great-looking opera singer. She fell for him directly. The cheating soon started after discovering that he couldn't perform in bed, and she was glad that Mathew Panduro supplied sex whenever she needed it.

She didn't know that Lucio had a son, which he was unaware of. On the other hand, Lucio was a great cook, so there were never problems when food was concerned. He usually took care of that. They were together on paper but living separate lives sanctioned by both.

***

All of this was happening on the 8th and 9th floor, which was a unique musical compound of sorts (except for Boris Duchovny and his brother and their folks and one small apartment being host to an insignificant clerk), assembling three apartments with tenants that had diametrically different views and taste in music: Hard Metal Rock, Jazz and Classical Opera. Such a concentration of musical talent nearby was hard to find anywhere else. It was often brought up that living close to the 8th floor was impossible due to the constant repetitions of these people. Either it was the piano – one jazzy – the other classical- or a heavy metal band plus an additional Hi-Fi 500W speaker system that could blow your mind out. One was never prepared for any of that, and the ones living on the 8th and 9th floor and not being musicians knew that as they always had ear props ready!

***

All of this was completed by a jazzy piano player, Bran Herznagel, and his neurotic, psychotic wife, Mathilda. Aside from Lucio and Diksha and Diksha's son from his first marriage or so, Andrew Somun (who played loud music all the time), Yevgenij lived there with his parents. This was complemented by the 9th floor, where you had Lana Chester, a brilliant and beautiful young classical pianist, on her way up in the music world. Mathew Panduro also lived on that floor in one room apartment; handsome and bohemian fellow, unconventional in appearance and behavior, he was fulfilling Diksha's sexual desires regularly and slowly but surely, building up a stable career as a folk singer and recording artist. He and Lucio would sometimes meet in public and private and had a mutual understanding regarding sharing the same woman. Mathew also met with Bran for some jamming jazz sessions. He used to play the trumpet before floating into folk music waters. He and Bran became close friends.

"What does it mean to be an Opera Singer, a performer, a musician, or an artist"? That was the question Lucio Tassone posed many times in different forums, i.e., various parties, just after-work gatherings, or simply everyday chat with peers and acquaintances from his intellectual circles. He would continue by saying that "To be a true master performer means to devote oneself utterly to a set of moral and ascetic principles, to seek a stillness of your mind in your music world and to master the way of the voice and the way of life the profession brings." A handsome young man that caught Lucio's eye was standing in the corner of the room and listening to everything Lucio was talking about. He nodded and couldn't take his eyes off the opera singer. Lucio considered himself a genuinely Bohemian man, a veritably nonconformist artist who lived an unconventional life. He understood that these two things might not be in sync; on one side, rules and codex; on the other, no standards and very few rules. Nonetheless, he found a harmonic convergence and a life filled with balance and ease, at least professionally, sleeping around and not getting emotionally involved with anyone until he met Yevgenij Makarov, the young man whose gaze at the party he couldn't forget. That meeting and moment changed many lives in so many different ways.

***

Yevgenij Makarov's "The Thorn Path" vocalist was 25 and gay. He had the looks of a D&G model and an extremely high IQ but was lazy. Somehow, he got it into his head that he was born for music and the career of a brutal rock star was his destiny. His hard rock-metal band was an utter failure. Being classically trained, Yevgenij wanted to make some fusion with heavy metal via long instrumental parts of the songs, which resulted in bizarre compositional layouts. The Thorn Path" consisted of him on vocals & guitars, his geek friend Mike on bass, Derek the drummer, who was always under drugs influence, and Lana Chester on Keyboards. Lana was out of place there but was so crazy after Yevgenij that she begged him for this though she thought little of the band and its music and had very little time as classical music took her on the road a lot. She could not understand why Yevgenij was wasting his valuable talent on this. He obliged to get her in the band as Lana was damn good, a girl that finished a music conservatory and could play Chopin and Debussy like the masters themselves, plus she was good on Hammond Organ, Korg, Yamaha keyboards, and MOOG. When she was not around, they just took the keyboards out. They tried a couple of pure disaster singles and a mini-LP album that became the laughingstock of the music community. It sold 75 copies out of 5000 printed, and the record company banned "The Thorn Path" from coming close to their building. This knocked down Yevgenij, but he didn't give up, continuing to record and sing. Lana's heart was bleeding and going out to this young man, a conservatorium graduate from Graz, Austria but somehow went into different musical paths that didn't seem to work. She could not help at all. Their music sucked. On the private side, things were going in a different direction. Yevgenij met Lucio Tassone at a bohemian music party thrown by some mutual music acquaintance, a record producer. They soon hooked up, finding common interests in art, film, and good wine and…discovering they were both very gay. Thanks to his excellent connections, Lucio promised Yevgenij he would soon open some doors in the record business. He was already mesmerized by this handsome and knowledgeable young man. Soon they became passionate lovers, meeting in different hotels in the city at different times until they started having sneaking meetings in their apartments.

***

Lana Chester's mom Melissa died when she was at the age of seven. She always had difficulty remembering her and was afraid not to erase her from her vision as time affected people ultimately. She had a younger sister Dana. Lana was now 25 years old, the same as Yevgenij, and had an education from the famous Julliard and St. Petersburg conservatorium behind her and some 30 awards and 100 performances. Her performance of Schumann's famous Piano Concerto in A Minor was hailed as something extraordinary, and DECCA recorded this immediately with the Berlin Philharmonic. None of that made any difference as after all that success, they kept on the road a lot, and she always returned to her apartment in the skyscraper keeping out of the limelight and being close to her sister and Yevgenij. Love was more robust than anything imaginable for her and kept burning inside her like an eternal flame.

Growing up and discovering her talent, she spent much time with their neighbor, Bran Herznagel, a fantastic jazzman who gave her first piano lessons. Bran took graduate studies at the Berklee College of Music in Boston, and it was there where my father met him while also being at Harvard in a different field. Later they became friends when physical proximity, like the skyscraper, brought them closer again. Bran was a brilliant pianist and used to jam with some great jazz musicians in clubs in New York, Detroit, and Chicago. Keith Jarrett once said to him, after he heard him jam in a Chicago club: "Not bad man, not bad at all. Call me up when you are in town next time, and let's do some jammin' together!" in 1975 he was there at the famous Live Concert in Cologne and later did a double piano jam session with Keith the following evening in a jazz club in Berlin. At that time, he had a promising career. For some strange reason, he returned home and continued playing in clubs but never really made a name for himself, just playing for the fun. There seems to be another reason: a woman he met in States and then returned with her, Lana's mom Melissa. It was Lana's mom's idea to put her close to this man, as she saw him as a close friend. Her mom had a short but passionate relationship with Bran as they were high school sweethearts, and Lana was conceived there. Suddenly she married someone else and never told Bran that Lana was his child. What made Melissa end that relationship and suddenly jump into someone else's arms nobody knew? Bran was shocked; after that, he lost interest in dating, marriage, and women in general. Still, he married Melissa's sister Mathilda as she saw an opportunity to grab the man, and in the end, he was forced to say yes.

Bizarrely enough, Melissa confided in Mathilda that Lana was his daughter. This was just a month before she died of an aneurysm. As if by some premonition, she knew her days were coming to a very early end. They were the closest friends, not just because of age but also because they were sisters. Melissa had only Mathilda and Lana. Mathilda didn't take this well, although she didn't show. She had no kids with Bran and hated her sister and daughter Lana. Melissa never knew that and loved her sister and had a special place in her heart for Bran, as after him, she never felt love again. Lana's father (or stepfather) was a neurosurgeon and was rarely at home, especially when Lana's mom died. There was a constant stream of nannies until both girls reached the age of maturity, and this got terminated. Then they took care of themselves, Lana on the road a lot and Dana working as a nurse in dad's hospital. Bran was like a father figure to her; she always felt a solid closeness to him and could see that her mom did the same. Her aunt Mathilda, Mom's sister, didn't particularly like that much and could see that the woman hated her. When Mom passed away, she even felt closer to Bran, though Mathilda started hating Lana even more and couldn't stand the sight of her. It was the same with Lucio's wife, Dasha. She could never understand why these two hated her so much. Mathilda decided to keep one secret but disclose another she knew from her sister, one that Dasha's son Yevgenij had another father, one called Lucio Tassone. She had to share this with Diksha Pathak and the gossip network.

For Lana Chester, passion is unlimited, and desire has infinite power. She could have had any man she desired, but Yevgenij stole her heart from the first moment she saw him as a 16-year-old girl, and when they got stuck in an elevator for three hours, discovering how a wonderful soul he was, very much like her own. He was into his music, which was not good, but she respected the choice and was where she was. Soon they became best of friends but never lovers as soon after the age of innocence passed, she found out the hard way that he was gay. Nothing she could do or say would change this, and if she persisted, she knew that Yevgenij would be lost forever, so she kept him close as a friend but was dying inside of the desire for him. Lana never gave hope that he might return to the 'other' side again and they could be together forever.

Yevgenij once gave her a hallmark card for her birthday that had written on it: "friend is someone who understands your past, believes in your future, and accepts you today the way you are." She kept this as the sacred relic you might find. She knew he would be her only love till the end of time. Yevgenij knew this but could not change inside, as that was what he was.

***

Lucio Tassone's stepson, Diksha's real son from the first capsized marriage, Andrew, was nothing. Nobody knew his father. He was conceived at a train station when some train conductor had sex with drunken Diksha in the lady's restroom. It was more a rape than anything else, but Diksha didn't mind. Later she found some guy and forced him into marriage to cover up this shameful act. Later she lies and tells everyone that it was her's and Lucius even before the first marriage as they were so in love and passionate even then, and finally, they find each other in the end. Lucio knew it was a lie, and this fellow was not his as he had never had sex with that woman during the 30 years of their marriage, but he let it pass. Andrew was an idiot, and the only music link he had to his parents was a 500W Hi-Fi stereo equipment which he used to the max when playing hip-hop music. He was a high-school dropout and was a bit of an embarrassment for the whole family.

Lucio didn't give a shit about that, but it was eating up Diksha, as she hated all others that looked better and were smarter, like Yevgenij. She also hated the bitch Lana Chester who had her heart for Yevgenij, not her son Andrew who was crazy about her. Lana never gave him the time of day. In the meantime, Mathew Panduro continued screwing Diksha Pathak but was getting fed off it and of her simultaneously. Diksha's singing in a jazzy, bohemian restaurant near the main square in the central city went well for several years until she started losing her voice even more due to some genetic fault, which gave her fewer performance opportunities. They didn't want her there or anywhere else. She became more evil, jealous, and engulfed in hatred. Even Mathew could not stand her anymore and was trying to find the first opportunity to end it all, but Diksha was like a black widow, weaving its web around everyone and everything she knew. Lucio didn't care as he had his life, and she hated him for that.

Thanks to Norrisa Guzinski's gossip skyscraper network (assembling some five of the evilest hags you can imagine), she found out by triangulating the information that Lucio and Yevgenij were seen entering a hotel together in one of the suburbs. She also found out that Yevgenij was his son. Suddenly she felt hatred, rage, jealousy, and lust for revenge. Lucio once said there are three types of women – those that love, those that think they are in love, and those that never feel love and are usually consumed by hatred and jealousy. Lana was in the first category, and Diksha was in the third. Diksha Pathak loved to gossip and do evil things at times. It was just her nature, and so were Norissa Guzinski's and others. If you turn to the Gossip, these women produced, it was not just idle talk or rumors, especially about the personal or private affairs of others in the skyscraper. Their sole purpose was to moralize and speak badly about others and then use these (in most cases unproven) facts and views to screw with people.

Additionally, they had a bad reputation for adding extra materials, lies, errors, and other variations to the information transmitted through the building. All of this carried specific and severe implications that the old hags' news and gossip were so transmitted that it had a harmful purpose as the end product. These women killed the extra time they had in their lives with cards, drinking coffee and other beverages, and gossiping. They would also call all kinds of people and tell them horrific things (anonymously, of course), that their closest ones died, ended up in jail, were raped, etc., or would just turn to private ads pages and screw with the sellers, having no intent to purchase or lease anything. This 'gossip network' was undoubtedly capable of everything, even black magic, if they knew how to use it. Though, one is not entirely sure they did not cast harmful spells on people. It was so true in this case 'that birds of a feather flock together' and that the 'end justifies the means. One day when they had their session, a decision came to ruin Lucio Tassone's life. Diksha Pathak made this decision, partly drunk, partly sober. She hated her husband now and hated Lana and Yevgenij. She hated just about anyone but wanted to ruin lives around her. It was just in her nature, and now that her life was so f**ked up with the singing career disappearing, her idiot son, her husband she hated, and the secrets around him, she wanted to f**k others' lives as well. She (they at the gossip session) decided to call Dasha's husband Viktor one day when he was away, and they knew that Lucio and Yevgenij would meet. How they knew, it beats the hell out of me! This way, she could crush two flies with one hit, revenge on Dasha for having a baby with Lucio (she hated that Lucio ever slept with a woman, and a beautiful one for that). Also, she would smear and destroy Yevgenij, so Lana would start to hate him and never forgive him when she found out. This would be a chance for Andrew to step in. In any case, misery would be spread, the pain would rule, and people's lives might be ruined. All of that felt good for Dasha and even Mathilda. Norissa and two other hags did not complain; on the contrary! Diksha Pathak called Viktor anonymously, and the ball was in motion, one that nobody could stop.

***

Bran Herznagel and Mathilda lived without passion, real love, or desire for each other. Mathilda was happy to snatch Bran from her sister Melissa, and Bran was satisfied he didn't have to think about marriage again. This was it. He didn't care. They had no children, as Mathilda couldn't. They never adopted as Bran would never allow it. Bran once had a passionate relationship that produced offspring he was unaware of. Mathilda and Melissa, Lana's mother, had nothing in common, and Mathilda was always jealous of her older sister, especially when she told her that Lana was Bran's daughter. She wished her dead. If she could, she would kill herself. After a month, Melissa died, not at the hand of Mathilda but from a nasty aneurysm, and Mathilda kept the secret about Lana from Bran.

Soon depression and anxiety began taking control of her, and as she was a housewife, sitting at home mostly doing nothing, it just worsened. Even the gossip daily network sessions did not help. She was increasingly closing herself inwards as if her sisters' death had something to do with it. Bran paid diligently for weekly shrink sessions, which seem to have no viable or visible result. The only time she was partly present was in the company of the gossip. Even though they shared a lot, she kept the secret about Lana's birth father from them. She knew Norissa Guzinski would spread this, and knowing how close Lana and Bran were already, it might bring a positive result but a negative for Mathilda. And she hated them both now. After her sister was gone, hatred was pointed toward Bran. She wished him dead too. She would never allow this secret to come out as that would bring joy to some and sorrow to her.

***

At that time, the Wines from the New World (USA, South Africa, Australia, New Zealand + Chile & Argentina) hadn't penetrated the markets, nor had they reached every household like they do today. Nonetheless, some Italian, Portuguese, and Spanish wines were out there. Still, none of them could compete with the French (or -and some Italians'), nor can they do that even today (according to my humble taste and personal opinion), as the fact of the matter remains that the best French wines are still the best in the world as they have this real sense of belonging to the soil in which they were produced, like no other wines in the world have nor will ever have the famous terroir. Lucio was sharing some of his ideas and thoughts on a great bottle of Bordeaux Margaux he was drinking with his lover.

Lucio and Yevgenij had magnificent sex that morning and were utterly in love. It was a weird feeling for Lucio as he had only slept with a woman with Yevgenij's mother, Dasha, some 25 years ago. Soon after, he discovered another side of the sexuality he preferred. After that, he slept with dozens of men, usually beautiful and intelligent. But no one could match Yevgenij or Lucio's feelings towards this young man. He could see in Yevgenij's eyes a deep sense of love, emotion, and devotion to the older man.

While still cuddling under the sheets in the bedroom and sipping the Claret, the apartment door opened, and someone came in. Yevgenij's stepfather came back early from a business trip as the phone call he received from the unknown woman threw him out of balance altogether. He had no clue that Dasha was at her sister's and Yevgenij was home. He hoped the damn bugger was dead of an overdose in some garage. Although he was his son, it felt like that kid had nothing of his gene pool, and he just wanted him dead all the time. He was too bright and too sophisticated for Viktor and unproductive. He and his damn music! But now the only thing in his mind was: "Who was Dasha screwing, And why? How could this happen?"

He would find one way or another, even if it had to be pulled by a crowbar out of her.

Yevgenij ran into the closet when he heard the keys rattle in the lock, and Lucio ran out like a rabbit naked onto the balcony, hoping that somehow he could get out of there in one piece. Viktor Makarov came into the apartment and saw something wrong: clothes thrown everywhere on the floor. He didn't notice that all the clothes were men's; there were no women's, especially ladies' underwear. Instinctively, instead of going to the living room to the right, he rushed left into the bedroom, and seeing the bed sheets all over the place as they have been used very recently, he flipped. He touched them, and they were still warm. A warm, red crimson color came to his face, and he started screaming his wife's name:

"Dasha, where are you? Where the f**k are you? Get over here, now! What the f**k is going on?" "Are you screwing around? I will kill you if you are!"

Suddenly he saw movement on the bedroom balcony, and the door was slightly opened. He went out and saw a man.

"What the f**k are you doing here?" Asked Viktor.

Lucio answered in a Bohemian way.

"I am waiting for the bus; what else."

"What?"

It took him a minute to figure out the lunacy of this situation and his moronic question. He was looking at a naked middle-aged man covering his penis with his hands, standing on his balcony, waiting for a bus. What bus? Now he recognized Lucio, and it finally got to him – bitch Dasha was f**king around with this guy. She always went about how fantastic a gentleman and performer Lucio was and what kind of bitch wife he had…" The motherf**ker was screwing his wife," thought Viktor instantly. It didn't take long for Viktor to punch Lucio in the face and then in the balls. Lucio fell and lost consciousness. Despite that, Dasha returned from her sisters earlier than she thought. Yevgenij decided to come out of the closet and confront Viktor. It was time.

After Yevgenij confessed to crying and Viktor tried to crush his head with a marble sculpture, Dasha intervened to save the son and told the truth about Yevgenij, that he was not his flesh & blood, but instead Lucio's son. When Lucio returned from the hard punch that knocked the living daylights out of him, he noticed that he was lying on the bedroom floor, obviously dragged in by Viktor. Viktor was sitting in the bed, covering his face with his hands and giggling weirdly. Dasha was beautiful, but now she looked completely out of sync, crying in the armchair and hysterically moving her hands. Yevgenij was naked, standing in the other corner, looking into nothing, not focused, not present, nor there. Lucio started to say something, muttering apologies, when Dasha cut him off, whispering in a sob…

"Yevgenij is your son Lucio; he is your son; how could you?"…How could you…he is your flesh & blood, and you slept with him, you dirty incestuous old man!"

"May you rot in hell, and I curse the day I slept with you, you filthy, dirty pig, you disgusting pervert, you…", She didn't finish the sentence. Guilt, Hate, Shame, Revenge, and Love probably swept into this room at the speed of light. Something snapped in Lucio when he realized what had transpired in front of his eyes. He looked at Yevgenij standing like a statue, naked in one corner, Viktor giggling like a madman on the bed, and Dasha hysterically screaming and yelling at him from the armchair. He stood up, went to Dasha, and slapped her hard across the face, making her numb. He dragged her quickly to the balcony getting her out and pressing her onto the railing. Viktor turned his head and didn't quite get what was happening. Before he could do anything, Lucio, with incredible strength, took Dasha in a wrestler's move and hurdled her over the balcony, throwing her from the 9th floor onto the construction site foundations. She was screaming in mid-air, her face in agonizing cramps, and when then fell, after a short flight, on the concrete, breaking her body and head. A pool of blood instantly formed underneath her. Viktor came to the balcony running, but it was too late. He wanted to throw Lucio down but didn't want to end up in jail. Dasha was not worth it. He just looked at Lucio, who was gone beyond normal. He was looking at her, crushed on the concrete, and uttered:

"I didn't know they put a concrete foundation there. I thought it was still grass, rocks, and rats. Hmm…strange, seems after so many years, things are beginning to happen here…at the construction site". Dasha was another 'jumper' from our skyscraper. She was a flyer without a desire to die this time, but circumstances changed that. Viktor dialed 911, and the Ambulance and Police came. Lucio was taken in handcuffed, and they took Viktor and Yevgenij to the station. Dasha died in the hospital of internal wounds. In all that, Yevgenij stayed silent. He never uttered a word.

Coda

Yevgenij Makarov/Tassone committed suicide in a small hotel on the outskirts of Naples while attending a summer music festival. He took an overdose of sleeping pills called Zomniac and was found the following day by housekeeping. Yevgenij could never get over the fact that he slept with his father, and soon after, Lucio ended up in jail, killing Dasha, and they released him from custody. Being gay was no crime, and Viktor gave the whole story. Yevgenij stayed silent and in some catatonic state. He packed his bags and left home for good in the middle of the night, not saying goodbye to anyone. He left a small note in the Naples hotel room "WHAT TO DO AFTER I AM NO MORE" (tiny wishes & requests). He didn't want any funeral, just cremation. "The Thorn Path" single "Security of Delusions" reached the Top 10 rock charts when the media got hold of the vocalist's tragic death. The album flopped, and the group dissolved soon after, never to reform again. Yevgenij was cremated, his ashes were given to Lana by his request, and a small letter should be opened on the 10th anniversary of his death. Many people showed up at the funeral, some from our skyscraper though no one knew him that well. They were there just for the kicks of it.

Lana could never get over Yevgenij and his premature death. She collapsed at the funeral a couple of times. She didn't blame him for what happened, for being gay, and for not knowing that Lucio was his father. It all broke him to such an extent that he killed himself. She would never be bitter about it and would have no reason to forgive him as there was none. Soon afterward, she left the city, took Yevgenij's ashes with her, and married a well-off Swiss conductor, a 30 older man, a sort of father figure that reminded her of a father she never knew, Bran Herznagel and displaced her from the young Yevgenij Makarov or Tassone she loved and could never have. She moved to Basel, Switzerland, never returning home except for one day a year. She also got her sister Dana to move and get a job in the nearby hospital. She had minimal contact with her father (her stepfather, actually). When he retired from medicine, he moved to Sicily and married a young Italian model. Lana gave birth to a baby girl and tried to find comfort in that. She was though constantly on anti-depressants. Later she got a son whom she named Yevgenij. He became her life now. She opened Yevgenij's letter and kept his 10-year wish. She read the finest love verses to imagine what was written on four pages. Even though he was gay, he loved Lana more than life; she was his only friend. Her heart broke once again and for the last time. She died of a heart attack at the precious age of 38.

Diksha Pathak took the news about Lucio in a frigid way. She started to wine hysterically, but it was more from her misery than some feelings towards Lucio. Later she got angrier and started to regret that she ever said anything. She remained where she was, in the skyscraper of her life, continuing to lament over her misfortunate destiny she had and drinking endless coffees and playing cards with Norissa Guzinski and other gossip hags. She never visited Lucio in jail and stayed married but separated for life. Her life was the most significant loss, but she never realized that. Thanks to her and Norissa Guzinski, the vicious circle of gossip, lies, innuendo, and finally, truths came together in a tragic finale ruining the lives of many and destroying the destiny of some. Mediocre people cannot tolerate the success of one of their own, in this case, of those living close by, even if they were superior in talent, work, and education or had better DNA. But Norissa, Diksha, and others like them could tolerate those rich & famous that did not belong here, were out of reach, and in some supermarket tabloids, oceans and continents away. Mathew Panduro finally stopped seeing Diksha and confronted her with what she had started, as she confided in him. He was able to get away. She soon slipped into heavy drinking, becoming a hard-core alcoholic in three years. It would take some more years for liver cirrhosis to work its way into her system and, ultimately, take her away from this world. She never felt bad for being an 'active' part in Lucio and Yevgenij's tragedy. She never regrets spreading the word about Lucio and Yevgenij, hoping it would damage Lana's relationship with Yevgenij so her son, idiot Andrew, might have a chance. She didn't know the consequences of that. Her son Andrew Somun (from her first marriage) also abandoned her after a few years, never spending quality time with Diksha and seeing her on the rarest occasions. He didn't care much that Lucio was not his father nor that he never found out who his birth father was, though he knew his name – Robert Somun. The boy did not care and had no clue what to do with his life. After two years, he joined the military and ended up on a UN mission in Angola, where he got killed in a tribal massacre of an opposing village. They never found his body.

Bran Herznagel continued smoking three packs or 60 cigarettes daily and playing piano wherever possible. Arthritis was slowly getting at him, so piano became difficult but not impossible. Music was his life; he would rather die at the keys than stop playing. Tragically enough, Bran never discovered that he was a father and that the fantastic woman named Lana Chester was his daughter. He died in a retirement home of lung cancer forgotten by many, remembered by very few. Nobody ever visited his grave except for Lana Chester and Mathew Panduro. They never missed the anniversary of his death. They would bring a portable piano, a trumpet, and jam for a half hour for Bran on the grave. Thanks to Bran, Mathew got a scholarship and finished his musical studies, which brought him to folk music. He could never forget that and always thought Bran was a good man with a good heart. Thanks to him, Lana got her first piano lessons and the warmth of this man for many years, the warmth that felt so close, real, and natural.

Bran Herznagel's wife Mathilda woke up one morning and was completely cured of neurosis and anxiety disorders she was suffering from. The whole murder thing and everything that followed the horrific death of Dasha Makarov woke her up from a depressive sleep she was in. She filed for divorce from Bran as she could never stand him or their marriage. She just felt great hatred and hoped he died. She also hoped Lana would die with him or after Yevgenij's suicide. She didn't have it to poison Ben or get rid of him in some other way. She left the skyscraper and the city and was never heard from again. She knew about his daughter but never said a word and kept it secret to her grave out of hatred for Bran and pathological jealousy of a much younger and more beautiful Lana. Nobody knew what became of her. Some say she opened a brothel in Romania, importing young girls from Eastern Europe after the wall fell; others say that she started a vineyard in New Zealand, and some others that she became a lesbian and secretly had a relationship with a nun in a convent somewhere in Bordeaux region, France. Most people would opt for the brothel scenario, which seemed most likely for her.

Lucio Tassone exited prison after serving seven out of 14 years, released on good behavior. He was charged with Homicide without malice aforethought or manslaughter. Murder in the first degree was stripped away as the testimony of a shrink that proclaimed him temporarily insane at the time of the crime. He stopped singing altogether, and his career and stature were ruined anyway. Staying around would be suicide and moral torture until the end of the days. He moved to Honduras and started working for an NGO to eradicate poverty in a local community. Usually, in such life tragedies and breakpoints, people find either death or God or rarely something in between. Well, for some, it is jail or some other institution.

In most cases, they walk the earth like zombies until actual death succumbs. Lucio Tassone became very different, finding God, Charity, and Penance in prison. He tried to kill himself once while inside but failed miserably, and thanks to a former priest that was doing time for some embezzlement, he regained strength in the spiritual. He never looked back, never talked about Opera, Music, Arts, Men, Women, Murder, etc., and turned to other things in life, more earthly, such as food, literacy, sewage, and water. Unfortunately, his consciousness ate slowly but surely at him. Sorrow for sin arising from fear of damnation – attrition, as he called it. That was the word he constantly used. He could never get over Yevgenij's death, role, and the horrific incest. He could never get over the murder of a woman who was a mother to their only child. Seven years of prison would never change anything for him. Naturally, he was already damned and waiting for a proper way to go out, as he did not believe in suicide. He died of cancer four years into charity work in the Americas.

Destiny chose to play its game with us, and it played a tough and ruthless one with these five individuals that lived physically and emotionally close to each other. Regardless of the unhappy and, in any respect, unbelievable epilogue, we all liked to think that they may have finally found some minor cadence of peace and tranquility that we all seek, and few of us ever find…in life or death…

Allegro, Andante, Adagio…Finale

30

Gabriel's Animal-Veggie Farm and Doomsday Inferno

And The Doomsday Inferno

Gabriel's Dream

[PART I]

It was not until 21:05 that evening that Gabriel Nash awoke from his deep, mystic, heavy, troublesome, and comatose-like sleep. It lasted almost 15 hours. He surely would not have woken so soon if he hadn't been disturbed by a distant voice in the beginning but a much more straightforward one now. He felt tired as if his long 15 hours of sleep were insufficient for an 80-year-old man with failing health. It was too much, and he knew it, but this was the first time he felt fully rested in years. The never-ending vaticination dream of Noah, the flood, and the animals finally ended, just moments before he woke up. It was almost hard to believe it was a dream, the details and characters were so vivid, and the message…the message was so accurate and timely. He woke up in a pool of water, i.e., the sheets were soaked, not with sweat but with water. Gabriel could not believe this. It was wet, and it also had the smell of rainwater. The voice was back again. He had the impression it was not human nor divine, either. He was wide awake now and not dreaming or sleeping. It was like…a voice …that sounded like a domestic animal. He finally lifted himself from the bed, sat on it, and turned on an old but still beautiful and gracious Art Deco lamp he and his late wife Frambruka bought at a Paris fair some 60 years ago. The lamp brought light to the stuffy room. Closed Venetian blinds prevented the light, now evening ones, from entering the room. He was glad he persuaded his son some years back to replace the dreadful German cloth shutters with these Italian beauties. He adjusted his eyes to the scene and looked before the bed. That's when he saw Hans, the duck.

Hans was your ordinary duck, a tiny, sturdy little bastard, neither wild nor domesticated fully, a web-orange-footed broad-billed swimming bird. He had a depressed body, short legs, and a kind, determined pair of eyes. What made him different from others in his animal race was that he had human elements. He liked to listen when there was talk; he followed Andy, Gabriel's grandson, everywhere, spending a lot of time with Gabriel himself. They brought him from their 'farm' (Nash's private weekend refuge place where domestic animals and fruit & vegetables were blooming) to see the veterinarian as he wasn't feeling all that well the last week, mostly sleeping and not eating at all. He also made the duck sound like he wanted to say something or make an important point. This time around, Hans was talking, or at least Gabriel thought so.

"Gabriel, you old fart, build the boat and bring us on it, as many pairs as you can. Seven pairs—14 of us! Don't forget the food, vegetables, and fruit! Your grandson brought them from the Farm and has them in the apartment; keep them here until the boat is done. Your grandson is good; he will be the Shepard and take care of them until the fire and rains come."

Hans continued.

"Build the boat, as floods and doomsday are near...I can smell the fire and smoke...just built the arc and made a difference Gabriel! "Build the boat before Halloween, do it, Gabriel, before Halloween, as then doomsday will arrive, and this tower of Babel we are in will perish in fire & water. Save thyself and our animals, Gabriel...it is your destiny; it is your task. Fulfill your dream Gabriel; fulfill it as Noah did. You are a righteous man, blameless among the people of your place and time, a pious man who believes; Save yourself and the animals, as these highrise sinners will be hit by fire and water by the wrath of the Almighty. Blasphemy will be washed away in rivers and floods...".

Gabriel watched Hans with a mesmerizing gaze. He wasn't sure why a duck was talking to him and telling him to build a boat, but he was sure this was no coincidence and that God had sent him the final message through Hans. This was the 5th sign he received and the one that sealed it all. It started with his late wife, Frambruka, who died five years ago (at the age of 85). On her death bed, she told Gabriel to take care of the farm, and its inhabitants, ones above the ground (animals) and underneath (she was talking of vegetables and fruit), as when the floods arrive, they will be washed away. She was lucid when she said this, and a spirit came to her in her sleep and told her this. She said the creature was like a tiny dark gray winged monster, but not dangerous, built in the shape of a dwarf with wings. She thought an angel spoke to her using her grandmother's voice. The second sign came in the form of a wooden boat called Genesis that was given to his son, Andy's father, Michael, as a gift from an old friend that died. The third sign came in the form of a Raven, a blackbird that landed every morning on their window sill, screamed like wild for a few minutes, and then left. The fourth sign was the sermon by a local priest in the little town outside the city, some 2 miles from the farm. He talked about doomsday, evil, fire, rain, and saving our souls and animals. It seemed the guy was nuts and was soon after committed to the crazy house, but he made complete sense to Gabriel. And the fifth sign was Hans, the voice of reason that spoke through the duck.

Gabriel, as well as all the Nashes, was very religious. He was a Christian but also an ecumenist, believing that all religions and we share one and only God in the inhabited world of humans and that the rest could be fixed easily. He always tried to promote unity amongst religions and believers, knowing the holy texts in detail. After his wife died and the signs kept coming, he knew that something horrible would happen, and he had to listen & save the souls of those bestowed upon him.

"So the dream was a prophecy, and the duck was the messenger!" Gabriel thought to himself while trying to regain his senses, strength, and control of the environment. Some hurried steps and the sound of the door leading into the front room being carefully opened took away his attention from Hans. Andy Nash, his grandson, walked into the room.

"Are you awake, Grandpa? I got worried; you slept as a log for almost 15 hours. Are you ok? What's Hans doing here?" Well, I could say that for all the 14 animals we have here."

"14 animals!" replied Gabriel. We have 14 animals – 7 pairs. Is that what you are saying, son?"

"Yes, I guess so, two pigs, two ducks, two hamsters, two dogs, two cats, two geese, and chickens. That's what we have in the apartment right now, but they won't stay long; why do you ask?"

"NO, we must keep them here; you cannot give them away, Andy!!!

"Because we are going to build a boat, my son, as in 14 days, the end of days will come, and we need our animals with us"!

Andy was sure his grandfather had finally, ultimately, and utterly lost his mind.

The (Ru-Uurban) Farm

Nothing surprised me in that apartment. Andy and his brother Bartholomew lived there with their parents, Jonathan and Emilia, and their Grandfather, Gabriel. After Gabriel's wife died five years ago, he moved, somewhat reluctantly, from the farm to the city apartment. The farm was their house, and they landed outside the city proper on a hilly, green top near a beautiful river overlooking a massive valley. They had excellent agricultural and domestic use life with organic farming and animals. Their grandchildren came with their parents every weekend. Gabriel and Frambruka were bottomless in their retirement, Gabriel after working 45 years on the railroad, and Frambruka after 35 years in the mill. After that, they just dedicated themselves to the farm altogether. Andy would sometimes bring some animals and their offspring and give

them to people he knew or persons that might want some small domesticated living creatures in their homes. Grandpa and Grandma
supported this effort and encouraged it strongly. Though Andy's
parents were not all that fond of the idea, they agreed. People in the
skyscraper will now definitely think they were full-blown farmers
and peasants.

After I visited the "Farm," what I saw there quickly prepared me
for the fact that the skyscraper apartment was filled with massive
amounts of vegetables and fruit in XXXL sizes, and seven pairs of
weird domestic animals were freely roaming around; oh yes, plus
the fact that Andy's grandpa was a weird bird that was talking to
the animals and himself most of the time, usually about the big
flood and the end of days that would come through a burning inferno. Nothing made sense. I went to Andy to pick up a little kitten, knowing he always had pairs of animals at hand. After that,
he insisted I follow him to the Farm one weekend. I remember
going to the Farm on one of the most unforgettable weekends. On
one of those lazy weekends in August, I rode with Andy and his
older brother Bartholomew, two very nice guys from a decent brutal, working, religious family. Their parents were among the finest
folks I knew in our skyscraper. I took a ride with Andy and his dad
and was forced to stay for lunch which could have satisfied a small
brigade of soldiers. Andy would pick up a pair of pigs, geese, and a
dog for some new hosts. His dad was going for the weekly vegetable and fruit intake. That saved them a lot on the economy as the
Farm produced better than ever, and Gabriel and Frambruka always
wanted their son to have the best products first. There was never a
discussion on that. A lot was also sold on the local farmers market
as organic food, but I always wondered who bought these giant
products. It must have been the price, which was low for the size of

these products. But of course, the fantastic place was the FARM. I gasped and closed and opened my eyes a few times. What came to mind was Charlie Brown's big Pumpkin Halloween thing. The difference here was that the pumpkins were not the only giants. The house was a typical Henzel and Grettel thing from Andersen's fairytales, meticulously kept in excellent shape. The other buildings were the hen house, a miniature cow house, something that looked like a combined dog and cat kennel, bee hives that were double the size of normal ones, and, of course, the planting grounds for vegetables and fruit plus some huge storage cabin and a small water tank with a friendly, fully functioning irrigation system. All of this was on a few acres of land, but nothing I witnessed in the vegetable and fruit garden. Andy was willing to give me a tour, and feeling like a Lilliputian was the understatement of the day!

I have never seen this before, neither have I read it in any book, nor has my imagination soared to such heights of unbelievable (sur) reality. There were Soooooooooo many vegetables and fruit in one space and neatly arranged in unique places. A gold mine of carrots, potatoes, corn, beans, zucchini, and God knows what else. Everything would be fine if not for the size. Was it the organic shit? Is it some mutation caused by extra fertile soil? Were they all crapping vast quantities of human manure here, or did all the animals contribute? Were the things being supplied from some deep underground source, or were the Nashes just doing bizarre food experiments here? None was a food expert, chemist, biologist, geologist, or anything else near vegetable and fruit science production. Something deeply wrong was happening with this ecosystem. I didn't know what, nor did I dare to ask. Andy's face was telling me all.

"I know what you are thinking, man; I have no f**king clue. Everything here has 'gone out of proportion, mutated, and seems out of this world. Grandpa has been working with this over the years. Grandma took care of animals", explained puzzled Andy, who has undoubtedly seen this a hundred times before.

I didn't even want to meet the animals. God knows what mutations happened there.

Andy continued.

"I harvested a few of the zucchinis and tomato lots, and they just came out big. Our tomatoes are ca five times bigger than normal ones, and see that in the corner some 3 meters away?"

I saw something that was massive and had a reddish-orange color.

"Oh, you mean the pumpkins, Andy?" That was a stupid and wrong exclamation.

"They are not pumpkins but our new breed of tomato man!"

Tomato, my ass…later, I almost fainted when I came close to it. I thought: what the f**k!!! It was tomato just ten times bigger than it should be, or was it 20?

"Hey, let's carry some of these vegetables into the house. We will need some for lunch and dinner later".

Andy was already in the field. And we did carry them. I was comfortably numb thinking about Lewis Carroll's novel Through the Looking-Glass and What Alice Found There. Was this happening? Where the f**k were we? Of course, there were no plausible answers; there never were when anything associated with our skyscraper came into question. When we carried them into the house, the zucchini and corn were out of control, looking like small rockets. At that moment, Gabriel came in.

"Great, they are as usual, but early this year because of the pig and cow manure. This is the wine of Bordeaux, the Nectar of the Gods, and the Grappa of Italy for our gardens! I am so glad our animals volunteered to add their extract contributions…we also crap there, or at least I tell everyone to do it…but the real magic is in the soil. Something magical, ecclesiastical, and epistemological in there… just amazing; of course, Frambruka and I did most of the work. We have harvested about thousands of these small guys through the years". Gabriel was looking proudly at his Zucchini, which was three times bigger than usual. The weird thing is that most vegetables had blossoms and some weird leaves still attached. I dared not to ask what these alien additions were. After hearing that this shitting ground has been used by human and animal kingdoms alike, I did not want to know.

"Hmmm, continued Gabriel, seems tomato has not been as strong as last year"! He was looking at the big thing I had in my arms. I just wondered how it looked last year.

Gabriel's wife, Frambruka, was also a religious woman but more of a strange world vegetable zealot. She must have been a horrifyingly ugly woman in her young days. A taller scarecrow woman, with metallic green eyes and long black—now it was white) hair that must have waited for 4.5 kilos at least tied up in sailors knots and was falling down her back; a face that, aside from all the horror that each piece produced (you couldn't decide what was worse, the ears, nose, chin or forehead) was radiating serenity and goodness, and that made her such an excellent site to see. The clothes made her look like a fortune teller woman from Azerbaijan, a modern scarecrow, or your worst nightmare; actually, the clothes were a horrible collection of patchwork and Red Cross leftovers with some weird materials sewn in. My grandma, God rest her soul, if she were alive today, would say: "She would f**k every Gypsy man's mother if she could in those clothes and with those looks"! Whatever that meant, it was right in place. To crown it all, she wore an old pair of stitched pieces of underwear as a hat; I heard from Andy that she was a carbon copy of her mother.

Frambruka's mom, Andy's grand-grandmother, died on this Farm and was buried near the bee hives. She and her husband were the first to start working here, and they dedicated their whole life to it. Frambruka's two sisters, Ingeborg and Spinacia, also helped out when they could, but they had their farm just 1 mile from this one. There they had a small double house, an east and west mirror of itself, also very much in the style of Gabriel's and Frambruka's. Ingeborg and Spinacia had no family, and their whole life was devoted to charity and farming. But one of them got married to a guy helping out in the fields…they were both in their 50s when that happened.

There was a rumor that he was a werewolf, as he only slept and drank during the day, worked in the fields at night, and did other nocturnal activities. Mind you, that was just a rumor. Otherwise, they produced wine aside from vegetable and fruit cultivation. I got that answer during lunch in the form of domestic wine. I had a weird feeling that the grapes were shaped differently than what one usually thinks. They also had a lot of carrots, and these orange things were the size of my arm – I kid you not! When I saw them being served during lunch, I could not believe my eyes. They called them fatty carrots. So, all of these people were into agricultural or organic farming, and the results of that activity, as you can see, were way out of this world.

As far as the animals went, all seemed normal though I have not seen the chickens and other furry things; most looked ok, except for the bees. According to Andy, the bees were double and some triple the size of normal ones…I would have probably thought that he was a liar until I saw some of them on the flowers and dared not to approach…the ones I saw were double the size of normal ones, and no wonder the bee houses were twice as big…they were on the fringe of the Farm…I was glad the tour did not include these flying monsters…Frambruka promised me a jar of the excellent nectar bee. She boasted that hers was much better than her sisters Spinacia's due to the bee size. I could not wait to try this, honey.

They have something special here. Before we had lunch, I found out how the owners of the Farm met. The way they met, Gabriel and Frambruka, I mean, was also something else, bizarre as this whole establishment was. Frambruka liked to tell this story while Gabriel would say: "The odds are good, but the goods are old." referring to the fact that Frambruka was ten years older than him. He just wanted to tease her as this woman was the only one in his life and the love of his life.

"Do you know how I met Frambruka, my wife?" Gabriel turned to me while I was looking nervously at arriving food and the size it had.

"No, I have no clue, Sir. I was curious. How did you?"

"Well, it's a long story, but I will give you the shortcut version." I knew this version would be at least a 1 hour long for sure, but there was little to do now after the humongous lunch;

Gabriel was a good storyteller, and the whole tale had a very romantic sound and feel, but the bottom line was that these things could not happen to ordinary folks. A sense of fear overtook him when he was getting into his late 30s – he was to remain a bachelor his whole life. It was horrible as the call of children and building a home was really what started pushing. Being a religious young man as he was and staying behind those that chased skirts and slept with just about anybody, Gabriel waited for the girl of his life. The years went on, and she didn't show up, nor was there anything on the horizon. He went to the Church and asked for help in finding a good, Christian woman with all shared beliefs as himself and someone that could bear him kids and would be satisfied with building a life, working on the Farm that they would inherit from his parents (he is the only son and that). The church was ready to jump in, and they found a lovely 28-year-old girl with the same values as Gabriel. The only thing missing was the picture, but the priest told him she was a sweet girl and there should be no worries. All was arranged for Saturday in the park near the Cathedral. She would sit on the bench reading the daily newspaper, and spotting her won't be difficult. Gabriel liked this shortcut to life, as, he thought, one never knew, this could be it, and this could be the one. Destiny can play games. Here it certainly did.

When Gabriel arrived that morning at the square, he saw two opposite sides and on each bench a woman. One was reading some books, and the other had newspapers in her hand. He went to that one and got slightly startled when he saw a rather uninviting and ugly woman. She indeed had more than 28 years, more like 40. It was hard to tell as she was so unspeakably unattractive. But something drew him to her, and after a while, he started a conversation speaking about life, love, his goals, the Farm he was to inherit, religion, food, just about it, and how he would like a partner for life and wondered if she would like to become his wife. In all that, he omitted to ask if she was the woman he was supposed to meet, one sent from the Church. She didn't say much, just nodded and said that she shared all his values and was looking for such a man her whole life and would love to become his wife. What made her do that and why she said it remains a mystery to this day, even to Gabriel. She thought God sent her this handsome young guy and made her dreams come true, but also, as her mother used to say, "put a bag over his head," so he could not see how ugly she was. Yes, Frambruka was aware of her physical situation but she had to believe that she possessed some other qualities. This young fellow thought so and was not blind; he could see. Later Gabriel's mother said, when she saw his bride, that "if he was digging in the worst dumpsters and trashcans of this world, he could never have found such a woman…." In any case, the two married, and the rest is history.

The girl he was supposed to meet was on the opposite side of Cathedral Square; a beautiful slender girl who looked like an angel with her classical face and Ashburn color long hair. She was sitting on the bench, but instead of reading the daily newspapers, she had a Bible in her hand. She forgot what the priest said. That morning nobody approached her except a drunken bum that left immediately, but she saw a young, handsome, tall man coming to some woman sitting on a bench on the other side of the square, and they started talking soon after. The person who was supposed to meet her never showed up, so she left in rather somber, foul mood after waiting 45 minutes. It was not meant to be. Gabriel later learned from the priest that the woman he met and offered a hand in marriage was not the one the church selected for him. Gabriel didn't care much as he thought destiny had brought him to Frambruka, to a kin soul…she was not much to look at, but that might change in some years. It didn't. She got even uglier, but their love grew even more robust, which produced two children, and the passion for the Farm blossomed, creating the animals and the vegetables I witnessed today. Gabriel rambled a bit more, but I wasn't listening. My attention turned to food. The lunch consisted of spinach soup, two grilled Roosters with zucchini, carrots, baked potatoes, and forest strawberry cake. The vegetables dominated the table-to-food space ratio, while the strawberries protruding from the cake were nothing like the small forest ones. These were the size of plums but tasted very well. The roosters were awesome. This vine, though, looked (or tasted) weird, very weird.

Thicker, much thicker than usual, one felt this was a sophisticated vampire blood drink. There were some small pieces of flesh coming off the vine. Not normal. I followed it to its trailing end, my throat, but the feeling when it went down the stomach was not that bad… God knows how Ingeborg and Spinacia did this thing. Did that werewolf husband of hers have anything to do with it? My heart stopped. Maybe this was made out of animal blood and remained, even worse, human. The vine thickened even more after a while, but it must have been the high % of alcohol that prevented me from asking any relevant questions about the nature of the taste and content. I just sipped it and enjoyed the moment. Gabriel's deep and enchanting voice and a hot pot of French solid taste coffee was the thing that would keep me awake. Besides, after seeing the Farm and its flora & fauna, nothing was weird anymore. Frambruka went to tend to her bees while Andy and his dad fixed the big chicken house. I was left alone with Gabriel, who first farted loudly and fell asleep after the hearty lunch. I dozed off soon after thinking of giant bees, mammoth watermelons, and mutated carrots. Frambruka waked me up.

"I want you to have this before you leave." She was holding a 5kg jar of honey with gold color.

"Nobody does it better than me, though my sister would have you believe otherwise. She chuckled like a scarecrow and showed the massive jar into my arms. When she turned around, I saw a small rat peeking under her underwear hat. He must have felt very comfortable up there. I did not blame him, not at all.

"You will love this, I am sure of it!" she said while returning to her bees.

Returning to the city and civilization, I thought of this establishment and its residents. I was holding my 5kg honey jar and wondering how long it took those monster bees to produce this and how long it would take me to consume it. When we were leaving the driveway, two ducks came out to, I guess, say goodbye to us. They were looking intensely at all of us, and the one called Hans (Andy told me that all animals had names) looked like he was opening his mouth. After lunch, I must have had hallucinations, and that thick wine was still in my head, but I was sure the duck was speaking, though the car windows were down. Good grief, this visit was something else!

After Frambruka's death (the cancer she carried for six years finally ate her away), Gabriel slowly stopped caring for the farm. Still, the younger forces took over, especially knowing how important this was for Gabriel and the memory of their mother. Andy was much more dedicated than his brother, and he found some weird passion in the animal kingdom, i.e., creating a donation farm for whoever wanted to become a host for these animals. Well, they did get rid of the cows as that didn't fit the bill, but the rest was ok. Later, when Gabriel moved into the city, the Farm looked after Frambruka's sisters and Andy's dad, Jonathan (who grew up on the farm with his sister Silvia who left for the US after her studies). He contemplated moving to the Farm as it was only 40min with the car from the city, which was not much commuting for work. He was spending so much time there any way that it wouldn't matter much. He decided on that firmly after the inferno night in our skyscraper and the events that unfolded.

The Ark

[PART II]

"I want to build the boat and you all to be there, together with all the animals – 7 pairs – 14 in total, and most of the vegetables and fruit we have…

After 40 days, the boat was made, not by Gabriel but by

Jonathan was sure by now that his father had lost his mind entirely but wanted to see where this might go.

We will build the boat on my farm, transport it here, and park it on a trailer outside the highrise!

"Dad, are you nuts?!?"

"No, I am perfectly sane, my son, and this is what your mother, God rest her soul, would have wanted!"

He was surprisingly lucid.

"I had five signs that the floods and fires are coming, so don't tell me I am nuts."

"You can't believe those signs, Dad." Jonathan was shaking his head.

"Why wouldn't I? I believed all the things that happened at the Farm as normal, giant bees, talking ducks, singing geese, mutated vegetables, voices in my head,"

"It has to be done, my son; trust me, it has to be done." Gabriel was firm as the 300-year-old Oak tree in the middle of the Farm ground.

Last few years, Gabriel started to change and was getting weirder and becoming a person that started living in another world, or at least preparing for one. When he became 80, everything abruptly changed, changed for the worse. He started claiming that the fifth sign from Hans the Duck was that the end of days is near and that a boat must be built. He was extremely persistent with the idea that the best of the Farm had to be assembled in the boat, ready to move beyond the fires & floods that would destroy us, destroy the very highrise we were living in. Of course, no one believed him in the family, but Jonathan could never say no to his father, even when the craziest ideas came to life. He was one of those Good Samaritan children who would subdue or even sacrifice the past, present, and future of their lives for one's parents. In this case, he was going to avoid this subject and try to persuade Gabriel if it was not for two reasons: firstly, his father's health was fragile, and pancreatic cancer he was diagnosed with gave him max a year or so if not even less; and secondly, Jonathan always fulfilled wishes of his parents no matter what. Even this time, however crazy it sounded, he would do it. But a third reason did not fit any bill but somehow made sense in this inverted reality. It was a letter he had received two days ago.

Dad, I think I might have something for you", exclaimed Jonathan with resignation in his voice.

"What is that?" asked curios Gabriel

"You remember Henry, don't you?

"Of course I do; I might have Cancer, but I don't have Alzheimer's yet."

"Well, Henry left you his sailing boat."

Gabriel looked with startled eyes at his son and wasn't sure who was the crazy one at the table. After a while, there was a spark in his eyes, and his face got a glow that Jonathan never saw before.

"Another sign, I knew it! The boat of salvation has arrived", exclaimed Gabriel triumphantly while Jonathan was utterly lost in translation.

Henry Perone was Gabriel's best friend. He was a priest that gave up his hood to have sex with one of the nuns from the nearby convent. The nun could not live with her shame and killed herself after the affair was made public. Henry was forced to leave the church for good at 60. Thanks to the inheritance he got from his deceased parents, he bought a Classic 55' Wooden Sailboat, S&S Hull Design. He decided to spend the rest of his life sailing in the Mediterranean and doing nothing except heavy drinking, eating, and occasional sex. He knew that life was not going to be the same ever again. The problem was that guilt got to him, not so much for leaving the church and doing what he had done, but for indirectly taking the nun's life. He sailed for several years, somehow eluding the destruction of his liver, but soon the heavy drinking caught up with him in another way, and one day, he slipped on the deck outside a deserted island, wholly drunk, and broke his neck. He was 80. All of this would not make for such significant information if it were not for the fact that Henry Perone was the priest that helped Gabriel find a wife. He was the same age as Gabriel. After seeing another woman on the bench, they became close friends and played chess often. After the incident, they stayed in touch, but sporadically, primarily due to Henry's weird living habits and regular sailing for the next two decades. Gabriel and Frambruka also felt angry at Henry for being an accomplice and causing the nun's death.

Gabriel never abandoned his excellent friend, but sailing winds took his destiny elsewhere. In any case, when Henry died and Jonathan broke the news to his dad, the fact was that there was a boat to handle. He left him nothing most minor of a monster sailing boat, a 1959 Ocean/Sea Cruiser—Liveaboard Ketch. The thing was delivered to a storage yard in the city on a big trailer left with the boat. One needed to rent a truck to move this thing. Jonathan could not believe his eyes when he got the letter, and the ship was delivered a week later. Storage place was paid for six months by Henry, just in case Gabriel needed time to think about what to do with the boat. He knew that Gabriel was fond of his Farm and staying put, but maybe this boat would do him good.

The man was dead, his friend passed away, and he never told him it was ok, as God would be the only judge and jury. When Jonathan told Gabriel, he was sad about the news, and what was even worse, he never had the chance to tell Henry that he forgave him for what he had done. Now in the aftermath of things, he should have done it sooner. He opened up the letter Jonathan had given him. It was from Henry, addressed to Gabriel, and sealed on the back. Gabriel opened it and read aloud to himself:

Dear Friend, if I can still call you that after all these years and all that has happened. A day has not passed since the horrible thing I did that I did not feel like a Flying Dutchman with no home, no harbor, or wish for life, but still, I live, until now. I thought that Escape was the solution and that my Boat Genesis would be my salvation. The only thing I realized is that I can not outrun life, I cannot hide from myself, and I cannot live with myself…guilt, shame, and pain have eaten my body much faster than alcohol, and somehow I feel now that my days will be over, call it a premonition or just a hunch…All in all, I try to remember people I care for and people that meant something, and I meant something to them; I can't think of many, not even a few…I left all I had for charity to the same monastery I brought so much shame…maybe that will bring them some comfort…the rest is in this boat…you are in my will, my dear friend, and the ship is yours…you do with it what you see fit…I know the decision will be the right one…I just felt that this has to go to you and your wife (I hope she is well)…call it another revelation or hunch…

I lived with nothing but pain, and the pleasure I found in the bottle and women made the pain even worse… Once again, forgive me for I have sinned, and I know God will judge me for what I have done, and maybe someday, my soul will be released from these torments… I hope I lost many years ago…but I might have a shoot at that yet…

Stay well, Gabriel…your friend to the end---Henry…

Sad man he was, sad man indeed, thought Gabriel. He felt the end and that some penance would bring him peace, but giving the boat to me? Why? This must have been another sign after all the five signs, the final sign that has arrived. God sent him a boat through Henry, a sinner who admitted to what he had done and was searching for salvation. Gabriel didn't need the 14 days anymore. The ship was here. Praise is the Lord, thought Gabriel. If only Frambruka were here to witness this. She never liked Henry, but this deed she would acknowledge. There was no turning back when the information on the boat broke out in the family. They all knew that this thing, a Classic 55' Wooden Sailboat, S&S Hull Design, was worth over 100.000 dollars. The money would do great wonders for the family and the Farm. But Jonathan wanted to do this for Gabriel and thought that one day he could fulfill the wish of the old bugger. He knew there would be no floods or fires and that Gabriel might get out from whatever he was going through; maybe the realization might help him through the last difficult weeks and perhaps months of battle with cancer. Besides, the only thing was renting a big Scania truck to hurdle this to our parking lot. There he would have to occupy ten places at least and get heat from the residents, but for one night, it might work. The problem would be the funny animals, but they could all be locked inside. The boat would be on a giant trailer with Gabriel inside, seven pairs of animals from the apartment, and various giant vegetables from the Farm. Jonathan's family would also be inside on the night of the 14th day. Jonathan was sure everyone would know that the whole family was certified crazy. His wife could not believe what was happening; Bartholomew, Andy's older brother, wanted nothing to do with this, while Andy thought that this was the best thing that had happened in years and that his Granddad was one crazy f**king son of a bitch, and a great one for that matter!

Doomsday Inferno

The form and identity of a town, city, or metropolis must remember the past, i.e., integrate history, context, culture, habit, memories and customs, unique ecologies, and all that is happening in the region. Brutally breaking with the past was never good. Pablo Sotomayor was thinking of that when looking at the cluster of some 100 skyscrapers in the distant, new suburb of the city. For him, it was a horrible but also troublesome site professionally. He was spending another dreadful and dull day at the local fire station when the call came in about the burning skyscraper. Nothing major happened for a week, which was good, but on the other hand, there were 16 false alarms and three small interventions that pissed him off. He loved the job and was hoping for improvements. Trucks were getting better. They just got a dozen new ones from Germany, and his station got a pair. One great Iveco and another Mercedes beauty with a turntable ladder, the first in the district. But that was half of the problem. There were others, and when the call came in that a skyscraper was on fire, Pablo could not stop thinking of helicopters and the damn towers that were destroying the city's image and silhouette day by day. Not to mention the poor souls in these bunny cages or bee hives. He was fortunate to live in a three-story apartment garden house. But the damn skyscrapers were a nightmare for people but a heaven for a potential fire. The firefighters' union, and especially his father and uncle that worked for 25 years fighting all kinds of blazes and flames one could imagine, have been calling for the City's Fire Department to get a helicopter to help put out towers, skyscrapers and all tall buildings, especially apartment skyscraper fires and help evacuate people trapped in them. They always got a no for various reasons, money, complicated affairs, operational concerns, etc. The Firefighters Association also joined the unions in condemning this behavior and saying that it is a disgrace that our city, with almost half a million inhabitants, does not have a helicopter to put water on a fire.

Most importantly, it could be used for evacuation, command, and control in many situations. Other cities have them, why not us? The answer was always that it is unsafe to use helicopters for highrise/skyscraper fires due to the complexity of things. Nobody knew what that meant. They know how much the new Canadian planes for forest fires were helping their brothers in arms on the sea coast. He also thought that even all highrises should get sprinklers, something unheard of. Alas, nothing was going to change.

As you know, a fire sprinkler system is an active fire protection measure consisting of a water supply system, providing adequate pressure and flow rate to a water distribution piping system, onto which fire sprinklers are connected. This is portrayed in textbooks, but that's how it works. Although historically only used in factories and large commercial buildings, home, and small building systems are now available at a cost-effective price. This was the case in the US and some other rich countries, but not here. But some new office buildings began to install this. He was more worried about housing estates. Those damn towers were a nightmare, but at least they had fire hoses on each floor; at least some of them. Suddenly he heard an explosion of some kind…it was massive and loud.

A few minutes passed, and a siren exploded in the station…chief yelled out:

"One of the towers is burning…one of those four yellow mother-f**kers in that…what was it? Yes, f**king donors of blood street…."

Pablo froze in place. He picked up his cell and called Suzy. A woman, Suzy Amlody, lived there, one that he had sex with and was cheating on his wife. She was in one of the towers, No.4. He feared the fire might have been in that last tower. If shit happened, it always happened there…On the other hand, he was happy that something was finally happening and that he would make a difference.

When Pablo and his colleagues arrived, the first crews at the scene, the building's top level, the attic storage spaces, elevator machinery, and some other parts were engulfed in thick red flames. Heavy smoke and fire could have been seen from afar, and some eyewitnesses said that the flames were shooting so high; they could be seen from the intercity road. Some people thought a rocket hit the tower or a Cessna crashed on it, or it was gas, though the tower was not supplied by natural gas, but rather a district heating... This was an 18+ skyscraper, and no f**king ladders would do the job here. Pablo thought of Helicopters, but that was Sci-Fi at this point. Crews had to use all their hoses to connect to the hoses in the building as the hydrophore or pressure booster for water that we had was dead as the power was dead. Usually, it manages to give water to the third floor without power, but the massive problem was it could not be used. It was a great device installed by an Italian firm when the towers were built. The most crucial demand is for the system to deliver the required flow at the proper pressure.

Robert Stevenson from Glasgow invented this in the 1800s or a bit later. The thing worked well in our building, but now it was dead. This tower was, with its 18 floors and attic, mezzanine and entry-level and cornice Ca 56/60 meters high, close to 200 feet.

Their trucks were tremendous, but your aerial ladder reaches only 75 feet or a structure more than 40 feet tall if your highest ladder is a 40-foot extension ladder. Forget it! One had to run up to the fire and connect the water on each floor, hook up the hoses (they were praying that all hoses worked), and then establish a major pressure booster with tracks. That's what they did. Joined by some new fire trucks and men, they were 25 on site to fight the blaze and redirect the evacuation – if needed.

Some people were already coming out of the skyscraper screaming. The Chief told Pablo and all others to start getting up and connecting the hoses, and if people went out of the building, 18+1 floors, six apartments, each bed with three people inside – some 300 people, they should assist them – it would be a damn nightmare, thought Pablo!

I think the praxis of firefighters, which is a general thing, is that they cannot order all the people in a highrise building like ours to leave during a fire. It is impossible for thousands or even hundreds of people to leave a burning building quickly with staircases, as the elevators were shut down for security reasons. It would take several hours, and time is not what they had. Highrise firefighting strategy is all about standing ground and 'defending in place,' as the firefighters call it: extinguish the fire while most occupants remain inside the building. At a low-rise building fire, the strategy can be to extinguish the fire and evacuate the people simultaneously. Here the deal was more complicated as the fire was only happening at the top, and due to the resilience of this tower and good fire preventive construction, it might be contained, but that was a gamble. The thing would be to get people out and fight the fire simultaneously, especially get the people from the top 4-5 floors closest to the attic space engulfed in flames. The chief was not a man of gambles, hypotheses, assumptions, assertions, or quasi-thinking bullshit. He was a doer and immediately ordered the 'water it down and empty it' strategy. The chief also knew that there was no such thing as a defense in place and that they just had to improvise on the go on the go, so to s. Even if they didn't want to, stepping into our highrise was the only thing they could do, as this was no ordinary place. Well, by now, even you know it!

The Escape

Although the whole tumult and fire lasted for hours, the scene that developed in the skyscraper would take months to describe as it resembled a scene before doomsday or before the fall of the Roman Empire and the entering of hordes of barbarians at the gate of Rome. What can be remembered from that was a landscape of utter confusion, fear, panic, selfishness, stampede, screaming, shouting, fighting, yelling, craziness, and God knows what else. When the fireman entered the building led by the Chief and Pablo and started climbing, they were startled by a horde of people coming down the stairwell. Everyone was running and screaming. Some people were shutting themselves inside and locking the apartments, as many poor souls did before Estonia sunk into the Baltic Sea. The fire-fighters have never seen a more tumultuous affair than that day at 19.00 hours that late afternoon/evening. The sky was so pitch black that it might have been midnight. When we, those of us that lived on the top 3 floors, heard the smoke and saw the fire blazes in the attic, we immediately went down the stairwell. Somewhere on the 14th floor, we were immediately blocked by people leaving their apartments and not just taking their personal belongings. Still, some carry TVs, paintings, glassware, and clothes, and some morons are trying to get some furniture out. We managed to get them out of the way, a pair that tried to get their favorite leather sofa out. Keke and Talis Tolleberg, my pals from the 15th floor, helped me overcome them with the help of my neighbor from the 17th floor, the strong airline mechanic Jusef Faros. He had to fist down one of the idiots that carried the sofa. A pair of nobody moved in just a month ago. Fortunately, we had Luke Petrowsky with us, a retired cop that was in deep depression but still in a functioning state. He was the one that sounded off the alarm to start with and called 911 and all that went with it. He had with him, not the usual 357 Magnum, but he took his SIG-Sauer P220. Luke often considered this Swiss marvel the best "out of the box" .45 caliber double action pistol. It was developed during the early 1970s by the famous Swiss company Sweizerishe Industrie-Gesellschaft or SIG, short for the Swiss Police and Army. Luke spent two years training with them and was damn proud of it. He took full control of the stairwell and started waving his gun and shouting orders. He also deputized a couple of lads in the process. As the man was not stable, the best thing was to run down as fast as possible. When we heard the explosion that shook the upper part and felt like a small earthquake, real panic erupted in the stairwell. Screams and shouting could be heard. Some people fell, got up continued, and others just trampled over each other. It was an incredible scene. Luke tried to control this as much as he could and managed a bit, apprehending some people he didn't like and bringing a dozen plastic restraints. This plastic zip-tie handcuff became very popular many years later; he was cuffing some people, making most of the noise and causing problems. On the 12th floor, we met the firefighters assembling hoses to meet the upstairs fire. They were swift and also directed this tumult. They looked at us with surprise as we were coming down in an organized manner led by Luke and his gun. Pablo was startled, but Luke announced himself as an officer on duty, though he had been retired for years. Elevators were still in motion, but they stopped when the electricity died out when the fire hit the transformers in the attic machinery. Fortunately, the small one stopped directly on the floor, but the big one was stuck in the middle. Thanks to Pablo, Luke, and some of us, we got it somehow down with mechanical help, so it opened on the 5th floor. What we saw inside was a shock to the system. It was filled with terrified folks and one cow. Bob Bondarenko, a fresh peasant from a village 60 miles from the city, recently moved into the highrise. He also brought a cow with him that he kept on the balcony and took her for grazing down with the big elevator daily. The crazy mother f**ker tried his best to defend this by the logic of livelihood – he needed milk every morning and could sell the leftover stuff. The cow was pissing liters daily and shitting tons…all came down from the balcony, and legal stuff was soon in play. The law was clear, but the hand of justice was slow: Having livestock in a city apartment was not allowed, but getting it done took time. Bob knew this somehow and played on the slowness of the judicial system claiming that his 12th-floor balcony was in the air and not in the city??!!! Several people called the police and started legal proceedings when Police didn't do anything against Bob and his cow Wilma. This soon became a circus point and foci of all gossip. He managed to get away with this for almost three months, but it seemed now there was a court order and animal health inspectors intervened, so Bob was close to defeat. In all that time, pissing and shitting continued to slide down the tower façade and hit some of the innocent apartment bystanders below. The cow was in the elevator, standing on its shit and pissing. It seems it got excited and just filled the elevator.

Somehow they all got out, and the cow descended five stairs. Amid this and the confusion, some firefighters were banging on the doors for people to know what was happening and for them to leave the building. Pablo and his colleague banged on two apartments on the same floor, calling people to get out. Kyle Gottfurcht, another new tenant on the 5th floor, a former biathlon national team member, and now a f**ked up pain-killer and alcohol misuse addict, took his shotgun when he heard the noise and tumult and someone banging on his door. His wife Satira Gottfurcht, an alcohol partner in crime, maiden name Meadowass, took the kitchen knife and ran to the door, followed closely by Kyle. When they opened the door, they were both cursing in the worst possible way and waiving with their weapons, ready to shoot and kill, if needed, to defend their turf. When Kyle pointed the gun at them, and Satira went for the attack, Luke appeared from nowhere. He shot Kyle in the leg as that was the only way to stop this lunatic, while Pablo hit Satira with his small firefighting shovel and brought her to the ground. Everything was happening fast, and in the greater scheme of things, this was just another episode in the escape. Sonny Lazarus, a publicist and a freelance journalist from the 8th floor, saw Norrisa Guzinski, the head of the gossip network, and her husband running with just pillows in their hands, and you could see some money bills and jewelry protruding from them. She was in disarray and screaming as the whole skyscraper echoed with booming sounds from the 9th floor. Namely, Andrew Somun, Diksha Pathak's son, was playing a tape recorded as a compilation of screams from horror movies combined with some thunder and explosions and added a flavor of sirens. He knew people were panicking, so he opened his apartment door and put one speaker and the other near the elevators. They were both more than 500W of power. He was enjoying the chaos in front of his eyes and ears. Norris and her husband were not the only ones running out of valuables. They were not the only ones. Others had small fat suitcases and some stuffed socks in their hands full of money and other valuables. Some people carried their animals, plants, and old parents. Sasha Balthazar was in the middle of her tarot séance on the 2nd floor when her cats started to run to the door like mad. She lived with no less than 18 cats in her apartment, and most of her pension and fortune-telling skills money fed the feline population. Suddenly the cats just wanted to run out of the place. She forgot to lock her door, and one of the firefighters banged and opened her door. All the cats ran out down the staircase like mad. She screamed and went after them. She soon caught up with them as they just ran some 40 meters to the trailer with the Genesis boat and sleeping Gabriel, assembling all under the trailer like a small wolf pack looking with wild eyes at the highrise but still feeling safe under this giant floating wooden piece. Safe was also the keyword for Luke Petrowsky. He went in and out many times, and the last time he got out, he screamed wildly, pointing with his gun and the shotgun he took from Kyle:

"Everything is under control and…."

He didn't finish the sentence as that moment was when the police got him down to the ground and handcuffed him, as the guy was out of control, plus he was not a cop anymore. Instead, Luke plastic zipped-cuffed the three cops. The mass started screaming outside for the cops to let him go and stormed the patrol that handcuffed him. In moments of turbulence and scuffles, the cops were beaten down to the ground and overwhelmed, and Luke was free.

"We cannot have chaos and anarchy. I am cuffing you for your good", proudly asserted Luke.

The crowd hailed him as a hero, shouting: "Luke, Luke, Luke…".

He held his P220 Sig and the Shotgun in the Air like a hero! Later three new patrols came, and Luke surrendered his weapons. It was getting close to Midnight, and the Inferno was ending as the Rain started falling heavily. After the initial thunders and lightning, the massive flood of rain started. The sky was becoming a black sea of angry water, ready to spill over onto the little people and drown them. The sky never had that color, nor did it look so ominous. The rain started coming down in liters and crushing the flames from the attic. Soon it becomes a small river that joins the fireman's water coming down the elevator shafts and the staircases, coming in small waterfalls through the core of the concrete base. Some people still coming out or stuck in the staircase shaft started falling and breaking arms and legs. Soon the ambulances arrived and took care of them.

The Ending

[PART III]

The brave firefighters fought the fire for 4 hours. It would have lasted a few more if it wasn't for the Biblical rain that came down and, in a matter of 50 minutes, helped to extinguish the blazes. The whole attic floor burned down, but thanks to the firefighters, it did not spread beyond the top 18th floor. Some four five top floors were completely black due to the smoke. The burning smell and ash tar stench stayed for months. Elevators took two months to get fully repaired and back on track, but they were never the same. The whole skyscraper was water-filled that day and looked like a mammoth fountain.

Miraculously no one died in the tumult; a gun wounded one person, some were beaten up, and one cow was saved intact. Three firefighters had some injuries and burns; a few had breathing problems due to smoke and toxic fumes inhalation. As to the residents, there were a lot of broken limbs and other minor physical problems, and some psychological ones as side effects of this drama, but that was about it. Suzy Amlody, his sex partner, was ok, and he was glad about it. Her f**ked-up son from the last marriage was not even in the building but with some friends. Pablo didn't like this strange guy that was a nut case, but he endured as sex with Suzy was awesome. He was sure the guy hated his guts. In any case, his ideas finally got a proper listen in some higher instances. The first helicopter will be purchased next year, and some new procedures will be implemented. All firefighters were commended for their excellent work and for saving lives. Luke was released and soon became the local hero. The only real casualty of the day & night was Gabriel, and he did not die from the fire. He naturally passed away in the Genesis ship, waiting for the floods to come. And sort of, they did arrive that day. As fast as they came, even faster they left. In those 50 minutes, the doors of heaven opened for Gabriel and his Boat, Genesis, to enter it forever.

Noah's Ark

The boat that Henry Perone left to Gabriel, Gabriel's ark that was named GENESIS, was a beauty. It was a stoutly constructed, Baltimore-built, "oak-on-oak" comfortable sea-cruising ketch on which Perone had lived for the past 20 years. Maynard Lowery built the boat in Tilghman, Maryland, in 1959. It was a perfectly and fully functioning little refuge from the world, i.e., a sound hull, a smooth-running Perkins 6.354 diesel engine, sound masts, new traditional rigging, and good sails. It had a 55' full-keel Sparkman & Stephens designed hull of bronze fastened 1 1/2" white oak planks on 3" steam bent oak frames spaced on 1' centers and bronze strapped throughout. This beauty weighed 32 tons and drew 7 feet. The beautiful cabin was constructed of mahogany and consisted of, fore to aft, a forecastle with one berth, followed by the galley with a Dickinson Atlantic stove, followed by the main salon with four berths and heated with a Dickinson Antarctic heater, then followed by the owner's stateroom with double berth to port, and a big head with stand-up shower to starboard, and followed lastly by the trunk cabin with double berth. The cabin top was an oak plank on oak beams covered with marine plywood. The nibbed laid deck is bronze fastened, sprung 1 1/2" teak strips with king plank and covering boards. The majority of the hardware is bronze and made by Merriman Bros. Company. With routine maintenance, none of which is beyond the scope of an aspiring and willing wooden boat owner, this beautiful boat could carry you anywhere. Henry knew this and cared for this beauty, even with his drinking problems. This is a quality craft of superior material. Now it was Gabriel's home. Jonathan arranged everything in days so that Gabriel could spend the 14th day, the exact day the fires engulfed our tower and the massive rain (hardest in 20 years) hit that evening. All seven pairs of animals were brought there with many vegetables and other stuff so Gabriel would be happy. He insisted that the whole family spend the day and night with him there. Even Bartholomew agreed though he knew the whole building would call him crazy the morning after. Rumors have already spread about the boat, and the whole family should be in an asylum. Some protested that the boat took too many parking spaces, but Jonathan fixed this with a big favor in the local police precinct. He knew the chief, and he agreed on this but, in return, wanted free vegetables and fruit for two years. Greedy bastard, thought Jonathan, but he went with it. What else was he going to do? Gabriel wanted to be in the parking space in the boat when the floods came, together with the livestock and his children; they were all with him on the boat when the fire erupted, and the biblical scene started to play out just 50m from the parking space. Gabriel insisted that he spend the previous night there and wait until Midnight that evening. He fell in and out of sleep, missing most of the fire, but he awoke just before the rains started. The Hebrew patriarch saved himself and his family and the animals by building an ark in which they survived for 40 days and 40 nights of rain; the story of Noah and the flood is told in the Book of Genesis. Our story is told here and now. The story of Noah was the story of Gabriel that evening did not last for forty days and forty nights but for 14 hours.

Nonetheless, the face of Noah was the face of Gabriel Nash. Gabriel awoke from a wet dream for the last time in his life. He was soaked in rainwater and felt reborn like a baby in the new, innocent, virgin world. That early morning, while fires were dying out in the tower attic, his eyes opened to what seemed like a beautiful rainbow emerging after the biblical rain mixed with fire. He remembered that God put the rainbow in the sky, saying, "Whenever I bring clouds over the earth, and the rainbow appears in the clouds, I will see it and remember the everlasting covenant between God and all living creatures of every kind on the earth." Gabriel looked at Hans the Duck standing by his side, intensely looking at him. Before he closed his eyes for the last time, Hans told him:

"You did well, Gabriel, you did well: 14 pairs were saved, vegetables and fruit were saved, your family is safe, and Frambruka rests in peace and awaits you, my old friend…now rest in peace, in eternal peace…"

Gabriel Nash smiled and thought of the next world. He closed his easy and saw his son and grandchildren standing by the boat looking at the tower, and then he saw the smiling face of his beloved wife approaching him in the distance. There was a shimmering light and rainbow colors all around and many animals around him…he saw fields of fruit and vegetables; he saw the light…Gabriel died peacefully in his sleep that late evening at precisely 11:45, lying on the wooden bench of the Genesis boat parked on the trailer outside the tower, his Arc, his refuge for all the creatures and food he gathered, in his own Noah's Ark. Gabriel left this earth in the belief that he has fulfilled the sacred mission he was given through the 5+1 signs and primarily through his wife's last words and the arrival of the boat Genesis given to him by his dear friend, a former priest. Five years he waited to be with her again, but he knew the task had to be done first. Now it was all over…He thought of his son and grandsons and how they would be fine and that the Farm with all the fruit and vegetables would rise & live on forever…he now started to see a white glowing light and Frambruka's face forming in front of him. He felt like he was being raised by something, and the warmth and light overtook him. He died with ease and smiled on his face. The rain stopped after Midnight, and the last blazes were gone…The folks were allowed to return soon after as some firemen, including Pablo, stayed to guard the attic, which was still letting out fumes, but no new fire was started. The inferno was over, and the skyscraper survived.

***

The Nashes were shocked to find Granddad dead. It must have happened just moments ago when they were not with him. Some consolation was found in the fact that he would not suffer the horrible last months of cancer and the physical pain it would bring. At least he died peacefully with a smile on his face. Jonathan was crying but was so glad he had brought the boat. The word spread fast, and rumors that some glowing thing from the fire came into the boat and took Gabriel. That was, of course, not confirmed. When the coroner came and took Gabriel, and things settled a bit, I approached Andy, standing still on the side of the boat and looking up at the sky.

"I am a sorry man; I knew how close you were to your Granddad."

"Thanks, he is at peace now," he continued to look at the sky.

"How did your grandfather know this was about to happen?" I asked Andy while watching the fantastic 6m long old wooden boat Genesis resting firmly on the trailer parked outside our building and the massive numbers of people, some 200 gathered outside the Tower waiting to go back inside after spending the late afternoon/evening in the parking lot or their cars. When this happened, some 50 people were not in the tower, and ca 50 never wanted to leave the building.

"I have no clue," answered Andy in puzzlement.

"I don't know if he knew. It was all in his mind; something happened to him after Grandma died. He spoke of signs and Ducks talking to him, and things that my Grandma saw and this boat that arrived…all of it seems unreal, surreal, you know what I mean?"

"Yes, I hear you so well" I couldn't believe any of it.

"Maybe the whole Farm deal, animals, vegetables, got to their head and…I don't know. This boat was just some incredible coincidence, but there were just too many of them…We could have burned down if the whole skyscraper exploded…you never know…."

"Well, Andy, at least you spent the whole night almost in the boat and felt a bit like Noah and got to spend the last night with your Granddad," I added.

"Yeah, true. Some animals crapped massively, and the two pigs farted all night, but Granddad was in heaven…I hope he is on his way there now…."

We both looked at the skies, which had a fantastic starry coverage like the rains and clouds never happened…and then we looked at our skyscraper that, yes, again, stood its ground…

"By the way, man, you need a pair of geese," Andy asked with a smile.

"These two geese don't need much for housing. Just shelter from the worst weather and wind, you know. They are fun having around". Besides, they are far from dumb, and Michael and Uriel (Gabriel gave them names of major Archangels) are pretty intelligent and funny". Andy was quite persistent, and I saw two heads looking from the stern of the Genesis boat.

Andy continued the sales pitch.

"What they lack in grace, they make up for in fervor, especially when it comes to putting someone in their place. I promise you, man, and you will see for yourself—it won't be a wild goose chase".

We both started laughing.

"Man, that was a great line! I think I will pass this time; I will have to think about it anyway as I have your cat now, but let's see…".

The two geese started honking, disapproving of what I had just said. Who knows, they might have been good watchdogs.

***

"The biggest thing you've got to do when occurrence like this happens is looking forward…not backward, so our first step is clean up what we've got," Mike Bartok, the chief fire investigator, said to the reporter from the local TV that evening.

"Later, we will see what has caused this fire. Was it some electrical failure, or theft or something…but speculation at this point is not good…"

Well, speculation was the only thing on the table. Already fairytales were forming as to what had happened, who caused it, and so on, and of course – what was that boat doing in the parking space, carrying now a dead man inside and a bunch of animals and other things. It took firefighters almost 3.5 hours and 15 minutes to control the fire at the tower. They might have been fighting with it if it wasn't for the Biblical rain. As to the cause—They are still investigating it as the case was never closed.

Author's Note

Well, that's not all of it, is it now? What happened in the tower had very little to do with the great flood & rains, a mythical story of a great flood sent to destroy civilization as an act of divine retribution. Even the Genesis boat, animals, Crazy vegetables, and fruit that might have been another sign that doomsday was coming seemed to be just another coincidence. That notwithstanding, I thought for sure, as many others did, that the days were numbered for our skyscraper and that the explosion and fires would take it down as the tragic collapse of the World Trade Canter on 9/11 some years back. They didn't. But, the explosion, fire, and massive firefighting affair had different interpretations, not least as some terrorist deeds. As to Gabriel's predictions, the only natural thing was the biblical rains that came down and helped extinguish the fires, so there could have been a divine intervention. At this point, I need to let you decide on your own, i.e., which of the four versions of the ending you prefer more. These four "plausible" endings came out from the collective gossip, massive drivel, baloney drooling, guessing games, and just pure imagination of the tower inhabitants…well there were some hard facts from the fire crime scene, CSI work, and various eyewitnesses that saw what allegedly preceded the events that evening. In any case, what led to the burning inferno that evening will never be known for sure, but who gives a shit. We survived, and the skyscraper, except for the attic, did not burn to the ground. What happened?

Any of the four strong endings might answer. I will give you the short-zipped versions; you can pick one or two.

If you don't like any of them, invent one of your own. I am sure it will fit the bill! When it comes to our skyscraper, the sky is the limit!

Here they are in the same order they came to the world in the days that followed the inferno:

1.   Bolt of Lightning Strikes

2.   The Barrel Deal Goes Sour

3.   Unexplained Phenomena

4.   A 'Reformed Pyromaniac'

1. Bolt of Lightning Strikes

The sky was getting dark, almost on the brink of coal-like color, but still some hours away from what most certainly seemed to be a rain of biblical proportions. Far away, thunder could be heard, and the wind picked up speed. Our skyscraper stood as a menacing fortress on the top of the hill, almost preparing for battle with an invisible enemy. Cloud-to-ground lightning was the choice of the day, and the skyscraper was the victim. This is the best-known and second-most common type of lightning we know of. The heavens decided it would be discharged that evening with a monstrous thunder that shook the whole place. Of all the different types of lightning, it poses this one posed the greatest threat to life and property since it struck the ground. In this case, it went first for the skyscraper, becoming cloud-to-tower lightning. In the atmospheric electrical discharge, a lightning bolt leader traveled at 60,000 m/s (130,000 mph), and temperatures were approaching 30,000 °C (54,000 °F). It found an opening in a skyscraper, and it struck. The lightning struck the three old pieces of household machinery: a dishwasher, stove, and refrigerator all at once! The bad thing was that they were all three in one storage cell with many wooden furniture parts in the two adjacent ones. To make things even worse, the proud owner of these three leftover pieces had piled up 25 aluminum pipes and 50 kilos of copper stored in an iron box. All of this provided that 'once in a lifetime-one in a million chance' opportunity for a thunderbolt to strike at the right spot at the right time. The whole attic cage was exposed as the window that faced it was broken and exposed to the sky. The explosion was real, surreal, unreal…the whole place burst into flames instantly, and in 30 minutes, the whole attic was a burning inferno.

The Rabbi of the main synagogue in the city was looking from the office tower in the center of the business district, visiting his son, whose company had its headquarters there. When he saw the lightning strike the tower, he uttered a blessing in Hebrew, "…He who does acts of creation," and recited it to the end. When the fire erupted in high red flames, He thought what Talmud spoke of the sky—"Shamaim"—as built from fire and water—"Esh Uma-im," and now saw with his own eyes the inexplicable mixture of fire and water that came together, during this incredible rainstorm. The priest in the central city Cathedral started crossing himself at vespers when a thunderstorm exploded and thought of an older man called Gabriel, whom he had met for confession many times. He spoke of the Biblical rains, floods, and fires and that the end of days was near. A nearby Imam of the local mosque, seeing the massive bolt of lightning come from dark clouds with wind and hail and crash into the tower, started to pray and remembered the words he read in the Qur'an: "And He sends down hail from mountains (clouds) in the sky, and He strikes with it whomever He wills, and turns it from whomever He wills. The vivid flash of its lightning nearly blinds the sight...."

2. The Barrel Deal Goes Sour

The sky was getting dark, almost on the brink of coal-like color, but still some hours away from what most certainly seemed to be a rain of biblical proportions. Far away, thunder could be heard, and the wind picked up speed. Our skyscraper stood as a menacing fortress on the top of the hill, almost preparing for battle with an invisible enemy. The skyscraper had district heating with hot water used in the radiators, but some people never had enough heat, nor did they trust the local companies with energy. They had their elements, furnaces, stoves, and who knows what else. But no one used Mazut. Mazut is a heavy, low-quality fuel oil for generating plants and similar applications. In the US and Western Europe, mazut is blended or broken down, with the end product being diesel. But this fuel was also used for heating houses in our part of the world. That was the case with some housing estates in 2-3 districts further from our towers. These housing estates were in shape and size similar to old USSR and far east compounds that were not connected, nor did they have the facility to blend or break it down into more traditional petrochemicals but had to use the 'waste oil' furnace. There was a shortage of Mazut in the city, and the price of it was pure gold at the moment. And some knew it!

Saki Dabanov, the local mobster and owner of the fish restaurant, got 20 barrels from mother Russia and would pay some good cash to Evan Kapadia to store 10 of these in our tower attic and to deliver it to a buyer a few days later. Evan had no clue what this was for or where it was going, nor did he care much. He was stoned most of the time during the day. Somehow he managed to get these massive barrels up to the attic with the help of one of his junky pals. They stored 9 of them in the attic corridor facing the west. They put the last one on the corridor's other side, just 5 meters away. They also stopped to rest there. The corridor went around the whole attic, which was a f**king maze. You had to have a map to find your way around. Even though there were arrows and numbers, it might take an average person some minutes to find the way out. It might be your hours or days if you are stoned like Evan and his friend. It took them 16 hours after they dozed off in one corridor. They stored the barrels just the night before the fire and were supposed to pick them up a few days later. They were both smoking pot and cigarettes, and finally, when the thunder woke them up, they recovered instantly, scrambling out of the cellar attic.

Unfortunately, Evan's friend threw a half-smoked cigarette on rags and paper close to the 10th barrel. After a while, the fire started forming in the cigarette but spread to the paper and some wood stuff to the plastic barrel, which was the first explosion that fueled the fire. In the later hours, the other nine exploded, also creating a burning inferno. Evan never got his money, except for a beating from Saki's goons when he told them they might have been responsible for this. As for Evan's pal, nobody heard of him again. He was probably floating in some sewer or was cemented under some foundation of one of Saki's Real Estate projects. Saki lost half of his barrel lot in the fire but at least had his restaurant intact as the fire somehow never spread. He never told the police or fire investigators what happened, nor did Evan.

3. Unexplained Phenomena

The sky was getting dark, almost on the brink of coal-like color, but still some hours away from what most certainly seemed to be a rain of biblical proportions. Far away, thunder could be heard, and the wind picked up speed. Our skyscraper stood as a menacing fortress on the top of the hill, almost preparing for battle with an invisible enemy. It was very dark and moist on the attic cellar floor, and currently, none of the residents was there leaving their old furniture or other junk. The fire was raging when Pablo and his colleagues reached the attic. Pablo remembered the first blast when another, much more robust, happened. Every firefighter's nightmare is the backdraft, an explosive surge in a fire produced by the sudden mixing of air with other combustibles. Fortunately, after the explosions, the sheer force blew away two of his injured colleagues, but he would be ok. They were all in shock just thinking of what the f**k was happening up there. A panicked firefighter could be heard on a police scanner asking dispatchers to send everyone available to the scene. Soon other firefighters came up and were ready to fight the blaze with water and other things.

Hala Kada, whose brother owns a phone shop in the nearby shopping street strip mall, told the local tabloid news: "Man, I was just getting off the phone from my bitch (that was sound covered on TV) in my brother's shop when I saw a huge tube fire out from the top of the tower man, it was f**king wild (this was covered too) man. This tube flew like a rocket, and then the fire started, but there was a massive blast before that man".

Several windows and pieces of cornice collapsed on several innocent bystanders standing on the pavement. Both statements coincided with what some of the other witnesses saw also or heard. Peter Petersson, who runs a nearby XXX Video Rental Store, told reporters he saw a portion of the building fly out with some sharp metal torpedoing. The investigators later tried to locate this canister or metal tube that allegedly flew out of the window. Some other witnesses spoke of a barrel flying out, and some residents spoke of WWII torpedoes being stored up there by some crazy fanatic that moved out of the building years ago but still had his storage cell left.

The two injured firefighters were taken to hospital later in the area, but there was no immediate word on their condition. Pablo found out later that they were good. It seemed they were good at the end. Local Television footage showed a large, billowing cloud of smoke coming out of the tower, obscuring the city's view in that part. Numerous fire engines, ambulances, and rescue vehicles were on the street outside the building. The reporters were talking about possible terrorist attacks, anarchists, diversion, torpedo storages, and other military options; the building did have 18 armies, navy, and air force families living inside. But no connections of any sort could be found. All of it just remained an unexplained phenomenon.

4. A 'Reformed Pyromaniac'

The sky was getting dark, almost on the brink of coal-like color, but still some hours away from what most certainly seemed to be a rain of biblical proportions. Far away, thunder could be heard, and the wind picked up speed. Our skyscraper stood as a menacing fortress on the top of the hill, almost preparing for battle with an invisible enemy. Three shadows climbed from the 18th floor to the attic maze storage ground. They wanted t have some fun, and they didn't belong in this skyscraper, but that did not stop them from entering & breaking into the place. The iron grind gate was easy to hack, and two were experts. Salihi Saaban and Tito Pantaglione have seen their share of locks and bolts, so this was a piece of cake. Both of them carried booze and homemade joints with inappropriate content. The intention was to drink and get high, and there were no other hidden agendas, at least not for these two. The third person was a long-time lost friend Hans Amlody. He just came out of the psychiatric ward as a 'rehabilitated pyromaniac arsonist.' He was responsible for 16 fires, one involving his elementary school. The kid was 15 but started the firestarter activities at 5 when he burned his cat alive. Allegedly rehabilitated, cured of an uncontrollable desire to set fire to things…especially buildings, the young pyromania-arsonist was ready to join the society.

They entered the skyscraper and went for one of the crossing hallways with a cozy spot for drinking. Hans was very much focused on the environment at hand, and when he saw a bunch of barrels stashed in the corridor and the smell coming from them, he knew this would be good. Plus, all the cells had wooden doors with wire, and they were in 80& cases filled with unnecessary furniture leftovers. He knew this environment was begging for a bonfire. He started shaking and got an erection just thinking about it. Hans had a violent disorder, as pyromania is an impulse to deliberately start fires to relieve tension. It typically includes feelings of gratification or relief afterward; for his, it was even sexual. There was also another thing. Pyromaniacs start fires to induce euphoria and often fixate on fire control institutions like fire stations and firefighters. Hans hated a guy called Pablo, who was screwing his mom. While he was locked up, she divorced his father, an alcoholic bum, and moved to the skyscraper on the 11th floor to the 1-room apartment. Somewhere along the way, she met Pablo and had sex with him all the time. When he came out a few months ago, he met the fireman and started to hate him, the skyscraper, and his mother. He just wanted to burn them alive, all of them. A burning flame inside Hans was an uncontrollable desire, mania, and 'Looney Toney's passion' to set fire to things. He was a burning cacoethes – an individual not cured at all but still with an irrational but irresistible motive for arson. That belief or action was one of the few things that made sense in Hans's brain and his life.

He was a combo of pyromaniac and arson; at least, that was the diagnosis he got from the hospital and the behavior modification treatment they gave him. They thought he was cured, but what did they know, thought Hans. This was going to be his masterpiece.

Most people want to avoid lightning, not Hans. He loved it! The irony is that attracting lightning is the easiest thing in the world for those that know how, and Hans knew. He moved a bunch of steel pipes and rods, standing on the side of one cell, close to the open window and pulling them outside so they protruded a lot. To this, he tied two long small kites of thin metal in the air, as Ben Franklin hoped for the best. The kites flew right away as the wind was picking. This was just for fun, as he knew that a massive thunderstorm was on the way, but the real thing was his gadget. A Thermite Fire Starter with a micro size of 2 inches tall by 1 1/2 wide. He bought this thing through a friend as soon as he came out. These small light wonders will light a fire in three feet of snow or pouring rain or blowing wind. The small container was shaped like a Kodak film canister with a snap-on lid. Hans knew it had 5 ounces of cast Thermite, and to ignite this little thing, you just needed some wood or cloth and paper – all of which were in abundance here. Voila! He would lay out some firewood, cloth, and paper, place his container on top of it, pull out the Visco fuse with his long extension, and then add some wood to ignite it.

"Let's just burn the house down! Yeah, I hate this f**king skyscraper anyway!" He knew this time he had to miss out on the best – watching this thing burn as he did not want to die here, and some pleasures had to be sacrificed for bigger ones, as he knew he would be watching, not from too afar, this tower burn for hours. He would stand back, and it will burn, burn baby burn!

"Well, well, what the hell," thought Hans, "It's worth it!"

Salihi and Tito were so stoned when they started heading out of the attic that they never realized Hans was left behind. He stayed behind preparing the Thermite gadget and using a long 10 meters slow, burning fuse. It took him 10 minutes to do this, ignite it, and run back before they closed the steel bar-grinded door to the attic behind him. He explained his absence on the account. He needed to take a leak. This was not necessary, as Salihi and Tito were barely conscious. Hans thought about how his gadget will work at 4500 degrees for 30 seconds producing 2 ounces of white-hot molten iron that remains red hot for several minutes after it is lit. He was shuddering excitedly and sweating all over his body as they descended the elevator. They crossed the street and went down to the factory wall on the other side of the road and slumbered in one half-ditch to light one more homemade joint and empty the last can of beer. Hans didn't tell them anything; he just huddled in his Puma pants and Champion sweatshirt hood and waited for the fire to start, thinking of his mom, Pablo, his father, and all the other assholes he met in his life…He started humming and singing a tune he composed while being 'rehabilitated' in the institution:

So now I see the fire and feel the heat,

I watch these f**kers choke, and bastards burn,

And I wonder what it takes for them to learn,

That, my friends, we are near the end of fire & urn.

My prophecy was written not long ago,

That fire, smoke, glow, and heat would rain,

And many would die in the sunlight of the sky.

But this is not some crazy arsonist tale of sorrow,

No, Sir, this is the man of light and borrows.

I will burn the house down long before dawn,

We need some f**king heat and action now,

And leave all the bad victims of this game.

Stand up, assholes – and stop the fire if you can,

As forever the counted one, I am sure you can't.

An old white Volkswagen Beetle was passing by, and an even older Methuselah Woodstock Hippy bastard with crazy eyes was driving it. He rolled down the driver's window and gave an 'Up yours' the finger to Hans, saying: "F**k you freak!" While speeding away, Hans saw that he had a giant bumper sticker on the back saying: "Too many freaks, not enough circuses!" He thought of that place and closed his eyes while continuing to sing.

And that's the END, folks…

Bonus Story

FLYMEAWAY.COM

As in all good music albums, there is always a bonus track usually left and reserved for the Japanese Market...well this one is for all markets and was relatively fresh when I unearthed it from my memory halls and mind vaults. I thought it would fit the bill for this storytelling moment and be a perfect extra ending to a weird bunch of tales...enjoy this lost & retrieved piece from the year 2000!

PROLOGUE—The African Affair

Somewhere in the summer of 1999

It was a f**king scorching heat with 80% humidity and 35C temperature and rising. The summer season begins in November and ends in March in this southern African country, and Bubba knew that so well. Still, this damn October felt like a furnace. Rain season was coming but not this week, not even this month. At least the rain would wash the misery of this African outing affair and hopefully get this enterprise moving somewhere else. Bubba would be gone before that, as their vacation in this place was soon ending. He didn't like any country with a hot climate, but most of these were the ones where smuggling blues ruled, and he and Memphis could smell them from miles away. Nonetheless, this week was an inferno on mother earth, and Bubba was dreaming of St. Moritz, some excellent small alpine hotel, and a beautiful blonde named Gretchen that would be running the place. Oh yeah, that was life. Soon with all the money saved on all these sleazy affairs, that just might become a reality. Who knows?

On the other hand, nothing might happen, and another stinky rat hole would be their next stop. In any case, a lot was riding on this load that was supposed to be delivered to Angola by a local drug lord Michael Masweze. The flight was ca 2 hours and always went over two borders and under the radar. We're working the ropes here in Memphis and that pilot Milton Onobanjo, whom Bubba disliked so much. He was just a frigging mechanic, and everything else on this airport that housed three ATR 42s, one Avro Jet BAe-146 they got from Ghana, was constantly under repair. He could never get any parts for it, nor anyone cared, as there was not a pilot ready to fly this plane. Bubba didn't blame them as to who would lift this thing, knowing that all kinds of things might go wrong, not due to the quality of the plane—as this baby was great—but more to the lack of parts that needed to be replaced and maintained. Bubba was the second mechanic at the airport. But the three ATRs were running passengers and goods, while #3 also ran stolen goods, ivory, snake skin, weapons, money, and drugs. The first guy Anton Jakande was stoned most of the time and was only good with small private planes. In any case, Milton Onobanjo was late, and there were running on a tight schedule. That asshole was a nut case, and he told this to Memphis on so many occasions—the guy was no good, Memphis should fly instead—though his smuggling brother-in-arms and boss thought that this was a blessing in disguise and that Milton knew the geography of this region of Africa better than anyone else and could land this plane in any weather or even if he was blind.

Bless my ass, thought Bubba. It was probably Memphis' Willy thinking as he was shagging Milton's pretty wife, Nuru, and that was not good, especially if you had a nut for a husband. No, sir, that was going to end up badly. Bubba was on his second packet of Gitanes cigarettes and looked at his old Atlantic Swiss watch. He remembered Jacques Laffite, a famous racing car dude he met in a bar in Marseilles, who introduced him to these beauties—the best cigarette in the world. His father gave him the watch, a brand that was the oldest Swiss watch company ever. He would never give away any of these two delicate possessions and vices.

Milton was 20min behind schedule. Bubba looked at the terminal building and saw Milton coming towards him. The dude looked angry. F**k, he was probably on all kinds of pills this morning. He looked more like a lunatic than a pilot that morning, and his clothes looked dirty and smelled of a combination of urine, bleach, and sweat embellished with a horrible leather smell. Milton just passed and brushed by Bubba, saying:

"When I see Memphis, I will kill that f**king son of a bitch, and I am through after this flight. You assholes can go and f**k yourselves..."

Then he pointed the finger to Bubba and turned away towards the ATR waiting on the Tarmac. This morning's flight would be without passengers as the plane needed maintenance in Angola, or so Bubba has falsified in the papers. The plane was loaded with drug money and some technical stuff the drug warlords needed for some local assault on something or someone. Bubba did not yet load a big metal case containing some valuable Swiss gold and diamonds. Bubba didn't want to know what Memphis handled and what Middle handled. Still, his cut was always excellent, so it must have been good stuff, and especially this flight was incredibly excellent as there were some frigging valuables in there. But seeing Milton in whatever stage of mental (in)sanity he was sent chills through Bubba's spine, and his beer gut belly feeling told him that this flight would go wrong. He started shouting at him, but Milton was deaf. Bubba turned to get the metal case and hoped this motherf**ker could land in Angola. If he got killed there or crashed on the way back, he wouldn't give a shit as they already got paid for whatever this plane was carrying, and Bubba knew there were several caskets and small packages that he wondered about, plus this metal case. The morning seemed terrible, and it just got even worse. Bubba started humming the Ambrosia 1978 hit Angola while getting the case at taking it to the ATR:

"Oh, living in Angola, I'm just living in Angola

I said living in Angola, living in Angola…"

Napoleon once said, ' History is a set of lies agreed upon.' Bubba was unsure if that was true, and not being a history scholar himself, he was still sure that whatever was transcribed and played out that morning was something no one would know. Still, all would find a plausible lie to put it all behind them as soon as possible. "Phakela Airways" was freshly painted on this ATR 42, and Bubba thoroughly checked the plane that morning. The cargo was way too valuable to mess around with this, though; after a couple of shots of bourbon, bubba wasn't sure if he checked the plane that well anymore. Ah f**k it; this lunatic might have lost his marbles, but it was a pretty good flyer. Neither Bubba nor Memphis did not know that Milton had been grounded that morning for medical reasons and was forbidden to fly at all, probably for good. Milton did not give a f**k about that and was about to fly one more time, or so he thought. His wife was cheating on him, his company did not respect him, his brother hated him, he hated the president of the country, and he thought these two motherf**kers cheated him on his money, always giving him less, plus one of them banged his wife. Oh yeah! Well, things were going to change that morning; he thought.

That morning they were changed because Milton single-handedly and very effectively crippled operations for the flag carrier and wiped out the whole fleet in one heat of the moment. Phakela Airways operations came to a complete standstill, as the airline temporarily had only one aircraft left, the BAe-146 Bubba could not repair without necessary parts, which was grounded at the time with technical problems. Phakela Airways Captain Milton Onobanjo commandeered one of the company's three ATR-42 aircraft. Fortunately, it was locked in a hangar some 700m from the main building and tarmac. The three planes were the only operational aircraft in the country's fleet. Oh yes, there was also an adorable Fairchild F-27J N2706J plane parked on the site, which was more than a relic than anything else, where Bubba and the other mechanic used to sleep. Of the 78 FH-227s built, 23 crashed, or so Bubba read somewhere. Nonetheless, this one didn't and was a perfect home for Bubba while Memphis was in the town's leading hotel coordinating business and sleeping with Milton's wife and other women. The other two pilots didn't like him much due to his strange human nature and shady deals and flights, but he was respected as a good flyer.

What happened on that day in October when Milton Onobanjo passed by Rick "Bubba" Orlando and went straight to commandeer an Aerospatiale ATR-42, forgetting to take the metal suitcase that Bubba did not give him in time before the departure, registration number A5-XZZ, from the Phakela Airways section of the terminal at "Alakija Ekwensi International Airport" (named after a former revolutionary and father of the nation) and took off. Bubba thought it would be the scheduled (unscheduled but maintained flight to Angola with goods for the drug and warlord) flight, but it was nothing more. For almost two and a half hours, Milton circled the airport, radioing the control tower and announcing his intention to kill his wife, commit suicide or crash the plane at the president's palace or the Airport Terminal. Complete panic erupted as the airport was evacuated as a precaution, and passengers later reported complete havoc in the terminal. The tower guys tried vainly convincing him to land, promising to bring his wife and even the president if needed. Efforts were led by the airline's CEO, the airport's director (same guy), and the army and police commanders on site. It seems Milton did not give a f**k, even when Memphis Kapadia tried to talk to him, and finally, when his wife arrived, there was a slight chance for something that he actually might change his mind, as he started to cry talking to her. But unfortunately, what the mother f**ker didn't know was that the plane was never fully fueled (this was not Bubba's responsibility but stoned bastard Anton's). The plane ran out of fuel. Bubba did the technical stuff and left the fueling to Anton, but neither knew nor had a clue the plane would circle instead of reaching the 2-hour destination where it was supposed to be refueled again.

Bubba called Memphis and told him what was happening, that Milton was heading nowhere and hovering over the airport with their cargo. He tried to reach through the tower communication with Milton and tell him to land though Milton refused, telling Memphis he would kill him and his wife for cheating on him. It was a grand f**kup! Memphis arrived in 30min and joined Bubba, cursing all the time and telling Bubba that their asses would be grass if this plane did not reach the destination.

As the aircraft began to run out of fuel, Milton Onobanjo realized he was f**ked, or he wanted to kill himself and destroy the cargo threatening to crash the ATR into the tower or terminal building of Phakela Airways Airport. He said that he wished to settle a grudge with the airline's management, demanding to speak to the company CEO, the President of the Country, and the Swiss Ambassador for some strange reason. His demands were never made clear. Most of all, he did not want to talk to Memphis Kapadia nor his cheating wife Nuru until they confessed their sex crimes, as he called them. He was screaming and saying he would destroy the cargo if Memphis and cheating Nuru did not confess to their sex affair on national TV that instant. He also wanted the airline to buy a proper Boeing or Airbus instead of these shitty mosquitos-looking ATR planes he was flying. He was saying many things, and too many people were listening, but very little had been done. Ian Fofan, the Country's vice prime minister and transportation minister, was about to be put through to him and promised changes and public sex confessions by his wife when the plane ran out of fuel.

Despite all the attempts to persuade him to land (including Memphis) and discuss his (crazy) grievances, and his unfaithful wife crying and telling him how much she loved him, he stated again and again that he was going to commit suicide by crashing the plane into different things and also maybe into some planes sitting on the apron. After a total flying time of about two hours+, mostly circling the airport, he made two final loops screaming when he found out the fuel was gone and then cutting off communication with the tower, crashing at 200 knots (230 mph) into Phakela Airways two other ATR 42s that were parked on the apron. He was killed instantly, but there were no other casualties except for Anton Jakande, the other mechanic who was stoned and fell asleep in one of the other ATRs while doing maintenance.

The central historical fact was that the ATR stopped working at the end, the props stopped turning, and the plane ran out of fuel. It crashed into the ramp area where the other two ATR aircraft were sitting waiting for their later scheduled flights and was destroyed in a way they would never fly and killed Milton, destroying his plane almost wholly. All three planes were destroyed in a fiery crash, and Phakela Airways were no more.

When Memphis and Bubba saw the plane crash and destroy the whole fleet, vast flames of fire engulfing the steel machines, their reflexes were fast as usual—"let's get the f**k out of here, Bubba, it's time to leave and forget about this. They both looked at the metal case Bubba did not deliver to Milton and thought: "F**k It,"; and so they did. So much was already lost in the plane that the drug lords paid them that this case won't help the cause; it's better to keep it.

All kinds of rumors started to resurface, such as repeatedly threatening the airport authorities and the airline's CEO, telling them that he would kill himself or them but never giving a reason for this weird and frantic behavior. On that morning, and at the time of the incident, he was supposed to go on medical leave from the airline, having failed 3-4 medical and psychological tests the week before and been declared unfit to fly; consequently, he was not authorized to take the ATR plane up in the air, definitely not the one with falsified maintenance scheduled that morning for a strange and obscure airstrip in western Angola. Airport security was reported to be more or less shit, as two policemen on duty were nowhere to be found that morning. It was said to be relatively easy for somebody to steal an aircraft, especially if that someone was a pilot of the airline. The tower people had no clue and never gave clearance for that flight when they discovered this. It was later revealed (without any proof) that Onobanjo had a brain tumor and AIDS and was a schizophrenic sociopath, although what part this may have played in his actions is unknown. Before his medical suspension, he had been flying well and was always cleared by the safety operations expert for the airline, former captain Memphis Kapadia. The airline company ad country was trying to save face at any cost.

While the initial investigation pointed to suicidal actions by the pilot, the police also turned to his strange radar and schedule— so-called maintenance and training flights to Angola and Namibia—all signed off by the first mechanic Joe "Bubba" Gershwin and the Airport's flight instructor and safety manager, former Canadian pilot Memphis Kapadia. Also, the leftovers in the cargo section, the part that was not destroyed by the crash and fire, revealed some strange artifacts, primarily illegal ones, including stolen Swiss gold, drugs, strange documents, destroyed electronic equipment, and a metal case that completely melted even possible diamonds could have been in the plane. The two in question, Bubba and Memphis, were supposed to be questioned, but it seemed they left the country, and the police issued a warrant for their arrest, though they were never found. Ian Fofan, the Country's vice prime minister and Milton's wife, began a sexual affair and got married after six months when Ian left his wife. Milton's wife shed some light on the whole affair but seemed to have known little except for her husband's unstable nature and the sexual affair she had with Memphis. Rest was an enigma.

Michael Masweze, The Western Angola Drug War Lord, was furious when he heard about this shit on TV but knew already something was wrong when the plane never landed on the small strip and Memphis's phone was out of order. His stash, which was well paid for, was all gone! He gave 1000s of orders, hits to be made, heads to roll, balls to be cut off. He even kidnapped Anton's wife and tried to get info from her, but there was little to be extracted. It seemed nothing was working, and after a while, he gave up. Bubba and Memphis had vanished from the face of the earth...or was it so?

The Main Thing—The Flymeaway.com Affair

Somewhere in the summer of 2000

I am unsure when the fear of flying entered my mind/life, i.e., the fear/concern of flying when the weather is unstable (all the result of natural climate change that is best seen in the fly zones). Probably when I took the 1999 flight from Miami to Zürich, and we got into a thunderstorm over the Atlantic, the Bermuda Triangle trying to lure us inside and swallow us forever. Any pilot with some sanity will not fly through a thunderstorm, and even one may sometimes think one is experiencing terrible turbulence; it's probably not that dangerous. In any case, our great Swissair Pilot that day flew fast. This time, it was not a mighty Airbus 330 that did but a mosquito-like insect called ATR 42, and it was not necessarily the weather and regular cloud formations that caused it, but the man and machine and the rest... We made it on the fringe of the thunderstorm clouds, but it was still shaking for some 35min, with stains of red wine on my khaki Miami pants. Wishing I was drunk, but after that Bermuda affair, I started to drink every time I flew; at least then, it was not a blue sky all the way…With all that has happened with climate change and the jet streams that are out of control at all altitudes, air pockets, and unexpected whirls, what remains in place to keep me calm is booze, sedatives, and tranquilizers. I would have forgotten that flight if it wasn't for the 'vacation' flight of 2000 to the Laffite Green Islands, which defiantly sealed my fate with the, ca 2-hour flight that affrighted me forever regarding wings in the sky.

The consortium ATR (Avions de Transport Régional) was formed as a partnership between France's Aerospatiale and Italy's Aeritalia. All of that wouldn't mean shit if it wasn't that the turboprops these guys produced soon enabled them to establish themselves as the market leader in this niche. SAAB of Sweden, Aerospace, not automobiles, also had great 340s and 2000s regional turboprop aircraft, but I think these guys expanded much more. In 1981, Aerospatiale and Aeritalia merged their designs for a turboprop regional aircraft and formed ATR as a 50-50 joint venture. The brilliant idea was developing, marketing, and supporting a regional transport aircraft. This shit took off very well, and they were the main actors for some time, ruling the skies with these conventional prop babies. As I said, Swedish SAAB soon followed with some Canadian actors behind, like Bombardier and the Brits. Several others, such as Koreans and Brazilians, with another approach—the regional jet jets entered the scene big time, with one of my favorite British Aerospace Avro jets leading the role. However, Turbo Props still prevailed, especially in the global developing countries domain. ATR developed a family of high-wing, twin-turboprop aircraft in the 40–70 seat range. This was the plane we were about to board that morning, an ATR 42, its first product (as the brochure stated, it entered service in 1985).

It was a complex little beast where Alenia Aeronautica's manufacturing facilities in Pomigliano near Naples, Italy, produced the aircraft fuselage and tail sections. At the same time, the wings were assembled at EADS Sogerma Services in Bordeaux in western France for Airbus France. Final assembly, flight testing, certification, and deliveries were responsible for ATR in Toulouse, France. So much for the specs and history, though none of that knowledge helped me when I saw the plane. This sorry little son of a bitch looked like she went through 30 years of war or a battle of the skies over England in WWII. I looked at it through the dirty window of the terminal building. It seems they were cleaning it and refueling before the boarding call came.

I guess that had priority. I could not see if anyone was in the cockpit, as that glass must have been cleaned when they produced the aircraft. The plane was white, with some red stripe going all the way on the body side and ending in tail wings with red painted letters FLYMEAWAY.COM, a newly established charter company running its life on a webpage domain, that I found out later, belonged to a porn site. It all seemed legit at the time, plus the offer was excellent. I had never been to these fantastic islands with a newly built small airport, some tremendous high-class bungalows and small hotels, and some mediocre and shitty hotels and motels...I was going to the latter ones. My friend that I was going to meet there insisted on it as she did not want to mingle or be associated with the rich people and, God forbid if he would be seen with them; instead, be with the typical tourist and folk, see nature, climb hills and save the fauna I guess...I didn't see the point of that type of vacation, nor was I keen on spending time with her; Augustine, as she was pretty boring, was the size of a whale and marched like a soldier on a war path. Good grief!

I Hate The F**king Tourists

This newly established charter was, flying from a small and obscure airport outside the city with a tiny runway and a terminal building that looked like a hut. We were crammed in this shitty want-be airport which had one terminal, if you could call that pig stale, horse stable, smoking chimney (yes, smoking was still permitted) terminal, swarmed by 300 people that were supposed to board four different charter planes, of companies with dubious names such as Flamingo Air, Here Comes the Sun, Freshair and our machine Flymeaway.com. I could not do the math as these ATRs (4) could not take more than 50 passengers...I guess they were waiting for other flights or? I was concerned, remembering not long ago an incident in some Greek islands with another obscure airline and bankrupt charter company where the plane was overbooked...That would have been enough to turn around and go home, but I was adamant about testing this 25 EUR ticket. The 300+ people around me, of course, looked like f**king tourists! But then again, so was I, and f**king ashamed for that!

A blogger and travel expert, Adrien Field, wrote recently, "Why is it that tourists, irrespective of their origin, are all fat, badly dressed, and generally abominable?" I don't know about that, some are ok, but in principle, he was right. I never considered myself a tourist, except for a few isolated incidents with a momentary lapse of reason or when I was small, and my parents took me on holiday. However, mind you—we were never tourists; not even then, we were visitors and travelers at best. These buggers (READ in CAPITAL LETTERS: "TOURISTS") here are the reason why globalization has a dark side, this being one of them, and is ruining all the great cities, natural places, townships, places in general and heritage we know of plus making it impossible for natives to exist and live everyday daily life. These abominations are set out with one, and only one goal in mind—to SEE and UNCHECK from their f**king bucket lists the sites, places, and monuments they can tell their asshole friends & absent extended families about or die peacefully thinking for example, that they know all about there is to know about the Incas, and their civilization as if they were born and raised on Machu Pichu, instead of being there 1.45min or how the cities of the USA came about if they climbed the Empire State Building or stood in the middle of Times Square, or knowing all about classical music if they took a photo of Vienna Concert Hall. For example, Americans spend more than $800 billion yearly on travel and recreational pursuits away from home. Other nations are also guilty, hell, all nations, for that matter! They set out—tourists of all nations and nationalities—on these cheap travels with their guidebooks and cameras and new phones and what else, reserved with things they must "see and note," without any sense or intention to feel and sense the places not least respect them—or God forbid to stay longer and learn them. Oh no, this pure and utter consumption and the false belief that they have become men and women of the world if one week has been spent in Egypt visiting all the monuments or traveling through France and Germany and England for 3.35 days, or climbing up Sugarloaf Mountain in Rio claiming to know Jesus or to have seen it all...

On the other hand, the authentic wayfarer, a sojourn traveler, has different intentions for studying & learn from these places. As Adrien points out, "they may travel to a place to see friends or for work, but they almost always integrate into the place they visit, and when approached from this perspective, the experience of travel is enriching both to the traveler and the local." I could not agree more fully with this statement! In contrast, the visitor has an entirely different intention, or as you genuinely, to enjoy a great cup of espresso doppio in the main square of Florence.

Mass Tourism, or as they call it these days over tourism, is a frigging disease. It is a trite sentiment that will be open to debate forever. Tourist Cities (ones with the natural predisposition and even once without it) all over the globe have sprawled with the local population and, of course, hotels. Traffic has increased, resulting in air pollution and congestion in most cities. Simultaneously infrastructure has developed, and cities have been revamped. As most of the ministers of tourism in Europe will tell you: "Tourism is an extraneous element that has significant economic benefits that need to be accommodated and managed." Yeah, but the other side of the coin is pretty dirty. Also ... no bullshit consumer non-citizens with checklists, no f**king fatties, no frigging tattoos, no infantile shorts; everyone dressed like grownups, women wearing lovely summer dresses, men smoking cigars or pipes, no mobile phones, no c=screaming kids. In other words, a snapshot of a time before the mass (over) tourism of Neanderthal hordes of virus infantilization of the Western World took off and took over the typical landscapes and lives.

So, when people say those tourists are those who travel for pleasure, they are partly right. I was not thinking of all that then in that shitty terminal, but instead letting my mind wander as it often does and wondering which poor mother f**kers will end in my plane and flight to the islands. I wasn't all that lucky that day, but then again, I had a "business class" ticket with seat A1...didn't know they sold those. Still, the option of internet booking was there with this one going 10 EUR more expensive, so you can imagine…while dozing off and thinking of the ordeal ahead, I saw in the crowd my long lost pal David Green, who was now living in Tel Aviv running a new startup with his dad who already had an IT company in Silicon Valley…David was one of the nicest and smartest guys in our tower, and I was sad when he left…heard he married our school friend Laura…I was hoping he was on my flight…he must have booked this thing too…I hoped he would sit close to me…

Airline Captain Kapadia & Who The F**k are these Passangers?

Memphis Kapadia or, as everyone called him, Bubba (later that nickname was gone, but instead worn by his best friend Joe "Bubba" Gershwin, whom he met in London, Canada) was a true legend for us. He was prone to only one of all imaginary substance abuse and that one of nicotine addiction and heavy sex; yes, I forgot that. While others, not least his brother Evan Kapadia, in his 'fine' company throughout the years, enjoyed alcoholism, drug abuse, cluster headache drugs, and senility – wait, that ain't an abuse! Still, they all ended up sooner than later in Alzheimer, senility, or marked by a tombstone. Not Memphis. His famous line was that God was his co-pilot, but the Devil was his bombardier. I guess this was about all the 'shady' and less shady business dealings and machinations he was involved in throughout the 4+ decades of his adult life. He must have been reaching his late 40s or early 50s' by now, but he still looked like a 25-year-old hipster with a f**king mission.

All possible urban legends existed and were neatly weaved into the social fabric of 2-3 generations about the escapades of Memphis Kapadia. The rumors that he smuggled weed in the corpses of dead people while working in the 'Last Resort' mortuary in s small town in Canada, smuggled stolen heritage artifacts with rubber boats off the coast of Venezuela, or used small planes to deliver guns to rebels in Congo were some of the legends that surrounded this guy. Some proved to be accurate, some not. In all weirdness, he always avoided life behind bars and somehow made a good life and living. Why am I telling this; well, I could not believe my eyes when I saw Captain Kapadia of the newly formed charter airline walking down the tarmac towards his plane. Flymeaway.com, which we found out very soon was Memphis´ latest enterprise and the chartering of two very used ATRs for this purpose. By his side was a stunning stewardess, and there was no sign of the other pilot...Man! Memphis was going to fly us to the islands! But then I started thinking: When did he take a license, let alone learn to fly a civil aviation plane?!? I knew he talked about flying Cessnas, but this! Were we safe? Will we survive? What the hell was this company all about if Memphis was their pilot? All those questions formed in my head when we started to board the plane for this adventurous journey...Little did I know that Memphis "owned" this enterprise and that plane we were about to board...

David and I finally met on the tarmac and hugged like we had not seen each other in decades! He looked great in his light blue slim-fit linen suit with a cream matching linen shirt, light brown loafers, and a light brown handkerchief in his pocket...looked like a f**king James Bond or Thomas Crown but probably with his tan physique even better, and a face that opened every possible door in life...We were super happy that we ended in "business class"...

We both could not wait until we got out of the shitty building and when the formalities were over at the counter—were checked and re-checked, the Flymeaway.com rep, who looked like he had 89 years and dementia, guided us through the jostling crowd and led us through a side gate to the tarmac and quickly locked it behind us. The other passengers looked like wild animals at us. The old timer said:

"The privileges of the business class...but I advise you to walk fast to the plane (some 150 meters away!) as I will soon have to release the cattle (he was referring to the rest of the passengers). It's a 48 seater, and your seats are at the front, but as we usually sell 80-100 tickets for each flight, it's first come, first serve...but you never know, animals might snitch your seats also..."

David and I looked at each other and could not believe our ears. We wanted to ask something more, but the old timer, which moved swiftly for his age, was closing the gate behind us and returning to the terminal. F**k, we almost started running to the plane and climbed the stairs into the ATR, where we saw the seats, but there were no numbers on them. The plane looked deserted, but we heard sounds from the cockpit, some moaning and muffled sounds. Suddenly the pretty stewardess/air hostess appeared from the cockpit, adjusting her small cap and fixing her mini skirt that was in the true meaning of the word MINI! She said something to the pilot and closed the door. She looked at us in surprise, "Aha, you are here, our business class passengers"! Good, now the others will arrive like beasts", she chuckled! The pretty air hostess ushered us inside the plane and sat us down in the front two seats. I got the window. "These are the business class seats, and it best to be seated until they all arrive!"

I looked out the window just in time to see about 70-80 people charging across the tarmac to get on the plane like wild animals chasing prey. A f**king stampede! Most made it, but some did not. They knew what was at stake, almost a tombola or lottery. Flymeaway.com had "oversold a bit" online and had no seat numbers. David and I were pretty concerned but laughing, passing/running by the four machines on the tarmac, trying to grab our seat, seeing these three aircraft that seemed and looked obsolete but flying and the primitive field with the almost unsurfaced runway, or it looked like that. It was dubious if this airport had any clearance to operate any flights, let alone these obscure companies. Now we were in this junk old machine being stormed by the horde that started to come into the machine, almost breaking their legs and climbing up the stairs. What David and I could not figure out was the heterogeneity of the passengers on this plane; an old lady with the chicken in her basket and her extended family of people that are even hard to find in books, some strange-looking tourists in the middle of the plane, some youngsters and hipsters, old-timers with a dark brown suntan and some workers and some ordinary folks of all kinds. All of that was on the way to the islands. Someone said we all have weird, strange things and habits about us. It is those people without them that should worry us. Maybe true, but this bunch of characters on the plane was bizarre.

I was looking outside the window and saw the other unlucky losers that didn't get seats screaming at the old timer, which now had two security guards of some kind with him, and they had pistols, and he had a shotgun!?! Ushering them back t the terminal building. The 2nd ATR would fly that evening, and then there would be 150 people competing for 50 seats...I wondered how long this company would exist until it got shut down or until the old timer or these shady security guards killed someone in the stampede. It won't be long, for sure!

The pilot, Memphis Kapadia, didn't care about passenger comfort; sadly, neither did Anna, the pretty stewardess. Not that I did care much for safety demos, as I knew them by heart, but that required thing did not exist, except for Anna Saying, "You know what you need to do...or you will all die..." and she just laughed, where she was joined in laughter by the rest of the passengers who didn't give a shit about security. Hand luggage was not stowed, of course (and that included all kinds of things, even a live chicken in the basket that the old lady was carrying, and tons of small and large bags), even on table-tops (yes, they did work!) during take-off and landing—nobody cared!

Just before start-up and lifting off, I turned to David:

"David, I know something about planes. And this thing has a Maximum Payload of 5,750kg, including all of us, and if you see that stuff they are putting inside the plane, that must weigh tons!" Outside the plane was a weird character, unshaven, obese, smoking a cigar (Great!) in brown clothes ushering all the massive packages—some black bags with massive tape, wooden crates, and metal boxes. One guy was helping him who certainly did not look like part of any ground crew, and all this was delivered in a massive truck with no signage or plates on it. This was not a catering or fuel truck; I wondered if we had any fuel in this metal can. The guy was sweating but very efficient. Our luggage was being thrown like rocks, and I wondered who and how delivered this and knew who would get seats. We had "business," so I didn't worry. The packages looked strange, and by the looks of this guy, so was the content. He was working fast, always watching over his shoulder.

"Ah, who cares, Haas," said David. I am sure the captain has this under control plus, if we are too heavy, we won't lift off, will we".

David laughed and was in an excellent mood. He told me he was meeting someone on the islands, and it was not Laura...seems their marriage was becoming history.

Speaking of the devil, just before take-off, Memphis Kapadia came out of the cockpit, and as soon as he saw David and me, he screamed and started hugging us: "Yesterday is history; today is a mystery, guys! F**king A! What a mystery to find you two! Tower kids, now men! Awesome, dudes...so glad you are on this happy flight with us! Anna and I will give you the best service! Enjoy doing nothing on this island; I intend to do so, and so should you! Anna said:

"He is the best captain in the world, and he grabbed her ass, "And she is the best flight attended in the atmosphere." They both laughed and kissed.

"I didn't know you were a pilot Memphis," I said innocently.

"Oh yeah, first-class man, Cambodian Flight Academy officer of the year! Rocking and rolling, bro! And I also fly all kinds of machines...Antonov, Airbus, Cessna, u name it!

David said, "good that you didn't ask him if he flew military jets; then you would get the real stuff!" We both knew this was far from the truth, but he knew how to fly as this company had been operating for a month with three weekly departures. Memphis didn't give a shit for the rest of the passengers, he just chatted with us, but then Memphis yelled to the rest of the congregation, i.e., 46 passengers left: Nobody got killed, and all the passengers came back in one piece...

"We will be soon off; we are just boarding some medical equipment, clothes, and help to the poor children of the island and the church and community groups. Everyone needs help, and we are here to help". He got great applause from the general population of the plane, who thought this was a genuine hero, so what the hell, 45 min delay is nothing. David and I just looked at each other: we knew better. Poor children, my ass! This was a different type of cargo...we just hoped it was not inflammable!

Memphis was making out with the stewardess. Well, no surprise there, knowing him. Our stewardess, Anna, was a gorgeous brunette woman in her mid-20s. Her lean body, thick waves of hair cascading over her shoulders with long legs, and super mini skirt and full breasts made her a quintessential poster girl for any airline. Even her little cap was like a sexy crown. She gives a flirtatious flick of her locks and tells us some non-essential things. She was trying to flirt with David, not so much with me, though David didn't care. David said to me: She is a typical example of lookism. Haas, "Lookism is a term used to refer to the positive stereotypes, prejudice, and preferential treatment given to physically attractive people, or more generally to people whose appearance matches cultural preferences." That's the book's definition, but it is real, I tell you. And even if she is not in any corporate business or otherwise, men are essentially pigs, are they will be slaves to this pattern for many years and some forever. David made a good point. It's a pigs' world, and we are pigs...and guess what? Pigs are flying!

Another final recollection of that morning, just before we took off from the tarmac and the last crates were thrown into the cargo— was the mechanics. The fat guy seemed to be a mechanic, also. He just viewed the control surfaces on the wings and checked superficially that all was okay. I looked at the plane, the wings, and the stuff under—I believe some of them were moved with machine screws rather than hydraulics, which seemed a bit scary, but I could be wrong on this technical issue. What did I know? I didn't know how old this ATR was and if these guys serviced it. I think I even saw a piece of cloth inside the mechanics of the wings, but then again, I must have been delusional, and fear was creeping into me like never before. The most bizarre thing was that after this inspection, the fat guy climbed into the cargo deck, which his buddy closed. I was sure I saw that, thinking there must be a good reason for that...or not!

In The Air, Above The Sea, On Land

While we were getting airborne (and here I thought we would never lift off), the flight attendant, Anna, stood in the cockpit doorway (a door covered by a used and dirty curtain) chatting to the pilot, our very own Mr. Kapadia, during take-off! She never buckled, but she did have an extra seat just in the eye line of David and me. She continued to wiggle at David and smile constantly, but David was in another dimension. Somehow, we lifted off with considerable noise and got to some altitude fairly steeply and fast. I wondered if Memphis even knew where the destination was. Once, a guy gave, can't remember who, a brilliant line on the Soviet Union carrier Aeroflot (not the Russian one today, I guess) that "it was the stone-faced dominatrix of the skies, a purgatory of execrable food, child-size seats, broken air-conditioning, and scowling service, all doled out in dank broom-closet planes." I just wondered, remembering these lines, what he would say for this entrepreneurial endeavor called Flymeaway.com, where the plane looked more like a diesel bus with an interior that resembled 1980s east Germany and an assemblage of people that not even Breughel could paint!

As soon as we reached the cruising altitude of, I guess, 25,000ft, the serving started, as Anna wanted to get rid o this task ASAP! She was alone, and the tray she rolled out was in such poor condition that I thought even rats would avoid it. I could see rust over the edges, which wasn't clean. The food was just plain awful. I don't know what those poor sods in the back received with 100% certainty, but it looked like a horrific sandwich that had seen much better days during the iron curtain flights in the 60s was served. The bread turned green, and some salami was inside with smelly cheese and old butter. That was accompanied by a cup of warm mineral water that lost its minerals and bubbles ages ago. Some complained over the quality but stopped very soon when Anna threatened to leave them without food for the two h flight. Service on this flight was a frigging disaster, but as we were privileged two individuals, we got a higher treatment. We were served last with all the engagement our flight attendants could put into this task. David and I got a decent warm ham and cheese open sandwich (although the meat was difficult to decipher), which looked ok, and wine in a hard-plastic glass. The wine bottle was a weird product, showing age with a cork that looked like it was made on Tortuga and a white label that could have been designed and drawn by my 3-year-old daughter if I had one. The wine was called "Evan Merlot," It portrayed a strange-looking guy badly drawn but still familiar. And some origin and other info but all handwritten; David and I tried the wine, and it tasted so spicy and sour but felt like it had never seen a natural grape in its content. Sugar was indeed present and had a strange ruby color. This could not have been wine. The label said 23.45% alcohol. What the hell was this?

David beat me to it, with a spasm in his face and mimicking by asking:

"Hmmm, interesting wine; what is this?"

Oh, I am glad you like the wine (Anna, the flight attendant, never figured out the sarcasm); It's homemade!

Homemade, I thought, what could that mean?

I said it aloud as she gave me the answer:

This is the captain's brother's wine, Evan Merlot's wine!

She turned her attention to David, who was mesmerized by this mysterious potion. Great wine; he is such a good wine producer! I will tell the captain you loved it!

"Interesting, I never tried this before."

"I understand it is terrific, and he uses goats and donkeys for production, and grapes are homemade even though he calls it a merlot, but there are other cool things inside like berries and goat blood and a lot of alcohol, she chuckled. It's supposed to be an aphrodisiac!"

Goat blood! I didn't even want to know what donkeys played in this process and how the wine was produced…

Anna went on:

"His mother crushes the graves, and the donkeys go over it and many other things…" I was about to ask something more when David intercepted me:

"L'Chayim Haas!" Said David holding the plastic cup of this homemade red wine, and drank one sip! He asked for another one.

"L'Chayim, David," let us enjoy this business-class earthly wine produced by no other than Evan Kapadia!"

Evan was probably stoned when he did this...we never found out where the vineyard and winery were and why was a homemade bottle in the plane at all...seems none of that mattered on this flight.

She is my Soulmate—in the Air Tonight

David opened up to me entirely on this trip, especially after three plastic glasses of "Merlot"!

"Oh man, I am so in love! I met this amazing woman on the business trip to Tel Aviv, and intimacy without intricacy got a different meaning".

This came out from nowhere, but probably after 3 cups of the mentioned Kapadia wine (we were moving to the 2nd bottle now), and Anna was also drinking with us, sitting in her chair doing her makeup. David was ecstatic...

"You have to understand one thing, Haas; Once you get into a stage when unsolved conflicts and everyday differences come to the point of no return and when respect for each other is more or less lost, adding a fact that nearness, romance, and love are almost all but gone then the only thing is left is friendship. And you know what? We don't even have that left! This is what happened to Laura and me. She was stuck in her 'Hollywood life of dreaming a stage-designed future' with a perfect profile of a man who believed, almost daily, in uncertainty and romanticized projected lifetimes of love & passion. In the end, it just broke as a balloon, and I tried t save it; God knows I did; we did counseling, group therapy, and other things... lying to each other along the way as the only truth that was said when she said she didn't love me anymore...I wanted to say the same and did at the end...even if I could have done it sooner, and it would not have made any difference whatsoever...so nobody changed after that. We spend tons of money and time on nothing—useless therapies and meetings with quack curators and shrinks; Nietzsche said once that "sometimes people don't want to hear the truth because they don't want their illusions destroyed," and he was right. That world never came! She never wanted to hear any truths about herself, and she was not perfect, far from it, man-. I had to work with every day like Sisyphus to make her happy; we were both lost souls swimming in a fish bowl, imagining a world from the other side of reality.

"People don't change, Haas," said David pointing in the air! "That is the frigging lie of the century that people can change. Some significant tremors in their lives might put them on a different course. Still, once you are formed with your DNA and the social environment you have been brought in and were formed from, only and maybe only taste, priorities change... momentary steps outside of your embedded human nature and true character are possible, but no leaps! Mark my words...we grow old, wiser, and more tired. And some of us adapt. Laura and I could not even adapt.

Now with Sarah, the love of my life, I have re-learned how to enjoy the simple pleasures of life, wine, food, and laughter, and also like a family, a home; aside from my dad and mom and my sister, I have a real partner, Sarah. I don't even feel I am cheating on Laura as we are done. Sarah and I just needed to look at the airport in Geneva, where we unexpectedly crashed into each other on the flight to Tel Aviv; Laura was never that, and she could never accept me for what I was and am. And you know what, Haas, f**k that! I feel and have all she wanted but not always...Not that I am not some parts of that, but I am also a pragmatist, innovator, you know...and I am well aware of my strengths and weaknesses as a person, professional, and friend...but that self-knowledge gives me an inner strength..."

I was listening to this and agreeing with him on all of it; knowing Laura very well and David, one could see this coming from miles away...they didn't have kids, which made things easier...

David went on.

"With Sarah, it's a different ball game...now I am all of that and more, she has found it all in me plus she is like me...so we have the best of both worlds...and now I want kids, for the first time in my life, and I am 30 with a woman like that...I think Laura needs to find a less intelligent man, even a rustic peasant-like chap with a grain of old-fashioned behavior and mannerism, with little or no initiative, mechanical working habits, and no opinion of his own, as she really doesn't need or want it regardless how much she asks for it. High-quality simpleton will do the job, day and night, with this character, uncomplicated man who will love and care for her and wake up every morning is the f**king same..."

"Laura, on the other hand, was sort of unapologetic believer in 'true love,' 'soul mates,' and other touchstones of hallmark greeting cards text and all those romantic movies mythology that she was immersed in. She was the first to say she didn't love me anymore, i.e., that love was lost. Everything I do is for a reason, not for some bloody emotional moment, or sentiments or for tradition – or God forbid for love, but that notwithstanding, I believe in all those things! And you know what, Haas, now I am fully and avidly in love with an amazing woman I want to stay with forever and ever!"

"I hear you so, brother!" I exclaimed! And we got back to the horrific wine that was now taking control of our bloodstream...the

Stewardess Anna was bringing us the 3rd bottle, which also had a white label with a home-painted figure of E van Kapadia holding a bucket in one hand and a bottle in the other...

I guess business class had some class after all...and I was ok with flying at this point though the plane was suddenly shaking and falling and going up at times, which was rather strange as the skies were clear. There were no turbulences, though air pockets and any jet winds are impossible to see...still! It felt like a 5-year-old flew it, or the pilot was drunk. I knew Memphis drank, but this was even weird for him. In the heat of the moment, the plane stabilized, and the cockpit opened; running came out the 7-year-old hill-Billy kid sitting behind us. The kid screamed, "Grandma, Grandma, I flew the plane, I flew it!" we never saw him entering the cockpit; I guess we were drinking too much; I guess the cockpit was never closed; for all we knew, there might have been even a goat inside.

Have All Your Eggs in One Basket

The definition of a "modern" primitive human being does not exist, at least not in its entirety. Still, some elements can create a stable definition or a term of reference for this complex phenomenon. These people are marked by primitive, gross, elemental, uncultivated simplicity, vulgarity, or just plain stupid, crude, and uncivilized. Both David and I realized the plane was full of them; don't get me wrong, we had nothing against them or their way of life and daily activities or state of mind, but when these people start to encroach on your private space and occupy the public realm entirely, then ones get pissed off, or slightly annoyed. The 4-5 rows behind us seemed to contain a massive vulgar family, made of grandparents, parents, kids, aunts, uncles, grandkids, cousins, and a cat and dog plus a chicken in a basket that the old lady was holding on the other side of David and me.

She had a face covered with facial wrinkles I had never seen before. It looked like someone planted some seed, and the plants grew, and then a massive harvester came over it. Though it was summer, she wore a typical Russian-style scarf over her head with floral patterns and red colors, a red sweater, and a blue wool cardigan underneath. There were strange rings on her fingers and a big old ring on her middle finger; the nails were uncut and long, containing all kinds of things underneath, everything from planting soil to food remnants and probably all in between. She had a long green wool skirt, red wool socks, and blue rubber shoes. A big crib basket in her lap contained a checkered cloth and a giant chicken surrounded by eggs, cheese, and other stuff. David and I watched in amusement, wondering if these eggs came from that chicken. Her family was so loud, shouting, screaming, producing massive rattle and hums, saying obscenities, eating like animals, not just the terrible airline food but theirs, which they brought in large amounts while kids were running up and down the "main street" of this plane. And now her grandson flew the plane – f**k a duck, thought we!

"Hey, you…" Grandma seemed to be referring either to David or me.

"Hey, you two bums, do you hear what I say?" I was sure she didn't say anything, but also, the noise of the propellers and the general super buzz of sounds in the plane muffled everything, including the old hag's voice. Finally, David turned to her and said:

"No, madam, we haven't heard anything; it is so loud in this plane, hard to hear anything from the screams of these kids."

David got an immediate response.

"F**k off, asshole, this is my family, and they can f**king do whatever they like; who gives a shit what you think!"

David was not sure what to say, and the combination of this poisonous wine we had and his excellent manners kept him from really replying. He only made a long face with a half-smile and a half-facial grimace that made an impression on the older woman.

"Man, your friend is some kind of a retard, isn't he?!" I was about to stand up angrily and set her in the right place, but she continued. She now turned to me, and I looked at her in amusement.

"Listen, boy, it's pretty frigging warm here, and my chicken and I need some fresh air. Can you open the windows on your side, as I don't want to catch a draft on my side and get a cold?"

I wasn't sure if she was kidding or if she was f**king serious. Her facial expression made any of those options plausible, but I went for the 2nd one. My assertions were correct in the end.

"No, I am sorry, these windows cannot be opened. If they could, we would all get sucked out and die, and the plane would crash. That's why we have an artificial environment inside created"…

"Artificial what…" said the old and then she and others around her started laughing.

"Boy, you just talk so much shit. I know; you don't want to get cold also, right"? She smiled with her "wonderful teeth." This was a rhetorical question, and I just drowsily said:

"Yeah, that must be it," but I added, "But I read in the instructions of how to fly in a plane that it is best not to open windows as they have no handles."

"Ah, doesn't matter," Then she said obscenity, lighted a cigarette afterward, and ignored me, which was perfect. Suddenly the paravane that separates the anteroom to the cockpit, the place where Anna prepared the strange thing we called food, opened up, and a big bloke in a lumberjack shirt and cow boots, who was the older woman's son, appeared carrying a cake and shouted:

"Mother, our mother, Happy Birthday, Dear Mother"

He gave the cake to Anna and took a sunbaked piece of paper from his left jean pocket, and started to give a speech:

"Dear Mother Varaminta! Greetings to you from your loved family. No matter how old you may be, you still look younger than your real age". Everyone broke into schizophrenic laughter, including Varaminta, who was deep into picking her nose and digging out whatever was available. She looked so amused.

  "To one of the weirdest people I've ever known – I am so happy you are my real mother. You surely had us fooled with your real age and all the strange men you had. So who knows who are fathers are." The congregation started to laugh wildly again.

"Another shitty year has been added to your marathon life, oh our mother and heart. Please relax and enjoy your day because you deserve it, and you are never old to have an adventure of a lifetime like this one today. You're still as strong as a bull and brave as a chicken! Happy Birthday, MOTHER!"

Varaminta stood up now, walked to the son, kissed him, turned to the rest of the family, us, and the whole plane, and raised her hand in appreciation. I guess the chicken was amused as we were. David and I expected some horrific "Happy Birthday to you…" tune to erupt, but instead of that, the whole family rose in the bliss of the moment and started to chant:

David and I were unsure what to do, but when her son looked at us wildly to rise from our seats, we followed suit and started chanting ourselves. "Mother, Mother, Mother, Mother…" As each moment passed, the noise was louder, and after 2 min of the chanting, the rest of the planer joined in; everyone was on their feet chanting "Mother, Mother, Mother" to this strange old hag and her vulgar family. Embarrassing moment!

Simply incredible!

After some time, the frigging commotion subsided, and everyone returned to their seats, trying to doze off while we got to the final destination in some 35min tops…David turned to me and started telling me all kinds of things…

"You know, Haas, I think about all kinds of different people I meet in my life and those included in wider and narrower circles of my extended friendships, acquaintances, colleagues, people I know and don't know, and of course, family. What I hate are the false, pretentious bastards that are also assholes in their human nature, psychopaths, greedy and selfish, stingy and parochial, and those that think they have a life. Still, they are lifeless, living in a constant demystification of their security of illusion and some weird satisfaction that lying to themselves will bring a sense of serenity and importance to their meaningless existences. You know, what I most like is good human nature and "fine" people, the most profound meaning of the word fine, as there are so many false and bad creatures out there that pretend they are fellow human beings…Just look at our parents, yours and mine: fine people with an unselfish and delicate human nature but still with some crosses to wear and DNA to account for, but still wonderful people that have lived their lives honestly and in helping others but also dealing with imperfect human beings, predators, jealous and selfish insects and vultures of all kinds…The horrible people don't change. They devise new ways to trick you into thinking they did. I don't know. I just met so many of these buggers, and more will come…

David turned around and pointed to the plane…

"Look at this congregation here, I guarantee you, 2/3 of these people are not what we call fine; sorry to say I feel there is only a 10% of this type of folk around, mark my words…" …with that, he kind of dozed off…wasn't sure where that was coming from or going (his comments). Still, I agreed with him…world was full of people who were not OK and did not have a lovely human souls…David drifted from that conversation into another on globalization and information society, how that will dominate the world, how AI will enter our lives more but will be problematic at some point, how there will be more wars and clashes of civilizations, how terror will get worse, and culture of fear will win, how with the rise of tolerance there will rise in the dark forces and conservativism, how some nations will do better than others, how the gap between the poor and rich will widen and finally, from his turf, how innovation, talent, technology, science, art, and networks will dominate our civilization and that ubiquitous information will be everywhere at all times…some 17 years ago he predicted a lot of things and in the year 2000. His company worked closely with Intel and Apple, which made him pretty rich in the coming years… finally he said:

"But you know, whatever happens, there will always be a place for a permanent open society in thinking, technology, and life in general; it just has to happen!

The Unexpected Pitstop and the Expected Landing

Of course, an unscheduled landing on some small shitty piece of rock was not what one expected, but nothing was expected on this trip. The plane was now descending fast, and Captain Kapadia came back on the loudspeakers:

"Dear passengers, we will make one stop to pick up some material and refuel before continuing to our far-off destination. Buckle up; it might be a rough landing as the airstrip is short."

We could not believe our ears and eyes, as what we saw outside the window was an approaching small island with little vegetation. In the middle, some make-believe airstrips and the run-down wooden hut were impersonating a terminal building. Besides, two persons were standing, waiting…The plane descended, and the airstrip seemed relatively short, but nobody had time to think about that… Kapadia took it down…We finally landed with several screams in the airplane. Kapadia emerged from the cockpit smiling… Even Anna was shit scared; one could see fear in her large black eyes.

"Wasn't that bad, ha? We will be in the air in no time" …He went back to the cockpit and started shouting something through the open window…the two guys came from nowhere and moved towards the cargo deck with some vehicle and particular escalator track…in less than 6,30sec they got three huge packages from the cargo. They took in one big aluminum case and three small wooden cases which had written "Ecuador Bandannas" misspelled…guess they meant bananas. God knows what was going on here. David and I just hoped it wouldn't explode; smuggled goods, rare animals, human organs, money, you name it…we had no clue…there was no sign of any refueling truck…in a matter of minutes, the plane was making a circle, as the props were on the whole time. We ascended, more or less the same way we landed, like a rocket…another round of screams (as we almost missed the end of the so-called tarmac and ended up in the sea) was silenced by Kapadia's deep voice saying that refueling was not needed as we have enough to reach our islands…

We soon lifted off exquisitely and with no problems. But suddenly, all became quiet in the plane, and David and I just looked at each other in amusement but also glad that we were still alive and flying in the air; we just wanted to get out of Dodge City and were happy to be on actual soil in 25min. Hopefully, there was not a 2nd pitstop lined up for this machine!

Just before landing, when all the meal trays were collected, and Anna disposed of all the trash, it was discovered that she and Memphis, who left the airplane on autopilot, that two pieces of cutlery that were not accounted for. Oh yes, this plane served metal forks and knives to all passengers, even though they ate sandwiches + plus, the stuff looked dirty and old – maybe even stolen. The concern for these missing pieces was so great that all the passengers got involved in the search until they were found! The old lady's grandson found the fork and knife under the 10th row…David and I could not believe our eyes, and the scene was almost from a burlesque… Memphis passed by carrying the missing piece and said, "This is

Austrian 18th-century shit, and I don't want to lose it" It…well, obviously stolen heritage goods, or maybe legit. Who knows…at this point, anything was possible.

When the dust settled down and our pilot took over the commands, I looked through the window. I saw the islands and the airport on one of them, which looked like a real thing, small but with an actual terminal building, runway, tower, and some other charter planes on the ground. David and I were shit scared by now… We hoped that Kapadia had permission to land or that we could make it on the first landing… Anna started a cigarette

The army of tourists was going to an inmate's paradise: An All-in-clusive resort where you could duly enjoy the life of a sheep in a flock tagged like an animal and fed like in a hospital with (free) generic food and beverages all day long. Generic hospitality, a false feeling of home and community, manufactured joviality, lightness of existence, security, and why ever leave? I could see these images pouring from the charter planes that landed…We were just about to land, and I could see David's face glowing, knowing his fantastic companion was waiting down there…

An Ending and a New Beginning

The condition of the planes, the service onboard, punctuality or lack thereof, safety, etc., all play a role. Every year there are lists of the worst airline companies in the world, and they usually include every possible airline from the likes of Afghanistan, Kyrgyzstan, Liberia, Mozambique, Bulgaria, Romania, Yemen, Turkmenistan, Sierra Leone, and Sudan, as well as dozens from Indonesia and some other corners of the globe. I bet you that Flymeaway.com would beat all those buggers by a large margin if you add adventure and smuggling of goods; then hey…who can compete with that shit? Kapadia mentioned they will start serving a few warm dishes and a "tailor-made lounge experience" with drinks and other things, especially for the so-called "business class," which was supposed to be called 'tiptop.' Yeah right! I would bet you if you surveyed the previous passengers. Including us, we would describe all kinds of weird things such as pro forma bullshit emergency procedures, i.e., lack of them and lack of safety in general, and then the unknown origin and fizzy drinks that are impossible to identify, whereas the food – which in the case of the sandwich or so-called warm meal we got—one dish on board, where no one is quite sure what it is or was. Uncomfortably loud engine noise of this bizarre plane that God only knows where and how it was assembled, and the age remained unknown. Seats that could fold backward are an urban legend.

Furthermore, my dear friends, the in-flight entertainment usually does not exist, of course, as for the cassette – tape player that was offered to us by Anna in business class. Well, who could complain? We didn't want this, and fortunately, the batteries were missing anyway, so we were saved from the pain of listening to only one rural folk band that she had.

We finally landed, and everyone was clapping, shouting, and standing up chaotically. Anna disappeared into the cockpit. We landed a bit further from the other planes and the main building…Anna and Memphis were ushering the folks out of the plane, down the stairs on the tarmac where some guy was standing and pointing towards the building: where folks should go. The only thing I could see outside my window was the emergence of the same fat guy from the cargo deck, moving around the plane in a brown mechanic uniform with another Asian-looking dude helping him, hurling the huge black bags and wooden and metal packages out from the cargo. At the same time, our luggage was being thrown onto the tarmac, not waiting for the terminal services to place them on the wagons. It was all going so fast, and they knew what they were doing. I just wondered who was that and what was going on, and did Memphis ever have a license, or this whole charter company existed? Such fundamental, existential questions did not have space and place at this moment; I just wanted to get out of this plane ASAP! Some smoke came out of the engine, and I saw oil leaking on the tarmac… Thank God we landed; as this machine was not in its prime and the way Memphis was treated in the air, it would not survive for long before it broke down or decommissioned. We said our goodbyes to Kapadia and Anna, and David and I started walking on the tarmac toward the terminal building, which was 100m away. The whole setting was a paradise island tropics, though it was the Mediterranean. David was smiling more and more and looking at someone waving to him. Then I noticed her when we came very close. Sarah appeared in the terminal, and I was mesmerized by how she looked like, simply amazing…chestnut brown hair that fell like waves onto her shoulders, stunningly dressed in a summer breezes dress that outlined the contour of a perfect model body and the face of a Cherubini angel with make just in the right amount and in right places and those luscious red lips….”David, David, my love..:” She shouted over the crowd. I was inert in my thoughts and completely blown away as David noticed and said, “She is something, isn't she?”

But Haas, it's the look, the eyes, and what's behind them, a universe of passion, love, and niceness you would not believe. I would give my love for this lady”.

I knew exactly what he meant, as this was real and infinite love that strikes you once, twice, or maybe never…David was a lucky man… and so was Sarah.

"My dear friend, we will see each other for sure, and why don't you and your friend join us during your stay here? You know where we are, which resort hotel. Give me a call, and e have dinner…otherwise, we meet again somewhere, or if you are passing by Tel Aviv, give me a call, brother…."

"I sure will, David; enjoy life and stay in love, my smart friend. Mazel tov"

"Mazel Tov Haas." He laughed. We hugged, and he ran to Sarah, who waved to me. They embraced and ran to the baggage pick-up area. Later they took off with their SUV for a lover's paradise vacation.

God bless her soul; my friend Augustine was waiting for me in her complete hiking and climbing gear, already sweating and seemingly more prominent than before, which made her look strange, dressed in a Tyrolian hat and camouflaged pants with glasses and red cheeks. She was nice, but her lifestyle and mannerism were eons away from me. We hugged, and she almost crushed me with her body weight and gadgets hanging from the fisherman swarf jacket she had on her. I shivered through my body, knowing we would need to explore, climb, and do all kinds of things I hated. I would probably get sick and stay in my room. A dinner with David and Sarah will never happen. After this bizarre flight and the prospects ahead, I wasn't looking forward to anything really; no expectations and no worries, as my friend was lesbian and was not interested in me in any romantic way. So I was going to make the best of these two weeks.

A minor dwarf popped up with a sign FLYMEAWAY.COM leading a large group of tourists to the tarmac, brushing past us. He screamed to the crowd to run, and they started in a frenzy stampede like the bulls in Pamplona towards the plane. Well…I thought to myself, "Haven't we seen this before."

The Final Act—The Mexican Affair

Somewhere in the summer of 2001

Joe "Bubba" Gershwin was sweating like a pig being prepared for slaughter. His favorite khaki mechanic trouser with extenders rapidly changed color due to the heat, sweat, and humidity. It almost felt that even the Decal named "BUBBA" sewed in was peeling off. What made it even worse was the most f**king terrible beer these people served, a warm bottle of piss, Corona! This one had a flat, tinny taste like it's been opened before, and someone purposely blended it with pee…guess that's why it's served with a lime or lemon. Montezuma's f**king revenge or what? He was munching some fried crap to get the horrid beer taste away. He hated being here; it was so frigging simple as that. But what the f**k? They needed this one! After the successful heist in Iceland and the less lucrative deals with the mobsters from the Romanian city of Brasov, where they almost contracted rabies being bitten by a bunch of wild junkyard dogs, things went f**king sour.

The disastrous African affair with that crazy pilot and the Angola Warlords, plus the big f**k-up that followed in the Corinthian Islands where they almost got wiped out by the local corrupt police sheriff. Fortunately, the Laffite Green Islands affair was good and prepared them for this last one; this was going to be the one, the affair that would be the end for both Bubba and Memphis, free from f**k-ups. They certainly didn't have nine lives though it felt like that. The only problem here is that this was a different story. Namely, they would work for Paco Guzmán Cardenas, leading the infamous cartel "Muerte Gloriosa"—Glorious Death. This was a ruthless consortium enterprise—almost a f**king country, composed of worse prison elements than you might imagine and sociopaths from the military plus other dangerous and lost souls but run by a strong family. These guys were dangerous as hell.

What started as major Mexican drug smugglers of marijuana soon became a major large-scale Mexican drug trafficking operation. They also became famous for pioneering the use of aircraft to smuggle drugs to the United States and other countries. That is where Bubba and Memphis came in. In a few years, this outfit became world-famous as an international drug trafficking, money laundering, and organized crime syndicate ruling 12 Mexican states, with important centers in Mexico City, Tepic, Toluca, Culiacán Rosales, Zacatecas, Guadalajara, and you name it! The cartel primarily got involved in the smuggling and distributing of Colombian cocaine, Mexican marijuana, methamphetamine, and Mexican and Southeast Asian heroin into the US, where the market for this was infinite. They always looked for a few good men and even more for a few good pilots without ethics, morals, and consciousness—and if things went sour—men that could fit plastic bags and fresh graves nicely. Bubba and Memphis undoubtedly had no problem with that, maybe not the last part of it.

Bubba was waiting for Javier Zambata's (Guzman's right-hand captain) first colonel Pedro Mexicante to meet him in this sleazy bar on the outskirts of Culiacán Rosales, where this cartel ran its operation. Memphis was on the other side of the street in a sleazy hotel room, watching with binoculars, inspecting the turf. Somehow, he always got Bubba to go in first. In five minutes, he would join Bubba, dressed in his standard dark blue linen shirt and gray linen jacket, black slacks, Japanese Toffler mocha shoes, and his signature black Ray Ban wayfarers plus a ponytail trying very much to look like a character from Miami Vice.

They had to offer a great piece: The DHC-6 Twin Otter, a 20-passenger STOL (Short Takeoff and Landing) utility aircraft developed by de Havilland Canada. It has often been called the most successful aircraft program in Canada's history and certainly now one for the Bubba/Kapadia smuggler's blues. This one, Bubba made an effort at it. Memphis won it on a card game in Guatemala with the daughter of the poor soul he skinned. He gave the daughter back after some time, but not this plane. The Twin Otter is truly the small airliner that does it all. Bubba modified this baby and eliminated all the passenger space, making it the ultimate machine as no aircraft can land on tarmac runways, mudflats, water, sand, snow, and ice as this superb machine. No aircraft does regularly scheduled flights in the Polar Regions, airports at extreme altitudes, or tropical islands (I wish they had this in the Corinthians instead of that crappy ATR). And now they owned one, had the expertise, and the Mexicans needed them.

Out of nowhere, Pedro arrived with his entourage, which was mean and ready to act if necessary. Although the first colonel for Javier, Pedro carried power like no one else. He was the nephew of the drug Lord Paco Guzmán Cardenas, and as he had no sons, Pedro was a like an adopted son. So Bubba and Memphis were meeting an up-and-raising star in the drug and criminal cartels world.

[Pedro Mexicante sits at the table and starts talking instantly]:

"I heard rumors, some good and some bad ones, about you two: Skilled and Stupid, Innovative and Naive, lucrative and cunning, but foremost greedy and sometimes stupid again."

Pedro Mexicante was a Mexican drug cartel, well-read philosopher. As he continued with an 'import' intellectual thought, false smile, and evil eyes:

Pedro: A wise Mexican man once said, 'When it comes to sorrow and pain, the standard rules of exchange do not apply because sorrow and pain transcend value. A man would give entire countries, nations, and families to lift sorrow and pain off his worried heart. And yet, you cannot buy anything with sorrow and pain because sorrow and pain are worthless, my friends.

Memphis: I am not sure...why are you telling us this?

Pedro: Oh, my friend, just in case you attempt to deny the reality of the world you're in now and will be while this venture lingers on. Do you love your lives so entirely that sorrow and pain could never enter the game? Would you exchange places with him (pointing at Bubba) upon the airline wheel? And I don't mean flying or dying because dying is easy, and flying is hard. You are a pilot at the crossing; you are the man at the water's edge and about to cross the Rubicon; you are him, he is you".

Memphis: Pardon my broken Mexican-Spanish, and with all due respect, but what are you talking about, Pedro?

Pedro: Well, that is good to hear, my pilot friend.

Bubba: Excuse me, are you saying what I think you are saying, that there will be problems, trouble or...?

Pedro: No. It's impossible. Trouble for whom and what? Not for me or us...but for you?

Bubba and Memphis had no f**king clue what this guy was saying. The motherf**ker was in some Seneca moment but always keeping eyes on both of them, analyzing, testing, and registering every facial and body movement they made.

Memphis: You said I was that man—at that crossing. Rubicon and all that shit...what do you mean?

Pedro: Yes. At the discernment, that life is not going to take you back. You two are the environment you have shaped for yourselves and the ambient that awaits and looks at you. And when you stop to realize that the ambient is the one that matters most, not your environment but the natural world that ceases to exist, one world that matters—the only one—then the f**king ambient you have created will also cease to exist.

[Pedro leaned towards Memphis and looked at him intensely}

Pedro: I sincerely hope that you understand that you might live great days of your lives, but at the same time, an infernal moment of bliss might replace that, and you would be living the last days of the world. If and when that happens, life will be replaced by death, day by night, fullness by emptiness, and death will undoubtedly acquire a different meaning. The old wise Mexican man also said, "The extinction of all reality is a concept no resignation can encompass. And then, all the grand designs and plans will be finally exposed and revealed". I hope you understand what I mean, Mr. Kapadia and Mr. Orlando. I will not be lenient or stupid like Mr. Masweze of Angola, will I now? Lucky for you, the bastard got decapitated by his brother, and then nobody gave a shit about you two. You got away from that mess pretty nicely, didn't you?

Their piss froze on the mention of the Angolan drug lord, but also relief that the bugger was gone and that these guys were not lurking in the shadows anymore. How in heaven did Pedro know about that? He must have checked everything.

Pedro: Now, Mr. Kapadia, I must go to meet people. Go places and do things. If I have any left, I might consider growing some oranges in my garden. Otherwise, it might be a small lemon tree.

[Pedro stands up to leave]

Pedro: I am not a Renaissance artist, nor do I have the profound wish and urge to paint this gray and screwed up world in colors more somber than those it wears, but as your world could give way to darkness and death, it becomes more and more difficult to dismiss the understanding that the world is oneself. So, gentlemen, it will be something you will have created, no more, no less, no far, no near. And if and when you cease to be, so will the world you know, the one you have shaped and composed for yourselves but not the ambient around you. There will be other worlds. Of course, there will be...many of them. But they are the worlds of other men that will take your place, and your understanding of them was never more than an illusion. I hope I made myself clear.

Bubba and Memphis just looked at each other in f**king bewilderment. What the hell were they supposed to say to this mumbo jumbo? Pedro filled in the blanks for them.

Pedro: Just in case you two bozos are not getting what I am delivering to you, I will say it in "plain" English: "Your world, the only one that doesn't matter to me or my bosses and associates, will seize to exist if you f**k this and us up in the process." He raised his hand in theatrical motion:

"It will be gone like a summer breeze or a breath from a virgin girl or post-mortem fart. And it will never come back again, that I can promise you". You are a damn good pilot with no scruples, he is a God damn good mechanic, and you have a great plane and are greedy with very little morale, ethics, compassion, or consciousness. That's all we need. I will see you in a week on the airstrip. Don't f**k this up or f**k with us as, because then, we will f**k you up, and that is going to be such a painful affair that you will never want to see or feel anything anymore; and if it goes well, who knows, you might have dinner at my place---Adios Amigos!

[With that, Pedro and his henchman left in the manner they arrived, as ghosts...]

After a few painful moments of silence, Memphis lighted a cigar and sighed, saying, "I am not afraid of this dude; we will fix this"... Bubba wondered how many times he had heard this quote before... His pee froze from this bastard, as he knew the guy would cut their balls if this job went sour and probably kill everyone they knew or wanted to know just to be sure or for the fun of it...

The plan is something that will never happen in reality. That was Bubba's sign of warning in the inner psyche. He was a pessimist, but there were grains of optimism deep down. But then again, Bubba thought: Optimist is simply uninformed or intellectually lagging, and Bubba was not that someone. Joe "Bubba" Gershwin took the last sip of the bottle with Corona on it but really contained piss and thought again of Gretchen, the beautiful German Alpine woman running a pretty nice small hotel in St. Moritz. How he would see her...he had to...but what Bubba's Beer belly gut was telling him was that this was not going to turn right, no Sir, the shit might just hit the fan...f**k! But on the other hand, if he was just lucky enough, he might save his head & balls and enjoy both of them in the Alpine world...

THE END

(Not to be Continued...for sure!)

Highrise

Written by Darren Wall, Birmingham (England),
Reprinted by Permission

Cold grey exterior,
Weeping acid rain,
Condensated glass,
Rotten window frame,

Drum and bass lines,
Speakers on the floor,
Tired mother screaming,
Kicking at their door,

Abuse laden vocals,
A wolf pack circle round,
Commotion on the stairwell,
Falling to the ground,

Blood soaked footsteps,
Muffled voices flee,
Sirens in the distance,
Mother cries for me.

Drum and Bass lines,
Speakers on the floor,
Orphaned son is weeping,
Mother screams no more.

Author's Bio

Tigran Haas was born in 1969 and raised primarily in Former Yugoslavia, Sarajevo, the Jerusalem of the Balkans. However, he has spent some of the best years in the USA. Tigran is a nostalgic storyteller, an avid movie fan, listens to ambient, new age, and melodic rock music, collects books, drinks scotch, loves Columbian coffee and Nespresso & daydreams. Dr. Haas is a Covid19 survivor, lives quietly, and works as a university professor in Stockholm, Sweden. This book is his first and maybe the last novel ever, written over the eternal span of twenty years in twenty European & American cities.